P9-ECS-831

THE AUDRAN SEQUENCE

ALSO BY GEORGE ALEC EFFINGER

WHAT ENTROPY MEANS TO ME

RELATIVES

NIGHTMARE BLUE
(with Gardner Dozois)

FELICIA

THOSE GENTLE VOICES

DEATH IN FLORENCE

HEROICS

THE WOLVES OF MEMORY

THE NICK OF TIME

THE BIRD OF TIME

SHADOW MONEY

THE RED TAPE WAR
(with Jack L. Chalker and Mike Resnick)

THE ZORK CHRONICLES

THE AUDRAN SEQUENCE

George Alec Effinger

SCIENCE FICTION

This is a work of fiction. All of the characters, organizations and events portrayed in this novel are either products of the author's imagination or are used fictitiously and are not to be construed as real. Any resemblance to actual events, locales, organizations, or persons, living or dead, is entirely coincidental.

WHEN GRAVITY FAILS   Copyright © 1986 by George Alec Effinger
   Publication History: Arbor House Publishing Company hardcover, 1986
     Bantam Books mass market paperback, 1988
     Orb trade paperback, November 2005
A FIRE IN THE SUN   Copyright © 1989 by George Alec Effinger
   Publication History: Doubleday hardcover, January 1989
     Spectra mass market paperback, March 1990
     Orb trade paperback, February 2006
THE EXILE KISS   Copyright © 1991 by George Alec Effinger
   Publication History: Doubleday Books hardcover, April 1991
     Spectra mass market paperback, February 1992
     Orb trade paperback, July 2006

First SFBC Science Fiction Printing: December 2008

All rights reserved, including the right to reproduce this book, or portions thereof, in any form.

Published by arrangement with
Orb Books
Published by Tom Doherty Associates, LLC
175 Fifth Avenue
New York, NY 10010

Visit The SFBC online at http://www.sfbc.com

ISBN # 978-1-60751-174-8

Printed in the United States of America.

Contents

When Gravity Fails

This book is dedicated to the memory of Amber.

"And some there be, which have no memorial."

. . . He must be the best man in his world and a good enough man for any world. . . . He is a lonely man and his pride is that you will treat him as a proud man or be very sorry you ever saw him. He talks as the man of his age talks—that is, with rude wit, a lively sense of the grotesque, a disgust for sham, and a contempt for pettiness.

—Raymond Chandler,
"The Simple Art of Murder"

When you're lost in the rain in Juarez and it's Eastertime too
And your gravity fails and negativity don't pull you through
Don't put on any airs when you're down on Rue Morgue
    Avenue
They got some hungry women there and they really make
    a mess out of you.

—Bob Dylan,
"Just Like Tom Thumb's Blues"

ᴏɴᴇ

Chiriga's nightclub was right in the middle of the Budayeen, eight blocks from the eastern gate, eight blocks from the cemetery. It was handy to have the graveyard so close-at-hand. The Budayeen was a dangerous place and everyone knew it. That's why there was a wall around three sides. Travelers were warned away from the Budayeen, but they came anyway. They'd heard about it all their lives, and they'd be damned if they were going home without seeing it for themselves. Most of them came in the eastern gate and started up the Street curiously; they'd begin to get a little edgy after two or three blocks, and they'd find a place to sit and have a drink or eat a pill or two. After that, they'd hurry back the way they'd come and count themselves lucky to get back to the hotel. A few weren't so lucky, and stayed behind in the cemetery. Like I said, it was a very conveniently situated cemetery, and it saved a lot of time and trouble all around.

I stepped into Chiri's place, glad to get out of the hot, sticky night. At the table nearest the door were two women, middle-aged tourists, with shopping bags filled with souvenirs and presents for the folks back home. One had a camera and was taking hologram snapshots of the people in the nightclub. The regulars usually don't take kindly to that, but they were ignoring these tourists. A man couldn't have taken those pictures without paying for it. Everyone was ignoring the two women except a tall, very thin man wearing a dark European suit and tie. It was as outrageous a costume as I'd seen that night. I wondered what his routine was, so I waited at the bar a moment, eavesdropping.

"My name is Bond," said the guy. "*James* Bond." As if there could be any doubt.

The two women looked frightened. "Oh, my God," one of them whispered.

My turn. I walked up behind the moddy and grabbed one of his wrists. I slipped my thumb over his thumbnail and forced it down and into his palm. He cried out in pain. "Come along, Double-oh-seven, old man," I murmured in his ear, "let's peddle it somewhere else." I escorted him to the door and gave him a hefty shove out into the muggy, rain-scented darkness.

The two women looked at me as if I were the Messiah returning with their personal salvations sealed in separate envelopes. "Thank you," said the one with the camera. She was speaking French. "I don't know what else to say except thanks."

"It's nothing," I said. "I don't like to see these people with their plug-in personality modules bothering anybody but another moddy."

The second woman looked bewildered. "A moddy, young man?" Like they didn't have them wherever she came from.

"Yeah. He's wearing a James Bond module. Thinks he's James Bond. He'll be pulling that trick all night, until someone raps him down and pops the moddy out of his head. That's what he deserves. He may be wearing Allah-only-knows-what daddies, too." I saw the bewildered look again, so I went on. "Daddy is what we call an add-on. A daddy gives you temporary knowledge. Say you chip in a Swedish-language daddy; then you understand Swedish until you pop it out. Shopkeepers, lawyers, and other con men all use daddies."

The two women blinked at me, as if they were still deciding if all that could be true. "Plugging right into the brain?" said the second woman. "That's horrifying."

"Where are you from?" I asked.

They glanced at each other. "The People's Republic of Lorraine," said the first woman.

That confirmed it: they probably had never seen a moddy-driven fool before. "If you ladies wouldn't mind a piece of advice," I said, "I really think you're in the wrong neighborhood. You're definitely in the wrong bar."

"Thank you, sir," said the second woman. They fluttered and squawked, scooping up their packages and bags, leaving behind their unfinished drinks, and hurried out the door. I hope they got out of the Budayeen all right.

Chiri was working behind the bar alone that night. I liked her; we'd been friends a long time. She was a tall, formidable woman, her black skin tattooed in the geometric designs of raised scars worn by her distant ancestors. When she smiled—which she didn't do very often—her teeth flashed disturbingly white, disturbing because she'd had her canines filed to sharp points. Traditional among cannibals, you know. When a stranger came into the club, her eyes were shrewd and black, as empty of interest as two bullet holes in the wall. When she saw me, though, she shot me that wide welcoming grin. *"Jambo!"* she cried. I leaned across the narrow bar and gave her a quick kiss on her patterned cheek.

"What's going on, Chiri?" I said.

"Njema," she said in Swahili, just being polite. She shook her head. "Nothing, nothing, same goddamn boring job."

I nodded. Not much changes on the Street; only the faces. In the club were twelve customers and six girls. I knew four of the girls, the other two were new. They might stay on the Street for years, like Chiri, or they might run. "Who's she?" I said, nodding at the new girl on stage.

"She wants to be called Pualani. You like that? Means 'Heavenly Flower,' she says. Don't know where she's from. She's a real girl."

I raised my eyebrows. "So you'll have someone to talk to now," I said.

Chiri gave me her most dubious expression. "Oh, yeah," she said. "You try talking to her for a while. You'll see."

"That bad?"

"You'll see. You won't be able to avoid it. So, did you come in here to waste my time, or are you buying anything?"

I looked at the digital clock blinking on the cash register behind the bar. "I'm meeting somebody in about half an hour."

It was Chiri's turn to raise her eyebrows. "Oh, business? We're working again, are we?"

"Hell, Chiri, this is the second job this month."

"Then buy something."

I try to stay away from drugs when I know I'm going to meet a client, so I got my usual, a shot of gin and a shot of bingara over ice with a little Rose's lime juice. I stayed at the bar, even though the client was coming, because if I sat at a table the two new girls would try to hustle. Even if Chiri warned them off, they'd still try. There was time enough to take a table when this Mr. Bogatyrev showed up.

I sipped my drink and watched the girl onstage. She was pretty, but they were all pretty; it went with the job. Her body was perfect, small and lithe and so sweet that you almost ached to run your hand down that flawless skin, glistening now with sweat. You ached, but that was the point. That's why the girls were there, that's why you were there, that's why Chiri and her cash register were there. You bought the girls drinks and you stared at their perfect bodies and you pretended that they liked you. And they pretended that they liked you, too. When you stopped spending money, they got up and pretended that they liked someone else.

I couldn't remember what Chiri had said this girl's name was. She'd obviously had a lot of work done: her cheekbones had been emphasized with silicone, her nose straightened and made smaller, her square jaw shaved down to a cute rounded point, oversized breast implants, silicone to round out her ass . . . they all left telltale signs. None of the customers would notice, but I'd seen a lot of women on a lot of stages in the last ten years. They all look the same.

Chiri came back from serving customers farther down the bar. We looked at each other. "She spill any money for brainwork?" I asked.

"She's just amped for daddies, I think," said Chiri. "That's all."

"She's spent so much on that body, you'd think she'd go the whole way."

"She's younger than she looks, honey. You come back in six months, she'll have her moddy plug, too. Give her time, and she'll show you the personality you like best, hardcore slut or tragic soiled dove, or anything in-between."

Chiri was right. It was just a novelty to see someone working in that nightclub using her own brain. I wondered if this new girl would have the stamina to keep working, or if the job would send her back where she came from, content with her perfectly modified body and her partially modified mind. A moddy and daddy bar was a tough place to make money. You could have the most dazzling body in the world, but if the customers were wired too, and paying more attention to their own intracranial entertainment, you might as well be home yourself, chipping in.

A cool, imperturbable voice spoke in my ear. "You are Marîd Audran?"

I turned slowly and looked at the man. I supposed this was Bogatyrev. He was a small man, balding, wearing a hearing aid—this man had no modifications at all. No visible ones, anyway. That didn't mean that he wasn't loaded with a module and add-ons I couldn't see. I've run into a few people like that over the years. They're the dangerous ones. "Yes," I said. "Mr. Bogatyrev?"

"I am glad to make your acquaintance."

"Likewise," I said. "You're going to have to buy a drink or this barmaid will start heating up her big iron cooking pot." Chiri gave us that cannibal leer.

"I'm sorry," said Bogatyrev, "but I do not consume alcohol."

"It's all right," I said, turning to Chiri. "Give him one of these." I held up my drink.

"But—" objected Bogatyrev.

"It's all right," I said. "It's on me, I'll pay for it. It's only fair—I'm going to drink it, too."

Bogatyrev nodded: no expression. Inscrutable, you know? The Orientals are supposed to have a monopoly on that, but these guys from Reconstructed Russia aren't bad, either. They practice at it. Chiri made the drink and I paid her. Then I steered the little man to a table in the back. Bogatyrev never glanced left or right, never gave the almost-naked women a moment of his attention. I've known men like that, too.

Chiri liked to keep her club dark. The girls tended to look better in the dark. Less voracious, less predatory. The soft shadows tended to clothe them with mystery. Anyway, that's what a tourist might think. Chiri was just keeping the lights off whatever private transactions might be occurring in the booths and at the tables. The bright lights on the stage barely penetrated the gloom. You could see the faces of the customers at the bar, staring, dreaming, or hallucinating. Everything else in the club was in darkness and indistinct. I liked it that way.

I finished my first drink and slid the glass to the side. I wrapped my hand around the second one. "What can I do for you, Mr. Bogatyrev?"

"Why did you ask me to meet you here?"

I shrugged. "I don't have an office this month," I said. "These people are my friends. I look out for them, they look out for me. It's a community effort."

"You feel you need their protection?" He was sizing me up, and I could tell that I hadn't won him over yet. Not all the way. He was intensely polite about it the whole time. They practice that, too.

"No, it isn't that."

"Do you not have a weapon?"

I smiled. "I don't carry a weapon, Mr. Bogatyrev. Not usually. I've never been in a situation where I needed one. Either the other guy has one, and I do what he says, or he doesn't, and I make him do what *I* say."

"But surely if you had a weapon and showed it first, it would avoid unnecessary risk."

"And save valuable time. But I have plenty of time, Mr. Bogatyrev, and it's *my* hide I'm risking. We all have to get our adrenaline flowing somehow. Besides, here in the Budayeen we work on kind of an honor system. They know I don't have a weapon, I know they don't. Anybody who breaks the rules gets broken right back. We're like one big, happy family." I didn't know how much of this Bogatyrev was buying, and it wasn't really important. I was just pushing a little, trying to get a sense of the man's temper.

His expression turned just a tiny bit sour. I could tell that he was thinking about forgetting the whole thing. There are lots of private strong arms listed in the commcodes. Big, strong types with lots of weapons to reassure people like Bogatyrev. Agents with shiny bright seizure guns under their jackets, with lush, comfortable suites in more attractive neighborhoods, with secretaries and computer terminals hooked into every data base in the known world and framed pictures of themselves shaking hands with people you feel you ought to recognize. That wasn't me. Sorry.

I saved Bogatyrev the trouble of asking. "You're wondering why Lieutenant Okking recommended me, instead of one of the corporations in the city."

Not a flicker out of Bogatyrev. "Yes," he said.

"Lieutenant Okking's part of the family," I said. "He tosses business my way, I toss business his way. Look, if you went to one of those chrome-plated agents, he'd do what you need done; but it would cost you five times more than my fee; it would take longer, I can guarantee you that; and the high-velocity guys have a tendency to thunder around with their expensive equipment and those attention-getting weapons. I do the job with less noise. Less likely that your interests, whatever they are, will end up decorated with laser burns themselves."

"I see. Now that you have brought up the subject of payment, may I ask your fee?"

"That depends on what you want done. There are certain kinds of work I don't do. Call it a quirk. If I don't want to take the job, though, I can refer you to someone good who will. Why don't you just start at the beginning?"

"I want you to find my son."

I waited, but Bogatyrev didn't seem to have anything further to say. "Okay," I said.

"You will want a picture of him." A statement.

"Of course. And all the information you can give me: how long he's been missing, when you last saw him, what was said, whether you think he ran away or was coerced. This is a big city, Mr. Bogatyrev, and it's very easy to dig in and hide if you want to. I have to know where to start looking."

"Your fee?"

"You want to haggle?" I was beginning to get annoyed. I've always had trouble with these New Russians. I was born in the year 1550—that would be 2172 in the calendar of the infidel. About thirty or forty years before my birth, Communism and Democracy died in their sleep from exhausted resources and rampant famine and poverty. The Soviet Union and the United States of America fractured into dozens of small monarchies and police states. All the other nations of the world soon followed suit. Moravia was an independent country now, and Tuscany, and the Commonwealth of the Western Reserve: all separate and terrified. I didn't know which Reconstructed Russian state Bogatyrev came from. It probably didn't make much difference.

He stared at me until I realized he wasn't going to say anything more until I quoted a price. "I get a thousand kiam a day and expenses," I said. "Pay me now for three days in advance. I'll give you an itemized bill after I find your son, *inshallah.*" If Allah wills, that is. I had named a figure ten times my usual fee. I expected him to haggle me down.

"That is entirely satisfactory." He opened a molded plastic briefcase and took out a small packet. "There are holotapes here, and a complete dossier on my son, all his interests, his vices, his aptitudes, his entire psychological profile, all that you will need."

I squinted at him across the table. It was odd that he should have that package for me. The Russian's tapes were natural enough; what struck me as fishy was the rest of it, the psych profile. Unless Bogatyrev was obsessively methodical—and paranoid to boot—I didn't see why he'd have that material prepared for me. Then I had a hunch. "How long has your son been missing?" I asked.

"Three years." I blinked; I wasn't supposed to wonder why he'd waited so long. He'd probably already been to the city jobbers and they hadn't been able to help him.

I took the package from him. "Three years makes a trail go kind of cool, Mr. Bogatyrev," I said.

"I would greatly appreciate it if you would give your full attention to the matter," he said. "I am aware of the difficulties, and I am willing to pay your fee until you succeed or decide that there is no hope of success."

I smiled. "There's always hope, Mr. Bogatyrev."

"Sometimes there is not. Let me give you one of your own Arab proverbs: Fortune is with you for an hour, and against you for ten." He took a thick roll of bills out of a pocket and sliced off three pieces. He put the money away again before the sharks in Chiri's club could sniff it, and held out the three bills to me. "Your three days in advance."

Someone screamed.

I took the money and turned to see what was happening. Two of Chiri's girls were throwing themselves down on the floor. I started to get out of my chair. I saw James Bond, an old pistol in his hand. I was willing to bet it was a genuine antique Beretta or Walther PPK. There was a single shot, as loud in the small nightclub as the detonation of an artillery shell. I ran up the narrow aisle between the booths and tables, but after a few steps I realized that I'd never get near him. James Bond had turned and forced his way out of the club. Behind him, the girls and the customers were shrieking and pushing and clawing their way to safety. I couldn't make my way through the panic. The goddamn moddy had taken his little fantasy to the ultimate tonight, firing a pistol in a crowded room. He'd probably replay that scene in his memory for years. He'd have to be satisfied with that, because if he ever showed his face around the Street again, he'd get jammed up so bad he'd have to be modified to hell and back just to pass as a human being again.

Slowly the club quieted down. There'd be a lot to talk about tonight. The girls would need plenty of drinks to soothe their nerves, and they'd need lots of comforting. They'd cry on the suckers' shoulders, and the suckers would buy them lots of drinks.

Chiri caught my eye. "Bwana Marîd," she said softly, "put that money in your pocket, and then get back to your table."

I realized that I was waving the three thousand kiam around like a handful of little flags. I stuffed the bills in a pocket of my jeans and went back to Bogatyrev. He hadn't moved an inch during all the excitement. It takes more than a fool with a loaded gun to upset these steely-nerved types. I sat down again. "I'm sorry about the interruption," I said.

I picked up my drink and looked at Bogatyrev. He didn't answer me. There was a dark stain spreading slowly across the front of his white silk Russian peasant blouse. I just stared at him for a long time, sipping my drink, knowing that the next few days were going to be a nightmare. At last I stood up and turned toward the bar, but Chiri was already there beside me, her phone in her hand. I took it from her without a word and murmured Lieutenant Okking's code into it.

two

the next morning, very early, the phone started to ring. I woke up, bleary and sick to my stomach. I listened to the ringing, waiting for it to stop. It wouldn't. I turned over and tried to ignore it; it just kept ringing and ringing. Ten, twenty, thirty—I swore softly and reached across Yasmin's sleeping body and dug for the phone in the heap of clothing. "Yeah?" I said when I found it at last. I didn't feel friendly at all.

"I had to get up even earlier than you, Audran," said Lieutenant Okking. "I'm already at my desk."

"We all sleep easier, knowing you're on the job," I said. I was still burned about what he'd done to me the night before. After the regular questioning, I'd had to hand over the package the Russian had given me before he died. I never even had a chance to peek inside.

"Remind me to laugh twice next time, I'm too busy now," Okking said. "Listen, I owe you a little something for being so cooperative."

I held the phone to my ear with one hand and reached for my pill case with the other. I fumbled it open and took out a couple of little blue triangles. They'd wake me up fast. I swallowed them dry and waited to hear the fragment of information Okking was dangling. "Well?" I said.

"Your friend Bogatyrev should have come to us instead. It didn't take us very long to match his tapes with our files. His missing son was killed accidentally almost three years ago. We never had an identification on the body."

There was a few seconds of silence while I thought about that. "So the poor bastard didn't have to meet me last night, and he didn't have to end up with that red, ragged hole in his shirt."

"Funny how life works out, isn't it?"

"Yeah. Remind me to laugh twice next time," I said. "Tell me what you know about him."

"Who? Bogatyrev or his son?"

"I don't care, either or both. All I know is some little man wanted me to do a job. He wanted me to find his son for him. I wake up this morning, and both he and the kid are dead."

"He should have come to us," said Okking.

"They have a history, where he came from, of not going to the police. Voluntarily, that is."

Okking chewed that over, deciding whether he liked it or not. He let it ride. "So there goes your income," he said, pretending sympathy. "Bogatyrev was some kind of political middleman for King Vyacheslav of Byelorussia and the Ukraine. Bogatyrev's son was an embarrassment to the Byelorussian legation. All the petty Russias are working overtime to establish their credibility, and the Bogatyrev boy was getting into one scandal after another. His father should have left him at home, then they'd both still be alive."

"Maybe. How'd the boy die?"

Okking paused, probably calling up the file on his screen to be certain. "All it says is that he was killed in a traffic accident. Made an illegal turn, was broadsided by a truck, the other driver wasn't charged. The kid had no identification, the vehicle he was driving was stolen. His body was kept in the morgue for a year, but no one claimed it. After that . . ."

"After that it was sold for scrap."

"I suppose you feel involved in this case, Marîd, but you're not. Finding that James Bond maniac is a police matter."

"Yeah, I know." I made a face; my mouth tasted like boiled fur.

"I'll keep you posted," said Okking. "Maybe I'll have some work for you."

"If I run into that moddy first, I'll wrap him up and drop him by your office."

"Sure, kid." Then there was a sharp click as Okking banged his phone down.

We're all one big, happy family. "Yeah, you right," I muttered to myself. I laid my head down on the pillow, but I knew I wasn't going back to sleep. I just stared at the peeling paint on the ceiling, hoping that I'd get through another week without it falling on me.

"Who was that? Okking?" murmured Yasmin. She was still turned away from me, curled up with her hands between her knees.

"Uh huh. You go back to sleep." She already *was* back to sleep. I scratched my head for a little while, hoping the tri-phets would hit before I gave in and got sick. I rolled off the mattress and stood up, feeling a pounding in my temples that hadn't been there a moment ago. After the friendly shakedown by Okking last night, I'd gone up the Street, knocking back drinks in one club after another. Somewhere along the line I must have run into Yasmin, because here she was. The proof was indisputable.

I dragged myself to the bathroom and stood under the shower until I ran out of hot water. The drugs still hadn't come on. I toweled myself mostly dry, debating whether to take another blue triangle or just blow off the whole day and go back to bed. I looked at myself in the mirror. I looked awful, but I always look awful in the mirror. I keep myself going with the firm belief that my real face is much better looking. I brushed my teeth and that took care of the terrible taste in my mouth. I started to brush my hair, but it seemed like too much effort, so I went back out into the other room and pulled on a clean shirt and my jeans.

It took me ten minutes to hunt down my boots. They were under Yasmin's clothes, for some reason. Now I was dressed. If only the god-damn *pills* would kick in, I could face the world. Don't talk to me about eating. I'd done that the day before yesterday.

I left Yasmin a note telling her to lock the door on her way out. Yasmin was one of the few people I trusted alone in my apartment. We always had a good time together, and I think we really cared about each other in some unspoken, fragile way. We were both afraid to push it, to test it, but we both knew it was there. I think it's because Yasmin hadn't been born a girl. Maybe spending half of your life one sex and half of your life the other does something to your perceptions. Of course, I knew lots of other sex-changes I couldn't get along with at all. Well, you just can't get away with generalizations. Not even to be kind.

Yasmin was fully modified, inside and out, body and mind. She had one of those perfect bodies, one of the ones you order out of a catalog. You sit down with the guy in the clinic and he shows you the book. You say, "How about these tits?" and he tells you how much, and you say, "This waist?" and he gives you an estimate for breaking your pelvic bones and resetting them, and you have your Adam's apple shaved down and you pick out your facial features and your ass and your legs. Sometimes you could even go for new eye color. They can help you with your hair, and the beard is a matter of drugs and one magical clinical procedure. You end up with a customized self, just like restoring an old gasoline automobile.

I looked across the room at Yasmin. Her long, straight, black hair— that's what I thought was her best asset, and she was born with it. It was hers all the way. There wasn't much else about her that was original equipment—even, when she was chipping in, her personality—but it all looked and functioned real nice. There was always something about a change, though, something that gave her away. The hands and feet, for instance; the clinics didn't want to touch them, there were too many bones. Female changes always had big feet, men's feet. And for some reason, they always had this slight nasal voice. I could always pick that up, even if nothing else told the T.

I thought I was an expert on reading people. What did I know? That's why I stuck myself out on a limb and handed down an ax to whoever felt like taking a whack.

Outside in the hall, the tri-phets finally flowered. It was like the whole world suddenly took a deep breath, expanding like a balloon. I caught my balance by grabbing at the railing, and then started downstairs. I didn't exactly know what I was going to do, but it was about time to start hustling up some money. The rent was coming due, and I didn't want to have to go to The Man to borrow it. I shoved my hands in my pockets and felt bills. Of course. The Russian had given me three big ones the night before. I took the money out and counted it; there was about twenty-eight hundred kiam left. Yasmin and I must have had some wild party on the other two hundred. I wished I remembered it.

When I hit the sidewalk, I was almost blinded by the sun. I don't function very well in the daytime. I shaded my eyes with a hand and looked up and down the street. No one else was about; the Budayeen hides from the light. I headed toward the Street with the vague idea of running a few errands. I could afford to run them now, I had money. I grinned; the drugs were pumping me up, and the twenty-eight hundred kiam lifted me the rest of the way. I had my rent made, all my expenses paid for the next three months or so. Time to lay in supplies: replenish the stock in the pill case, treat myself to a few luxury caps and tabs, pay off a couple of debts, buy a little food. The rest would go in the bank. I have a tendency to fritter away money if it sits around too long in my pocket. Better to salt it away, turn it into electronic credit. I don't allow myself to carry a credit charge-card—that way I can't bankrupt myself some night when I'm too loaded to know what I'm doing. I spend cash, or I don't spend at all. You can't fritter bytes, not without a card.

I turned toward the eastern gate when I got to the Street. The nearer I came to the wall the more people I saw—my neighbors going out into the city like me, tourists coming into the Budayeen during the slack time. The outsiders were just fooling themselves. They could get into just as much trouble in broad daylight.

There was a little barricade set up at the corner of Fourth Street, where the city was doing some street repair. I leaned against the posts to overhear the conversations of a couple of hustlers out for the early trade—or, if they hadn't yet made enough money to go home, it might still be last night for them. I'd listened to this stuff a million times before, but James Bond had got me pondering moddies, and so these negotiations took on a slightly new meaning today.

"Hello," said this short, thin mark. He was wearing European clothing, and he spoke Arabic like someone who had studied the language for three months in a school where no one, neither teacher nor pupils, had ever come within five thousand miles of a date palm.

The bint was taller than him by about a foot and a half, but give some of that to the black spike-heeled boots. She probably wasn't a real woman, but a change or a pre-op deb; but the guy didn't know or care. She was impressive. Hustlers in the Budayeen *have* to be impressive, just to be noticed. We don't have a lot of plain, mousy housewives living on the Street. She was dressed in a kind of short-skirted black frilly thing with no back or sleeves, lots of visibility down the front, cinched around the waist with a solid silver chain with a Roman Catholic rosary dangling from it. She wore dramatic purple and pink paints and a beautiful mass of auburn hair, artfully arranged to frame her face in defiance of all known laws of natural science. "Lookin' to go out?" she asked. When she spoke, I read her for someone who still had a masculine set of chromosomes in every one of her refurbished body's cells, whatever was beneath that skirt.

"Maybe," said the trick. He was playing it cagey.

"Lookin' for anybody special?"

The man licked his lips nervously. "I was hoping to find Ashla."

"Uh uh, baby, sorry. Lips, hips, or fingertips, I don't do no Ashla." She looked away for a second and spat. "You go by that girl, I think she got Ashla." She pointed to a deb I knew. The trick nodded his thanks and crossed the street. I accidentally caught the first whore's eyes. "Fuck, man," she said, laughing a little. Then she was watching the Street again, looking for lunch money. A couple of minutes later another man came up to her and had the same conversation. "Lookin' for anybody special?"

This guy, a little taller than the first and a lot heavier, said "Brigitte?" He sounded apologetic.

She dug in her black vinyl purse and brought out a plastic rack of moddies. A moddy is a lot bigger than a daddy, which usually just chips right into a socket on the side of the moddy you're using, or onto the cory plug in your skull if you're not wired for moddies or if you just feel like being yourself. The girl held a pink plastic moddy in one hand and put the rack back in her purse. "Here she go, your main woman. Brigitte, she be real popular, she get a lot of airplay. She cost you more."

"I know," said the trick. "How much?"

"You tell me," she said, thinking he might be a cop setting her up. That kind of thing still happened whenever the religious authorities ran out of infidels to persecute. "How much you got to spend?"

"Fifty?"

"For *Brigitte,* man?"

"A hundred?"

"An' fifteen for the room. You come with me, sugar." They walked off along Fourth Street. Ain't love grand.

I knew who Ashla was and who Brigitte was, but I wondered who all the other moddies in that rack might be. It wasn't worth a hundred kiam a throw to find out, though. Plus fifteen for the room. So this Titian-haired hustler goes off with her sweetheart and chips Brigitte in, and she *becomes* Brigitte, and she's everything he remembers her being; and it would always be the same, whoever used a Brigitte moddy, woman, deb, or sex-change.

I went through the eastern gate and I was halfway to the bank when I stopped suddenly in front of a jewelry store. Something was gnawing at the edge of my mind. There was some idea trying to burst its way into my consciousness. It was an uncomfortable, ticklish feeling; there didn't seem to be any way to help it, either. Maybe it was only the tri-phets I'd taken; I can get pretty carried away with meaningless thoughts when I'm humming like that. But no, it was more than just drug inspiration. There was something about Bogatyrev's murder or the conversation I'd had on the phone with Okking. There was something wrong.

I thought over as much of that business as I could remember. Nothing stood out in my memory as unusual; Okking's bit had been a brush-off, I realized, but it was just the standard cop brush-off: "Look, this is a matter for the police, we don't need you sticking your nose into it, you had a job last night but it blew up in your face, so thank you very much." I've heard the same line from Okking before, a hundred times. So why did it feel so wonky today?

I shook my head. If there was something to it, I'd figure it out. I filed it away in my backbrain; it would stew there and either boil away into nothing or simmer down into a cold, hard fact that I could use. Until then, I didn't want to bother about it. I wanted to enjoy the warmth and strength and confidence I was getting from the drugs. I'd pay for that when I crashed, so I wanted to get my money's worth.

Maybe ten minutes later, just as I was getting to the bank's sidewalk teller terminals, my phone rang again. I plucked it off my belt. "Yeah?" I said.

"Marîd? This is Nikki." Nikki was a crazy change, worked as a whore for one of Friedlander Bey's jackals. About a year ago I had been pretty friendly with her, but she was just too much trouble. When you were with her, you had to keep track of the pills and the drinks she was taking; one too many and Nikki got belligerent and completely incoherent. Every time we went out, it ended up in a brawl. Before her modifications, Nikki had been a tall, muscular male, I guess—stronger than I am. Even after the sex change, she was still impossible to handle in a fight. Trying to drag her off the people she imagined had insulted her was an ordeal. Getting her calmed down and safely home was exhausting. Finally I decided that I liked her when she was straight, but the rest of it just wasn't worth it. I saw her now and then, said hello and gossiped, but I didn't want to wade into any more of her drunken, screaming, senseless conflicts.

"Say, Nikki, where you at?"

"Marîd, baby, can I see you today? I really need you to do me a favor."

Here we go, I thought. "Sure, I guess. What's up?"

There was a short pause while she thought about how she was going to phrase this. "I don't want to work for Abdoulaye anymore." That was the name of Friedlander Bey's bottleholder. Abdoulaye had about a dozen girls and boys on wires all around the Budayeen.

"Easy enough," I said. I've done this kind of work a lot, picking up a few extra kiam now and then. I've got a good relationship with Friedlander Bey—within the walls we all called him Papa; he practically owned the Budayeen, and had the rest of the city in his pocket, as well. I always kept my word, which was a valuable recommendation to someone like Bey. Papa was an old-timer. The rumor was that he might be as much as two hundred years old, and now and then I could believe it. He had an archaic sense of what was honor and what was business and what was loyalty. He dispensed favors and punishments like an ancient idea of God. He owned many of the clubs, whorehouses, and cookshops in the Budayeen, but he didn't discourage competition. It was all right with him if some independent wanted to work the same side of the street. Papa operated on the understanding that he wouldn't bother you if you didn't bother him; however, Papa offered all kinds of attractive inducements. An awful lot of free agents ended up working for him after all, because they couldn't get those particular benefits for themselves. He didn't just *have* connections; Papa *was* connections.

The motto of the Budayeen was "Business is business." Anything that hurt the free agents eventually hurt Friedlander Bey. There was enough to go around for everybody; it might have been different if Papa had been the greedy type. He once told me that he used to be that way, but after a hundred and fifty or sixty years, you stop wanting. That was about the saddest thing anyone ever said to me.

I heard Nikki take a deep breath. "Thanks, Marîd. You know where I'm staying?"

I didn't pay that much attention to her comings and goings anymore. "No, where?"

"I'm staying by Tamiko for a little while."

Great, I thought, just great. Tamiko was one of the Black Widow Sisters. "On Thirteenth Street?"

"Yeah."

"I know. How about if I come by, say, two o'clock?"

Nikki hesitated. "Can you make it one? I've got something else I need to do."

It was an imposition, but I was feeling generous; it must have been the blue triangles. For old times' sake I said, "All right, I'll be there about one, *inshallah.*"

"You're sweet, Marîd. I'll see you then. Salaam." She cut the connection.

I hung the phone on my belt. It didn't feel, at that moment, like I was getting into something over my head. It never does, before you take the leap.

Three

It was twelve forty-five when I found the apartment building on Thirteenth Street. It was an old two-story house, broken up into separate flats. I glanced up at Tamiko's balcony overlooking the street. There was a waist-high iron railing on three sides, and in the corners were lacy iron columns twined with ivy, reaching up toward the overhanging roof. From an open window I could hear her damn koto music. Electronic koto music, from a synthesizer. The shrieking, high-pitched singing that accompanied it gave me chills. It might have been a synthetic voice, it might have been Tami. Did I tell you that Nikki was a little crazy? Well, next to Tami, Nikki was just a cuddly little white bunny. Tamiko'd had one of her salivary glands replaced with a plastic sac full of some high-velocity toxin. A plastic duct led the poison down through an artificial tooth. The toxin was harmless if swallowed, but loose in the bloodstream, it was horribly, painfully lethal. Tamiko could uncap that tooth anytime she needed to—or wanted to. That's why they called her and her friends the Black Widow Sisters.

I punched the button by Tami's name, but no one responded. I rapped on the small pane of Plexiglas set into the door. Finally I stepped into the street and shouted. I saw Nikki's head pop out of the window. "I'll be right down," she called. She couldn't hear anything over that koto music. I've never met anybody else who could even *stand* koto music. Tamiko was just bughouse nuts.

The door opened a little, and Nikki looked out at me. "Listen," she said worriedly, "Tami's in kind of a bad mood. She's a little loaded, too. Just don't do or say anything to set her off."

I asked myself if I really wanted to go through with this, after all. I didn't really need Nikki's hundred kiam that much. Still, I'd promised her, so I nodded and followed her up the stairs to the apartment.

Tami was sprawled on a heap of brightly patterned pillows, with her head propped against one of the speakers of her holo system. If that music had sounded loud down in the street, I was now learning what "loud" meant. The music must have been throbbing in Tami's skull like the world's worst migraine, but she didn't seem to mind. It must have been throbbing in time to whatever drug she had in her. Her eyes were half-closed and she was slowly nodding. Her face was painted white, as stark white as a geisha's, but her lips and eyelids were flat black. She looked like the avenging specter of a murdered Kabuki character.

"Nikki," I said. She didn't hear me. I had to walk right up next to her and shout into her ear. "Why don't we get out of here, where we can talk?" Tamiko was burning some kind of incense, and the air was thick with its overwhelming sweet scent. I really wanted some fresh air.

Nikki shook her head and pointed to Tami. "She won't let me go."

"Why not?"

"She thinks she's protecting me."

"From what?"

Nikki shrugged. "Ask *her*."

As I watched, Tami canted over alarmingly and toppled in slow motion, until her white-daubed cheek was pressed against the bare, dark-varnished wood of the floor. "It's a good thing you can take care of yourself, Nikki."

She laughed weakly. "Yeah, I guess so. Look, Marîd, thanks for coming over."

"No problem," I said. I sat in an armchair and looked at her. Nikki was an exotic in a city of exotics: her long, pale blond hair fell to the small of her back. Her skin was the color of young ivory, almost as white as the paint on Tami's face. Her eyes were unnaturally blue, however, and glittered with a flickering hint of madness. The delicacy of her facial features contrasted disconcertingly with the bulk and strength of her frame. It was a common enough error; people chose surgical modifications that they admired in others, not realizing that the changes might look out of place in the context of their own bodies. I glanced at Tami's inert form. She wore the emblem of the Black Widow Sisters: immense, incredible breast implants. Tami's bust probably measured fifty-five or sixty inches. It was funny to see the stunned expression on a tourist's face when he accidentally bumped into one of the Sisters. It was funny unless you thought a little about what was likely to happen.

"I just don't want to work for Abdoulaye anymore," said Nikki, watching her fingers twist a lock of her champagne-colored hair.

"I can understand that. I'll call and arrange a meeting with Hassan. You know Hassan the Shiite? Papa's mouthpiece? That's who we have to deal with."

Nikki shook her head. Her bright gaze flicked about the room. She was worried. "Will it be dangerous or anything?" she asked.

I smiled. "Not a chance," I said. "There'll be a table set up, and I'll sit on one side with you, and Abdoulaye will sit on the other. Hassan sits between us. I present your side of the story, Abdoulaye gives his, and Hassan thinks about it. Then he makes his judgment. Usually you have to make some kind of payment to Abdoulaye. Hassan will name the figure. You'll have to grease Hassan a little afterward, and we ought to bring some kind of gift for Papa. That helps."

Nikki didn't look reassured. She stood up and tucked her black T-shirt into her tight black jeans. "You don't know Abdoulaye," she said.

"You bet your ass I do," I said. I probably knew him better than she did. I got up and crossed the room to Tami's Telefunken holo. With a stiff forefinger I silenced the koto music. Peace flooded in; the world thanked me. Tamiko moaned in her sleep.

"What if he doesn't keep his part of the agreement? What if he comes after me and forces me to go back to work for him? He likes to beat up girls, Marîd. He likes that a lot."

"I know all about him. But he has the same respect for Friedlander Bey's influence that everyone else does. He won't dare cross Hassan's decision. And you better not, either. If you skip out without paying, Papa will send his thugs after you. You'll be back to work for sure, then. After you heal."

Nikki shuddered. "Has anybody ever skipped out on you?" she asked.

I frowned. It had happened just one time: I remembered the situation all too well. It had been the last time I'd ever been in love. "Yeah," I said.

"What did Papa and Hassan do?"

It was a lousy memory, and I didn't like calling it up. "Well, because I represented her, I was responsible for the payment. I had to come up with thirty-two hundred kiam. I was stone broke, but believe me, I got the money. I had to do a lot of crazy, dangerous things to get it, but I owed it to Papa because of what this girl did. Papa likes to be paid quickly. Papa doesn't have a lot of patience at times like that."

"I know," said Nikki. "What happened to the girl?"

It took me a few seconds to get the words out. "They found out where she'd split to. It wasn't difficult for them to trace her. They brought her back with her legs fractured in three places each, and her face was ruined. They put her to work in one of their filthiest whore-houses. She could earn only one or two hundred kiam a week in a place like that, and they let her keep maybe ten or fifteen. She's still saving up to get her face fixed."

Nikki couldn't say anything for a long time. I let her think about what I told her. Thinking about it would be good for her.

"Can you call to make the appointment now?" she asked at last.

"Sure," I said. "Is next Monday soon enough?"

Her eyes widened. "Can't we do it tonight? I need to get it finished tonight."

"What's your hurry, Nikki? Going somewhere?"

She gave me a sharp look. Her mouth opened and closed. "No," she said, her voice shaky.

"You can't just set up appointments with Hassan whenever you want."

"Try, Marîd. Can't you just call him and try?"

I made a little gesture of surrender. "I'll call. I'll ask. But Hassan will make the appointment at his convenience."

Nikki nodded. "Sure," she said.

I unclipped my phone and unfolded it. I didn't have to ask Info for Hassan's commcode. The phone rang once and was answered by one of Hassan's stooges. I told him who I was and what I wanted, and I was told to wait; they always tell you to wait, and you *wait*. I sat there, watching Nikki twisting her hair, watching Tamiko breathing slowly, listening to her snoring softly on the floor. Tamiko was wearing a light cotton kimono, dyed matte black. She never wore any kind of jewelry or ornament. With the kimono, her ornately arranged black hair, her sur-gically altered eyelids, and the painted face, she looked like an assassin-geisha, which is what she was, I guess. Tamiko looked very convincing, with the epicanthic folds and all, for someone who hadn't been born an Oriental.

A quarter of an hour later, with Nikki fidgeting nervously around the apartment, the stooge spoke into my ear. We had an appointment for that evening, just after sunset prayers. I didn't bother to thank Has-san's flunky; I have a certain amount of pride, after all. I clipped the phone back on my belt. "I'll come by and get you about seven-thirty," I said to Nikki.

I got that nervous eye-flick again. "Can't I meet you there?" she asked.

I let my shoulders sag. "Why not? You know where?"

"Hassan's shop?"

"You go straight back through the curtain. There's a storeroom behind there. Go through the storeroom, through the back door into the alley. You'll see an iron door in the opposite wall. It'll be locked, but they'll be expecting you. You won't have to knock. Get there on *time*, Nikki."

"I will. And thanks, Marîd."

"The hell with thanks. I want my hundred kiam now."

She looked startled. Maybe I'd sounded a little too tough; too bad. "Can't I give it to you after—"

"*Now*, Nikki."

She took some money out of her hip pocket and counted off a hundred. "Here." There was a new coldness between us.

"Give me another twenty for Papa's little gift. And you're responsible for Hassan's *baksheesh*, too. I'll see you tonight." And then I got out of that place before the rampant craziness began to seep into *my* skull.

I went home. I hadn't slept enough, I had a splitting headache, and the edge of the tri-phet glow had disappeared somewhere in the summer afternoon. Yasmin was still asleep, and I climbed onto the mattress next to her. The drugs wouldn't let me nap, but I really wanted to have a little peace and quiet with my eyes shut. I should have known better; as soon as I relaxed, the tri-phets began thrumming in my head louder than ever. Behind my closed eyelids, the red darkness began to flash like a strobe light. I felt dizzy; then I imagined patterns of blue and dark green, swirling like microscopic creatures in a drop of water. I opened my eyes again to get rid of the strobing. I felt involuntary twitches in my calf muscles, in my hand, in my cheek. I was strung tighter than I thought: no rest for the wicked.

I stood up again and crumpled the note I'd left for Yasmin. "I thought you wanted to go out today," she said sleepily.

I turned around. "I did go out. Hours ago."

"What time is it?"

"About three o'clock."

"*Yaa salaam!* I'm supposed to be at work at three today!"

I sighed. Yasmin was famous all over the Budayeen for being late for just about everything. Frenchy Benoit, the owner of the club where Yasmin worked, fined her fifty kiam if she came in even a minute late. That didn't get Yasmin to move her pretty little ass; she took her sweet old time, paid Frenchy the fifty nearly every day, and made it back in drinks and tips the first hour. I've never seen anyone who could separate a sucker from his money so fast. Yasmin worked hard, she wasn't lazy. She just loved to sleep. She would have made a great lizard, basking on a hot rock in the sun.

It took her five minutes to leap out of bed and get dressed. I got an abstract kiss that landed off-center, and she was going out the door, digging in her purse for the module she'd use at work. She called something over her shoulder in her barbaric Levantine accent.

Then I was alone. I was pleased with the turn my fortunes had taken. I hadn't been this flush in many months. As I was wondering if there was something I wanted, something I could blow my sudden wealth on, the image of Bogatyrev's bloodstained blouse superimposed itself over the spare, shabby furnishings of my apartment. Was I feeling guilty? Me? The man who walked through the world untouched by its corruption and its crude temptations. I was the man without desire, the man without fear. I was a catalyst, a human agent of change. Catalysts caused change, but in the end they remained unchanged themselves. I helped those who needed help and had no other friends. I participated in the action, but was never stung. I observed, but kept my own secrets. That's how I always thought of myself. That's how I set myself up to get hurt.

In the Budayeen—hell, in the whole world, probably—there are only two kinds of people: hustlers and marks. You're one or the other. You can't act nice and smile and tell everybody that you're just going to sit on the sidelines. Hustler or mark or sometimes a little of each. When you stepped through the eastern gate, before you'd taken ten steps up the Street, you were permanently cast as one or the other. Hustler or mark. There was no third choice, but I was going to have to learn that the hard way. As usual.

I wasn't hungry, but I forced myself to scramble some eggs. I ought to pay more attention to my diet, I know that, but it's just too much trouble. Sometimes the only vitamins I get are in the lime slices in my gimlets. It was going to be a long, hard night, and I was going to need all my resources. The three blue triangles would be wearing off before my meeting with Hassan and Abdoulaye; in fact, it figured that I'd show up at my absolute worst: depressed, exhausted, in no shape at all to represent Nikki. The answer was stunningly obvious: *more* blue triangles. They'd boost me back up. I'd be operating at superhuman speed, with computer precision and a prescient knowledge of the rightness of things. Synchronicity, man. Tapped into the Moment, the Now, the convergence of time and space and life and the holy fuckin' tide in the affairs of men. At least, it would seem that way to me; and across the table from Abdoulaye, putting up a good front was every bit as good as the real thing. I would be mentally alert and morally straight, and that son of a bitch Abdoulaye would *know* I hadn't shown up just to get my ass kicked. These were the persuasive arguments I gave as I crossed my crummy room and hunted for my pill case.

Two more tri-phets? Three, to be on the safe side? Or would that wind me too tight? I didn't want to go spanging off the wall like a snapping guitar string. I swallowed two, pocketed the third just in case.

Man, tomorrow was going to be one godawful scurvy day. Better Living Through Chemistry didn't mind lending me the extra energy up front, in the form of pretty pastel pills; but, to use one of Chiriga's favorite phrases, paybacks are a bitch. If I managed to survive the stupifying crash that was coming due, it would be an occasion for general rejoicing all around the throne of Allah.

The pace picked up again in about half an hour. I showered, washed my hair, trimmed my beard, shaved the little places on my cheeks and neck where I don't want the beard, brushed my teeth, washed out the sink and the tub, walked naked through my apartment searching for other things to clean or rearrange or straighten up—and then I caught myself. "Hold on, kid," I muttered. It was good that I took the two extra bangers so early; I'd settle down before it was time to leave.

Time passed slowly. I thought of calling Nikki to remind her to get going, but that was pointless. I thought of calling Yasmin or Chiri, but they were at work now, anyway. I sat back against the wall and shivered, almost in tears: Jesus, I really *didn't* have any friends. I wished I had a holo system like Tamiko's; it would have killed some time. I've seen some holoporn that made the real thing seem fetid and diseased.

At seven-thirty I dressed: an old, faded blue shirt, my jeans, and my boots. I couldn't have looked pretty for Hassan if I'd wanted to. As I was leaving my building, I heard the crackle of static, and the amplified voice of the muezzin cried *"laa 'illaha 'illallaahu"*—it is a beautiful sound, that call to prayer, alliterative and moving even to a blaspheming dog of an unbeliever like myself. I hurried through the empty streets; hustlers stopped their hustling for prayer, marks overcame their cullibility for prayer. My footsteps echoed on the ancient cobblestones like accusations. By the time I reached Hassan's shop, everything had returned to normal. Until the final, evening call to prayer, the hustlers and the marks could return to their rock 'n' roll of commerce and mutual exploitation.

Minding Hassan's shop at that hour was a young, slender American boy everyone called Abdul-Hassan. Abdul means "the slave of," and is usually rounded out with one of the ninety-nine names of God. In this case, the irony was that the American boy was Hassan's, in every respect you could think of except, perhaps, genetically. The word around the Street was that Abdul-Hassan had not been born a boy, in exactly the same way that Yasmin had not been born a girl; but no one I knew had the time or the inclination to launch a full-scale investigation.

Abdul-Hassan asked me something in English. It was a mystery to the casual bargain hunter just what Hassan's shop dealt in. That was because it was virtually empty; Hassan's shop dealt in everything, and so there was no vital reason to display anything. I couldn't understand English, so I just jerked my thumb toward the stained, block-printed curtain. The boy nodded and went back to his daydreaming.

I passed through the curtain, the storeroom, and the alley. Just as I came to the iron door, it swung outward almost silently. "Open sesame," I whispered. Then I stepped into a dimly lighted room and looked around. The drugs made me forget to be afraid. They made me forget to be cautious, too; but my instincts are my livelihood, and my instincts are firing away morning and evening, drugs or no drugs. Hassan reclined on a small mountain of cushions, puffing on a narjîlah. I smelled the tang of hashish; the burbling of Hassan's water pipe was the only sound in the room. Nikki sat stiffly on the edge of a rug, evidently terrified, with a cup of tea in front of her crossed legs. Abdoulaye rested on a few cushions, whispering into Hassan's ear. Hassan's expression was as empty as a handful of wind. This was his tea party; I stood and waited for him to speak.

"Ahlan wa sahlan!" he said, smiling briefly. It was a formal greeting, meaning something like "you have come to your people and level ground." It was intended to set the tone for the rest of this parley. I gave the proper response, and was invited to be seated. I sat beside Nikki; I noticed that she was wearing a single add-on in the midst of her pale blond hair. It must have been an Arabic-language daddy, because I knew she couldn't understand a word of it without one. I accepted a small cup of coffee, heavily spiced with cardamom. I raised the cup to Hassan and said, "May your table last forever."

Hassan wafted a hand in the air and said, "May Allah lengthen your life." Then I was given another cup of coffee. I nudged Nikki, who had not drunk her tea. You just can't expect business to start immediately, not until you'd drunk at least three cups of coffee. If you declined sooner, you risked insulting your host. All the while the coffee- and tea-drinking was going on, Hassan and I asked after the health of the other's family and friends, and called on Allah to bless this one and that one and protect all of us and the whole Muslim world from the depredations of the infidel.

I murmured under my breath to Nikki to keep downing the odd-tasting tea. Her presence here was distasteful to Hassan for two reasons: she was a prostitute, and she wasn't a real woman. The Muslims have never made up their minds about that. They treated their women as second-class citizens, but they weren't exactly sure what to do with men who became women. The Qur'ân evidently makes no provisions for such things. The fact that I myself wasn't exactly a devotee of the Book in which there is no doubt didn't help matters. So Hassan and I kept drinking and nodding and smiling and praising Allah and trading pleasantries tit for tat, like a tennis match. The most frequent expression in the Muslim world is *inshallah*, if God wills. It removes all guilt: blame it on Allah. If the oasis dries up and blows away, it was Allah's will. If you get caught sleeping with your brother's wife, it was Allah's will. Getting your hand or your cock or your head chopped off in reprisal is Allah's will, too. Nothing much gets done in the Budayeen without discussing how Allah is going to feel about it.

The better part of an hour passed this way, and I could tell that both Nikki and Abdoulaye were getting antsy. I was doing fine. Hassan was smiling broader every minute; he was inhaling hashish in heroic quantities.

At last, Abdoulaye couldn't stand it any longer. He wanted the conversation to get around to money. Specifically, how much Nikki was going to have to pay him for her freedom.

Hassan wasn't pleased by this impatience. He raised his hands and looked wearily heavenward, reciting an Arab proverb that meant "Greed lessens what is gathered." It was a ludicrous statement, coming from Hassan. He looked at Abdoulaye. "You have been this young woman's protector?" he asked. There are many ways of expressing "young woman" in this ancient language, each with its own subtle undertone and shade of meaning. Hassan's careful choice was *il-mahroosa*, your daughter. The literal meaning of *il-mahroosa* is "the guarded one," and seemed to fit the situation nicely. That's how Hassan got to be Papa's ace strongarm, by threading his way unerringly between the demands of culture and the necessities of the moment.

"Yes, O Wise One," replied Abdoulaye. "For more than two years."

"And she displeases you?"

Abdoulaye's forehead wrinkled up. "No, O Wise One."

"And she has not harmed you in any way?"

"No."

Hassan turned to me; Nikki was beneath his notice. "The guarded one wishes to live in peace? She plots no malice against Abdoulaye Abu-Zayd?"

"I swear this is true," I said.

Hassan's eyes narrowed. "Your oaths mean nothing here, unbeliever. We must leave aside the honor of men, and make a contract of words and silver."

"Those who hear your words, live," I said.

Hassan nodded, pleased by my manners, if by nothing else about me or Nikki. "In the name of Allah, the Beneficent, the Merciful," declared Hassan, his hands raised, palms upward, "I render now my judgment. Let all who are present hear and obey. The guarded one shall return all jewelry and ornaments given to her by Abdoulaye. She shall return all gifts of value. She shall return all costly clothing, keeping for herself only that clothing seemly for daily attire. On his part, Abdoulaye Abu-Zayd must promise to let the guarded one pass about her business unhindered. If some dispute arises in this, I shall decide." He glared from one to the other, making it clear that there would be no dispute. Abdoulaye nodded, Nikki looked unhappy. "Further, the guarded one shall pay unto Abdoulaye Abu-Zayd the sum of three thousand kiam before noon prayer tomorrow. This is my word, Allah is Most Great."

Abdoulaye grinned. "May you be healthy and happy!" he cried.

Hassan sighed. "Inshallah," he murmured, fitting the mouthpiece of the narjîlah between his teeth again.

I was forced by convention to thank Hassan, too, although he'd stung Nikki pretty badly. "I am obliged to you," I said, standing and dragging Nikki to her feet. Hassan waved a hand, as if shooing a buzzing fly out of his presence. As we passed through the iron door, Nikki turned and spat.

She shouted the worst insults her add-on could supply: "Himmar oo ibn-himmar! Ibn wushka! Yil'an 'abook!" I grabbed her more firmly and we ran. Behind us came the laughter of Abdoulaye and Hassan. They'd hustled their share for the evening and were feeling generous, letting Nikki escape unpunished for her obscenities.

When we got back to the Street, I slowed down, out of breath. "I need a drink," I said, leading her into the Silver Palm.

"Bastards," Nikki growled.

"Don't you have the three thousand?"

"I've got it. I just don't want to give it to them, that's all. I had other plans for it."

I shrugged. "If you want to get out from under Abdoulaye bad enough . . ."

"Yeah, I know." She still didn't look happy about it.

"Everything will be all right," I told her, steering her through the dark, cool bar.

Nikki's eyes opened wide, she threw up her hands. "Everything will be all right," she said, laughing. *"Inshallah."* Her mockery of Hassan sounded hollow. She tore off the Arabic daddy. That's about the last I remember of that night.

four

You know what a hangover is. You know about the pounding headache, the vague and persistent sick stomach, the feeling that you'd just rather lose consciousness entirely until the hangover went away. But do you know what a massive hypnotic-drug hangover is like? You feel as if you're in somebody else's dream; you don't feel real. You tell yourself, "I'm not actually going through all this now; this happened to me years and years ago, and I'm just remembering it." Every few seconds you realize that you *are* going through it, that you *are* here and now, and the dissonance starts a cycle of anxiety and an even greater feeling of unreality. Sometimes you're not sure where your arms and legs are. You feel like someone carved you out of a block of wood during the night, and if you behave, someday you'll be a real boy. "Thought" and "motion" are foreign concepts; they are attributes of *living* people. Add all *that* on top of a booze hangover, and throw in the abysmal depression, bone-breaking fatigue, more nausea, more anxiety, tremors, and cramps that I owed from all the tri-phets I'd taken the day before. That's how I felt when they woke me up at dawn. Death warmed over—ha! I hadn't been warmed over at all.

Dawn, yet. The loud banging on my door started just as the muezzin was crying, "Come to prayer, come to prayer. Prayer is better than sleep. Allah is Most Great!" I might have laughed at the "prayer is better than sleep" part, if I'd been able. I rolled over and faced the cracked green wall. I regretted that simple action immediately; it had felt like a slow-motion film with every other frame missing. The universe had begun to stutter around me.

The banging on the door wouldn't go away. After a few moments, I realized that there were several fists trying to slam their way in.

"Yeah, wait a minute," I called. I crawled slowly out of bed, trying not to jar any part of my body that might still be alive. I made it to the floor and rose up very slowly. I stood there and wobbled a little, waiting to feel real. When I didn't, I decided to go to the door anyway. I was halfway there when I realized I was naked. I stopped. All this decision-making was getting on my nerves. Should I go back to the bed and throw on some clothes? Angry shouts joined the pounding fists. The hell with the clothes, I thought.

I opened the door and saw the most frightening sight since some hero or other had to face Medusa and the other two Gorgons. The three monsters that confronted me were the Black Widow Sisters, Tamiko, Devi, and Selima. They all had their preposterous breasts crammed into thin black pullovers; they were wearing tight black leather skirts and black spike-heeled shoes; their working outfits. My sluggish mind wondered why they were dressed for work so early. Dawn. I don't ever see dawn, unless I'm coming at it from the other side, going to bed after the sun rises. I supposed the sisters hadn't been to—

Devi, the refugee from Calcutta, shoved me backward into my room. The other two followed, slamming the door. Selima—Arabic for "peace"—turned, drew her right arm up and, snarling, jabbed the hard point of her elbow up into my gut just below my breastbone. All the air was forced out of my lungs, and I collapsed to my knees, gasping. Someone's foot kicked my jaw viciously, and I went over backward. Then one of them picked me up and the other two worked me over, slowly and carefully, not missing a single tender and unprotected spot. I had been dazed to begin with; after a few deft and punishing blows, I lost all track of what was happening. I hung limply in someone's grasp, almost grateful that this wasn't really happening to me, that it was some terrible nightmare that I was merely remembering, safely in the future.

I don't know how long they beat me. When I came to, it was eleven o'clock. I just lay on the floor and breathed; some ribs must have been cracked, because even breathing caused agony. I tried to order my thoughts—at least the drug hangover had abated a little. My pill case. Got to find my pill case. Why can't I ever find my damn pill case? I crawled very slowly to the bed. The Black Widow Sisters had been thorough and efficient; I learned that with every movement. I was badly bruised almost everywhere, but they hadn't shed a drop of blood. It occurred to me that if they'd wanted to kill me, one playful nip would have done the job. This was all supposed to mean something. I'd have to ask them about it the next time I saw them.

I hauled myself onto the bed and across the mattress to my clothes.

My pill case was in my jeans, where it usually was. I opened it, knowing I had some escape-velocity painkillers in there. I saw that my entire stash of beauties—butaqualide HCI—was gone. They were illegal as hell all over and just as plentiful. I'd had at least eight. I must have taken a handful to get me to sleep over the screaming tri-phets; Nikki must have taken the rest. I didn't care about them now. I wanted *opiates*, any and all opiates, *fast*. I had seven tabs of Sonneine. When I got them down, it would be like the sun breaking through the gloomy clouds. I would bask in a buzzy, warm respite, an illusion of well-being rushing to every hurt and damaged part of my body. The notion of crawling to the bathroom for a glass of water was too ridiculous to consider. I summoned both spit and courage, and downed the chalky sunnies, one by one. They'd take twenty minutes or so to hit, but the anticipation was enough to ease the throbbing torment just a little.

Before the sunnies ignited, there was a knock on my door. I made a little, involuntary cry of alarm. I didn't move. The knock, polite but firm, came again. *"Yaa shabb,"* called a voice. It was Hassan. I closed my eyes and wished I believed in something enough to pray to it.

"A minute," I said. I couldn't shout. "Let me get dressed." Hassan had used a more-or-less friendly form of address, but that didn't mean a damn thing. I made it to the door as quickly as I could, wearing only my jeans. I opened the door and saw that Abdoulaye was with Hassan. Bad news. I invited them in. *"Bismillah,"* I said, asking them to enter in God's name. It was a formality only, and Hassan ignored it.

"Abdoulaye Abu-Zayd is owed three thousand kiam," he said simply, spreading his hands.

"Nikki owes it. Go bother *her*. I'm in no mood for any of your greasy nattering."

It was probably the wrong thing to say. Hassan's face clouded like the western sky in a simoom. "The guarded one has fled," he said flatly. "You are her representative. You are responsible for the fee."

Nikki? I couldn't believe that Nikki'd do this to me. "It isn't noon yet," I said. It was a lame maneuver, but it was all I could think of.

Hassan nodded. "We will make ourselves comfortable." They sat on my mattress and stared at me with fierce eyes and voracious expressions I didn't like at all.

What was I going to do? I thought of calling Nikki, but that was pointless; Hassan and Abdoulaye had certainly already visited the building on Thirteenth Street. Then I realized that Nikki's disappearance and the working-over I'd gotten from the Sisters were very likely related in some way. Nikki was their pet. It made some sort of sense, but not to me, not yet. All right, I thought, it looked as if I was going to have to come across with Abdoulaye's money, and wring it out of Nikki when I caught up with her. "Listen, Hassan," I said, wetting my swollen split lips, "I can give you maybe twenty-five hundred. That's all I have in the bank right now. I'll pay the other five hundred tomorrow. That's the best I can do."

Hassan and Abdoulaye exchanged glances. "You will pay me the twenty-five hundred today," said Abdoulaye, "and another *thousand* tomorrow." Another exchange of glances. "I correct myself: another *fifteen hundred* tomorrow." I got it. Five hundred to repay Abdoulaye, five hundred juice to him, and five hundred juice to Hassan.

I nodded sullenly. I had no choice at all. Suddenly, all my pain and anger were focused on Nikki. I couldn't wait to run into her. I didn't care if it was in front of the Shimaal Mosque, I was going to put her through every copper fiq's worth of hell she'd caused me, with the Black Widow Sisters and these two fat bastards.

"You seem to be in some discomfort," said Hassan pleasantly. "We will accompany you to your bank machine. We will use my car."

I looked at him a long time, wishing there was some way I could excise that condescending smile from his face. Finally I just said, "I am quite unable to express my thanks."

Hassan gave me his negligent wave of the hand. "No thanks are needed when one performs a duty. Allah is Most Great."

"Praise be to Allah," said Abdoulaye.

"Yeah, you right," I said. We left my apartment, Hassan pressed close against my left shoulder, Abdoulaye close against my right.

Abdoulaye sat in the front, beside Hassan's driver. I sat in the back with Hassan, my eyes closed, my head pressed back against the genuine leather upholstery. I'd never in my life before been in such a car, and at that moment I couldn't care less. The pain was grinding and growing. I felt droplets of sweat run slowly down my forehead. I must have groaned. "When we have concluded our transaction," Hassan murmured, "we must see to your health."

I rode the rest of the way to the bank wordlessly, without a thought. Halfway there the sunnies came on, and suddenly I was able to breathe comfortably and shift my weight a little. The rush kept coming until I thought I was going to faint, and then it settled into a wonderful, lambent aura of promise. I barely heard Hassan when we arrived at the teller machine. I used my card, checked my balance, and withdrew twenty-five hundred and fifty kiam. That left me with a grand total of six kiam in my account. I handed the twenty-five big ones to Abdoulaye.

"Fifteen hundred more, tomorrow," he said.

"*Inshallah*," I said mockingly.

Abdoulaye raised a hand to strike me, but Hassan caught it and restrained him. Hassan muttered a few words to Abdoulaye, but I couldn't make them out. I shoved the remaining fifty in my pocket, and realized that I had no other money with me. I should have had *some*— the money I'd had the day before plus Nikki's hundred, less whatever I'd spent last night. Maybe Nikki had clipped it, or one of the Black Widow Sisters. It didn't make any difference. Hassan and Abdoulaye were having some sort of whispered consultation. Finally Abdoulaye touched his forehead, his lips, and his chest, and walked away. Hassan grasped my elbow and led me back into his luxurious, glossy black automobile. I tried to speak; it took a moment. "Where?" I asked. My voice sounded strange, hoarse, as if I hadn't used it in decades.

"I will take you to the hospital," said Hassan. "If you will forgive me, I must leave you there. I have pressing obligations. Business is business."

"Action is action," I said.

Hassan smiled. I don't think he bore me any personal animosity. *"Salaamtak,"* he said. He was wishing me peace.

"Allah yisallimak," I replied. I climbed out of the car at the charity hospital, and went to the emergency clinic. I had to show my identification and wait until they called up my records from their computer memory. I took a seat on a gray steel folding chair with a printed copy of my records on my lap, and waited for my name to be called. I waited eleven hours; the sunnies faded after ninety minutes. The rest of the time was a delirious hell. I sat in a huge room filled with sick and wounded people, all poor, all suffering. The wail of pain and the shrieks of babies never ended. The air reeked of tobacco smoke, the stink of bodies, of blood and vomit and urine. A harried doctor saw me at last, muttered to himself as he examined me, asked me no questions at all, taped my ribs, wrote out a prescription, and ordered me away.

It was too late to get the scrip filled at a pharmacy, but I knew I could score some expensive drugs on the Street. It was now about two in the morning; the action would be strong. I had to limp all the way back to the Budayeen, but my rage at Nikki fueled me. I had a score to settle with Tami and her friends, too.

When I got to Chiriga's club, it was half-empty and oddly quiet. The girls and debs sat listlessly; the customers stared into their beers. The music was blaring as loud as usual, of course, and Chiri's own voice cut through that noise with her shrill Swahili accent. But laughter was missing, the undercurrent of double-edged conversations. There was no action. The bar smelled of stale sweat, spilled beer, whiskey, and hashish.

"Marîd," said Chiri when she saw me. She looked tired. It had evidently been a long, slow night with little money in it for anybody.

"Let me buy you a drink," I said. "You look like you could use one." She managed a tired smile. "When have I ever said no to that?"

"Never that I can recall," I said.

"Never will, either." She turned and poured herself a drink out of a special bottle she kept under the bar.

"What's that?" I asked.

"Tende. An East African speciality."

I hesitated. "Let me have one of those."

Chiri's expression became very mock-serious. "Tende no good for white bwana. Knock white bwana on his mgongo."

"It's been a long, rotten day for me, too, Chiri," I said. I handed her a ten-kiam note.

She looked sympathetic. She poured me some tende, and raised her glass in a toast. *"Kwa siha yako,"* she said in Swahili.

I picked up my drink. *"Sahtayn,"* I said in Arabic. I tasted the tende. My eyebrows went up. It tasted fiery and unpleasant; still I knew that if I worked at it, I could develop a taste for it. I drained the glass.

Chiri shook her head. "This nigger girl scared for white bwana. Wait for white bwana to throw up all over her nice, clean bar."

"Another one, Chiri. Keep 'em coming."

"Your day's been that bad? Honey, step over here by the light."

I went around the edge of the bar where she could see me better. My face must have looked ghastly. She reached up gently to touch the bruises on my forehead, around my eyes, my purple, swollen lips and nostrils. "I just want to get drunk fast, Chiri," I said, "and I'm broke, too."

"You couped three thousand off that Russian, didn't you tell me about that? Or did I hear that from somebody else? Yasmin, maybe. After the Russian ate that bullet, you know, both of my new girls quit, and so did Jamila." She poured me some more tende.

"Jamila is no great loss." She was a deb, a pre-op transsexual who never intended to get the operation. I started on my second drink. It seemed to be on the house.

"Easy for you to say. Let's see *you* lure tourists in here without naked boobies shaking on stage. You want to tell me what happened to you?"

I shook the glass of liquor back and forth, gently. "Another time."

"You looking for anybody in particular?"

"Nikki."

Chiri gave a little laugh. "That explains some of it, but Nikki couldn't bust you up that bad."

"The Sisters."

"All three?"

I grimaced. "Individually and in concert."

Chiri glanced upward. "Why? What did you do to them?"

I snorted. "I haven't figured that out yet."

Chiri cocked her head and looked at me sideways for a moment. "You know," she said softly, "I did see Nikki today. She came by my place about ten this morning. She said to tell you 'thank you.' She didn't say why, but I suppose you know. Then she went off looking for Yasmin."

I felt my anger starting to bubble up again. "Did she say where she was going?"

"No."

I relaxed again. If anyone in the Budayeen knew where Nikki was, it would be Tamiko. I didn't like the thought of facing that crazy bitch again, but I was sure as hell going to. "You know where I can seize some stuff?"

"What you need, baby?"

"Oh, say, half a dozen sunnies, half a dozen tri-phets, half a dozen beauties."

"And you say you're broke, too?" She reached down under the bar again and found her bag. She rummaged through it and came up with a black plastic cylinder. "Take this into the men's room and pocket what you need. You can owe me. We'll work something out—maybe I'll take you home with me tonight."

That was an exciting though daunting thought. I haven't been intimidated by many women, changes, debs, or boys in my time; I mean, I'm no superhuman sex machine, but I get along. Chiri, though, was a scary proposition. Those evil, patterned scars and filed teeth . . . "I'll be right back," I said, palming the black cylinder.

"I just got Honey Pílar's new module," Chiri called after me. "I'm dying to try it out. You ever want to jam Honey Pílar?"

It was a very tempting suggestion, but I had other business for the next hour or so. After that . . . with Honey Pílar's personality module plugged in, Chiri would *become* Honey Pílar. She'd jam the way Honey had jammed when the module was recorded. You close your eyes and you're in bed with the most desirable woman in the world, and the only man she wants is you, begging for *you* . . .

I took some tabs and caps from Chiri's caddy and came back out into the club. Chiri looked down along the bar casually as I put the black cylinder in her hand. "Nobody's making no money tonight," she said dully. "Another drink?"

"Got to run. Action is action," I said.

"Business is business," said Chiri. "Such as it is. It *would* be if these cheap motherfuckers would spend a little money. Remember what I said about my new moddy, Marîd."

"Listen, Chiri, if I get finished and you're still here, we'll break it in together. *Inshallah*."

She gave me that grin of hers that I liked so much. "*Kwa heri*, Marîd," she said.

"*As-salaam alaykum*," I said. Then I hurried out into the warm, drizzling night, taking a deep breath of the sweet scent of some flowering tree.

The tende had lifted my spirits, and I had swallowed a tri-phet and a sunny. I'd be doing all right when I booted my way into Tamiko's phony geisha rat's nest. I practically ran the whole way up the Street to Thirteenth, except I discovered I couldn't. I used to be able to run a lot farther than that. I decided it wasn't age that had slowed me down, it was the abuse my body had taken that morning. Yeah, that was it. Sure.

Two-thirty, three in the morning, and koto music is coming out of Tami's window. I pounded on her door until my hand started to hurt.

She couldn't hear me; it was either the loud music or her drugged state. I tried to force the door and found that it was unlocked. I went slowly and quietly up the stairs. Almost everyone around me in the Budayeen is modified somehow, with personality modules and add-ons wired down deep into their brains, giving them skills and talents and inputs of information; or even, as with the Honey Pílar moddy, entirely new personalities. I alone walked among them unaltered, relying on nerve and stealth and savvy. I outhustled the hustlers, pitting my native wits against their computer-boosted awareness.

Right now, my native wits were yelling at me that something was wrong. Tami wouldn't have left her door open. Unless she did it for Nikki, who'd left her key behind. . . .

At the top of the stairs I saw her, in much the same position I'd seen her in the day before. Tamiko's face was painted the same stark white with the same gruesome black highlights. She was naked, though, and her unnatural, surgically enhanced body was pale against the hardwood floor. Her skin had a wan, sick pallor to it, except for the dark burn marks and the bruises around her wrists and throat. There was a wide slash from her right carotid artery to the left, and a great pool of blood had formed, into which her white makeup had run off a little. This Black Widow would never sting anyone again.

I sat near her on the cushions and looked at her, trying to understand it. Maybe Tami had just picked up the wrong trick, and he'd pulled his weapon before she could uncap hers. The burn marks and the bruises spelled torture, long, slow, painful torture. Tami had been paid back many times over for what she'd done to me. *Qadaa oo qadar*—a judgment of God and fate.

I was about to call Lieutenant Okking's office when my phone rang on my belt. I was so lost in thought, staring at Tami's corpse, that the ringing startled me. Sitting in a room with a staring dead woman is scary enough. I answered the phone. "Yeah?" I said.

"Marîd? You've got to—" And then I heard the line go dead. I wasn't even sure whose voice it had been, but I thought I recognized it. It sounded like Nikki's.

I sat there a little longer, wondering if Nikki had been trying to ask me for something or warn me. I felt cold, unable to move. The drugs took effect, but this time I barely noticed. I took a couple of deep breaths and spoke Okking's commcode into the phone. No Honey Pílar tonight.

ƒIVE

ῖ leαƦnεδ an interesting fact.

It didn't make up for the particularly foul day I'd had, but it was a fact I could file in my highly regarded cerebrum: police lieutenants are rarely enthusiastic about homicides reported less than half an hour before they're supposed to go off duty. "Your second cadaver in less than a week," Okking observed, when he showed up at the Thirteenth Street apartment. "We're not going to start paying you commissions on these, if that's what you're after. On the whole, we try to discourage this sort of thing, if we can."

I looked at Okking's tired, florid face and guessed that in the middle of the night, this passed for wry cop humor. I don't know where Okking was from—one or another dilapidated, bankrupt European country I guess, or one of the North American federations—but he had a genuine gift for getting along with the innumerable squabbling factions residing under his jurisdiction. His Arabic was the worst I'd ever heard—he and I usually held our acerbic conversations in French—yet he was able to handle the several Muslim sects, the devoutly religious and the non-practicing, Arab and non-Arab, the rich and poor, honest and slightly bent, all with the same elegant touch of humanity and impartiality. Believe me, I hate cops. A lot of people in the Budayeen fear cops or distrust cops or just plain don't like them. I *hate* cops. My mother had been forced into prostitution when I was very young, to keep us both fed and sheltered. I remember with painful clarity the games the cops had played with her then. That had been in Algeria a long time ago, but cops were cops to me. Except for Lieutenant Okking.

The medical examiner's usually stoic expression showed a little distaste when he saw Tamiko. She had been dead about four hours, he said. He could get a general description of the murderer from the hand-prints on her neck and other clues. The killer had plump, stubby fingers, and mine are long and tapered. I had an alibi, too: I had the receipt from the hospital stamped with the time of my treatment, and the written prescription. "Okay, friend," said Okking, still jovial in his sour way, "I guess it's safe to let you back out on the streets."

"What do you think?" I asked, indicating Tami's body.

Okking shrugged. "It looks like we've got some kind of maniac. You know these whores end up like this every so often. It's part of their overhead, like face paint and tetracycline. The other whores write it off and try not to think about it. They'd *better* think about it, though, because whoever did this is likely to do it again; that's been my experience. We might end up with two or three or five or ten dead people before we catch up with him. You go tell your friends what you saw. You tell it to them so they listen. Get the word around. Spread it among the six or eight sexes we've got in these walls not to accept dates with men about five and a half feet tall, heavyset, with short, fat fingers and a yen for the ultimate sadism while he's getting laid." Oh, yeah: the M.E. found that the killer had taken a trip around the world while he'd been beating Tami, branding her naked skin, and strangling her. Traces of semen had been found in all three orifices.

I did my best to get the word out. Everyone agreed with my own secret opinion: whoever had killed Tami had better watch his *own* ass. Anybody who jammed with the Black Widow Sisters usually got *himself* jammed up, and trashed. Devi and Selima would be picking up every guy they could find who fit the general description, just in the hope he was the right one. I had the feeling they wouldn't slip the toxin to him at the first chance, either. I'd learned how much they enjoyed what *they* thought of as foreplay.

The next day was Yasmin's day off, and about two in the afternoon I gave her a call. She hadn't been home all night; it was none of my business where she'd been. I was amused and startled to find out that I was, however, just the least bit jealous. We made a date for dinner at five at our favorite café. You can sit at a table on the terrace and watch the traffic on the Street. Only two blocks from the gate, the Street isn't so tawdry. The restaurant was a good place to relax. I didn't tell Yasmin about any of the previous day's trouble over the phone. She would have kept me talking all afternoon, and she needed the three hours to make the dinner date on time.

As it was, I had two drinks while I waited for her at the table. She arrived about quarter to six. Three quarters of an hour late is about average for Yasmin; in fact, I hadn't really expected her until after six o'clock. I wanted to get a couple of drinks ahead. I'd had only about four hours of sleep, and I struggled with terrible nightmares the whole time. I wanted to get some liquor into me, and a good meal, and have Yasmin hold my hand while I told her of my ordeal.

"Marhaba!" she called gaily as she wove her way between the iron tables and chairs.

I signaled to Ahmad, our waiter, and he took Yasmin's drink order and left menus. I looked at her as she studied her menu. She was wearing a light cotton European-style summer dress, yellow with white butterflies. Her black hair was brushed down sleek and lustrous. She wore a silver crescent on a silver chain around her darkly tanned neck. She looked lovely. I hated to bother her now with my news. I decided to put it off as long as I could.

"So," she said, looking up at me and grinning, "how was your day?"

"Tamiko's dead," I said. I felt like a fool. There must have been a way to begin the story with less of an awful thud.

She sort of goggled at me. She murmured an Arabic superstitious phrase to ward off evil.

I took a deep breath and let it out. Then I started with dawn, yesterday morning, and my enthusiastic wake-up call from the Sisters. I went through the whole day, ending with my dismissal by Okking and my weary and lonely walk home.

I saw a tear slide slowly down one of her carefully blushed cheeks. She wasn't able to speak for several seconds. I didn't know she'd be so upset; I berated myself for my clumsiness.

"I wish I'd been with you last night," she said at last. She didn't realize how hard she was squeezing my hand. "I had a date, Marîd, some guy from the club. He's been coming in to see me for weeks, and finally last night he offered me two hundred kiam to go out with him. He's a nice guy, I suppose, but—"

I raised a hand. I didn't need to hear this. I didn't care how she paid her rent. I would have liked to have had her with me last night, too. I would have liked to have held her between the nightmares. "It's all over now, I guess," I said. "Let me blow the rest of my fifty kiam on this dinner, and then let's go for a long walk."

"Do you really think it's all over?"

I chewed my lip. "Except for Nikki. I wish I knew what that phone call meant. I just can't understand her running out on me like that, sticking me for Abdoulaye's three thousand. I mean, in the Budayeen, you can never be sure how loyal your friends are; but I'd gotten Nikki out of one or two scrapes before. I thought that might have counted for something with her."

Yasmin's eyes opened wider, then she laughed. I couldn't see what she thought was so humorous. My face still looked swollen and bruised, and my ribs still hurt like the devil. The day before had been anything but clownish. "I saw Nikki yesterday morning," said Yasmin.

"You did?" Then I remembered that Chiriga had seen Nikki about ten o'clock, and that Nikki had left Chiri's to find Yasmin. I hadn't connected that visit to Chiri with Nikki's later skip-out.

"Nikki looked very nervous," said Yasmin, "and she told me she'd quit her job and had to move out of Tami's apartment. She wouldn't tell me why. She said she'd tried to call you again and again, but there wasn't any answer." Of course not; when Nikki was trying to call me, I was lying unconscious on my floor. "She gave me this envelope and told me to be sure you got it."

"Why didn't she just leave it with Chiri?" That would have saved a lot of mental and physical anguish.

"Don't you remember? Nikki worked in Chiri's club, oh, a year ago, maybe longer. Chiri caught Nikki shortchanging customers and stealing from the other girls' tip jars."

I nodded; now I recalled that Nikki and Chiri left each other pretty much alone. "So Nikki went to Chiri just to get your address?"

"I asked her a lot of questions, but she wouldn't answer a thing. She just kept saying, 'Make sure Marîd gets this,' over and over."

I hoped it was a letter, an apology maybe, with an address where I could reach her. I wanted my money back. I took the envelope from Yasmin and tore it open. Inside was my three thousand kiam, and a note written in French. Nikki wrote:

My dearest Marîd:

   I so much wanted to give you the money in person. I called many times, but you did not answer. I am leaving this with Yasmin, but if you never get it, how will you know? You will hate me forever, then. When we meet again, I will not understand. My feelings are so confused.

   I am going to live with an old friend of my family. He is a wealthy businessman from Germany, who always brought me presents whenever he visited. That was when I was a shy, introverted little boy. Now that I am, well, what I am, the German businessman has discovered that he is even more inclined to give me presents. I was always fond of him, Marîd, although I can't love him. But being with him will be so much more pleasant than staying with Tamiko.

   The gentleman's name is Herr Lutz Seipolt. He lives in a

*magnificent house on the far side of the city, and you must
ask the driver to take you to (I have to copy this down for
you) Bayt il-Simsaar il-Almaani Seipolt. That ought to get
you to the villa.*

*Give my love to Yasmin and to everyone. I will visit the
Budayeen when I can, but I think I will enjoy playing the mis-
tress of such an estate for a while. I am sure you, of all people,
Marîd, will understand: Business is business, mush hayk? (And
I'll bet you thought I never learned a single word of Arabic!)*

*With much love,
Nikki*

When I finished reading the letter, I sighed and handed it to Yasmin. I'd forgotten that she couldn't read a word of French, and so I
translated it for her.

"I hope she'll be happy," she said when I folded the letter up.

"Being kept by some old German bratwurst? Nikki? You know
Nikki. She needs the action as much as I do, as much as you do. She'll
be back. Right now, I guess, it's sugar-daddy time on the Princess Nikki
Show."

Yasmin smiled. "She'll be back, I agree; but in her own time. And
she'll make that old bratwurst pay for every minute of it." We both
laughed, and then the waiter brought Yasmin's drink, and we ordered
dinner.

As we finished the meal, we lingered over a last glass of champagne.
"What a day yesterday was," I said bemusedly, "and now everything is
back to normal. I have my money, except I'll be out a thousand kiam in
interest. When we leave here, I want to find Abdoulaye and pay him."

"Sure," said Yasmin, "but even then, everything won't be back to
normal. Tami's still dead."

I frowned. "That's Okking's problem. If he wants my expert
advice, he knows where to find me."

"Are you really going to talk to Devi and Selima about why they
beat you?"

"You bet your pretty plastic tits. And the Sisters better have a damn
good reason."

"It must have something to do with Nikki."

I agreed, although I couldn't imagine what. "Oh," I said, "and let's
stop by Chiriga's. I owe her for the stuff she let me have last night."

Yasmin gazed at me over the rim of her champagne glass. "It
sounds like we might not get home until late," she said softly.

"And when we do get home, we'll be lucky to find the bed."

Yasmin made a sweeping, mildly drunken gesture. "Fuck the bed," she said.

"No," I said, "I have more worthy goals."

Yasmin giggled a little shyly, as if our relationship were beginning all over again from the very first night together. "Which moddy do you want me to use tonight?" she asked.

I let out my breath, taken by her loveliness and her quiet, unaffected charm. It *was* as if I were seeing her again for the first time. "I don't want you to use any moddy," I said quietly. "I want to make love with *you*."

"Oh, Marîd," she said. She squeezed my hand, and we stayed like that, staring into each other's eyes, inhaling the perfume of the sweet olive, hearing the songs of thrushes and nightingales. The moment lasted almost forever . . . and then . . . I remembered that Abdoulaye was waiting. I had better not forget Abdoulaye; there is an Arabic saying that a clever man's mistake is equal to the mistakes of a thousand fools.

Before we left the café, however, Yasmin wanted to consult the book. I told her that the Qur'ân didn't contain much solace for me. "Not the Book," she said, "the wise mention of God. The *book*." She took out a little device about the size of a pack of cigarettes. It was her electronic *I Ching*. "Here," she said, giving it to me, "switch it on and press H."

I didn't have a lot of faith in the *I Ching*, either; but Yasmin had this fascination with fate and the unseen world and the Moment and all of that. I did as she told me, and when I pressed the square white spot marked H, the little computer played a reedy, tinkling tune, and a woman's tinny voice spoke up. "Hexagram Eighteen. Ku. Work on that which has been spoiled. Changes in the fifth and sixth lines."

"Now hit J, for Judgment," said Yasmin.

I did, and the calculator peeped out its goddamn little song again and said, "Judgment:

Putting effort into what has been ruined
Brings great success.
It profits one to cross the great water.
Heed three days before beginning.
Heed three days before completing.

"What has been ruined can be made good again through effort. Do not fear danger—crossing the great water. Success depends on forethought; be cautious before beginning. A return of ruin must be avoided; be cautious before completing.

"The superior man arouses the people and renews their spirit."

I looked at Yasmin. "I hope you're getting something out of all of this," I said, "because it doesn't mean a camel's glass eye to me."

"Oh, sure," said Yasmin in a hushed voice. "Now, go on. Press L for the Lines."

I did as I was told. The spooky machine continued: "A six in the fifth place means:

Repairing what the father has ruined.
One's actions are praiseworthy.

"A nine at the top means:

He does not serve kings and princes,
Sets himself higher goals."

"Who's it talking about, Yasmin?" I asked.

"You, darling, who else?"

"Now what do I do?"

"You find out what the changing lines turn the hexagram into. Another hexagram. Push CH for Change."

"Hexagram Forty-seven. K'un. Oppression."

I pressed J.

"Judgment:

Oppression. Success. Perseverance.
The great man causes good fortune.
There is no blame.
When one has something to say,
It is not believed.

"A great man remains confident through adversity, and this confidence leads to later success. It is a strength greater than fate. It must be accepted that for a time he is not granted power, and his counsel is ignored. In times of adversity, it is important to maintain confidence and speak but little.

"If one is weak in adversity, he remains beneath a bare tree and falls more deeply into sorrow. This is an inner delusion that must be overcome at all costs."

That was it: the oracle had spoken. "Can we go now?" I asked plaintively.

Yasmin was looking dreamily into some other Chinese dimension. "You're destined for great things, Marîd," she murmured.

"Right," I said, "but the important thing is, can that talking box guess my weight? What good is it?" I didn't even have the motherless good sense to know when I'd been told off by a book.

"You've got to find something to believe in," she said seriously.

"Look, Yasmin, I keep trying. Really, I do. Was that some kind of prediction? Was it reading my future?"

Her brow furrowed. "It's not really a prediction, Marîd. It's kind of an echo of the Moment we're all part of. Because of who you are and what you think and feel, and what you've done and plan to do, you could have drawn no other hexagram than Number Eighteen, with the changes in just those two lines. If you did it again, right this very second, you'd get a different reading, a different hexagram, because the first one changed the Moment and the pattern is different. See?"

"Synchronicity, right?" I said.

She looked puzzled. "Something like that."

I sent Ahmad off with the check and a stack of kiam notes. It was a warm, lush, dry evening, and it would be a beautiful night. I stood up and stretched. "Let's go find Abdoulaye," I said. "Business is business, damn it."

"And afterward?" She smiled.

"Action is action." I took her hand, and we started up the Street toward Hassan's shop.

The good-looking American boy was still sitting on his stool, still gazing off toward nowhere. I wondered if he was actually having thoughts, or if he was some kind of electronically animated figure that only came to life when someone approached or he caught the crackle of a few kiam. He looked at us and smiled, and asked some question in English again. Maybe a lot of the customers who came into Hassan's place spoke English, but I doubted it. It wasn't a place for tourists; it wasn't that kind of souvenir shop. The boy must have been all but helpless; unable to speak Arabic and without a language daddy. He must have been helpless; that is, dependent. On Hassan. For so *many* things.

I know a little simple English; if it's spoken slowly enough, I can understand a few words. I can say, "Where is the toilet?" and "Big Mac and fries" and "Fuck you," but that's about the extent of my vocabulary. I stared at the boy; he stared back. He smiled slowly. I think he liked me.

"Where is the Abdoulaye?" I asked in English. The kid blinked and rattled off some indecipherable reply. I shook my head, letting him know that I hadn't understood a word. His shoulders slumped. He tried another language; Spanish, I think. I shook my head again.

"Where is the Sahîb Hassan?" I asked.

The boy grinned and rattled off another string of harsh-sounding words, but he pointed at the curtain. Great: we were communicating.

"*Shukran,*" I said, leading Yasmin to the back of the shop.

"You're welcome," said the boy. That stumped me. He knew that I'd said "thanks" in Arabic, but he didn't know how to say "you're welcome." Dumb kid. Lieutenant Okking would find him in an alleyway some night. Or *I* would, with my kind of luck.

Hassan was in the storeroom, checking some crates against an invoice. The crates were addressed to him in Arabic script, but other words were stenciled in some European language. The crates could have contained anything from static pistols to shrunken heads. Hassan didn't care what he bought and sold, as long as he turned a profit. He was the Platonic ideal of the crafty merchant.

He heard us come through the curtain, and greeted me like a long-lost son. He embraced me and asked, "You are feeling better today?"

"Praise be to Allah," I replied.

His eyes flicked from me to Yasmin and back. I think he may have recognized her from the Street, but I don't think he knew her personally. I saw no need to introduce her. It was a breach of etiquette, but tolerated in certain situations. I made the determination that this was one of those times. Hassan extended a hand. "Come, join me in some coffee!"

"May your table last forever, Hassan, but we've just dined; and I am in a hurry to find Abdoulaye. I owe him a debt, you recall."

"Yes, yes, quite so." Hassan's brow creased. "Marîd, my darling, clever one, I haven't seen Abdoulaye for hours. I think he's entertaining himself elsewhere." Hassan's tone implied Abdoulaye's entertainment was any of several possible vices.

"Yet I have the money now, and I wish to end my obligation."

Hassan pretended to mull this problem over for a moment. "You know, of course, that a portion of that money is indirectly to be paid to me."

"Yes, O Wise One."

"Then leave the whole sum with me, and I will give Abdoulaye his portion when next I see him."

"An excellent suggestion, my uncle, but I would like to have Abdoulaye's written receipt. Your integrity is beyond reproach, but Abdoulaye and I do not share the same bond of love as you and I."

That didn't sit well with Hassan, but he could make no objection. "I think you will find Abdoulaye behind the iron door." Then he rudely turned his back on us and continued his labor. Without turning to face us, he spoke again. "Your companion must remain here."

I looked at Yasmin, and she shrugged. I went through the store-room quickly, across the alley, and knocked on the iron door. I waited a few seconds while someone identified me from somewhere. Then the door opened. There was a tall, cadaverous, bearded old man named Karîm. "What do you wish here?" he asked me gruffly.

"Peace, O Shaykh, I have come to pay my debt to Abdoulaye Abu-Zayd."

The door closed. A moment later, Abdoulaye opened it. "Let me have it. I need it now." Over his shoulder, I could see several men engaged in some high-spirited gambling.

"I have the whole sum, Abdoulaye," I said, "but you're going to write me out a receipt. I don't want you claiming that I never paid you."

He looked angry. "You dare imagine I'd do such a thing?"

I glared back at him. "The receipt. Then you get your money."

He called me a couple of foul names, then ducked back into the room. He scrawled out the receipt and showed it to me. "Give me the fifteen hundred kiam," he said, growling.

"Give me the receipt first."

"Give me the accursed money, you pimp!"

For a second I thought about hitting him hard with the edge of my hand across the flat of his nose, breaking his face for him. It was a deli-cious image. "Christ, Abdoulaye! Get Karîm back here. Karîm!" I called. When the gray-bearded old man returned, I said to him, "I'm going to give you some money, Karîm, and Abdoulaye is going to give you that piece of paper in his hand. You give him the money, and give me the paper."

Karîm hesitated, as if the transaction were too complicated for him to follow. Then he nodded. The trade was made in silence. I turned and went back across the alley. "Son of a whore!" cried Abdoulaye. I smiled. That is one hell of an insult in the Muslim world; but, as it happened to be true, it's never offended me very much. Still, because of Yasmin and our plans for the evening, I had let Abdoulaye abuse me beyond my usual limit. I promised myself that soon there would be a settling of that account, as well. In the Budayeen, it is not well to be thought of as one who meekly submits to insolence and intimidation.

As I passed through the storeroom and went to Yasmin, I said, "You can collect your cut from Abdoulaye, Hassan. You'd better do it fast: I think he's losing big." Hassan nodded but said nothing.

"I'm glad that's taken care of," said Yasmin.

"Not any more than I am." I folded the receipt and pushed it down into a hip pocket.

We went to Chiri's, and I waited until she'd finished serving three

young men in Calabrian naval uniforms. "Chiri," I said, "we can't stay
long, but I wanted to give you this." I counted out seventy-five kiam
and put the money on the bar. Chiri didn't make a move toward it.
"Yasmin, you look beautiful, honey. Marîd, what's this for? The
stuff last night?" I nodded. "I know you make a thing about keeping
your word and paying your debts and all that honorable choo. I wouldn't
charge you Street prices, though. Take some of this back."

I grinned at her. "Chiri, you risk causing offense to a Muslim."

She laughed. "Muslim, my black ass. Then you two have a drink
on me. There's a lot of action tonight, a lot of loose money. The girls
are in a good mood, and so am I."

"We're celebrating, Chiri," said Yasmin. They exchanged some
kind of secret signal—maybe that kind of occult, gender-specific
transfer of knowledge goes along with the sex-change operation. Anyway, Chiri understood. We took the free drinks she'd offered, and got
up to go.

"You two have a good night," she said. The seventy-five kiam had
long since disappeared. I don't remember seeing it happen, though.

"*Kwa heri*," I said as we left.

"*Kwa herini ya kuonana*," she said. Then, "All right, which one of
you lazy, fat-assed whores is supposed to be up on stage dancing?
Kandy? Well, get your fuckin' clothes off and get to work!" Chiri
sounded happy. All was well with the world.

"We could pass by Jo-Mama's," said Yasmin. "I haven't seen her in
weeks." Jo-Mama was a huge woman, nearly six feet tall, somewhere
between three and four hundred pounds, with hair that changed according to some esoteric cycle: blonde, redhead, brunette, midnight black;
then a dull brown would start to grow out, and when it was long enough,
it was transformed by some sorcery into blonde hair again. She was a
tough, strong woman, and no one caused trouble in *her* bar, which
catered to Greek merchant seamen. Jo-Mama had no scruples against
pulling her needle gun or her Solingen perforator and creating general
peace in gory heaps all around her. I'm sure Jo-Mama could easily
have handled *two* Chirigas at the same time, and simultaneously still
have the unruffled calm to mix a Bloody Mary from scratch for a customer. Jo-Mama either liked you a lot or she hated your guts. You *really*
wanted her to like you. We stopped in; she greeted both of us in her
usual loud, fast-talking, distracted way. "Marîd! Yasmin!" She said
something to us in Greek, forgetting that neither of us understood that
language; I can say even less in Greek than I can in English. All that I
know I've picked up from hanging out in Jo-Mama's: I can order ouzo
and retsina; I can say *kalimera* (hello); and I can call somebody

maláka, which seems to be their favorite insult (as far as I can make out, it means "jerk-off").

I gave Jo-Mama the best hug I could manage. She's so plentiful that Yasmin and I together probably couldn't circumscribe her. She included us in a story she was telling to another customer ". . . so Fuad comes running back to me and says, 'That black bitch clipped me!' Now, you and I both know that nothing gives Fuad a thrill like being clipped by some black whore." Jo-Mama looked questioningly at me, so I nodded. Fuad was this incredibly skinny guy who had this fascination with black hookers, the sleazier and the more dangerous, the better. Nobody liked Fuad, but they used him to run and fetch; and he was so desperate to be liked that he'd run and fetch all night, unless he ran into the girl he happened to be in love with that week. "So I asked him how he managed to get clipped this time, because I was figuring he knew all the angles by now, I mean, God, even Fuad isn't as stupid as Fuad, if you know what I mean. He says, 'She's a waitress over by Big Al's Old Chicago. I bought a drink, and when she brought my change back, she'd wet the tray with a sponge and held the tray up above where I could see it, see? I had to reach up and slide my change off the tray, and the bottom bill stuck on the wet part.' So I grabbed him by the ears and shook his head back and forth. 'Fuad, Fuad,' I said, 'that's the oldest scam in the book. You must have seen that one worked a million times. I remember when Zainab pulled that one on you last year.' And the stupid skeleton nods his head, and his big lump of an Adam's apple is going up and down and up and down, and he says to me, he says, 'Yeah, but all those other times they was one-kiam bills. Nobody ever done it with a ten before!' As if that made it all different!" Jo-Mama started to laugh, the way a volcano starts to rumble before it goes blam, and when she really got into the laugh, the bar shook, and the glasses and bottles on it rattled, and we could feel the vibrations clear across the bar on our stools. Jo-Mama laughing could cause more damage than a smaller person throwing chairs around. "So what you want, Marîd? Ouzo, and retsina for the young lady? Or just a beer? Make up your mind, I don't have all night, I got a crowd of Greeks just in from Skorpios, their ship's carrying boxes full of high explosives for the revolution in Holland and they got a long way to sail with it and they're all nervous as a goldfish at a cat convention and they're drinking me dry. What the hell do you want to drink, goddamn it! Getting an answer out of you is like prying a tip out of a Chink."

She paused just long enough for me to cram a few words in. I got myself my gin and bingara with Rose's, and Yasmin had a Jack Daniels with a Coke back. Then Jo-Mama started in on another story, and I watched her like a hawk, because sometimes she starts the stories so you'll get all caught up in them and forget you've got change coming. I never forget. "Let me have the change all in singles, Mama," I said, interrupting her story and reminding her, in case my change had slipped her mind. She gave me an amused look and made the change, and I kicked her a whole kiam for a tip. She stuffed it into her bra. There was plenty of room in there for all the money I'd ever see in my lifetime. We finished our drinks after two or three more stories, kissed her good-bye, and wandered further up the Street. We stopped in Frenchy's and a few other places, and we were satisfactorily loaded by the time we got home.

We didn't say a word to each other; we didn't even pause to turn on a light or go to the bathroom. We had our clothes off and were lying close together on the mattress. I ran my fingernails up the back of Yasmin's thighs; she loves that. She was scratching my back and chest; that's what I like. I used the tips of my thumb and fingers to touch her skin very lightly, just barely tickling her, from her armpit up her arm to her hand, and then I tickled her palm and her fingers. I ran my fingertips back down her arm, down her side, and across her sexy little ass. Then I began touching the sensitive creases of her groin the same way. I heard her start to make soft sounds, and she didn't realize her own hands had fallen beside her; then she began touching her breasts. I reached over and grabbed her wrists, pinning her arms to the bed. She opened her eyes in surprise. I grunted softly and kicked her right leg aside, a little roughly, then I spread her left leg with mine. She gave a little shudder and moan. She tried to reach down to touch me, but I wouldn't let go of her wrists. I held her immobile, and I felt a strong, almost cruel sense of control, yet it was expressed in the most caring and tender way. It sounds like a contradiction; if you don't feel the same thing sometimes, I can't explain it to you. Yasmin was giving herself to me wordlessly, completely; at the same time I was taking her, and she *wanted* me to take her. She liked me to get a little wild now and then; the moderate force I permitted myself to use only aroused her more. Then I entered her, and we let out our breath together in a sigh of pleasure. We began to move slowly, and her legs lifted; she put her heels on my hips, digging in and holding on, as close to me as she could get, while I was driving into her as close to *her* as possible. We jammed like that, slowly, drawing out every gentle touch, every surprise shock of roughness, for a long while. Yasmin and I still clung to each other, our hearts thumping and our breath ragged and quick. We clung until our bodies quieted, and still we held each other, both satisfied, both exhilarated by this restatement of our mutual need and our mutual trust and, above all else, our mutual love. I suppose at some time we separated, and I suppose at some time we fell asleep; but in the late morning when I awoke, our legs were still entwined, and Yasmin's head was on my shoulder.

Everything had been fixed, everything had indeed returned to normal. I had Yasmin to love, I had money in my pocket to last a few months, and whenever I wanted it, there was action. I smiled softly and slowly drifted back into untroubled dreams.

six

It was one of those rare times of shared happiness, of perfect contentment. We had a feeling of expectation, that what was already wonderful would only get better and better as time went on. These moments are one of the rarest, most fragile things in the world. You have to seize the day; you have to recall all the rotten, dirty things you endured to earn this peace. You have to remember to enjoy each minute, each hour, because although you may feel like it's going to last forever, the world plans otherwise. You want to be grateful for every precious second, but you simply can't do it. It's not in human nature to live life to the fullest. Haven't you ever noticed that equal amounts of pain and joy are not, in fact, equal in duration? Pain drags on until you wonder if life will ever be bearable again; pleasure, though, once it's reached its peak, fades faster than a trodden gardenia, and your memory searches in vain for the sweet scent.

Yasmin and I made love again when we woke at last, this time on our sides, with her back to me. We held each other close when we finished, but only for a few moments, because Yasmin wanted to live life to the fullest again. I reminded her that this, too, was just not in human nature—at least as far as I was concerned. I wanted a little longer to savor the gardenia, which was still pretty fresh in my mind. Yasmin really wanted another gardenia. I told her to wait another minute or two.

"Sure," she said, "tomorrow, with the apricots." That's the Levantine equivalent of "when pigs fly."

I would have loved to jam her right then until she cried for mercy, but my flesh was still weak. "This is the part they call the afterglow," I said. "Sensitive, voluptuous people like me value it as much as the jamming itself."

"Fuck that, man," she said, "you're just getting old." I knew she wasn't being serious, that she was just riding me—or trying to. Actually, I was beginning to feel my weak flesh beginning to stir already, and was almost ready to proclaim my remaining youth, when there was a knock at the door.

"Uh oh, there goes your surprise," I said. For a recluse, I was sure entertaining a lot of visitors lately.

"I wonder who it is. You don't owe anyone any money."

I grabbed my jeans and crammed myself into them. "Then it's got to be somebody trying to borrow," I said, heading for the peephole in the door.

"From you? You wouldn't give a copper fîq to a beggar who knew the Secret of the Universe."

As I got to the door, I looked back at Yasmin. "The universe doesn't have secrets," I said cynically, "only lies and swindles." My indulgent mood vanished in a split second when I looked through the peephole. "Son of a bitch," I said under my breath. I went back to the bed. "Yasmin," I said softly, "give me your bag."

"Why? Who is it?" She found her purse and passed it to me.

I knew she always carried a low-grade seizure gun for protection. I don't carry a weapon like that; alone and unarmed I walked among the cutthroats of the Budayeen, because I was special, exempt, proud, and stupid. I had these delusions, you see, and I lived a kind of romantic fallacy. I was no more eccentric than your average raving loon. I took the gun and went back to the door. Yasmin watched me, silently and anxiously.

I opened the door. It was Selima. I held the seizure gun pointed between her eyes. "How nice to see you," I said. "Come on in. There's something I've been wanting to ask you."

"You won't need the gun, Marîd," said Selima. She brushed by me, seemed unhappy to see Yasmin, and looked in vain for somewhere to sit. She was extremely uncomfortable, I noticed, and very upset about something.

"So," I said cruelly, "you just want to get in a few last whacks before somebody lays you out like Tami?"

Selima glowered, reached back, and slapped me hard across the face. I'd earned it.

"Sit on the bed, Selima. Yasmin will move over. As for the gun, it would have come in handy when you and your friends dropped by and started my morning with such a bang. Or don't you remember about that?"

"Marîd," she said, licking her glossy red lips, "I'm sorry about that. It was a mistake."

"Oh, well, that makes it all better, then." I watched Yasmin cover herself with the sheet and crawl as far away from Selima as she could, with her knees drawn up and her back in the corner. Selima had the immense breasts that was the trademark of the Black Widow Sisters, but otherwise she was almost unmodified. She was naturally prettier than most sex-changes. Tamiko had turned herself into a caricature of the modest and demure geisha; Devi accentuated her East Indian heritage, complete with a caste mark on her forehead to which she was not entitled, and when she was not working, she wore a brightly colored silk sari, embroidered in gold. Selima, on the contrary, wore the veil and the hooded cloak, a subtle fragrance, and the demeanor of a middle-class Muslim woman of the city. I think, but I'm not sure, that she was religious; I can't imagine how she squared her thievery and frequent violence with the teachings of the Prophet, may prayers and peace be upon him. I'm not the only self-deluded fool in the Budayeen.

"Please, Marîd, let me explain." I'd never seen Selima—or either of her Sisters, for that matter—in such a state of near-panic. "You know that Nikki left Tami's." I nodded. "I don't think she wanted to go. I think someone forced her."

"That isn't the message *I* got. She wrote me a letter about some German guy and what a wonderful life she was going to have, and that she had a real fish on the line here and she was going to play him for everything he had."

"We all got the same letter, Marîd. Didn't you notice anything suspicious about it, though? Maybe you don't know Nikki's handwriting as well as I do. Maybe you didn't pay attention to her choice of words. There were clues in the note that made us think she was trying to get something across between the lines. I think someone was standing over her, making her write the letters so no one would think twice when she disappeared. Nikki was right-handed, and the letters were written with her left hand. The script was awful, nothing like her usual writing. She wrote our notes in French, although she knows perfectly well that none of us understands that language. She spoke English, and both Devi and Tami could have read that; that's the language she used with them. She never mentioned an old German friend of her family; there may well have been such a man when she was younger, but the way she called herself 'a shy, introverted little boy,' well, that just underlined the bad feeling we had about the whole letter. Nikki told lots of stories about her life before she had her change. She was vague about most of the details—where she was really from, things like that—but she always laughed about what a terror she—he—had been. She wanted to be just like us, and so she went into these biographical accounts of her hell-raising. She was anything but shy and introverted. Marîd, that letter smelled from beginning to end."

I let my hand with the gun drop. Everything Selima had said made sense, now that I thought about it. "That's why you're so shaken up," I said thoughtfully. "You think Nikki's in some kind of trouble."

"I think Nikki's in trouble," said Selima, "but that's not why I'm so rabbity. Marîd, Devi's dead. She's been murdered, too."

I closed my eyes and groaned. Yasmin gave a loud gasp; she uttered another superstitious formula—"far from you"—to protect us from the evil that had just been mentioned. I felt weariness, as if I'd overdosed on shocking news and just couldn't work up the proper reaction. "Don't tell me," I said, "let me guess: just like Tami. Burn marks, bruises around her wrists, jammed coming and going, strangled, and her throat cut. And you think someone's out to get all three of you, and you're next."

I was astonished by her reply. "No, you're wrong. I found her lying in her bed, almost like she was peacefully asleep. She'd been shot, Marîd, with an old-fashioned gun, the kind that used metal bullets. There was a bullet hole exactly centered on her caste mark. No signs of a fight or anything. Nothing disturbed in her apartment. Just Devi, part of her face blown away, a lot of blood splattered on the bedclothes and the walls. I threw up. I've never seen anything like it. Those old weapons were so bloody and, well, brutal." This from a woman who'd slashed enough faces in her time. "I'll bet no one's been shot with a bullet in fifty years." Selima evidently didn't know about my Russian, whatever his name had been; dead bodies didn't cause much scandal and gossip in the Budayeen; they weren't all that rare. Corpses were more of an inconvenience than anything else. Getting large quantities of blood-stains out of nice silk or cashmere is a tedious job.

"Have you called Okking yet?" I asked.

Selima nodded. "It wasn't his shift. Sergeant Hajjar came and asked all the questions. I wish it'd been Okking instead."

I knew what she meant. Hajjar was the kind of cop I think of when I think of "cop." He walked around as if he had a cork up his ass, look-ing for petty rowdies to blast into grand mal seizures. He had a partic-ular hard-on for Arabs who were inattentive to their spiritual duties: people like me and almost everyone else in the Budayeen.

I put the gun back in Yasmin's bag. My mood had changed entirely; now suddenly, and for the first time, I felt sympathy for

Selima. Yasmin put her hand on Selima's shoulder in a comforting gesture. "I'll make some coffee," I said. I looked at the last Black Widow Sister. "Or would you rather have tea?"

She was grateful for our kindness, and our company, too, I think. "Tea, thank you," she said. She had begun to calm down.

I put the kettle on to boil. "So just tell me one thing: why *did* the three of you work out your kinks on my body the other day?"

"Allah have mercy on me," said Selima. She took a folded scrap of paper from her bag and brought it to me. "This is Nikki's usual handwriting, but it's obvious she was in a terrible hurry." The words were written in English, scrawled quickly on the back of an envelope.

"What does it say?" I asked.

Selima glanced at me and quickly looked back down at the paper. "It says, 'Help. Hurry. Marîd.' That's why we did what we did. We misunderstood. We thought you were responsible for whatever trouble she was in. Now I know that you had done her the service of negotiating her release from that pig Abdoulaye, and that she owed you money. She wanted us to let you know that she needed help, but didn't have time to write anything more. She was probably lucky just to scribble this down."

I thought about the beating they'd given me; the hours of unconsciousness; the pain I'd suffered and still suffered; the long, nightmarish wait at the hospital; the anger I'd felt toward Nikki; the thousand kiam it had cost me. I added all that up and tried to cancel it. I couldn't. I still felt an unaccustomed rage inside me, but now it seemed I had no one to vent it on. I looked at Selima. "Just forget it," I said.

Selima wasn't moved. I thought she'd meet me halfway at least, but then I remembered who I was dealing with. "It isn't all right, you know," she reminded me. "I'm still worried about Nikki."

"The letter she wrote *might* be true, after all," I said, pouring tea into three cups. "Those clues you mentioned, they might all have some innocent explanation." I didn't believe a word of it, even as I said it. It was only to make Selima feel better.

She took her cup of tea and held it. "I don't know what to do now," she said.

"It may be some crazy trick is after all three of you," Yasmin suggested. "Maybe you ought to hide out for a while."

"I thought of that," Selima said. Yasmin's theory didn't sound likely to me: Tamiko and Devi had been killed in such completely different ways. Of course, that didn't rule out the possibility of a creative murderer. Despite all the old cop truisms about a criminal's modus operandi, there wasn't a reason in the world why a killer couldn't use two offbeat techniques. I kept quiet about this, too.

"You could stay in my apartment," said Yasmin. "I could stay here with Marîd." Both Selima and I were startled by Yasmin's offer.

"That's good of you to offer," said Selima. "I'll think about it, sugar, but there are a couple of other things I want to try. I'll let you know."

"You'll be all right if you just keep your eyes open," I said. "Don't do any business for a few days, don't mix with strangers." Selima nodded. She handed me her tea, which she hadn't even tasted.

"I have to go," she said. "I hope everything is straight now between us."

"You have more important things to worry about, Selima," I said. "We've never been very close before. In a morbid way, maybe we'll end up better friends because of this."

"The price has been high," she said. That was all too true. Selima started to say something else, then stopped. She turned and went to the door, let herself out, and closed the door quietly behind her.

I stood by the stove with three cups of tea. "You want one of these?" I asked.

"No," said Yasmin.

"Neither do I." I dumped the tea into the sink.

"There's either one mighty twisted bastard out there killing people," mused Yasmin, "or what's worse, two different motherfuckers working the same side of the street. I'm almost afraid to go to work."

I sat down beside her and stroked her perfumed hair. "You'll be all right at work. Just listen to what I told Selima: don't pick up any trick you don't already know. Stay here with me instead of going home alone."

She gave me a little smile. "I couldn't bring a trick here to your apartment," she said.

"You're damn straight about *that*," I said. "Forget about turning tricks at all until this business is over and they've caught the guy. I've got enough money to support both of us for a little while."

She put her arms around my waist and laid her head on my shoulder. "You're all right," she said.

"You're okay, too, when you're not snoring like a go-devil," I said. In reprisal, she raked my back hard with her long, claret-colored fingernails. Then we stretched out on the bed and played around again for half an hour.

I got Yasmin out of bed about two-thirty, made her something to eat while she showered and dressed, and urged her to get to work without getting fined for being late: fifty kiam is fifty kiam, I always reminded her. Her answer to that was, "So why worry? One fifty-kiam bill looks just like all the others. If I don't bring home one, I'll bring home another." I couldn't quite get her to see that if she just hustled her bustle a little more, she could bring them *both* home.

She asked me what I was going to do that afternoon. She was a little jealous because I'd earned my money for the next few weeks; I could sit around in some coffeehouse all day, bragging and gossiping with the boyfriends of the other dancers and working girls. I told her that I had some errands to run, and that I'd be busy, too. "I'm going to see what the story is with Nikki," I said.

"You didn't believe Selima?" Yasmin asked.

"I've known Selima a long time. I know she likes to go overboard in these situations. I'd be willing to bet that Nikki is safe and happy with this Seipolt guy. Selima just had to invent some story to make her life sound exotic and risky."

Yasmin gave me a dubious look. "Selima doesn't *have* to make up stories. Her life *is* exotic and risky. I mean, how can you exaggerate a bullet hole through the forehead? Dead is *dead*, Marîd."

She had a point there, but I didn't feel like awarding it to her out loud. "Go to work," I said, kissing her and fondling her and booting her out of the apartment. Then I was all alone. "Alone" was much quieter now than ever before; I think I almost preferred having a lot of noise and people and provocation around. That's a bad sign for a recluse. It's even worse for a solitary agent, for a tough character who lives for action and menace, the kind of bold, competent guy I liked to think I was. When the silence starts to give you the nervous jimjams, that's when you find out you're *not* a hero, after all. Oh, sure, I knew a lot of truly dangerous people, and I'd done a lot of dangerous things. I was on the inside, one of the sharks rather than one of the minnows; and I had the respect of the other sharks as well. The trouble was that having Yasmin around all the time was getting to be enjoyable, but that didn't fit the lone wolf's profile.

I said all of this to myself while I shaved my throat, looking in the bathroom mirror. I was trying to persuade myself of something, but it took me a while to do it. When I did, I wasn't happy about my conclusion: I hadn't accomplished very much during the last several days; but three times now, people had dropped dead near me, people I knew, people I didn't know. If this trend went on, it could endanger Yasmin.

Hell, it could endanger *me*.

I had said that I thought Selima was getting excited over nothing. That was a lie. While Selima was telling me her story, I was recalling the brief, frantic phone call I'd gotten: "Marîd? You've got to—" I hadn't been sure before that it had been from Nikki; but I was certain now, and I was feeling guilty because I hadn't acted on it. If Nikki had been hurt in any way, I was going to have to live with that guilt for the rest of my life.

I put on a white cotton *gallebeya*; covered my head with the familiar Arab headdress, the white *keffiya*, and held it in place with a rope *akal*. I put some sandals on my feet. Now I looked like every other poor, scruffy Arab in the city, one of the *fellahîn*, or peasants. I doubt if I'd dressed like this more than ten times in all the years I'd lived in the Budayeen. I've always affected European clothing, in my youth in Algeria and later when I'd wandered eastward. I did not now look like an Algerian; I wanted to be taken for a local *fellah*. Maybe only my reddish beard whispered a discordant note, but the German would not know that. As I left my apartment and walked along the Street toward the gate, I didn't hear my name called once or catch a glance of recognition. As I walked among my friends, they did not know me, so unusual was it for me to dress this way. I felt invisible, and with invisibility goes a certain power. My uncertainty of a few minutes before evaporated, replaced by my old confidence. I was dangerous again.

Just beyond the eastern gate was the broad Boulevard il-Jameel, lined with palm trees on both sides. A spacious neutral ground separated the north- and southbound traffic, and was planted with several varieties of flowering shrub. There was something blooming every month of the year, filling the air along the boulevard with sweet scents, distracting the eyes of those who passed by with their blossoms' startling colors: luscious pink, flaming carmine, rich pansy purple, saffron yellow, pristine white, blue as varied as the restless sea, and still more. In the trees and lodged high above the street on rooftops sang a multitude of warblers, larks, and ringdoves. The combined beauties moved one to thank Allah for these lavish gifts. I paused on the neutral ground for a moment; I had emerged from the Budayeen dressed as what I truly was—an Arab of few kiam, no great learning, and severely limited prospects. I had not anticipated the feeling of excitement this aroused in me. I felt a new kinship with the other scurrying *fellahîn* around me, a kinship that extended—for the moment—to the religious part of daily life that I had neglected for so long. I promised myself that I would tend to those duties very soon, as soon as I had the opportunity; I had to find Nikki first.

Two blocks north of the Budayeen's eastern gate in the direction of the Shimaal Mosque, I found Bill. I knew he'd be near the walled quarter, sitting behind the steering wheel of his taxi, watching the people passing by on the sidewalk with patience, love, curiosity, and cold fear. Bill was almost my size, but more muscular. His arms were covered with blue-green tattoos, so old that they had blurred and become indistinct; I wasn't even certain what they had once represented. He hadn't cut his sandy-colored hair or beard in years, many years; he looked like a Hebrew patriarch. His skin, where it was exposed to the sun as he drove around the city, was burned a bright red, like forbidden crayfish in a pot. In his red face, his pale blue eyes stared with an insane intensity that always made me look quickly away. Bill was crazy, with a craziness he'd chosen for himself as carefully as Yasmin had chosen her high, sexy cheekbones.

I met Bill when I first came to the city. He had already learned to live among the outcasts, wretches, and bullies of the Budayeen years before; he helped me fit myself easily into that questionable society. Bill had been born in the United States of America—that's how old he was—in the part that is now called Sovereign Deseret. When the North American union broke into several jealous, balkanized nations, Bill turned his back on his birthplace forever. I don't know how he earned a living until he learned the way of life here; Bill doesn't remember, either. Somehow he acquired enough cash to pay for a single surgical modification in his body. Rather than wiring his brain, as many of the lost souls of the Budayeen choose to do, Bill selected a more subtle, more frightening bodmod: He had one of his lungs removed and replaced with a large, artificial gland that dripped a perpetual, measured quantity of some fourth-generation psychedelic drug into his bloodstream. Bill wasn't sure which drug he'd asked for, but judging from his abstracted speech and the quality of his hallucinations, I'd guess it was either *l*-ribopropylmethionine—RPM—or acetylated neocorticine.

You can't buy RPM or acetylated neocorticine on the street. There isn't much of a market for either drug. They both have the same long-term effect: After repeated doses of these drugs, a person's nervous system begins to degenerate. They compete for the binding sites in the human brain that are normally used by acetylcholine, a neurotransmitter. These new psychedelics attack and occupy the binding sites like a victorious army swooping down upon a conquered city; they cannot be removed, either by the body's own processes or by any form of medical therapy. The hallucinatory experiences are unparalleled in pharmacological history, but the price in terms of damage is exorbitant. The user, more literally than ever before, burns out his brain, synapse by synapse. The resulting condition is symptomatically indistinguishable from advanced Parkinson's and Alzheimer's diseases. Continued use, when the drugs begin interfering with the autonomic nervous system, probably proves fatal.

Bill hadn't reached that state yet. He was living a day-long, night-long dreamlife. I remembered what it had been like sometimes, when I had dropped a less-dangerous psychedelic and had been struck by the crippling fear that "I would never come down," a common illusion that you use to torture yourself. You feel as if this time, this particular drug experience, unlike all the pleasant experiences in the past, *this time* you've gone and broken something in your head. Trembling, terrified, promising that you'll never take another pill again, you huddle up against the onslaught of your own darkest dreams. At last, however, you do recover; the drug wears off, and sooner or later you forget just how bad the horror was. You do it again. Maybe this time you'll be luckier, maybe not.

There were no maybes with Bill. Bill was *never* coming down, ever. When those moments of utter, absolute dread began, he had no way to lessen the anxiety. He couldn't tell himself that if he just held out long enough, in the morning he'd be back to normal. Bill would never be back to normal. That's the way he wanted it. As for the cell-by-cell death of his nervous system, Bill only shrugged. "They all gonna die someday, right?"

"Yes," I replied, clinging nervously to the rear seat of his taxi as he plunged through narrow, twisting alleys.

"And if they go all at once, everybody *else* has a party at your funeral. You don't get *nothin'*. You get *buried*. This way, I get to say good-bye to my brain cells. They all done a lot for me. Good-bye, good-bye, farewell, it's been good to know ya. Give each goddamn little fucker its own little send-off. If you die like a regular person, bam! you're dead, violent stopping of every goddamn part of you, sugar in the gas tank, water in the carburetor, come to a grinding halt, you get one second, maybe two seconds, to scream to God that you're on your way. Awful way to come to an end. Live a violent life, live a violent death. Me, I'm sneaking across the bar one neuron at a time. If I have to go into that good night, I'm goin' *gentle*; the hell with whoever said not to. That sucker's *dead*, man, so what did he know? Not even the courage of his convictions. Maybe after I'm dead the *afrit* won't know I'm there if I keep my mouth shut. Maybe they'll leave me alone. I don't want to be fucked with after I'm dead, man. How can you protect yourself after you're dead? Think about *that*, man. I'd like to get my hands on the guy who invented demons, man. And they call *me* crazy."

I didn't want to discuss it any further.

Bill drove me out to Seipolt's. I always had Bill drive me when I went into the city for any reason. His insanity distracted me from the pervasive normalness all around, the lack of chaos imposed on everything. Riding with Bill was like carrying a little pocket of the Budayeen around with me for security. Like taking a tank of oxygen with you when you went into the deep, dark depths.

Seipolt's place was far from the center of the city, on the southeast edge. It was within sight of the realm of the everlasting sand, where the dunes waited for us to relax just a little, and then they'd cover us all like ashes, like dust. The sand would smooth out all conflicts, all works, all hopes. It would swoop down, a victorious army upon a conquered city, and we would all lie in the deep, dark depths beneath the sand forever. The good night would come—but not just yet. No, not here, not yet.

Seipolt saw that order was maintained and the desert held back; date palms arched around the villa, and gardens bloomed because water was forced to flow in this inhospitable place. Bougainvillea flowered and the breeze was perfumed with enticing aromas. Iron gates were kept in repair, painted and oiled; long, curving drives were kept clean and raked; walls were whitewashed. It was a magnificent residence, a rich man's home. It was a refuge against the creeping sand, against the creeping night that waits so patiently.

I sat in the back of Bill's taxi. His engine idled roughly, and he muttered and laughed to himself. I felt small and foolish—Seipolt's mansion awed me, despite myself. What was I going to say to Seipolt? The man had power—why, I couldn't hold back even a handful of sand, not if I tried with all my might and prayed to Allah at the same time.

I told Bill to wait, and I watched him until I saw that somewhere down in his careening mind he understood. I got out of the taxi and walked through the iron gate, up the white-pebbled drive toward the front entrance to the villa. I knew that Nikki was crazy; I knew that Bill was crazy; I was now learning that *I* wasn't entirely well, either.

As I listened to my feet crunching the small stones, I wondered why we all just didn't go back where we'd come from. That was the real treasure, the greatest gift: to be where you truly belonged. If I was lucky, someday I would find that place. *Inshallah*. If Allah willed.

The front door was a massive thing made of some kind of blond wood, with great iron hinges and an iron grille. The door was swinging open as I raised my hand to grasp the brass knocker. A tall, lean, blond European stared down at me. He had blue eyes (unlike Bill's, this man's eyes were the kind you always hear described as "piercing" and, by the Prophet's beard, I felt pierced); a thin, straight nose with flaring nostrils; a square chin; and a tight-lipped mouth that seemed set in a permanent expression of mild revulsion. He spoke to me in German.

I shook my head. " *'Anaa la 'afham,"* I said, grinning like the stupid Arab peasant he took me for.

The man with the blond hair looked impatient. He tried English. I shook my head again, grinning and apologizing and filling his ears with Arabic. It was obvious that he couldn't make any sense out of my language, and he wasn't going to try any harder to find another that I might understand. He was just on the point of slamming the heavy door in my face, when he saw Bill's taxi. That made him think. I looked like an Arab; to this man, all Arabs were pretty much the same, and one of their shared qualities was poverty. Yet I had hired a taxi to drive out to the residence of a rich and influential man. He was having trouble making sense of that, so now he wasn't so ready to dismiss me out of hand. He pointed at me and muttered something; I supposed it was "Wait here." I grinned, touched my heart and my forehead, and praised Allah three or four times.

A minute later, Blondie returned with an old man, an Arab in the employ of the household. The two men spoke together briefly. The old *fellah* turned to me and smiled. "Peace be upon you!" he said.

"And upon you," I said. "O neighbor, is this man the honored and excellent one, Lutz Seipolt Pasha?"

The old man laughed a little. "You are mistaken, my nephew," he said. "He is but the doorman, a menial even as I am." I really doubted that they were all *that* equal. Evidently the blond man was part of Seipolt's retinue, brought from Germany.

"On my honor, I am a fool!" I said. "I have come to ask an important question of His Excellency." Arabic terms of address frequently make such use of elaborate flattery. Seipolt was a businessman of some sort; I had already called him Pasha (an obsolete title used in the city for ingratiation) and His Excellency (as if he were some sort of ambassador). The old, leather-skinned Arab understood what I was doing well enough. He turned to the German and translated the conversation.

The German seemed even less pleased. He replied with a single, curt sentence. The Arab spoke to me. "Reinhardt the doorman wishes to hear this question."

I grinned into Reinhardt's hard eyes. "I'm only looking for my sister, Nikki."

The Arab shrugged and relayed the information. I saw Reinhardt blink and make the beginning of some gesture, then catch himself. He said something to the old *fellah*. "There is no one by that name here," the Arab told me. "There are no women at all in this household."

"I am certain that my sister is here," I said. "It is a matter of my family's honor." I sounded threatening; the Arab's eyes opened wide.

Reinhardt hesitated. He was undecided whether to slam the door in my face, after all, or kick this problem upstairs. I figured him for a coward; I was right. He didn't want to take the responsibility for the decision, so he agreed to convey me somewhere inside the cool, lavishly furnished house. I was glad to get out of the hot sun. The old Arab disappeared, returning to his duties. Reinhardt did not deign to look at me or address a word in my direction; he merely walked deeper into the house, and I followed. We came to another heavy door, this one of a fine-grained dark hardwood. Reinhardt rapped; a gruff voice called out, and Reinhardt answered. There was a short pause, then the gruff voice gave an order. Reinhardt turned the doorknob, pushed the door open just a little, and walked away. I entered the room, putting the dumb-Arab look back on my face. I pressed my hands together in supplication and dipped my head a few times for good measure. "You are His Excellency?" I asked in Arabic.

I was looking at a heavy, coarse-featured, bald man in his sixties, with a moddy and two or three daddies plugged into his sweat-shiny skull. He sat behind a heavily littered desk, holding a telephone in one hand and a large, blued-steel needle gun in the other. He smiled at me. "Please do me the honor of coming closer," he said in unaccented Arabic; it was probably a language daddy speaking for him.

I bowed again. I was trying to think, but my mind was like a blank parchment. Needle guns do that to me sometimes. "O Excellent One," I said, "I beg your pardon for intruding."

"To hell with all that 'Excellent One' bull. Tell me why you're here. You know who I am. You know I don't have a lot of time to waste."

I pulled Nikki's letter from my shoulder bag and gave it to him. I guessed he'd figure it out quickly enough.

He read it through and then put down the telephone—but not the needle gun. "You're Marîd, then?" he said. He'd stopped smiling.

"I have that privilege," I said.

"Don't get smart with me," said Seipolt. "Sit down in that chair." He waved me aside with the pistol. "I've heard one or two things about you."

"From Nikki?"

Seipolt shook his head. "Here and there in the city. You know how Arabs like to gossip."

I smiled. "I didn't realize I had such a reputation."

"It's nothing to get excited about, kid. Now, what makes you think this Nikki, whoever she is, is here? This letter?"

"Your house seemed like a good place to start looking. If she's not here, why is your name so prominent in her plans?"

Seipolt looked genuinely bewildered. "I don't have any idea, and that's the truth. I've never heard of your Nikki, and I don't have the least interest in her. As my staff will attest, I haven't had an interest in *any* woman in many years."

"Nikki's not just any woman," I said. "She's a simulated woman built on a customized boy's chassis. Maybe that's what's been stirring your interest during those years."

Seipolt's expression grew impatient. "Let me be blunt, Audran. I no longer have the apparatus to get sexually interested in anyone or anything. I no longer have the desire to have that condition repaired. I have found that I prefer business. *Versteh'?*"

I nodded. "I don't suppose you'd allow me to search your lovely home," I said. "I needn't disturb you while you work: don't mind me, I'll be quiet as a jerboa."

"No," he said, "Arabs steal things." His smile grew slowly until it was an evil thing.

I don't taunt easily, so I just shook that one off. "May I have the letter back?" I asked. Seipolt shrugged; I went to his desk and picked up Nikki's note, tucked it back in my shoulder bag. "Import-export?" I asked.

Seipolt was surprised. "Yes," he said. He looked down at a stack of bills of lading.

"Anything in particular, or the usual odds and ends?"

"What the hell difference does it make to you *what* I—" I waited for him to reach the middle of his outraged reply, then swiftly hit the inside of his right forearm with my left hand, swinging the muzzle of the needle gun away, and slapped him across his plump, white face with my right hand. Then I tightened my grip on his left wrist. We struggled silently for a moment. He was sitting, and I was standing over him, balanced, with momentum and surprise on my side. I twisted his wrist outward, abusing the small bones in his forearm. He grunted and dropped the needle gun to the desk, and with my right hand I swept it all the way across the room with one motion. He made no attempt to retrieve it. "I have other weapons," he said softly. "I have alarms to summon Reinhardt and the others."

"I do not doubt that," I said, not relaxing my hold on his wrist. I felt my little sadistic streak beginning to enjoy this. "Tell me about Nikki," I said.

"She's never been here, I don't know a damn thing about her," said Seipolt. He was starting to suffer. "You can hold the gun on me, we can fight and wrestle around the room, you can battle my men, you can search the house. Goddamn it, I don't know *who* your Nikki is! If you don't believe me now, there isn't a damn thing in the world I can say that will change your mind. Now, let's see how smart you really are."

"At least four people received that same letter," I said, thinking out loud. "Two of them are dead now. Maybe the police could find some clue here, even if I couldn't."

"Let go of my wrist." His voice was icy and commanding. I let go of his wrist; there didn't seem to be much point in holding it any longer, anyway. "Go ahead and call the police. Let them search. Let *them* persuade you. Then after they leave, I will make you sorry you ever stepped onto my property. If you don't get out of my office right now, you uncivilized idiot, you may never get another chance. *Versteh'?*"

"Uncivilized idiot" was a popular insult in the Budayeen that doesn't translate well. I was doubtful that it had been included in Seipolt's daddy vocabulary; I was amused that he had picked up the idiom in his years among us.

I cast a quick glance at his needle gun, lying on the carpet about a dozen feet from me. I would have liked to take it with me, but that would be bad manners. I wasn't going to fetch it for Seipolt, though; let him have Reinhardt pick it up. "Thanks for everything," I said, with a friendly look on my face. Then I changed my expression to the very respectful, dumb Arab. "I am obliged to you, O Excellent One. May your day be happy, may you awaken tomorrow in health!" Seipolt only stared at me hatefully. I backed away from him—not because of any wariness, but only to exaggerate the Arabic courtesy I was mocking him with. I passed through the office door and closed it softly. Then I stared up into Reinhardt's face again. I grinned and bowed; he showed me out. I paused on my way to the front door to admire some shelves filled with various kinds of rare artworks: pre-Columbian, Tiffany glass, Lalique crystal, Russian religious icons, ancient Egyptian and Greek statuary fragments. Among the hodgepodge of periods and styles was a ring, obscure and inconspicuous, a simple band of silver and lapis lazuli. I had seen that ring before, around one of Nikki's fingers while she played endlessly, twisting the locks of her hair. Reinhardt was studying me too closely; I wanted to grab the ring, but it was impossible.

At the door, I turned and began to give Reinhardt some Arabic formula of gratitude, but I didn't have the chance: this time, with great relish, the blond Aryan bastard flung the door shut, almost breaking my nose. I went back along the pebble drive, lost in thought. I got into Bill's cab. "Home," I said.

"Huh," Bill grunted. "Play hurt, play with pain. Easy for *him* to say, the son of a bitch. And there's the best defensive line in history waiting for me to twitch my little pink ass, waiting to tear my head off and hand it to me, right? 'Sacrifice.' So I hoped they'd call some dinky pass play and let me rest; but no, not today. The quarterback was an *afrit*, he only looked like a human being. I had him spotted, all right. When he handed it off, the ball was always hot as coals. I should have guessed something was up, even back then. Fire demons. A little bit of burning brimstone and smoke, see, and the referee can't see them grabbing at your facemask. *Afrits* cheat. *Afrits* want you to know what it's going to be like for you after you're dead, when they can do anything they want to you. They like to play with your mind like that. *Afrits*. Kept calling off-tackle plunges all afternoon. Hot as hell."

"Let's go home, Bill," I said more loudly.

He turned to look at me. "Easy for *you* to say," he muttered. Then he started his old taxi and backed out of Seipolt's drive.

I called Lieutenant Okking's commcode during the ride back to the Budayeen. I told him about Seipolt and Nikki's note. He didn't seem to be very interested. "Seipolt's nobody," said Okking. "He's a rich nobody from reunited Neudeutschland."

"Nikki was scared, Okking," I told him.

"She probably lied to you and the others in those letters. She lied about where she was going, for some reason. Then it didn't work out the way she'd planned, and she tried to get in touch with you. Whoever she'd gone with didn't let her finish." I could almost hear him shrug. "She didn't do a smart thing, Marîd. She's probably been hurt because of it, but it wasn't Seipolt."

"Seipolt may be nobody," I said bitterly, "but he lies very well under pressure. Have you figured out anything about Devi's murder? Some connection with Tamiko's killing?"

"There probably isn't any connection, buddy, as much as you and your criminal colleagues want there to be. The Black Widow Sisters are the kind of people who get themselves murdered, that's all. They ask for it, so they get it. Just coincidence that the two of them were postmarked so close together."

"What kind of clues did you find at Devi's?"

There was a brief silence. "What the *hell*, Audran, all of a sudden I have a new partner? Who the fuckin' hell do you think you *are*? Where do you get off questioning *me*? As if you didn't know I couldn't talk police business with you like that, even if I wanted to, which is not in the most minute sense true. Go away, Marîd. You're bad luck." Then he snapped the connection.

I put my phone in my bag and closed my eyes. It was a long, dusty, hot ride back to the Budayeen. It would have been quiet, except for

Bill's constant monologue; and it would have been comfortable, except for Bill's dying taxi. I thought about Seipolt and Reinhardt; Nikki and the sisters; Devi's killer, whoever he was; Tamiko's mad torturer, whoever *he* was. None of it made any sense to me at all.

Okking had just been telling me that very thing: it didn't make sense because there *was* no sense. You can't find a point in a pointless killing. I had just become aware of the random violence in which I had lived for years, part of it, ignoring it, believing myself immune to it. My mind was trying to take the unrelated events of the last several days and make them fit a pattern, like making warriors and mythical beasts out of scattered stars in the night sky. Senseless, pointless; yet the human mind seeks explanations. It demands order, and only something like RPM or Sonneine can quiet that clamoring or, at least, distract the mind with something else.

Sounded like a great idea to me. I took out my pill case and swallowed four sunnies. I didn't bother offering anything to Bill; he'd paid in advance, and anyway he had a private screening.

I had Bill let me out at the eastern gate of the Budayeen. The fare was thirty kiam; I gave him forty. He stared at the money for a long time until I took it back and pushed it into the pocket of his shirt. He looked up at me as if he'd never met me before. "Easy for *you* to say," he murmured.

I needed to learn a few things, so I went directly to a modshop on Fourth Street. The modshop was run by a twitchy old woman who'd had one of the first brain jobs. I think the surgeons must have missed what they'd been aiming for just slightly, or else Laila had always made you feel like getting out of her presence as quickly as possible. She couldn't talk to you without whining. She crooked her head and stared up at you as if she were some kind of garden mollusk and you were about to step on her. You sometimes considered stepping on her, but she was too quick. She had long, straggly gray hair; bushy gray eyebrows; yellow eyes; bloodless lips and depopulated jaws; black skin, scaled and scabrous; and the same crooked, clawed fingers that a witch ought to have. She had one moddy or another plugged in all day, but her own personality—and it wasn't a likable personality at all—bled through as if the moddy weren't exciting the right cells, or enough of them, or strongly enough. You'd get Janis Joplin with static-like flashes of Laila, you'd get the Marquise Josephine Rose Kennedy with Laila's nasal whine, but it was her shop and her merchandise, and if you didn't want to put up with her, you went elsewhere.

I went to Laila because even though I wasn't wired, she let me "borrow" any moddy or daddy she had in stock, by plugging it into herself. If I needed to do a little research, I went to Laila and hoped that she didn't distort what I had to learn in any lethal way.

This afternoon she was being herself, with only a bookkeeping add-on and an inventory-management add-on plugged in. It was that time of the year again; how the months fly when you take a lot of drugs.

"Laila," I said. She was so much like the old hag in *Snow White* that you couldn't think of more to say to her. Laila was one person with whom you didn't make small talk, whatever you wanted from her.

She looked up, her lips mumbling stock numbers, quantities, markups, and markdowns. She nodded.

"What do you know about James Bond?" I asked.

She put her microrecorder down and tapped it off. She stared at me for a few seconds, her eyes getting very round, then very narrow. "Marîd," she said. She managed to whine my name.

"What do you know about James Bond?"

"Videos, books, twentieth-century power fantasies. Spies, that kind of action. He was irresistible to women. You want to be irresistible?" She whined at me suggestively.

"I'm working on that on my own, thanks. I just want to know if anybody's bought a James Bond moddy from you lately."

"No, I'm sure of it. Haven't even had one in stock for a long time. James Bond is kind of ancient history, Marîd. People are looking for new arms. Cloak-and-dagger is too quaint for words." When she stopped talking, numbers formed on her lips as her daddies went on speaking to her brain.

I knew about James Bond because I'd read the books—actual, physical books made out of paper. At least, I'd read *some* of them, four or five. Bond was a Eur-Am myth like Tarzan or Johnny Carson. I wished Laila had had a Bond moddy; it might have helped me understand what Devi's killer was thinking. I shook my head; something was tickling my mind again. . . .

I turned my back on Laila and left her shop. I glanced at a holographic advertisement playing on the sidewalk outside her display window. It was Honey Pílar. She looked about eight feet tall and absolutely naked. When you're Honey Pílar, naked is the only way to go. She was running her lascivious hands over her superluminally sexy body. She shook her pale hair out of her green eyes and stared at me. She slid the pink tip of her tongue across her unnaturally full, luscious lips. I stood watching the holoporn, mesmerized. That was what it was for, and it was working just fine. At the edge of my consciousness, I was aware that several other men and women had stopped in their tracks and were staring, too. Then Honey spoke. Her voice, enhanced electronically to send chills of desire through my already lust-ridden body, reminded me of adolescent longings I hadn't thought of in years. My mouth was dry; my heart was pounding.

The hologram was selling Honey's new moddy, the one Chiri already owned. If I bought one for Yasmin. . . .

"My moddy lies over the ocean," said Honey in a breathy, soft voice, while her hands slid slowly down the copious upper slopes of her perfect breasts. . . .

"My moddy lies over the sea." Her hands tweaked her nipples hard, then found their way to the delicious undersides of those breasts and continued southward.. . . .

"Now someone is jamming my moddy," she confided, as her fiery fingernails lightly touched her flat belly, still searching, still seeking. . . .

"Now he knows what it's like to jam *me*!" Her eyes were half-closed with ecstasy. Her voice became a drawn-out moan, pleading for the continuation of that pleasure. She was begging *me* as her hands at last slipped out of sight between her suntanned thighs.

As the hologram faded, another woman's voice overdubbed the details of manufacturer and cost. "Haven't you tried modular marital aids? Are you still using holoporn? Look, if using a rubber is like kissing your sister, then holoporn is like kissing a *picture* of your sister! Why stare at a holo of Honey Pílar, when with her new moddy you can jam the livin' daylights out of her again and again, whenever you want! Come on! Give your girlfriend or boyfriend the new Honey Pílar moddy today! Modular marital aids are sold as novelty items only."

The voice faded away and let me have my mind back. The other spectators, similarly released, went on about their business a little unsteadily. I turned toward the Street, thinking first about Honey Pílar, then about the moddy I would give Yasmin as an anniversary present (as soon as possible, for the anniversary of *anything*. Hell, I didn't care), and at last the tantalizing thing that had been bothering me. I'd thought of it first after I spoke with Okking about the shooting in Chiriga's nightclub, and again today.

Someone who just wanted to have a little Fun With Murder wouldn't have used a James Bond moddy. No, a Bond moddy is too specialized and too sterile. James Bond didn't get pleasure from killing people. If some psychotic wanted to use a personality module to help him murder more satisfyingly, he might have chosen any of a dozen rogues. There were underground moddies, too, that weren't on sale in the respectable modshops: for a big enough pile of kiam, you could probably get your hands on a Jack the Ripper moddy. There were moddies of fictional characters, or real people, recorded right from their brains or reconstructed by clever programmers. I felt ill as I thought about the perverse people who wanted the illicit moddies, and the black-market industry that catered to them with Charles Manson modules or Nosferatu modules or Heinrich Himmler modules.

I was sure that whoever had used the Bond module had done so for a different purpose, knowing in advance that it wouldn't give him much pleasure. It wasn't pleasure the false James Bond had been after. His goal had not been excitement, but execution.

Devi's death—and, of course, the Russian's—had not been the work of a mad slasher among the dregs of society. Both murders had been, in fact, assassinations. Political assassinations.

Okking would not listen to any of this without proof. I had none. I wasn't even certain in my own mind what this all meant. What connection could there be between Bogatyrev, a minor functionary in the legation of a weak and indigent Eastern European kingdom, and Devi, one of the Black Widow Sisters? Their worlds didn't intersect at all.

I needed more information, but I didn't know where it was going to come from. I found myself walking determinedly somewhere. Where was I going? I asked myself. Devi's apartment, of course. Okking's men would still be combing the premises for clues. There'd be barriers up, and a cordon with signs warning CRIME SCENE. There'd be—

Nothing. No barriers, no cordon, no police. A light was on in the window. I went up to the green shutters that were used to cover the doorway. They were thrown open, so that Devi's front room was clearly visible from the sidewalk. A middle-aged Arab was down on his hands and knees, painting a wall. We greeted each other, and he wanted to know if I wanted to rent the place; it would be fixed up in another two days. That's all the memorial Devi got. That's all the effort Okking would put into finding her killer. Devi, like Tami, didn't deserve much of the authorities' time. They hadn't been good citizens; they hadn't earned the right to justice.

I looked up and down the block. All the buildings on Devi's side of the street were the same: low, whitewashed, flat-roofed houses with green-shuttered doors and windows. There would have been no place for "James Bond" to hide, to waylay Devi. He could only have concealed himself inside her apartment in some way, waiting for her to come home after work; or else he'd waited someplace nearby. I crossed the old, cobbled street. On the opposite side, some of the houses had low stoops with iron handrails. Directly across from Devi's house, I sat on the topmost step and looked around. On the ground below me, to the right of the stairs, were a few cigarette butts. Someone had sat on this stoop, smoking; maybe it was the person who lived in the house, maybe not. I squatted down and looked at the butts. There were three gold bands on each, around the filters.

In the James Bond books, he smoked cigarettes made up specially for him of some particular mixture of tobaccos, and his blend was marked with the three gold bands. The assassin took his job seriously; he used a small-caliber pistol, probably a Walther PPK, like Bond's. Bond kept his cigarettes in a gunmetal cigarette case that held fifty; I wondered if the assassin had one of those, too.

I put the cigarette butts in my shoulder bag. Okking wanted proof, I had proof. That didn't mean Okking would agree. I looked up into the sky; it was getting late, and there would be no moon tonight. The slender sliver of the new moon would appear tomorrow night, bringing with it the beginning of the holy month of Ramadân.

The already-frantic Budayeen would get more hysterical after nightfall tomorrow. Things would be deathly quiet during the day, though. Deathly quiet. I laughed softly as I walked in the direction of Frenchy Benoit's bar. I'd seen enough of death, but the notion of peace and quiet sounded very inviting.

What a fool I was.

SEVEN

bismillah ar-Rahman ar-Raheem. In the name of Allah, the Compassionate, the Merciful.

In the month of Ramadân, in which was revealed the Qur'ân, a guidance for mankind, and clear proofs of the guidance, and the Criterion of right and wrong. And whosoever of you is present, let him fast the month, and whosoever of you is sick or on a journey, let him fast the same number of days. Allah desireth for you ease; He desireth not hardship for you; and He desireth that ye should complete the period, and that ye should magnify Allah for having guided you, and that it may be that ye be thankful.

That was the one hundred eighty-fifth verse of the sûrah Al-Baqarah, The Cow, the second sûrah in the noble Qur'ân. The Messenger of God, may the blessing of Allah be on him and peace, gave directions for the observance of the holy month of Ramadân, the ninth lunar month of the Muslim calendar. This observance is considered one of the five Pillars of Islam. During the month, Muslims are prohibited from eating, drinking, and smoking from dawn until sunset. The police and the religious leaders see that even those like myself, who are negligent at best about spiritual duties, comply. Nightclubs and bars are closed during the day, and the cafés and restaurants. It is forbidden to take so much as a sip of water until after dusk. When night falls, when it is proper to serve food, the Muslims of the city enjoy themselves. Even those who shun the Budayeen the rest of the year may come and relax in a café.

Night would replace day completely in the Muslim world during the month, were it not for the five-times-daily call to prayer. These must be heeded as usual, so the respectful Muslim rises at dawn and prays, but does not break his fast. His employer may let him go home for a few hours in the afternoon to nap, to catch up on the sleep he loses by staying awake into the early hours of the morning, taking his meals and enjoying what he cannot enjoy during the day.

In many ways, Islam is a beautiful and elegant faith; but it is the nature of religions to put a higher premium on your proper attention to ritual than on your convenience. Ramadân can be very inconvenient to the sinners and scoundrels of the Budayeen.

Yet at the same time, it made some things simpler. I merely shifted my schedule several hours later on the clock, and I wasn't put out at all. The nightclubs made the same alteration in their hours. It might have been worse if I had other things to attend to during the day; say, for instance, facing Mecca and praying every now and then.

The first Wednesday of Ramadân, after I'd settled myself into the changed daily scheme, I sat in a small coffeehouse called the Café Solace, on Twelfth Street. It was almost midnight, and I was playing cards with three other young men, drinking small cups of thick coffee without sugar, and eating small bites of *baqlaawah*. This was just what Yasmin had been envious of. She was over at Frenchy's, shaking her fine little behind and charming strangers into buying her champagne cocktails; I was eating sweet pastries and gambling. I didn't see anything wrong with taking it easy when I could, even if Yasmin still had to put in a long, exhausting ten hours. It seemed to be the natural order of things.

The three others at my table were a mixed collection. Mahmoud was a sex-change, shorter than me but broader through the shoulders and hips. He had been a girl until five or six years ago; he'd even worked for Jo-Mama for a while, and now he lived with a real girl who hustled in the same bar. It was an interesting coincidence.

Jacques was a Moroccan Christian, strictly heterosexual, who felt and acted as if he had special privileges because he was three-quarters European, therefore beating me out by a full grandparent. Nobody listened to Jacques very much, and whenever celebrations and parties were planned, Jacques learned about them just a little too late. Jacques was included in card games, however, because somebody has to be there to lose, and it might as well be a miffy Christian.

Saied the Half-Hajj was tall and well-built, rich, and strictly homosexual; he wouldn't be seen in the company of a woman, real, renovated, or reconverted. He was called the Half-Hajj because he was so scatterbrained that he could never start one project without getting distracted in the middle by two or three others. Hajj is the title one gets after completing the holy pilgrimage to Mecca, which is one of the other Pillars of Islam. Saied had actually begun the journey several years ago, made about five hundred miles, and then turned back because he'd had a magnificent money-making idea that he forgot before he reached home again. Saied was somewhat older than I was, with a carefully trimmed mustache that he was very proud of. I don't know why; I've never thought of a mustache as an achievement, unless you'd started out life like Mahmoud. Female, that is. All three of my companions had had their brains wired. Saied was wearing a moddy and two daddies. The moddy was just a general personality module; not a particular person but a particular type—he was being strong, silent, rough trade today, and neither of the add-ons could have been giving him card-playing help. He and Jacques were making me and Mahmoud richer.

These three ill-assorted louts were my best male friends. We wasted a lot of afternoons (or, during Ramadân, late evenings) together. I had two prime sources of information in the Budayeen: these three, and the girls in the clubs. The information I got from one person often contradicted the version I heard from another, so I'd long ago gotten into the habit of trying to hear as many different stories as I could and averaging them all out. The truth was in there somewhere, I knew it; the problem was coaxing it into the open.

I had won most of the money on the table, and Mahmoud the rest. Jacques was about to throw in his cards and quit the game. I wanted something more to eat, and the Half-Hajj agreed. The four of us were just about to leave the Solace and find somewhere else to have lunch, when Fuad ran up to us. This was the scrawny, spindle-legged son of a camel who was called (among other things) Fuad il-Manhous, or Fuad the Chronically Unlucky. I knew right off that I wasn't going to get anything to eat for a while. The look on il-Manhous's face told me that a little adventure was about to begin.

"Praise Allah that I found you all here," he said, snapping quick glances at each of us.

"Go with Allah, my brother," said Jacques tartly. "I think I see Him heading that way, toward the north wall."

Fuad ignored him. "I need some help," he said. He sounded more frantic than usual. He has little adventures fairly often, but this time he seemed really upset.

"What's wrong, Fuad?" I asked.

He looked at me gratefully, like a child. "Some black bitch clipped me for thirty kiam." He spat on the ground.

I looked at the Half-Hajj, who only looked heavenward for strength. I looked at Mahmoud, who was grinning. Jacques looked exasperated.

"Them bitches get you pretty regularly, don't they, Fuad?" asked Mahmoud.

"You just think so," he replied defensively.

"What happened this time?" asked Jacques. "Where? Anybody we know?"

"New girl," he said.

"It's always a new girl," I said.

"She works over at the Red Light," said the Cursed One.

"I thought you were banned out of there," said Mahmoud.

"I was," Fuad tried to explain, "and I still can't spend any money in there, Fatima won't let me, but I'm working for her as a porter, so I'm in there all the time. I don't live by Hassan's shop anymore, he used to let me sleep in his storeroom, but Fatima lets me sleep under the bar."

"She won't give you a drink in her place," said Jacques, "but she lets you carry out her garbage."

"Uh huh. And sweep up and clean off the mirrors."

Mahmoud nodded wisely. "I've always said that Fatima has a soft heart," he said. "You've all heard me."

"So what *happened*?" I asked. I hate having to listen to Fuad circumambulate the point for half an hour every time.

"I was in the Red Light, see," he said, "and Fatima had just told me to bring in another couple bottles of Johnny Walker and I'd gone back and told Nassir and he gave me the bottles and I brought them up to Fatima and she put them under the bar. Then I asked her, I said, 'What do you want me to do now?' and she said, 'Why don't you go drink lye?' and I said, 'I'm going to go sit down for a while,' and she said, 'All right,' so I sat down by the bar and watched for a while, and this girl came over and sat down next to me—"

"A black girl," said Saied the Half-Hajj.

"Uh huh—"

The Half-Hajj gave me a look and said, "I have a special sensitivity in these matters." I laughed.

Fuad went on. "Uh huh, so this black girl was real pretty, never saw her before, she said she just started working for Fatima that night, and I told her it was a pretty rowdy bar and that sometimes you have to watch yourself because of the crowd they get in there, and she said she was real grateful because I gave her the advice and she said people in the city were real cold and didn't care about anybody but themselves, and it was nice to meet a nice guy like me. She gave me a little kiss on my cheek, and she let me put my arm around her, and then she started—"

"To feel you up," said Jacques.

Fuad blushed furiously. "She wanted to know if she could have a drink, and I said I only had enough money to live on for the next two weeks, and she asked me how much I had, and I said I wasn't sure. She said she bet I probably had enough to get her *one* drink and I said, 'Look, if I've got more than thirty, I will, but if I've got less than thirty, I can't,' and she said that sounded fair, so I took out my money and guess what? I had exactly thirty, and we hadn't said what we were going to do if I had exactly thirty, so she said it was okay, I didn't have to buy her a drink. I thought that was real nice of her. And she kept kissing on me and hugging me and touching me, and I thought she really liked me a lot. And then, guess what?"

"She took your money," said Mahmoud. "She wanted you to count it just to see where you kept it."

"I didn't know she done it until later, when I wanted to get something to eat. It was all gone, like she reached into my pocket and took it."

"You've been clipped before," I said. "You *knew* she was going to do it. I think you *like* being clipped. I think you get off on it."

"That's not true," said Fuad stubbornly. "I really thought she liked me a lot, and I liked her, and I thought maybe I could ask her out or something later, after she got off work. Then I saw my money was gone, and I knew she done it. I can put two and two together, I'm no dummy."

We all nodded without saying anything.

"I told Fatima, but she wouldn't do anything, so I went back to Joie—that's what she calls herself, but she told me it wasn't her real name—and she got real mad, saying she never stole nothing in her life. I said I knew she done it, and she got madder and madder, and then she pulled a razor out of her purse, and Fatima told her to put it away, I wasn't worth it, but Joie was still real mad and come at me with the razor, and I got out of there and looked all over the place for you guys."

Jacques closed his eyes wearily and rubbed them. "You want us to go get your thirty kiam back. Why the hell *should* we, Fuad? You're an imbecile. You want us to walk up to some screaming crazy flatbacker who's waving a razor around, just because you can't hang on to your own roll."

"Don't argue with him, Jacques," said Mahmoud, "it's like talking to a brick wall." The actual Arabic phrase is, "You talk in the east, he answers in the west," which is a very perceptive description of what was happening with Fuad il-Manhous.

The Half-Hajj, though, was wearing this moddy that made him

into a Man of Action, so he just twirled his mustache and gave Fuad a small, rugged smile. "Come on," he said, "you show me this Joie."

"Thanks," said the skinny Fuad, fawning all over Saied, "thanks a whole lot. I mean, I don't have another goddamn fîq, she has all the money I had saved for the next—"

"Just shut up about it," said Jacques. We got up and followed Saied and Fuad to the Red Light. I shook my head; I didn't want to be involved in this at all, but I had to go along. I hate eating by myself, so I told myself to be patient; we'd all go by the Café de la Fée Blanche afterward and have lunch. All of us except the Cursed One, I mean. In the meantime, I swallowed two tri-phets, just for luck.

The Red Light Lounge was a rough place, and you went into it knowing it was a rough place, so if you got rolled or clipped in there, it was hard to find someone to give you a little sympathy. The police figured you were a fool to be there in the first place, so they would just laugh in your face if you made a complaint to them. Both Fatima and Nassir are interested only in how much profit they make on each bottle of liquor they sell and how many champagne cocktails their girls push; they couldn't be bothered keeping track of what the girls were doing on their own. It was free enterprise in its purest, most unhindered form.

I was reluctant to set foot in the Red Light because I didn't get along with either Fatima or Nassir, so I was last in our little group to sit down. We took a table away from the bar. They kept it as dark in there as Chiri kept her place. There was a heavy, sour smell of spilled beer. A hatchet-faced redhaired girl was dancing onstage. She had a nice little body unless your gaze strayed up past her neck. What she did on stage was designed to keep your attention away from her defects and focused intently on what she had to sell. Fanya, her name was, I remembered. They called her "Floor-show Fanya," because her notion of dance was mostly horizontal, rather than in the customary upright position.

It was still early in the night, so we ordered beers, but virile old Saied the Half-Hajj, still listening to his manly moddy, got himself a double shot of Wild Turkey to go with his beer. No one asked the undernourished Fuad if he wanted anything. "That's her over there," he said in a loud whisper, pointing to a short, plain girl who was working on a European in a business suit.

"She's no girl," said Mahmoud. "Fuad, she's a deb."

"Don't you think I can tell the difference between a boy and a girl?" responded Fuad hotly. No one wanted to voice an opinion about that; as far as I was concerned, it was too dark for me to read her yet. I'd know later, when I saw her better.

Saied didn't even wait for his drink. He stood up and sort of strolled over to Joie. You know, "nothing can touch me because, deep inside, I'm Attila the Hun, and all you other faggots better watch your asses." He engaged Joie in conversation; I couldn't hear a word, and I didn't want to. Fuad followed the Half-Hajj like a pet lamb, piping up in his shrill voice now and then, agreeing vigorously with Saied or denying vigorously the new whore.

"I don't know nothing about this chump's thirty kiam," she said.

"She's got it, look in her purse," screeched the Unlucky One.

"I got more than that, you son of a bitch," cried Joie. "How you gonna prove some of it is yours?"

Tempers were igniting fast. The Half-Hajj had the sense to turn and send Fuad back to our table, but Joie followed the scrawny *fellah*, pushing him and calling him all kinds of foul names. I thought Fuad was almost on the verge of tears. Saied tried to pull Joie away, and she turned on him. "When my people gets here, he's gonna climb into your ass," she shouted.

The Half-Hajj gave her one of his little, heroic smiles. "We'll see about that when he gets here," he said calmly. "In the meantime, we're giving my friend here his money back, and I don't want to hear about you shaving him or any of my other friends again, or you'll have so many cuts on your face you'll have to turn tricks with a bag over your head."

It was at just this moment, with Saied holding Joie's wrists together, with Fuad standing on her other side, blithering loudly into her ear, that Joie's pimp came into the bar. "Here we go," I murmured.

Joie called to him and quickly told him what was happening. "These cocksuckers are trying to take my money!" she cried.

The pimp, a big, one-eyed Arab named Tewfik whom everybody called Courvoisier Sonny, didn't need to hear a word from anyone. He slapped Fuad aside without so much as a glance. He put one hand around Saied's right wrist and made him release Joie's hands. Then he shoved the Half-Hajj's shoulder and sent him backward, staggering. "Messing with my girl like that can get you cut, my brother," he said in a deceptively soft voice.

Saied strolled back to our table. "She *is* a deb," he said, "Just a man in a dress." He and Sonny were standing right above me, and I wished they'd take their negotiations outside. The disturbance hadn't seemed to draw the attention of either Fatima or Nassir. Meanwhile, Fanya had ended her turn on stage, and a tall, lanky black sex-change, American, began to dance.

"Your ugly, thieving, syphilitic whore took thirty kiam of my friend's money," said Saied in the same soft voice as Sonny.

"You gonna let him call me names, Sonny?" demanded Joie. "In front of all these other bitches?"

"Praise Allah," said Mahmoud sadly, "it has turned into an affair of honor. It was a lot simpler when it was just larceny."

"I won't let nobody call you nothing, girl," said Sonny. He had put a little growl into his soft voice. He turned to Saied. "I'm telling you now to shut the fuck up."

"Make me," said Saied, smiling.

Mahmoud, Jacques, and I grabbed our beers and got halfway out of our seats; we were too late. Sonny had a knife in the rope belt around his *gallebeya*; he reached for it. Saied got his knife out quicker. I heard Joie cry a warning to Sonny. I saw Sonny's eyes get narrow as he backed away a step. Saied swung his left fist hard at Sonny's jaw, and Sonny ducked away. Saied took a step forward, blocked Sonny's right arm, bent a little, and drove his knife into Sonny's side.

I heard Sonny make a little sound, a quiet, gurgling, surprised groan. Saied had slashed Sonny's chest and cut some big vessels. Blood spurted in all directions, more blood than you would think possible for one person to carry around. Sonny stumbled one step to his left, then two steps forward, and fell onto the table. He grunted, jerked and thrashed a few times, and slipped off the table to the floor. We were all staring at him. Joie hadn't made another sound. Saied hadn't moved; he was still in the same position he'd been in when his knife had cut open Sonny's heart. He slowly rose up straight, his knife-hand falling to his side. He was breathing heavily, loudly. He turned around and grabbed his beer; his eyes were glassy and expressionless. He was soaked with blood. His hair, his face, his clothing, his hands and arms, all were covered with Sonny's blood. There was blood all over the table. There was blood all over us. I was almost drenched in blood. It had taken me a moment, but now I realized how much blood I had on me, and I was horrified. I stood up, trying to pull my blood-soaked shirt away from my body. Joie began to scream, again and again; someone finally slapped her a few times, and she shut up. At last Fatima called Nassir out of the back room, and he called the police. The rest of us just sat down at another table. The music stopped, the girls went into their dressing room, the customers slipped out of the bar before the police could arrive. Mahmoud went to Fatima and got a pitcher of beer for us.

Sergeant Hajjar took his time coming around to see the aftermath.

When he arrived at last, I was surprised to see that he'd come alone. "What's that?" he asked, indicating Sonny's corpse with the toe of a boot.

"Dead pimp," said Jacques.

"They all look the same, dead," said Hajjar. He noticed the blood splashed all over everything. "Big guy, huh?"

"Sonny," said Mahmoud.

"Oh, *that* motherfucker."

"He died for thirty lousy kiam," said Saied, shaking his head unbelievingly.

Hajjar looked around the bar thoughtfully, then looked straight at me. "Audran," he said, stifling a yawn, "come with me." He turned to walk back out of the bar.

"Me?" I cried. "I didn't have anything to do with it!"

"With what?" asked Hajjar, puzzled.

"With that knifing."

"The hell with the knifing. You got to come with me." He led me to his patrol car. He didn't care at all about this murder. If some rich-bitch tourist gets done in, the police break their buns lifting fingerprints and measuring angles and interrogating everybody twenty or thirty times. But let someone nip this gorilla one-eyed stable-boss or Tami or Devi, and the cops act as bored as an ox on a hill. Hajjar wasn't going to question anybody or take pictures or anything. It wasn't worth his time. To the officials, Sonny had only gotten what he had coming; in Chiriga's philosophy, "Paybacks are a motherfucker." The police didn't mind if the whole Budayeen decimated itself, one worthless degenerate at a time.

Hajjar locked me into the back seat, then slid behind the steering wheel. "Are you arresting me?" I asked.

"Shut up, Audran."

"Are you arresting me, you son of a bitch?"

"No."

That brought me up short. "Then what the hell are you holding me for? I told you I didn't have a goddamn thing to do with that killing in the bar."

Hajjar glanced back over his shoulder. "Will you forget about that pimp already? This doesn't have anything to do with that."

"Where are you taking me?"

Hajjar looked around again and gave me a sadistic grin. "Papa wants to talk to you."

I felt cold. "Papa?" I'd seen Friedlander Bey here and there, I knew all about him, but I'd never actually been summoned into his presence before.

"And from what I hear, Audran, he's spitting mad. You'd be better off if I *did* bring you in for murder."

"Mad? At me? What for?"

Hajjar just shrugged. "I don't know. I was just told to fetch you. Let Papa do his own talking."

Just at this moment of growing fear and menace, the tri-phets decided to kick in and race my heart even harder. It had started out to be such a nice evening, too. I'd won some money, I was looking forward to a pleasant meal, and Yasmin was going to spend the night again. Instead I was in the back of a police cruiser, my shirt and jeans still damp with Sonny's blood, my face and arms beginning to itch as the blood dried on them, heading toward some foreboding meeting with Friedlander Bey, who owned everybody and everything. I was sure it was some sort of accounting, but I couldn't imagine for what. I've always been extremely careful not to tread on Papa's toes. Hajjar wouldn't tell me any more; he only grinned wolfishly and said that he wouldn't want to be in my boots. I didn't want to be in my boots, either, but that's where I'd found myself too often lately. "It is the will of Allah," I murmured anxiously. Nearer My God to Thee.

Eight

fRiedlander bey lived in a large, white, towered mansion that might almost have qualified as a palace. It was a large estate in the middle of the city only two blocks from the Christian Quarter. I don't think anyone else had such a great expanse of property walled off. Papa's house made Seipolt's look like a Badawi tent. But Sergeant Hajjar didn't drive me to Papa's house: we were going in the wrong direction. I mentioned this to Hajjar, the bastard.

"Let *me* do the driving," he said in a surly voice. He called me "il-Maghrîb." Maghrîb may mean sunset, but it also refers to the vast, vague part of North Africa to the west, where the uncivilized idiots come from—Algerians, Moroccans, semihuman creatures like that. Lots of my friends will call me il-Maghrîb, or Maghrebi, and then it's only a nickname or an epithet; when Hajjar used it, it was definitely an insult.

"The house is back the other way about two and a half miles," I said.

"Don't you think I know that? Jesus Christ, would I love to have you handcuffed to a pole for fifteen minutes."

"Where on Allah's good, green earth are you taking me?"

Hajjar wouldn't answer any more questions, so I just gave up and watched the city go by. Riding with Hajjar was a lot like riding with Bill: you didn't learn very much and you weren't sure where you were going or how you were going to get there.

The cop pulled into an asphalt driveway behind a cinder-block motel on the eastern outskirts of the city. The cinder blocks were painted a pale green, and there was a small handlettered sign that said simply MOTEL NO VACANCY. I thought a motel with a permanent No

Vacancy sign was a trifle unusual. Hajjar got out of the cop car and opened the back door. I slid out and stretched a little; the tri-phets had me humming in a high-velocity way. The combination of the drugs and my nervousness added up to a headache, a very sick stomach, and fidgeting that flirted with total emotional collapse.

I followed Hajjar to room nineteen of the motel. He rapped on the door in some kind of signal. The door was opened by a hulking Arab who looked like a block of sandstone that walked. I didn't expect him to be able to talk or think; when he did, I was astonished. He nodded to Hajjar, who didn't acknowledge it; the sergeant went back toward his car. The Stone looked at me for a moment, probably wondering where I'd come from; then he realized that I must have come with Hajjar, and that I was the one he was waiting to let into the damn motel room. "In," he said. His voice sounded like sandstone that spoke.

I shuddered as I passed by him. There were two more men in the room, another Stone That Speaks on the far side, and Friedlander Bey, sitting at a folding table set up between the king-sized bed and the bureau. All the furnishings were European, but a little worn and shabby.

Papa stood when he saw me come in. He was about five feet two inches tall, but almost two hundred pounds. He wore a plain, white cotton shirt, gray trousers, and slippers. He wore no jewelry. He had a few wisps of graying hair brushed straight back on his head, and soft brown eyes. Friedlander Bey didn't look like the most powerful man in the city. He raised his right hand in front of his face, almost touching his forehead. "Peace," he said.

I touched my heart and my lips. "And on you be peace."

He did not look happy to see me. The formalities would protect me for a short while and give me time to think. What I needed to plan was a way to bowl over the two Stones and get out of that motel room. It was going to be a challenge.

Papa seated himself at the table again. "May your day be prosperous," he said. He indicated the chair across from him.

"May your day be prosperous and blessed," I said. As soon as I could, I was going to ask for a glass of water, and take as many Paxium as I had with me. I sat down.

His brown eyes caught mine and held them. "How is your health?" he asked. His voice was unfriendly.

"Praise Allah," I said. I felt the fear growing.

"We have not seen you in some time," said Friedlander Bey. "You have made us lonely."

"May Allah never let you feel lonely."

The second Stone served coffee. Papa took a cup and sipped from it to show me it wasn't poisoned. Then he handed it to me. "Be pleased," he said. There was little hospitality in his voice.

I took the cup. "May coffee be found forever in your house."

We drank some coffee together. Papa sat back and regarded me for a moment. "You have honored us," he said at last.

"May Allah preserve you." We had come to the end of the short form of the amenities. Things would begin to happen now. The first thing that happened was that I took out my pill case, dug up every tranquilizer I could find, and swallowed them with some more coffee. I took fourteen Paxium; some people would find that a large quantity. It wasn't, for me. I know lots of people in the Budayeen who can drink me under the table—Yasmin, for one—but I bow to no one in my capacity for pills and caps. Fourteen 10-milligram Paxium, if I was lucky, would only unscrew the tension a little; they wouldn't even begin to make me really tranquil. Right then, I'd need something with a little more velocity to it for that. Fourteen Paxium was barely Mach 1.

Friedlander Bey held out his coffee cup to his servant, who refilled it. Papa sipped a little of it, watching me over the rim of the small cup. He set it down precisely and said, "You understand that I have a great number of people in my employ."

"Indeed yes, O Shaykh," I said.

"A great number of people who depend on me, not only for their livelihoods, but for much more. I am a source of security in their difficult world. They know that they may depend on me for wages and certain favors, as long as they perform their work for me in a satisfactory way."

"Yes, O Shaykh." The blood drying on my face and arms irritated me.

He nodded. "So when I learn that one of my friends has, indeed, been welcomed by Allah into Paradise, I am distressed. I am concerned for the well-being of all who represent me in the city, from my trusted lieutenants down to the poorest and most insignificant beggar who aids me however he can."

"You are the people's shield against calamity, O Shaykh."

He waved a hand, tired of my interruptions. "Death is *one* thing, my nephew. Death comes to all, there is no one who can run from it. The jar cannot remain whole forever. We must learn to accept our eventual demise; and more, we must look forward to our eternal delight and refreshment in Paradise. Yet death before death is due is unnatural. That is *another* thing completely; it is an affront to Allah, and must be set right. One cannot recall the dead to life, but one can avenge a murder. Do you understand me?"

"Yes, O Shaykh." It hadn't taken Friedlander Bey long to hear about Courvoisier Sonny's premature end. Nassir probably called Papa even before he called the police.

"Then, let me put this question to you: How does one revenge a murder?"

There was a long, glacial silence. There was only one answer, but I took a while to frame my reply in my mind. "O Shaykh" I said at last, "a death must be met with another death. That is the only revenge. It is written in the Straight Path, 'Retaliation is prescribed for you in the matter of the murdered'; and also, 'One who attacketh you, attack him in like manner as he attacked you.' But it also says elsewhere, 'The life for the life, and the eye for the eye, and the nose for the nose, and the ear for the ear, and the tooth for the tooth, and for wounds retaliation. But whoso forgoeth it in the way of charity, it shall be expiation for him.' I am innocent of this murder, O Shaykh, and to seek revenge wrongfully is a crime worse than the killing itself."

"Allah is Most Great," murmured Papa. He looked at me in surprise. "I had heard that you were an infidel, my nephew, and it caused me pain. Yet you have a certain knowledge of the noble Qur'ân." He stood up from the table and rubbed his forehead with his right hand. Then he crossed to the large bed and laid down on the bedspread. I turned to face him, but a huge brown hand clamped itself on my shoulder and forced me to turn around again. I could only stare across the table, at Friedlander Bey's empty chair. I could not see him, but I could hear him when he spoke. "I have been told that of all people in the Budayeen, you had most reason to want to murder this man."

I thought back over the recent months; I couldn't even remember the last time I'd even said hello to Sonny. I stayed out of the Red Light; I had nothing to do with the kind of debs, changes, and girls Sonny ran on the street; our circles of friends didn't seem to intersect at all, except for Fuad il-Manhous—and Fuad was no friend of mine and, I'm sure, no friend of Sonny's, either. Yet the Arab's concept of revenge is as fully developed and patient as the Sicilian's. Maybe Papa was thinking of some incident that had happened months, even years, ago, something I had forgotten completely, that could be construed as a motive to kill Sonny. "I had no reason at all," I said shakily.

"I do not enjoy evasions, my nephew. It happens very often that I must ask someone these difficult questions, and he always begins by making evasive answers. This continues until one of my servants persuades him to stop. The next stage is a series of answers that do not sound so evasive, but are clearly lies. Once again, my guest must be persuaded not to waste valuable time this way." His voice was tired and low. I tried to turn to face him again, and once more the huge hand grasped my shoulder, more painfully this time. Papa went on. "After a while, one is at last brought to the point where truth and cooperation seem far the most reasonable course, yet it often makes me sad to see in what state my guest is in when he makes this discovery. My advice, then, is to pass through evasion and lies quickly—better still, not at all—and proceed directly to truth. We will all benefit."

The stone hand did not leave my shoulder. I felt as if my bones were slowly being crushed into white powder inside my skin. I made no sound.

"You owed this man a sum of money," said Friedlander Bey. "You owe him no longer, because he is dead. I will collect that sum, my nephew, and I will do that which the Book allows."

"I didn't owe him any money!" I cried. "Not one goddamn fîq!"

A second stone hand began to crush my other shoulder. "The dog's tail is still bent, O Lord," murmured the Stone That Speaks.

"I do not lie," I said, gasping a little. "If I tell you that I owed Sonny nothing, it is the truth. I am known everywhere in the city as one who does not lie."

"It is true that I have never had cause to doubt you before, my nephew."

"Perhaps he has found reasons to take up the practice, O Lord," murmured the Stone That Speaks.

"Sonny?" said Friedlander Bey, returning to the table. "No one cares about Sonny. He is no friend of mine, or of anyone; to that I can attest. If he is dead, too, then it but makes the air over the Budayeen more pleasant to breathe. No, my nephew, I have asked you to join me here to talk about the murder of my friend, Abdoulaye Abu-Zayd."

"Abdoulaye," I said. The pain was immense; I was beginning to see little flecks of red before my eyes. My voice was hoarse and barely audible. "I did not even know that Abdoulaye was dead."

Papa rubbed his forehead again. "There have been several deaths recently among my friends. More deaths than is natural."

"Yes," I said.

"You must prove to me that you did not kill Abdoulaye. No one else has such a reason to wish him ill fortune."

"And what reason do you think I have?"

"The obligation I mentioned. Abdoulaye was not well-loved, that is true; and he may well have been disliked, even hated. Yet everyone knew that he had my protection, and that a harmful thing done to him was a harmful thing done to me. His murderer will die, just as he died."

I tried to raise my hand, but I could not. "How did he die?" I asked.

Papa looked at me through lowered eyelids. "You must tell *me* how he died."

"I—" The stone hands left my shoulders; that only made the pain there get worse. Then I felt the fingers wrap themselves around my throat.

"Answer quickly," said Papa gently, "or very soon you will not be able to answer at all, ever again."

"Shot," I croaked. "Once. Small lead bullet."

Papa made a slight, flicking gesture with one hand; the stone fingers released my throat. "No, he was not shot. Yet two other people have been killed with just such an antique weapon in the last fortnight. It is interesting to me that you know of that matter. One of them was under my protection." He paused, a thoughtful look on his face. His coarse, trembling hands played with his empty coffee cup.

The pain receded quickly, although my shoulders would be sore for days. "If he was not shot," I said, "how *was* Abdoulaye murdered?"

His eyes jerked back to my face. "I am not yet certain that you are not his killer," he said.

"You have said that I have the only motive, that I had an obligation to him. That obligation was paid several days ago. I owed him nothing."

Papa's eyes opened wider. "You have some proof?"

I rose out of my chair just a bit, to get the receipt that was still in my hip pocket. The stone hands returned to my shoulders instantly, but Papa waved them away again. "Hassan was there," I said. "He'll tell you." I dug into my pocket and took out the paper, opened it, and passed it across the table. Friedlander Bey glanced at it, then studied it more closely. He looked beyond me, over my shoulder, and made a small motion with his head. I turned around, and the Stone had gone back to his post by the door.

"O Shaykh, if I may ask," I said, "who is it that told you of this debt? Who suggested to you that I was Abdoulaye's murderer? It must be someone who did not know that I paid the debt in full."

The old man nodded slowly, opened his mouth as if to tell me, then thought better of it. "Ask no more questions," he said.

I took a deep breath and let it out. I wasn't out of this room safely yet; I had to remember that. I couldn't feel anything from the Paxium. Those tranquilizers had been a goddamn waste of money.

Friedlander Bey looked down at his hands, which were toying again with his coffee cup. He signaled to the second Stone, who filled the cup with coffee. The servant looked at me, and I nodded; he gave me another cupful. "Where were you," asked Papa, "about ten o'clock tonight?"

"I was in the Café Solace, playing cards."

"Ah. What time did you begin playing cards?"

"About half past eight."

"And you were in that café until midnight?"

I thought back a few hours. "It was about half past twelve when we all left the Solace and went over to the Red Light. Sonny was stabbed somewhere between one o'clock and one-thirty, I'd say."

"Old Ibrihim at the Solace would not dispute your story?"

"No, he would not."

Papa turned and nodded to the Stone That Speaks behind him. The Stone used the room's telephone. A short time later, he came to the table and murmured in Papa's ear. Papa sighed. "I'm very glad for you, my nephew, that you can account for those hours. Abdoulaye died between ten and eleven o'clock. I accept that you did not kill my friend."

"Praise Allah the protector," I said softly.

"So I will tell you how Abdoulaye died. His body was found by my subordinate, Hassan the Shiite. Abdoulaye Abu-Zayd was murdered in a most foul manner, my nephew. I hesitate to describe it, lest some evil spirit seize the notion and prepare the same fate for me."

I recited Yasmin's superstitious formula, and that pleased the old man. "May Allah preserve you, my nephew," he said. "Abdoulaye lay in the alley behind Hassan's shop, his throat slashed and blood smeared over him. There was little blood in the alley, however, so he was murdered in some other place and removed to the spot where Hassan found him. There were the horrible signs that he had been burned many times, on his chest, on his arms, on his legs, on his face, even upon his organs of procreation. When the police examined the body, Hassan learned that the filthy dog who murdered Abdoulaye had first used my friend's body as a woman's, in the mouth and in the forbidden place of the sodomite. Hassan was quite distraught, and had to be sedated." Papa looked deeply agitated himself as he told me this, as if he had never seen or heard anything so profoundly unnerving. I knew that he had become accustomed to death, that he had caused people to die and that other people had died because of their association with him. Abdoulaye's case, though, affected him passionately. It wasn't really the killing; it was the absolute and appalling disregard for even the most elementary code of conscience. Friedlander Bey's hands were shaking even worse than before.

"It is the same way that Tamiko was killed," I said.

Papa looked at me, unable to speak for a moment. "How did you come to be in possession of that information?" he asked.

I could sense that he was playing again with the notion that I might be responsible for these killings. I seemed to have facts and details that otherwise shouldn't have been known to me. "I discovered Tami's body," I said. "I reported it to Lieutenant Okking."

Papa nodded and looked down again. "I cannot tell you how filled with hatred I am," he said. "It makes me grieve. I have tried to control such feelings, to live graciously as a prosperous man, if that is the will of Allah, and to give thanks for my wealth and do Allah honor by harboring neither anger nor jealousy. Yet my hand is always forced, someone always tries to probe for my weakness. I must respond harshly or lose all I have worked to attain. I wish only peace, and my reward is resentment. I will be avenged on this most abominable of butchers, my nephew! This mad executioner who defiles the holy work of Allah will die! By the sacred beard of the Prophet, I will have my vengeance!"

I waited a moment until he had calmed himself a little. "O Shaykh," I said, "there have been two people murdered by leaden bullets, and two who have been tortured and bled in this same way. I believe there may be more deaths to come. I have been seeking a friend who has disappeared. She was living with Tamiko, and she sent me a frightened message. I fear for her life."

Papa frowned at me. "I have no time for your troubles," he muttered. He was still preoccupied with the outrage of Abdoulaye's death. In some ways, from the old man's point of view, it was even more frightening than what the same killer had done to Tamiko. "I was prepared to believe that you were responsible, my nephew; if you had not proven your innocence, you would have died a lingering and terrible death in this room. I thank Allah that such an injustice did not occur. You seemed to be the most likely person upon whom to direct my wrath, but now I must find another. It is only a matter of time until I discover his identity." His lips pressed together into a cruel, bloodless smile. "You say you were playing cards at the Café Solace. Then the others with you will have the same alibi. Who were these men?"

I named my friends, glad to provide an explanation of their whereabouts; they would not have to face such an inquisition as this.

"Would you like some more coffee?" asked Friedlander Bey wearily.

"May Allah guide us, I have had enough," I said.

"May your times be prosperous," said Papa. He gave a heavy sigh. "Go in peace."

"By your leave," I said, rising.

"May you arise in the morning in health."

I thought of Abdoulaye. "*Inshallah,*" I said. I turned, and the Stone That Speaks had already opened the door. I felt a great relief flood through me as I left the room. Outside, beneath a clear black sky pricked with bright stars, was Sergeant Hajjar, leaning against his patrol car. I was surprised; I thought he'd gone back to the city long ago.

"I see you made it out all right," he said to me. "Go around the other side."

"Sit in front?" I asked.

"Yeah." We got into the car; I'd never sat in the front of a police car before. If my friends could only see me now. . . . "You want a smoke?" Hajjar asked, taking out a pack of French cigarettes.

"No, I don't do that," I said.

He started the car and whipped it around in a tight circle, then headed back to the center of town, lights flashing and siren screaming. "You want to buy some sunnies?" he asked. "I know you do *that.*"

I would have loved to get some more sunnies, but buying them from a cop seemed odd. The drug traffic was tolerated in the Budayeen, the way the rest of our harmless foibles were tolerated. Some cops don't enforce every law; there were undoubtedly plenty of officers one could safely buy drugs from. I just didn't trust Hajjar, not as far as I could kick him uphill in the dark.

"Why are you being so nice to me all of a sudden?" I asked.

He turned to me and grinned. "I didn't expect you to get out of that motel room alive," he said. "When you walked through that door, you had Papa Bey's Okay mark stamped on your forehead. What's okay with Papa is okay with me. Get it?"

I got it. I had thought that Hajjar worked for Lieutenant Okking and the police force, but Hajjar worked for Friedlander Bey, all the way.

"Can you take me to Frenchy's?" I said.

"Frenchy's? Your girlfriend works there, right?"

"You keep up on things."

He turned and grinned at me again. "Six kiam apiece, the sunnies."

"Six?" I said. "That's ridiculous. I can get them for two and a half."

"Are you crazy? There's nowhere in the city you can get them less than four, and you can't get them."

"All right," I said, "I'll give you three kiam each."

Hajjar rolled his eyes upward. "Don't bother," he said in a disgusted voice. "Allah will grant me a sufficient living without you."

"What is your lowest price? I mean your lowest."

"Offer whatever you think is fair."

"Three kiam," I said again.

"Because it's between you and me," said Hajjar seriously, "I'll go as low as five and a half."

"Three and a half. If you won't take my money, I can find some-body who will."

"Allah will sustain me. I hope your dealing goes well."

"What the hell, Hajjar? Okay, four."

"What, you think I'm making you a present of these?"

"They're no present at these prices. Four and a half. Does that sat-isfy you?"

"All right, I'll take my consolation from God. No gain to me, but give me the money and that ends it." And that is the way Arabs in the city bargain, in a souk over a beaten-brass vase, or in the front seat of a cop car.

I gave him a hundred kiam, and he gave me twenty-three sunnies. He reminded me three times on the way to Frenchy's that he had thrown in one free, as a gift. When we got to the Budayeen, he didn't slow down. He squealed through the gate and shot up the Street, predicting amiably that everyone would get out of his way; almost everyone did. When we got to Frenchy's, I started to get out of the car. "Hey," he said in a hurt tone of voice, "aren't you going to buy me a drink?"

Standing in the street, I slammed the door closed and leaned down to look in through the window. "I just can't do that, as much as I would like to. If my friends saw me drinking with a cop, well, think what that would do to my reputation. Business is business, Hajjar."

He grinned. "And action is action. I know, I hear that all the time. See you around." And he whipped the patrol car around again and bel-lowed off down the Street.

I was already sitting down at Frenchy's bar when I remembered all the blood on my clothes and my body. It was too late; Yasmin had already spotted me. I groaned. I needed something to set me up for the scene that was fast approaching. Fortunately, I had all these sunnies. . . .

⊼iⴖ℮

i was wakened once again by the ringing of my telephone. It was simpler to find it this time; I no longer owned the jeans it had been clipped to the previous night, or the shirt I'd been wearing. Yasmin had decided that it would be much easier to dispose of them entirely than to try to wash the stains out. Besides, she said, she didn't want to think about Sonny's blood every time she ran her fingernails up my thigh. I had other shirts; the jeans were another matter. Finding a new pair was the first order of business for that Thursday.

Or so I had planned. The phone call changed that. "Yeah?" I said.

"Hello! Welcome! How are you?"

"Praise Allah," I said, "who *is* this?"

"I ask your pardon, O clever one, I thought you would recognize my voice. This is Hassan."

I squeezed my eyes shut and opened them. "Hello, Hassan," I said. "I heard about Abdoulaye last night from Friedlander Bey. The consolation is that you are well."

"May Allah bless you, my dear. Indeed, I am calling you to relay an invitation from Friedlander Bey. He desires that you come to his house and take breakfast with him. He will send a car and driver."

This was not my favorite way to begin a day. "I thought I persuaded him last night that I was innocent."

Hassan laughed. "You have nothing to worry yourself about. This is purely a friendly invitation. Friedlander Bey would like to make amends for the anxiety he may have caused you. Also, there are one or two things he would like to ask of you. There may be a large amount of money in it for you, Marîd, my son."

I had no interest in taking Papa's money, but I could not turn down his invitation; that was just not done in Papa's city. "When will the car be here?" I asked.

"Very soon. Refresh yourself, and then listen closely to whatever suggestions Friedlander Bey makes. You will profit from them if you are wise."

"Thank you, Hassan," I said.

"No thanks are needed," he said, hanging up.

I laid back on the pillow and thought. I had promised myself years ago that I would never take Papa's money; even if it represented legitimate pay for a service rendered, accepting it put you in that broad category of his "friends and representatives." I was an independent operator, but if I wanted to maintain that status, I'd have to walk carefully this afternoon.

Yasmin was still asleep, of course, and I did not disturb her—Frenchy's did not open until after sundown. I went to the bathroom and washed my face and brushed my teeth. I would have to go to Papa's dressed in the local costume. I shrugged; Papa would probably interpret that as a compliment. That reminded me that I ought to take some small gift with me; this was an entirely different sort of interview than last night's. I finished my brief toilet and dressed, leaving off the *keffiya* and wearing instead the knitted skullcap of my birthplace. I packed my shoulder bag with money, my telephone, and my keys, looked around the apartment with a vague feeling of foreboding, and went outside. I should have left a note telling Yasmin where I was going, but it occurred to me that if I never came home, the note wouldn't do me any good.

There was a warm, late-afternoon sun-shower falling. I went to a shop nearby and bought a basket of mixed fruits, then walked back to my apartment building. I enjoyed the fresh, clean smell of the rain on the sidewalk. I saw a long black limousine waiting for me, its engine thrumming. A uniformed driver stood in the doorway of my building, out of the light rain. He saluted me as I got nearer, and he opened the expensive car's rear door. I got in, addressed a silent prayer to Allah, and heard the door slam. A moment later the car was in motion, heading toward Friedlander Bey's great house.

There was a uniformed guard at the gate in the high, ivy-covered wall, who passed the limousine through. The pebble-paved driveway curved gracefully through carefully tended landscaping. There was a profusion of bright tropical flowers blooming all around and, behind them, tall date palms and banana plants. The effect was more natural and more cheering than the artificial arrangements around Lutz Seipolt's place. We drove slowly, the tires of the car making loud popping sounds on the gravel. Inside the wall, everything was quiet and still, as if Papa had succeeded in keeping out the city's noise and clamor as well as unwanted visitors. The house itself was only two stories high, but it rambled over quite an expensive plot of midtown real estate. There were several towers—no doubt with guards in them, too—and Friedlander Bey's home had its own minaret. I wondered if Papa kept his own, private muezzin to call him to his devotions.

The driver pulled to a stop before the wide marble stairs of the front entrance. Not only did he open the car's rear door for me, but he also accompanied me up the stairs. It was he who rapped on the estate's polished mahogany door. A butler or some other servant opened the door, and the driver said, "The master's guest." Then the driver went back to the car, the butler bowed me in, and I was standing in Friedlander Bey's house. The beautiful door closed softly behind me, and the cool, dry air caressed my perspiring face. The house was faintly perfumed with incense.

"This way, please," said the butler. "The master is at his prayers just now. You may wait in this antechamber."

I thanked the butler, who sincerely wished that Allah do all sorts of wonderful things for me. Then he disappeared, leaving me alone in the small room. I walked about casually, admiring the lovely objects Papa had acquired during his long, dramatic life. At last, a communicating door opened, and one of the Stones signaled to me. I saw Papa inside, folding his prayer rug and putting it away in a cabinet. There was a mîhrab in his office, the semicircular recess you find in every mosque indicating the direction of Mecca.

Friedlander Bey turned to face me, and his plump, gray face brightened with a genuine smile of welcome. He came toward me and greeted me; we proceeded through all the formalities. I offered him my gift, and he was delighted. "The fruits look succulent and tempting," he said, putting the basket on a low table. "I will enjoy them after the sun sets, my nephew; it was kind of you to think of me. Now, will you make yourself comfortable? We must talk, and when it is proper, I beg that you will join me at breakfast." He indicated an antique lacquered divan that looked like it was worth a small fortune. He relaxed on its mate, facing me across several feet of exquisite pale blue and gold rug. I was waiting for him to begin the conversation.

He stroked his cheek and looked at me, as if he hadn't done enough of that last night. "I can see by your coloring that you are a Maghrîb," he said. "Are you Tunisian?"

"No, O Shaykh, I was born in Algeria."

"One of your parents was surely of Berber heritage."

That rankled me a little. There are long-standing, historical reasons for the irritation, but they're ancient and tedious and of no relevance now. I avoided the whole Berber-Arab question by saying, "I am a Muslim, O Shaykh, and my father was French."

"There is a saying," said Friedlander Bey, "that if you ask a mule of his lineage, he will say only that one of his parents was a horse." I took that as a mild reproof; the reference to mules and asses is more meaningful if you consider, as all Arabs do, the donkey, like the dog, to be among the most unclean of animals. Papa must have seen that he had only irked me more, because he laughed softly and waved a hand. "Forgive me, my nephew. I was only thinking that your speech is accented heavily with the dialect of the Maghrîb. Of course, here in the city our Arabic is a mixture of Maghrîb, Egyptian, Levantine, and Persian. I doubt if anyone speaks a pure Arabic, if such a thing exists at all anywhere but in the Straight Path. I meant no offense. And I must extend a further apology, for my treatment of you last night. I hope you can understand my reasons."

I nodded grimly, but I did not reply.

Friedlander Bey went on. "It is necessary that we return to the unpleasant subject we discussed briefly at the motel. These murders must stop. There is no acceptable alternative. Of the four victims thus far, three have been connected to me. I cannot see these killings as anything other than a personal attack, direct or indirect."

"Three of the four?" I asked. "Certainly Abdoulaye Abu-Zayd was one of your people. But the Russian? And the two Black Widow Sisters? No pimp would dare try to coerce the Sisters. Tamiko and Devi were famous for their fierce independence."

Papa made a small gesture of distaste. "I did not interfere with the Black Widow Sisters in regard to their prostitution," he said. "My concerns are on a higher plane than that, although many of my associates find profit in purveying all manner of vice. The Sisters were allowed to keep every kiam they earned, and they were welcome to it. No, they performed other services for me, services of a discreet, dangerous, and necessary nature."

I was astonished. "Tami and Devi were . . . . your assassins?" I asked.

"Yes," said Friedlander Bey. "And Selima will continue to take on such assignments when no other solution is possible. Tamiko and Devi were paid well, they had my complete trust and confidence, and they always gave excellent results. Their deaths have caused me no little anguish. It is not a simple matter to replace such artists, particularly ones with whom I enjoyed such a satisfactory working partnership."

I thought this over for a little while; it wasn't hard to accept, although the information had come as quite a surprise. It even answered a few questions I'd entertained from time to time concerning the open daring of the Black Widow Sisters. They worked as secret agents of Friedlander Bey, and they were protected; or they were *supposed* to be protected. Yet two had died. "It would be simpler to understand this situation, O Shaykh," I said, musing out loud, "if both Tami and Devi had been murdered in the same way. Yet Devi was shot with the old pistol, and Tami was tortured and slashed."

"Those were my thoughts, my nephew," said Papa. "Please continue. Perhaps you will shed light on this mystery."

I shrugged. "Well, even that fact could be dismissed, if other victims hadn't been found slain in these same ways."

"I will find both killers," said the old man calmly. It was a flat statement of fact, neither an emotional vow nor a boast.

"It occurred to me, O Shaykh," I said, "that the murderer who uses the pistol is killing for some political reason. I saw him shoot the Russian, who was a minor functionary in the legation of the Byelorussian-Ukrainian Kingdom. He was wearing a James Bond personality module. The weapon is the same type of pistol the fictional character used. I think a common murderer, killing out of spite or sudden anger or in the course of a robbery, would chip in some other module, or none at all. The James Bond module might provide a certain insight and skill in the business of quick, clean assassination. That would be of value only to a dispassionate killer whose acts were part of some larger scheme."

Friedlander Bey frowned. "I am not convinced, my nephew. There isn't the slightest connection between your Russian diplomat and my Devi. The assassination idea occurred to you only because the Russian worked in some political capacity. Devi had no idea of world affairs at all. She was of no help or hindrance to any party or movement. The James Bond theme merits further inspection, but the motives you suggest are without substance."

"Do you have any ideas about either killer, O Shaykh?" I asked.

"Not yet," he said, "but I have only just begun to collect information. That is why I wanted to discuss this situation with you. You should not think that my involvement is solely a matter of revenge. It is that, of course, but it is a great deal larger than that. To put it simply, I must protect my investments. I must demonstrate to my associates and my friends that I will not permit such a threat to their safety to continue. Otherwise I will begin to lose the support of the people who make up the foundation and framework of my power. Taken individually, these four murders are repellent but not unheard-of occurrences: murders take place every day in the city. Together, however, these four killings are an immediate challenge to my existence. Do you understand me, my nephew?"

He was making himself very clear. "Yes, O Shaykh," I said. I waited to hear the suggestions Hassan said would be made.

There was a long pause while Friedlander Bey regarded me pensively. "You are very different from most of my friends in the Budayeen," he said at last. "Almost everyone has had some modification made on his body."

"If they can afford it," I said, "I think they should have whatever mod they want. As for me, O Shaykh, my body has always been fine just the way it is. The only surgery I've ever had has been for therapeutic reasons. I am pleased with the form I was given by Allah."

Papa nodded. "And your mind?" he asked.

"It runs a little slow sometimes," I said, "but, on the whole, it's served me well. I've never felt a desire to have my brain wired, if that's what you mean."

"Yet you take prodigious quantities of drugs. You did so in my presence last night." I had nothing to say to that. "You are a proud man, my nephew. I've read a report about you that mentions this pride. You find excitement in contests of wit and will and physical prowess with people who have the advantage of modular personalities and other software add-ons. It is a dangerous diversion, but you seem to have emerged unscathed."

A few painful memories flashed through my mind. "I've been scathed, O Shaykh, more than a few times."

He laughed. "Even that has not prompted you to modify yourself. Your pride takes the form of presenting yourself—as the Christians say in some context—as being *in* the world but not *of* it."

"Untempted by its treasures and untouched by its evils, that's me." My ironic tone was not lost on Papa.

"I would like you to help me, Marîd Audran," he said. There it was, take it or leave it.

The way he put it, I was left in an extremely uncomfortable position: I could say, "Sure, I'll help you," and then I'd have compromised myself in precisely the way I swore I never would; or I could say, "No, I won't help you," and I'd have offended the most influential person in my world. I took a couple of long, slow breaths while I sorted out my answer. "O Shaykh," I said at last, "your difficulties are the difficulties of everyone in the Budayeen; indeed, in the city. Certainly, anyone who cares about his own safety and happiness will help you. I will help you all that I can, but against the men who have murdered your friends, I doubt that I can be of much use."

Papa stroked his cheek and smiled. "I understand that you have no wish to become one of my 'associates.' Be that as it may. You have my guarantee, my nephew, that if you agree to aid me in this matter, it will not mark you as one of 'Papa's men.' Your pleasure is in your freedom and independence, and I would not take that from one who does me a great favor."

I wondered if he was implying that he might take away the freedom from one who refused to perform the favor. It would be child's play for Papa to steal my liberty; he could accomplish that by simply planting me forever, deep beneath the tender grass in the cemetery where the Street comes to its end.

Baraka: an Arabic word that is very difficult to translate. It can mean magic or charisma or the special favor of God. Places can have it; shrines are visited and touched in the hope that some of the *baraka* will rub off. People can have *baraka;* the derwishes, in particular, believe that certain fortunate people are specially blessed by Allah, and are therefore worthy of singular respect in the community. Friedlander Bey had more *baraka* than all the stone shrines in the Maghrîb. I can't say if it was *baraka* that made him what he was, or if he attained the *baraka* as he attained his position and influence. Whatever the explanation, it was very difficult to listen to him and deny him what he asked. "How can I help you?" I said. I felt hollow inside, as if I had made a great surrender.

"I want you to be the instrument of my vengeance, my nephew," he said.

I was shocked. No one knew better than I how inadequate I was to the task he was giving me. I had tried to tell him that already, but he'd only brushed aside my objections as if they were just some form of false modesty. My mouth and throat were dry. "I have said that I will help you, but you ask too much of me. You have more capable people in your employ."

"I have stronger men," said Papa. "The two servants you met last night are stronger than you, but they lack intelligence. Hassan the Shiite has a certain shrewdness, but he is not otherwise a dangerous man. I have considered each of my friends, O my beloved nephew, and I have made this decision: none but you offers the essential combination of qualities I seek. Most important, I trust you. I cannot say the same of many of my associates; it is a sad thing to admit. I trust you because you do not care to rise in my esteem. You do not try to ingratiate yourself with me for your own ends. You are not a truckling leech, of which I have more than my share. For the important work we must do, I must have someone about whom I have no doubts; that is one of the reasons our meeting last night was so difficult for you. It was an examination of your inner worth. I knew when we parted that you were the man I sought."

"You do me honor, O Shaykh, but I am afraid I do not share your confidence."

He raised his right hand, and it trembled visibly. "I have not finished my speech, my nephew. There are further reasons why you must do as I ask, reasons that benefit you, not me. You tried to speak of your friend Nikki last night, and I would not permit it. I ask your forgiveness again. You were quite correct in your concern for her safety. I am certain that her disappearance was the work of one or the other of these murderers; perhaps she herself has already been slain, Allah grant that it not be true. I cannot say. Yet if there is any hope of finding her alive, it is in you. With my resources, together we will find the killers. Together we will deal with them, as the Wise Mention of God directs. We will prevent Nikki's death if we can, and who can say how many other lives we may save? Are these not worthy goals? Can you still hesitate?"

It was all very flattering, I suppose; but I wished like hell that Papa had picked somebody else. Saied would have done a good job, especially with his ass-kicking moddy chipped in. There was nothing I could do now, though, except agree. "I will do my best for you, O Shaykh," I said reluctantly, "but I do not abandon my doubts."

"That is well," said Friedlander Bey. "Your doubts will keep you alive longer."

I really wished he hadn't added that last word; he sounded as if I couldn't survive, no matter what I did, but my doubts would keep me around to watch myself suffer. "It will be as Allah wills," I said.

"May the blessing of Allah be on you. Now we must discuss your payment."

That surprised me, too. "I had no thought of payment," I said.

Papa acted as if he did not hear. "One must eat," he said simply. "You shall be paid a hundred kiam a day until this affair is concluded." Concluded is right: until either we put an end to the two murdering sons of bitches, or one of them puts an end to me.

"I did not ask for such a wage," I said. A hundred a day; well, Papa had said one must eat. I wondered what he thought I was accustomed to eating.

Again he ignored me. He gestured to the Stone That Speaks, who approached and handed Friedlander Bey an envelope. "Here is seven hundred kiam," Papa said to me, "your pay for the first week." He gave the envelope back to the Stone, who brought it to me.

If I took the envelope, it was a symbol of my complete acceptance of Friedlander Bey's authority. There would be no turning back, no quitting, no ending but the ending. I looked at the white envelope in the sandstone-colored hand. My own hand rose a little, sank a little, rose again and took the money. "Thank you," I said.

Friedlander Bey looked pleased. "I hope it brings you pleasure," he said. It had damn well better; I was certainly going to earn every fuckin' fîq of it.

"O Shaykh, what are your instructions?" I asked.

"First, my nephew, you must go to Lieutenant Okking and put yourself at his disposal. I will inform him that we will cooperate completely with the police department in this matter. There are circumstances that my associates can manage with greater efficiency than the police; I'm sure the lieutenant will acknowledge that. I think that a temporary alliance of my organization with his will best serve the needs of the community. He will give you all the information he has on the killings, a probable description of the one who cut the throats of Abdoulaye Abu-Zayd and Tamiko, and whatever else he has so far withheld. In return, you will assure him that we will keep the police informed of such facts as we uncover."

"Lieutenant Okking is a good man," I said, "but he cooperates only when he feels like it, or when it's clearly to his advantage."

Papa gave me a brief smile. "He will cooperate with you now, I will make sure of that. He will soon learn that it is, indeed, in his own best interest." The old man would be as good as his word; if anyone could persuade Okking to help me, it was Friedlander Bey.

"And then, O Shaykh?"

He cocked his head and smiled again. For some reason I felt cold, as if a bitter wind had found its way into Papa's fortress. "Do you foresee a time, my nephew," he asked, "or can you imagine a circumstance, in which you would seek the modifications you have so far rejected?"

The icy wind blew more fiercely. "No, O Shaykh," I said, "I can't foresee such a time or imagine such a situation; that doesn't mean that it may not happen. Perhaps sometime in the future I'll have need to choose some modification."

He nodded. "Tomorrow is Friday, and I observe the Sabbath. You will need time to think and plan. Monday is soon enough."

"Soon enough? Soon enough for what?"

"To meet with my private surgeons," he said simply.

"No," I whispered.

Suddenly, Friedlander Bey ceased being the kindly uncle. He became, instantly, the commander of men's allegiance, whose orders cannot be questioned. "You have accepted my coin, my nephew," he said sternly. "You will do as I say. You cannot hope to succeed against our enemies unless your mind is improved. We know that at least one of the two has an electronically augmented brain. You must have the same, but to an even greater degree. My surgeons can give you advantages over the murderers."

The two sandstone hands appeared on my shoulders, holding me firmly in place. Now, truly, there was no way out. "What sort of advantages?" I asked apprehensively. I began to feel the cold sweat of utter fear. I had avoided having my brain wired more out of profound dread than principle. The idea produced terror in me, amounting to an irrational, paralyzing phobia.

"The surgeons will explain it all to you," said Papa.

"O Shaykh," I said, my voice breaking, "I do not wish this."

"Events have moved beyond your wishing," he replied. "You will change your mind on Monday."

No, I thought, it won't be me; it will be Friedlander Bey and his surgeons who will change my mind.

Ten

"Lieutenant Okking's out of his office at the moment," said a uniformed officer. "Can I help you with something?"

"Will the lieutenant be back soon?" I asked. The clock above the officer's desk said almost ten o'clock. I wondered how late Okking was going to work tonight; I had no desire to talk to Sergeant Hajjar, whatever his connection to Papa. I still didn't trust him.

"The lieutenant said he'd be right back, he's just gone downstairs for something."

That made me feel better. "Is it all right if I wait in his office? We're old friends."

The cop looked at me dubiously. "Can I see some identification?" he asked. I gave him my Algerian passport; it's expired, but it's the only thing I own with my photograph on it. He punched my name into his computer, and a moment later my whole history began spilling across his screen. He must have decided that I was an upright citizen, because he gave me back my passport, stared up into my face for a moment, and said, "You and Lieutenant Okking go back a ways together."

"It's a long story, all right," I said.

"He won't be another ten minutes. You can take a seat in there."

I thanked the cop and went into Okking's office. It was true, I *had* spent a lot of time here. The lieutenant and I had formed a curious alliance, considering that we worked opposite sides of the legal fence. I sat in the chair beside Okking's desk and waited. Ten minutes passed, and I began to get restless. I started looking at the papers piled in hefty stacks, trying to read them upside-down and sideways. His *Out* box was half-filled with envelopes, but there was even more work crammed into the *In* box. Okking earned whatever meager wages he got from the department. There was a large manila envelope on its way to a small-arms dealer in the Federated New England States of America; a hand-written envelope to some doctor in the city; a neatly addressed envelope to a firm called Universal Exports with an address near the waterfront—I wondered if it was one of the companies Hassan dealt with, or maybe it was one of Seipolt's; and a heavily stuffed packet being sent to an office-supplies manufacturer in the Protectorate of Brabant.

I had glanced at just about everything in Okking's office when, an hour later, the man himself appeared. "Hope I haven't kept you waiting," he said distractedly. "What the hell do you want?"

"Nice to see you too, Lieutenant. I've just come from a meeting with Friedlander Bey."

That caught his attention. "Oh, so now you're running errands for sand-niggers with delusions of grandeur. I forget: is that a step up or a step down for you, Audran? I suppose the old snake charmer gave you a message?"

I nodded. "It's about these murders."

Okking seated himself behind his desk and gazed at me innocently. "What murders?" he asked.

"The two with the old pistol, the two throat-slashings. Sure, *you* remember. Or have you been too busy rounding up jaywalkers again?"

He shot me an ugly look and ran a finger along a heavy jaw that badly needed shaving. "I remember," he said bluntly. "Why does Bey think this concerns him?"

"Three of the four victims did odd jobs for him, back in the days when they had a little more spring in their step. He just wants to make sure that none of his other employees get the same treatment. Papa has a lot of civic consciousness that way. I don't think you appreciate that about him."

Okking snorted. "Yeah, you right," he said. "I always thought those two sex-changes worked for him. They looked like they were trying to smuggle cantaloupes under their sweaters."

"Papa thinks these murders are aimed at him."

Okking shrugged. "If they are, those killers are lousy marksmen. They haven't so much as nicked Papa yet."

"He doesn't see it that way. The women who work for him are his eyes, the men are his fingers. He said that himself, in his own warm and wonderful way."

"What was Abdoulaye, then, his asshole?"

I knew that Okking and I could go on like that all night. I briefly explained the unusual proposition Friedlander Bey had asked me to deliver. As I expected, Lieutenant Okking had as little faith as I. "You know, Audran," he said dryly, "official law-enforcement groups worry a lot about their public image. We get enough beating-up in the news media as it is, without having to go out on the front steps and kiss ass with somebody like Friedlander Bey because nobody thinks we can do a damn thing about these murders without him."

I patted the air to make it all better between us. "No, no," I said, "it isn't that at all. You're misunderstanding me, you're misunderstanding Papa's motives. No one's saying you couldn't nail these murderers without help. These guys aren't any more clever or dangerous than the scruffy, beetle-headed crumbs you pull in here every day. Friedlander Bey only suggests that because his own interests are directly involved, teamwork might save everybody time and effort, as well as lives. Wouldn't it be worth it, Lieutenant, if we keep just one of your uniformed cops from stopping a bullet?"

"Or one of Bey's whores from annexing a butcher knife? Yeah, listen, I already got a call from Papa, probably while you were on your way over here. We went through this whole song-and-dance already, and I agreed to a certain point. A *certain point,* Audran. I don't like you or him trying to make police policy, telling me how to run my investigation, interfering in any way. Understand?"

I nodded. I knew both Lieutenant Okking and Friedlander Bey, and it didn't make any difference what Okking *said* he didn't want; Papa'd get his way anyhow.

"Just so we understand each other on this," said the lieutenant. "The whole thing is unnatural, like rats and mice going to church to pray for the recovery of a cat. When it's over, when we have those two killers, don't expect any more honeymoon. Then it will be seizure guns and batons and the same old harassment on both sides."

I shrugged. "Business is business," I said.

"I'm real tired of hearing that line," he said. "Now get out of my sight."

I got out and took the elevator down to the ground floor. It was a nice, cool evening, a swelling moon slipping in and out of gleaming metal clouds. I walked back to the Budayeen, thinking. In three days I was going to have my brain wired. I'd avoided that fact since I left Friedlander Bey's; now I had all the time in the world to think about it. I felt no excitement, no anticipation, only dread. I felt that, somehow, Marîd Audran would cease to be and someone new would awaken from that surgery, and that I'd never be able to put my finger on the difference; it would bother me forever, like a popcorn hull wedged permanently between my teeth. Everyone else would notice the change, but I wouldn't because I was on the inside.

I went straight to Frenchy's. When I got there, Yasmin was working on a young, thin guy wearing white baggy pants with drawstrings around the ankles and a gray salt-and-pepper sport coat about fifty years old. He probably bought his whole wardrobe in the back of some antique shop for one and a half kiam; it smelled musty, like your great-grandmother's quilt that has been left in the attic too long.

The girl on stage was a sex-change named Blanca; Frenchy had a policy about not hiring debs. Girls were all right with him, and debs who'd had their full changes, but the ones stuck indecisively in the middle made him feel that they might get stuck sometime in the middle of some other important transaction, and he just didn't want to be held responsible. You knew when you went into Frenchy's that there wasn't going to be anybody in there with a cock bigger than yours unless it was Frenchy himself or one of the other customers, and if you found out that awful truth you had nobody to blame but yourself.

Blanca danced in a peculiar, half-conscious way that was common among dancers all up and down the Street. They moved vaguely in time to the music, bored and tired and waiting to get out from under the hot lights. They stared at themselves incessantly in the smeared mirrors behind them, or they turned and stared at their reflections across the room behind the customers. Their eyes were fixed forever in some empty space about a foot and a half above the customers' heads. Blanca's expression was a faint attempt to look pleasant—"attractive" and "alluring" weren't in her professional vocabulary—but she looked as if she'd just had a lot of nerve-deadening drug pumped into her lower jaw and she hadn't decided if she liked it yet. While Blanca was on stage she was selling herself—she was promoting herself as a product entirely separate from her own self-image, herself as she would be when she came down from the stage. Her movements—mostly weary, half-hearted imitations of sexual motions—were supposed to titillate her watchers, but unless the customers had had a lot to drink or were otherwise fixated on this particular girl, the dancing itself would have little effect. I'd watched Blanca dance dozens, maybe hundreds, of times; it was always the same music, she always made the same gyrations, the same steps, the same bumps, the same grinds at the same instants of each song.

Blanca finished her last number and there was a scattering of applause, mostly from the mark who had been buying her drinks and thought he was in love with her. It takes a little longer for you to establish an acquaintance in a place like Frenchy's—or any of the other bars along the Street. That seems like a paradox, because the girls rushed up to grab any single man who strayed into the place. The conversation was so limited, though: "Hi, what's your name?"

"Juan-Javier."

"Oh, that's nice. Where you from?"

"Nuevo Tejas."

"Oh, that's interesting. How long have you been in the city?"

"A couple of days."

"Want to buy me a drink?"

That's all there is, there ain't no more. Even a top-notch international secret agent couldn't relay more information in that small amount of time. Beneath it all was a constant undercurrent of depression, as if the girls were locked into this job, although the illusion of absolute freedom hovered almost visibly in the air. "Any time you want to quit, honey, you just walk out that door." The way out the door, though, led to one of only two places: another bar just like Frenchy's, or the next step down the ladder toward the deadly bottom of the Life: "Hi, handsome, looking for some company?" You know what I mean. And the income gets lower and lower as the girl gets older, and pretty soon you get people like Maribel turning tricks for the price of a shot glass of white wine.

After Blanca, a real girl called Indihar came on stage; it might even have been her real name. She moved the same as Blanca, hips and shoulders swaying, feet almost motionless. As she danced, Indihar mouthed the words to the songs silently, completely unaware that she was doing it. I asked a few girls about that; they all mouthed the lyrics, but none of them realized they did it. They all got self-conscious when I mentioned the fact, but the next time they got up to dance, they sang to themselves just as they always had. Made the time go quicker, I guess, gave them something to do besides look at the customers. Back and forth the girls swayed, their lips moving, their hands making empty gestures, their hips swirling where habit told them to swirl their hips. It might have been sexy to some of the men who'd never seen such things before, it might have been worth what Frenchy charged for his drinks. I could drink for free because Yasmin worked there and because I kept Frenchy amused; if I'd had to pay, I would have found something more interesting to do with my time. Anything would have been more interesting; sitting alone in the dark in a soundless room would have been more interesting.

I waited through Indihar's set, and then Yasmin came out of the dressing room. She gave me a wide smile that made me feel special. There was some applause from two or three men scattered along the bar: she was mixing well tonight, making money. Indihar threw on a gauzy top and started hitting up the customers for tips. I kicked in a kiam and she gave me a little kiss. Indihar's a good kid. She plays by the rules and doesn't hassle anybody. Blanca could go to hell, as far as I was concerned, but Indihar and I could be good friends.

Frenchy caught my eye and motioned me down to the end of the bar. He was a big man, about the size of two average Marseilles enforcers, with a big, black, bushy beard that made mine look like the fuzz in a cat's ear. He glowered at me with his black eyes. "Where ya at, cap?" he asked.

"Nothing happening tonight, Frenchy," I said.

"Your girl's doing all right for herself."

"That's good," I said, "because I lost my last fîq through a hole in my pocket."

Frenchy squinted and looked at my *gallebeya*. "You don't have any pockets in that outfit, *mon noraf*."

"That was days ago, Frenchy," I said solemnly. "We've been living on love since." Yasmin had some orbital-velocity moddy chipped in, and her dancing was something to watch. People all up and down the bar forgot their drinks and the other girls' hands in their laps, and stared at Yasmin.

Frenchy laughed; he knew that I was never as flat-out broke as I always claimed to be. "Business is bad," he said, spitting into a small plastic cup. With Frenchy, business is always bad. Nobody ever talks prosperity on the Street; it's bad luck.

"Listen," I said, "there's some important thing I have to talk over with Yasmin when she's finished this set."

Frenchy shook his head. "She's working on that mark down there wearing the fez. Wait until she milks him dry, then you can talk to her all you want. If you wait until the mark leaves, I'll get someone else to take her next turn on stage."

"Allah be praised," I said. "Can I buy you a drink?"

He smiled at me. "Buy two," he said. "Pretend one's for me, one's for you. Drink them both. I can't stomach the stuff anymore." He patted his belly and made a sour face, then got up and walked down the bar, greeting his customers and whispering in the ears of his girls. I bought two drinks from Dalia, Frenchy's short, round-faced, informative barmaid; I'd known Dalia for years. Dalia, Frenchy, and Chiriga were very likely fixtures on the Street when the Street was just a goat-path from one end of the Budayeen to the other. Before the rest of the city decided to wall us in, probably, and put in the cemetery.

When Yasmin finished dancing, the applause was loud and long. Her tip jar filled quickly, and then she was hurrying back to her enamored mark before some other bitch stole him away. Yasmin gave me a quick, affectionate pinch on the ass as she passed behind me.

I watched her laughing and talking and hugging that cross-eyed bastard son of a yellow dog for half an hour; then his money ran out, and both he and Yasmin looked sad. Their affair had come to a premature end. They waved fond, almost passionate farewells and promised they'd never forget this golden evening. Every time I see one of those goddamn wogs climbing all over Yasmin—or any of the other girls, for that matter—I remember watching nameless men grabbing at my mother. That was a hell of a long time ago, but for certain things my memory works just too well. I watched Yasmin and I told myself it was just her job; but I couldn't help the sick, acid feeling that climbed out of my gut and made me want to start breaking things.

She scooted down beside me, drenched with perspiration, and gasped, "I thought that son of a slut would never leave!"

"It's your charming presence," I said sourly. "It's your scintillating conversation. It's Frenchy's needled beer."

"Yeah," said Yasmin, puzzled by my annoyance, "you right."

"I have to talk to you about something."

Yasmin looked at me and took a few deep breaths. She mopped her face with a clean bar towel. I suppose I sounded unusually grave. Anyway, I went through the events of the evening for her: my second meeting with Friedlander Bey; our—that is, *his*—conclusions; and how I had failed to impress Lieutenant Okking. When I finished, there was stunned silence from all around.

"You're going to do it?" asked Frenchy. I hadn't noticed him returning. I wasn't aware that he'd been eavesdropping, but it was his place and nobody knew his eaves better.

"You're going to get *wired*?" asked Yasmin breathlessly. She found the whole idea vastly exciting. *Arousing,* if you get my meaning.

"You're crazy if you do," said Dalia. Dalia was as close to being a true conservative as you could find on the Street. "Look what it does to people."

"What *does* it do to people?" shouted Yasmin, outraged, tapping her own moddy.

"Oops, sorry," said Dalia, and she went to mop up some imaginary spilled beer at the far, far end of the bar.

"Think of all the things we could do together," said Yasmin dreamily.

"Maybe it's not good enough for you the way it is," I said, a little hurt.

Her expression fell. "Hey, Marîd, it's not that. It's just—"

"This is *your* problem," said Frenchy, "it's none of my business. I'm going in the back and count tonight's money. Won't take me very long." He disappeared through a ratty gold-colored cloth that served as a flimsy barrier to the dressing room and his office.

"It's permanent," I said. "Once it's done, it's done. There's no backing out."

"Have you ever heard me say that I wanted to have my wires yanked?" asked Yasmin.

"No," I admitted. It was just the *irrevocableness* of it that prickled my skin.

"I haven't regretted it for an instant, and neither has anybody else I know who's had it done."

I wet my lips. "You don't understand," I said. I couldn't finish my argument; I couldn't put into words what she didn't understand.

"You're just afraid," she said.

"Yeah," I said. That was a good starting point.

"The Half-Hajj has *his* brain wired, and he's not even a quarter of the man you are."

"And all it got him was Sonny's blood all over everything. I don't need moddies to make me act crazy, I can do that on my own."

Suddenly she got a faraway, inspired look in her eyes. I knew something fascinating had occurred to her, and I knew it most likely meant bad news for me. "Oh, Allah and the Virgin Mary in a motel room," she said softly. That had been a favorite blasphemy of her father's, I think. "This is working out just like the hexagram said."

"The hexagram." I had put that *I Ching* business out of my mind almost before Yasmin had finished explaining it to me.

"Remember what it said?" she asked. "About not being afraid to cross the great water?"

"Yeah. What great water?"

"The great water is some major change in your life. Getting your brain wired, for instance."

"Uh huh. And it said to meet the great man. I did that. Twice."

"It said to wait three days before beginning, and three days before completing."

I counted up quickly: tomorrow, Saturday, Sunday. Monday, when I was going to have this thing done, would be after three days. "Oh, hell," I muttered.

"And it said that nobody would believe you, and it said that you had to keep up your confidence during adversity, and it said that you didn't serve kings and princes but higher principles. That's my Marîd." And she kissed me; I felt ill. There was absolutely no way I could get out of the surgery now, unless I started running and began a new life in some new country, shoving goats and sheep around and eating a few figs every couple of days to stay alive like the other *fellahîn*.

"I'm a hero, Yasmin," I said, "and we heroes sometimes have secret business to attend to. Got to go." I kissed her three or four times, squeezed her right silicone tit for luck, and stood up. On the way out of Frenchy's I patted Indihar's ass, and she turned and grinned at me. I waved good-night to Dalia. Blanca I pretended didn't even exist.

I walked down the Street to the Silver Palm, just to see what people were doing and what was going on. Mahmoud and Jacques were sitting at a table, having coffee and sopping up *hummus* with pita bread. The Half-Hajj was absent, probably out kicking gigantic heterosexual stone cutters around for the hell of it. I sat down with my friends. "May your and so forth, and so forth," said Mahmoud. He was never one to worry about formalities.

"Yours too," I said.

"Getting yourself wired, I hear," said Jacques. "A crucial decision. A major undertaking. I'm sure you've considered both sides of the matter?"

I was a little astonished. "News travels fast, doesn't it?"

Mahmoud raised his eyebrows. "That's what news is for," he said, around a mouthful of bread and *hummus*.

"Permit me to buy you some coffee," said Jacques.

"Praise Allah," I said, "but I feel like something stronger."

"Just as well," said Jacques to Mahmoud. "Marîd has more money than the two of us together. He's on Papa's payroll now."

I didn't like the sound of that rumor at all. I went to the bar and ordered my gin, bingara, and Rose's. Behind the bar, Heidi grimaced, but she didn't say anything. She was pretty—hell, she was one of the most beautiful real women I'd ever met. She always fitted into her well-chosen clothing the way some of the debs and changes wished they could, with their store-bought bodies. Heidi had wonderful blue eyes and soft, pale bangs. I don't know why, but bangs on young women always make me jittery. I think it's the hebephile in me; if I examine myself closely enough, I find hints of every objectionable quality known to man. I'd always wanted to get to know Heidi *really* well, but I guess I wasn't her type. Maybe her type was available on a moddy, and after I got my brain wired . . .

While I was waiting for her to mix my drink, another voice spoke up about twenty feet away, beyond a group of Korean men and women who would soon learn, no doubt, that they were in the wrong part of town. "Vodka martini, dry. Pre-war Wolfschmidt's if you've got it, shaken and not stirred. With a twist of lemon peel."

Well, now, I said to myself. I waited until Heidi came back with my drink. I paid her and swirled the liquor and ice in tight, counterclockwise circles. Heidi brought my change; I tipped her a kiam, and she started some polite conversation. I interrupted her rather rudely; I was more interested in the vodka martini.

I picked up my glass and stepped back from the bar, just enough to get a good look at James Bond. He was just as I remembered him from the brief encounter in Chiri's place, and from Ian Fleming's novels; black hair parted on one side, a heavy lock of it falling in an unruly comma over the right eye, the scar running down the right cheek. He had straight, black brows and a long, straight nose. His upper lip was short and his mouth, though relaxed, somehow gave the impression of cruelty. He looked ruthless. He had paid a great deal of money to a team of surgeons to make him look ruthless. He glanced at me and smiled; I wondered if he recalled our previous meeting. His gray-blue eyes crinkled a bit at their edges as he observed me; I had the distinct feeling that I was, in fact, being observed. He was wearing a plain cotton shirt and tropical worsted trousers, no doubt of British manufacture, with black leather sandals suitable to the climate. He paid for his martini and came toward me, one hand extended. "Nice to see you again, old man," he said.

I shook hands with him. "I don't believe I've been granted the honor of making the gentleman's acquaintance," I said in Arabic.

Bond answered me in flawless French. "Another bar, another circumstance. It was of no great consequence. Everything turned out satisfactorily in the end." It had been satisfactory for him, at least. At the moment, the dead Russian had no opinion at all.

"May Allah forgive me, my friends are waiting," I said.

Bond smiled his famous half-smile. He gave me back an Arabic saying—in perfect local Arabic. "What has died has passed," he said, shrugging, meaning either that bygones were bygones, or that it would be good policy for me to begin forgetting all the recently dead; I wasn't sure which interpretation Bond intended. I nodded, disconcerted more by his facility with my language. Then I remembered that he was wearing a James Bond moddy, probably with an Arabic-language daddy chipped in. I took my drink to the table where Mahmoud and Jacques were sitting, and chose a chair from which I could keep an eye on the bar and its single entrance. By the time I'd seated myself, Bond had downed his martini and was going out into the cobbled Street. I felt a chilly wave of indecision: what was I supposed to do? Could I hope to

bring him down now, before I had my brain wired? I was unarmed.
What possible good could come of attacking Bond prematurely? Yet
surely Friedlander Bey would consider this an opportunity lost, one that
might well mean the death of someone else, someone dear to me. . . .

I decided to follow. I left my drink untasted on the table and gave
my friends no explanation. I got out of my chair and went to the open
doorway of the Silver Palm, just in time to see Bond turn left into a
side street. I crept along carefully behind. Evidently I wasn't careful
enough, because when I stopped at the corner and peered cautiously
around, James Bond was gone. There were no other streets parallel to
the Street for him to have turned onto; he must have entered one of the
low, whitewashed, flat-roofed dwellings on the block. That was *some*
information, at least. I turned around again to walk back to the Silver
Palm, when a flare of pain detonated behind my left ear. I crumpled to
my knees, and a strong, tanned hand grabbed the light material of my
gallebeya and dragged me back to my feet. I muttered some curses and
raised my fist. The edge of his hand chopped at the point of my shoulder, and my arm dropped, numb and useless.

James Bond laughed softly. "Every time you see a well-setup European in one of your grimy, quaint rumshops, you think you can come
along behind and relieve him of his pocketbook. Well, my friend,
sometimes you choose to rob the wrong European." He slapped me
across the face, not very hard, threw me away from himself against the
rough face of the wall behind me, and stared at me as if I owed him an
explanation or apology. I decided he was right.

"A hundred thousand pardons, *effendi,*" I murmured. Somewhere
in my mind arose the thought that this James Bond was handling himself a good sight better than he had when he let me escort him out of
Chiri's a couple of weeks ago. Tonight, his goddamn black comma of
hair wasn't even out of place. He wasn't even breathing hard. There
was some logical explanation for all that, too; I'd let Papa or Jacques or
the *I Ching* figure it out: my head was throbbing too hard and my ears
were chiming.

"And you needn't bother with that '*effendi*' bunk," he said grimly.
"That's a Turkish flattery, and I still have more than one grudge against
the Turks. You're no Turk, anyway, by the looks of you." His slightly
cruel mouth gave me a slightly vicious sneer and he walked by me as if
I were no threat at all to his safety or his wallet. That, in point of fact,
was the plain truth. I had just had my second run-in with the man who
called himself James Bond. At the moment, we each had a score of
one, out of a possible two; I was in no hurry at all to play the rubber
match. He seemed to have learned a lot since our last meeting, or for

some reason of his own he had allowed me to chuck him so easily out of Chiri's. I knew I was badly outclassed here.

As I walked slowly and painfully back to the Silver Palm, I came to an important decision: I was going to tell Papa that I wouldn't help him. It wasn't merely a matter of being afraid to have my brain wired; hell, even with it goosed from here to the Prophet's Birthday, I was no competition for these killers. I couldn't even follow James Bond down one goddamn block in my own neighborhood without getting my ass kicked around. I didn't have a single doubt that Bond could have dealt more harshly with me, if he'd chosen to. He thought I was just a robber, a common Arab thief, and he merely treated me the way he treated all common Arab thieves. It must have been a daily occurrence for him.

No, there was nothing that could persuade me otherwise. I didn't need the three days to think about it—Papa and his wonderful scheme could just go to hell.

I went back to the Silver Palm and threw down my drink in two great gulps. Over the protestations of Mahmoud and Jacques, I said that I had to be going. I kissed Heidi on the cheek and whispered a licentious suggestion in her ear, the same suggestion I always whispered; and she replied with the same amused rejection. I walked thoughtfully back to Frenchy's to explain to Yasmin that I was not going to be a hero, that I was not going to serve higher principles than kings and princes and all the rest of that foolishness. Yasmin would be disappointed in me, and I probably wouldn't get into her pants for a week; but that was better than getting my throat slashed and having my ashes strewn over the sewage treatment plant.

I would have a lot of explaining to do to everybody. I would have a lot of apologizing to do, too. Everyone from Selima to Chiri to Sergeant Hajjar to Friedlander Bey himself would be after my balls, but I had made my decision. I was my own man, and I wouldn't be pressured into accepting a terrifying fate, however morally right and public-spirited they all made it sound. The drink at the Silver Palm, the two at Frenchy's, a couple of tri-phets, four sunnies, and eight Paxium all agreed with me. Before I found my way back to Frenchy's, the night was warm and safe and wholly on my side, and everybody who was urging me to wire my brain was stuffed down deep in a dark pit into which I planned never again to peek. They could all jam each other silly, for all I cared. I had my own life to lead.

ELEVEN

friday was a day of rest and recuperation. My body had been bruised and beaten by a lot of people lately, some of whom had been friends and acquaintances, some of whom I was just chafing to catch in a dark alley real soon. One of the best things about the Budayeen is the prevalence of dark alleys. They were planned purposefully, I think. Somewhere in somebody's sacred scripture it says, "And there shall be caused to be built dark alleys wherein the mockers and the unrighteous shall in their turn have their heads laid open and in like wise their fat lips busted; and even this shall be pleasing in the sight of Heaven." I couldn't quote you exactly where that verse comes from. I might have dreamt it up early Friday morning.

The Black Widow Sisters had had first crack at me; various lackeys of Lutz Seipolt, Friedlander Bey, and Lieutenant Okking had caused me grief, as had their smugly smiling masters; and just last night I'd been briefly chastized by this James Bond lunatic. My pill case was now completely empty: nothing but pastel-colored dust on the bottom that I could lick from my fingertips, hoping for a milligram of help. The opiates were the first to go; my supply of Sonneine, bought from Chiriga and then Sergeant Hajjar, had been downed in rapid succession as each of my body's movements brought new twinges and spasms of pain. When the sunnies were gone I tried Paxium, the little lavender pills that some people believe is the ultimate gift of the organic chemical universe, the Answer to All of Life's Little Worries, but which I'm coming to the conclusion aren't worth their weight in jackal snot. I ate them anyway and washed them down with about six ounces of Jack Daniels that Yasmin brought home from work with her. Okay, that left the full-throttle blue triangles. I didn't really know what they'd do for pain, but I was certainly willing to use myself as a research volunteer. Science Marches On. I dropped three tri-phets, and the effect was fascinating from a pharmacological standpoint: in about half an hour, I began taking a tremendous interest in my heartbeat. I measured my pulse rate at something like four hundred and twenty-two per minute, but I kept getting distracted by phantom lizards crawling around just at the edges of my peripheral vision. I'm almost certain that my heart wasn't really pumping that hard.

Drugs are your friends, treat them with respect. You wouldn't throw your friends in the garbage. You wouldn't flush your friends down the toilet. If that's the way you treat your friends or your drugs, you don't deserve to have either. Give them to me. Drugs are wonderful things. I won't listen to anybody trying to get me to give them up. I'd rather give up food and drink—in fact, on occasion, I have.

The effect of all the pills was to make my mind wander. Actually, any sign of life on its part was heartening. Life was taking on a kind of bleak, pungent, really penetrating, and awfully *huge* quality that I didn't enjoy at all.

On top of that, I remembered that I'd collected a couple of caps of RPM from Saied the Half-Hajj. This is the same junk that Bill the taxi driver has coursing through his bloodstream all the time, *all* the time, at the cost of his immortal soul. I've got to remember not to ride with Bill anymore. Jesus, that stuff is just really scary, and the worst part was that I actually *paid* cash money for the privilege of feeling so lousy. Sometimes I'm disgusted by the things I do, and I make resolutions to clean myself out. I promised, when that RPM wore off, if it ever did . . .

Friday was the Sabbath, a day of rest except for everybody in the Budayeen who went right back to work as soon as the sun went down. We observed the holy month of Ramadân, but the city's cops and the mosque's bullies let up on us a little on Fridays. They were happy to get whatever cooperation they could. Yasmin went to work and I stayed in bed, reading a Simenon I think I had read when I was about fifteen and again when I was about twenty and again a couple of other times. It's hard to tell with Simenon. He wrote the same book a dozen times, but he had so many different books that he wrote a dozen times each that you have to read all of them and then sort them out in some kind of rational order according to a logical, thematic basis that's always been far beyond me. I just start at the back (if it's printed in Arabic) or the front (if it's printed in French) or the middle (if I'm in a hurry or too full of my friends, the drugs).

Simenon. Why was I talking about Simenon? It was going to lead to a vital and illuminating point. Simenon suggests Ian Fleming: they're both writers; they both clawed out thrillers in their individual fashions; they're both dead; and neither one of them knew the first thing about making a good martini—Fleming's "shaken and not stirred," my holy whoring mother's ineffable left tit; and Ian Fleming leads neatly and directly to James Bond. The man with the Bond moddy never again left another 007 trace in the city, not so much as the stub of a Morlands Special with the gold rings around the filter or a chomped-on slice of lemon peel or a Beretta bullet hole. Yeah, it was the Beretta he'd used on Bogatyrev and Devi. The Beretta was Bond's choice of pistols in the early Fleming novels, until some hotshot reader pointed out that it was a "lady's gun" with no stopping power; so Fleming had Bond switch to the Walther PPK, a smallish but reliable automatic. If our James Bond had used the Walther, it would have left a messier indentation in Devi's face; the Beretta made a rather tidier little hole, like the pop-top slot in a can of beer. That slapping-around I got from him was the last anyone saw or heard of James Bond in the city. He had a low tolerance for boredom, I guess.

That's another first-rate reason for getting to know your medicines and correctives. Boredom can be tedious, but not when you're counting your pulse at over four hundred a minute. By the life of my beard and the sacred shifting balls of the Apostle of God, may the blessings of Allah be on him and peace, I really just wanted to go to sleep! Every time I closed my eyes, though, a black-and-white strobe effect started flashing, and purple and green things swam by, gigantic things. I cried, but they wouldn't leave me alone. I couldn't see how Bill could drive his taxi through them all.

So that was Friday, in brief summary. Yasmin came home with the Jack Daniels, I killed the rest of my drug supply, passed out sometime near noon, and awoke to find Yasmin gone. It was now Saturday. I had two more days to enjoy my brain.

Early Saturday evening, I noticed my money seemed to have vaporized. I should have had a few hundred kiam left; I'd spent a little, of course, and I'd probably blown even more that I couldn't account for. Yet I had the feeling that I ought to have more than the ninety kiam I found in my shoulder bag. Ninety kiam wasn't going to get me much of anything; a new pair of jeans was going to cost me forty or more.

I began to suspect that Yasmin had been dipping into my finances. I hate that about women, even the ones whose genetic threads in their cells still said they were male. Jo-Mama says, "Just 'cause the cat had her kittens in the oven don't make them biscuits." Take a pretty boy, nip off his *couilles* and buy him a silicone balcony that could comfortably seat an underfed family of three, and before you know it, she's digging around in your wallet. They eat up all your pills and caps, spend your money, bitch about the goddamn sheet and the blanket, stare rapturously all afternoon at themselves in the bathroom mirror, make innocent little remarks about the devastating young plushes passing by in the other direction, want to be held for an hour after you've exhausted yourself jamming them into the floorboards, and then they climb up your back because you look out the window with a slightly irked expression on your face. What could you possibly be annoyed about, with a virtually perfect goddess hanging around the apartment, decorating your floor with her dirty underwear? You might take something to elevate your mood, but the precious bitch already consumed all that, remember?

Only another day and a half of Marîd Audran's brain as Allah the Protector in His wisdom had designed it. Yasmin was not speaking to me: she thought I was a coward and a selfish son of a clapped-up ass for not going along with Papa's plan. One minute, it was all set—on Monday morning, I was going to meet with Friedlander Bey's surgeons and have my thoughts electrified. The next minute, I was a rotten bastard who didn't care what happened to his friends. She couldn't remember if I was going to get my brain wired or not; she couldn't think back far enough to recall the last argument (*I* could: I was *not* going to get my brain wired, and that was the end of it). I didn't get out of bed all day Friday or Saturday. I watched shadows get longer and shorter and longer. I heard the muezzin call the faithful to prayer; and then, what seemed to me like a few minutes later, he called again. I stopped paying attention to Yasmin and her moods sometime on Saturday evening, before she started to get ready for work.

She slammed her way back and forth across my room, calling me all kinds of innovative foul names, some of which I'd actually never heard before, despite my years of wandering. It just made me love the little slut even more. I didn't get out of bed until Yasmin left for Frenchy's. My body alternated between rattling chills and flashes of fever so bad I had to cool off in the shower. Then I'd lie back in bed and shiver and sweat. I soaked the sheets and the mattress cover, and clung with white-knuckled fingers to the blanket. The phantom lizards were on my face and arms now, but crawling around less frequently. I felt safe enough to go to the bathroom again, something I'd been thinking about for a long while. I wasn't hungry, but I was pretty thirsty. I drank a couple of glasses of water, then slid shakily back into bed. I wished Yasmin would come home.

Despite the waning effects of the drug overdose and my growing fear, I had made up my mind about Monday morning. Saturday night passed with more cold sweats and remittent fever, and I stared wakefully at the ceiling, even after Yasmin came back and went drunkenly to sleep. Sunday, just before sunset, while she was getting herself ready to go to work again, I got out of bed and stood naked behind her. She was putting on her eye makeup, screwing her face into crazy expressions and glossing her eyelids with loveliness from some rich-bitch department store beyond the Budayeen. She wouldn't use inexpensive paint from the bazaars like everyone else, as if anyone in Frenchy's could get a good look at her in that dimness. The same makeup was on the racks in the souks, but Yasmin paid top prices for it across town. She wanted to look heartbreaking on stage, when not a juiced-up fool in the place would be looking at her *eyes*. She was going for a layered effect of blue and green below her narrow, sketched-in eyebrows. Then she worked on a tasteful sprinkle of gold glittery sparkles. The sparkles were the hard part. She put them on one by one. "Get to bed early," she said.

"Why?" I asked innocently.

"Because you have a busy day tomorrow," she said.

I shrugged.

"Your brain," she said, "remember?"

"My brain, I remember," I said. "It's not going anywhere unusual. I don't have anything particularly taxing lined up for it."

"You're getting the worthless thing wired!" She turned on me like a nesting falcon on a hawk.

"Not the last time I thought it over," I said.

She grabbed up her small blue overnight case. "Well, you son-of-a-bitching mother-ugly *kaffir*," she cried, "fuck you *and* the horse you rode in on!" She made more noise leaving my apartment than I thought was possible, and that was before she even slammed the door. After she slammed the door it got very quiet, and I was able to think. I couldn't think of anything to think about, though. I walked around the room a few times, put one or two things away, kicked some of my clothes from the right to the left and back again, and laid down on the bed. I'd been in the bed so long that it wasn't diverting to be there again now, but there wasn't that much else to do. I watched the darkness in the room stretch and reach out toward me. That wasn't so exciting anymore, either.

The pain had gone, the overdose-induced hysteria had gone, my money had gone, Yasmin had gone. This was peace and contentment. I hated every goddamn second of it.

In this silent center of motionlessness and mindlessness, free of all the frenzy that had surrounded me for many days, I surprised myself with a piece of genuine intuition. It began by congratulating myself for figuring that the man with the James Bond moddy had a Beretta rather than a Walther. Then the Bond thought linked up to something else, and they hooked together with one or two more ideas, and it all illuminated an inexplicable detail that had been simmering in my memory for a couple of days, at least. I recalled my last visit to Lieutenant Okking. I remembered the way he didn't seem to be at all interested in my theories or Friedlander Bey's proposition. That wasn't so unusual; Okking resisted interference from anyone. He disliked positive interference, in the form of authentic assistance, just as much. It wasn't Okking himself to whom my thoughts kept returning; it was something in his office.

One of the envelopes had been addressed to Universal Export. I recalled wondering idly if Seipolt ran that firm, or if Hassan the Shiite ever received any curious crates from them. The company's name was so commonplace that there were probably a thousand "Universal Exports" all around the world. Maybe Okking was just sending off a mail order for some rattan patio furniture to put next to his backyard barbecue.

Of course, the very ordinariness of "Universal Export" was the reason that M., the head of James Bond's special 00 section, used it as a false cover and code name in Ian Fleming's books. The forgettable name would never have stuck in my memory without that connection to the Bond stories. Maybe "Universal Export" was a disguised reference to the man who'd worn the James Bond moddy. I wished that I had memorized the address on that envelope.

I sat up, startled. If the Bond explanation had any truth to it, why was that envelope in Lieutenant Okking's *Out* box? I told myself that I was getting as jumpy as a grasshopper on a griddle. I was probably looking for honey where there were no bees. Still, I felt my stomach turn sick again. I felt myself being drawn unwillingly into a morass of tortuous and deadly paths.

It was time for action. I had spent Friday, Saturday, and most of Sunday paralyzed between my worn and grimy sheets. It was the moment to get moving, to leave the apartment, to rid myself of this clinging morbidity and fear. I had ninety kiam; I could buy myself some butaqualides and get some decent sleep.

I threw on my *gallebeya*, which was getting a little on the soiled side, my sandals, and my *libdeh*, the close-fitting cap. I grabbed my shoulder bag on the way out the door, and hurried downstairs. Suddenly I really wanted to score some beauties; I mean, I *really* wanted them. I'd just gotten over three horrible days of sweating too much of everything out of my system, and already I was rushing out to buy more. I made a mental note to slow down my drug intake; crumpled the mental note; and tossed it into my mental wastebasket.

Beauties, it seemed, were scarce. Chiriga didn't have any, but she gave me a free drink of tende while she told me about how much trouble she was having with a new girl working for her, and that she was still saving her Honey Pílar moddy for me. I remembered the holoporn ad outside old Laila's shop. "Chiri," I said, "I'm just getting over the flu or something; but I promise, we'll go have dinner some night next week. Then, *inshallah*, we'll burn your moddy out."

She didn't even smile. She looked at me as if she were watching a wounded fish flopping in the water. "Marîd, honey," she said sadly, "now really, listen to me: you got to cut out all these pills. You're wrecking yourself."

She was right, but you don't ever want to hear that kind of advice from anybody else. I nodded, gulped the rest of the tende, and left her club without saying good-bye.

I caught up with Jacques, Mahmoud, and Saied at Big Al's Old Chicago. They said they were all tapped out, financially and medicinally. I said, "Fine, see you around."

"Marîd," said Jacques, "maybe it's none of my—"

"It's not," I said. I passed by the Silver Palm: no action there, either. I passed by Hassan's shop, but he wasn't in the back and his American chicken just gazed at me with sultry eyes. I ducked into the Red Light—that's how desperate I was beginning to feel—and Fatima told me that one of the white girls' boyfriends had a whole suitcase full of different stuff, but that he wouldn't be in until maybe five in the morning. I said that if nothing else turned up by then, I'd come back. No free drink from Fatima.

Finally, at Jo-Mama's Hellenic hideaway, I ran into a little luck. I bought six beauties from Jo-Mama's second barmaid, Rocky, another hefty woman with short, brushy black hair. Rocky stung me a little on the price, but at that point I didn't care. She offered me a beer on the house to wash them down, but I told her I was just going to go home and take them and climb back into bed.

"Yeah, you right," said Jo-Mama, "you got to get to sleep early. You got to get up in the morning, dawlin', and have your skull drilled."

I shut my eyes briefly and sighed. "Where did you hear about that?" I asked her.

Jo-Mama pasted a slightly offended, wholly innocent look on her face. "*Everybody's* been knowin' it, Marîd. Ain't that the truth, Rocky?

It's what everybody's been having trouble believing. I mean, *you* getting your brain wired. F'sure, the next thing we be hearing, Hassan'll be giving away free rugs or rifles or handjobs to the first twenty callers."

"I'll take that beer," I said, very tired. Rocky drew one; for a moment nobody knew if this was the free beer or if I'd turned that one down and this was another one that I had to pay for.

"It's on me," said Jo-Mama.

"Thanks, Mama," I said. "I'm not getting my brain wired." I took a big gulp of the beer. "I don't care *who* told *who*, I don't care who *they* heard it from. This is me, Marîd, talking: I am *not* getting my brain wired. *Comprendez?*"

Jo-Mama shrugged like she didn't believe me; after all, what was *my* word against the word of the Street? "I got to tell you what happened in here last night," she said, about to launch into one of her endless but entertaining stories. I half-wanted to hear it because I had to keep up with the news, but I was rescued.

"*There* you are!" shouted Yasmin, banging into the bar and whacking a vicious swipe at me with her purse. I ducked my head, but she cracked me in the side.

"What the hell—" I started to say.

"Take it outside," said Jo-Mama automatically. She looked as astonished as I felt.

Yasmin wasn't in the mood to listen to either of us. She grabbed me around the wrist—her hand was as strong as mine, and my wrist was *grabbed*. "You come with me, you cocksucker," she said.

"Yasmin, shut the fuck up and leave me alone," I said. Jo-Mama got off her stool; that ought to have been a warning, but Yasmin paid her no attention. She still had my wrist, and her fingers closed even tighter. She yanked on my arm.

"You're going to come with me," she said in an ominous voice, "because I got something pretty to show you, you goddamn yellow-bellied pussy."

I was really angry; I'd never been this angry with Yasmin before, and I still didn't know what she was talking about. "Slap her face for her," said Rocky from behind the bar. That always works in the holoshows for excitable heroines and panicking junior officers; I didn't think, though, that it would quiet Yasmin down. She'd probably just beat the living hell out of me, and then we'd go do whatever she wanted in the first place. I raised the arm she was still clutching, turned it outward a little, broke her grasp, and grabbed *her* wrist. Then I twisted her arm and forced it up behind her back in a tight hammerlock. She cried out in pain. I pushed her arm further, and she yelped again.

"That's for calling me those names," I said, growling softly, close to her ear. "You can do that at home if you want, but not in front of my friends."

"You want me to hurt you bad?" she said angrily.

"You can try."

"Later," she said. "I still got something to show you."

I let go of her arm, and she rubbed it for a moment. Then she snatched up her purse and kicked open Jo-Mama's door. I raised my eyebrows at Rocky; Jo-Mama was giving me an amused little smile, because all of this would eventually make a better story than the one she never got to tell me. Jo-Mama, at least, was going to come out ahead.

I followed Yasmin outside. She turned to me; before she could say a word, I put my right hand tightly around her throat and flung her up against an ancient brick wall. I didn't care how much I hurt her. "You're *never* going to do that again," I said in a dangerously calm voice. "You understand me?" And just for the pure sadistic pleasure of it, I knocked her head roughly against the bricks.

"*Fuck you*, asshole!"

"Anytime you think you're man enough, you mutilated, gelded son of a bitch," I said. And then Yasmin started to cry. I felt myself collapse inside. I felt I had done the worst thing I could ever do, and there was no way I could make up for it. I might crawl on my knees all the way to Mecca to pray for forgiveness, and Allah would forgive me, but Yasmin wouldn't. I would have given anything I had, anything I could steal, if the last few minutes hadn't happened; but they had, and they would be difficult for either of us to forget.

"Marîd," she whispered between sobs. I held her. Right then, there wasn't a damn thing in the world to say. We clasped each other that way, close together, Yasmin weeping, me wanting to but unable, for five or ten or fifteen minutes. A few people passed by on the sidewalk and pretended they didn't see us. Jo-Mama stuck her head out of the door and ducked back inside. A moment later, Rocky looked out as if she were just casually counting the crowd that didn't exist on this dark street. I wasn't thinking anything, I wasn't feeling anything. I just clung to Yasmin, and she clung to me.

"I love you," I murmured at last. When you find the appropriate time, it's always the best and only thing to say.

She took my hand and we started walking slowly toward the back of the Budayeen. I thought we were just wandering, but after a few minutes I realized that Yasmin was leading me somewhere. The grim certainty grew in me that I didn't want to see what she was going to show me.

A body had been stuffed into a large plastic trash bag, but someone had disturbed the pile of bags, Nikki's bag had split open, and she lay sprawled on the damp, filthy bricks of a tight blind alley. "I thought it was your fault she was dead," said Yasmin with a little whimper. "Because you didn't do very much to try and find her." I held Yasmin's hand and we just stood there for a while, staring down at Nikki's corpse, not saying anything more for a while. I *knew* that I'd see Nikki like this sometime, finally. I think I knew it from the beginning, when Tamiko had been murdered and Nikki made that short, frantic phone call.

I let go of Yasmin's hand and knelt down beside Nikki. There was a lot of blood all over her, in the dark green trash bag, on the moss-covered bricks of the pavement. "Yasmin, baby," I said, looking up into her bleak face, "you don't want to see this anymore. Why don't you call Okking, then go home? I'll be there in a little while."

Yasmin made a vague, meaningless gesture. "I'll call Okking," she said in a toneless voice, "but I got to go back to work."

"Frenchy can go fuck himself tonight," I said. "I want you to go home. Listen, honey, I *need* to have you there."

"All right," she said, smiling a little through the tears. Our relationship hadn't been destroyed, after all. With a little care it would be just as good as new, maybe even better. It was a relief to feel hopeful again.

"How did you know she was here?" I asked, frowning.

"Blanca found her," said Yasmin. "Her back door's down there, and she passes by here on her way to work." She pointed further up the alley, where a peeling, gray-painted door was set into the blank brick wall.

I nodded and watched Yasmin walk slowly toward the Street. Then I turned back to Nikki's ruined body. It had been the throat-slasher, and I could see the bruises on Nikki's wrists and neck, the burn marks, and a lot of small cuts and wounds. The killer had invested more time and expertise in finishing Nikki than he had with Tami or Abdoulaye. I was sure the medical examiner would find the traces of rape, too.

Nikki's clothing and purse had been thrown into the trash bag with her. I looked through her clothes, but I didn't find anything. I reached for the purse, but I had to lift Nikki's head. She had been clubbed cruelly and savagely until her skull and hair and blood and brains were all crushed together into a repellent mass. Her throat had been cut so brutally that her head was almost severed. I had never seen such profane, desecrating, perverse savagery in my life. I cleared the strewn refuse from a space and rested Nikki's corpse gently on the broken bricks. Then I walked away a few steps, knelt, and vomited. I heaved and retched until my stomach muscles began to ache. When the sickness passed, I made myself go back to look through her purse. I found two curious and noteworthy objects: a brass reproduction that I'd seen in Seipolt's house of an ancient Egyptian scarab; and a crude, almost homemade-looking moddy. I put both in my shoulder bag, chose the trash bag with the least stench surrounding it, and made myself as comfortable as I could. I addressed a prayer to Allah on behalf of Nikki's soul. Then I waited.

"Well," I said quietly, looking around at the squalid, mucky place where Nikki had been abandoned, "I guess I get up in the morning and get my brain wired." *Maktoob*, all right: it was written.

Twelve

muslims are often, by nature, very superstitious. Our co-travelers through Allah's bewildering creation include all sorts of *djinn, afrit,* monsters, and good and bad angels. Then there are legions of sorcerous people armed with dangerous powers, the evil eye being the most frequently encountered. All of this makes the Muslim culture no more irrational than any other; every group of people has its own set of unfriendly, unseen things waiting to pounce on the unwary human being. Commonly there are far more enemies in the spirit world than there are protectors, although there are supposed to be uncountable armies of angels and the like. Maybe they've all been on R&R since the deparadisation of Shaitan, I don't know.

Anyway, one of the superstitious practices clung to by some Muslims, particularly the nomadic tribes and the uncivilized *fellahîn* of the Maghrîb—i.e., my mother's people—is to name a newborn with an affliction or a dreadful quality to ward off the envy of whatever spirit or witch might be paying too much attention. I'm told that this is done all over the world by people who have never even heard of the prophet, may peace be on his name. I am called Marîd, which means "illness," and I was given it in the hope that I would not, in fact, suffer much illness in my lifetime. The charm seems to have had a certain positive effect. I had a burst appendix removed a few years ago, but that's a common, routine operation, and it is the only serious medical problem I've ever had. I guess that may be due to the improved treatments available in this age of wonders, but who can say? Praise Allah, and all that.

So I haven't had much experience with hospitals. When the voices woke me, it took me quite some time to figure out where I was, and then another while to recall why the hell I was there in the first place. I opened my eyes; I couldn't see anything but a dim blur. I blinked again and again, but it was like someone had tried to paste my eyelids closed with sand and honey. I tried to raise my hand to rub my eyes, but my arm was too weak; it wouldn't travel the negligible distance from my chest to my face. I blinked some more and squinted. Finally I could make out two male nurses standing near the foot of my bed. One was young, with a black beard and a clear voice. He held a chart and was briefing the other man. "Mr. Audran shouldn't give you too much trouble," he said.

The second man was a good deal older, with gray hair and a hoarse voice. He nodded. "Meds?" he asked.

The younger man frowned. "It's unusual. He can have almost anything he wants, with approval from his doctors. The way I understand it, he'll get that approval just by asking. As much and as often as he wants."

The gray-haired man let out an indignant breath. "What did he do, win a contest? An all-expense-paid drug holiday in the hospital of his choice?"

"Lower your voice, Ali. He isn't moving, but he may be able to hear you. I don't know who he is, but the hospital has been treating him like a foreign dignitary or something. What's being spent to ablate every little twinge of his discomfort could relieve the pain of a dozen suffering poor people on the charity wards."

Naturally, that made me feel like a filthy pig. I mean, *I* have feelings, too. I didn't ask for this kind of treatment—I didn't remember asking for it, at least—and I planned to put an end to it as soon as I could. Well, if not an *end* to it, that is, maybe ease it off a little. I didn't want to be handled like a feudal shaykh.

The younger man went on, consulting his chart. "Mr. Audran was admitted for some elective intracranial work. Elaborate circuit implants, very experimental, I understand. That's why he's been on bed rest this long. There may be some unforeseen side effects." That made me a little uneasy: *what* side effects? Nobody had ever mentioned them to me before.

"I'll take a look at his chart this evening," said the gray-haired man.

"He sleeps most of the time, he shouldn't bother you too much. Merciful Allah, between the etorphin bubble and the injections, he should sleep for the next ten or fifteen years." Of course, he was underestimating my wonderfully efficient liver and enzyme system. Everyone always thinks I'm exaggerating about that.

They began to leave the room. The older man opened the door and stepped out. I tried to speak; nothing came out, as if I hadn't used my voice for months. I tried again. There was a whispered croaking sound. I swallowed a little saliva and murmured, "Nurse."

The man with the black beard put my chart on the console beside my bed and turned to me, his expression blank. "Be right with you, Mr. Audran," he said in a cool voice. Then he went out and shut the door behind him.

The room was clean and plain and almost bare of decoration, but it was also comfortable. It was much more comfortable than the charity wards, where I had been treated after my appendix burst. That had been an unpleasant time; the only bright spots were the saving of my life, all thanks be to Allah, and my introduction to Sonneine, once again may Allah be praised. The charity wards were not wholly philanthropic— I mean, the *fellahîn* who could not afford private doctors were, indeed, given free medical attention; but the hospital's principle motive was to provide a wide range of unusual problems for the interns, residents, and student nurses to practice upon. Everyone who examined you, everyone who performed some sort of test, everyone who did some minor surgery at your bedside, had only a modest familiarity with his job. These people were earnest and sincere, but inexperienced: they could make the simple taking of blood an ordeal, and a more painful procedure a hellish torture. It was not so in this private room. I had comfort and ease and freedom from pain. I had peace and rest and competent care. Friedlander Bey was giving this to me, but I would repay him. He would see to that.

I suppose that I dozed off for a little while, because when the door opened again I awoke with a start. I expected to see the nurse, but it was a young man in a green surgical outfit. He had dark, sunburnt skin and bright brown eyes, with one of the largest black mustaches I've ever seen. I imagined him trying to contain the thing within a surgical mask, and that made me smile. My doctor was a Turk. I had a little trouble understanding his Arabic. He had trouble understanding me, too.

"How are we today?" he said without looking at me. He glanced through the nurse's notes and then turned to the data terminal beside my bed. He touched a few keys, and displays changed on the terminal's screen. He made no sounds at all, neither the doctor's concerned clucking nor the encouraged humming. He stared at the scrolling parade of numbers and twirled the ends of his mustache. At last he faced me and said, "How are you feeling?"

"Fine," I said noncommittally. When I deal with doctors I always figure that they're after certain specific information; but they won't ever come out and ask you just what they need to know because they're afraid you'll distort the truth and give them what you think they *want* to

hear, so they go about it in this circular way as if you're not still trying
to guess what they want to know and distorting the truth anyway.

"Any pain?"

"A little," I said. It was a lie: I was drifted to the hairline—my former hairline, that is. You never tell a doctor that you're not suffering,
because that might encourage him to lower your dosage of anodynes.

"Sleeping?"

"Yes."

"Had anything to eat?"

I thought for a moment. I was ravenously hungry, although the IV
was dripping a glucose solution directly into the back of my hand.
"No," I said.

"We might start you on some clear liquids in the morning. Been
out of bed?"

"No."

"Good. Stay there for another couple of days. Dizzy? Numbness in
your hands or feet? Nausea? Unusual sensations, bright lights, hearing
voices, phantom limbs, anything like that?"

Phantom limbs? "No." I wouldn't tell him that if it *was* true.

"You're doing just fine, Mr. Audran. Coming along right on
schedule."

"Allah be thanked. How long have I been here."

The doctor gave me a glance, then looked at my chart again. "A little over two weeks," he said.

"When did I have the surgery?"

"Fifteen days ago. You were in the hospital for two days of preparation before that."

"Uh huh." There was less than a week of Ramadân remaining. I
wondered what had happened in the city during my absence. I certainly hoped a few of my friends and associates were left alive. If anyone had been hurt—killed, that is—it would be Papa who would have
to bear the responsibility. That was just about as effective as blaming it
on God, and as practical, too. You couldn't get a lawyer to sue either of
them.

"Tell me, Mr. Audran, what is the last thing you remember?"

That was a tough one. I thought for a few moments; it was like diving into a dark, stormy cloudbank: there was nothing there but a grim
feeling of foreboding down below. I had vague impressions of stern
voices and the memory of hands rolling me over on the bed, and bolts
of blazing pain. I remembered someone saying "Don't pull on that," but
I didn't know who had said it or what it meant. I searched further and
realized that I couldn't remember going into surgery or even leaving my

apartment and coming to the hospital. The very last thing I could see clearly was . . .

Nikki. "My friend," I said, my mouth suddenly dry and my throat tight.

"The one who was murdered," said the doctor.

"Yes."

"That happened almost three weeks ago. You don't remember anything since?"

"No. Nothing."

"Then you don't recall meeting me before today? Our conversations?"

The dark cloudwall was rushing up to blot me out, and I figured now was a good time for it, too. I hated these gaps in my consciousness. They're a nuisance, even the little twelve-hour holes; a three-week slice missing from my mental pie was more trouble than I wanted to deal with. I just didn't have the energy to work up a decent panic. "I'm sorry," I said, "I just don't remember."

The doctor nodded. "My name is Dr. Yeniknani. I assisted your surgeon, Dr. Lisân. In the last several days you've gradually recovered some self-awareness. If, however, you've lost the content of our talks, it is very important that we discuss that information again."

I just wanted to go back to sleep. I rubbed my eyes with a weary hand. "And if you do explain it all to me again, I'll probably forget it and you'll just have to do it all over tomorrow or the next day."

Dr. Yeniknani shrugged. "That is possibly so, but you have nothing else to occupy your time, and I am paid well enough that I am more than willing to do what must be done." He gave me a broad smile to let me know he was joking—these fierce types have to do that or you'd never guess; the doctor looked like he ought to be shouldering a rifle in some mountain ambush rather than wielding clipboards and tongue depressors, but that's just my shallow mind making stereotypes. It keeps me amused. The doctor showed me his huge, crooked, yellow teeth again and said, "Besides, I have an overwhelming love for mankind. It is the will of Allah that I should begin to end all human suffering by having this same uninteresting interview with you each day until you at last remember it. It is for us to do these things; it is for Allah to understand them." He shrugged again. He was very expressive, for a Turk.

I blessed the name of God and waited for Dr. Yeniknani to launch into his bedside manner.

"Have you looked at yourself?" he asked.

"No, not yet." I'm never in a hurry to see my body after it's been offended in any serious way. I do not find wounds particularly fascinating, especially when they are my own. When I had my appendix taken out, I couldn't look at myself below the navel for a month. Now, with my brain newly wired and my head shaved, I didn't want to look in a mirror; that would make me think about what had been done, and why, and where all this might lead. If I were careful and clever, I might stay in that hospital bed, pleasantly sedated, for months or even years. It didn't sound like so terrible a fate. Being a numb vegetable was preferable to being a numb corpse. I wondered how long I could malinger here before I was rudely dumped back on the Street. I was in no hurry, that's for sure.

Dr. Yeniknani nodded absently. "Your . . . *patron*," he said, choosing the word judiciously, "your patron specified that you were to be given the most comprehensive intracranial reticulation possible. That is why Dr. Lisân performed the surgery himself: Dr. Lisân is the finest neurosurgeon in the city, one of the most respected in the world. Quite a lot of what he has given you he invented or refined himself, and in your case Dr. Lisân has tried one or two new procedures that might be called . . . experimental."

That didn't soothe me, I didn't care how great a surgeon Dr. Lisân might be. I am of the "better safe than sorry" school. I could be just as happy with a brain lacking one or two "experimental" talents, but one that didn't run the risk of turning to tahini if I concentrated too long. But what the hell. I grinned a crooked, devil-may-care grin and realized that poking hot wires into unknown corners of my brain to see what happened was not much worse than gunning around the city in the back of Bill's taxi. Maybe I did have some kind of death wish, after all. Or some kind of plain stupidity.

The doctor raised the lid of the tray-table beside my bed; there was a mirror under there, and he rolled the table so that I could see my reflection. I looked awful. I looked like I'd died and started off toward hell and then got lost, and now I was stuck nowhere at all, definitely not alive but not decently deceased, either. My beard was neatly trimmed, and I had shaved every day or someone had done it for me; but my skin was pale, an unhealthy color like smudged newsprint, and there were deep shadows under my eyes. I stared into the mirror for a long moment before I even noticed that my head was indeed bald, just a fine growth of fuzz covering my scalp like lichen clinging to a senseless stone. The implanted plug was invisible, hidden beneath protective layers of gelstrip bandages. I raised a tentative hand as if to touch the crown of my head, but I couldn't bring myself to do it. I felt a strange, unpleasant tingling shoot up through my bowels, and I shuddered. My hand fell away and I looked at the doctor.

"When we take the gelstrips off," he said, "you'll notice that you have two plugs, one anterior and the second plug posterior."

"Two?" I'd never heard of anyone with two plugs before.

"Yes. Dr. Lisân has given you twice the augmentation of a conventional corymbic implantation."

That much capacity hooked into my brain was like putting a rocket engine on an oxcart; it would never fly. I closed my eyes feeling more than a little frightened. I started murmuring Al-Fâtihah, the first sûrah of the noble Qur'ân, a comforting prayer that always comes to me at times like this. It is the Islamic equivalent of the Christian Lord's Prayer. Then I opened my eyes and stared at my reflection. I was still afraid, but at least I had made my uncertainty known in heaven, and from here on I'd just accept everything as the will of Allah. "Does that mean I can chip in two different moddies at the same time, and be two people at once?"

Dr. Yeniknani frowned. "No, Mr. Audran, the second plug will accept only software add-ons, not a full personality module. You wouldn't want to try two modules at once. You might end up with a pair of charred cerebral hemispheres and a backbrain that would be completely useless except as a paperweight. We have given you the augmentation as—" (he almost committed an indiscretion and mentioned a name) "your patron directed. A therapist will instruct you in the proper use of your corymbic implants. How you choose to employ them after you leave the hospital is, of course, your own affair. Just remember that you're dealing directly with your central nervous system now. It isn't a matter of taking a few pills and staggering around for a while until you recover your sobriety. If you do something ill-advised with your implants, it may well have permanent effects. Permanent, frightening effects."

Okay, he had me sold. I did what Papa and everybody else wanted: my brain was wired. Good old Dr. Yeniknani had put the fear into me, though, and I told myself right there in the hospital bed that I'd never promised that I'd *use* the damn thing. I'd get out of the hospital as soon as I could, go home, forget about the implants, and go about my business as usual. It would be a cold day in Jiddah before *I* chipped in. Let the plugs sit there for decoration. When it came to Marîd Audran's subskullular amplification, pal, the batteries had definitely not been included, and I intended to leave it that way. Zinging my little gray cells with chemicals now and then didn't incapacitate them permanently, but

I wasn't going to sizzle them in any electric frying pan. Only so far can I be pushed, and then my inborn perversity asserts itself.

"So," said Dr. Yeniknani more encouragingly, "with that mandatory warning out of the way, I suppose you're looking forward to hearing about what your improved mind and body are capable of doing for you."

"You bet," I said, without enthusiasm.

"What do you know about the activities of the brain and the nervous system?"

I laughed. "About as much as any hustler from the Budayeen who can barely read and write his name. I know that the brain is in the head, I've heard that it's a bad idea to let some thug spill it on the sidewalk. Beyond that, I don't know much." I did, truthfully, know some more, but I always hold something in reserve. It's a good policy to be a little quicker, a little stronger, and a little smarter than everybody thinks you are.

"Well, then, the posterior corymbic implant is completely conventional. It will enable you to chip in a personality module. You know that the medical profession is not unanimous in its sanction of these modules. Some of our colleagues feel that the potential for abuse far outweighs the benefits. Those benefits, actually, were very limited at first; the modules were produced on a limited basis as therapeutic aids for patients with certain severe neurological disturbances. However, the modules have been taken over by the popular media and are used for purposes grossly different from those their inventors originally intended." He shrugged again. "It's too late to do anything about that now, and those few who are outraged and would prohibit the modules' use can barely get an audience for their views. So you will have access to the entire range of personality modules for sale to the public, modules that are extremely serviceable and can save a good deal of drudgery as well as those that many people might find offensive." I thought immediately of Honey Pílar. "You can walk into any shop and become Salâh ad-Dîn, a genuine hero, the great sultan who drove out the Crusaders; or become the mythical Sultan Shahryar, and entertain yourself with the beautiful storyteller and the entire *Thousand Nights and a Night*. Your posterior implant can also accommodate up to six software add-ons."

"That's just the same kind of implant all my friends have," I said. "What about the experimental advantages you mentioned? How dangerous will they be to chip in?"

The doctor smiled briefly. "That's difficult to say, Mr. Audran; they are, after all, experimental. They've been tested on many animal subjects and just a few human volunteers. The results have been satisfactory, but not unanimously. A lot will depend on you, if Allah pleases. Let me explain by first describing the sort of controls we're talking about. Personality modules alter your consciousness, and make you believe temporarily that you are someone else. The add-ons feed directly into your short-term memory, and give you an instant knowledge of any subject; that vanishes when you remove the chip. The add-ons you can use with the anterior implant affect several other, more specialized diencephalic structures." He took a black felt-tip pen and sketched a rough map of the brain. "First, we have inserted an extremely thin silver, plastic-sheathed wire into your thalamus. The wire is less than a thousandth of an inch in diameter, too delicate to be manipulated by hand. This wire will connect your reticular system to a unique add-on we will provide you; it will enable you to damp out the neural network that catalogs sensory detail. If, for instance, it is vital for you to concentrate, you may choose to block out disturbing visual, audible, tactile, and other signals."

I raised my eyebrows. "I can see how that may come in handy," I said.

Dr. Yeniknani smiled. "It is only a tenth part of what we have given you—there are other wires, to other areas. Near the thalamus, in the center of your brain, is the hypothalamus. This organ is small, but it has many varied and vital functions. You will be able to control, augment, or override most of them. For example, you may decide to ignore hunger, if you wish; using the proper add-on, you will feel no hunger at all, however long you fast. You will have the same control over thirst and the sensation of pain. You may consciously regulate your body temperature, blood pressure, and the state of sexual arousal. Perhaps most usefully, you will be able to suppress fatigue."

I just sat and looked at him, wide-eyed, as if he had unwrapped for me a fabulous treasure or a real wishing-lamp. But Dr. Yeniknani was no enslaved *djinn*. What he offered was not magic, but as far as I was concerned it might as well have been: I didn't even know if I entirely believed him, except that I tended to believe fierce Turks in positions of authority. I humor them, at least, so I let him continue.

"You will find it simpler to learn new skills and information. Of course, you will have electronic add-ons to feed these things into your short-term memory; but if you want to transfer them permanently to your long-term memory, your hippocampus and other associated areas have been circuited for this. If you need to, you may alter your circadian and lunar clocks. You'll be able to fall asleep when you wish, and awaken automatically according to the chips you're using. The circuit to your pituitary will give you indirect control over your other endocrines, such as your thyroid and adrenal glands. Your therapist will go into more detail about just how you can take advantage of these functions. As you see, you may devote total attention to your tasks, without needing to interrupt them quite so often for the normal bodily necessities. Now, of course, one can't go indefinitely without sleep or taking in water or emptying one's bladder; but if you choose, you may dismiss the insistent and increasingly unpleasant warning signs."

"My patron doesn't want me distracted," I said dryly.

Dr. Yeniknani sighed. "No, he doesn't. Not by anything."

"Is there anything more?"

He chewed his lip for a moment. "Yes, but your therapist will cover all of it, and we'll give you the usual brochures and booklets. I may say that you'll be able to control your limbic system, which influences your emotions. That is one of Dr. Lisân's new developments."

"I'll be able to choose my feelings? Like I was choosing what clothes to wear?"

"To some extent. Also, in wiring these areas of the brain, we were often able to affect more than one function at one location. For instance, as a positive bonus, your system will be able to burn alcohol more efficiently, quicker than the standard ounce an hour. If you choose." He gave me a brief, knowing look, because of course a good Muslim does not drink alcohol; he must have been aware that I wasn't the most devout person in the city. Yet the subject was still a delicate one between two relative strangers.

"My patron will be pleased by that, too, I'm sure. Fine. I can't wait. I'll be a force for good among the unrighteous and corrupt."

"*Inshallah,*" said the doctor. "As God wills."

"Praise Allah," I said, humbled by his honest faith.

"There is still one thing more, and then I wish to give you a personal word, a little of my own philosophy. The first thing is that as you must know, the brain—the hypothalamus, actually—has a pleasure center that can be electrically stimulated."

I took a deep breath. "Yes, I've heard about that. The effect is supposed to be absolutely overwhelming."

"Animals and people who have leads into that area and are permitted to stimulate the pleasure center often forget everything else—food, water, every other need and drive. They may continue exciting the pleasure center to the point of death." His eyes narrowed. "*Your* pleasure center has not been wired. Your patron felt it would have been too great a temptation for you, and you have more to accomplish than spending the rest of your life in some dream heaven."

I didn't know if I felt glad about that news or not. I didn't want to waste away as the result of some never-ending mental orgasm; but if the choice was between that or going up against two savage, mad assassins, I think, in a moment of weakness, I might pick exquisite pleasure that didn't fade or pall. It might take a little getting used to, but I'm sure I would get the hang of it.

"Near the pleasure center," said Dr. Yeniknani, "there is an area that causes rage and ferociously aggressive behavior. It is also a punishment center. When it is stimulated, subjects experience torment as great as the ecstasy of the pleasure center. This area *was* wired. Your sponsor felt that this might prove useful in your undertaking for him, and it gives him a measure of influence over you." He said this in a clearly disapproving tone of voice. I wasn't crazy about the news, either. "If you choose to use it to your advantage, you can become a raging, unstoppable creature of destruction." He stopped, evidently not liking how Friedlander Bey had exploited the neurosurgical art.

"My . . . patron gave this all a lot of thought, didn't he?" I said sardonically.

"Yes, I suppose he did. And so should you." Then the doctor did an unusual thing: he reached over and put his hand on my arm; it was a sudden change in the formal atmosphere of our talk. "Mr. Audran," he said solemnly, looking directly into my eyes, "I have a rather good idea of why you had this surgery."

"Uh huh," I said, curious, waiting to hear what he had to say.

"In the name of the Prophet, may peace be on his name and blessings, you need not fear death."

That rocked me. "Well," I said, "I don't think about it very much, I guess. Anyway, the implants aren't that dangerous, are they? I admit that I was afraid they'd roast my wits if something went wrong, but I didn't think they could kill me."

"No, you don't understand. When you leave the hospital, when you are in that situation for which you underwent this augmentation, you need not be afraid. The great English shâ'ir, Wilyam al-Shaykh Sebîr, in his splendid play, *King Henry the Fourth, Part II,* says, 'We owe God a death . . . and, let it go which way it will, he that dies this year, is quit for the next.' So you see, death comes to us all. Death is inescapable. Death is desirable as our passage to paradise, may Allah be praised. So do what you must, Mr. Audran, and do not be hindered by an undue fear of death in your search for justice."

Wonderful: my doctor was some kind of Sufi mystic or something. I just stared at him, unable to think of a damn thing to say. He squeezed my arm and stood up. "With your permission," he said.

I gestured vaguely. "May your day be prosperous," I said.

"Peace be on you."

"And on you be peace," I replied. Then Dr. Yeniknani left my room. Jo-Mama would get a big kick out of this story. I couldn't wait to hear the way *she'd* tell it.

Just after the doctor went out, the young male nurse returned with an injection. "Oh," I said, starting to tell him that earlier I hadn't meant that I wanted a shot; I had only wanted to ask him a few questions.

"Roll over," said the man briskly. "Which side?"

I jiggled a little in bed, feeling the soreness in each hip, deciding that both were pretty painful. "Can you give it to me someplace else? My arm?"

"Can't give it to you in your arm. I can give it to you in your leg, though." He pulled back the sheet, swabbed the front of my thigh about halfway down toward the knee, and jabbed me. He gave the leg another quick swipe with the gauze, capped the syringe, and turned away without a word. I wasn't one of his favorite patients, I could see that.

I wanted to say something to him, to let him know that I wasn't the self-indulgent, vice-ridden, swinish person he thought I was. Before I could speak a word, though, before he'd even reached the door to my room, my head began to swirl and I was sinking down into the familiar warm embrace of numbness. My last thought, before I lost consciousness, was that I had never had so much fun in my life.

thirteen

I did not expect to have many visitors while I was in the hospital. I'd told everyone that I appreciated their concern but that it was no big deal, and that I'd rather be left in peace until I felt better. The response I usually got, carefully considered and tactfully phrased, was that nobody was planning to visit me, anyway. I said, "Good." The real reason I didn't want people coming to look at me was that I could imagine the aftereffects of major brain surgery. The visitors sit on the foot of your bed, you know, and tell you how great you look, and how quickly you'll feel all better, and how everybody misses you, and—if you can't fall asleep fast enough—all about *their* old operations. I didn't need any of that. I wanted to be left alone to enjoy the final, straggling, time-released molecules of etorphin planted in a bubble in my brain. Sure, I was prepared to play a stoic and courageous sufferer for a few minutes every day, but I didn't have to. My friends were as good as their word: I didn't have a single, goddamn visitor, not until the last day, just before I was discharged. All that time, no one came to see me, no one even called or sent a card or a crummy plant. Believe me, I've got all that written down in my book of memories.

I saw Dr. Yeniknani every day, and he made sure to point out at least once each visit that there were worse things to fear than death. He kept dwelling on it; he was the most morbid doctor I've ever known. His attempt to calm my fearful spirit had absolutely the wrong effect. He should have stuck with his professional resources: pills. They—I mean the kind I got in the hospital, made by real pharmaceutical houses and all—are very dependable and can make me forget about death and suffering and anything else just like *that*.

So as the next few days passed, I realized that I had a clear idea of

how vital my well-being was to the tranquility of the Budayeen: I could
have died and been buried inside a brand-new mosque in Mecca or
some Egyptian pyramid thrown together in my honor, and nobody
would even know about it. Some friends! The question arises: Why did
I even entertain the notion of sticking my own neck out for their well-
being? I asked myself that over and over, and the answer was always:
Because who else did I have? *Triste, non?* The longer I observe the
way people really act, the happier I am that I never pay attention to
them.

The end of Ramadân came, and the festival that marks the close of
the holy month. I was sorry I was still in the hospital, because the festival, Îd el-Fitr, is one of my favorite times of the year. I always cele-
brate the end of the fast with towers of *ataïf*, pancakes dipped in syrup
and sprinkled with orange-blossom water, layered with heavy cream,
and covered with chopped almonds. Instead, this year I took some
farewell shots of Sonneine, while some religious authority in the city
was declaring that he'd sighted the new crescent moon, the new month
had begun, and life could now return to normal.

I went to sleep. I woke up early the next morning, when the blood
nurse came around for his daily libation. Everyone else's life may have
gone back to normal, but mine was permanently doglegged in a direction I could not yet imagine. My loins were girded, and now I was
needed on the field of battle. Unfurl the banners, O my sons, we will
come down like a wolf on the fold. I come not to send peace, but a
sword.

Breakfast came and went. We had our little bath. I called for a shot
of Sonneine; I always liked to take one after all the heavy work of the
morning was finished, while I had a couple of hours before lunch. A
drifty little nap, then a tray of food: good stuffed grape leaves; *hamûd*;
skewered *kofta* on rice, perfumed with onions, coriander, and allspice.
Prayer is better than sleep, and food is better than drugs . . . sometimes. After lunch, another shot and a second nap. I was awakened by
Ali, the older, disapproving nurse. He shook my shoulder. "Mr.
Audran," he murmured.

Oh no, I thought, they want more blood. I tried to force myself
back to sleep.

"You have a visitor, Mr. Audran."

"A visitor?" Surely there had been some mistake. After all, I was
dead, laid to rest on some mountaintop. All I had to do now was wait
for the grave robbers. Could it be that they were here already? I didn't
even feel stiff, yet. They wouldn't even let me get cold in the tomb, the
bastards. Ramses II was shown more respect, I'll bet. Haroun al-

Raschîd. Prince Saalih ibn Abdul-Wahîd ibn Saud. Everybody but me. I struggled up to a sitting position.

"O clever one, you are looking well." Hassan's fat face was resting in its shabby business smile, the unctuous look that even the stupidest tourist could spot as too deceitful by half.

"It is as God pleases," I said groggily.

"Yes, praise Allah. Very soon you will be wholly recovered, *inshallah*."

I didn't bother to respond. I was just glad he wasn't sitting on the foot of my bed.

"You must know, my nephew, that the entire Budayeen is desolate without your presence to light our weary lives."

"So I understand," I said. "From the flood of cards and letters. From the crowds of friends that mob the hospital corridors day and night, anxious to see me or just hear word of my condition. From all your many little thoughtfulnesses that have made my stay here bearable. I cannot thank you enough."

"No thanks are necessary—"

"—for a duty. I know, Hassan. Anything else?"

He looked a little uncomfortable. It might have crossed his mind that *just possibly* I was mocking him, but usually he was impervious to that sort of thing. He smiled again. "I am happy that you will be among us again tonight."

I was startled. "I will?"

He turned over one fat palm. "Is it not so? You are to be discharged this afternoon. Friedlander Bey sent me with a message: you must visit him as soon as you feel well. Tomorrow will be soon enough. He does not wish for you to hurry your recuperation."

"I didn't even know that I was being released, and I'm supposed to see Friedlander Bey tomorrow; but he doesn't want to hurry me. I suppose your car is waiting to take me home."

Now Hassan looked unhappy. He didn't like my suggestion at all. "Oh darling, I wish it were so, but it cannot be. You must make other arrangements. I have business elsewhere."

"Go in safety," I said quietly. I laid my head back on the pillow and tried to find my dream again. It was long gone.

"*Allah yisallimak*," murmured Hassan, and he was gone, too.

All the peace of the last few days disappeared, and it happened with disturbing suddenness. I was left with a pervasive feeling of self-loathing. I remembered one time a few years ago, when I had pursued a girl who worked sometimes at the Red Light and sometimes at Big Al's Old Chicago. I had worked my way into her consciousness by being funny and fast and, I suppose, contemptible. I finally got her to go out with me, and I took her to dinner—I don't remember where—and then back to my apartment. We were on the bed five minutes after I locked the front door, and we jammed for maybe another ten or fifteen minutes, and then it was all over. I lay back and looked at her. She had bad teeth and sharp bones and smelled as if she carried sesame oil around with her in an aerosol. "My God," I thought. "Who *is* this girl? And how am I going to get rid of her *now*?" After sex, all animals are sad; after *any* kind of pleasure, really. We're not built for pleasure. We're built for agony and for seeing things too clearly, which is often a terrible agony in itself. I loathed myself then, and I loathed myself now.

Dr. Yeniknani knocked lightly on my door and came in. He glanced briefly at the nurse's daily notes.

"Am I going home?" I asked.

He turned his bright, black eyes on me. "Hmm? Oh, yes. Your discharge orders have already been written. You have to arrange for someone to come and get you. Hospital policy. You can leave anytime."

"Thank God," I said, and I meant it. That surprised me.

"Praise Allah," said the doctor. He looked at the plastic box of daddies beside my bed. "Have you tried all of these?" he asked.

"Yes," I said. That was a lie. I had tried a few, under the supervision of a therapist; the data add-ons had been pretty much of a disappointment. I don't know what I'd expected. When I chipped in one of the daddies, its information was sitting there in my mind, as if I'd known all of it all my life. It was like staying up all night and cramming for an exam, without having to lose any sleep and without the possibility of forgetting any of the material. When I popped the chip out, it all vanished from my memory. No big deal. Actually, I was looking forward to trying some of the daddies that Lalla had in her shop. The daddies would come in very handy now and then.

It was the moddies I was afraid of. The full personality modules. The ones that crammed you away in some little tin box inside your head, and someone you didn't know took over your mind and body. They still spooked the hell out of me.

"Well, then," said Dr. Yeniknani. He didn't wish me luck, because everything was in the hands of Allah, Who knew what the outcome was going to be anyway, so luck hardly entered into it. I'd learned gradually that my doctor was an apprentice saint, a Turkish derwish. "May God provide a successful conclusion to your undertaking," he said. Very well spoken, I thought. I had come to like him a lot.

"*Inshallah*," I said. We shook hands, and he left. I went to the closet, took out my street clothes, threw them on the bed—there was a shirt and my boots and socks and underwear and a new pair of jeans that I didn't remember buying. I dressed quickly and spoke Yasmin's commcode into my phone. It rang and rang. I spoke my own, thinking she might be at my apartment; there was no answer there, either. Maybe she was at work, although it wasn't two o'clock. I called Frenchy's, but no one had seen her yet. I didn't bother leaving a message. I called a cab instead.

Hospital policy or not, nobody gave me a hard time about leaving unescorted. They wheeled me downstairs and I got into the cab, holding a bag of toilet articles in one hand and my rack of daddies in the other. I rode back to my apartment feeling a bewildering emptiness, no emotions at all.

I unlocked my front door and went in. I figured the place would be a mess. Yasmin had probably stayed here a few times while I was in the hospital, and she was never great at picking up after herself. I expected to see little mounds of her clothes all over the floor, monuments of dirty dishes in the sink, half-eaten meals and open jars and empty cans all around the stove and table; but the room was as clean as when I'd last seen it. *Cleaner*, even; I'd never done such a thorough job of sweeping, dusting, and washing the windows. That made me suspicious: some skillful lockpicker with a yen for neatness had broken into my home. I saw three envelopes beside the mattress on the floor, stuffed fat. I bent over and picked them up. My name was typed on the outside of the envelopes; on the inside of each was seven hundred kiam, all in tens, seventy new bills fastened together with a rubber band. Three envelopes, twenty-one hundred kiam; my wages for the weeks I spent in the hospital. I didn't think I was getting paid for that time. I would have done it for free—the Sonneine on top of the etorphin had been quite pleasant.

I lay down on the bed and tossed the money to the side, where Yasmin sometimes slept. I still felt a curious hollowness, as if I was waiting for something to come along and fill me up and give me a hint about what to do next. I waited, but I didn't get the word. I looked at my watch; it was now almost four o'clock. I decided not to put off the hard stuff. I might as well get it over with.

I got up again, stuck a wad of a few hundred kiam in my pocket, found my keys, and went back downstairs. I began to feel just the beginning of some kind of emotional reaction. I paid close attention: I was nervous, not pleasantly so; and I was sure that I was fighting my way up the thirteen steps of the gallows, intent on putting my head in some as-yet-unseen noose. I walked down the Street to the east gate of the Budayeen and looked for Bill. I didn't see him. I got into another cab. "Take me to Friedlander Bey's house," I said.

The driver turned around and looked at me. "No," he said flatly. I got out and found another driver who didn't mind going there. I made sure we agreed on the cabfare first, though.

When we got there I paid the driver and climbed out. I hadn't let anyone know I was coming; Papa probably didn't expect to see me for another day. Nevertheless, his servant was holding the polished mahogany door open before I reached the top of the white marble stairs. "Mr. Audran," he murmured.

"I'm surprised you remember," I said.

He shrugged—I couldn't say if he smiled or not—and said, "Peace be upon you." He turned away.

I said "And upon you be peace" to his back and followed. He led me to Papa's offices, to the same waiting room I had seen before. I went in, sat down, stood up again restlessly, and began to pace. I didn't know why I'd come here. After "Hello, how are you?" I was depressed to find I had nothing else to say to Papa at all. But Friedlander Bey was a good host when it served his purposes, and he wouldn't let a guest feel uncomfortable.

In a while the communicating door opened and one of the sandstone giants gestured. I passed by him and came again into Papa's presence. He looked very tired, as if he had been handling urgent financial, political, religious, judicial, and military matters without rest for many hours. His white shirt was stained with perspiration, his fine hair mussed, his eyes weary and bloodshot. His hand trembled as he gestured to the Stone That Speaks. "Coffee," he said, in a hoarse and peculiarly soft voice. He turned to me. "Come, my nephew, be seated. You must tell me if you are well. It pleases Allah that the surgery was successful. I have had several reports from Dr. Lisân. He was quite satisfied with the results. In that regard I am also satisfied, but of course the true proof of the value of the implants will be in how you use them."

I nodded, that's all.

The Stone arrived with the coffee, and it gave me a few minutes to settle my nerves while we sipped and chatted. I realized that Papa was looking at me rather closely, his brows drawn together, his expression mildly displeased. I closed my eyes in exasperation: I had come in my usual street clothes. The jeans and boots were fine in Chiri's club or for hanging out with Mahmoud, Jacques, and Saied, but Papa preferred to see me in the *gallebeya* and *keffiya*. Too late now, I told myself; I'd started off in the hole, and I was going to have to climb out of it and gain some more ground to get back in his good graces.

I shook my cup back and forth a little after the second refilling, indicating that I had had enough. The coffee things were cleared away, and Papa murmured something to the Stone. The huge man left the room also. This was the first time, I believe, that I'd been alone with Papa. I waited.

The old man pressed his lips together while he thought. "I am glad that you thought enough of my wishes to undergo the surgery," he said.

"O Shaykh," I said, "it is—"

He shut me up with a quick gesture. "However, merely having the surgery will not solve our problems. That is unfortunate. I have had other reports that told me you were reluctant to explore the full benefits of my gifts. You may be thinking that you can satisfy our arrangement by wearing the implants, but not using them. If you are thinking that, you are deluding yourself. Our mutual problem cannot be solved unless you agree to use the weapon I have given you, and use it to the utmost. I have not had such augmentation myself because I believe my religion forbids it; therefore, one might argue that I am not the proper person to advise you on this matter. Yet I think I know a thing or two about personality modules. Would you care to discuss a proper choice with me?"

The man was reading my mind, but that was his job. The odd thing was that the deeper in I got, the easier it seemed to be to talk to Friedlander Bey. I wasn't even properly terrified when I heard myself declining his offer. "O Shaykh," I said, "we do not even agree on the identity of our enemy. How then can we hope to choose a suitable personality as an instrument of our vengeance?"

There was a brief silence during which I heard my heart give one good bam! and start on another. Papa's eyebrows raised a little and fell back into place. "Once again, my nephew, you prove to me that I was not mistaken in my choice of you. You are correct. How then do you propose to begin?"

"O Shaykh, I will begin by making a closer ally of Lieutenant Okking, and getting all the information he has in the police files. I know certain things about some of the victims that I'm sure he does not. I see no reason to give him this information now, but he may require it later. I will then interview all our mutual friends; I think I will find further clues. A careful, scientific examination of all the available data should be the first step."

Friedlander Bey nodded thoughtfully. "Okking has information you do not have. You have information he does not have. Someone should assemble all that information in one place, and I would rather that person be you, and not the good lieutenant. Yes, I am pleased with your suggestion."

"All who see you, live, O Shaykh."

"May Allah grant that you go and come in safety."

I saw no reason to tell him that what I truly planned to do was make a closer scrutiny of Herr Lutz Seipolt. What I knew of Nikki and her death made the whole affair more sinister than either Papa or Lieutenant Okking were willing to admit. I still had the moddy I'd found in Nikki's purse. I'd never mentioned that moddy to anyone. I would have to find out what was recorded on it. I also hadn't mentioned the ring or the scarab.

It took me another few minutes to ease myself out of Friedlander Bey's villa, and then I couldn't find a taxi. I ended up walking, but I didn't mind because I was having a fierce argument with myself all the way. The argument went like this:

Self$_1$ (afraid of Papa): "Well, why not do what he wants? Just collect all the information and let him suggest the next step. Otherwise, you'll just be asking for a broken body. If not a dead one."

Self$_2$ (afraid of death and disaster): "Because every step I take is directly toward two—not one, but two—psychopathic murderers who don't care half a chickpea if I live or die. As a matter of fact, either or both of them would probably give considerably more than that just for the chance to put a bullet between my eyes or slit my throat. That's why."

Both selves had considerable stores of logical, reasonable things to say. It was like being at a mental tennis match: one would bash a statement across the net, and the other would bash a refutation right back. They were too evenly matched, the rally would go on forever. After a while I got bored and stopped watching. I had all the equipment, after all, to become El Cid or Khomeini or anybody else, and why was I still hesitating? Nobody else around here had any of my qualms. I didn't think of myself as a coward, either. What would it take to get me to chip in that first moddy?

I got the answer to that the very same night. I heard the sunset call to prayer as I passed through the gate and headed up the Street. Outside the Budayeen, the muezzin sounded almost ethereal; inside the gate, the same man's voice had somehow gained a reproachful note. Or was that my imagination? I wandered over to Chiriga's nightclub and sat down at the bar. She wasn't there. Behind the bar was Jamila, who had worked for Chiri a few weeks ago and then quit after my Russian was shot in the club. People come and go around the Budayeen; they'll work in one club and get fired or quit over some dumb-ass little thing, go work someplace else, eventually make the circuit and end up back where they started. Jamila was one of those people who can make the

circuit faster than most. She was lucky to hang onto a job in one place
for seven days running.

"Where's Chiri?" I asked.

"She's coming in at nine. You want something to drink?"

"Bingara and gin over ice, with a little Rose's." Jamila nodded and
turned away to mix it. "Oh," she said, "you had a call. They left a message. Let me find it."

That surprised me. I couldn't imagine who would leave a message
for me, how they'd known I'd come in here tonight.

Jamila returned with my drink and a cocktail napkin with two
words scrawled across it. I paid her and she left without another word.
The message was *Call Okking*. What a fitting beginning to my new life
as a superman: urgent police business. No rest for the wicked; it was
becoming my motto. I unclipped my phone and growled Okking's
commcode, then waited for him to answer. "Yeah?" he said at last.

"Marîd Audran," I said.

"Wonderful. I called the hospital, but they said you'd been discharged. I called your house, but there wasn't any answer. I called your
girlfriend's boss, but you weren't there. I called your usual hangout, the
Café Solace, but they hadn't seen you. So I tried a few other places,
and left messages. I want you here in half an hour."

"Sure, Lieutenant. Where are you?"

He gave me a room number and the address of a hotel run by a
Flemish conglomerate, in the most affluent section of the city. I'd never
been in the hotel, or within so much as ten blocks of it. That wasn't my
part of town.

"What's the situation?" I asked.

"A homicide. Your name has come up."

"Ah. Anyone I know?"

"Yes. It's odd that as soon as you went into the hospital, these
bizarre killings stopped. Nothing unusual for almost three weeks. And
the day you're released, we're right back in the Reign of Terror."

"Okay, Lieutenant, you've got me and I'll have to confess. If I'd
been smart, I would have arranged a murder or two while I was in the
hospital, to throw off suspicion."

"You're a wise guy, Audran. That just makes your predicament
worse, all the way around."

"Sorry. So you never told me: who's the victim?"

"Just get here fast," he said, and hung up.

I gulped my drink, left Jamila half a kiam tip, and hurried out into
the warm night air. Bill was still missing from his usual place on the

wide Boulevard il-Jameel outside the Budayeen. Another cab driver agreed to the fare I offered him, and we rumbled across town to the hotel. I went straight up to the room, and was stopped by a police officer standing inside the yellow tape "crime scene" barrier. I told him Lieutenant Okking was expecting me. He asked me my name, and then let me pass.

The room was like the inside of a slaughterhouse. There was blood everywhere—pools of blood, streaks of blood on the walls, blood spattered on the bed, on the chairs and bureau, all over the carpet. A murderer would have had to spend a lot of time and energy making certain his victim was sufficiently dead to splash all that blood so much, thoroughly soaking the room. He'd have to kill the wretch with stab after stab, like a ritual human sacrifice. It was inhuman, grotesque, and demented. Neither James Bond nor the nameless torturer had worked this way. This was either a third maniac, or one of the first two with a brand-new moddy. In both cases our scanty clues were now obsolete. That's all we needed at this point.

The police were completing the job of bundling the corpse into a body bag on a stretcher, and moving it out the door. I found the lieutenant. "So who the hell got the business tonight?" I asked.

He looked at me closely, as if he could gauge my guilt or innocence from my reaction. "Selima," he said.

My shoulders slumped. I felt immensely exhausted all of a sudden. "Allah be merciful," I murmured. "So why did you want me here? What does this have to do with me?"

"You're investigating all this for Friedlander Bey. And besides, I want you to look in the bathroom."

"Why?"

"You'll see. Be prepared, though; it's pretty sickening."

That just made me less eager to go into the bathroom. I did, though. I had to, there was no choice. The first thing I saw was a human heart, hacked from Selima's chest, sitting in the bathroom sink. That made me retch right there. The sink was fouled with her dark blood. Then I saw the blood smeared all over the mirror above the sink. There were uneven borders and geometric patterns and unintelligible symbolic marks drawn on the glass. The most unsettling part was the few words written in blood in a dripping handwriting, that said *Audran, you next.*

I felt a faint, unreal sensation. What did this insane butcher know about me? What connection did I have with the monstrous slaying of Selima, and of the other Black Widow Sisters as well? The only thought I had was that my motivation up until now had been a kind of gallant desire to help protect my friends, those who might be future victims of the unknown mad murderers. I had had no personal interest, except possibly a desire for revenge, for Nikki's killing and for the others. Now, though, with my name written in congealing blood on that mirror, it *had* been made personal. My own life was at stake.

If anything in the world could induce me to take the final step and chip in my first moddy, this was it. I knew absolutely that from now on, I'd need every bit of help I could get. Enlightened self-interest, I called it; and I cursed the vile executioners who had made it necessary.

fourteen

first thing the next morning, I paid a call on Laila at her modshop on Fourth Street. The old woman was just as creepy as ever, but her costume had undergone some slight revision. She had her dirty, thin gray hair shoved under a blond wig full of ringlets; it didn't look so much like a hairpiece as something your great-aunt would slip over a toaster to hide it from view. Laila couldn't do much with her yellowed eyes and wrinkled black skin, but she sure tried. She had so much pale powder on her face that she looked like she'd just busted out of a grain elevator. Over that she had smeared bright cerise streaks on every available surface; to me it appeared that her eye shadow, cheek blush, and lipstick had all come out of the same container. She wore a sparkly pair of plastic sunglasses on a grimy string around her neck—cat's-eye sunglasses, and she had chosen them with care. She hadn't bothered to find herself some false teeth, but she had swapped her filthy black shift for an indecently tight, low-cut slit-skirted gown in blazing dandelion yellow. It looked like she was trying to shove her head and shoulders free of the maw of the world's biggest budgie. On her feet she wore cheap blue fuzzy bedroom slippers. "Laila," I said.

"Marîd." Her eyes weren't quite focused. That meant that she was just her own inimitable self today; if she had been chipping in some moddy, her eyes would have been focused and the software would have sharpened up her responses. It would have been easier to deal with her if she *had* been someone else, but I let it go.

"Had my brain wired."

"I heard." She snickered, and I felt a ripple of disgust.

"I need some help choosing a moddy."

"What you want it for?"

I chewed my lip. How much was I going to tell her? On one hand, she might repeat everything I said to anyone who came into her shop; after all, she told me what everybody else said to her. On the other hand, nobody paid any attention to her in the first place. "I need to do a little work. I got wired because the job might be dangerous. I need something that will jack up my detective talent, and also keep me from getting hurt. What do you think?"

She muttered to herself for a while, wandering up and down the aisles, browsing through her bins. I couldn't make out what she was saying, so I just waited. Finally she turned around; she was surprised that I was still there. Maybe she'd already forgotten what I'd asked. "Is a made-up character good enough?" she said.

"If the character is smart enough," I said.

She shrugged and mumbled some more, snagged a plastic-wrapped moddy in her clawlike fingers, and held it out to me. "Here," she said.

I hesitated. I recalled thinking that again she reminded me of the witch from *Snow White*; now I looked at the moddy like it was a poisoned apple. "Who is it?"

"Nero Wolfe," she said. "Brilliant detective. Genius for figuring out murders. Didn't like to leave his own house. Someone else did all his legwork and took the beatings."

"Perfect," I said. I sort of remembered the character, although I don't think I ever read any of the books.

"You'll have to get somebody to go ask the questions," she said. She held out a second moddy.

"Saied'll do it. I'll just tell him he'll get to knock some heads together whenever he wants, and he'll jump at the chance. How much for both of them?"

Her lips moved for a long time while she tried to add two figures together. "Seventy-three," she whined. "Forget the tax."

I counted out eighty kiam and took my change and the two moddies. She looked up at me. "Want to buy my lucky beans?" I didn't even want to *hear* about them.

There was still one little item troubling me, and it may have been the key to the identity of Nikki's killer, the torturer and throat-slasher who still needed silencing. It was Nikki's underground moddy. She may have been wearing it when she died, or the killer may have been wearing it; as far as I knew, goddamn *nobody* may have been wearing it. It may just be a big nothing. But then why did it give me such a sick, desperate feeling whenever I looked at it? Was it only the way I recalled Nikki's body that night, stuffed into trash bags, dumped in that alley? I took two or three deep breaths. Come on, I told myself, you're a damn good stand-in for a hero. You've got all the right software ready to whisper and chuckle in your brain. I stretched my muscles.

My rational mind tried to tell me thirty or forty times that the moddy didn't mean anything, nothing more than a lipstick or a crumpled tissue I might have found in Nikki's purse. Okking wouldn't have been pleased to know that I'd withheld it and two other items from the police, but I was getting to the point where I was beyond caring about Okking. I was growing weary of this entire matter, but it was succeeding in pulling me along in its wake. I had lost the will even to bail out and save myself.

Laila was fiddling with a moddy. She reached up and chipped it in. She liked to visit with her ghosts and phantoms. "Marîd!" She whined this time in the thrilling voice of Vivien Leigh from *Gone with the Wind*.

"Laila, I've got a bootleg moddy here and I want to know what's on it."

"Sure, Marîd, nevah you mind. Just you give me that little ol'—"

"Laila," I cried. "I don't have time for any of that goddamn Southern belle! Either pop your own moddy or force yourself to pay attention."

The idea of popping out her moddy was too horrifying for her to consider. She stared at me, trying to distinguish me in the crowd. I was the one between Ashley, Rhett, and the doorway. "Why, Marîd! What's come ovah you? You seem so feverish an' all!"

I turned my head away and swore. For the love of Allah, I really wanted to hit her. "I have this moddy," I said, and my teeth didn't move apart a fraction of an inch. "I have to know what's on it."

"Fiddle-dee-dee, Marîd, what's so important?" She took the moddy from me and examined it. "It's divided into three bands, honey."

"But how can you tell what's recorded on it?"

She smiled. "Why, that's just the easiest thing in the world." With one hand, she popped the Scarlett O'Hara moddy and tossed it carelessly somewhere beside her; it hit a rack of daddies and skittered into a corner. Laila might never find her Scarlett again. With the other hand she centered my suspect moddy and chipped it in. Her slack face tightened just a bit. Then she dropped to the floor.

"Laila?" I said.

She was twisting into grotesque positions, her tongue protruding, her eyes wide and staring and sightless. She was making a low, sobbing sound, as if she'd been beaten and maimed for hours and didn't even have the strength left to cry out. Her breathing was harsh and shallow, and I heard it rasp in her throat. Her hands were bundles of dry black sticks, scrabbling uselessly at her head, desperate to pop the moddy out, but she couldn't control her muscles. She was crying deep in her throat, and rocking back and forth on the floor. I wanted to help her, but I didn't know what to do. If I'd come any closer, she might have clawed me.

She wasn't human anymore, it was horribly easy to see that. Whoever had designed that moddy liked animals—liked to *do* things to animals. Laila was behaving like a large creature; not a housecat or small dog, but a caged, furious, tormented jungle animal. I could hear her hiss, I could see her snapping at the legs of the furniture and striking out at me with her nonexistent fangs. When I stooped near her, she swung on me quicker than I thought possible. I tried to grab at the moddy and came away with three long, bloody slashes down my arm. Then her eyes locked on mine. She crouched, pulling her knees forward.

Laila leaped, her thin, black body launched toward me. She gave a shrieking, wailing cry and stretched out her hands for my neck. I was sickened by the sight, by the change that had come over the old woman. It wasn't just Laila attacking me: it was the old hag's body possessed by the corrupt influence of the moddy. Ordinarily, I could have held Laila away with one hand; today, however, I found myself in mortal danger. This beast-Laila would not be happy merely with cornering me or wounding me. It wanted me dead.

As she flew toward me, I sidestepped as neatly as I could, giving her a lot of movement with my arms the way a matador fools the eye of the bull. She crashed into a bin of used daddies, flipped on her back, and drew her legs up as if to disembowel me. I brought my right fist down hard on the side of her face. There was a muffled crack of bone, and she collapsed limply in the bin. I bent down and chipped out the bootleg moddy and tucked it away with my other software. Laila wasn't unconscious long, but she was stunned. Her eyes wouldn't focus, and she was muttering deliriously. When she felt better she was going to be very unhappy. I looked quickly around her shop for something to fit her vacant implant. I ripped open a new moddy package—it was an instructional unit, I think, because it came with three daddies. Something about giving dinner parties for Anatolian bureaucrats. I was sure Leila would find that one fascinating.

I unclipped my phone and called the hospital where I'd had my own amping done. I asked for Dr. Yeniknani; when he answered at last, I explained what had happened. He told me an ambulance would be on its way to Laila's shop in five minutes. He wanted me to give the moddy to one of the paramedics. I told him that whatever he learned about the moddy was confidential, that he shouldn't divulge the information to

the police or even Friedlander Bey. There was a long pause, but finally
Dr. Yeniknani agreed. He knew and trusted me more than he trusted
Okking and Papa put together.

The ambulance arrived within twenty minutes. I watched the two
male paramedics carefully lift Laila on a stretcher and put her into the
wagon. I committed the moddy to one of them and reminded him to
give it to no one but Dr. Yeniknani. He nodded hurriedly and climbed
back behind the steering wheel. I watched the ambulance drive off, out
of the Budayeen, toward whatever medical science might or might not
be able to do for Laila. I clutched my own two purchases and locked
and shut the door to the old woman's shop. Then I got the hell out of
there. I shuddered on the sidewalk.

I'd be jammed if I knew what I'd learned. First—granting the huge
condition that the bootleg moddy originally belonged to the throat-
cutter—did *he* wear it or did he give it to his victims? Would a timber
wolf or a Siberian tiger know how to burn a helpless person with cigarettes? No, it made better sense to picture the moddy chipped into a
raging but well-secured victim. That accounted for the wrist bruises—
and Tami, Abdoulaye, and Nikki had all had their skulls socketed.
What did the assassin do if the victim wasn't a moddy? Probably just
iced the sucker and sulked all afternoon.

All I could figure was that I was looking for a pervert who needed
a savage, caged carnivore to get his juices flowing. The notion of
resigning flashed through my mind, the often-played scene of quitting
despite Friedlander Bey's soft-spoken threats. This time I went as far
as to imagine myself beside the cracked roadway, waiting for the
ancient electric bus with its crowd of peasants on top. My stomach was
turning, and it had only just so much room to move.

It was too early to find the Half-Hajj and talk him into being my
accomplice. Maybe about three or four o'clock he'd be at the Café
Solace, along with Mahmoud and Jacques; I hadn't seen or spoken to
any of them in weeks. I hadn't seen Saied at all since the night he'd
sent Courvoisier Sonny on the Great Circle Route to paradise, or
somewhere. I went back home. I thought I might take the Nero Wolfe
moddy out and look at it and turn it over in my hand a couple of dozen
times and maybe peel off the shrinkwrap and find out if I'd have to
swallow a few pills or a bottle of tende to get the nerve to chip the
damn thing in.

Yasmin was in my apartment when I got there. I was surprised;
she, however, was upset and hurt. "You got out of the hospital yesterday, and you didn't even *call* me," she cried. She dropped down on the
corner of the bed and scowled at me.

"Yasmin—"

"Okay, you said you didn't want me to visit you in the hospital, so I didn't. But I thought you'd see me as soon as you came home."

"I did want to, but—"

"Then why didn't you *call* me? I'll bet you were here with somebody else."

"I went to see Papa last night. Hassan told me that I was supposed to report in."

She gave me a dubious look. "And you were there all night long?"

"No," I admitted.

"So who else did you see?"

I took a deep breath and let it out. "I saw Selima."

Yasmin's scowl turned into a grimace of utter contempt. "Oh, is that what trigs you these days? And how was she? As good as her advertisements?"

"Selima's on the list now, Yasmin. With her sisters."

She blinked at me for a moment. "Tell me why I'm not surprised. We *told* her to be careful."

"You just can't be that careful," I said. "Not unless you go live in a cave a hundred miles from your nearest neighbor. And that wasn't Selima's style."

"No." There was silence for a while; I guess Yasmin was thinking that it wasn't her style, either, that I was suggesting that the same kind of thing might happen to her. Well, I hope she was thinking that, because it's true. It's always true.

I didn't tell her about the blood-o-gram Selima's killer left for me in the hotel suite's bathroom. Somebody had figured Marîd Audran for an easy mark, so it was time for Marîd Audran to play things close to the chest. Besides, mentioning it wouldn't improve Yasmin's mood, or mine, either. "I got a moddy I want to try," I said.

She raised an eyebrow. "Anybody I know?"

"No, I don't think so. It's a detective out of some old books. Thought he might help me stop these murders."

"Uh huh. Did Papa suggest it?"

"No. Papa doesn't know what I'm really going to do. I told him I was just going to follow along after the police and look at the clues through a magnifying glass and all that. He believed me."

"Sounds like a waste of time to me," said Yasmin.

"It *is* a waste of time, but Papa likes things orderly. He operates in a steady, efficient, but dreary and minimal-velocity way."

"But he gets things done."

"Yes, I have to admit that he gets things done. Still, I don't want him looking over my shoulder, vetoing every other step I take. If I'm going to do this job for him, I have to do it my way."

"You're not doing the job just for him, Marîd. You're doing it for us. All of us. And besides, remember the *I Ching*? It said no one would believe you. This is that time evil, patterned scars and filed teeth . . . 'I'll be right you think is right, and you'll be vindicated in the end.' "

"Sure," I said, smiling grimly, "I only hope my fame doesn't come posthumously."

" 'And covet not that which Allah hath made some of you excel others. Unto men a fortune from that which they have earned, and unto women a fortune from that which they have earned. Do not envy one another, but ask Allah of His bounty. Behold! Allah is the Knower of all things.' "

"Right, Yasmin, quote at me. Suddenly you're all religious."

"*You're* the one worrying about where your devotions lie. I *already* believe; I just don't practice."

"Fast without prayer is like a shepherd without a crook, Yasmin. And you don't even fast, either."

"Yeah, but—"

"But nothing."

"You're evading the subject again."

She was right about that, so I changed evasions. "To be or not to be, sweetheart, *that* is the question." I tossed the moddy a few inches into the air and caught it. "Whether 'tis nobler in the mind—"

"Will you plug the goddamn thing in already?"

So I took a deep breath, murmured "In the name of God," and plugged it in.

The first frightening sensation was of being suddenly engulfed by a grotesque glob of flesh. Nero Wolfe weighed a seventh of a ton, 285 pounds or more. All Audran's senses were deceived into believing he had gained a hundred and thirty pounds in an instant. He fell to the floor, stunned, gasping for breath. Audran had been warned that there would be a time lag while he adjusted to each moddy he used; whether it had been recorded from a living brain or programmed to resemble a fictional character, it had probably been intended for an ideal body unlike Audran's own in many ways. Audran's muscles and nerves needed a little while to learn to compensate. Nero Wolfe was grossly fatter than Audran, and taller as well. When Audran had the moddy chipped in he would walk with Wolfe's steps, take things with Wolfe's reach and grasp, settle his imaginary corpulence into chairs with Wolfe's care and delicacy. It hit Audran harder than he had even expected.

After a moment Wolfe heard a young woman's voice. She sounded worried. Audran was still writhing on the floor, trying to breathe, trying merely to stand up again. "Are you all right?" the young woman asked.

Wolfe's eyes narrowed to little slits in the fat pouches that surrounded them. He looked at her. "Quite all right, Miss Nablusi," he said. He sat up slowly, and she came toward him to help him stand. He waved at her impatiently, but he did lean on her a bit as he got to his feet.

Wolfe's recollections, artfully wired into the moddy, mixed with Audran's submerged thoughts, feelings, sensations, and memories. Wolfe was fluent in many languages: English, French, Spanish, Italian, Latin, Serbo-Croatian, and others. There wasn't room to pack so many language daddies into a single moddy. Audran asked himself what the French word for al-kalb was, and he knew it: le chien. Of course, Audran spoke perfect French himself. He asked for the English and Croatian words for al-kalb, but they eluded him, right on the tip of the tongue, a mental tickle, one of those frustrating little memory lapses. They—Audran and Wolfe—couldn't remember which people spoke Croatian, or where they lived; Audran had never heard of the language before. All this made him suspect the depth of this illusion. He hoped they wouldn't hit bottom at some crucial moment when Audran was depending on Wolfe to get them out of some life-threatening situation. "Pfui," said Wolfe.

Ah, but Nero Wolfe rarely got himself into life-threatening situations. He let Archie Goodwin take most of those risks. Wolfe would uncover the Budayeen's assassins by sitting behind his familiar old desk—figuratively, of course—and ratiocinating his way to the killers' identities. Then peace and prosperity would descend once more upon the city, and all Islam would resound with Marîd Audran's name.

Wolfe glanced again at Miss Nablusi. He often showed a distaste for women that bordered on open hostility. How did he feel toward a sex-change? After a moment's reflection, it seemed the detective had only the same mistrust he held for organically grown, nothing artificially added, lo-cal, high-fiber females in general. On the whole, he was a flexible and objective evaluator of people; he could hardly have been so brilliant a detective otherwise. Wolfe would have no difficulty interviewing the people of the Budayeen, or comprehending their outré attitudes and motivations.

As their body grew more comfortable with the moddy, Marîd Audran's personality retired even further into passivity, able to do little more than make suggestions, while Wolfe assumed more control. It became clear that wearing a moddy could lead to the expenditure of a lot of money. Just as the murderer who'd worn the James Bond moddy had reshaped his physical appearance and his wardrobe to match his adopted personality, so too did Audran and Wolfe suddenly want to invest in yellow shirts and yellow pajamas, hire one of the world's finest chefs, and collect thousands of rare and exotic orchid plants. All that would have to wait. "Pfui," grumbled Wolfe again.

They reached up and popped the moddy out.

There was another dizzy swirl of disorientation; and then I was standing in my own room, staring stupidly down at my hand and at the module it held. I was back in my own body and my own mind.

"How was it?" asked Yasmin.

I looked at her. "Satisfactory," I said, using Wolfe's most enthusiastic expression. "It might do," I admitted. "I have the feeling that Wolfe will be able to sort through the facts and find the explanation, after all. If there is one."

"I'm glad, Marîd. And remember, if this one isn't good enough, there are thousands of other moddies you can try, too."

I put the moddy on the floor beside the bed and lay down.

Maybe I ought to have had my brain boosted a long time ago. I suspected that I'd been missing a bet, that I'd been wrong and everybody else had been right. Well, I was all grown up and I could admit my mistakes. Not out loud, of course, and never to someone like Yasmin, who'd never let me forget about it: but deep down inside I knew, and that's what counted. It had only been my pride and fear, after all, that had kept me from getting wired sooner—my feeling that I could show up any moddy with my own native good sense and one cerebral hemisphere tied behind my back. I unclipped my phone and called the Half-Hajj at home; he hadn't gone out yet for lunch, and he promised to pass by my apartment in a few minutes. I told him I had a little gift for him.

Yasmin lay down beside me while we waited for Saied to arrive. She put a hand across my chest and rested her head on my shoulder. "Marîd," she said softly, "you know that I'm really proud of you."

"Yasmin," I said slowly, "you know that I'm really scared out of my wits."

"I know, honey; I'm scared, too. But what if you hadn't done your part in all this? What about Nikki and the others? What if more people are killed, people you could have saved? What could I think about you then? What would *you* think?"

"I'll make a deal with you, Yasmin: I'll go on and do what I can and take whatever chances I can't avoid. Just stop telling me all the time that I'm doing the right thing and that you're so glad I may be dead in the next half-hour. All the cheering in the reserved seats is great for your morale; but it doesn't help me in the least, after a while it gets kind of tiresome, and it won't make bullets or knives bounce off my hide. Okay?"

She was, of course, hurt, but I meant exactly what I'd said; I wanted to nip all this "Go out there and get 'em, boy!" choo in the bud. I was sorry that I'd been so hard on Yasmin, though. To cover it, I got up and went to the bathroom. I closed the door and ran a glass of water. The water is always warm in my apartment, summer or winter, and I rarely have ice in the little freezer. After a while you can drink the tepid water with its swirling, suspended particles in it. Not me, though. I'm still working on that. I like a glass of water that doesn't stare back at you.

I took my pill case from my jeans and scrabbled out a cluster of Sonneine. These were the first sunnies I'd taken since I got out of the hospital. Like some kind of addict I was celebrating my abstinence by breaking it. I dropped the sunnies into my mouth and took a gulp of warm water. There, I thought, *that's* what will keep me going. A couple of sunnies and a few tri-phets are worth a stadium full of well-wishers with their bedsheet banners. I closed the pill case quietly—was I trying to keep Yasmin from hearing? Why?—and flushed the toilet. Then I went back into the big room.

I was halfway across the floor when Saied knocked on the door. *"Bismillah,"* I called, and swung it open.

"Yeah, you right," said the Half-Hajj. He came into the room and dropped himself on the corner of the mattress. "What you got for me?"

"He's amped now, Saied," said Yasmin. He turned toward her slowly and gave her that rough-and-tough glare of his. He was in that hitter frame of mind again. A woman's place is in *certain areas* of the home, seen and not heard, maybe not even seen if she knows what's good for her.

The Half-Hajj looked back at me and nodded. "*I* was wired when I was thirteen years old," he said.

I wasn't going to arm-wrestle with him about anything. I reminded myself that I was asking him to help me, and that it would truly be dangerous for him. I flipped the Archie Goodwin moddy to him, and he caught it easily with one hand. "Who is it?" he asked.

"A detective from some old books. He works for the greatest detective in the world. The boss is big and fat and never leaves his home, so Goodwin does all the legwork for him. Goodwin is young and good-looking and smart."

"Uh huh. And I suppose this moddy is just an end-of-Ramadân gift, a little late, right?"

"No."

"You took Papa's money, and you took his wire-job, and so you're really going out after whoever's been disenfranchising our friends and neighbors. Now you want me to chip in sturdy, reliable Goodwin and ride along with you after adventure or something."

"I need someone, Saied," I said. "You were the first person I thought of."

He looked a little flattered by that, but he was still far from enthusiastic. "This just isn't my line," he said.

"Chip it in, and it will be."

He looked at that one from both sides and realized I was right. He took off his *keffiya*, which he'd shaped into a kind of turban, popped out the moddy he was wearing, and plugged in Archie Goodwin.

I walked by him, toward the sink. I watched as his expression lost focus and then reformed subtly into something else. He seemed more relaxed, more intelligent now. He gave me a wry, amused smile, but he was measuring me and the new contents of his mind. His eyes took in everything in the room, as if he'd have to make an item-by-item catalog of it all later. He waited, giving me a look that was part insolence and part devotion. He wasn't seeing me, I knew; he was seeing Nero Wolfe.

Goodwin's attitudes and personality would appeal to Saied. He'd love the chance to jazz me with Goodwin's sardonic remarks. He liked the idea of being devastatingly attractive; wearing that moddy, he'd even be able to overcome his own aversion to women. "We'd have to discuss the matter of salary," he said.

"Of course. You know that Friedlander Bey is underwriting my expenses."

He grinned. I could see visions of expensive suits and intimate dinners and dancing at the Flamingo whirl through his rectified mind.

Then, suddenly, the grin receded. He was riffling through Goodwin's artificial memories. "I've been punched around more than a little, working for you," he said, thoughtfully.

I wiggled a finger at him, in Wolfe's manner. "That is part of your job, Archie, and you are well aware of it. I surmise it is the part you enjoy most."

The grin filled his face again. "And you enjoy surmising about me and *my* surmising. Well, go ahead, it's the only exercise you get. And you might be right about that. Anyway, it's been a long time since we had a case to work on."

Maybe I should have had my Wolfe moddy chipped in, too; without it, watching the Half-Hajj do his sidekick imitation solo was almost embarrassing. I gave a Wolfe grunt because it was expected, and paused. "Then you'll help me?" I asked.

"Just a minute." Saied popped the moddy out and chipped in his old one. It took less time for him to get used to going from a moddy to his own naked brain and into a second moddy. Of course, as he said, he'd been doing it since he'd been thirteen; I'd only done it once, a few minutes ago. He looked me over sourly, from my face down to the floor and back up again. When he started talking, I knew immediately that he wasn't in a good mood. Without Goodwin's moddy to make it all seem fun and romantic and excitingly risky, the Half-Hajj was having none of it. He stepped closer to me and spoke with his jaws clenched tightly together. "Look," he said, "I'm real sorry Nikki got killed. It bothers me that somebody's aced out the Black Widow Sisters, too, though they were never friends of mine; it's just a bad thing all the way around. As for Abdoulaye, he got what was coming to him and, if you ask me, he got it later than he deserved. So it comes down to a grudge match between you and some blazebrain on account of Nikki. I say *wonderful*, you got the whole Budayeen and the city and Papa himself on your side. But I don't see where you get the goddamn nerve"—and he poked me real hard in the chest with a forefinger that was like a heavy iron rod—"to ask me to screen you from everything bad that might happen. You'll take the reward, all right, but the bullet holes and the stab wounds you figure you can palm off onto me. Well, Saied can see what you're doing, Saied isn't as crazy as you think he is." He snorted, almost amazed at my audacity. "Even if you get out of all this alive, Maghrebi, even if everybody in the world thinks you're some kind of hero, we're going to have to settle this business between us." He looked at me, his face fierce and red, his jaw muscles working, trying to cool down enough to get his rage out coherently. At last he gave up; for a few seconds I thought he was going to slug me. I didn't move an inch. I waited. He raised his fist, hesitated, then grabbed the Archie Goodwin moddy from his other hand. He threw the moddy to the floor, chased it a few yards as it skidded across the room, then raised one foot and brought it down, crushing the plastic moddy beneath the heavy wooden stacked heel of his leather boot. Shattered pieces of the plastic case and bright, colored bits of the circuitry within flew in all directions. The Half-Hajj stared down at the ruined moddy for a moment, his eyes blinking stupidly. Then he slowly looked up at me again. "You know what that guy *drinks*?" he shouted. "He drinks *milk*, goddamn it!" Deeply offended, Saied headed toward the door.

"Where are you going?" asked Yasmin timidly.

He glanced at her. "I'm going to find the biggest porterhouse steak in the city and put it where it belongs. I'm going to have a hell of a good time in honor of how close I came to getting conned to death by your boyfriend here." Then he threw open the front door and stalked out, slamming the door shut behind him.

I laughed. It had been a great performance, and just the release I had been needing. I wasn't looking forward to the reckoning Saied had threatened; but if the two assassins didn't make the matter trivial, I was sure that the Half-Hajj would get over his anger soon enough. If I did end up a hero, unlikely as it seemed, he'd be in an unpopular minority, sounding spiteful and envious. I was sure that Saied would never stay in any unpopular group if he could do anything about it. I'd just have to keep breathing long enough, and the Half-Hajj would eventually be my friend again.

My good humor, I guessed, coincided with the rising of the sunnies. See, I told myself, how already they're helping you stay in control? What good would it have done to get into a fistfight with Saied?

"Now what?" asked Yasmin.

I wished she hadn't asked that. "I'll go find another moddy, as you suggested. In the meantime, I have to put all the information together the way Papa wants, and try to sort all this out and see if there's a definite pattern or line of investigation to follow."

"You weren't being a coward, were you, Marîd? About getting the brain implants?"

"Sure, I was afraid. You know that. I wasn't being a coward about it, though. It's more as if I was putting off the inevitable. I've felt like Hamlet a lot lately. Even when you admit that the thing you fear *is* inevitable, you're not sure it's still the correct thing to do. Maybe Hamlet could have solved things with less bloodshed another way, without forcing his uncle's hand. Maybe getting my brain amped only seems right. Maybe I'm overlooking something obvious."

"If you just diddle with yourself like this, more people will die, maybe even yourself. Don't forget, if half the Budayeen knows you're on the killers' trail, the killers know it, too."

That hadn't yet occurred to me. Even the sunnies couldn't buoy me up after that piece of news.

An hour later I was in Lieutenant Okking's office. As usual, he didn't show much enthusiasm when I looked in on him. "Audran," he said. "Collected another dead body for me? If all's right with the world, then you're dragging yourself in here mortally wounded, desperate for my forgiveness before you kick off."

"Sorry, Lieutenant," I said.

"Well, I can dream, can't I?"

Ya salaam, he was always so goddamn amusing. "I'm supposed to work more closely with you, and you're supposed to cooperate willingly with me. Papa thinks it best if we pool all our information."

He looked like he'd just sniffed something decomposing nearby. He muttered a few words unintelligibly under his breath. "I don't like his high-handed butting in, Audran, and you can tell him that for me. He's going to make it harder for me to close this case. Friedlander Bey's only endangering himself more by having you interfere with police business."

"He doesn't see it that way."

Okking nodded glumly. "All right, what do you want me to tell you?"

I sat back and tried to look casual. "Everything you know about Lutz Seipolt and the Russian who was killed in Chiri's club."

Okking was startled. It took him a moment to compose himself. "Audran, what possible connection could there be between the two?" he asked.

We'd been through this before; I knew he was just stalling. "There have to be overlapping motives or some broad conflict we don't understand, being played out in the Budayeen."

"Not necessarily," said the lieutenant. "The Russian wasn't part of the Budayeen. He was a political nobody who set foot in your quarter only because you asked him to meet you there."

"You're doing a good job of changing the subject, Okking. Answer the question: Where is Seipolt from and what does he do?"

"He came to the city three or four years ago, from someplace in the Fourth Reich, Frankfurt, I think. He set himself up as an import-export agent—you know how vague a description that is. His main business is food and spices, coffee, some cotton and fabrics, Oriental rugs, junk copper and brass pieces, cheap jewelry, Muski glass from Cairo, and other minor things. He's big in the European community, he seems to turn a nice profit, and he has never shown any signs of being involved in any high-level illicit international trade. That's about all I know."

"Can you imagine why he pulled a gun on me when I asked him a few questions about Nikki?"

Okking shrugged. "Maybe he just likes his privacy. Look, you aren't the most innocent-looking guy in the world, Audran. Maybe he thought you were there to put the arm on him and run off with his collection of ancient statuary and scarabs and mummified mice."

"Then you've been to his place?"

Okking shook his head. "I get reports," he said. "I'm an influential police administrator, remember?"

"That's right, I keep forgetting. So the Nikki-Seipolt angle is a dead end. What about the Russian, Bogatyrev?"

"He was a mouse working for the Byelorussians. First his kid went missing, and then he had the bad luck to stop this James Bond's slug. He has even less of a connection to the other murders than Seipolt does."

I smiled. "Thanks, Lieutenant. Friedlander Bey wanted me to make sure you hadn't turned up any new evidence lately. I really don't want to disrupt your investigation. Just tell me what I should do next."

He made a face. "I'd suggest that you go on a fact-finding mission to Tierra del Fuego or New Zealand or somewhere out of my hair, but you'd only laugh and not take me seriously. So check on anyone who had a grudge against Abdoulaye, or if anyone particularly wanted to kill the Black Widow Sisters. Find out if any of the Sisters had been seen with an unknown or suspicious person just before she was killed."

"All right," I said, standing up. I'd just been given a first-class runaround, but I wanted Okking to think he had me snowed. Maybe he had some definite leads that he didn't want to share with me, despite what Papa had said. That might explain his offhand lying. Whatever the reason, I planned to come back soon—when Okking wasn't around—and use the computer records to dig a little deeper into the backgrounds of Seipolt and Bogatyrev.

When I got home, Yasmin pointed to the table. "Somebody left a note for you."

"Oh yeah?"

"Just slipped it under the door and knocked. I went to the door, but there wasn't anybody there. I went downstairs, but there was nobody on the sidewalk, either."

I felt a chill. I tore open the envelope. There was a short message printed out on computer paper. It said:

AUDRAN:
YOU'RE NEXT!
JAMES BOND IS GONE.
I'M SOMEONE ELSE NOW. CAN YOU GUESS WHO?

THINK ABOUT SELIMA AND YOU'LL KNOW.
IT WON'T DO YOU ANY GOOD, BECAUSE
YOU'LL BE DEAD SOON!

"What does it say?" asked Yasmin.
"Oh, nothing," I said. I felt a little tremor in my hand. I turned
away from Yasmin, crumpled the paper, and stuffed it in my pocket.

fifteen

since the night Bogatyrev had been killed in Chiriga's place, I had
felt almost every strong emotion a person can. There had been disgust
and terror and elation. I had known hate and love, hope and despair. I
had been by turns timid and bold. Yet nothing had filled me so completely as the fury that surged in me now. The preliminary jostling was
over, and ideas like honor, justice, and duty were submerged beneath
the overpowering need to stay alive, to keep from being killed. The
time for doubt had passed. I had been threatened—*me,* personally. That
anonymous message had gotten my attention.

My rage was directed immediately at Okking. He was hiding information from me, maybe covering up something, and he was endangering my life. If he wanted to endanger Abdoulaye or Tami, well, I guess
that's police business. But endangering me—that's *my* business. When
I got to his office, Okking was going to learn that. I was going to teach
it to him the hard way.

I was striding fiercely up the Street, seething and rehearsing what
I was going to say to the lieutenant. It didn't take me long to get it
all worked out. Okking would be surprised to see me again, only an
hour after I'd left his office. I planned to storm in, slam his door so
hard the glass would rattle, shove the death threat into his face, and
demand a complete recitation of facts. Otherwise I would haul him
down to one of the interrogation rooms and bounce him off his own
walls for a while. I bet Sergeant Hajjar would give me all the help I
wanted, too.

As I got to the gate at the eastern end of the Budayeen, I faltered
a bit between steps. A new thought had rammed its way into my mind.
I had felt that little tickle of unfinished business this morning when I'd

talked to Okking; I'd felt it after seeing Selima's corpse, too. I always let my unconscious mind work on those tickles, and sooner or later it puzzled them out. Now I had my answer, like an electric buzzer going off in my head.

Question: What is missing from this picture?

Answer: Let's take a close look. First, we've had several unsolved murders in the neighborhood in the last several weeks. How many? Bogatyrev, Tami, Devi, Abdoulaye, Nikki, Selima. Now, what do the police do when they hit a brick wall in a homicide investigation? Police work is repetitive, tedious, and methodical; they bring in all the witnesses again and make them go over their statements in case some vital clue has been neglected. The cops ask the same questions five, ten, twenty, a hundred times. You get dragged down to the station, or they wake you up in the middle of the night. More questions, more of the same dull answers.

With a scoreboard showing six unsolved, apparently related killings, why hadn't the police been doing more plodding and inspecting and badgering? I hadn't had to go through my stories a second time, and I doubt that Yasmin or anyone else had to, either.

Okking and the rest of the department had to be laying off. By the life of my honor and my eyes, why weren't they pursuing this thing? Six dead already, and I was sure that the count would go higher. I had been personally promised at least one more corpse—my own.

When I got to the copshop I went by the desk sergeant without a word. I wasn't thinking about procedures and protocol, I was thinking about blood. Maybe it was the look on my face or a midnight-black aura I was carrying with me, but no one stopped me. I went upstairs and cut through the maze of corridors until I came to Hajjar, sitting outside Okking's meager headquarters. Hajjar must have noticed my expression, too, because he just jerked a thumb over his shoulder. He wasn't going to stand in my way, and he wasn't going to take his chances with the boss, either. Hajjar wasn't smart, but he was tricky. He was going to let Okking and me beat on each other, but he wasn't going to be nearby himself. I don't remember if I said anything to Hajjar or not. The next thing I recall, I was leaning over Okking's desk with my right fist wrapped tightly in the bunched cotton cloth of his shirt. We were both screaming.

"What the hell does this mean?" I shouted, waving the computer paper in front of his eyes. That's all I could get out before I was spun around, dropped, and pinned to the floor by two policemen, while three more covered me with their needle guns. My heart was already racing, it couldn't beat any faster without exploding. I stared at one of the cops, looking into the tiny black mouth of his pistol. I wanted to kick his face in, but my mobility was restricted.

"Let him go," said Okking. He was breathing hard, too.

"Lieutenant," objected one of the men, "if—"

"Let him go. *Now*."

They let me go. I got to my feet and watched the uniforms holster their weapons and leave the room. They were all muttering. Okking waited for the last one to cross the threshold, then he slowly closed the door, ran a hand through his hair, and returned to his desk. He was spending a lot of time and effort calming himself. I suppose he didn't want to talk to me until he got himself under control. Finally he sat down in his swivel chair and looked at me. "What is it?" he asked. No bantering, no sarcasm, no cop's veiled threats or wheedling. Just as my time for fear and uncertainty had passed, so had Okking's time for professional disdain and condescension.

I laid the note on his blotter and let him read it. I sat down in a hard, angular plastic chair beside Okking's desk and waited. I saw him finish reading. He closed his eyes and rubbed them wearily. "Jesus," he murmured.

"Whoever that James Bond was, he traded in that moddy for another one. He said I'd know which one if I thought about it. Nothing rings any bells with me."

Okking stared at the wall behind me, calling up the scene of Selima's murder in his mind. First his eyes got a little wider, then his mouth fell open a bit, and then he groaned. "Oh my God," he said.

"What?"

"How does Xarghis Moghadhîl Khan sound?"

I'd heard the name before, but I wasn't sure who Khan was. I knew that I wasn't going to like him, though. "Tell me about him," I said.

"It was about fifteen years ago. This psychopath proclaimed himself the new prophet of God in Assam or Sikkim or one of those places to the east. He said a gleaming blue angel presented him with revelations and divine proclamations, the most urgent being that Khan go out and jam every white woman he could find and murder anybody who got in his way. He bragged about settling two or three hundred men, women, and children before he was stopped. Killed four more in prison before they executed him. He liked to hack organs out of his victims as sacrifices to his blue metal angel. Different organs for different days of the week or phases of the moon or some goddamn thing."

There was anxious silence for a few seconds. "He's going to be a lot worse as Khan than he was as Bond," I said.

Okking nodded grimly. "Xarghis Moghadhîl Khan by himself

makes the whole of the Budayeen's collection of thugs look like car-
toon cats and mice."

I closed my eyes, feeling helpless. "We've got to find out if he's
just some lunatic hatchet man or if he's working for somebody."

The lieutenant stared past me at the far wall for a moment, turning
some idea over in his mind. His right hand toyed nervously with a
cheap bronze figure of a mermaid on his desk. Finally he looked at me.
"I can help you there," he said softly.

"I was sure you knew more than you were telling. You know who
this Bond-Khan guy is working for. You know I was right about the
murders being assassinations, don't you?"

"We don't have time for back-patting and medal-pinning. That can
come later."

"You'd better come across with the whole story now. If Friedlander
Bey hears that you're holding back this information, he'll have you out
of your job before you have time to say you're sorry."

"I don't know that for sure, Audran," said Okking. "But I don't
want to test it."

"So spell it out: Who was James Bond working for?"

The cop turned away again. When he glanced back at me, there
was anguish in his expression. "He was working for me, Audran."

The plain truth is, that wasn't what I was expecting to hear. I didn't
know how to react. _"Wallâhî il-'azîm,"_ I murmured. I just let Okking
take care of explaining it however he wanted.

"You're stumbling around in something bigger than a few serial
murders," he said. "I guess you know that, but you don't have any idea
how _much_ bigger. All right. I was getting money from a European government to locate somebody who had fled to the city. This person was
in line to rule another country. A political faction in the fugitive's
homeland wanted to assassinate him. The government I work for wanted
to find him and bring him back unharmed. You don't need to know all
the details of the intrigue, but that's the basic idea. I hired 'James
Bond' to find the man, and also to disrupt the other party's attempt to
assassinate him."

I took a few seconds to take that all in. It was a pretty good sized
chunk to swallow. "Bond killed Bogatyrev. And Devi. And Selima,
after he became Xarghis Khan. So I was on the right track from the
beginning—Bogatyrev was iced on purpose. It wasn't an unfortunate
accident, as you and Papa and everybody else kept insisting. And that's
why you haven't been digging deeper into these murders. You know
exactly who killed them all."

"I wish I did, Audran." Okking looked tired, and a little sick. "I don't have the slightest idea who's working for the other side. I have enough clues—the same awful M.O., the bruises and handprints on the tortured bodies, a pretty good description of the killer's size and weight, a lot of little forensic details like that. But I don't know who it is, and it scares me."

"*You're* scared? You got a hell of a lot of nerve. Everybody in the Budayeen has been hiding under their covers for weeks, wondering if these two psychos would tap them next, and *you're* scared. What the hell are you scared of, Okking?"

"The other side won, the prince was assassinated; but the murders didn't stop. I don't know why. The assassination should have ended the matter. The killers are probably eliminating anyone who might identify them."

I chewed my lip and thought. "I need to back up a little," I said. "Bogatyrev worked for the legation of one of the Russian kingdoms. How does he tie up with Devi and Selima?"

"I told you I didn't want to give out all the details. This gets dirty, Audran. Can't you be satisfied with what I've already told you?"

I felt myself getting furious again. "Okking, your fucking hit man is coming after *me* next. I've got a goddamn *right* to know the whole story. Why can't you tell your killer to lay off now?"

"Because he's disappeared. After the prince was killed by the other side, Bond dropped out of sight. I don't know where he is or how to get in contact with him. He's working on his own, now."

"Or else someone else has given him a new set of instructions." I couldn't suppress a shudder when the first name that crossed my mind was not Seipolt's—the logical choice—but Friedlander Bey's. I knew then that I'd been kidding myself about Papa's motives: fear for his own life, and a laudable interest in protecting the other citizens of the city. No, Papa was never so straightforward. But could he somehow be behind these terrible events? It was a possibility I could neglect no longer.

Okking was lost in thought, too, a glint of fear in his eyes. He played with his little mermaid some more. "Bogatyrev wasn't just a minor clerk with that Russian legation. He was the Grand Duke Vasili Petrovich Bogatyrev, the younger brother of King Vyacheslav of Byelorussia and the Ukraine. His nephew, the crown prince, had gotten to be too much of an embarrassment at court and had to be sent away. Neofascist parties in Germany wanted to find the prince and bring him back to Byelorussia, thinking that they could use him to topple his father from the throne and replace the monarchy with a German-controlled 'protectorate.' Remnants of the Soviet Communists supported them; they wanted the monarchy destroyed, too, but they planned to replace it with their own sort of government."

"A temporary alliance of the far right wing and the far left," I said. Okking smiled wanly. "It's happened before."

"And you were working for the Germans."

"That's right."

"Through Seipolt?"

Okking nodded. He wasn't enjoying any bit of this. "Bogatyrev wanted you to find the prince. When you did, the duke's man, whoever he is, would kill him."

I was astonished. "Bogatyrev was setting up the murder of his own nephew? His brother's son?"

"To preserve the monarchy at home, yes. They'd decided it was unfortunate but necessary. I told you it was dirty. When you wander into the highest level of international affairs, it's almost always dirty."

"Why did Bogatyrev need me to find his nephew?"

Okking shrugged. "In the past three years of the prince's exile, he'd managed to disguise himself and hide pretty well. Sooner or later, he must have realized his life was in danger."

"Bogatyrev's 'son' wasn't killed in a traffic accident, then. You lied to me; he was still alive when you told me the matter was closed. But you say the Byelorussians *did* kill him, after all."

"He was that sex-change friend of yours. Nikki. Nikki was really the Crown Prince Nikolai Konstantin."

"Nikki?" I said in a flat voice. I was unnerved by the accumulated weight of the truths I'd demanded to hear, and by the weight of regret. I remembered Nikki's terrified voice during that short, interrupted telephone call. Could I have saved her? Why hadn't she trusted me more? Why didn't she tell me the truth, tell me what she must have suspected? "Then Devi and the other two Sisters were killed—"

"Just because they were too close to her. It didn't make any difference whether or not they really knew anything dangerous. The German killer—Khan, now—and the Russian guy aren't taking any chances. That's why you're on the list, too. That's why . . . this." The lieutenant opened a drawer and took something out, flipped it across his desk toward me.

It was another note on computer paper, just like mine. Only it was addressed to Okking.

"I'm not leaving the police station until this is all over," he said. "I'm staying right here with a hundred fifty friendly cops watching my back."

"I hope none of them is Bogatyrev's knifeman," I said. Okking winced. The idea had already occurred to him, too.

I wished I knew how long the hit lists were, how many names followed mine and Okking's. It was a shock when I realized that Yasmin could very well be on them. She knew at least as much as Selima had; more, because I'd told her what I knew and what I guessed. And Chiriga, was her name there? What about Jacques, Saied, and Mahmoud? And how many other people that I knew? Thinking about Nikki, who'd gone from prince to princess to dead, thinking about what I had ahead of me, I felt crushed; I looked at Okking and realized that he was crushed, too. Far worse than I. His career in the city was over, now that he had admitted to being a foreign agent.

"I don't have any more to tell you," he said.

"If you learn something, or if I need to get in touch with you . . ."

"I'll be here," he said in a dead voice. *"Inshallah."* I got up and left his office. It was like escaping from prison.

Outside the station house, I unclipped my phone and spoke into it as I walked. I called the hospital and asked for Dr. Yeniknani.

"Hello, Mr. Audran," came his deep voice.

"I wanted to find out about the old woman, Laila."

"It's too soon to tell, to be quite frank. She may recover with the passage of time, but it doesn't seem likely. She is old and frail. I have her sedated and she's under constant observation. I'm afraid she might fall into an irreversible coma. Even if that doesn't happen, there's an extremely high probability that she will never regain her intelligent faculties. She will never be able to care for herself or perform the simplest tasks."

I took a deep breath and let it out. I felt that I was to blame.

"All is as Allah ordains," I said numbly.

"Praise be to Allah."

"I will ask Friedlander Bey to take upon himself the cost of her medical expenses. What happened to her was a result of my investigations."

"I understand," said Dr. Yeniknani. "There is no need to speak to your sponsor. The woman is being treated as a charity case."

"I speak for Friedlander Bey as well as myself: we cannot adequately express our thanks."

"It is a sacred duty," he said simply. "Our technicians have determined what was recorded on that module. Do you wish to know?"

"Yes, of course," I said.

"There are three bands. The first, as you know, is a recording of the responses of a large, powerful, but starved, maltreated, and ruthlessly provoked cat, apparently a Bengal tiger. The second band is the brain impression of a human infant. The last band is the most repellent of all. It is the captured, fading consciousness of a very recently murdered woman."

"I knew I was looking for a monster, but I've never heard anything so depraved in all my life." I was thoroughly disgusted. This lunatic had no moral restraints on him at all.

"A piece of advice, Mr. Audran. Never use such a cheaply manufactured module. They are crudely recorded, with a great deal of harmful 'noise.' They lack the safeguards built into the industrially made modules. Too frequent use of underground moddies results in damage to your central nervous system, and through it, your whole body."

"I wonder where it will end?"

"Simple enough to predict: the killer will get a duplicate module made."

"Unless Okking or I or someone else gets to him first."

"Take heed, Mr. Audran. He is, as you say, a monster."

I thanked Dr. Yeniknani and returned the phone to my belt. I couldn't stop thinking about how wretched and miserable a life Laila had remaining to her. I thought also about my nameless foe, who used a commission from the Byelorussian royalists as a license to indulge his repressed desire to commit atrocities. The news from the hospital changed my half-formed plans entirely. Now I knew precisely what I had to do, and I had some good ideas about how to get it done.

Going up the Street, I met Fuad the Terminally Witless. *"Marhaba,"* he said. He squinted up at me, one hand shading his weak eyes.

"How's it goin', Fuad?" I said. I wasn't in the mood to stand around and talk with him. I had some preparations to make.

"Hassan wants to see you. Something to do with Friedlander Bey. Said you'd know what he meant."

"Thanks, Fuad."

"Do you? Know what he means?" He blinked at me, hungry for gossip.

I sighed. "Yeah, right, I know. Got to run." I tried to tear myself away from him.

"Hassan said it was really important. What's it all about, Marîd? You can tell me. I can keep a secret."

I didn't answer; I doubted that Fuad could keep *anything*, least of all a secret. I just clapped him on the shoulder like a pal, and gave him my back. I stopped in Hassan's shop before I went home. The American kid was still sitting on his stool in the empty room. He gave me a chilling come-hither smile. I was sure now: this boy liked me. I didn't say a word, but ducked into the back and found Hassan. He was doing what he was always doing, checking invoices and packing lists against his cartons and crates. He saw me and smiled. Apparently he and I were on good terms now: it was so hard keeping track of Hassan's moods that I had stopped trying. He set down his clipboard, put one hand on my shoulder, and kissed my cheek in the Arabic manner. "Welcome, O my darling nephew!"

"Fuad said you had something to tell me from Papa."

Hassan's face grew serious. "That is only what I told Fuad. I tell you this from *myself*. I am worried, O Maghrebi. I am *more* than worried—I am terrified. I have not slept soundly for four nights, and when I do nap, I have the most horrible dreams. I thought nothing could be worse than when I found Abdoulaye . . . when I found him . . . His voice faltered. "Abdoulaye was not a good man, we both know that; yet he and I were closely associated for a number of years. You know that I employed him, even as Friedlander Bey employs me. Now I have been warned by Friedlander Bey that—" Hassan's voice broke and he was unable to say anything for a moment. I was afraid that I would have to watch this bloated pig go to pieces right in front of me. The idea of patting his hand and saying "There, there," was absolutely loathsome. He got himself collected, though, and went on. "Friedlander Bey warned me that more of his friends may yet be in danger. That includes you, O clever one, and myself as well. I am sure you understood the risks weeks ago, but I am not a brave man. Friedlander Bey did not choose me to perform your task because he knows I have no courage, no inner resources, no honor. I must be harsh with myself, because now I can see the truth. *I have no honor*. I think only of myself, of the danger that may confront me, of the possibility that I may suffer and end up just as—" At that point Hassan did break down. He wept. I waited patiently for the shower to pass; slowly the clouds parted, but even then no sun glimmered through.

"I'm taking my own precautions, Hassan. We all should take precautions. Those who've been killed died because they were foolish or too trusting, which is the same thing."

"I trust no one," said Hassan.

"I know. That may keep you alive, if anything will."

"How reassuring," he said dubiously. I don't know what he wanted—a written promise that I would guarantee his scabrous, pitiful little life?

"You'll be all right, Hassan; but if you're so afraid, why not ask Papa for asylum until these killers are caught?"

"Then you think there *are* more than one?"

"I know it."

"That makes it all twice as bad." He struck his chest with his fist several times, appealing to Allah for justice: what had Hassan ever done to deserve this? "What will you do?" the plump, fat-faced merchant said.

"I don't know yet," I said.

Hassan nodded thoughtfully. "Then may Allah protect you," he said.

"Peace be upon you, Hassan," I said.

"And upon you be peace. Take with you this gift from Friedlander Bey." The "gift" was another envelope thick with crisp currency.

I went back out through the cloth hanging and the bare shop without giving Abdul-Hassan a glance. I decided to stop in to see Chiri, to give her a warning and some advice; I also wanted to hide out there for half an hour and forget that I was running for my life.

Chiriga greeted me with her characteristic enthusiasm. *"Habari gani?"* she cried, the Swahili equivalent of "What's up?" Then she narrowed her eyes when she saw my implants. "I heard, but I was waiting to see you before I believed. Two?"

"Two," I admitted.

She shrugged. "Possibilities," she murmured. I wondered what she was thinking. Chiri was always a couple of steps ahead of me when it came to figuring out ways to pervert and corrupt the best-intentioned of legal institutions.

"How've you been?" I asked.

"All right, I guess. No money, nothing happening, same old goddamn boring job." She showed me her sharpened teeth to let me know that while the club might not be making money and the girls and changes weren't making money, *Chiri* was making money. And she wasn't bored, either.

"Well," I said, "we're all going to have to work to keep it all right." She frowned. "Because of the, uh . . ." She waved a hand in a little circle.

I waved a hand in a little circle, too. "Yeah, because of the 'uh.' Nobody but me wants to believe these killings aren't over and that just about everybody we know is a possible slabsitter."

"Yeah, you right, Marîd," said Chiri in a soft voice. "What the hell you think I should do?"

She had me there. As soon as I talked her into agreeing, she next wanted me to explain the logic the assassins were using. Hell, I'd wasted a lot of time running up and down looking for that, too. Anybody could get bumped, anytime, for any reason. Now when Chiriga asked for practical advice, all I could say was "Be careful." It looked like you had two choices: you went about things just the same but with more eyes open, or you could go live on another continent just to be on the safe side. The latter is assuming you didn't pick the wrong continent and walk right into the heart of the matter, or let it follow along with you.

So I shrugged and told her it looked like a gin and bingara kind of afternoon. She poured herself a big drink, poured me a double on the house, and we sat around and looked into each other's unhappy eyes for a while. No kidding, no flirting, no mentioning the Honey Pílar moddy. I didn't even look at her new girls, and Chiri and I were huddled together too closely for the others to barge in and say hello. When I killed my drink I took a glass of her tende—it was starting to taste better. The first time I'd tried it, it was like I'd bitten into the side of some animal that had died under a log a week ago. I stood up to go, but then some true tenderness that I wasn't quick enough to hide made me touch Chiri's scarred cheek and pat her hand. She flashed me a smile that was almost back to full strength. I got out of there before we both decided to retire to Free Kurdistan or somewhere.

Back at my apartment, Yasmin was working on being late to work. She had got up early that morning to drop her pain and suffering on me, so to get to Frenchy's late she just about had to go back to sleep and start all over again. She gave me a drowsy smile from the mattress. "Hi," she said in a small voice. I think she and the Half-Hajj were the only people in the city who weren't completely terrified. Saied had his moddy to simulate courage, but Yasmin just had me. She was absolutely confident that I was going to protect her. That made her even dumber than Saied.

"Yasmin, look, I got a million things to do, and you're going to have to stay at your own place for a few days, okay?"

She looked hurt again. "You don't want me around?" Meaning: you got somebody else now?

"I don't want you around because I'm a big, shiny target now. This apartment is going to be too dangerous for anybody. I don't want you getting into the line of fire, understand?"

She liked that better; it meant I still cared for her, the dizzy bitch. You have to keep telling them that every ten minutes or they think you're sneaking out the back. "Okay, Marîd. You want your keys back?"

I thought about that a second. "Yeah. That way I know where they are, I know somebody won't lift them from you to get into my place." She took them out of her purse and tossed them toward me. I scooped them up. She made going-to-work motions, and I told her twenty or thirty times that I loved her, that I'd be extra crafty and sly, and that I'd call her a couple times a day just to check in. She kissed me, took a quick glance at the time and gave a phony gasp, and hurried out the door. She'd have to pay Frenchy his big fifty again today.

As soon as Yasmin was gone, I started putting together what I had, and I soon saw how little that was. I didn't want either of the freezers to pop me in my own house, so I needed a place to stay until I felt safe again. For the same reason, I wanted to look different on the street. I still had a lot of Papa's money in my bank account, and the cash I'd just gotten from Hassan would let me move around with a little freedom and security. It never took me long to pack. I stuffed some things into a black nylon zipper bag, wrapped my case of special daddies in a T-shirt and put it on top, then zipped the bag and left my apartment. When I hit the sidewalk, I wondered if Allah would be pleased to let me come back to this place. I knew I was just worrying myself for no good reason, the way you keep pushing at a sore tooth. Jesus, what a nuisance it was, being desperate to stay alive.

I left the Budayeen and crossed the big avenue into a rather pricey collection of shops; these were more like boutiques than like the souks you'd expect. Tourists found just the souvenirs they were looking for here, despite the fact that most of the junk was made in other countries many thousands of miles away. There probably aren't any native arts and crafts in the city at all, so the tourists browsed happily through gaily colored straw parrots from Mexico and plastic folding fans from Kowloon. The tourists didn't care, so nobody had any kick coming. We were all very civilized out here on the edge of the desert.

I went into a men's clothing store that sold European business suits. Usually I didn't have the money to buy half a pair of socks, but Papa was staking me to a whole new look. It was so different, I didn't even know what I needed. I told the clerk I was looking for someone genuinely interested in helping customers. I let him know I was serious—sometimes *fellahîn* go into these shops just to get their sweat all over the Oxford suits. I told him I wanted to be outfitted completely from the ground up, I told him how much I was willing to spend, and let him put the wardrobe together. I didn't know how to match shirts and ties—I didn't know how to *tie* a tie, I got a printed brochure about different knots—so I really needed the clerk's help. I figured he was getting a commission, so I let him oversell me by a couple of hundred kiam or so. He wasn't just putting on an act about being friendly, the way most shopkeepers do. He didn't even shrink away from touching me, and I was about as scruffy then as you could get. In the Budayeen alone, that takes in a wide range of shabbiness.

I paid for the clothes, thanked the clerk, and carried my packages a couple of blocks to the Hotel Palazzo di Marco Aurelio. It was part of a large international Swiss-owned chain: all of them looked alike, and none of them had any of the elegance that had made the original so charming. I didn't care. I wasn't looking for elegance or charm, I was looking for a place to sleep where no one would sizzle me in the night. I wasn't even curious enough to ask why the hotel in this Islamic stronghold was named after some Roman son of a bitch.

The guy at the desk didn't have the attitude of the salesman at the clothing store; I knew immediately that the room clerk was a snob, that he was paid to be a snob, that the hotel had trained him to raise his natural snobbery to ethereal heights. There was nothing I could say to crack his contempt; he was as set in his ways as a sidewalk. There was something I could do, though, and I did it. I took out all the money I had with me and spread it out on the pink marble counter. I told him I needed a good single room for a week or two, and I'd pay in cash in advance.

His expression didn't change—he still hated my guts—but he called over an assistant and instructed him to find me a room. It didn't take long. I carried my own packages up in an elevator and dumped them on the bed in my room. It was a nice room, I guess, with a good view of the back ends of some buildings in the business district. I had my own holo set, though, and a tub instead of just a shower. I emptied the zipper bag onto the bed, too, and changed into my Arab costume. It was time to pay another call on Herr Lutz Seipolt. This time I took a few daddies along with me. Seipolt was a shrewd man, and his boy Reinhardt might give me problems. I chipped in a German-language daddy and took along some of the body-and-mind controls. From now on I was only going to be a blur to normal people. I didn't plan to hang around anywhere long enough for someone to draw a bead on me. Marîd Audran, the superman of the sands.

Bill was sitting in his beat-up old taxi, and I got in beside him on the front seat. He didn't notice me. He was waiting for orders from the inside, as usual. I called his name and shoved his shoulder for almost a minute before he turned and blinked at me. "Yeah?" he said.

"Bill, will you take me out to Lutz Seipolt's place?"

"I know you?"

"Uh huh. We went out there a few weeks ago."

"That's easy for *you* to say. Seipolt, huh? The German guy with the thing for blondes with legs? I can tell you right now, you're not his type at all."

Seipolt had told me he didn't have a thing for *anybody* anymore.

My God, Seipolt had lied to me, too; I tell you, I was shocked. I sat back and watched the city scream by the car as Bill forced his way through it. He always made the trip a little more difficult than it had to be. Of course, he was avoiding things in the road most people can't even *see*, and he did it well, too. I don't think he smacked a single *afrit* all the way out to Seipolt's.

I got out of the cab and walked slowly to Seipolt's massive wooden door. I knocked and rang the bell and waited, but no one came. I started to go around the house, hoping to run into the old *fellah* caretaker I'd met the first time I'd come out here. The grass was lush and the plants and flowers ticked along on their botanical timetables. I heard the chirping of birds high in a tree, a rare enough sound in the city, but I didn't hear anything that might mean the presence of people in the estate. Maybe Seipolt had gone to the beach. Maybe Seipolt had gone shopping for brass storks in the *medînah*. Maybe Seipolt and blue-eyed Reinhardt had taken the afternoon and evening off to make the rounds of the city's hot spots, dining and dancing under the moon and stars.

Around the big house to the right, between two tall palmettos, was a side door set into the whitewashed wall. I didn't think Seipolt ever used it; it looked like a convenience for whoever had to carry the groceries in and the garbage out. This side of the house was landscaped with aloes and yucca and flowering cactus, different from the front of the villa and its tropical rain-forest blossoms. I grabbed the doorknob, and it turned in my hand. Somebody had probably just gone into town for the newspaper. I let myself in and found myself looking down a flight of stairs into an arid darkness, and up a shorter flight into a pantry. I went up, through the pantry, through a well-equipped and gleaming kitchen, and into an elaborate dining room. I didn't see anyone or hear anyone. I made a little noise to let Seipolt or Reinhardt know I was there; I wouldn't want them to shoot me down, thinking I was spying or something.

From the dining room I passed through a parlor and down a corridor to Seipolt's collection of ancient artifacts. I was on familiar ground now. Seipolt's office was just . . . over . . .

. . . there. The door was closed, so I crossed to it and rapped on it loudly. I waited and rapped again. Nothing. I opened the door and stepped into Seipolt's office. It was dim; the drapes were closed across the window. The air was stifling and stale, as if the air-conditioning wasn't working and the room had been shut up for a while. I wondered if I dared go through the stuff on Seipolt's desk. I went up to it and riffled quickly through some reports on the top of a stack of papers.

Seipolt lay in a kind of alcove formed by the bay window behind his desk and two file cabinets against the left-hand wall. He was wearing a dark suit, stained darker now with blood, and when I first glanced over the desktop I thought he was a charcoal-gray throw rug on the light brown carpet. Then I saw a bit of his pale blue shirt and one hand. I took a few steps toward him, not really interested in seeing just how badly cut to pieces he was. His chest was opened from his throat to his groin, and a couple of dark, bloody things were spilled out on the carpet. One of his own internal organs had been crammed into his other stiff hand.

Xarghis Moghadhil Khan had done this. That is to say, James Bond, who worked for Seipolt. Until just recently. Another witness and lead obliterated.

I found Reinhardt in his own upstairs suite, in the same shape. The nameless old Arab had been murdered on the lawn in back of the house, as he worked among the lovely flowers he nurtured in defiance of nature and climate. All had been killed quickly, then dismembered. Khan had crept from one victim to the next, killing fast and quiet. He moved more silently than a ghost. Before I went back into the house, I chipped in a few daddies that suppressed fear, pain, anger, hunger, and thirst; the German daddy was already in place, but it looked as if it wouldn't be very useful this afternoon.

I headed toward Seipolt's office. I intended to go back in there and search through the desk. Before I got to the room, though, someone called out to me. *"Lutz?"*

I turned to look. It was the blonde with the legs.

"Lutz?" she asked. *"Bist du noch bereit?"*

"Ich heisse Marîd Audran, Fräulein. Wissen Sie wo Lutz ist?" At that point my brain swallowed the German add-on whole; it wasn't as if I could just translate the German into Arabic, but as if I was speaking a language I'd known since early childhood.

"Isn't he down here?" she asked.

"No, and I can't find Reinhardt either."

"They must have gone into the city. They were saying something about that over lunch."

"I'll bet they've gone to my hotel. We had a dinner engagement, and I understood that I was to meet him here. I hired a car all the way out here. What a damn stupid thing. I guess I'll just give the hotel a ring and leave a message for Lutz, and then call another taxi. Would you like to come along?"

She bit her thumbnail. "I don't know if I should," she said.

"Have you seen the city yet?"

She frowned. "I haven't seen *anything* but this house since I've *been* here," she said grumpily.

I nodded. "That's how he is, he drives himself too hard. He always says he'll take it easy and enjoy himself, but he works himself and he works everybody around him. I don't want to say anything against him—after all, he's one of my oldest business associates and dearest friends—but I think it's bad for him to keep going the way he does. Am I right?"

"That's just what I tell him," she said.

"Then why don't we go back to the hotel? Maybe once we're there together, the four of us, we'll get him to relax a little tonight. Dinner and a show, as my guests. I insist."

She smiled. "Just let me—"

"We must hurry," I said. "If we don't get back quickly, Lutz will turn around and come back here. He's an impatient man. Then I'll have to make still another trip out here. It's an awful ride you know. Come along, we don't have any time to spare."

"But if we're going out to dinner—"

I should have guessed. "I think that dress suits you perfectly, my dear; but if you prefer, why I beg that you allow me to accommodate you with another outfit of your choice, and whatever accessories you feel are necessary. Lutz has given me many gifts over the years. It would give me great pleasure to acknowledge his generosity in this small way. We can go shopping before dinner. I know several very exclusive English, French, and Italian shops. I'm sure you'd enjoy that. Indeed, you might choose your garments for the evening while Lutz and I take care of our little business. It will all work out beautifully."

I had her by the arm and out the front door. We were walking up the gravel drive to Bill's taxi. I opened one of the car's rear doors and helped her in, then I walked around the back of the cab and got in the other side. "Bill," I said in Arabic, "back to the city. The Hotel Palazzo di Marco Aurelio."

Bill looked at me sourly. "Marcus Aurelius is dead, too, you know," he said as he started up the taxi. I got a frosty feeling wondering what he meant by "too."

I turned to the beautiful woman beside me. "Pay no attention to the driver," I said in German. "Like all Americans, he is mad. It is the will of Allah."

"You didn't phone the hotel," she said, giving me a sweet smile. She liked the idea of a new suit of clothes and jewelry just because we were going to dinner. I was just a crazy Arab with too much money. She liked crazy Arabs, I just knew it.

"No, I didn't. I'll have to call as soon as we get there."

She wrinkled up her nose in thought. "But if we're *there*—"

"You don't understand," I told her. "For the common run of guests, the desk clerk is capable of handling matters like this. But when the guests are, shall we say, special—like Herr Seipolt or myself—then one must speak directly with the manager.

Her eyes got bigger. "Oh," she said.

I looked back at the freshly watered garden that Seipolt's money had imposed on the very edge of the creeping dunes. In a couple of weeks, that place would look as dry and dead as the middle of the Empty Quarter. I turned to my companion and smiled easily. We chatted all the way back to the city.

sixteen

At the hotel, I left the blonde in a comfortable chair in the lobby. Her name was Trudi. Trudi Nothing, she told me blithely, just Trudi. She was a close personal friend of Lutz Seipolt. She'd been at his house for more than a week. They'd been introduced by a mutual friend. Uh huh. That Trudi, she was just the nicest, most outgoing girl—and Seipolt, you couldn't *ask* for a sweeter man, down under all that murder and intrigue he wore just to fool people.

I went to make my phone call, but it wasn't to anyone in the hotel that I needed to talk—it was Okking. He told me to babysit Trudi until he could get his fat ass moving. I popped out the daddies I was wearing, then put back the German-language one; I wouldn't be able to say a word to Trudi without it. That's when I learned Vital Important Fact #154 about the special add-ons Papa had given me:

You Pay For Everything In This World.

See, I *knew* that. I learned it many years ago at my mama's knee. It's just that it's something you keep forgetting and have to relearn every once in a while. Don't Nobody Get Nothing For Free.

All the time I'd been out at Seipolt's, the daddies were holding my hormones in check. When I went back into the house to search Seipolt's desk, I would have been helpless with nausea, knowing that the hacked-up bodies hadn't been dead very long, knowing that bastard Khan might *still* be around the place somewhere. When Trudi called out "Lutz?" I would have split my skin jumping in twenty directions at once.

When I popped the daddies out, I found out that I hadn't avoided those terrible feelings, I'd only postponed them. Suddenly my brain and my nerves were tied in an agonizing jumble, like a tangled ball of yarn. I couldn't untwist the separate emotional currents: there was wide-eyed, gasping horror, stifled by the daddies for a few hours; there was sudden fury directed at Khan, for the satanic method he had chosen to remain unknown, and for making me witness the results of his heinous acts; there was physical pain and utter weariness, as the fatigue poisons in my muscles rendered me almost helpless (the daddy had told my brain and the meat part of me to ignore injury and fatigue, and I was suffering from both now); I realized that I was awfully thirsty and I was getting pretty damn hungry; and my bladder, which the daddies had ordered not to communicate with any other part of my body, was near bursting. ACTH was pouring into my bloodstream, making me even more upset. Epinephrine pumped out of my adrenals, making my heart beat faster still, getting me ready for fight or flight; it made no difference that the threat was long gone. I was getting the entire reaction I would normally have experienced over a period of three or four hours, condensed into a solid, crippling blow of emotion and deprivation.

I chipped those daddies back in as fast as I could, and the world stopped lurching. In a minute, I was smoothly back in control. My breathing became normal, my heartbeat slowed down, the thirst, hunger, hatred, tiredness, and the sensation of my full bladder all vanished. I was grateful, but I knew that I was only postponing the payback yet again; when it came due at the end of all this, it would make the worst drug hangover I'd ever known seem like a quick kiss in the dark. Paybacks, *ils sont un motherfucker, n'est-ce pas, monsieur?*

I would have to agree with that.

As I was going back to the lobby and Trudi, someone called my name. I was glad I had the daddies back in; I never liked having my name called in public places anyway, particularly when I was in disguise. "Monsieur Audran?"

I turned and gave one of the hotel clerks a cool look. "Yes?" I said.

"A message for you, monsieur. Left in your box." I could tell he was having trouble with my *gallebeya* and *keffiya*. He was under the impression that only Europeans stayed in his nice, clean hotel.

It was moderately impossible that anyone had left a message for me, on two counts: the first was that no one knew I was staying here, and the second was that I'd checked in under a made-up name. I wanted to see what kind of foolish mistake had been made, and then throw it in the faces of the hotel's stuffed shirts. I took the message.

Computer paper, right?

AUDRAN:
SAW YOU AT SEIPOLT'S, BUT THE TIME WASN'T RIGHT.
SORRY.
I WANT YOU ALL TO MYSELF, ALONE AND QUIET.
I DIDN'T WANT ANYONE TO THINK YOU WERE JUST PART OF
A RANDOM GROUP OF VICTIMS.
WHEN THEY FIND YOUR BODY,
I WANT TO BE SURE THEY KNOW
YOU RECEIVED INDIVIDUAL ATTENTION.

KHAN

My knees were trying to buckle, brain implants or no. I folded the note and put it in my shoulder bag.

"Are you all right, monsieur?" asked the clerk.

"The altitude," I said. "It always takes me a while to adjust."

"But there is none," he said, bewildered.

"That's just what I mean." I went back to Trudi.

She smiled at me as if life had lost its savor while I was away. I wondered what she thought about all by herself. All "alone and quiet." I winced.

"I'm sorry to have been gone so long," I murmured. I gave her a little bow and took the chair beside her.

"I was just fine," she said. She took a long time uncrossing her legs and crossing them the other way. Everyone between here and Osaka must have watched her do it. "Did you speak to Lutz?"

"Yes. He *was* here, but he had some urgent matter to clear up. Something official, with Lieutenant Okking."

"Lieutenant?"

"He's in charge of making sure nothing awkward happens in the Budayeen. You've heard of that part of our city?"

She nodded. "But why would the lieutenant want to talk with Lutz? Lutz doesn't have anything to do with the Budayeen, does he?"

I smiled. "Forgive me, my dear, but you sound a trifle naive. Our friend is a very busy, very industrious man. I doubt if anything happens in the city without Lutz Seipolt knowing about it."

"I suppose so."

That was all bull; Seipolt was middle-management, at best. He was certainly no Friedlander Bey. "They are sending a car for us, so we'll all meet together just as we planned. Then we can decide what we'll do for the rest of the evening."

Her face lit up again. She wasn't going to miss out on her new outfit and the free night on the town, after all.

"Would you care for a drink while we wait?" I asked. That's how we passed the time until a couple of plain-clothes gold shields shuffled tiredly across the thick blue carpet toward us. I stood up, made some introductions, and we all left the hotel lobby the best of friends. We continued our pleasant little conversation all the way to the precinct station. We went upstairs, but I was stopped by Sergeant Hajjar. The two plainclothesmen escorted Trudi in to see Okking.

"What happened?" asked Hajjar grimly. I think he was being all cop now. Just to show me he could still do it.

"What do you think happened? Xarghis Khan, who worked for Seipolt and your boss, covered a few more of his tracks. Very thorough, this guy is. If I were Okking, I'd be nervous as hell. I mean, the lieutenant is a stand-out uncovered track himself."

"He knows it; I've never seen him so shook. I made him a present of thirty or forty Paxium. He took a bunch of 'em for lunch." Hajjar grinned.

One of the uniformed cops came out of Okking's office. "Audran," he said, and jerked his head at me. I was just part of the team, they all had a lot of respect for me.

"In a minute." I turned back to Hajjar. "Listen," I said, "I'm going to want to look through what you pull out of Seipolt's desk and file cabinets."

"I figured," said Hajjar. "The lieutenant's too busy to worry about all that, so he'll tell me to take care of it. I'll make sure you get first crack at it."

"All right. It's important, I hope." I went into Okking's glass-walled enclosure just as the two soft-clothes guys led Trudi out. She smiled at me and said *"Marhaba."* That's when I guessed that she spoke Arabic, too.

"Sit down, Audran," said Okking. His voice was hoarse. I sat down. "Where's she going?"

"We're just going to question her in a little more depth. We're going to sift her brain thoroughly. Then we'll let her go home, wherever the hell that is."

It sounded like good police work to me; I just wondered if Trudi would be in any shape to go when they got done sifting her. They'd use hypnosis and drugs and electrical brain stimulation, and it all left you feeling kind of wrung out. That's what I've heard.

"Khan is getting closer," said Okking, "but the other one hasn't made a peep since Nikki."

"I don't know what that means. Say, Lieutenant, Trudi isn't Khan, is she? I mean, could she ever have been James Bond?"

He looked at me like I was crazy. "How the hell would I know? I never met Bond in person, we just dealt over the phone, by mail. As far as I know, *you're* the only living person who ever saw him face-to-face. That's why I can't get over this little, nagging suspicion I have, Audran. There's something not quite right about you."

About *me*, I thought; a lot of damn nerve again, coming from a foreign agent cashing checks from the National Socialists. I was unhappy to hear that Okking wouldn't be able to pick Khan out of a lineup, if we should get so lucky. I didn't know if the lieutenant was lying, but he was probably telling the truth. He knew he was high on the list, if not next, to be slashed. He'd been serious about not leaving that room, too: he'd set up a cot in the office, and there was a tray with an unfinished meal on it on his desk.

"The only thing we probably know for sure is that both of them use their moddies not only to kill but to spread a little terror. It's working fine, too," I said. "Your guy—" Okking shot me an ugly look, but hell, it was the truth. "Your guy's changed from Bond to Khan. The other guy is the same as he was, as far as we know. I just hope the Russians' bumper has gone home. I wish we could know for sure that we don't have to worry about him anymore."

"Yeah," said Okking.

"Did you get anything useful out of Trudi before you sent her downstairs?"

Okking shrugged and flipped over half a sandwich on the tray. "Just the polite information. Her name and all that."

"I'd like to know how she got involved with Seipolt in the first place."

Okking raised his eyebrows. "Easy, Audran. Seipolt was the highest bidder this week."

I let out an exasperated breath. "I figured that much, Lieutenant. She told me she'd been introduced to Seipolt by somebody."

"Mahmoud."

"Mahmoud? My friend, Mahmoud? The one who used to be a girl over by Jo-Mama's before his sex change?"

"You right."

"What's Mahmoud got to do with this?"

"While you were in the hospital, Mahmoud got promoted. He took over the position that was left vacant when Abdoulaye got creased."

Mahmoud. Gone from sweet young thing working in the Greek clubs to petty shakedown artist to big-time white slaver in a couple of easy steps. All I could think was "Where else but in the Budayeen?"

You talk about equal opportunity for all. "I'll have to talk to Mahmoud," I muttered.

"Get in line. He's coming in here in a little while, as soon as my boys can roust him."

"Let me know what he tells you."

Okking sneered. "Of course, friend; didn't I promise you? Didn't I promise Papa? Anything else I can do for you?"

I got up and leaned over his desk. "Look, Okking, you're used to looking at pieces of bodies splashed around nice peoples' living rooms, but I can't do it without throwing up." I showed him my latest message from Khan. "I want to know if I can get myself a gun or something."

"What the hell do I care?" he said softly, almost hypnotized by Khan's note. I waited. He looked up at me, caught my eye, and sighed. Then he pulled open a lower drawer in his desk and took out some weapons. "What do you want?"

There were a couple of needle guns, a couple of static pistols, a big seizure gun, and even a large automatic projectile pistol. I chose a small Smith & Wesson needle gun and the General Electric seizure cannon. Okking put a box of formatted needle clips on his blotter for me, twelve needles to a magazine, a hundred magazines in the box. I scooped them all up and tucked them away. "Thanks," I said.

"Feel protected now? They give you a sense of invulnerability?"

"You feel invulnerable, Okking?"

His sneer tilted over and crashed. "The hell," he said. He waved me out of there; I went, as grateful as ever.

By the time I got out of the building, the sky was getting dusky in the east. I heard the recorded cries of muezzins from minarets all over the city. It had been a busy day. I wanted a drink, but I still had some things to do before I could let myself ease off a little. I walked into the hotel and went up to my room, stripped off my robe and head-gear, and took a shower. I let the hot water pound against my body for a quarter of an hour; I just rotated under it like lamb on a spit. I washed my hair and soaped my face two or three times. It was regrettable but necessary: the beard had to come off. I had gotten clever, but Khan's reminder in my mailbox made it plain that I still wasn't clever enough. First, I cut my long reddish-brown hair short.

I hadn't seen my upper lip since I was a teenager, so the short, harsh swipes with the razor gave me some twinges of regret. They passed quickly; after a while I was actually curious about what I looked like under it all. In another fifteen minutes I had eliminated the beard completely, going back over every place on my neck and face until the skin stung and blood stood out along bright red slashes.

When I realized what I reminded myself of, I couldn't look at my reflection any longer. I threw cold water on my face and toweled off. I imagined thumbing my nose at Friedlander Bey and the rest of the sophisticated undesirables of the city. Then I could find my way back to Algeria and spend the rest of my life there, watching goats die.

I brushed my hair and went into the bedroom, where I opened the packages from the men's store. I dressed slowly, turning some thoughts over in my mind. One notion eclipsed everything else: whatever happened, I wasn't going to chip in a personality module again.

I would use every daddy that offered help, but they just extended my own personality. No human thinking machine of fact or fiction was any good to me—none of them had ever faced this situation, none of them had ever been in the Budayeen. I needed to keep my own wits about me, not those of some irrelevant construct.

It felt good to get that settled. It was the compromise I'd been searching for ever since Papa first told me I'd volunteered to get wired. I smiled. Some weight—negligible, a quarter-pound, maybe—lifted from my shoulders.

I won't say how long it took me to get my necktie on. There were clip-on ties, but the shop where I'd bought everything frowned on their existence.

I tucked my shirt into my trousers, fastened everything, put on my shoes, and threw on the suit jacket. Then I stepped back to look at my new self in the mirror. I cleaned some dried blood from my neck and chin. I looked good, faster than light with a little money in my pocket. You know what I mean. *I* was the same as always: the *clothes* looked first-rate. That was fine, because most people only look at the clothes, anyway. It was more important that for the first time, I believed the whole nightmare was close to resolution. I had gone most of the way through a dark tunnel, and only one or two obscure shapes hid the welcome light at the end of it.

I put the phone on my belt, invisible beneath the suit coat. As an afterthought, I slipped the little needle gun into a pocket; it barely made a bulge, and I was thinking "better safe than sorry." My malicious mind was telling me "safe *and* sorry"; but it was too late at night to listen to my mind, I'd been doing that all day. I was just going down to the hotel's bar for a little while, that's all.

Nevertheless, Xarghis Khan knew what I looked like, and I knew nothing about him except that he probably didn't look anything like James Bond. I remembered what Hassan had said only a few hours ago: "I trust nobody."

That was the plan, but was it practical? Was it even possible to go through a single day being totally suspicious? How many people did I trust without even thinking about it—people who, if they felt like getting rid of me, could have murdered me quickly and simply? Yasmin, for one. The Half-Hajj, I'd even invited him up to my apartment; all he needed to be the assassin was the wrong moddy. Even Bill, my favorite cabbie; even Chiri, who owned the hugest collection of moddies in the Budayeen. I'd go crazy if I kept thinking like that.

What if Okking himself was the very murderer he was pretending to track down? Or Hajjar?

Or Friedlander Bey?

Now I was thinking like the Maghrebi bean-eater they all thought I was. I shook it off, left the hotel room, and rode the elevator down to the mezzanine and the dimly lighted bar. There weren't many people there: the city had few enough tourists to begin with, and this was an expensive and quiet hotel. I looked along the bar and saw three men on the stools, all leaning together and talking quietly. To my right there were four more groups, mostly men, sitting at tables. Recorded European or American music played softly. The theme of the bar seemed to be expressed in potted ferns and stucco walls painted pastel pink and orange. When the bartender raised his eyebrows at me, I ordered a gin and bingara. He made it just the way I liked, down to the splash of Rose's. That was a point for the cosmopolitans.

The drink came and I paid for it. I sipped at it, asking myself why I'd thought sitting here would help me forget my problems. Then she drifted up to me, moving in an unhuman slow-motion as if she were half-asleep or drugged. It didn't show in her smile or her speech, though. "Do you mind if I sit with you?" Trudi asked.

"Of course not." I smiled graciously at her, but my mind was roiling with questions.

She told the barman she wanted peppermint schnapps. I would have put fifty kiam on that. I waited until she got her drink; I paid for it, and she thanked me with another languorous smile.

"How do you feel?" I asked.

She wrinkled her nose. "What do you mean?"

"After answering questions all day for the lieutenant's men."

"Oh, they were all as nice as they could be."

I didn't say anything for a few seconds. "How did you find me?"

"Well," she gestured vaguely, "I knew you were staying here. You brought me here this afternoon. And your name—"

"I never told you my name."

"—I heard it from the policemen."

"And you recognized me? Though I don't look anything like the way I did when you met me? Even though I've never worn clothes like these before or been without my beard?"

She gave me one of those smiles that tell you that men are such fools. "Aren't you glad to see me?" she asked, with that glaze of hurt feelings that the Trudies do so well.

I went back to my gin. "One of the reasons I came down to the bar. Just on the chance you'd come in."

"And here I am."

"I'll always remember that," I said. "Would you excuse me? I'm a couple drinks ahead of you."

"Sure, I'll be fine."

"Thanks." I went off to the men's room, got myself in a stall, and unclipped my phone. I called Okking's number. A voice I didn't recognize told me he was in his office, asleep for the night, and he wasn't going to be awakened except for an emergency. Was this an emergency? I said I didn't think so, but that if it was I'd get back to him. I asked for Hajjar, but he was out on an investigation. I got Hajjar's number and punched it.

He let his phone ring a while. I wondered if he were really investigating anything or just soaking up ambience. "What is it?" he snarled.

"Hajjar? You sound out of breath. Lifting weights or something?"

"Who is this? How'd you get—"

"Audran. Okking's out for the night. Listen, what did you learn from Seipolt's blonde?"

The phone went mute for a moment, then Hajjar's voice came back on, a little more friendly. "Trudi? We knocked her out, dug around as deep as we could, and brought her back up. She didn't know anything. That worried us, so we put her out a second time. Nobody should know as much nothing as she does and still be alive. But she's clean, Audran. I've known tent stakes that had more going for them than she does, but all she knows about Seipolt is his first name."

"Then why is she still alive and Seipolt and the others aren't?"

"The killer didn't know she was there. Xarghis Khan would have jammed the living daylights out of her, then maybe killed her. As it happened, our Trudi was in her room taking a nap after lunch. She doesn't remember if she locked her door. She's alive because she'd only been there a few days and she wasn't part of the regular household."

"How'd she react to the news?"

"We fed her the facts while she was under, and took out all the horribleness for her. It's like she read about it in the papers."

"Praise Allah, you cops are nice. Did you put anybody on her when she left?"

"You *see* anybody?"

That stung me. "What makes you so sure I'm with her?"

"Why else would you be calling me about her this time of night? She's clean, sucker, as far as we could tell. As for anything else, well, we didn't give her a blood test, so you're on your own." The line went dead.

I grimaced, clipped the phone back on my belt, and went out to the bar. I spent the rest of that gin and tonic looking for Trudi's shadow, but I didn't see a likely candidate. We went out to have something to eat, to give me the chance to ease my mind. By the end of the supper, I was sure no one was following either Trudi or me. We went back to the bar and had a few more drinks and got to know each other. She decided we knew each other well enough just before midnight.

"It's kind of noisy in here, isn't it?" she said.

I nodded solemnly. There were only three other people in the bar now, and that included the block of wood who was making our drinks. It was just that time when either Trudi or I had to say something stupid, and she beat me to it. It was right then that I simultaneously misplaced my caution and decided to teach Yasmin a lesson. Listen, I was mildly drunk, I was depressed and lonely, Trudi was really a sweet girl and absolutely gorgeous—how many do you need?

When we went upstairs, Trudi smiled at me and kissed me a few times, slowly and deeply, as though morning wasn't coming until after lunch some time. Then she told me it was her turn to use the bathroom. I waited for her to close the door, then I called down to the desk and asked them to be sure I was awake by seven the next morning. I took out the small plastic needle gun, threw back the bedspread, and hid the weapon quickly. Trudi came out of the bathroom with her dress hanging loosely, its fastenings left undone. She smiled at me, a lazy, knowing smile. As she came toward me, my only thought was that this would be the first time I'd ever gone to sleep with a gun under my pillow.

"What are you thinking about?" she asked.

"Oh, just that you don't look bad, for a real girl."

"You don't like real girls?" she whispered in my ear.

"I just haven't been with one for a while. It's just worked out that way."

"You like toys better?" she murmured, but there was no more room for discussion.

SEVENTEEN

When the phone rang, I was dreaming that my mother was shouting at me. She was screaming so loud that I couldn't recognize her, I just knew it was her. We started arguing about Yasmin, but that changed; we fought about living in the city, and we fought about how I could never be expected to understand anything because the only thing I ever thought about was myself. My part was limited to crying "I am not!" while my heart thudded in my sleep.

I thrashed awake, bleary and still tired. I squinted at the phone, then picked it up. A voice said, "Good morning. Seven o'clock." Then there was a click. I put the phone back and sat up in bed. I took a deep breath that hesitated and hitched two or three times on the way in. I wanted to go back to sleep, even if it meant nightmares. I didn't want to get up and face another day like yesterday.

Trudi wasn't in bed. I swung my feet to the floor and walked naked around the small hotel room. She wasn't in the bathroom, either, but she had written a note for me and left it on the bureau. It said:

Dear Marîd—
Thanks for everything. You're a dear, sweet man. I hope we meet again sometime.
I have to go now, so I'm sure you won't mind if I borrow the fare from your wallet.

Love ya,
Trudi
(My real name is Gunter
Erich von S.

You mean you really
didn't know, or were you just
being nice?)

There is very little I've missed in my life, as far as sex goes. My secret fantasies don't concern what, they concern who. I'd seen and heard everything, I thought. The only thing I'd never heard faked— until, evidently, last night—was that involuntary animal catch in a woman's breathing, the very first one, before the lovemaking has even had time to become rhythmical. I glanced down at Trudi's note again, remembering all the times Jacques, Mahmoud, Saied, and I had sat at a table at the Solace, watching people walk by. "Oh, her? She's a female-to-male sex-change in drag." I could read *everybody*. I was famous for it.

I swore I'd never tell anyone anything ever again. I wondered if the world ever got tired of its jokes; no, that was too much to hope for. The jokes would go on and on, getting worse and worse. Right now I was certain that if age and experience couldn't stop the jokes, there was nothing about death that would make them stop, either.

I folded my new clothing carefully and packed it in the zipper bag. I wore my white robe and *keffiya* again today, making yet another new look—Arab costume but clean-shaven. The man of a thousand faces. Today I wanted to take Hajjar up on his promise to let me use the police computer files. I wanted to fill in a little background, on the police themselves. I wanted to find out as much as I could about Okking's link to Bond/Khan.

Instead of walking, I took a cab to the police station. It wasn't that I was getting spoiled by the luxury Papa was paying for; I just felt the urgent pressing of events. I was killing time as fast as it was killing me. The daddies were buzzing in my head, and I didn't feel muscle-weary, hungry, or thirsty. I wasn't angry or afraid, either; some people might have warned me that not being afraid was dangerous. Maybe I should have been afraid, a little.

I watched Okking eat a late breakfast in his flimsy fortress while I waited for Hajjar to get back to his desk. When the sergeant came in, he gave me a distracted look. "You're not the only bakebrain I have to worry about, Audran," he said in a surly voice. "We've got thirty other jerks giving us fantasy information and inside words they dig out of dreams and teacups."

"You'll be glad I don't have a goddamn piece of information for you, then. I came to get some from you. You said I could use your files."

"Oh, yeah, sure; but not here. If Okking saw you, he'd split my skull. I'll call downstairs. You can use one of the terminals on the second floor."

"I don't care where it is," I said. Hajjar made the phone call, typed out a pass for me, and signed it. I thanked him and found my way down to the data bank. A young woman with Southeast Asian features led me to an unused screen, showed me how to get from one menu to the next, and told me that if I had any questions, the machine itself would answer them. She wasn't a computer expert or a librarian; she just managed traffic flow in the big room.

First I checked the general files, which were much like a news agency's morgue. When I typed in a name, the computer gave me every fact available to it concerning the person. The first name I entered was Okking's. The cursor paused for a second or two, then lettered steadily across the display in Arabic, right to left. I learned Okking's first name, his middle name, his age, where he'd been born, what he'd done before coming to the city, all the stuff that gets put on a form above the important double line. Below that line comes the really vital information; depending on whose form it is, that can be the subject's medical record, arrest record, credit history, political involvement, sexual preference(s), or anything else that may one day be pertinent.

As for Okking, below that double line there was nothing. Absolutely nothing. *Al-Sifr*, zero.

At first I assumed there was some kind of computer problem. I started over again, returning to the first menu, choosing the sort of information I was looking for, and typing in Okking's name. And waited.

Mâ shî. Nothing.

Okking had done this, I was sure. He had covered his tracks, just as his boy Khan was now covering his own. If I wanted to travel to Europe, to Okking's birthplace, I might learn more about him, but only to the point when he left there to come to the city. Since then, he did not exist at all, not officially speaking.

I typed in Universal Export, the code name of James Bond's espionage group. I had seen it on an envelope on Okking's desk once. Again, there were no entries.

I tried James Bond without hope, and turned up nothing. Similarly with Xarghis Khan. The real Khan and the "real" Bond had never visited the city, so there was no file on either of them.

I thought about other people I might spy on—Yasmin, Friedlander Bey, even myself—but I decided to leave my curiosity unsatisfied until a less urgent occasion. I entered Hajjar's name and was not astonished by what I read. He was about two years younger than I was, Jordanian, with a moderately long arrest record before coming to the city. A psychological profile agreed point for point with my own estimation of him; you didn't dare trust him as far as he could run with a camel on his back. He was suspected of smuggling drugs and money to prisoners. He was once investigated in connection with the disappearance of a good deal of confiscated property, but nothing definite came of it. The official file put forth the possibility that Hajjar might be profiting from his position on the police force, that he might be selling his influence to private citizens or criminal organizations. The report suggested that he might not be above such abuses of authority as extortion, racketeering, and conspiracy, among other law-enforcement frailties.

Hajjar? Come now, what ever gave you that idea? Allah forfend.

I shook my head ruefully. Police departments all over the world are identical in two respects: they all have a fondness for breaking your head open with little or no provocation, and they can't see the simple truth if it's lying in front of them naked with its legs spread. The police don't enforce laws; they don't even get busy until after the laws are broken. They solve crimes at a pitifully low rate of success. What the police are, to be honest, is a kind of secretarial pool that records the names of the victims and the statements of the witnesses. After enough time passes, they can safely shove this information to the back of the filing system to make room for more.

Oh yeah, the police help little old ladies across the street. So I'm told.

One by one, I entered the names of everyone who'd been connected to Nikki, beginning with her uncle, Bogatyrev. The entries on the old Russian and on Nikki matched exactly what Okking had finally told me about them. I figured that if Okking could excise himself from this system, he could alter its remaining records in other ways, too. I wouldn't find anything useful here except by accident or Okking's oversight. I went on with a diminished hope of success.

I had none. At last I changed my mind and read the entries on Yasmin, Papa, and Chiri, on the Black Widow Sisters, on Seipolt and Abdoulaye. The files told me that Hassan was likely a hypocrite, because he would not use brain implants for his business, on religious grounds, yet he was a known pederast. That wasn't news to me. The only thing that I might suggest to Hassan someday was that the American boy, who already had his skull wired, might be more useful as an accounting tool than just sitting on a stool in Hassan's bare shop.

The only person I knew on whom I didn't peep was myself. I didn't want to know what they thought about me.

After I searched the files for my friends' histories, I looked at telephone company records for the phones in the police station. There was nothing enlightening there, either; Okking wouldn't have used his office phone to call Bond. It was like I was standing at the hub of a lot of radiating roads, all of them dead ends.

I walked out of there with food for thought but no new facts. I liked knowing what the files had to say about Hajjar and the others; and the reticence it showed toward Okking—and, not so mysteriously, toward Friedlander Bey—was provocative if not informative. I thought about it all as I wandered into the Budayeen. In a few minutes I was back at my apartment building.

Why had I come here? Well, I didn't want to sleep in the hotel room another night. At least one assassin knew I was there. I needed another base of operations, one that would be safe for at least a day or two. As I got more accustomed to letting the daddies help me in my planning, my decision making got faster and less influenced by my emotions. I now felt completely in control, cool and assured. I wanted to get a message to Papa, and then I would find another temporary place to sleep.

My apartment was just the way I'd left it. Truthfully, I hadn't been away long, although it felt like weeks; my time sense was all distorted. Tossing the zipper bag onto the mattress, I sat down and murmured Hassan's commcode into my phone. It rang three times before he answered. *"Marhaba,"* he said. He sounded tired.

"Hello, Hassan, this is Audran. I need to have a meeting with Friedlander Bey, and I was hoping you could fix it for me."

"He will be glad that you are showing interest in doing things the proper way, my nephew. Certainly, he will want to see you and learn from you what progress you are making. Do you wish an appointment for this afternoon?"

"As soon as you can, Hassan."

"I will take care of it, O clever one, and I will call you back to tell you of the arrangements."

"Thanks. Before you go, I want to ask you a question. Do you know if there's any connection between Papa and Lutz Seipolt?"

There was a long silence while Hassan framed his reply. "Not any longer, my nephew. Seipolt is dead, is he not?"

"I know that," I said impatiently.

"Seipolt was involved only in the import-export trade. He dealt only in cheap trinkets, nothing that would be of interest to Papa."

"Then so far as you know, Papa never tried to cut himself a piece of Seipolt's business?"

"My nephew, Seipolt's business was barely worth mentioning. He was just a small businessman, like myself."

"But, also like yourself, he felt he needed a secondary income to make ends meet. You work for Friedlander Bey, and Seipolt worked for the Germans."

"By the life of my eyes! Is that so? Seipolt, a spy?"

"I'd be willing to bet you already knew that. Never mind. Did *you* ever have any dealings with him?"

"What do you mean?" Hassan's voice became harsh.

"Business. Import-export. You have that in common."

"Oh, well, I bought items from him now and then, if he offered some particularly interesting European goods; but I don't think he ever bought anything from me."

That didn't get me anywhere. At Hassan's request, I gave him a quick rundown of the events since my discovery of Seipolt's body. By the time I finished, he was thoroughly frightened again. I told him about Okking and the doctored police records. "That's why I need to see Friedlander Bey," I said.

"You suspect something?" asked Hassan.

"It isn't only the missing information in the files, and the fact that Okking's a foreign agent. I just can't believe that he has the full resources of the department looking into these murders, and yet he hasn't come forward with a single useful piece of information for me. I'm sure he knows much more than he's telling me. Papa promised that he'd pressure Okking into sharing what he knows. I need to hear all that."

"Of course, my nephew, don't worry about that. It shall be done, *inshallah*. Then you have no true idea of how much the lieutenant actually knows?"

"That is the way of the *flic*. He might have the whole case wrapped up, or he may know even less than I do. He's a master at giving you the runaround."

"He cannot give Friedlander Bey the runaround."

"He'll try."

"He won't succeed. Do you need more money, O clever one?"

Hell, I could always use more money. "No, Hassan, I'm doing fine for now. Papa has been more than generous."

"If you need cash to further your investigation, you have only to contact me. You are doing an excellent job, my son."

"At least I'm not dead yet."

"You have the wit of a poet, my darling. I must go now. Business is business, you know."

"Right, Hassan. Call me back after you've spoken with Papa."

"Praise be to Allah for your safety."

"Allah yisallimak," I said. I stood up and tucked the phone away again; then I began looking for the one other object that I'd found in Nikki's purse: the scarab she had taken from Seipolt's collection. That brass reproduction tied Nikki directly to Seipolt, as did her ring that I'd seen in the German's house. Of course, with Seipolt now among the dear departed, these items were of questionable value. True, Dr. Yeniknani still had the homemade moddy; that might be an important piece of evidence. I thought it was time to begin preparing a presentation of all I'd learned, so that I could eventually turn it all in to the authorities. Not Okking, of course, and not Hajjar. I wasn't sure who the proper authorities were, but I knew there had to be some somewhere. The three items were not enough to convict anyone in a European court of law, but according to Islamic justice, they were plenty.

I found the scarab under the edge of the mattress. I unzipped my bag and stuffed Seipolt's tourist's souvenir down under my clothing. I packed carefully, wanting to be sure that everything I owned was out of the apartment. Then I kicked a lot of scraps and rubbish into low piles here and there. I didn't feel like spending a lot of time cleaning. When I finished, there was nothing in the room that showed that I'd ever lived there. I felt a stinging sadness: I'd lived in that apartment longer than in any other single place in my life. If anywhere could truly be called my home, this little apartment should be it. Now, though, it was a big, abandoned room with dirty windows and a torn mattress on the floor. I went out, shutting the door behind me.

I returned my keys to Qasim, the landlord. He was surprised and upset that I was going. "I've liked living in your building," I told him, "but it pleases Allah that now I must move on."

He embraced me and called on Allah to lead each of us in righteousness unto Paradise.

I went to the bank and used the card to withdraw my entire account, closing it. I stuffed the bills into the envelope Friedlander Bey had sent me. When I got myself another place to stay, I'd take it out and see how much I had altogether; I was kind of teasing myself by not peeking now.

My third stop was the Hotel Palazzo di Marco Aurelio. I was dressed now in my *gallebeya* and *keffiya*, but with my short haircut and clean-shaven face. I don't think the desk clerk recognized me.

"I paid for a week in advance," I said, "but business matters force me to check out earlier than I planned."

The desk man murmured. "We're sorry to hear that, sir. We've enjoyed having you." I nodded and tossed my room's tag onto the counter. "Just let me look at . . ." He keyed the room number into his terminal, saw that the hotel did indeed owe me a little money, and began getting the voucher printed out.

"You've all been very kind," I said.

He smiled. "It is our pleasure," he said. He handed me the voucher and pointed to the cashier. I thanked him again. A few moments later I crammed the partial refund in my zipper bag with the rest of my money.

Carrying my cash, my moddies and daddies, and my clothing in the zipper bag, I walked south and west, away from the Budayeen and away from the expensive shopping district beside the Boulevard il-Jameel. I came to a *fellahîn* neighborhood of twisting streets and alleys, where the houses were small, flat-topped, needing whitewash, with windows covered by shutters or thin wooden lattices. Some were in better repair, with attempts at gardening in the dry earth at the base of the walls. Others looked derelict, their gap-toothed shutters hanging in the sun like tongues of panting dogs. I went up to a well-kept house and rapped on the door. I waited a few minutes until it opened. A large, heavily muscled man with a full black beard glared down at me. His eyes were narrowed suspiciously, and in the corner of his mouth his teeth were chewing away at a splinter of wood. He waited for me to speak.

With no confidence at all, I launched into my story. "I have been stranded in this city by my companions. They stole all our merchandise and my money, too. I must beg in the name of Allah and the Apostle of God, may the blessings of Allah be upon him and peace, your hospitality for today and for this evening."

"I see," said the man in a surly voice. "The house is closed."

"I will give you no cause for offense. I will—"

"Why don't you try begging where the hospitality is more generous? People tell me there are families here and about with enough to eat for themselves and also for dogs and strangers, as well. Me, I'm lucky to earn a little money for beans and bread for my wife and my four children."

I understood. "I know you don't need trouble. When I was robbed, my companions didn't know that I always keep a little extra cash in my bag. They greedily took everything in plain sight, leaving me with enough to live on for one or two days, until I can make my way back and demand a lawful accounting of them."

The man just stared at me, waiting for something magical to appear. I unslung my zipper bag and opened it. I let him watch me shove the clothing aside—my shirts, my trousers, socks—until I reached down and pulled out a paper bank note. "Twenty kiam," I said sadly, "that's all they left me with."

My new friend's face went through a rapid selection of emotions. In this neighborhood, twenty-kiam notes made their presence felt with noise and shouting. The man may not have been sure of me, but I knew what *he* was thinking.

"If you would give me the benefit of your hospitality and protection for the next two days," I said, "I will let you have all the money you see here." I thrust the twenty closer to his widening eyes.

The man wavered visibly; if he'd had big, flat leaves, he would have rustled. He didn't like strangers—hell, *no one* likes strangers. He didn't like the idea of inviting one into his house for a couple of days. Twenty kiam, though, was equal to several days' pay for him. When I looked closely at him again, I knew that he wasn't sizing me up anymore—he was spending the twenty kiam a hundred different ways. All I had to do was wait.

"We are not wealthy people, O sir."

"Then the twenty kiam will ease your life."

"It would, indeed, O sir, and I desire to have it; however, I am shamed to permit such an excellent one as you to witness the squalor of my house."

"I have seen squalor greater than any you can imagine, my friend, and I have risen above it even as you may. I was not always as I appear to you. It was only the will of Allah that I be flung down to the deepest pits of misery, in order that I might return to take back what has been torn from me. Will you help me? Allah will bring good fortune to all who are generous to me on my way."

The *fellah* looked at me in confusion for a long while. At first, I knew he thought I was just crazy, and the best thing was to run as far away from me as possible. My babbling sounded like some kidnapped prince's speech from the old tales. The stories were fine for late at night, for murmuring around the fire after a simple supper and before sleep and troubled dreams. In the light of day, however, a confrontation like this had nothing to make it seem plausible. Nothing except the money, waving like the frond of a date palm in my hand. My friend's eyes were fixed on the twenty kiam, and I doubt that he could have described my face to anyone.

In the end, I was admitted into the house of my host, Ishak Jarir. He maintained a strict discipline, and I saw no women. There was a second floor above, where the family members slept, and where there were a few small closets for storage. Jarir opened a plain wooden door to one of these and roughly shoved me inside. "You will be safe here," he said in a whisper. "If your treacherous friends come and inquire about you, no one in this house has seen you. But you may stay only until after morning prayers tomorrow."

"I thank Allah that in His wisdom He has guided me to so generous a man as you. I have yet an errand to run, and if everything occurs as I foresee, I will return with a bank note the twin of that you hold in your hand. The twin shall be yours, as well."

Jarir didn't want to hear any of the details. "May your undertaking be prosperous," he said. "Be warned, though: if you come back after last prayers, you will not be admitted."

"It is as you say, honorable one." I looked over my shoulder at the pile of rags that would be my home that night, smiled innocently at Ishak Jarir, and got out of his house suppressing a shudder.

I turned down the narrow, stone-paved street that I thought would take me back to the Boulevard il-Jameel. As the street began a slow curve to the left, I knew that I'd made a mistake, but it was going in the right direction anyway, so I followed it. When I got around the turn, however, there was nothing but the blank brick rear walls of buildings hedging in a reeking, dead-end alley. I muttered a curse and turned around to retrace my steps.

There was a man blocking my way. He was thin, with a patchy, slovenly kept beard and a sheepish smile on his face. He was wearing an open-necked yellow knit shirt, a rumpled and creased brown business suit, a white *keffiya* with red checks, and scuffed brown oxford shoes. His foolish expression reminded me of Fuad, the idiot from the Budayeen. Evidently he had followed me up the dead-end street; I hadn't heard him come up behind me.

I don't like people catfooting up behind me; I unzipped my bag while I stared at him. He just stood there, shifting his weight from one foot to the other and grinning. I took out a couple of daddies and zipped the bag closed again. I started to walk by him, but he stopped me with a hand on my chest. I looked down at the hand and back up at his face. "I don't like being touched," I said.

He shrank back as if he had defiled the holy of holies. "A thousand pardons," he said weakly.

"You following me for some reason?"

"I thought you might be interested in what I have here." He indicated an imitation-leather briefcase he carried in one hand.

"You a salesman?"

"I sell moddies, sir, and a wide selection of the most useful and interesting add-ons in the business. I'd like to show them to you."

"No, thanks."

He raised his eyebrows, not so sheepish now, as if I'd asked him to go right ahead. "It won't take a moment, and very possibly I have just the thing you're looking for."

"I'm not looking for anything in particular."

"Sure you are, sir, or you wouldn't have gotten wired, now, would you?"

I shrugged. He knelt down and opened his sample case. I was determined that he wasn't going to sell me anything. I don't do business with weasels.

He was taking moddies and daddies out of the case and lining them up in a neat row in front of his briefcase. When he was finished he looked up at me. I could tell how proud he was of his merchandise. "Well," he said. There was an anticipatory hush.

"Well what?" I asked.

"What do you think of them?"

"The moddies? They look like every other moddy I've ever seen. What are they?"

He grabbed the first moddy in the line. He flipped it to me and I caught it; a quick glimpse told me it was unlabeled, made of tougher plastic than the usual moddies I saw at Laila's and in the souks. Bootleg. "You know that one already," the man said, giving me that sorry smile again.

That earned him a sharp look.

He pulled off his *keffiya*. He had thinning brown hair hanging down and covering his ears. It looked like it hadn't been washed in a month. One hand popped out the moddy he'd been wearing. The timid salesman vanished. The man's jaws went slack and his eyes lost their focus, but with practiced speed he chipped in another of his homemade moddies. Suddenly his eyes narrowed and his mouth set in a hard, sadistic leer. He had transformed himself from one man to another; he didn't need the usual physical disguises: the entirely different set of postures, mannerisms, expressions, and speech patterns was more effective than any combination of wigs and makeup could be.

I was in trouble. I held James Bond in my hand, and I was staring into the cold eyes of Xarghis Moghadhîl Khan. I was staring into madness. I reached up and chipped in the two daddies. One would let me get unnatural, desperate strength from my muscles, without weariness or pain, until the tissue actually tore apart. The second cut out all sound; I needed to concentrate. Khan snarled at me. There was a long, vicious dagger in his hand now, its hilt of silver decorated with colored stones, its guard of gold. "Sit down," I read his lips. "On the ground."

I wasn't going to sit down for him. My hand moved about four inches, seeking the needle gun under my robes. My hand moved a little and stopped, because I remembered that the needle gun was still beneath the pillow in the hotel room. By now the chambermaid would have found it. And the seizure gun was zipped away safely in my bag. I backed away from Khan. "I've been following you for a long time, Mr. Audran. I watched you at the police station, at Friedlander Bey's, at Seipolt's house, at the hotel. I could have killed you that night when I pretended you were just a goddamn robber, but I didn't want to be interrupted. I waited for the right moment. *Now*, Mr. Audran, now you will die." It was wonderfully simple to read his lips: the whole world had relaxed and was moving only half as fast as normal. He and I had all the time we needed. . . .

Khan's mouth twisted. He enjoyed this part. He stalked me back deeper into the alley. My eyes were fixed on his gleaming knife, with which Khan intended not only to kill me but also to hack my body to pieces. He meant to drape my bowels over the filthy stones and the refuse like holiday garlands. Some people are terrified of death; others are even more terrified of the agony that might come first. To be honest, that's me. I knew that some day I'd have to die, but I hoped it would be quick and painless—in my sleep, if I was lucky. Tortured first by Khan: that was definitely not how I wanted to go out.

The daddies kept me from panicking. If I let myself get too scared, I'd be souvlaki in five minutes. I backed away further, scanning the alley for something that would give me a chance against this maniac and his dagger. I was running out of time.

Khan's lips pulled back from his teeth and he charged me, uttering wordless cries. He held the dagger overhand at shoulder height, coming at me like Lady Macbeth. I let him take three steps, then I moved to my left and rushed him. He expected me to flee backward, and when I went at him he flinched. My left hand reached for his right wrist, my right arm swung behind his forearm and held his hand steady. I bent his knife hand back with my left hand, against the fulcrum of my right arm. Usually you can disarm an attacker like that, but Khan was strong. He was stronger than that nearly emaciated body should have been; the insanity gave him a little extra power, and so did his moddy and daddies.

Khan's free hand had me by the throat, and he was forcing my head back. I got my right leg behind his and pulled his feet out from under him. We both went down; and as we fell I covered his face with my right hand. I made sure to slam the back of his head into the ground as hard as I could. I landed on his wrist with my knee, and his hand opened. I threw his dagger as far as I could, then used both hands to beat Khan's head on the slimy pavement a few more times. Khan was dazed, but it didn't last long. He rolled out of my grasp and flung himself back on me, tearing and biting at my flesh. We wrestled, each trying to get an advantage, but we were grappling so tightly that I couldn't swing my fists. I couldn't even work my arms free. Meanwhile, he was hurting me, raking me with his black nails, drawing blood with his teeth, bludgeoning me with his knees.

Khan shrieked and heaved me to the side; then he leaped, and before I could get away, he landed on top of me again. He held my arms pinned with one knee and one hand. He raised a fist, ready to smash it down on my throat. I cried out and tried to roll him off, but I couldn't move. I struggled, and I saw the lunatic light of victory in his eyes. He was crooning some inarticulate prayer. With a wild bellow, he slammed his fist down and caught the side of my face. I almost lost consciousness.

Khan ran for his knife. I forced myself to sit up and search wildly for my zipper bag. Khan found the dagger and was coming at me. I got my bag open and threw everything out on the ground. Just as Khan was three feet from me, I nailed him with one long burst from the seizure gun. Khan gave a gurgling cry and toppled beside me. He would be out for hours.

The daddies blocked most of my pain, but not all; the rest they held at a distance. Still, I couldn't move yet, and it would be a few minutes before I could do anything useful. I watched Khan's skin turn a cyanotic blue as he fought to draw air into his lungs. He went into convulsions and then suddenly relaxed completely, only a few inches from me. I sat and gasped until I was able to shake off the effects of the fight. Then the first thing I did was pop the Khan moddy out of his head. I called Lieutenant Okking to give him the good news.

Eighteen

i found my pill case in the zipper bag and took seven or eight sunnies. I was trying something new. My body was aching after the fight with Khan, but it wasn't the pain so much; purely in the interest of science, I wanted to see how the opiate would affect my augmented sensations. While I waited for Okking, I learned the truth empirically: the daddy that cleared alcohol from my system at a faster rate also kicked out the sunnies, too. Who needs that? I popped that moddy and took another hit of Sonneine.

When Okking arrived he was buoyant. That was the only word to describe him. I'd never seen him so pleased. He was attentive and gracious to me, concerned for my wounds and pain. He was so nice, I figured the holo news people were around taping, but I was wrong. "I guess you're one up on me now, Audran," he said.

I figured he owed me a lot more than that. "I've done your whole goddamn job for you, Okking."

Even that didn't puncture his elation. "Maybe, maybe. At least now I can get some sleep. I couldn't even eat without imagining Selima, Seipolt, and the others."

Khan roused; without a moddy in his socket, however, he began to scream. I recalled how awful I felt when I took the daddies out after just a few days. Who knows how long Khan—whatever his real name was—had gone, hiding beneath first one moddy and then another. Maybe without a false personality chipped in, he wasn't able to confront the inhuman acts he'd performed. He lay on the pavement, his hands cuffed behind him and his ankles chained together, thrashing and thundering curses at us. Okking watched him for a few seconds. "Drag him out of here," he said to a couple of uniformed officers.

They were none too gentle about it, but Khan got no sympathy from me. "Now what?" I asked Okking.

He sobered up a little. "I think it's about time for me to offer my resignation," he said.

"When the news gets around that you've accepted money from a foreign government, you're not going to be very popular. You've dented your credibility."

He nodded. "The word has already gotten around, at least in the circles that count. I've been given the choice of finding employment out of the city or spending the rest of my life behind bars in one of your typical wog hellholes. I don't see how they can fling people into those prisons, they're right out of the Dark Ages."

"You've put the numbers on your share of the population, Okking. You'll have a big welcoming committee waiting for you."

He shivered. "I think as soon as I get my personal affairs tied up, I'll just pack my bags and slip away into the night. I wish they'd give me a character reference, though. I mean, foreign agent or no, I've done good work for the city. I never compromised my integrity, except a few times."

"How many other people can honestly say the same? You're one of a kind, Okking." He was just the kind of guy who would walk away from this and turn it into a recommendation on his resume. He'd find work somewhere.

"You like seeing me in trouble, don't you, Audran?"

As a matter of fact, I did. Rather than answer, though, I turned to my zipper bag and repacked it; I'd learned my lesson, so I tucked the seizure gun under my robe. From Okking's conversation, I gathered that the formal questioning was finished, that I could go now. "Are you going to stay in the city until Nikki's killer is caught?" I asked. "Are you at least going to do that much?" I turned to face him.

He was surprised. "Nikki? What are you talking about? We got the killer, he's on his way to the chopping block right now. You're obsessed, Audran. You don't have any proof of your second killer. Lay off or you'll learn how fast heroes can become ex-heroes. You're getting boring."

If *that* wasn't a cop's way of thinking! I caught Khan and turned him over to Okking; now Okking was going to tell everybody that Khan had bumped them all, from Bogatyrev to Seipolt. Of course, Khan *had* killed Bogatyrev and Seipolt; but I was sure that he hadn't killed Nikki, Abdoulaye, or Tami. Did I have any proof? No, nothing tangible; but none of it hung together any other way. This was an international rat's nest; one side tried to kidnap Nikki and bring her alive to her father's country, and the other side wanted to kill her to prevent the scandal. If

Khan had murdered agents of both parties, it made sense only if he was merely a psychotic who cut up people senselessly, in no pattern. That just wasn't true. He was an assassin whose victims had been put away to further his employers' scheme and to protect his own anonymity. The man who cut Seipolt up was not a madman, he was not really Khan—he only wore a Khan moddy.

And that man had nothing to do with Nikki's death.

There was still another killer loose in the city, even if Okking found it convenient to forget him.

About ten minutes after Okking and his crew and I went our separate ways, the telephone rang. It was Hassan, calling back to tell me what Papa had said. "I've got some news, too, Hassan," I said.

"Friedlander Bey will see you shortly. He will send a car for you in fifteen minutes. I trust you are at home?"

"No, but I'll be waiting outside the building. I had some interesting company, but they've all gone away now."

"Good, my nephew. You deserved some pleasant relaxation with your friends."

I stared up at the cloud-covered sky, thinking about my confrontation with Khan, wondering if I should laugh at Hassan's words. "I didn't get much relaxing done," I said. I told him what had happened from the time I'd last talked to him until they carted Okking's hired killer away.

Hassan stammered at me in amazement. "Audran," he said when he finally regained control, "it pleases Allah that you are safe, that the maniac has been captured, and that Friedlander Bey's wisdom has triumphed."

"You right," I said. "Give all the credit to Papa. He was giving me the benefit of his wisdom, all right. Now that I think about it, I didn't get a hell of a lot more help from him than I got from Okking. Sure, he backed me into a corner and made me go along with having my head opened; but after that he just sat back and tossed money my way. Papa knows everything that goes on in the Budayeen, Hassan. You mean to tell me both he and Okking have been standing around with their thumbs in their ears, absolutely baffled? I don't buy that. I found out what Okking's part in all this was; I'd like even better to know what Papa's been doing behind the scenes."

"Silence, son of a diseased dog!" Hassan dropped his ingratiating manner and let his real self peek out, something he didn't do very often. "You still have much to learn about showing respect to your elders and betters." Then, just as suddenly, the old Hassan, Hassan the mendacious near-buffoon, returned. "You are still feeling the strain of the conflict. Forgive me for losing my patience with you, it is I who must be more understanding. All is as Allah wills, neither more nor less. So, my nephew, the car will call for you soon. Friedlander Bey will be well pleased."

"There isn't time to get him a little gift, Hassan."

He chuckled. "Your news will be gift enough. Go in peace, Audran."

I didn't say anything, but broke the connection. I resettled my zipper bag on my shoulder and walked toward my old apartment building. I would meet with Papa, and then I would hide in Ishak Jarir's closet. The bright side was that Khan was now out of the picture. Khan had been the only one of the two murderers who'd shown any desire to eliminate me. That meant the other one probably felt like letting me live. At least, I hoped so.

While I waited for Papa's limo to come, I thought about my battle with Khan. I hated the man violently—all I had to do was call to mind the horror of Selima's mutilated corpse, the revulsion I had felt while stumbling upon the dismembered bodies at Seipolt's house. First he had killed Bogatyrev, Nikki's own uncle who wanted her dead. Nikki was the key; all the other homicides were part of the frantic coverup that was supposed to keep the Russian scandal secret. I suppose it worked—oh, a lot of people here in the city knew about it, but without a live crown prince to embarrass the monarchy, there was no scandal back in White Russia. King Vyacheslav was safe on his throne, the royalists had won. In fact, with some clever and careful work on their part, they could use Nikki's murder to strengthen their grip on the unstable nation.

I didn't care about any of that. Following the brawl with Khan, I'd let him live—for a little while. He had a date now with the headsman in the courtyard of the Shimaal Mosque. Let him relive his brutalities in terror of Allah in the meantime.

The limo arrived and carried me to Friedlander Bey's estate. The butler escorted me to the same waiting room I'd seen twice before. I waited for Papa to complete his prayers. Friedlander Bey didn't make a great show of his devotion, which in a way made it all the more remarkable. Sometimes his belief shamed me; on those occasions I called up memories of the cruelties and crimes he was responsible for. I was only fooling myself; Allah knows none of us is perfect. I'm sure Friedlander Bey had no such illusions about himself. At least he asked his God to forgive him. Papa had explained it to me once before: he had to take care of a great number of relatives and associates, and sometimes the only way to protect them was to be unduly hard on outsiders. In that light, he was a great leader and a stern but loving father to his people. I, on the other hand, was a nobody who did a lot of illicit things myself, to no one's benefit; and I didn't even have the saving grace to beg Allah's pardon.

At last one of the two huge men who guarded Papa motioned to me. I entered the inner office; Friedlander Bey was waiting for me, seated on his antique lacquered divan. "Once again you do me great honor," he said. He indicated that I should be seated across the table from him, on the other divan.

"It is my honor to wish you good evening," I said.

"Will you take a morsel of bread with me?"

"You are most generous, O Shaykh," I said. I didn't feel wary or self-conscious, as I had on my previous meetings with Papa. After all, I had done the impossible for him. I had to keep reminding myself that the great man was now in my debt.

The servants brought the first course of the meal, and Friedlander Bey steered the conversation from one trivial subject to another. We sampled a little of many different dishes, everything succulently prepared and fragrant; I decided to chip out the hunger-override daddy, and when I did, I realized just how hungry I was. I was able to do justice to Papa's banquet. I wasn't, however, ready to pop the other daddies out. Not quite yet.

The servants brought platters of lamb, chicken, beef, and fish, served with delicately seasoned vegetables and savory rice. We ended with a selection of fresh fruit and cheeses; when all the dishes were cleared away, Papa and I relaxed with strong coffee flavored with spices.

"May your table last forever, O Shaykh," I said. "That was the finest meal I've ever enjoyed."

He was pleased. "I give thanks to God it was to your liking. Will you drink some more coffee?"

"Yes, thank you, O Shaykh."

The servants were gone and so, too, were the Stones Who Speak. Friedlander Bey poured my coffee himself, a gesture of sincere respect. "You must agree now that my plans for you were all in order," he said softly.

"Yes, O Shaykh. I am grateful."

He waved that aside. "It is we, the city and myself, who are grateful to you, my son. Now we must speak of the future."

"Forgive me, O Shaykh, but we cannot safely think of the future until we are secure in the present. One of the murderers who menaced us has been accounted for, but there is yet another at large. That evil one may have returned to his homeland, it is true; it is some time now since he struck down his victims. Yet it would be prudent for us to consider the possibility that he is still in the city. We would be well advised to learn his identity and his whereabouts."

The old man frowned and pulled at his gray cheek. "O my son, you alone believe in the existence of this other assassin. I do not see why the man who was James Bond, who was also Xarghis Khan, could not also be the torturer who slew Abdoulaye in so unspeakable a manner. You mentioned the many personality modules Khan had in his possession. Could not one of them make him the demon who also murdered the Crown Prince Nikolai Konstantin?"

What did I have to do to persuade these people? "O Shaykh," I said, "your theory requires that one man was working for both the fascist-communist alliance *and* the Byelorussian loyalists. He would, in effect, be neutralizing himself at every turn. It would postpone the outcome, which might be to his advantage although I don't understand how; and he would be able to report positive results to both sides for a time. Yet if all that were true, how would he resolve the situation? He would finally be rewarded by one side and punished by the other. It's foolish to think that one man might simultaneously be protecting Nikki *and* trying to murder her. In addition, the police examiner determined that the man who killed Tami, Abdoulaye, and Nikki was shorter and heavier than Khan, with thick, stubby fingers."

Friedlander Bey's face flickered with a weak smile. "Your vision, respected one, is acute but limited in scope. I myself have sometimes found it worthwhile to support both sides of a quarrel. What else can one do when one's beloved friends dispute a matter?"

"With your forgiveness, O Shaykh, I point out that we are speaking of many cold-blooded homicides, not quarrels or disputes. And neither the Germans nor the Russians are our beloved friends. Their internal bickerings are of no importance to us here in the city."

Papa shook his head. "Limited scope," he repeated softly. "When the infidel lands of the world break apart, we are revealed in our strength. When the great Shaitans, the United States and the Soviet Union, each fell into separate groups of states, it was a token from Allah."

"A token?" I asked, wondering what all this had to do with Nikki and the wires in my skull and the poor, forgotten people of the Budayeen.

Friedlander Bey's brows drew together, and he looked suddenly like a desert warrior, like the mighty chieftains who had come before him, all wielding the irresistible Sword of the Prophet. "Jihad," he murmured.

Jihad. Holy war.

I felt a prickle on my skin, and the blood roared in my ears. Now that the once-great nations were growing helpless in their poverty and dissension, it was time for Islam to complete the conquest that had begun so many centuries before. Papa's expression was very much like the look I had seen in the eyes of Xarghis Khan.

"It is what pleases Allah," I said. Friedlander Bey let out his breath and gave me a benevolent, approving smile. I was humoring the man. He was more dangerous now than I ever suspected. He had almost dictatorial power in the city; that, coupled with his great age and this delusion, made me walk carefully in his presence.

"You will do me a great favor if you will accept this," he said, leaning over the table with still another envelope. I suppose someone in his position thinks money is the perfect gift for the man who has everything. Anyone else might have found it offensive. I took the envelope.

"You overwhelm me," I said. "I cannot adequately express my thanks."

"The debt is mine, my son. You have done well, and I reward those who carry out my wishes."

I didn't look in the envelope—even I knew that would have been a breach of manners anywhere. "You are the father of generosity," I said.

We were getting along just fine. He liked me a lot better now than at our first meeting, so long ago. "I grow tired, my son, and so you must forgive me. My driver will return you to your home. Let us visit together again soon, and then we shall speak of your future."

"On the eyes and head, O lord of men. I am at your disposal."

"There is no might or power save in Allah the exalted and great." That sounds like a formula reply, but it's usually reserved for moments of danger or before some crucial action. I looked at the gray-haired man for some clue, but he had dismissed me. I made my farewells and left his office. I did a lot of thinking during the ride to the Budayeen.

It was a Monday evening, and Frenchy's was already getting crowded. There was a mix of naval and merchant marine types, who'd come fifty miles from the port; there were five or six male tourists, looking for one kind of action and about to find another; and there were a few tourist couples looking for racy, colorful stories they could take home with them. There was a sprinkling of businessmen from the city, too, who probably knew the score but came in anyway to have a drink and look at naked bodies.

Yasmin was sitting between two sailors. They were laughing and winking at each other over her head—they must have thought they'd found what they were looking for. Yasmin was sipping a champagne cocktail. She had seven empty glasses in front of her. Very definitely, *she* had found what she was looking for. Frenchy charged eight kiam for a cocktail, which he split with the girl who ordered it. Yasmin had cleared thirty-two kiam already off those two jolly sea rovers, and from the look of it there was more to come, the night was still young. And that's not including tips, either. Yasmin was wonderful at pulling tips. She was a joy to watch; she could separate a mark from his money faster than anyone I knew, except maybe Chiriga.

There were several seats open at the bar, one near the door and a few in the back. I never liked to sit near the door, you looked like some kind of tourist or something. I headed for the shadowy interior of the club. Before I got to the stool, Indihar came up to me. "You'll be more comfortable in a booth, sir," she said.

I smiled. She didn't recognize me in my robes and without my beard. She suggested the booth because if I sat on the stool, she wouldn't be able to sit next to me and work on my wallet. Indihar was a nice enough person, I'd never gotten into any kind of hassle with her. "I'll sit at the bar," I said. "I want to talk to Frenchy."

She gave me a little shrug, then turned and sorted out the rest of the crowd. Like a hunting hawk she sighted three affluent-looking merchants sitting with one girl and one change. There was always room for one more. Indihar pounced.

Frenchy's barmaid, Dalia, came over to me, trailing her wet towel on the counter. She made a couple of passes at the spot just in front of me and plopped a cork coaster down. "Beer?" she asked.

"Gin and bingara with a hit of Rose's," I said.

She squinted her eyes at me. "Marîd?"

"My new look," I said.

She dropped her towel onto the bar and stared at me. She didn't say a word. That went on until I started to get self-conscious. "Dalia?" I said.

She opened her mouth, closed it, then opened it again. "Frenchy," she cried, "here he is!"

I didn't know what that meant. People all around turned to look at me. Frenchy got up from his seat near the cash register and lumbered over to me. "Marîd," he said, "heard about you taking on that guy that wiped the Sisters."

It dawned on me that I was a bigshot now. "Oh," I said, "it was more like *he* took *me* on. He was doing pretty well, too, until I decided to get serious."

Frenchy grinned. "You were the only one that had the balls to go after him. Even the city's finest were ten steps behind you. You saved a lot of lives, Marîd. You drink free in here and every other place on the Street from now on. No tips, either, I'll give the word to the girls."

It was the only meaningful gesture Frenchy could make, and I appreciated it. "Thanks, Frenchy," I said. I learned how quickly being a big shot can get embarrassing.

We talked for a while. I tried to get him to see that there was still another killer around, but he didn't want to know about it. He preferred to believe the danger was over. I had no proof that the second assassin was still in the city, after all. He hadn't used a cigarette on anybody since Nikki's death. "What are you looking for?" asked Frenchy.

I stared up at the stage, where Blanca was dancing. She was the one who had actually discovered Nikki's corpse in the alley. "I have one clue and an idea of what he likes to do to his victims." I told Frenchy about the moddy Nikki had in her purse, and about the bruises and cigarette burns on the bodies.

Frenchy looked thoughtful. "You know," he said, "I do remember somebody telling me about a trick they turned."

"What about it? Did the trick try to burn her or something?"

Frenchy shook his head. "No, not that. Whoever it was said that when she got the trick's clothes off, he was all covered with the same kind of burns and marks."

"Whose trick was it, Frenchy? I need to talk to her."

He gazed off toward the middle of next week, trying to remember. "Oh," he said, "it was Maribel."

"Maribel?" I said in disbelief. Maribel was the old woman who occupied a stool at the angle of the bar. She always took that stool. She was somewhere between sixty and eighty years old, and she'd been a dancer half a century ago, when she still had a face and a body. Then she stopped dancing and concentrated on the aspects of the industry that brought more immediate cash benefits. When she got even older, she had to lower her retail markup in order to compete with the newer models. Nowadays she wore a red nylon wig that had all the body and bounce of the artificial lawns in the European district. She had never had the money for physical or mental modifications. Surrounded by the most beautiful bodies money could buy, her face looked even older than it was. Maribel was at a distinct disadvantage. She overcame that, however, through shrewd marketing techniques that stressed personalized attention and customer satisfaction: for the price of one champagne cocktail, she would give the man next to her the benefit of her manual dexterity and her years of experience. Right at the bar, sitting and chatting as if they were all alone in a motel room somewhere. Maribel subscribed to the classical Arab proverb: the best kindness is done quickly. She had to carry most of the conversation, of course; but unless you watched closely—or the guy couldn't keep the glazed look off his face—you'd never know that an intimate encounter was taking place.

Most girls wanted you to buy them seven or eight cocktails before they'd even begin to negotiate. Maribel's clock was running out, she didn't have time for that. If Yasmin was the Neiman-Marcus—and she was, in my opinion—then Maribel was the Crazy Abdul's Discount Mart of hustlers.

That's why I found Frenchy's story hard to believe. Maribel would never have the opportunity to see scars on her trick. Not sitting at the corner of the bar like that.

"She took this guy home," said Frenchy, grinning.

"Who'd go home with Maribel?" It was hard to believe.

"Someone who needed the money."

"Son of a bitch. *She* pays men to jam her?"

"Money cycles through this world like anything else."

I thanked Frenchy for the information and told him I needed to talk to Maribel. He laughed and went back to his stool. I moved over to the seat beside her. "Hi, Maribel," I said.

She had to look at me a while before she recognized me. "Marîd," she said happily. Between the first syllable and the second, her hand plopped in my lap. "Buy me a cocktail?"

"All right." I signaled to Dalia, who put a champagne cocktail in front of the old woman. Dalia gave me a crooked smile and I just shrugged helplessly. The girls and changes in Frenchy's club always got a tall stainless-steel cup of ice water with their drinks. They said it was because they didn't like the taste of liquor, and to get all that alcohol down they had to drink ice water with it. They sipped some champagne or some hard liquor, then went to the ice water. The marks thought it was tough on these poor girls, having to guzzle two or three dozen drinks every night if they didn't enjoy the stuff. The truth was that they never swallowed the drink; they spit it out into the metal cup. Every so often Dalia would take the cup away and empty it on the pretext of freshening up the ice water. Maribel didn't want the spit-back cup. She liked her booze.

I had to admit, Maribel's hand was as skilled as any silversmith's. Practice makes perfect, I guess. I was about to tell her to stop, but then I said to myself, what the hell. It was a learning experience. "Maribel," I said, "Frenchy told me you saw somebody with burn marks and bruises all over his body. Do you remember who?"

"I did?"

"Somebody you went home with."

"When?"

"I don't know. If I could find that person, he might be able to tell me something that would save some lives."

"Really? Would I get some kind of reward for that?"

"A hundred kiam, if you can remember."

That stopped her. She hadn't seen a hundred kiam in one lump since her glory days, and they belonged to another century. She hunted through her disordered memories, desperately trying to come up with a mental picture. "I'll tell you," she said, "there *was* somebody like that, I remember that much; but I can't for the life of me remember who. I'll get it, though. Will the reward still be good—"

"Whenever you remember, give me a call or tell Frenchy."

"I won't have to split the money with him, will I?"

"No," I said. Yasmin was on stage now. She saw me sitting with Maribel, she saw Maribel's arm moving up and down. Yasmin gave me a disgusted look and turned away. I laughed. "Thanks, but that's all right, Maribel."

"Going, Marîd?" asked Dalia. "That didn't take very long."

"Rotate, Dalia," I said. I left Frenchy's, worried that my friends, like Okking, Hassan, and Friedlander Bey, believed they were all safe now. I knew they weren't, but they didn't want to listen to me. I almost wished something terrible would happen, just so they'd know I was right; but I didn't want to bear the guilt for it.

In the midst of their relief and celebration, I was more alone than ever before.

nineteen

"You do not wish it."

Audran looked at him. Wolfe sat there like a self-satisfied statue, his eyes half-closed, his lips pushing out a little, pulling in, then pushing out again. He turned his head a fraction of an inch and gazed at me. "You do not wish it," he said again.

"But I do!" cried Audran. "I just want all of this to be over."

"Nevertheless." He raised a finger and wiggled it. "You continue to hope that there will be some simple solution, some way that doesn't threaten danger or, what is yet worse to your way of thinking, ugliness. If Nikki had been murdered cleanly, simply, then you might have tracked her killer down relentlessly. As it is, the situation becomes ever more repellent, and you desire only to hide from it. Consider where you are now: huddled in the linen closet of some impoverished, nameless fellah." He frowned disapprovingly.

Audran felt condemned. "You mean I didn't go about it the right way? But you're the detective, not me. I'm just Audran, the sand-nigger who sits on the curb with the plastic cups and the rest of the garbage. You always say yourself that any spoke will lead the ant to the hub."

His shoulders raised a quarter of an inch in a shrug, and then fell. He was being compassionate. "Yes, I say that. However, if the ant walks all the way around the rim three-quarters of the circumference before choosing a spoke, he may lose more than merely time."

Audran spread his hands helplessly. "I'm getting near the hub in my own clumsy way. So why don't you use your eccentric genius and tell me where I can find this other killer?"

Wolfe put his hands on the arms of his chair and levered himself up. His expression was set and he barely noticed me as he walked by. It was time to go up to his orchids.

ᴡɦᴇɴ ī chipped out the moddy and replaced the special daddies, I was sitting on the floor of Jarir's closet, my head on my drawn-up knees. With the daddies back in, I was invincible—not hungry, not tired, not thirsty, not afraid, not even angry. I set my jaw, I ran my hand through my rumpled hair, I did all those valiant things. Step aside buddy, this is a job for . . .

For me, I guess.

I glanced at my watch and saw that it was early evening. That was all right, too; all the little throat-slashers and their victims would be out.

I wanted to show that bloated Nero Wolfe that real people have their own low cunning, too. I also wanted to live the rest of my life without feeling forever like I had to throw up in the next few seconds. That meant catching Nikki's killer. I took out the envelope of money and counted it. There was over fifty-seven thousand kiam. I had expected a little more than five. I stared at all that money for a long time. Then I put it away, took out my pill case, and swallowed twelve Paxium without water. I left the little room and passed Jarir. I didn't say a word to him going out.

The streets in that part of town were deserted already, but the nearer I got to the Budayeen, the more people I saw. I passed through the eastern gate and went up the Street. My mouth was dry despite the daddies that were supposed to keep the lid clamped down on my endocrines. It was a good thing I wasn't afraid, because I was scared stiff. I passed the Half-Hajj and he said a few words; I just nodded and went by as if he'd been a total stranger. There may have been a convention or a tour group in town, because I remember little knots of strangers standing in the Street, staring into the clubs and the cafés. I didn't bother walking around them. I just shoved my way through.

When I got to Hassan's shop, the front door was closed. I stood there and stared at it stupidly. I couldn't remember it ever being closed before. If it had just been me, I'd have reported it to Okking; but it wasn't just me. It was me and my daddies, so I kicked the door beside the lock, one, two, three, and it finally sprang open.

Naturally, Abdul-Hassan, the street-american kid, wasn't on his stool in the empty shop. I crossed the shop in two or three strides and ripped the cloth hanging aside. There was no one in the storeroom in the back, either. I hurried across the dark area between the stacks of wooden crates, and went out the heavy iron door into the alley. There was another iron door in the building across the way; behind it was the room in which I'd bargained for Nikki's short-lived freedom. I went up to it and pounded on it loudly. There was no response. I pounded again. Finally a small voice called out something in English.

"Hassan," I yelled.

The small voice said something, went away for a few seconds, then shouted something else. I promised myself that if I lived through this, I was going to buy that kid an Arabic-language daddy. I took out the envelope of money and waved it, yelling "Hassan! Hassan!"

After a few seconds, a small crack opened. I took out a thousand-kiam note, put it in the kid's hand, showed him all the rest of the cash, and said "Hassan! Hassan!" The door shut with a whuff and my thousand kiam disappeared.

A moment later the door opened again, and I was all ready for it. I grabbed the edge and pulled, wrenching the door out of the kid's grasp. He cried out and swung with it, but he let go. I flung the door open, then doubled over as the kid kicked me as hard as he could. He was too short to reach where he was aiming, but he still hurt me pretty bad. I grabbed a fistful of his shirt and slapped him a few times, then whacked the back of his head against the wall and let him fall into the refuse-strewn alley. I let my breathing catch up; the daddies were doing a fine job, my heart was pumping away as if I were just humming along with Fazluria, not running for my life. I paused only to bend down and snap back the thousand-K bill the 'ricain kid was still holding. "Take care of the fiqs," my mother always taught me.

There was no one in the ground-floor room. I thought about slamming and locking the iron door behind me, so that the American kid or any other bogeyman couldn't sneak up without my knowing, but I decided instead that I might need a handy exit in a hurry. I made no noise as I walked carefully and slowly toward the stairway against the wall to my left. Without the daddies I would have been elsewhere, whispering into a stranger's ear in some romantic language. I took out my rack of daddies and considered them. The two corymbic implants I had were not fully loaded; I could still chip in another three, but I was already wearing everything I thought I might need in a crisis. All but one, to tell the truth: there was still the special black daddy that plugged directly into my punishment cells. I didn't think I'd ever use that one voluntarily; but, if I had to face somebody like Xarghis Moghadhîl Khan again with nothing but a butter knife, I'd rather go out a snarling, vicious beast than a rational, whimpering human being. I held the black daddy in my left hand and went on up the stairs.

In the room above there were two people. Hassan, smiling faintly and looking just a little distracted, was standing in a corner and rubbing his eyes. He looked sleepy. "Audran, my nephew," he said.

"Hassan," I said.

"Did the boy let you in?"

"I gave him a thousand and took the decision out of his hands. Then I took the thousand out of his hands, too."

Hassan gave me his little ingratiating laugh. "I am fond of the boy, as you know, but he's an American." I'm not sure what he meant by that, "He's an American, so he's a little stupid," or "He's an American, there are plenty more."

"He won't be bothering us," I said.

"Good, O excellent one," said Hassan. His eyes flicked down to Lieutenant Okking, who was spread-eagled on the floor, his wrists and ankles tied with nylon cords to rings set into the walls. It was obvious that Hassan had used this set-up before—often. Okking's back, legs, arms, and head were marked with cigarette burns and streaked with long, bright slashes of blood. If he was screaming I didn't notice, because the daddies had my senses concentrated on Hassan. Okking was still alive, though. I could see that much.

"You finally got around to the cop," I said. "Are you sorry his brain isn't wired? You like to use your bootleg moddy, don't you?"

Hassan raised an eyebrow. "It is a pity," he said. "But, of course, *your* implant will suffice. I am already looking forward to that with pleasure. I owe you thanks, my nephew, for suggesting the policeman. It was my belief that my guest here was as witless a fool as he acted. You insisted that he was withholding information. I couldn't take the chance that you were correct." I frowned and looked at Okking's writhing body. I promised myself that later, when I was in my own mind, I'd get sick.

"All along," I said, as if we were merely discussing the price of beauties, "I thought there were two killers wearing moddies. I've been so stupid: it turned out to be one moddy and one old-fashioned crackpot. Here I was trying to outthink some international high-tech hoodlum, and it turns out to be the neighborhood dirty old man. What a waste of time, Hassan! I should be ashamed to take Papa's money for this." As I was saying all this, of course, I was edging slowly closer to him, looking down at Okking and shaking my head, and generally acting like a kindly police sergeant in a movie, trying to soft-talk a frantic slob from jumping off a ledge. Take my word for it: it's harder than it looks.

"Friedlander Bey has paid you the last kiam you'll ever see." Hassan actually sounded sad.

"Maybe, maybe not," I said, still moving slowly. My eyes were on Hassan's thick, stubby fingers wrapped around a cheap, curved Arab knife. "I've been so blind. You were working for the Russians."

"Of course," Hassan snapped.

"And you kidnapped Nikki."

He looked up at me, surprised. "No, my nephew, it was Abdoulaye who took her, not me."

"But he was following your orders."

"Bogatyrev's."

"Abdoulaye took her from Seipolt's villa."

Hassan only nodded.

"So she was still alive the first time I questioned Seipolt. She was somewhere in his house. He wanted her alive. Then when I went back to demand answers from him, he was dead."

Hassan stared at me, fingering the blade.

"After Bogatyrev died, you killed her and dumped her body. Then you killed Abdoulaye and Tami to protect yourself. Who made her write those notes?"

"Seipolt, O clever one."

"Okking's the last, then. The only one left who can link you to the murders."

"And yourself, of course."

"Of course," I said. "You're a hell of a good actor, Hassan. You had me fooled. If I hadn't found your underground moddy"—his teeth flashed in a startled snarl—"and some things that connected Nikki to Seipolt, I would never have had anything to go on. Both you and the Germans' assassin did first-rate work. I would never have guessed you until I realized that every goddamn important piece of information passed through you. From Papa to me, from me to Papa. It was right in front of me the whole time, all I had to do was see it. Finally, I just *had* to figure it out—it was you, you and your goddamn fat, short, stubby fingers." I was only about ten feet from Hassan, ready to take another cautious step, when he shot me.

He had a small, white plastic pistol and he stitched a row of needles in the air in a big, looping arc. The last two needles in the clip caught me in the side, just below my left arm. I felt them faintly, almost as if they'd happened to someone else. I knew they'd hurt bad in a little while, and part of my mind beneath the daddies wondered if the needles were juiced or if they were just sharp bits of metal to tear my body apart. If they were drugged or poisoned, I'd find out soon enough. It had become time for desperation. I completely forgot I had my seizure gun with me; I had no intention of having a sharp-shooting match with Hassan, anyway. I took the black daddy and slapped it into place even as I was collapsing from the wounds.

It was like . . . it was like being strapped to a table and having a dentist drilling up through the roof of my mouth. It was like being right on the edge of an epileptic fit and not quite making it, wishing that it would either go away or seize me and get it over with. It was like having the brightest lights in the world blazing in my eyes, the loudest noises exploding in my ears, demons sandpapering my flesh, unnameable vile odors clogging my nose, the foulest muck in my throat. I would gladly have died then just to have it all stop.

I would kill.

I grabbed Hassan by his wrists and fastened my teeth in his throat. I felt his hot blood spurting in my face; I remember thinking how wonderful it tasted. Hassan howled with pain. He beat on my head, but he couldn't free himself from the purely insane, purely animal hold I had on him. He thrashed, and we fell to the floor. He got loose and slammed another clip into his pistol and shot me again, and again I leaped on his throat. I tore at his windpipe with my teeth, and my stiff fingers dug into his eyes. I felt his blood running down my arms, too. Hassan's shrieks were horrible, maddened, but they were almost drowned out by my own. The black daddy was still torturing me, still burning like acid inside my head. All my screaming, all the infuriated, savage ferocity of my attack, did nothing to lessen my torment. I slashed and clawed and ripped at Hassan's bloody body.

Much later, I woke up, heavily tranquilized, in the hospital. Eleven days had passed. I learned that I had mangled Hassan until he was no longer alive, and even then I did not stop. I had avenged Nikki and all the others, but I had made every crime of Hassan's look like the gentlest of children's games. I had bitten and torn Hassan's body until there was barely enough left to identify.

And I had done the same to Okking.

twenty

it was Doc Yeniknani, the gentle Sufi Turk, who released me from the hospital at last. I had taken my share of hurts from Hassan, but I don't remember getting them, for which I thank Allah. The needle wounds, lesions, and lacerations were the easy part. The med staff just crammed me back together and covered me all over with gelstrips. My medication was taken care of by computer this time—no snippy nurses. The doctor programmed a list of drugs into the machine, along with the quantity and how often I was allowed to request them. Every time I wanted a jolt, I just punched a button. If I punched it too often, nothing happened. If I waited just the right amount of time, the computer slipped me intravenous Sonneine right through my feeding tube. I was in the hospital for almost three months; and when I got out, my ass felt as nice and smooth as the day I was born. I will have to get one of those mechanical drug-pushers for myself. It could revolutionize the street narcotics industry. Oh, they'll put a few people out of work, but that's always been the price of free enterprise and progress.

The physical beating I took while I was reducing the former Hassan the Shiite to soup bones wasn't bad enough to keep me in bed so long. Actually, those wounds could have been treated in the emergency room, and I could have been out dining and dancing a few hours later. The real problem was inside my head. I had seen and done too many terrible things, and Dr. Yeniknani and his colleagues considered the possibility that if they just disconnected the punishment daddy and the other override daddies, when all the facts and memories hit my poor, unbuffered brain, I'd end up as crazy as a spider on ice skates.

The American kid found me—found us, I mean, me and Hassan and Okking—and called the cops. They got me to the hospital, and apparently the highly paid, highly skilled specialists didn't want any part of me. No one wanted to risk his reputation by taking charge. "Do we leave the add-ons in? Do we take them out? If we take them out, he might go permanently insane. If we leave them in, they might burn their way right down into his belly." All those hours that black daddy was still juicing the punishment center in my brain. I passed out again and again, but I wasn't dreaming about Honey Pílar, you can bet on that.

They popped the punishment chip first, but left the others in to leave me in a kind of insensible limbo. They brought me back to full, unaugmented consciousness slowly, testing me every step of the way. I'm proud to say that I'm as sane today as I ever was; I have all the daddies in their plastic box in case I get nostalgic.

I didn't have any visitors in the hospital this time, either. I guessed that my friends had good memories. I took the opportunity to grow my beard back, and my hair was getting long again. It was a Tuesday morning when Dr. Yeniknani signed my releases. "I pray to Allah that I never see you here again," he said.

I shrugged. "From now on, I'm going to get myself a quiet little business selling counterfeit coins to tourists. I don't want any more trouble."

Dr. Yeniknani smiled. "No one wants trouble, but there is trouble enough in the world. You cannot hide from it. Do you remember the shortest sûrah in the noble Qur'ân? It is actually one of the earliest revealed by the Prophet, may blessings be upon his name and peace. 'Say: I seek refuge in the Lord of mankind, the King of mankind, the God of mankind, from the evil of the sly whisperer, who whispers in the hearts of mankind, of the *djinn* and of mankind.' "

"*Djinn* and mankind and guns and knives," I said.

Dr. Yeniknani shook his head slowly. "If you look for guns, you will find guns. If you look for Allah, you will find Allah."

"Well, then," I said wearily, "I will just have to start my life fresh when I get out of here. I'll just change all my ways and how I think and forget all the years of experience I've had."

"You mock me," he said sadly, "but some day you will listen to your own words. I pray to Allah that when that day comes, you will yet have time to do as you say." Then he signed my papers, and I was free again, me again, with nowhere to go.

I didn't have an apartment anymore. All I had was a zipper bag with a lot of money in it. I called a cab from the hospital and rode over to Papa's. This was the second time I'd dropped by without an appointment, but this time I had the excuse that I couldn't phone Hassan to make an arrangement. The butler recognized me, even favoring me with a minute change in his expression. Evidently I had become a celebrity. Politicians and sex stars may cuddle up to you and it doesn't prove a thing, but when the butlers of the world notice you, you realize that some of what you believe about yourself is true.

I even got to give the waiting room a miss. One of the Stones That Speak appeared in front of me, did an about-face, and marched off. I followed. We went into Friedlander Bey's office, and I took a few steps toward Papa's desk. He stood up, his old face so shriveled up in smiles that I was afraid it would snap into a million pieces. He hurried toward me, took my face, and kissed me. "O my son!" he cried. Then he kissed me again. He couldn't find the words to express his joy.

For my part, I was a little uncomfortable. I didn't know whether I should play the brick-fronted hero or the awshucks kid who just happened to be in the right place at the right time. The truth was, I only wanted to get out of there as fast as I could with another thick envelope of reward money, and never have anything to do with the old son of a bitch again. He was making it difficult. He kept kissing me.

At last it got thick, even for an old-fashioned Arab potentate like Friedlander Bey. He let me go and retreated behind the formidable bastion of his desk. It seemed that we weren't going to share a pleasant lunch or tea and swap stories of mangled corpses while he told me how terrific I was. He just stared at me for a long time. One of the Stones crept up beside me, just behind my right shoulder. The other Stone planted himself behind my left shoulder. It felt eerily reminiscent of my first interview with Friedlander Bey, in the motel. Now, in these grander surroundings, I was somehow reduced from the conquering hero to some slimy miscreant who'd been caught with his hand in someone else's pocket, and was now on the carpet. I don't know how Papa did it, but it was part of his magic. Uh oh, I thought, and my stomach started to grumble. I still hadn't learned what his motives had been.

"You have done well, O excellent one," said Friedlander Bey. His tone was thoughtful and not wholly approving.

"I was granted good fortune by Allah in His greatness, and by you in your foresight," I said.

Papa nodded. He was used to being yoked together with Allah that way. "Take, then, the token of our gratitude." One of the Stones shoved an envelope against my ribs, and I took it.

"Thank you, O Shaykh."

"Thank not me, but Allah in His beneficence."

"Yeah, you right." I pushed the envelope into a pocket. I wondered if I could go now.

"Many of my friends were slain," mused Papa, "and many of my valued associates. It would be well to guard against such a thing ever happening again."

"Yes, O Shaykh."

"I have need of loyal friends in positions of authority, on whom I can rely. I am shamed when I recall the trust I put in Hassan."

"He was a Shiite, O Shaykh."

Friedlander Bey waved a hand. "Nevertheless. It is time to repair the injuries that have been done to us. Your task is not finished, not yet, my son. You must help build a new structure of security."

"I will do what I can, O Shaykh." I didn't like the way this was going at all, but once again I was helpless.

"Lieutenant Okking is dead and gone to his Paradise, *inshallah*. His position will be filled by Sergeant Hajjar, a man whom I know well and whose words and deeds I need not fear. I am considering a new and essential department—a liaison between my friends of the Budayeen and the official authorities."

I never felt so small and so alone in my life.

Friedlander Bey went on. "I have chosen you to administer that new supervisory force."

"Me, O Shaykh?" I asked in a quavery voice. "You don't mean me."

He nodded. "Let it be done."

I felt a surge of rage and stepped toward his desk. "The hell with you and your plans!" I shouted. "You sit there and manipulate—you watch my friends die—you pay this guy and that guy and don't give a good goddamn what happens to them as long as your money rolls in. I wouldn't doubt that you were behind Okking and the Germans *and* Hassan and the Russians." Suddenly I shut up quick. I hadn't been thinking fast, I'd just been letting my anger out; but I could tell by the sudden tightness around Friedlander Bey's mouth that I'd touched something pretty goddamn sensitive. "You *were*, weren't you?" I said softly. "You didn't give a flying fuck *what* happened to anybody. You were playing *both* sides. Not against the middle—there *wasn't* any middle. Just *you*, you walking cadaver. You don't have a human atom in you. You don't love, you don't hate, you don't care. For all your kneeling and praying, you got nothing in you. I've seen handfuls of sand with more conscience than you."

The really strange thing was that during that whole speech, neither of the Stones That Speak came any nearer or shoved me around or broke my face for me. Papa must have given them a signal to let me have my little oration. I took another step toward him, and he lifted the corners of his mouth in a pitiful, ancient man's attempt at a smile. I stopped short, as if I'd walked into an invisible glass wall.

Baraka. The charismatic spell that surrounds saints and tombs and mosques and holy men. I couldn't have harmed Friedlander Bey and he knew it. He reached into a desk drawer and brought out a gray plastic device that fitted nicely into the palm of his hand. "Do you know what this is, my son?" he asked.

"No," I said.

"It is a portion of you." He pressed a button, and the screaming nightmare that had made an animal of me, that had driven me to rend and tear Okking and Hassan, flooded my skull in its full, unstoppable fury.

I came to in a fetal position on Papa's rug.

"That was only fifteen seconds," he told me calmly.

I stared at him sullenly. "That's how you're going to make me do what you want?"

He gave me that piece of a smile again. "No, my son." He tossed the control device in a gentle arc, and I caught it. I looked at him. "Take it," he said. "It is your loving cooperation I desire, not your fear."

Baraka.

I pocketed the remote control unit and waited. Papa nodded. "Let it be done," he said again. And just like that, I was a cop. The Stones That Speak moved closer toward me. In order to breathe, I had to keep skipping a couple of feet in front of them. They squeezed me out of the room and down the hall and out of Friedlander Bey's house altogether. I didn't have another chance to say anything. I was standing in the street, a lot richer. I was also some kind of imitation law-enforcement agent with Hajjar as my immediate boss. Even in my worst drug-induced half-crazed nightmares, I'd never concocted anything as horrible as that.

As the word does, it got around fast. They probably knew about it before I did, while I was still recuperating and playing solitaire with the Sonneine. When I went into the Silver Palm, Heidi wouldn't serve me. At the Solace, Jacques, Mahmoud, and Saied stared about six inches above my shoulder into humid air and talked about how much garlic was enough; they never even acknowledged my presence. I noticed that Saied the Half-Hajj had inherited custody of Hassan's American kid. I hoped they'd be very happy together. I finally went into Frenchy's, and Dalia set a coaster in front of me. She looked very uncomfortable. "Where you at, Marîd?" she asked.

"I'm all right. You still talking to me?"

"Sure, Marîd, we been friends a long time." She gave a long, worried look down at the end of the bar, though.

I looked, too. Frenchy stood up from his stool and came slowly toward me. "I don't want your business, Audran," he said gruffly.

"Frenchy, after I caught Khan, you told me I could drink free in here for the rest of my life."

"That was before what you done to Hassan and Okking. I never had no use for either of them, but what you did . . ." He turned his head aside and spat.

"But Hassan was the one who—"

He cut me off. He turned to the barmaid. "Dalia, if you ever serve this bastard in here again, you're fired. You got that?"

"Yeah," she said, looking nervously from Frenchy to me.

The big man turned back to me. "Now get out," he said.

"Can I talk to Yasmin?" I asked.

"Talk to her and get out." Then Frenchy turned his back on me and walked away, the way he'd walk away from something he didn't want to have to see or smell or touch.

Yasmin was sitting in a booth with a mark. I went up to her, ignoring the guy. "Yasmin," I said, "I don't—"

"You best go away, Marîd," she said in an icy voice. "I heard what you did. I heard about your sleazy new job. You sold out to Papa. I'd have expected that from anybody else; but you, Marîd, I couldn't believe it at first. But you did it, didn't you? Everything they say?"

"It was the daddy, Yasmin, you don't know how it made me feel. Anyway, *you're* the one who wanted me to—"

"I suppose it was the daddy that made you a cop, too?"

"Yasmin . . ." Here I was, the man whose pride sufficeth, who needed nothing, who expected nothing, who wandered the lonely ways of the world unappalled because there were no more surprises. How long ago had I believed that, actually been conned by it, seen myself that way? And now I was pleading with her. . . .

"Go away, Marîd, or I'll have to call Frenchy. I'm working."

"Can I call you later?"

She made a small grimace. "No, Marîd. No."

So I went away. I'd been on my own before, but this was something new in my experience. I suppose I should have expected it, but it still hit me harder than all the terror and ugliness I'd gone through. My own friends, my former friends, found it simpler to draw a line through my name and cut me out of their lives than to deal with the truth. They didn't want to admit to themselves the danger they'd been in, the danger they might be in again someday. They wanted to pretend that the world was nice and healthy and worked according to a few simple rules that somebody had written down somewhere. They didn't need to know what the rules were, precisely; they just needed to know they were there just in case. I was now a constant reminder that there *were* no rules, that insanity was loose in the world, that their own safety, their own lives, were always in jeopardy. They didn't want to think about that, so they made a simple compromise: I was the villain, I was the scapegoat, I took all the honor and all the punishment. Let Audran do it, let Audran pay for it, fuck Audran.

Okay, if that's how it was going to be. I thundered into Chiri's place and threw a young black man off my usual stool. Maribel got off a stool down at the end of the bar and wobbled drunkenly toward me. "Been looking for you, Marîd," she said in a thick voice.

"Not now, Maribel. I'm not in the mood."

Chiriga looked from me to the young black man, who was thinking about starting something with me. "Gin and bingara?" she asked, raising her eyebrows. That's as much expression as she showed me. "Or tende?"

Maribel sat down next to me. "You got to listen, Marîd."

I looked at Chiri; it was a tough decision. I went with vodka gimlets.

"I remember who it was," Maribel said. "The one I went home with. With the scars, who you was looking for. It was Abdul-Hassan, the American kid. See? Hassan must have put them scars on him. I *told* you I'd remember. Now you owe me."

She was pleased with herself. She tried to sit up straight on the stool.

I looked at Chiri, and she gave me just the merest hint of a smile.

"What the hell," I said.

"What the hell," she said.

The young black man was still standing there. He gave us each a puzzled look and walked out of the club. I probably saved him a small fortune.

A Fire in the Sun

My grandfather, George Conrad Effinger, whom I never knew, was a police officer in the city of Cleveland during the Depression. He was killed in the line of duty. This book is dedicated to his memory, growing fainter now each year in the minds of those people who did know him, except for his policeman's shield, Badge #374, hung with pride in a station house in Cleveland.

Children begin by loving their parents; after a time they judge them; rarely, if ever, do they forgive them.

—Oscar Wilde
The Picture of Dorian Gray

ONE

WE'D RIDDEN for many days out the coast highway toward Mauretania, the part of Algeria where I'd been born. In that time, even at its
lethargic pace, the broken-down old bus had carried us from the city to
some town forsaken by Allah before it even learned what its name was.
Centuries come, centuries go: In the Arab world they arrive and depart
loaded on the roofs of shuddering, rattling buses that are more trouble
to keep in service than the long parades of camels used to be. I remembered what those bus rides were like from when I was a kid, sitting or
standing in the aisle with fifty other boys and men and maybe another
two dozen clinging up on the roof. The buses passed by my home then.
I saw turbaned heads, heads wearing fezes or knit caps, heads in white
or checked *keffiyas*. All men. That was something I planned to ask my
father about, if I ever met him. "O my father," I would say, "tell me
why everyone on the bus is a man. Where are their women?"

And I always imagined that my father—I pictured him tall and lean
with a fierce dark beard, a hawk or an eagle of a man; he was, in my
vision, Arab, although I had my mother's word that he had been a
Frenchman—I saw my father gazing thoughtfully into the bright sunlight, framing a careful reply to his young son. "O Marîd, my sweet
one," he would say—and his voice would be deep and husky, issuing
from the back of his throat as if he never used his lips to speak,
although my mother said he wasn't like that at all—"Marîd, the women
will come later. The men will send for them later."

"Ah," I would say. My father could pierce *all* riddles. I could not
pose a question that he did not have a proper answer for. He was wiser
than our village shaykh, more knowledgeable than the man whose face

filled the posters pasted on the wall we were pissing on. "Father," I would ask him, "why are we pissing on this man's face?"

"Because it is idolatrous to put his face on such a poster, and it is fit only for a filthy alley like this, and therefore the Prophet, may the blessing of Allah be on him and peace, tells us that what we are doing to these images is just and right."

"And Father?" I would always have one more question, and he'd always be blissfully patient. He would smile down at me, put one hand fondly behind my head. "Father? I have always wanted to ask you, what do you do when you are pissing and your bladder is so full it feels like it will explode before you can relieve it and while you are pissing, *just then*, the muezzin—"

Saied hit me hard in the left temple with the palm of his hand. "You sleeping out here?"

I looked up at him. There was glare everywhere. I couldn't remember where the hell we were. "Where the hell are we?" I asked him.

He snorted. "*You're* the one from the Maghreb, the great, wild west. You tell me."

"Have we got to Algeria yet?" I didn't think so.

"No, stupid. I've been sitting in that goddamn little coffeehouse for three hours charming the warts off this fat fool. His name is Hisham."

"Where are we?"

"Just crossed through Carthage. We're on the outskirts of Old Tunis now. So listen to me. What's the old guy's name?"

"Huh? I don't remember."

He hit me hard in the right temple with the palm of his other hand. I hadn't slept in two nights. I was a little confused. Anyway, he got the easy part of the job: Sitting around the bus stops, drinking mint tea with the local ringleaders and gossiping about the marauding Christians and the marauding Jews and the marauding heathen niggers and just in general being goddamn smooth; and I got the piss-soaked alleys and the flies. I couldn't remember why we divided this business up like that. After all, I was supposed to be in charge—it was my idea to find this woman, it was my trip, we were using my money. But Saied took the mint tea and the gossip, and I got—well, I don't have to go into that again.

We waited the appropriate amount of time. The sun was disappearing behind a western wall; it was almost time for the sunset call to prayer. I stared at Saied, who was now dozing. Good, I thought, now I get to hit *him* in the head. I had just gotten up and taken one little step, when he looked up at me. "It's time, I guess," he said, yawning. I nodded, didn't have anything to add. So I sat back down, and Saied the Half-Hajj went into his act.

Saied is a natural-born liar, and it's a pleasure to watch him hustle. He had the personality module he liked best plugged into his brain— his heavy-duty, steel-belted, mean mother of a tough-guy moddy. Nobody messed with the Half-Hajj when he was chipping that one in.

Back home in the city, Saied thought it was beneath him to earn money. He liked to sit in the cafés with me and Mahmoud and Jacques, all day and all evening. His little chicken, the American boy everybody called Abdul-Hassan, went out with older men and brought home the rent money. Saied liked to sneer a lot and wear his *gallebeya* cinched with a wide black leather belt, which was decorated with shiny chrome-steel strips and studs. The Half-Hajj was always careful of his appearance.

What he was doing in this vermin-infested roadside slum was what he called fun. I waited a few minutes and followed him around the corner and into the coffeehouse. I shuffled in, unkempt, filthy, and took a chair in a shadowy corner. The proprietor glanced at me, frowned, and turned back to Saied. Nobody ever paid any attention to me. Saied was finishing the tail end of a joke I'd heard him tell a dozen times since we'd left the city. When he came to the payoff, the shopkeeper and the four other men at the long counter burst into laughter. They liked Saied. He could make people like him whenever he wanted. That talent was programmed into an add-on chip snapped into his bad-ass moddy. With the right moddy and the right daddy chips, it didn't matter where you'd been born or how you'd been raised. You could fit in with any sort of people, you could speak any language, you could handle yourself in any situation. The information was fed directly into your short-term memory. You could literally become another person, Ramses II or Buck Rogers in the 25th century, until you popped the moddy and daddies out.

Saied was being rough and dangerous, but he was also being charming, if you can imagine that combination. I watched the shop owner reach and grab the teapot. He poured some into the Half-Hajj's glass, slopping some more on the wooden counter. Nobody moved to mop it up. Saied raised the glass to drink, then slammed it down again. "*Yaa salaam!*" he roared. He leaped up.

"What is it, O my friend?" asked Hisham, the proprietor.

"My ring!" Saied shouted. He was wearing a large gold ring, and he'd been waving it under the old man's nose for two solid hours. It had had a big, round diamond in its center.

"What's the matter with your ring?"

"Look for yourself! The stone—my diamond—it's gone!"

Hisham caught Saied's flapping arm and saw that, indeed, the diamond was now missing. "Must have fallen out," the old man said, with the sort of folk wisdom you find only in these petrified provincial villages.

"Yes, fallen out," said Saied, not calmed in the least. "But where?"

"Do you see it?"

Saied made a great show of searching the floor around his stool. "No, I'm sure it's not here," he said at last.

"Then it must be out in the alley. You must've lost it the last time you went out to piss."

Saied slammed the bar with his heavy fist. "And now it's getting dark, and I must catch the bus."

"You still have time to search," said Hisham. He didn't sound very confident.

The Half-Hajj laughed without humor. "A stone like that, worth four thousand Tunisian dinars, looks like a tiny pebble among a million others. In the twilight I'd never find it. What am I to do?"

The old man chewed his lip and thought for a moment. "You're determined to leave on the bus, when it passes through?" he asked.

"I must, O my brother. I have urgent business."

"I'll help you if I can. Perhaps I can find the stone for you. You must leave your name and address with me; then if I find the diamond, I'll send it to you."

"May the blessings of Allah be on you and on your family!" said Saied. "I have little hope that you'll succeed, but it comforts me to know you will do your best for me. I'm in your debt. We must determine a suitable reward for you."

Hisham looked at Saied with narrowed eyes. "I ask no reward," he said slowly.

"No, of course not, but I insist on offering you one."

"No reward is necessary. I consider it my duty to help you, as a Muslim brother."

"Still," Saied went on, "should you find the wretched stone, I'll give you a thousand Tunisian dinars for the sustenance of your children and the ease of your aged parents."

"Let it be as you wish," said Hisham with a small bow.

"Here," said my friend, "let me write my address for you." While Saied was scribbling his name on a scrap of paper, I heard the rumbling of the bus as it lurched to a stop outside the building.

"May Allah grant you a good journey," said the old man.

"And may He grant you prosperity and peace," said Saied, as he hurried out to the bus.

I waited about three minutes. Now it was my turn. I stood up and staggered a couple of steps. I had a lot of trouble walking in a straight line. I could see the shopkeeper glaring at me in disgust. "The hell do you want, you filthy beggar?" he said.

"Some water," I said.

"Water! Buy something or get out!"

"Once a man asked the Messenger of God, may Allah's blessings be on him, what was the noblest thing a man may do. The reply was 'To give water to he who thirsts.' I ask this of you."

"Ask the Prophet. I'm busy."

I nodded. I didn't expect to get anything free to drink out of this crud. I leaned against his counter and stared at a wall. I couldn't seem to make the place stand still.

"*Now* what do you want? I told you to go away."

"Trying to remember," I said peevishly. "I had something to tell you. Ah, yes, I know." I reached into a pocket of my jeans and brought out a glittering round stone. "Is this what that man was looking for? I found this out there. Is this—?"

The old man tried to snatch it out of my hand. "Where'd you get that? The alley, right? *My* alley. Then it's mine."

"No, I found it. It's—"

"He said he wanted me to look for it." The shopkeeper was already gazing into the distance, spending the reward money.

"He said he'd pay you money for it."

"That's right. Listen, I've got his address. Stone's no good to you without the address."

I thought about that for a second or two. "Yes, O Shaykh."

"And the address is no good to me without the stone. So here's my offer: I'll give you two hundred dinars for it."

"Two hundred? But he said—"

"He said he'd give me a thousand. *Me*, you drunken fool. It's worthless to you. Take the two hundred. When was the last time you had two hundred dinars to spend?"

"A long time."

"I'll bet. So?"

"Let me have the money first."

"Let me have the stone."

"The money."

The old man growled something and turned away. He brought a rusty coffee can up from under the counter. There was a thick wad of money in it, and he fished out two hundred dinars in old, worn bills. "Here you are, and damn your mother for a whore."

I took the money and stuffed it into my pocket. Then I gave the stone to Hisham. "If you hurry," I said, slurring my words despite the fact that I hadn't had a drink or any drugs all day, "you'll catch up with him. The bus hasn't left yet."

The man grinned at me. "Let me give you a lesson in shrewd business. The esteemed gentleman offered me a thousand dinars for a four-thousand dinar stone. Should I take the reward, or sell the stone for its full value?"

"Selling the stone will bring trouble," I said.

"Let me worry about that. Now you go to hell. I don't ever want to see you around here again."

He needn't worry about that. As I left the decrepit coffeehouse, I popped out the moddy I was wearing. I don't know where the Half-Hajj had gotten it; it had a Malaccan label on it, but I didn't think it was an over-the-counter piece of hardware. It was a dumbing-down moddy; when I chipped it in, it ate about half of my intellect and left me shambling, stupid, and just barely able to carry out my half of the plan. With it out, the world suddenly poured back into my consciousness, and it was like waking from a bleary, drugged sleep. I was always angry for half an hour after I popped that moddy. I hated myself for agreeing to wear it, I hated Saied for conning me into doing it. *He* wouldn't wear it, not the Half-Hajj and his precious self-image. So I wore it, even though I'm gifted with twice the intracranial modifications as anybody else around, enough daddy capacity to make me the most talented son of a bitch in creation. And still Saied persuaded me to damp myself out to the point of near vegetability.

On the bus, I sat next to him, but I didn't want to talk to him or listen to him gloat.

"What'd we get for that chunk of glass?" he wanted to know. He'd already replaced the real diamond in his ring.

I just handed the money to him. It was his game, it was his score. I couldn't have cared less. I don't even know why I went along with him, except that he'd said he wouldn't come to Algeria with me unless I did.

He counted the bills. "Two hundred? That's all? We got more the last two times. Oh well, what the hell—that's two hundred dinars more we can blow in Algiers. 'Come with me to the Kasbah.' Little do those gazelle-eyed boys know what's stealing toward them even now, through the lemon-scented night."

"This stinking bus, that's what, Saied."

He looked at me with wide eyes, then laughed. "You got no romance in you, Marîd," he said. "Ever since you had your brain wired, you been no fun at all."

"How about that." I didn't want to talk anymore. I pretended that I was going to sleep. I just closed my eyes and listened to the bus thumping and thudding over the broken pavement, with the unending arguments and laughter of the other passengers all around me. It was crowded and hot on that reeking bus, but it was carrying me hour by hour nearer to the solution of my own mystery. I had come to a point in my life where I needed to find out who I really was.

The bus stopped in the Barbary town of Annaba, and an old man with a grizzled gray beard came aboard selling apricot nectar. I got some for myself and some for the Half-Hajj. Apricots are the pride of Mauretania, and the juice was the first real sign that I was getting close to home. I closed my eyes and inhaled that delicate apricot aroma, then swallowed a mouthful of juice and savored the thick sweetness. Saied just gulped his down with a grunt and gave me a blunt "Thanks." The guy's got all the refinement of a dead bat.

The road angled south, away from the dark, invisible coast toward the city of Constantine. Although it was getting late, almost midnight, I told Saied that I wanted to get off the bus and grab some supper. I hadn't eaten anything since noon. Constantine is built on a high limestone bluff, the only ancient town in eastern Algeria to survive through centuries of foreign invasions. The only thing I cared about, though, was food. There is a local dish in Constantine called *chorba beïda bel kefta*, a meatball soup made with onions, pepper, chick-peas, almonds, and cinnamon. I hadn't tasted it in at least fifteen years, and I didn't care if it meant missing the bus and having to wait until tomorrow for another, I was going to have some. Saied thought I was crazy.

I had my soup, and it was wonderful. Saied just watched me wordlessly and sipped a glass of tea. We got back on the bus in time. I felt good now, comfortably full and warmed by a nostalgic glow. I took the window seat, hoping that I'd be able to see some familiar landscape as we passed through Jijel and Mansouria. Of course, it was as black as the inside of my pocket beyond the glass, and I saw nothing but the moon and the fiercely twinkling stars. Still, I pretended to myself that I could make out landmarks that meant I was drawing closer to Algiers, the city where I had spent a lot of my childhood.

When at last we pulled into Algiers sometime after sunrise, the Half-Hajj shook me awake. I didn't remember falling asleep. I felt terrible. My head felt like it had been crammed full of sharp-edged broken glass, and I had a pinched nerve in my neck, too. I took out my pillcase and stared into it for a while. Did I prefer to make my entrance into Algiers hallucinating, narcotized, or somnambulant? It was a difficult decision. I went for pain-free but conscious, so I fished out eight tabs of Sonneine. The sunnies obliterated my headache—and every other mildly unpleasant sensation—and I more or less floated from the bus station in Mustapha to a cab.

"You're stoned," said Saied when we got to the back of the taxi. I told the driver to take us to a public data library.

"Me? Stoned? When have you ever known me to be stoned so early in the morning?"

"Yesterday. The day before yesterday. The day before that."

"I mean *except* for then. I function better with a ton of opiates in me than most people do straight."

"Sure you do."

I stared out the taxi's window. "Anyway," I said, "I've got a rack of daddies that can compensate." There isn't another blazebrain in the Arab world with the custom-made equipment I've got. My special daddies control my hypothalamic functions, so I can tune out fatigue and fear, hunger and thirst and pain. They can boost my sensory input too.

"Marîd Audran, Silicon Superman."

"Look," I said, annoyed by Saied's attitude, "for a long time I was terrified of getting wired, but now I don't know how I ever got along without it."

"Then why the hell are you still decimating your brain cells with drugs?" asked the Half-Hajj.

"Call me old-fashioned. Besides, when I pop the daddies out, I feel terrible. All that suppressed fatigue and pain hit me at once."

"And you don't get paybacks with your sunnies and beauties, right? That what you're saying?"

"Shut up, Saied. Why the hell are you so concerned all of a sudden?"

He looked at me sideways and smiled. "The religion has this ban on liquor and hard drugs, you know." And this coming from the Half-Hajj who, if he'd ever been inside a mosque in his life, was there only to check out the boys' school.

So in ten or fifteen minutes the cab driver let us out at the library. I felt a peculiar nervous excitement, although I didn't understand why. All I was doing was climbing the granite steps of a public building; why should I be so wound up? I tried to occupy my mind with more pleasant thoughts.

Inside, there were a number of terminals vacant. I sat down at the gray screen of a battered Bab el-Marifi. It asked me what sort of search I wanted to conduct. The machine's voice synthesizer had been designed in one of the North American republics, and it was having a lot of trouble pronouncing Arabic. I said, "Name," then "Enter." When the cursor appeared again, I said, "Monroe comma Angel." The data deck thought about that for a while, then white letters began flicking across its bright face:

> Angel Monroe
> 16, Rue du Sahara
> (Upper) Kasbah
> Algiers
> Mauretania
> 04-B-28

I had the machine print out the address. The Half-Hajj raised his eyebrows at me and I nodded. "Looks like I'm gonna get some answers."

"*Inshallah*," murmured Saied. If God wills.

We went back out into the hot, steamy morning to find another taxi. It didn't take long to get from the library to the Kasbah. There wasn't as much traffic as I remembered from my childhood—not vehicular traffic, anyway; but there was still the slow, unavoidable battalions of heavily laden donkeys being cajoled through the narrow streets.

The Rue du Sahara is a mistake. I remember someone telling me long ago that the true name of the street was actually the Rue N'sara, or Street of the Christians. I don't know how it got corrupted. Very little of Algiers has any real connection to the Sahara. After all, it's a hell of a long hike from the Mediterranean port to the desert. It doesn't make any difference these days, though; the new name is the only one anyone ever uses. It's even found its way onto all the official maps, so that closes the matter.

Number 16 was an exhausted, crumbling brick pile with two bulging upper stories that hung out over the cobbled street. The apartment house across the way did the same, and the two buildings almost kissed above my head, like two dowdy old matrons leaning across a back fence. There was a jumble of mail slots, and I found Angel Monroe's name scrawled on a card in fading ink. I jammed my thumb on her buzzer. There was no lock on the front door, so I went in and climbed the first flight of stairs. Saied was right behind me.

Her apartment turned out to be on the third floor, in the rear. The hallway was carpeted, if that's the right word, with a dull, gritty fabric that had at one time been maroon. The traffic of uncountable feet had completely worn through the material in many places, so that the dry gray wood of the floor was visible through the holes. The walls were covered with a filthy tan wallpaper, hanging down here and there in forlorn strips. The air had an odd, sour tang to it, as if the building were occupied by people who had come there to die, or who were certainly sick enough to die but instead hung on in lonely misery. From behind one door I could hear a family battle, complete with bellowed threats and crashing crockery, while from another apartment came insane, high-pitched laughter and the sound of flesh loudly smacking flesh. I didn't want to know about it.

I stood outside the shabby door to Angel Monroe's flat and took a deep breath. I glanced at the Half-Hajj, but he just gave me a shrug and pointedly looked away. Some friend. I was on my own. I told myself that nothing weird was going to happen—a lie just to get myself to take the next step—and then I knocked on the door. There was no response. I waited a few seconds and knocked again, louder. This time I heard the rattle and squeak of bedsprings and the sound of someone coming slowly to the door. The door swung open. Angel Monroe stared out, trying very hard to focus her eyes.

She was a full head shorter than me, with bleached blond hair curled tightly into an arrangement I would call "ratty." Her black roots looked as if no one had given them much attention since the Prophet's birthday. Her eyes were banded with dark blue and black makeup, in a manner that brought to mind the more colorful Mediterranean saltwater fish. The rouge she wore was applied liberally, but not quite in the right places, so she didn't look so much wantonly sexy as she did feverishly ill. Her lipstick, for reasons best known to Allah and Angel Monroe, was a kind of pulpy purple color; her lips looked like she'd bought them first and forgot to put them in the refrigerator while she shopped for the rest of her face.

Her body led me to believe that she was too old to be dressed in anything but the long white Algerian *haïk,* with a veil conservatively and firmly in place. The problem was that this body had never seen the inside of a *haïk.* She was clad now in shorts so small that her well-rounded belly was bending the waistband over. Her sagging breasts were not quite clothed in a kind of gauzy vest. I knew for certain that if she sat in a chair, you could safely hide the world's most valuable gem in her navel and it would be completely invisible. Her legs were patterned with broken veins like the dry *chebka* valleys of the Mzab. On her broad, flat feet she wore tattered slippers with the remains of pink fuzzy bows dangling loose.

To tell the truth, I felt a certain disgust. "Angel Monroe?" I asked. Of course that wasn't her real name. She was at least half Berber, as I am. Her skin was darker than mine, her eyes as black and dull as eroded asphalt.

"Uh huh," she said. "Kind of early, ain't it?" Her voice was sharp and shrill. She was already very drunk. "Who sent you? Did Khalid send you? I told that goddamn bastard I was sick. I ain't supposed to be working today, I told him last night. He said it was all right. And then he sends you. *Two* of you, yet. Who the hell does he think I am? And it ain't like he don't have no other girls, either. He could have sent you to Efra, that whore, with her plug-in talent. If I ain't feeling good, it don't bother me if he sends you to her. Hell, I don't care. How much you give him, anyway?"

I stood there, looking at her. Saied gave me a jab in the side. "Well, uh, Miss Monroe," I said, but then she started chattering again.

"The hell with it. Come on in. I guess I can use the money. But you tell that son of a bitch Khalid that—" She paused to take a long gulp from the tall glass of whiskey she was holding. "You tell him if he don't care enough about my health, I mean, making me work when I already told him I was sick, then hell, you tell him there are plenty of others I can go work for. Anytime I want to, you can believe that."

I tried twice to interrupt her, but I didn't have any success. I waited until she stopped to take another drink. While she had her mouth full of the cheap liquor, I said, "Mother?"

She just stared at me for a moment, her filmy eyes wide. "No," she said at last, in a small voice. She looked closer. Then she dropped her whiskey glass to the floor.

two

later, after the return trip from Algiers and Mauretania, when I got back home to the city the first place I headed was the Budayeen. I used to live right in the heart of the walled quarter, but events and fate and Friedlander Bey had made that impossible now. I used to have a lot of friends in the Budayeen too, and I was welcome anywhere; but now there were really only two people who were generally glad to see me: Saied the Half-Hajj, and Chiriga, who ran a club on the Street halfway between the big stone arch and the cemetery. Chiri's place had always been my home-away-from-home, where I could sit and have a few drinks in peace, hear the gossip, and not get threatened or hustled by the working girls.

Once upon a time I'd had to kill a few people, mostly in self-defense. More than one club owner had told me never to set foot in his bar again. After that, a lot of my friends decided that they could do without my company, but Chiri had more sense.

She's a hard-working woman, a tall black African with ritual facial scars and sharply filed cannibal teeth. To be honest, I don't really know if those canines of hers are mere decoration, like the patterns on her forehead and cheeks, or a sign that dinner at her house was composed of delicacies implicitly and explicitly forbidden by the noble Qur'ân. Chiri's a moddy, but she thinks of herself as a smart moddy. At work, she's always herself. She chips in her fantasies at home, where she won't bother anyone else. I respect that.

When I came through the club's door, I was struck first by a welcome wave of cool air. Her air conditioning, as undependable as all old Russian-made hardware is, was working for a change. I felt better already. Chiri was deep in conversation with a customer, some bald guy with a bare chest. He was wearing black vinyl pants with the look of real leather, and his left hand was handcuffed behind him to his belt. He had a corymbic implant on the crest of his skull, and a pale green plastic moddy was feeding him somebody else's personality. If Chiri was giving him the time of day, then he couldn't have been dangerous, and probably he wasn't even all that obnoxious.

Chiri doesn't have much patience with the crowd she caters to. Her philosophy is that *somebody* has to sell them liquor and drugs, but that doesn't mean she has to socialize with them.

I was her old pal, and I knew most of the girls who worked for her. Of course, there were always new faces—and I mean *new*, carved out of dull, plain faces with surgical skill, turning ordinary looks into enthralling artificial beauty. The old-time employees got fired or quit in a huff on a regular basis; but after working for Frenchy Benoit or Jo-Mama for a while, they circulated back to their former jobs. They left me pretty much alone, because I'd rarely buy them cocktails and I didn't have any use for their professional charms. The new girls could try hustling me, but Chiri usually told them to lay off.

In their unforgiving eyes I'd become the Creature Without A Soul. People like Blanca and Fanya and Yasmin looked the other way if I caught their eye. Some of the girls didn't know what I'd done or didn't care, and they kept me from feeling like a total outcast. Still, it was a lot quieter and lonelier for me in the Budayeen than it used to be. I tried not to care.

"*Jambo*, Bwana Marîd!" Chiriga called to me when she noticed that I was sitting nearby. She left the handcuffed moddy and drifted slowly down her bar, plopping a cork coaster in front of me. "You come to share your wealth with this poor savage. In my native land, my people have nothing to eat and wander many miles in search of water. Here I have found peace and plenty. I have learned what friendship is. I have found disgusting men who would touch the hidden parts of my body. You will buy me drinks and leave me a huge tip. You will tell all your new friends about my place, and they will come in and want to touch the hidden parts of my body. I will own many shiny, cheap things. It is all as God wills."

I stared at her for a few seconds. Sometimes it's hard to figure what kind of mood Chiri's in. "Big nigger girl talk dumb," I said at last.

She grinned and dropped her ignorant Dinka act. "Yeah, you right," she said. "What is it today?"

"Gin," I said. I usually have a shot of gin and a shot of bingara over ice, with a little Rose's lime juice. The drink is my own invention, but I've never gotten around to naming it. Other times I have vodka gimlets, because that's what Philip Marlowe drinks in *The Long Goodbye*. Then on those occasions when I just really want to get loaded fast, I drink from Chiri's private stock of *tende*, a truly loathsome African liquor from the Sudan or the Congo or someplace, made, I think, from fermented yams and spadefoot toads. If you are ever offered *tende*, DO NOT TASTE IT. You *will* be sorry. Allah knows that I am.

The dancer just finishing her last number was an Egyptian girl named Indihar. I'd known her for years. She used to work for Frenchy Benoit, but now she was wiggling her ass in Chiri's club. She came up to me when she got offstage, wrapped now in a pale peach-colored shawl that had little success in concealing her voluptuous body. "Want to tip me for my dancing?" she asked.

"It would give me untold pleasure," I said. I took a kiam bill from my change and stuffed it into her cleavage. If she was going to treat me like a mark, I was going to act like one. "Now," I said, "I won't feel guilty about going home and fantasizing about you all night."

"That'll cost you extra," she said, moving down the bar toward the bare-chested guy in the vinyl pedal pushers.

I watched her walk away. "I like that girl," I said to Chiriga.

"That's our Indihar, one fine package of suntanned fun," said Chiri.

Indihar was a real girl with a real personality, a rarity in that club. Chiri seemed to prefer in her employees the high-velocity prettiness of a sexchange. Chiri told me once that changes take better care of their appearance. Their prefab beauty is their whole life. Allah forbid that a single hair of their eyebrows should be out of place.

By her own standards, Indihar was a good Muslim woman too. She didn't have the head wiring that most dancers had. The more conservative imams taught that the implants fell under the same prohibition as intoxicants, because some people got their pleasure centers wired and spent the remainder of their short lives amp-addicted. Even if, as in my case, the pleasure center is left alone, the use of a moddy submerges your own personality, and that is interpreted as insobriety. Needless to say, while I have nothing but the warmest affection for Allah and His Messenger, I stop short of being a fanatic about it. I'm with that twentieth-century King Saud who demanded that the Islamic leaders of his country stop dragging their feet when it came to technological progress. I don't see any essential conflict between modern science and a thoughtful approach to religion.

Chiri looked down the bar. "All right," she called out loudly, "which one of you motherfuckers' turn is it? Janelle? I don't want to have to tell you to get up and dance again. If I got to remind you to play your goddamn music one more time, I'm gonna fine you fifty kiam. Now move your fat ass." She looked at me and sighed.

"Life is tough," I said.

Indihar came back up the bar after collecting whatever she could pry out of the few glum customers. She sat on the stool beside me. Like Chiri, she didn't seem to get nightmares from talking with me. "So what's it like," she asked, "working for Friedlander Bey?"

"You tell me." One way or another, everybody in the Budayeen works for Papa.

She shrugged. "I wouldn't take his money if I was starving, in prison, and had cancer."

This, I guessed, was a dig, a not-very-veiled reference to the fact that I had sold out to get my implants. I just swallowed some more gin and bingara.

Maybe one of the reasons I went to Chiri's whenever I needed a little cheering up is that I grew up in places just like it. My mother had been a dancer when I was a baby, after my father ran off. When the situation got real bad, she started turning tricks. Some girls in the clubs do that, some don't. My mother had to. When things got even harder, she sold my little brother. That's something she won't talk about. I won't talk about it, either.

My mother did the best she knew how. The Arab world has never put much value on education for women. Everybody knows how the more traditional—that is to say, more backward and unregenerate— Arab men treat their wives and daughters. Their *camels* get more respect. Now, in the big cities like Damascus and Cairo, you can see modern women wearing Western-style clothing, holding down jobs outside the home, sometimes even smoking cigarettes on the street.

In Mauretania, I'd seen that the attitudes there were still rigid. Women wore long white robes and veils, with hoods or kerchiefs covering their hair. Twenty-five years ago, my mother had no place in the legitimate job market. But there is always a small population of lost souls, of course—people who scoff at the dictates of the holy Qur'ân, men and women who drink alcohol and gamble and indulge in sex for pleasure. There is always a place for a young woman whose morals have been ground away by hunger and despair.

When I saw her again in Algiers, my mother's appearance had shocked me. In my imagination, I'd pictured her as a respectable, moderately well-to-do matron living in a comfortable neighborhood. I hadn't seen or spoken to her in years, but I just figured she'd managed to lift herself out of the poverty and degradation. Now I thought maybe she was happy as she was, a haggard, strident old whore. I spent an hour with her, hoping to hear what I'd come to learn, trying to decide how to behave toward her, and being embarrassed by her in front of the Half-Hajj. She didn't want to be troubled by her children. I got the impression that she was sorry she hadn't sold me too, when she'd sold Hussain Abdul-Qahhar, my brother. She didn't like me dropping back into her life after all those years.

"Believe me," I told her, "I didn't like hunting you up, either. I only did it because I have to."

"Why do you have to?" she wanted to know. She reclined on a musty-smelling, torn old sofa that was covered with cat hair. She'd made herself another drink, but had neglected to offer me or Saied anything.

"It's important to me," I said. I told her about my life in the far-away city, how I'd lived as a subsonic hustler until Friedlander Bey had chosen me as the instrument of his will.

"You live in the city now?" She said that with a nostalgic longing. I never knew she'd been to the city.

"I lived in the Budayeen," I said, "but Friedlander Bey moved me into his palace."

"You work for him?"

"I had no choice." I shrugged. She nodded. It surprised me that she knew who Papa was too.

"So what did you come for?"

That was going to be hard to explain. "I wanted to find out everything I could about my father."

She looked at me over the rim of her whiskey glass. "You already heard everything," she said.

"I don't think so. How sure are you that this French sailor was my dad?"

She took a deep breath and let it out slowly. "His name was Bernard Audran. We met in a coffee shop. I was living in Sidi-bel-Abbès then. He took me to dinner, we liked each other. I moved in with him. We came to live in Algiers after that, and we were together for a year and a half. Then after you was born, one day he just left. I never heard from him again. I don't know where he went."

"*I* do. Into the ground, that's where. Took me a long time, but I traced Algerian computer records back far enough. There was a Bernard Audran in the navy of Provence, and he was in Mauretania when the French Confederate Union tried to regain control over us. The problem is that his brains were bashed out by some unidentified *noraf* more than a year before I was born. Maybe you could think back and see if you can get a clearer picture of those events."

That made her furious. She jumped up and flung her half-full glass of liquor at me. It smashed into the already stained and streaked wall to my right. I could smell the pungent, undiluted sharpness of the Irish whiskey. I heard Saied murmuring something beside me, maybe a prayer. My mother took a couple of steps toward me, her face ugly with rage. "You calling me a *liar?*" she shrieked.

Well, I was. "I'm just telling you that the official records say something different."

"Fuck the official records!"

"The records also say that you were married seven times in two years. No mention of any divorces."

My mother's anger faltered a bit. "How did that get in the computers? I never got officially married, not with no license or nothing."

"I think you underestimate the government's talent for keeping track of people. It's all there for anybody to see."

Now she looked frightened. "What else'd you find out?"

I let her off her own hook. "Nothing else. There wasn't anything more. You want something else to stay buried, you don't have to worry." That was a lie; I had learned plenty more about my mom.

"Good," she said, relieved. "I don't like you prying into what I done. It don't show respect."

I had an answer to that, but I didn't use it. "What started all this nostalgic research," I said in a quiet voice, "was some business I was taking care of for Papa." Everybody in the Budayeen calls Friedlander Bey "Papa." It's an affectionate token of terror. "This police lieutenant who handled matters in the Budayeen died, so Papa decided that we needed a kind of public affairs officer, somebody to keep communications open between him and the police department. He asked me to take the job."

Her mouth twisted. "Oh yeah? You got a gun now? You got a badge?" It was from my mother that I learned my dislike for cops.

"Yeah," I said, "I got a gun *and* a badge."

"Your badge ain't any good in Algiers, *salaud.*"

"They give me professional courtesy wherever I go." I didn't even know if that was true here. "The point is, while I was deep in the cop comp, I took the opportunity to read my own file and a few others. The funny thing was, my name and Friedlander Bey's kept popping up together. And not just in the records of the last few years. I counted at least eight entries—hints, you understand, but nothing definite—that suggested the two of us were blood kin." That got a loud reaction from the Half-Hajj; maybe I should have told him about all this before.

"So?" said my mother.

"The hell kind of answer is that? So what does it mean? You ever jam Friedlander Bey, back in your golden youth?"

She looked raving mad again. "Hell, I jammed *lots* of guys. You expect me to remember all of them? I didn't even remember what they looked like while I was jamming them."

"You didn't want to get involved, right? You just wanted to be good friends. Were you ever friends enough to give credit? Or did you always ask for the cash up front?"

"Maghrebi," cried Saied, "this is your *mother!*" I didn't think it was possible to shock him.

"Yeah, it's my mother. Look at her."

She crossed the room in three steps, reached back, and gave me a hard slap across the face. It made me fall back a step. "Get the fuck *out* of here!" she yelled.

I put my hand to my cheek and glared at her. "You answer one thing first: Could Friedlander Bey be my real father?"

Her hand was poised to deliver another clout. "Yeah, he could be, the way practically *any* man could be. Go back to the city and climb up on his knee, sonny boy. I don't ever want to see you around here again."

She could rest easy on that score. I turned my back on her and left that repulsive hole in the wall. I didn't bother to shut the door on the way out. The Half-Hajj did, and then he hurried to catch up with me. I was storming down the stairs. "Listen, Marîd," he said. Until he spoke, I didn't realize how wild I was. "I guess all this is a big surprise to you—"

"You do? You're very perceptive today, Saied."

"—but you can't act that way toward your mother. Remember what it says—"

"In the Qur'ân? Yeah, I know. Well, what does the Straight Path have to say about prostitution? What does it have to say about the kind of degenerate my holy mother has turned into?"

"You've got a lot of room to talk. If there was a cheaper hustler in the Budayeen, I never met him."

I smiled coldly. "Thanks a lot, Saied, but I don't live in the Budayeen anymore. You forget? And I don't hustle anybody or anything. I got a steady job."

He spat at my feet. "You used to do nearly anything to make a few kiam."

"Anyway, just because I used to be the scum of the earth, it doesn't make it all right for my mother to be scum too."

"Why don't you just shut up about her? I don't want to hear about it."

"Your empathy just grows and grows, Saied," I said. "You don't know everything I know. My alma mater back there was into renting herself to strangers long before she had to support my brother and me.

She wasn't the forlorn heroine she always said she was. She glossed over a lot of the truth."

The Half-Hajj looked me hard in the eye for a few seconds. "Yeah?" he said. "Half the girls, changes, and debs we know do the same thing, and you don't have any problem treating *them* like human beings."

I was about to say "Sure, but none of them is my mother." I stopped myself. He would have jumped on that sentiment too, and besides, it was starting to sound foolish even to me. The edge of my anger had vanished. I think I was just greatly annoyed to have to learn these things after so many years. It was hard for me to accept. I mean, now I had to forget almost everything I thought I knew about myself. For one thing, I'd always been proud of the fact that I was half-Berber and half-French. I dressed in European style most of the time—boots and jeans and work shirts. I suppose I'd always felt a little superior to the Arabs I lived among. Now I had to get used to the thought that I could very well be half-Berber and half-Arab.

The raucous, thumping sound of mid-twenty-first-century hispo roc broke into my daydream. Some forgotten band was growling an ugly chant about some damn thing or other. I've never gotten around to learning any Spanish dialects, and I don't own a Spanish-language daddy. If I ever run into any Columbian industrialists, they can just damn well speak Arabic. I have a soft spot in my liver for them because of their production of narcotics, but outside of that I don't see what South America is for. The world doesn't need an overpopulated, starving, Spanish-speaking India in the Western Hemisphere. Spain, their mother country, tried Islam and said a polite no-thank-you, and their national character sublimed right off into nothingness. That's Allah punishing them.

"I hate that song," said Indihar. Chiri had given her a glass of Sharâb, the soft drink the clubs keep for girls who don't drink alcohol, like Indihar. It's exactly the same color as champagne. Chiri always fills a cocktail glass with ice and pours in a few ounces of soda—which should be a tip-off to the mark: you don't get ice in your champagne in the real world. But the ice takes up a lot of space where the more expensive stuff would go. That'll cost a sucker eight kiam and a tip for Chiri. The club kicks three bills back to the girl who got the drink. That motivates the employees to go through their cocktails at supersonic speed. The usual excuse is that it's thirsty work whirling like a derwish to the cheers of the crowd.

Chiri turned to watch Janelle, who was on her last song. Janelle doesn't really dance, she flounces. She takes five or six steps to one end of the stage, waits for the next heavy-footed bass drum beat, then does a kind of shrugging, quivering thing with her upper body that she must think is torridly sexy. She's wrong. Then she flounces back the other way to the opposite end of the stage and does her spasm number again. The whole time she's lip-synching, not to the lyrics, but to the wailing lead keypad line. Janelle the Human Synthesizer. Janelle the Synthetic Human is closer to the truth. She wears a moddy every day, but you have to talk to her to find out which one. One day she's soft and erotic (Honey Pílar), the next day she's cold and foulmouthed (Brigitte Stahlhelm). Whichever personality she's chipped in, though, is still housed in the same unmodified Nigerian refugee body, which she also thinks is sexy and about which she is also mistaken. The other girls don't associate with her very much. They're sure she lifts bills out of their bags in the dressing room, and they don't like the way she cuts in on their customers when they have to go up to dance. Someday the cops are going to find Janelle in a dark doorway with her face pulped and half the bones in her body broken. In the meantime, she flounces in time to the ragged screams of keypads and guitar synths.

I was bored as hell. I knocked back the rest of my drink. Chiri looked at me and raised her eyebrows. "No thanks, Chiri," I said. "I got to go."

Indihar leaned over and kissed me on the cheek. "Well, don't be a stranger now that you're a fascist swine cop."

"Right," I said. I got up from my stool.

"Say hello to Papa for me," said Chiri.

"What makes you think I'm going there?"

She gave me her filed-tooth grin. "Time for good boys and girls to check in at the old *kibanda.*"

"Yeah, well," I said. I left the rest of my change for her hungry register and went back outside.

I walked down the Street to the arched eastern gate. Beyond the Budayeen, along the broad Boulevard il-Jameel, a few taxis waited for fares. I saw my old friend, Bill, and climbed into the backseat of his cab. "Take me to Papa's, Bill," I said.

"Yeah? You talk like you know me. I know you from somewhere?"

Bill didn't recognize me because he's permanently fried. Instead of skull wiring or cosmetic bodmods, he's got a large sac where one of his lungs used to be, dripping out constant, measured doses of light-speed hallucinogen into his bloodstream. Bill has occasional moments of lucidity, but he's learned to ignore them, or at least to keep functioning until they go away and he's seeing purple lizards again. I've tried the drug he's got pumping through him day and night; it's called RPM, and even though I'm pretty experienced with drugs of all nations, I never want to take that stuff again. Bill, on the other hand, swears that it has opened his eyes to the hidden nature of the real world. I guess so: he can see fire demons and I can't. The only problem with the drug—and Bill will be the first to admit this—is that he can't remember a goddamn thing from one minute to the next.

So it wasn't surprising that he didn't recognize me. I've had to go through the same conversation with him a hundred times. "It's me, Bill. Marîd. I want you to take me to Friedlander Bey's."

He squinted back at me. "Can't say I ever seen you before, buddy."

"Well, you have. Lots of times."

"That's easy for *you* to say," he muttered. He jabbed the ignition and pulled away from the curb. We were headed in the wrong direction. "Where did you say you wanted to go?" he asked.

"Papa's."

"Yeah, you right. I got this *afrit* sitting up here with me today, and he's been tossing hot coals in my lap all afternoon. It's a big distraction. I can't do nothing about it, though. You can't punch out an *afrit*. They like to mess with your head like that. I'm thinking of getting some holy water from Lourdes. Maybe that would spook 'em. Where the hell *is* Lourdes, anyway?"

"The Caliphate of Gascony," I said.

"Hell of a long drive. They do mail orders?"

I told him I didn't have the slightest idea, and sat back against the upholstery. I watched the landscape slash by—Bill's driving is as crazy as he is—and I thought about what I was going to say to Friedlander Bey. I wondered how I should approach him about what I'd found out, what my mother had told me, and what I suspected. I decided to wait. There was a good chance that the information in the computers linking me to Papa had been planted there, a devious means of winning my cooperation. In the past, I'd carefully avoided any direct transactions with Papa, because taking his coin for any reason meant that he owned you forever. But when he paid for my cranial implants, he made an investment that I'd be paying back for the rest of my life. I didn't *want* to be working for him, but there was no escape. Not yet. I maintained the hope that I'd find a way to buy my way out, or coerce him into giving me my freedom. In the meantime, it pleased him to pile responsibility on my unwilling shoulders, and gift me with ever-larger rewards.

Bill pulled through the gate in the high white wall around Friedlander Bey's estate and drove up the long, curved driveway. He came to a stop at the foot of the wide marble stairs. Papa's butler opened the polished front door and stood waiting for me. I paid the fare and slipped

Bill an extra ten kiam. His lunatic eyes narrowed and he glanced from the money to me. "What's this?" he asked suspiciously.

"It's a tip. You're supposed to keep that."

"What's it for?"

"For your excellent driving."

"You ain't trying to buy me off, are you?"

I sighed. "No. I admire the way you steer with all those red-hot charcoals in your drawers. I know I couldn't do it."

He shrugged. "It's a gift," he said simply.

"So's the ten kiam."

His eyes widened again. "Oh," he said, smiling, "*now* I get it!"

"Sure you do. See you around, Bill."

"See ya, buddy." He gunned the cab and the tires spat gravel. I turned and went up the stairs.

"Good afternoon, *yaa Sidi*," said the butler.

"Hello, Youssef. I'd like to see Friedlander Bey."

"Yes, of course. It's good to have you home, sir."

"Yeah, thanks." We walked along a thickly carpeted corridor toward Papa's offices. The air was cool and dry, and I felt the gentle kiss of many fans. There was the fragrance of incense on the air, subtle and inviting. The light was muted through screens made of narrow strips of wood. From somewhere I heard the liquid trickle of falling water, a fountain splashing in one of the courtyards.

Before we got to the waiting room, a tall, well-dressed woman crossed the hall and went up a flight of stairs. She gave me a brief, modest smile and then turned her head away. She had hair as black and glossy as obsidian, gathered tightly into a chignon. Her hands were very pale, her fingers long and tapered and graceful. I got just a quick impression, yet I knew this woman had style and intelligence; but I felt also that she could be menacing and hard, if she needed.

"Who was that, Youssef?" I asked.

He turned to me and frowned. "That is Umm Saad." I knew immediately that he disapproved of her. I trusted Youssef's judgment, so my first intuition about her was most likely correct.

I took a seat in the outer office and killed time by finding faces in the pattern of cracks in the ceiling. After a while, one of Papa's two huge bodyguards opened the communicating door. I call the big men the Stones That Speak. Believe me, I know what I'm talking about. "Come in," said the Stone. Those guys don't waste breath.

I went into Friedlander Bey's office. The man was about two hundred years old, but he'd had a lot of body modifications and transplants. He was reclining on cushions and drinking strong coffee from a

golden cup. He smiled when I came in. "My eyes live again, seeing you
O my nephew," he said. I could tell that he was genuinely pleased.

"My days apart from you have been filled with regret, O Shaykh,"
I said. He motioned, and I seated myself beside him. He reached forward to tip coffee from the golden pot into my cup. I took a sip and
said, "May your table always be prosperous."

"May Allah grant you health," he said.

"I pray that you are feeling well, O Shaykh."

He reached out and grasped my hand. "I am as fit and strong as a
sixty-year-old, but there is a weariness that I cannot overcome, my
nephew."

"Then perhaps your physician—"

"It is a weariness of the soul," he said. "It is my appetite and ambition that are dying. I keep going now only because the idea of suicide
is abhorrent."

"Perhaps in the future, science will restore you."

"How, my son? By grafting a new zest for living onto my exhausted
spirit?"

"The technique already exists," I told him. "You could have a
moddy and daddy implant like mine."

He shook his head ruefully. "Allah would send me to Hell if I did
that." He didn't seem to mind if *I* went to Hell. He waved aside further
speculation. "Tell me of your journey."

Here it was, but I wasn't ready. I still didn't know how to ask him if
he figured in my family tree, so I stalled. "First I must hear all that happened while I was gone, O Shaykh. I saw a woman in the corridor. I've
never seen a woman in your house before. May I ask you who she is?"

Papa's face darkened. He paused a moment, framing his reply.
"She is a fraud and an impostor, and she is beginning to cause me great
distress."

"Then you must send her away," I said.

"Yes," he said. His expression turned stonelike. I saw now not a
ruler of a great business empire, not the controller of all vice and illicit
activity in the city, but something more terrible. Friedlander Bey might
truly have been the son of many kings, because he wore the cloak of
power and command as if he'd been born to it. "I must ask you this
question, O my nephew: Do you honor me enough to fill your lungs
again with fire?"

I blinked. I thought I knew what he was talking about. "Did I not
prove myself just a few months ago, O Shaykh?"

He waved a hand, just that easily making nothing of the pain and
horror I'd suffered. "You were defending yourself from danger then,"

he said. He turned and put one old, clawlike hand on my knee. "I need you now to defend *me* from danger. I wish you to learn everything you can about this woman, and then I want you to destroy her. And her child also. I must know if I have your absolute loyalty."

His eyes were burning. I had seen this side of him before. I sat beside a man who was gripped more and more by madness. I took my coffee cup with a trembling hand and drank deeply. Until I finished swallowing, I wouldn't have to give him an answer.

three

before i had my skull amped, I used to have an alarm clock. In the morning when it went off, I liked to stay in bed a little while longer, bleary and yawning. Maybe I'd get up and maybe I wouldn't. Now, though, I don't have a choice. I chip in an add-on the night before, and when that daddy decides it's time, my eyes snap open and I'm *awake*. It's an abrupt transition and it always leaves me startled. And there's no way in hell that chip will let me fall back asleep. I hate it a lot.

On Sunday morning I woke up promptly at eight o'clock. There was a black man I'd never seen before standing beside my bed. I thought about that for a moment. He was big, much taller than me and well built without going overboard about it. A lot of the blacks you see in the city are like Janelle, refugees from some famine-stricken, arid African wasteland. This guy, though, looked like he'd never missed a sensible, well-balanced meal in his life. His face was long and serious, and his expression seemed to be set in a permanent glower. His stern brown eyes and shaven head added to his grim demeanor. "Who are you?" I asked. I didn't get out from under the covers yet.

"Good morning, *yaa Sidi*," he said. He had a soft, low-pitched voice with a touch of huskiness. "My name is Kmuzu."

"That's a start," I said. "Now what in the name of Allah are you doing here?"

"I am your slave."

"The hell you are." I like to think of myself as the defender of the downtrodden and all that. I get prickly at the idea of slavery, an attitude that runs counter to the popular opinion among my friends and neighbors.

"The master of the house ordered me to see to your needs. He thought I'd be the perfect servant for you, *yaa Sidi,* because my name means 'medicine' in Ngoni."

In Arabic, my own name means "sickness." Friedlander Bey knew, of course, that my mother had named me Marîd in the superstitious hope that my life would be free of illness. "I don't mind having a valet," I said, "but I'm not gonna keep a slave." Kmuzu shrugged. Whether or not I wanted to use the word, he knew he was still *somebody's* slave, mine or Papa's.

"The master of the house briefed me in great detail about your needs," he said. His eyes narrowed. "He promised me emancipation if I will embrace Islam, but I cannot abandon the faith of my father. I think you should know that I'm a devout Christian." I took that to mean that my new servant wholeheartedly disapproved of almost everything I might say or do.

"We'll try to be friends anyway," I said. I sat up and swung my legs out of the bed. I popped out the sleep control and put it in the rack of daddies I keep on the nightstand. In the old days, I spent a lot of time in the morning scratching and yawning and rubbing my scalp; but now when I wake up, I'm denied even those small pleasures.

"Do you truly need that device?" asked Kmuzu.

"My body has sort of gotten out of the habit of sleeping and waking up on its own."

He shook his head. "It is a simple enough problem to solve, *yaa Sidi.* If you just stay awake long enough, you will fall asleep."

I saw that if I expected to have any peace, I was going to have to murder this man, and soon. "You don't understand. The problem is that after three days and nights without sleep, when I do doze off at last I have bizarre dreams, really gruesome ones. Why should I put myself through all that, when I can just reach for pills or software instead?"

"The master of the house instructed me to limit your drug use."

I was starting to get aggravated. "Fine," I said, "you can just fucking *try.*" The drug situation was probably behind Friedlander Bey's "gift" of this slave. I'd made a bad mistake on my very first morning *chez* Papa: I showed up late for breakfast with a butaqualide hangover. I was moderately dysfunctional for a couple of hours, and that earned me his disapproval. So that first afternoon I passed by Laila's modshop on Fourth Street in the Budayeen and invested in the sleep control.

My preference is still a half-dozen beauties, but these days I'm always looking over my shoulder for Papa's spies. He's got a million of 'em. Let me make it clear: You *don't* want his disapproval. He never forgets these things. If he needs to, he hires other people to carry his grudges for him.

The advantages of the situation, however, are many. Take the bed, for instance. I've never had a bed before, just a mattress thrown on the floor in the corner of a room. Now I can kick dirty socks and underwear under something, and if something falls on the floor and gets lost I know just where it'll be, although I won't be able to reach it. I still fall out of the damn bed a couple of times a week, but because of the sleep control, I don't wake up. I just lie there in a heap on the floor until morning.

So I got out of bed on this Sunday morning, took a hot shower, washed my hair, trimmed my beard, and brushed my teeth. I'm supposed to be at my desk in the police station by nine o'clock, but one of the ways I assert my independence is by ignoring the time. I didn't hurry getting dressed. I chose a pair of khaki trousers, a pale blue shirt, a dark blue tie, and a white linen jacket. All the civilian employees in the copshop dress like that, and I'm glad. Arab dress reminds me too much of the life I left behind when I came to the city.

"So you've been planted here to snoop on me," I said while I tried to get the ends of my necktie to come out even.

"I am here to be your friend, *yaa Sidi*," said Kmuzu.

I smiled at that. Before I came to live in Friedlander Bey's palace, I was lonely a lot. I lived in a bare one-room flat with nothing but my pillcase for company. I had some friends, of course, but not the kind who dropped over all the time because they missed me so much. There was Yasmin, whom I suppose I loved a little. She spent the night with me occasionally, but now she looked the other way when we bumped into each other. I think she held it against me that I've killed a few people.

"What if I beat you?" I asked Kmuzu. "Would you still be my friend?"

I was trying to be sarcastic, but it was definitely the wrong thing to say. "I would make you stop," said Kmuzu, and his voice was as cold as any I've ever heard.

I think my jaw dropped. "I didn't mean that, you know," I said. Kmuzu gave a slight nod of his head, and the tension passed. "Help me with this, will you? I think the necktie is winning."

Kmuzu's expression softened a little, and he seemed glad to perform this little service for me. "It is fine now," he said when he finished. "I will get your breakfast."

"I don't eat breakfast."

"*Yaa Sidi,* the master of the house directed me to make sure that you eat breakfast from now on. He believes that breakfast is the most important meal of the day."

Allah save me from nutrition fascists! "If I eat in the morning, I feel like a lump of lead for hours."

It didn't make any difference to Kmuzu what I thought. "I will get your breakfast," he said.

"Don't you have to go to church or something?"

He looked at me calmly. "I have already been to worship," he said. "Now I will get your breakfast." I'm sure he'd note every calorie I took in and file a report with Friedlander Bey. It was just another example of how much influence Papa exerted.

I may have felt a little like a prisoner, but I'd certainly been given compensations. I had a spacious suite in the west wing of Friedlander Bey's great house, on the second floor near Papa's own private quarters. My closet was filled with many suits of clothes in different styles and fashions—Western, Arab, casual, formal. Papa gave me a lot of sophisticated high-tech hardware, from a new Chhindwara constrained-AI data deck to an Esmeraldas holo system with Libertad screens and a Ruy Challenger argon solipsizer. I never worried about money. Once a week, one of the Stones That Speak left a fat envelope stuffed with cash on my desk.

All in all, my life had changed so much that my days of poverty and insecurity seemed like a thirty-year nightmare. Today I'm well fed, well dressed, and well liked by the right people, and all it's cost me is what you'd expect: my self-respect and the approval of most of my friends.

Kmuzu let me know that breakfast was ready. "*Bismillah,*" I murmured as I sat down: in the name of God. I ate some eggs and bread fried in butter, and swallowed a cup of strong coffee.

"Would you like anything more, *yaa Sidi?*" asked Kmuzu.

"No, thank you." I was staring at the far wall, thinking about freedom. I wondered if there was some way I could buy my way out of the police-liaison job. Not with money, anyway, I was sure of that. I don't think it's possible to bribe Papa with money. Still, if I paid very close attention, I just might find some other means of leverage. *Inshallah.*

"Then shall I go downstairs and bring the car around?" Kmuzu asked. I blinked and realized that I had to get going. I didn't have Friedlander Bey's long black limousine at my disposal, but he'd given me a comfortable new electric automobile to use. After all, I was his official representative among the guardians of justice.

Kmuzu, of course, would be my driver now. It occurred to me that I'd have to be very clever to go anywhere without him. "Yes, I'll be down in a minute," I said.

I ran a hand through my hair, which was getting long again. Before

I left the house, I put a rack of moddies and daddies in my briefcase. It was impossible to predict what sort of personality I'd need to have when I got to work, or which particular talents and abilities. It was best just to take everything I had and be prepared.

I stood on the marble stairs and waited for Kmuzu. It was the month of Rabi al-Awwal, and a warm drizzle was falling from a gray sky. Although Papa's estate was carved out of a crowded neighborhood in the heart of the city, I could almost pretend that I was in some quiet garden oasis, far from urban grime and noise. I was surrounded by a green lushness that had been coaxed into existence solely to soothe the spirit of one weary old man. I heard the quiet, peaceful trickling of cool fountains, and some energetic birds warbled nearby from the carefully tended fruit trees. On the still air drifted a heavy, sweet perfume of exotic flowers. I pretended that none of this could seduce me.

Then I got into the cream-colored Westphalian sedan and rode out through the guarded gate. Beyond the wall I was thrown suddenly into the bustle and clamor of the city, and with a shock I realized how sorry I was to leave the serenity of Papa's house. It occurred to me that in time I could come to be like him.

Kmuzu let me out of the car on Walid al-Akbar Street, at the station house that oversaw the affairs of the Budayeen. He told me that he'd be back to drive me home promptly at four-thirty. I had a feeling that he was one of those people who was never late. I stood on the sidewalk and watched as he drove away.

There was always a crowd of young children outside the station house. I don't know if they were hoping to see some shackled criminal dragged in, or waiting for their own parents to be released from custody, or just loitering in the hopes of begging loose change. I'd been one of them myself not so very long ago in Algiers, and it didn't hurt me any to throw a few kiam into the air and watch them scramble for it. I reached into my pocket and grabbed a clutch of coins. The older, bigger kids caught the easy money, and the smaller ones clung to my legs and wailed "*Baksheesh!*" Every day it was a challenge to shake my young passengers loose before I got to the revolving door.

I had a desk in a small cubicle on the third floor of the station house. My cubicle was separated from its neighbors by pale green plasterboard walls only a little taller than I was. There was always a sour smell in the air, a mixture of stale sweat, tobacco smoke, and disinfectant. Above my desk was a shelf that held plastic boxes filled with dated files on cobalt-alloy cell-memories. On the floor was a big cardboard box crammed with bound printouts. I had a grimy Annamese data deck on my desk that gave me trouble-free operation on two out of every three jobs. Of course, my work wasn't very important, not according to Lieutenant Hajjar. We both knew I was there just to keep an eye on things for Friedlander Bey. It amounted to Papa having his own private police precinct devoted to protecting his interests in the Budayeen.

Hajjar came into my cubicle and dropped another heavy box on my desk. He was a Jordanian who'd had a lengthy arrest record of his own before he came to the city. I suppose he'd been an athlete ten years ago, but he hadn't stayed in shape. He had thinning brown hair and lately he'd tried to grow a beard. It looked terrible, like the skin of a kiwi fruit. He looked like a mother's bad dream of a drug dealer, which is what he was when he wasn't administering the affairs of the nearby walled quarter.

"How you doin', Audran?" he said.

"Okay," I said. "What's all this?"

"Found something useful for you to do." Hajjar was about two years younger than me, and it gave him a kick to boss me around.

I looked in the box. There were a couple of hundred blue cobalt-alloy plates. It looked like another really tedious job. "You want me to sort these?"

"I want you to log 'em all into the daily record."

I swore under my breath. Every cop carries an electronic log book to make notes on the day's tour: where he went, what he saw, what he saw, what he said, what he did. At the end of the day, he turns in the book's cell-memory plate to his sergeant. Now Hajjar wanted me to collate all the plates from the station's roster. "This isn't the kind of work Papa had in mind for me," I said.

"What the hell. You got any complaints, take 'em to Friedlander Bey. In the meantime, do what I tell you."

"Yeah, you right," I said. I glared at Hajjar's back as he walked out.

"By the way," he said, turning toward me again, "I got someone for you to meet later. It may be a nice surprise."

I doubted that. "Uh huh," I said.

"Yeah, well, get movin' on those plates. I want 'em finished by lunchtime."

I turned back to my desk, shaking my head. Hajjar annoyed the hell out of me. What was worse, he knew it. I didn't like giving him the satisfaction of seeing me irked.

The funny thing was that Hajjar was in Friedlander Bey's pocket too, but he liked to pretend he was still his own man. Since he'd been promoted and given command, though, Hajjar had gone through some startling changes. He'd begun to take his work seriously, and he'd cut back on his intrigues and profiteering schemes. It wasn't that he'd suddenly discovered a sense of honor; he just realized he'd have to work his tail off to keep from getting fired as a crook and an incompetent.

I selected a productivity moddy from my rack and chipped it onto my posterior plug. The rear implant functions the same as everybody else's. It lets me chip in a moddy and six daddies. The anterior plug, however, is my own little claim to fame. This is the one that taps into my hypothalamus and lets me chip in my special daddies. As far as I know, no one else has ever been given a second implant. I'm glad I hadn't known that Friedlander Bey told my doctors to try something experimental and insanely dangerous. I guess he didn't want me to worry. Now that the frightening part is over, though, I'm glad I went through it. It's made me a more productive member of society and all that.

When I had boring police work to do, which was almost every day, I chipped in an orange moddy that Hajjar had given me. It had a label that said it was manufactured in Helvetia. The Swiss, I suppose, have a high regard for efficiency. Their moddy could take the most energetic, inspired person in the world and transform him instantly into a drudge. Not into a stupid drudge, like what the Half-Hajj's dumbing-down hardware did to me, but into a mindless worker who isn't aware enough to be distracted before the whole assignment is in the Out box. It's the greatest gift to the office menial since conjugal coffee breaks.

I sighed and took the moddy, then reached up and chipped it in.

The immediate sensation was as if the whole world had lurched and then caught its balance. There was an odd, metallic taste in Audran's mouth and a high-pitched ringing in his ears. He felt a touch of nausea, but he tried to ignore it because it wouldn't go away until he popped the moddy out. The moddy had trimmed down his personality like the wick of a lamp, until there was only a vague and ineffectual vestige of his true self left.

Audran wasn't conscious enough even to be resentful. He remembered only that he had work to do, and he pulled a double handful of cobalt-alloy plates out of the box. He slotted six of them into the adit ports beneath the battered data deck's comp screen. Audran touched the control pad and said, "Copy ports one, two, three, four, five, six." Then he stared blankly while the deck recorded the contents of the plates. When the run was finished, he removed the plates, stacked them on one side of the desk, and loaded in six more. He barely noticed the morning pass as he logged in the records.

"Audran." Someone was saying his name.

He stopped what he was doing and glanced over his shoulder.

*Lieutenant Hajjar and a uniformed patrolman were standing in the
entrance to his cubicle. Audran turned slowly back to the data deck.
He reached into the box, but it was empty.*

"Unplug that goddamn thing."

*Audran faced Hajjar again and nodded. It was time to pop the
moddy.*

There was a dizzy swirl of disorientation, and then I was sitting at
my desk, staring stupidly at the Helvetian moddy in my hand. "Jeez," I
murmured. It was a relief to be fully conscious again.

"Tell you a secret about Audran," Hajjar said to the cop. "We didn't
hire him because of his wonderful qualities. He really don't have any.
But he makes a great spindle for hardware. Audran's just a moddy's
way of gettin' its daily workout." The cop smiled.

"Hey, you gave me this goddamn moddy in the first place," I said.

Hajjar shrugged. "Audran, this is Officer Shaknahyi."

"Where you at?" I said.

"All right," said the cop.

"You got to watch out for Audran," Hajjar said. "He's got one of
those addictives personalities. He used to make a big deal out of not
havin' his brain wired. Now you never see him without some kind of
moddy stuck in his head."

That shocked me. I hadn't realized I'd been using my moddies so
much. I was surprised anyone else had noticed.

"Try to overlook his frailties, Jirji, 'cause you and him are gonna
be workin' together."

Shaknahyi gave him a sharp look. I did the same. "What do you
mean, 'working together'?" said the cop.

"I mean what I said. I got a little assignment for you two. You're
gonna be workin' very closely for a while."

"You taking me off the street?" asked Shaknahyi.

Hajjar shook his head. "I never said that. I'm pairin' Audran with
you on patrol."

Shaknahyi was so outraged, I thought he was going to split down
the middle. "Shaitan take my kids first!" he said. "You think you're
teaming me up with a guy with no training and no experience, you're
goddamn crazy!"

I didn't like the idea of going out on the street. I didn't want to
make myself a target for every loon in the Budayeen who owned a
cheap needle gun. "I'm supposed to stay here in the station house," I
said. "Friedlander Bey never said anything about real cop work."

"Be good for you, Audran," said Hajjar. "You can ride around and see all your old buddies again. They'll be impressed when you flash your badge at them."

"They'll hate my guts," I said.

"You're both overlooking one small detail," said Shaknahyi. "As my partner, he's supposed to guard my back every time we walk into some dangerous situation. To be honest, I don't have a lick of faith in him. You can't expect me to work with a partner I don't trust."

"I don't blame you," said Hajjar. He looked amused by the cop's opinion of me. My first impression of Shaknahyi wasn't so good, either. He didn't have his brain wired, and that meant he was one of two kinds of cop: Either he was a strict Muslim, or else he was one of those guys who thought his own naked, unaugmented brain was more than a match for the evildoers. That's the way I used to be, but I learned better. Either way, I wouldn't get along with him.

"And I don't want the responsibility of watching his back," I said. "I don't need that kind of pressure."

Hajjar patted the air in a kind of soothing motion. "Well, forget about that. You're not gonna be chasin' down bad guys on the street. You're gonna be conductin' an unofficial investigation."

"What kind of investigation?" asked Shaknahyi suspiciously.

Hajjar waved a dark green cobalt-alloy plate. "Got a big file here on Reda Abu Adil. I want you two to learn it backwards and forwards. Then you're gonna meet the man and stick to him like shadows."

"His name's come up a couple of times at Papa's house," I said. "Who is he?"

"He's Friedlander Bey's oldest rival." Hajjar leaned against the pale green wall. "They got a competition goes back a hundred years."

"I know about him," said the cop gruffly.

"Audran only knows about small-time thugs in the Budayeen. Abu Adil don't come near the Budayeen. Keeps his interests far away from Papa's. Carved out a little kingdom for himself on the north and west sides of town. Even so, I got a request from Friedlander Bey to put him under surveillance."

"You're doing this just because Friedlander Bey asked you to?" asked Shaknahyi.

"You bet your ass. He's got a suspicion that Abu Adil is thinkin' about breakin' their truce. Papa wants to be ready."

Well, until I found my leverage with Friedlander Bey, I was his puppet. I had to do whatever he and Hajjar told me to do.

Shaknahyi, however, didn't want any part of it. "I wanted to be a cop because I thought I could help people," he said. "I don't make a lot of money, I don't get enough sleep, and every day I mix into one goddamn crisis after another. I never know when somebody's gonna pull a gun on me and use it. I do it because I believe I can make a difference. I didn't sign on to be some rich bastard's personal spy. How long has this outfit been for sale, anyway?" He glowered at Hajjar until the lieutenant had to look away.

"Listen," I said to Shaknahyi, "what's your problem with me?"

"You're not a cop, for one thing," he said. "You're worse than a rookie. You'll hang back and let some creep nail me, or else you'll get itchy and shoot a little old lady. I don't want to be teamed with somebody unless I think I can count on him."

I nodded. "Yeah, you right, but I can wear a moddy. I've seen plenty of rookies wearing police officer moddies to help them through the routines."

Shaknahyi threw up his hands. "He just makes it worse," he muttered.

"I said not to worry about a rough time on the street," said Hajjar. "This is just an investigation. Mostly desk-job stuff. I don't know what's got you so spooked, Jirji."

Shaknahyi rubbed his forehead and sighed. "All right, all right. I just wanted to have my objection on the record."

"Okay," said Hajjar, "it's been noted. I want to hear regular reports from both of you, 'cause I got to keep Friedlander Bey happy. That's not as easy as it sounds, either." He tossed the cell-memory plate to me.

"Want us to start on this right away?" I asked.

Hajjar gave me a wry look. "If you can fit it into your busy social calendar."

"Make a copy for me," said Shaknahyi. "I'll study the file today, and tomorrow we'll take a ride by Abu Adil's place."

"Fine," I said. I slipped the green plate into my data deck and copied it onto a blank.

"Right," said Shaknahyi, taking the copy and walking out of my cubicle.

"You two didn't hit it off real well," said Hajjar.

"We just have to get the job done," I said. "We don't have to go dancing together."

"Yeah, you right. Why don't you take the rest of the afternoon off? Go home and look through the report. I'm sure you got any questions, Papa can answer them for you."

He left me alone too, and I called Friedlander Bey's house through the data deck. I spoke to one of the Stones That Speak. "Yeah?" he said bluntly.

"This is Audran. Tell Kmuzu to pick me up at the police station in about twenty minutes."

"Yeah," said the Stone. Then I was listening to a dial tone. The Stones make up in curtness what they lack in eloquence.

Twenty minutes later on the dot, Kmuzu swung the electric sedan in toward the curb. I got into the backseat, and he began driving home.

"Kmuzu," I said, "you know anything about a businessman named Reda Abu Adil?"

"A little, *yaa Sidi*," he said. "What do you wish to know?" He never looked away from the road.

"Everything, but not right now." I closed my eyes and let my head fall back against the seat. If only Friedlander Bey would tell me as much as he told Kmuzu and Lieutenant Hajjar. I hated to think that Papa still didn't entirely trust me.

"When we get back to the estate," said Kmuzu, "you'll want to talk with Friedlander Bey."

"That's right," I said.

"I warn you that the woman has put him in a surly mood."

Wonderful, I thought. I'd forgotten about the woman. Papa was going to want to know why I hadn't murdered her yet. I spent the rest of that ride thinking up a plausible excuse.

four

If I'd known just how difficult things were going to be, I might have had Kmuzu drive me straight out of the city and on to some distant, peaceful place. When I got home—by this time I was used to thinking of Friedlander Bey's palace as home—it was about four o'clock in the afternoon. I decided that I could use a nap. After that, I planned to have a brief meeting with Papa and then go out and spend some time in Chiriga's club. Unfortunately, my slave Kmuzu had other ideas.

"I will be quite comfortable in the small room," he announced.

"I'm sorry?" I said. I didn't know what the hell he was talking about.

"The small room that you use for storage. It will be sufficient for my needs. I will bring a cot."

I looked at him for a moment. "I assumed you'd be sleeping in the servant's wing."

"Yes, I have quarters there, *yaa Sidi*, but I will be better able to look after you if I have a room here also."

"I'm not really interested in having you look after me every minute of the day, Kmuzu. I put a certain value on my privacy."

Kmuzu nodded. "I understand that, but the master of the house directed me—"

I'd heard enough of that. "I don't care *what* the master of the house directed you," I shouted. "Whose slave *are* you, mine or his?"

Kmuzu didn't answer me. He just stared at me with his big, solemn eyes.

"Yeah, well, never mind," I said. "Go ahead and make yourself at home in the storage room. Stack up all my stuff and drag in a mattress if you want." I turned away, deeply irritated.

"Friedlander Bey has invited you to dine with him after he speaks to you," said Kmuzu.

"I suppose it doesn't mean anything that I have other plans," I said. All I got was the same silent stare. Kmuzu was awful good at that.

I went into my bedroom and undressed. Then I took a quick shower and thought about what I wanted to say to Friedlander Bey. First, I was going to tell him that this slave-spy thing with Kmuzu was going to have to end pretty goddamn quick. Second, I wanted to let him know that I wasn't happy about being teamed with Officer Shaknahyi. And third, well, that's when I realized that I probably didn't have the nerve to mention anything at all about items one and two.

I got out of the shower and toweled myself dry. Standing under the warm water had made me feel a lot better and I decided that I didn't need a nap after all. Instead, I stared into a closet deciding what to wear. Papa liked it when I wore Arab dress. I figured what the hell and picked a simple maroon *gallebeya*. I decided that the knitted skullcap of my homeland wasn't appropriate, and I'm not the turban type. I settled on a plain white *keffiya* and fixed it in place with a simple black rope *akal*. I tied a corded belt around my waist, supporting a ceremonial dagger Papa'd given me. Also on the belt, pulled around behind my back, was a holster with my seizure gun. I hid that by wearing an expensive tan-colored cloak over the *gallebeya*. I felt I was ready for anything: a feast, a debate, or an attempted assassination.

"Why don't you stay here and get yourself settled in?" I said to Kmuzu, but instead he followed me downstairs. I just knew he'd do that. Papa's offices were on the ground floor in the main part of the house connecting the two wings. When we got there, one of the Stones That Speak was in the corridor, guarding the door. He glanced at me and nodded; but when he looked at Kmuzu, his expression changed. His lip curled just a little. That was the most emotion I'd ever seen from one of the Stones.

"Wait," he said.

"I will go in with my master," said Kmuzu.

The Stone struck him in the chest and shoved him back a step. "Wait," he said.

"It's all right, Kmuzu," I said. I didn't want the two of them wrestling on the floor here outside Friedlander Bey's office. They could settle their little dominance dispute on their own time.

Kmuzu gave me a cool glance, but said nothing. The Stone bowed his head slightly as I went past him into Papa's waiting room, and then he closed the door behind me. If he and Kmuzu went at it out in the hall, I'd be at a loss to know what to do. What's the proper etiquette when your slave is getting beaten up by your boss's slave? Of course, that wasn't giving Kmuzu the benefit of the doubt. Maybe he had a trick or two of his own. Who knows, he might have been able to handle the Stone That Speaks.

Anyway, Friedlander Bey was in his inner office. He was sitting behind his gigantic desk. He didn't look well. His elbows were on the desktop, and his head was in his hands. He was massaging his forehead. He stood up when I came in. "I am pleased," he said. He didn't sound pleased. He sounded exhausted.

"It's my honor to wish you good evening, O Shaykh," I said. He was wearing an open-necked white shirt with the sleeves rolled up and a pair of baggy gray trousers. He probably wouldn't even notice the trouble I'd taken to dress conservatively. You can't win, right?

"We will dine soon, my son. In the meantime, sit with me. There are matters that need our attention."

I sat in a comfortable chair beside his desk. Papa took his seat again and fiddled with some papers, frowning. I wondered if he was going to talk about the woman, or why he'd decided to saddle me with Kmuzu. It wasn't my place to question him. He'd begin when he was ready.

He shut his eyes for a moment and then opened them, sighing. His sparse white hair was rumpled, and he hadn't shaved that morning. I guessed he had a lot on his mind. I was a little afraid of what he was going to order me to do this time.

"We must speak," he said. "There is the matter of alms-giving."

Okay, I'll admit it: Of all the possible problems he could have chosen, alms-giving was pretty low on my list of what I expected to hear. How foolish of me to think he wanted to discuss something more to the point. Like murder.

"I'm afraid I've had more important things on my mind, O Shaykh," I said.

Friedlander Bey nodded wearily. "No doubt, my son, you truly believe these other things are more important, but you are wrong. You and I share an existence of luxury and comfort, and that gives us a responsibility to our brothers."

Jacques, my infidel friend, would've had trouble grasping his precise point. Sure, other religions are all in favor of charity too. It's just good sense to take care of the poor and needy, because you never know when you're going to end up poor and needy yourself. The Muslim attitude goes further, though. Alms-giving is one of the five pillars of the religion, as fundamental an obligation as the profession of faith, the daily prayer, the fast of Ramadan, and the pilgrimage to Mecca.

I gave the same attention to alms-giving that I gave the other duties. That is, I had profound respect for them in an intellectual sort of way, and I told myself that I'd begin practicing in earnest real soon now.

"Evidently you've been considering this for some time," I said.

"We have been neglecting our duty to the poor and the wayfarers, and the widows and orphans among our neighbors."

Some of my friends—my old friends, my former friends—think Papa is nothing but a murderous monster, but that's not true. He's a shrewd businessman who also maintains strong ties to the faith that created our culture. I'm sorry if that seems like a contradiction. He could be harsh, even cruel, at times; but I knew no one else as sincere in his beliefs or as glad to meet the many obligations of the noble Qur'ân.

"What do you wish me to do, O my uncle?"

Friedlander Bey shrugged. "Do I not reward you well for your services?"

"You are unfailingly gracious, O Shaykh," I said.

"Then it would not be a hardship for you to set aside a fifth part of your substance, as is suggested in the Straight Path. Indeed, I desire to make a gift to you that will swell your purse and, at the same time, give you a source of income independent of this house."

That caught my attention. Freedom was what I hungered for every night as I drifted off to sleep. It was what I thought of first when I woke in the morning. And the first step toward freedom was financial independence.

"You are the father of generosity, O Shaykh," I said, "but I am unworthy." Believe me, I was panting to hear what he was going to say. Proper form, however, required me to pretend that I couldn't possibly accept his gift.

He raised one thin, trembling hand. "I prefer that my associates have outside sources of income, sources that they manage themselves and whose profits they need not share with me."

"That is a wise policy," I said. I've known a lot of Papa's "associates," and I know what kind of sources they had. I was sure he was about to cut me into some shady vice deal. Not that I had scruples, you understand. I wouldn't mind getting my drugs wholesale. I've just never had much of a mind for commerce.

"Until recently the Budayeen was your whole world. You know it well, my son, and you understand its people. I have a great deal of influence there, and I thought it best to acquire for you some small commercial concern in that quarter." He extended to me a document laminated in plastic.

I reached forward and took it from him. "What is this, O Shaykh?" I asked.

"It is a title deed. You are now the owner of the property described upon it. From this day forward it is your business to operate. It is a profitable enterprise, my nephew. Manage it well and it will reward you, *inshallah*."

I looked at the deed. "You're—" My voice choked. Papa had bought Chiriga's club and was giving it to me. I looked up at him. "But—"

He waved his hand at me. "No thanks are necessary," he said. "You are my dutiful son."

"But this is Chiri's place. I can't take her club. What will she do?"

Friedlander Bey shrugged. "Business is business," he said simply.

I just stared at him. He had a remarkable habit of giving me things I would have been happier without: Kmuzu and a career as a cop, for instance. It wouldn't do any good at all to refuse. "I'm quite unable to express my thanks," I said in a dull voice. I had only two good friends left, Saied the Half-Hajj and Chiri. She was really going to hate this. I was already dreading her reaction.

"Come," said Friedlander Bey, "let us go in to dinner." He stood up behind his desk and held out his hand to me. I followed him, still astonished. It wasn't until later that I realized I hadn't spoke to him about my job with Hajjar or my new assignment to investigate Reda Abu Adil. When you're in Papa's presence, you go where he wants to go, you do what he wants to do, and you talk about what he wants to talk about.

We went to the smaller of the two dining rooms, in the back of the west wing on the ground floor. This is where Papa and I usually ate when we dined together. Kmuzu fell into step behind me in the corridor, and the Stone That Speaks followed Friedlander Bey. If this were a sentimental American holoshow, eventually they'd get into a fight and afterward they'd become the best of friends. Fat chance.

I stopped at the threshold of the dining room and stared. Umm Saad and her son were waiting for us inside. She was the first woman I'd ever seen in Friedlander Bey's house, but even so she'd never been permitted to join us at the table. The boy looked about fifteen years old, which in the eyes of the faith is the age of maturity. He was old enough to meet the obligations of prayer and ritual fasting, so under other circumstances he might have been welcome to share our meal. "Kmuzu," I said, "escort the woman back to her apartment."

Friedlander Bey put a hand on my arm. "I thank you, my son, but I've invited her to meet with us."

I looked at him, my mouth open, but no intelligent reply occurred to me. If Papa wanted to initiate major revolutions in attitude and behavior at this late date, that was his right. I closed my mouth and nodded.

"Umm Saad will have her dinner in her apartment after our discussion," Friedlander Bey said, giving her a stern look. "Her son may then retire with her or remain with the men, as he wishes."

Umm Saad looked impatient. "I suppose I must be grateful for whatever time you can spare me," she said.

Papa went to his chair, and the Stone assisted him. Kmuzu showed me to my seat across the table from Friedlander Bey. Umm Saad sat on his left, and her son sat on Papa's right. "Marîd," said Papa, "have you met the young man?"

"No," I said. I hadn't even seen him before. He and his mother were keeping a very low profile in that house. The boy was tall for his age, but slender and melancholy. His skin had an unnatural yellowish tint, and the whites of his eyes were discolored. He looked unhealthy. He was dressed in a dark blue *gallebeya* with a geometric print, and he wore the turban of a young shaykh—not a tribal leader, but the honorary turban of a youth who has committed the entire Qur'ân to memory.

"*Yaa Sidi*," said the woman, "may I present to you my handsome son, Saad ben Salah?"

"May your honor be increased, sir," said the boy.

I raised my eyebrows. At least the kid had manners. "Allah be gracious to you," I said.

"Umm Saad," said Friedlander Bey in a gruff voice, "you have come into my house and made extravagant claims. My patience is at an end. Out of respect for the way of hospitality I have suffered your presence, but now my conscience is clear. I demand that you trouble me no more. You must be out of my house by the call to prayer tomorrow morning. I will instruct my servants to give you any assistance you require."

Umm Saad gave him a little smile, as if she found his anger amusing. "I don't believe you've given sufficient thought to our problem. And you've made no provision for the future of your grandson." She covered Saad's hand with her own.

That was like a slap across the face. She was claiming to be Friedlander Bey's daughter or daughter-in-law. It explained why he wanted *me* to get rid of her, instead of doing it himself.

He looked at me. "My nephew," he said, "this woman is not my daughter, and the boy is no kin of mine. This is not the first time a stranger has come to my door claiming blood ties, in the hope of stealing some of my hard-won fortune."

Jeez, I should have taken care of her when he first asked me, before he dragged me into all this intrigue. Someday I'm going to learn to deal with things before they get too complicated. I don't mean that I really would have murdered her, but I might have had a chance to cajole or threaten or bribe her to leave us in peace. I could tell that it was too late now. She wasn't going to accept a settlement; she wanted the ball of wax whole, without any little chunks missing.

"You are certain, O Shaykh?" I said. "That she's not your daughter, I mean?"

For a moment I thought he was going to hit me. Then in a tightly controlled voice he said, "I swear it to you upon the life of the Messenger of God, may blessings be upon him and peace."

That was good enough for me. Friedlander Bey isn't above a little manipulation if it furthers his purposes, but he doesn't swear false oaths. We get along so well partly because he doesn't lie and I don't lie. I looked at Umm Saad. "What proof do you have of your claim?" I said.

Her eyes grew wider. "Proof?" she cried. "Do I need proof to embrace my own father? What proof do *you* have of your father's identity?"

She couldn't have known what a touchy subject that was. I ignored the remark. "Papa—" I stopped myself. "The master of the house has shown you courtesy and kindness. Now he properly requests that you bring your visit to an end. As he said, you may have the help of any of the servants of the house in your departure." I turned to the Stone That Speaks, and his head nodded once. He'd make sure that Umm Saad and her son would be out on the doorstep by the last syllable of the muezzin's morning call.

"Then we have preparations to make," she said, standing. "Come, Saad." And the two of them left the small dining room with as much dignity as if it were their own palace and they the aggrieved party.

Friedlander Bey's hands were pressed flat on the table in front of him. His knuckles were white. He took two or three deep, deliberate breaths. "What do you propose to do, to end this annoyance?" he said.

I looked up, from Kmuzu to the Stone That Speaks. Neither slave seemed to show the least interest in the matter. "Let me understand something first, O Shaykh," I said. "You want to be rid of her and her son. Is it essential that she die? What if I take another, less violent way to discourage her?"

"You saw her and heard her words. Nothing short of violence will bring her scheme to an end. And further—only her death will discourage other leeches from trying the same strategy. Why do you hesitate, my son? The answer is simple and effective. You've killed before. Killing again should not be so difficult. You need not even make it seem accidental. Sergeant Hajjar will understand. He will not proceed with an investigation."

"Hajjar is a lieutenant now," I said.

Papa waved impatiently. "Yes, of course."

"You think Hajjar will overlook a homicide?" Hajjar was bought off, but that didn't mean he'd sit still while I made him look like a fool. I could get away with a lot now, but only if I was careful to preserve Hajjar's public image.

The old man's brow creased. "My son," he said slowly so I wouldn't misunderstand, "if Lieutenant Hajjar balks, he too can be removed. Perhaps you will have better luck with his successor. You can continue this process until the office is filled at last with a police supervisor of sufficient imagination and wit."

"Allah guide you and me," I murmured. Friedlander Bey was pretty damn casual these days about off-bumping as a solution to life's little setbacks. I was struck again by the fact that Papa himself was in no rush to pull any triggers himself. He had learned at an early age to delegate responsibility. And I had become his favorite delegatee.

"Dinner?" he asked.

I'd lost my appetite. "I pray that you'll forgive me," I said. "I have a lot of planning to do. Maybe after your meal, you'll answer some questions. I'd like to hear what you know about Reda Abu Adil."

Friedlander Bey spread his hands. "I don't imagine that I know much more than you," he said.

Now, hadn't Papa twisted Hajjar's arm to start an official investigation? So why was he playing dumb now? Or was this just another test? How many goddamn tests did I have to pass?

Or maybe—and this made it all *real* interesting—maybe Hajjar's curiosity about Abu Adil didn't come from Papa, after all. Maybe Hajjar had sold himself more than once: to Friedlander Bey, and also to the second-highest bidder, and to the third-highest, and to the fourth . . .

I remembered when I was a hot-blooded fifteen-year-old. I promised my girlfriend, Nafissa, that I wouldn't even look at another girl. And I made the same pledge to Fayza, whose tits were bigger. And to Hanuna, whose father worked in the brewery. Everything was just fine until Nafissa found out about Hanuna, and Fayza's father found out about both of the others. The girls would have cut my balls off and scratched out my eyes. Instead, I slipped out of Algiers while the enemy slept, and so began the odyssey that brought me to this city.

That's a dead, dry story and of little relevance here. I'm just suggesting how much trouble Hajjar was looking at if Friedlander Bey and Reda Abu Adil ever caught on to his two-timing.

"Isn't Abu Adil your chief competitor?" I asked.

"The gentleman may think we compete. I do not think that we are in conflict in any way. Allah grants Abu Adil the right to sell his beaten brass where I am selling my beaten brass. If someone chooses to buy from Abu Adil rather than from me, then both customer and merchant have my blessing. I will get my livelihood from Allah, and nothing Abu Adil can do will help or hinder me."

I thought of the vast sums of money that passed through Friedlander Bey's house, some of it ending up in fat envelopes on my own desk. I was confident that none of it derived from the sale of beaten brass. But it made a pleasant euphemism; I let it go.

"According to Lieutenant Hajjar," I said, "you think Abu Adil is planning to put you out of business altogether."

"Only the Gatherer of Nations shall do that, my son." Papa gave me a fond look. "But I am pleased by your concern. You needn't worry about Abu Adil."

"I can use my position down at the copshop to find out what he's up to."

He stood up and ran a hand through his white hair. "If you wish. If it will ease your mind."

Kmuzu pulled my chair away from the table and I stood up also. "My uncle," I said, "I beg you to excuse me. May your table be pleasant to you. I wish you a blessed meal."

Friedlander Bey came to me and kissed me on each cheek. "Go in safety, my darling," he said. "I am most pleased with you."

As I left the dining room, I turned to see Papa sitting once again in his chair. There was a grim look on the old man's face, and the Stone That Speaks was bending low to hear something Papa was saying. I wondered just what Friedlander Bey shared with his slave, but not yet with me.

"You've got to finish moving in, don't you?" I said to Kmuzu as we walked back to my apartment.

"I will bring a mattress, *yaa Sidi*. That will be enough for tonight."

"Good. I have some work to do on the data deck."

"The report on Reda Abu Adil?"

I looked at him sharply. "Yes," I said, "that's right."

"Perhaps I can help you get a clearer picture of the man and his motives."

"How is it that you know so much about him, Kmuzu?" I asked.

"When I was first brought to the city, I was employed as a body-guard for one of Abu Adil's wives."

I thought that information was remarkable. Consider: I begin an investigation of a total stranger, and my brand-new slave turns out to have once worked for that same man. This wasn't a coincidence, I could feel it. I had faith that it'd all fit together eventually. I just hoped I'd still be alive and healthy when it did.

I paused outside the door to my suite. "Go get your bedding and your belongings," I told Kmuzu. "I'll be going through the file on Abu Adil. Don't worry about disturbing me, though. When I'm working, it takes a bomb blast to distract me."

"Thank you, *yaa Sidi*. I will be as quiet as I can."

I began to turn the color lock on the door. Kmuzu gave a little bow and headed toward the servant's quarters. When he'd turned the corner, I hurried away in the opposite direction. I went down to the garage and found my car. It felt strange, sneaking away from my own servant, but I just didn't feel like having him tagging along with me tonight.

I drove through the Christian quarter and then through the upper-class shopping district east of the Budayeen. I parked the car on the Boulevard il-Jameel, not far from where Bill usually sat in his taxi. Before I left the car, I took out my pillcase. It seemed like it had been a long time since I'd treated myself to some friendly drugs. I was well supplied, thanks to my higher income and the many new contacts I'd met through Papa. I selected a couple of blue tri-phets; I was in such a hurry that I swallowed them right there, without water. In a little while I'd be ramping with energy and feeling indomitable. I was going to need the help, because I had an ugly scene ahead of me.

I also thought about chipping in a moddy, but at the last moment I decided against it. I needed to talk with Chiri, and I had enough respect for her to show up in my own head. Afterward, though, things might be different. I might feel like going home as someone else entirely.

Chiri's club was crowded that night. The air was still and warm inside, sweet with a dozen different perfumes, sour with sweat and spilled beer. The sexchanges and pre-op debs chatted with the customers with false cheerfulness, and their laughter broke through the shrill music as they called for more champagne cocktails. Bright bolts of red and blue neon slashed down slantwise behind the bar, and brilliant points of light from spinning mirror balls sparkled on the walls and ceiling. In one corner there was a hologram of Honey Pílar, writhing alone upon a blond mink coat spread on the white sands of some romantic beach. It was an ad for her new sex moddy, *Slow, Slow Burn*. I stared at it for a moment, almost hypnotized.

"Audran," came Chiriga's hoarse voice. She didn't sound happy to see me. "Mr. Boss."

"Listen, Chiri," I said. "Let me—"

"Lily," she called to one of the changes, "get the new owner a drink. Gin and bingara with a hit of Rose's." She looked at me fiercely. "The *tende* is mine, Audran. Private stock. It doesn't go with the club, and I'm taking it with me."

She was making it hard for me. I could only imagine how she felt. "Wait a minute, Chiri. I had nothing to do with—"

"These are the keys. This one's for the register. The money in there's all yours. The girls are yours, the hassles are yours from now on too. You got any problems you can go to Papa with 'em." She snatched her bottle of *tende* from under the bar. "*Kwa heri*, motherfucker," she snarled at me. Then she stormed out of the club.

Everything got real quiet then. Whatever song had been playing came to an end and nobody put on another one. A deb named Kandy was on stage, and she just stood there and stared at me like I might start slavering and shrieking at any moment. People got up from their stools near me and edged away. I looked into their faces and I saw hostility and contempt.

Friedlander Bey wanted to divorce me from all my connections to the Budayeen. Making me a cop had been a great start, but even so I still had a few loyal friends. Forcing Chiri to sell her club had been another brilliant stroke. Soon I'd be just as lonely and friendless as Papa himself, except I wouldn't have the consolation of his wealth and power.

"Look," I said, "this is all a mistake. I got to settle this with Chiri. Indihar, take charge, okay? I'll be right back."

Indihar just gave me a disdainful look. She didn't say anything. I couldn't stand to be in there another minute. I grabbed the keys Chiri'd dropped on the bar and I went outside. She wasn't anywhere in sight on the Street. She might have gone straight home, but she'd probably gone to another club.

I went to the Fée Blanche, old man Gargotier's café on Ninth Street. Saied, Mahmoud, Jacques, and I hung out there a lot. We liked to sit on the patio and play cards early in the evening. It was a good place to catch the action.

They were all there, all right. Jacques was the token Christian in our crowd. He liked to tell people that he was three-quarters European. Jacques was strictly heterosexual and smug about it. Nobody liked him much. Mahmoud was a sexchange, formerly a slim-hipped, doe-eyed dancing girl in the clubs on the Street. Now he was short, broad, and mean, like one of those evil *djinn* you had to sneak past to rescue the enchanted princess. I heard that he was running the organized prostitution in the Budayeen for Friedlander Bey these days. Saied the Half-Hajj glared at me over the rim of a glass of Johnny Walker, his usual drink. He was wearing his tough-guy moddy, and he was just looking for me to give him an excuse to break my bones.

"Where y'at?" I said.

"You're scum, Audran," said Jacques softly. "Filth."

"Thanks," I said, "but I can't stay long." I sat in the empty chair. Monsieur Gargotier came over to see if I was spending any money tonight. His expression was so carefully neutral, I could tell he hated my guts now too.

"Seen Chiri pass by here in the last few minutes?" I asked. Monsieur Gargotier cleared his throat. I ignored him and he went away.

"Want to shake her down some more?" asked Mahmoud. "Think maybe she walked out with some paper clips that belong to you? Leave her alone, Audran."

I'd had enough. I stood up, and Saied stood up across the table from me. He took two quick steps toward me, grabbed my cloak with one hand, and pulled his other fist straight back. Before he could slug me, I chopped quickly at his nose. A little blood came out of his nostril. He was startled, but then his mouth began to twist in pure rage. I grabbed the moddy on his corymbic implant and ripped it loose. I could see his eyes unfocus. He must have been completely disoriented for a moment. "Leave me the hell alone," I said, pushing him back down in his chair. "All of you." I tossed the moddy into the Half-Hajj's lap.

I headed back down the Street, seething. I didn't know what to do next. Chiri's club—my club, now—was packed with people and I couldn't count on Indihar to keep order. I decided to go back there and try to sort things out. Before I'd walked very far, Saied came up behind me and put his hand on my shoulder. "You're making yourself real unpopular, Maghrebi," he said.

"It's not all my doing."

He shook his head. "You're letting it happen. You're responsible."

"Thanks," I said. I kept walking.

He took my right hand and slapped his badass moddy into it. "You take this," he said. "I think you're gonna need it."

I frowned. "The kind of problems I got call for a clear head, Saied. I got all these moral questions to think about. Not just Chiri and her club. Other things."

The Half-Hajj grunted. "Never understand you, Marîd," he said.

"You sound like a tired old relic. You're as bad as Jacques. If you just choose your moddies carefully, you never have to worry about moral questions. God knows I never do."

That's all I needed to hear. "See you around, Saied," I said.

"Yeah, you right." He turned and headed back to the Fée Blanche.

I went on to Chiri's where I shooed everybody out, closed up the place, and drove back to Friedlander Bey's. I climbed the stairs wearily to my apartment, glad that the long, surprise-filled day was finally over. As I was getting ready for bed, Kmuzu appeared quietly in the doorway. "You shouldn't deceive me, *yaa Sidi.*"

"Your feelings hurt, Kmuzu?"

"I am here to help you. I'm sorry you refused my protection. A time may come when you will be glad to call on me."

"That's quite possibly true," I said, "but in the meantime, how about leaving me alone?"

He shrugged. "Someone is waiting to see you, *yaa Sidi.*"

I blinked at him. "Who?"

"A woman."

I didn't have the energy to deal with Umm Saad now. Then again, it might be Chiri—

"Shall I show her in?" asked Kmuzu.

"Yeah, what the hell." I was still dressed, but I was getting very tired. I promised myself that this was going to be a very short conversation.

"Marîd?"

I looked around. Framed in the door, wearing a ragged brown cloth coat, holding a battered plastic suitcase, was Angel Monroe. Mom.

"Thought I'd come spend a few days with you in the city," she said. She grinned drunkenly. "Hey, ain't you glad to see me?"

fivε

when my admirable add-on woke me on Monday morning, I lay in bed for a few moments, thinking. I was willing to admit that maybe I'd made a few mistakes the night before. I wasn't sure how I might have repaired the situation with Chiri, but I should have tried. I owed that much to her and our friendship. I wasn't happy about seeing my mother at the door later, either. I'd solved that problem by digging out fifty kiam and packing her off into the night. I sent Kmuzu with her to find a hotel room. At breakfast, Friedlander Bey offered me some constructive criticism on that decision.

He was furious. There was a husky, hoarse quality to his voice that let me know he was trying like hell not to shout at me. He put his hands on my shoulders, and I could feel him tremble with emotion. His breath was perfumed with mint as he quoted the noble Qur'ân. " 'If one of your parents or both of them attain old age with thee, say not fie unto them nor repulse them, but speak unto them a gracious word. And lower unto them the wing of submission through mercy, and say: My Lord! Have mercy on them both as they did care for me when I was little.' "

I felt shaken. Being inundated by Friedlander Bey's wrath was kind of like practicing for The Day of Judgment. He'd think that comparison was sacrilegious, of course, but he's never been the target of his own fury.

I couldn't keep from stammering. "You mean Angel Monroe." Jeez, that was a lame thing to say, but Papa'd surprised me with this tirade. I still wasn't thinking clearly.

"I'm talking about your mother," he said. "She came to you in need, and you turned her away from your door."

"I provided for her the best way I knew how." I wondered how Papa had heard about the incident in the first place.

"You do not cast your mother out to abide with strangers! Now you must seek the forgiveness of Allah."

That made me feel a little better. This was one of those times when he said "Allah" but he meant "Friedlander Bey." I had sinned against his personal code; but if I could find the right things to say and do, it would be all right again. "O Shaykh," I said slowly, choosing my words carefully, "I know how you feel about women in your house. I hesitated to invite her to stay the night under your roof, and it was too late to consult with you. I balanced my mother's need against your custom, and I did what I thought best." Well, hell, that was almost true.

He glared at me, but I could see that he'd lost the edge of his anger. "Your action was a worse affront to me than having your mother as a guest in my home," he said.

"I understand, O Shaykh, and I beg you to forgive me. I did not mean to offend you or disregard the teaching of the Prophet."

"May the blessing of Allah be upon him and peace," Papa murmured automatically. He shook his head ruefully, but with each passing second his grim expression lightened. "You are still young, my son. This is not the last error of judgment you will make. If you are to become a righteous man and a compassionate leader, you must learn from my example. When you are in doubt, never be afraid to seek my counsel, whatever the time or place."

"Yes, O Shaykh," I said quietly. The storm had passed.

"Now you must find your mother, return her here, and make her welcome in a suitable apartment. We have many unused rooms, and this house is yours as well as mine."

I could tell by his tone that this conversation was over, and I was pretty damn glad. It had been like crossing between the minarets of the Shimaal Mosque on a tightrope. "You are the father of kindness, O Shaykh," I said.

"Go in safety, my nephew."

I went back up to my suite, my breakfast forgotten. Kmuzu, as usual, went with me. "Say," I said, as if the thought had just occurred to me, "*you* didn't happen to let Friedlander Bey know about last night, did you?"

"*Yaa Sidi,*" he said with a blank expression, "it is the will of the master of the house that I tell him of these things."

I chewed my lip thoughtfully. Talking to Kmuzu was like addressing a mythical oracle: I had to be sure to phrase my questions with absolute precision, or I'd get nonsense for an answer. I began simply. "Kmuzu, you are my slave, aren't you?"

"Yes," he said.

"You obey me?"

"I obey you and the master of the house, *yaa Sidi*."

"Not necessarily in that order, though."

"Not necessarily," he admitted.

"Well, I'm gonna give you a plain, unambiguous command. You won't have to clear it with Papa because he suggested it to me in the first place. I want you to find a vacant apartment somewhere in the house, preferably far away from this one, and install my mother comfortably. I want you to spend the entire day seeing to her needs. When I get home from work, I'll need to talk to her about her plans for the future, so that means she gets no drugs and no alcohol."

Kmuzu nodded. "She could not get those things in this house, *yaa Sidi*."

I'd had no problem smuggling my pharmaceuticals in, and I was sure Angel Monroe had her own emergency supply hidden somewhere too. "Help her unpack her things," I said, "and take the opportunity to make sure she's checked all her intoxicants at the door."

Kmuzu gave me a thoughtful look. "You hold her to a stricter standard than you observe yourself," he said quietly.

"Yeah, maybe," I said, annoyed. "Anyway, it's not your place to mention it."

"Forgive me, *yaa Sidi*."

"Forget it. I'll drive myself to work today."

Kmuzu didn't like that, either. "If you take the car," he said, "how can I bring your mother from the hotel?"

I smiled slowly. "Sedan chair, oxcart, hired camel caravan, I don't care. You're the slave, you figure it out. See you tonight." On my desk was yet another thick envelope stuffed with paper bills. One of Friedlander Bey's little helpers had let himself into my apartment while I'd been downstairs. I took the envelope and my briefcase and left before Kmuzu could come up with another objection.

My briefcase still held the cell-memory file on Abu Adil. I was supposed to have read through it last night, but I never got around to it. Hajjar and Shaknahyi were probably going to be griped, but I didn't care. What could they do, fire me?

I drove first to the Budayeen, leaving my car on the boulevard and walking from there to Laila's modshop on Fourth Street. Laila's was small, but it had character, crammed between a dark, grim gambling den and a noisy bar that catered to teenage sexchanges. The moddies and daddies in Laila's bins were covered with dust and fine grit, and generations of small insects had met their Maker among her wares. It wasn't pretty, but what you got from her most of the time was good old honest value. The rest of the time you got damaged, worthless, even dangerous merchandise. You always felt a little rush of adrenalin before you chipped one of Laila's ancient and shopworn moddies directly into your brain.

She was always—*always*—chipped in, and she never stopped whining. She whined hello, she whined goodbye, she whined in pleasure and in pain. When she prayed, she whined to Allah. She had dry black skin as wrinkled as a raisin, and straggly white hair. Laila was not someone I liked to spend a lot of time with. She was wearing a moddy this morning, of course, but I couldn't tell yet which one. Sometimes she was a famous Eur-Am film or holo star, or a character from a forgotten novel, or Honey Pílar herself. Whoever she was, she'd yammer. That was all I could count on.

"How you doing, Laila?" I said. There was the acrid bite of ammonia in her shop that morning. She was squirting some ugly pink liquid from a plastic bottle up into the corners of the room. Don't ask me why.

She glanced at me and gave me a slow, rapturous smile. It was the look you get only from complete sexual satisfaction or from a large dose of Sonneine. "Marîd," she said serenely. She still whined, but now it was a serene whine.

"Got to go out on patrol today, and I thought you might have—"

"Marîd, a young girl came to me this morning and said, 'Mother, the eyes of the narcissus are open, and the cheeks of the roses are red with blushing! Why don't you come outside and see how beautifully Nature has adorned the world!'"

"Laila, if you'll just give me a minute—"

"And I said to her, 'Daughter, that which delights you will fade in an hour, and what profit will you then have in it? Instead, come inside and find with me the far greater beauty of Allah, who created the spring.'" Laila finished her little homily and looked at me expectantly, as if she were waiting for me either to applaud or collapse from enlightenment.

I'd forgotten religious ecstasy. Sex, drugs, and religious ecstasy. Those were the big sellers in Laila's shop, and she tested them all out personally. You had her personal Seal of Approval on every moddy.

"Can I talk now? Laila?"

She stared at me, swaying unsteadily. Slowly she reached one scrawny arm up and popped the moddy out. She blinked a couple of times, and her gentle smile disappeared. "Get you something, Marîd?" she said in her shrill voice.

Laila had been around so long, there was a rumor that as a child she'd watched the imams lay the foundation of the Budayeen's walls. But she knew her moddies. She knew more about old, out-of-print moddies than anyone else I've ever met. I think Laila must have had one of the world's first experimental implants, because her brain had never worked quite right afterward. And the way she still abused the technology, she should have burnt out her last gray cells years ago. She'd withstood cerebral torture that would have turned anyone else into a drooling zombie. Laila probably had a tough protective callus on her brain that prevented anything from penetrating. Anything at all.

I started over from the beginning. "I'm going out on patrol today, and I was wondering if you had a basic cop moddy."

"Sure, I got everything." She hobbled to a bin near the back of the store and dug around in it for a moment. The bin was marked "Prussia/Poland/Breulandy." That didn't have anything to do with which moddies were actually in there; Laila'd bought the battered dividers and scuffed labels from some other kind of shop that was going out of business.

She straightened up after a few seconds, holding two shrink-wrapped moddies in her hand. "This is what you want," she said.

One was the pale blue Complete Guardian moddy I'd seen other rookie cops wearing. It was a good, basic piece of procedural programming that covered almost every conceivable situation. I figured that between the Half-Hajj's mean-mother moddy and the Guardian, I was covered. "What's this other one?" I asked.

"A gift to you at half price. Dark Lightning. Only this version's called Wise Counselor. It's what I was wearing when you came in."

I found that interesting. Dark Lightning was a Nipponese idea that had been very popular fifty or sixty years ago. You sat down in a comfortable padded chair, and Dark Lightning put you instantly into a receptive trance. Then it presented you with a lucid, therapeutic dream. Depending on Dark Lightning's analysis of your current emotional state, it could be a warning, some advice, or a mystical puzzle for your conscious mind to work on.

The high price of the contraption kept it a curiosity among the wealthy. Its Far Eastern fictions—Dark Lightning usually cast you as a contemptuous Nipponese emperor in need of wisdom, or an aged Zen monk begging sublimely in the snow—limited its appeal still further. Lately, however, the Dark Lightning idea had been revived by the growth of the personality module market. And now apparently there was an Arabic version, called Wise Counselor.

I bought both moddies, thinking that I wasn't in a position to turn down any kind of help, friend or fantasy. For someone who once hated the idea of having his skull amped, I was sure building up a good collection of other people's psyches.

Laila had chipped in Wise Counselor again. She gave me that tranquil smile. It was toothless, of course, and it made me shiver. "Go in safety," she said in her nasal wail.

"Peace be upon you." I hurried out of her shop, walked back down the Street, and passed through the gate to where the car was parked. It wasn't far from there to the station house. Back at my desk on the third floor, I opened my briefcase. I put my two purchases, the Complete Guardian and Wise Counselor, in the rack with the others. I grabbed the green cobalt-alloy plate and slotted it into the data deck, but then I hesitated. I really didn't feel like reading about Abu Adil yet. Instead I took Wise Counselor, unwrapped it, then reached up and chipped it in.

After a moment of dizziness, Audran saw that he was reclining on a couch, drinking a glass of lemon sherbet. Facing him on another couch was a handsome man of middle years. With a shock, he recognized the man as the Apostle of God. Quickly, Audran popped the moddy out.

I sat there at my desk, holding Wise Counselor and trembling. It wasn't what I'd expected at all. I found the experience deeply disturbing. The quality of the vision was absolutely realistic—it wasn't like a dream or a hallucination. It didn't feel as if I'd only imagined it; it felt as if I'd truly been in the same room with Prophet Muhammad, blessings and peace be on him.

It should be clear that I'm not a terribly religious person. I've studied the faith and I have tremendous respect for its precepts and traditions, but I guess I just don't find it convenient to practice them. That probably damns my soul for eternity, and I'll have plenty of time in Hell to regret my laziness. Even so, I was shocked by the pure arrogance of the moddy's manufacturer, to presume to depict the Prophet in such a way. Even illustrations in religious texts are considered idolatrous; what would a court of Islamic law make of the experience I'd just had?

Another reason I was shaken, I think, was because in the brief moment before I'd popped the moddy, I'd gotten the distinct impression that the Prophet had something intensely meaningful to tell me.

I started to toss the moddy back into my briefcase, when I had a flash of insight: The manufacturer hadn't depicted the Prophet, after all. The visions of Wise Counselor or Dark Lightning weren't preprogrammed vignettes written by some cynical software scribbler. The moddy was psychoactive. It evaluated my own mental and emotional states, and enabled *me* to create the illusion.

In that sense, I decided, it wasn't a profane mockery of the religious experience. It was only a means of accessing my own hidden feelings. I realized I'd just made a world-class rationalization, but it made me feel a lot better. I chipped the moddy in again.

After a moment of dizziness, Audran saw that he was reclining on a couch, drinking a glass of lemon sherbet. Facing him on another couch was a handsome man of middle years. With a shock, he recognized the man as the Apostle of God.

"As-salaam alaykum," said the Prophet.

"Wa alaykum as-salaam, yaa Hazrat," replied Audran. He thought it was odd that he felt so comfortable in the Messenger's presence.

"You know," said the Prophet, "there is a source of joy that leads you to forget death, that guides you to an accord with the will of Allah."

"I don't know exactly what you mean," Audran said.

Prophet Muhammad smiled. "You have heard that in my life there were many troubles, many dangers."

"Men repeatedly conspired to kill you because of your teachings, O Apostle of Allah. You fought many battles."

"Yes. But do you know the greatest danger I ever faced?"

Audran thought for a moment, perplexed. "You lost your father before you were born."

"Even as you lost yours," said the Prophet.

"You lost your mother as a child."

"Even as you were without a mother."

"You went into the world with no inheritance."

The Prophet nodded. "A condition forced upon you, as well. No, none of those things were the worst, nor were the efforts of my enemies to starve me, to crush me with boulders, to burn me in my tent, or to poison my food."

"Then, yaa Hazrat," asked Audran, "what was the greatest danger?"

"Early in my season of preaching, the Meccans would not listen to my word. I turned to the Sardar of Tayef and asked his permission to preach there. The Sardar gave permission, but I did not know that secretly he plotted to have me attacked by his hired villains. I was

*badly hurt, and I fell unconscious to the ground. A friend carried me
out of Tayef and lay me beneath a shady tree. Then he went into the village again to beg for water, but no one in Tayef would give him any."*

"You were in danger of dying?"

*Prophet Muhammad raised a hand. "Perhaps, but is a man not
always in danger of dying? When I was again conscious, I lifted my
face to Heaven and prayed, 'O Merciful, You have instructed me to
carry Your message to the people, but they will not listen to me. Perhaps it is my imperfection that prevents them from receiving Your blessing. O Lord, give me the courage to try again!'*

*"Then I noticed that Gabriel the Archangel lay upon the sky over
Tayef, waiting for my gesture to turn the village into a blasted wasteland. I cried out in horror: 'No, that is not the way! Allah has chosen
me among men to be a blessing to Mankind, and I do not seek to chas-
tise them. Let them live. If they do not accept my message, then perhaps
their sons or their sons' sons will.'*

*"That awful moment of power, when with a lifted finger I might
have destroyed all of Tayef and the people who lived there, that was the
greatest danger of my life."*

*Audran was humbled. "Allah is indeed Most Great," he said. He
reached up and popped the moddy out.*

Yipe. Wise Counselor had sifted through my subskullular impulses,
then tailored a vision that both interpreted my current turmoil and suggested solutions. But what was Wise Counselor trying to tell me? I was
just too dull and literal-minded to understand what it all meant. I
thought it might be advising me to go up to Friedlander Bey and say,
"I've got the power to destroy you, but I'm staying my hand out of
charity." Then Papa would be overcome with guilt, and free me of all
obligations to him.

Then I realized that it couldn't be that simple. In the first place, I
didn't have any such power to destroy him. Friedlander Bey was protected from lesser creatures like me by *baraka,* the almost magical
presence possessed by certain great men. It would take a better person
than I to lift a finger against him, even to sneak in and pour poison in
his ear while he slept.

Okay, that meant I'd misunderstood the lesson, but it wasn't something I was going to worry about. The next time I met an imam or a
saint on the street, I'd have to ask him to explain the vision to me. In
the meantime I had more important things to do. I put the moddy back
in my briefcase.

Then I loaded the file on Abu Adil and spent about ten minutes

glancing through it. It was every bit as boring as I was afraid it would
be. Abu Adil had been brought to the city at an early age, more than a
century and a half ago. His parents had wandered for many months
after the disaster of the Saturday War. As a boy, Abu Adil helped his
father, who sold lemonade and sherbets in the Souk of the Tanners. He
played in the narrow, twisting alleys of the *medînah,* the old part of
town. When his father died, Abu Adil became a beggar to support himself and his mother. Somehow, through strength of will and inner
resources, he rejected his poverty and miserable station and became
a man of respect and influence in the *medînah.* The report gave no
details of this remarkable transformation, but if Abu Adil was a serious
rival to Friedlander Bey, I had no trouble believing it had happened. He
still lived in a house at the western edge of the city, not far from the
Sunset Gate. By all reports it was a mansion as grand as Papa's, surrounded by ghastly slums. Abu Adil had an army of friends and associates in the hovels of the *medînah,* just as Friedlander Bey had his own
in the Budayeen.

That was about as much as I'd learned when Officer Shaknahyi
ducked his head into my cubicle. "Time to roll," he said.

It didn't bother me in the least to tell my data deck to quit. I wondered why Lieutenant Hajjar was so worked up about Reda Abu Adil. I
hadn't run across anything in the file that suggested he was anything
but another Friedlander Bey: just a rich, powerful man whose business
took on a gray, even black character now and then. If he was like
Papa—and the evidence I'd seen indicated that's just what he was—he
had little interest in disturbing innocent people. Friedlander Bey was
no criminal mastermind, and I doubted that Abu Adil was, either. You
could rouse men like him only by trespassing on their territory or by
threatening their friends and family.

I followed Shaknahyi downstairs to the garage. "That's mine,"
he said, pointing to a patrol car coming in from the previous shift.
He greeted the two tired-looking cops who got out, then slid behind
the steering wheel. "Well?" he said, looking up at me.

I wasn't in a hurry to start this. In the first place, I'd be stuck in the
narrow confines of the copcar with Shaknahyi for the duration of the
shift, and that prospect didn't excite me at all. Second, I'd really rather
sit upstairs and read boring files in perfect safety than follow this
battle-hardened veteran out into the mean streets. Finally, though, I
climbed into the front seat. Sometimes there's only so much stalling
you can do.

"What you carrying?" he said, looking straight out the windshield
while he drove. He had a big wad of gum crammed into his right cheek.

"You mean this?" I held up the Complete Guardian moddy, which I hadn't chipped in yet.

He glanced at me and muttered something under his breath. "I'm talking about what you're gonna use to save me from the bad guys," he said. Then he looked my way again.

Under my sport coat I was wearing my seizure gun. I took it out of the holster and showed him. "Got this last year from Lieutenant Okking," I said.

Shaknahyi chewed his gum for a few seconds. "The lieutenant was always all right to me," he said. His eyes slid sideways again.

"Yeah, well," I said. I couldn't think of anything terribly meaningful to add. I'd been responsible for Okking's death, and I knew that Shaknahyi knew it. That was something else I'd have to overcome if we were going to accomplish anything together. There was silence in the car for a little while after that.

"Look, that weapon of yours ain't much good except for maybe stunning mice and birds up close. Take a look on the floor."

I reached under my seat and pulled out a small arsenal. There was a large seizure cannon, a static pistol, and a needle gun that looked like its flechettes could strip the meat from the bones of an adult rhinoceros. "What do you suggest?" I asked.

"How do you feel about splashing blood all over everything?"

"Had enough of that last year," I said.

"Then forget the needle gun, though it's a dandy side arm. It alternates three sedative barbs, three iced with nerve toxin, and three explosive darts. The seizure cannon may be too hefty for you too. It's got four times the power of your little sizzlegun. It'll stop anybody you aim at up to a quarter of a mile away, but it'll kill a mark inside a hundred yards. Maybe you ought to go with the static gun."

I stuffed the needle gun and the seizure cannon back under the seat and looked at the static gun. "What kind of damage will this do?"

Shaknahyi shrugged. "Hit 'em in the head with that two or three times and you've crippled 'em for life. The head's a small target, though. Get 'em in the chest and it's Heart Attack City. Anywhere else, they can't control their muscles. They're helpless for half an hour. That's what you want."

I nodded and tucked the static gun into my coat pocket. "You don't think I'll—" My telephone began warbling, and I unclipped it from my belt. I figured it was one of my other problems checking in. "Hello?" I said.

"Marîd? This is Indihar."

It seemed like they just weren't making good news anymore. I closed my eyes. "Yeah, how you doing? What's up?"

"You know what *time* it is? You own a club now, Maghrebi. You got a responsibility to the girls on the day shift. You want to get down here and open up?"

I hadn't given the club a goddamn thought. It was something I really didn't want to worry about, but Indihar was right about my responsibility. "I'll get there as soon as I can. Everybody show up today?"

"I'm here, Pualani's here, Janelle quit, I don't know where Kandy is, and Yasmin's here looking for a job."

Now Yasmin too. Jeez. "See you in a few minutes."

"*Inshallah,* Marîd."

"Yeah." I clipped the phone back on my belt.

"Where you got to go now? We don't have time for no personal errands."

I tried to explain. "Friedlander Bey thought he was doing me this big favor, and he bought me my own club in the Budayeen. I don't know a damn thing about running a club. Forgot all about it until now. I got to pass by there and open the place."

Shaknahyi laughed. "Beware of two-hundred-year-old kingpins bearing gifts," he said. "Where's this club?"

"On the Street," I said. "Chiriga's place. You know which one I mean?"

He turned and studied me for a moment without saying anything. Then he said, "Yeah, I know which one you mean." He swung the patrol car around and headed for the Budayeen.

You might think it'd be a kick to zip through the eastern gate in an official car, and drive up the Street when other vehicular traffic is forbidden. My reaction was just the opposite. I scrunched myself down in the seat, hoping no one I knew would see me. I'd hated cops all my life and now I was one; already my former friends were giving me the same treatment I used to give Hajjar and the other police around the Budayeen. I was grateful that Shaknahyi had the sense not to turn on the siren.

Shaknahyi dropped the car right in front of Chiriga's club, and I saw Indihar standing on the sidewalk with Pualani and Yasmin. I was unhappy to see that Yasmin had cut her long, beautiful black hair, which I'd always loved. Maybe since we'd broken up, she felt she had to change things. I took a deep breath, opened the door, and got out. "How y'all doing?" I said.

Indihar glowered at me. "We lost about an hour's tips already," she said.

"You gonna run this club or not, Marîd?" said Pualani. "I can go work by Jo-Mama's real easy."

"Frenchy'd take me back in a Marrakesh minute," said Yasmin. Her expression was cold and distant. Riding around in copcars wasn't improving my status with her at all.

"Don't worry," I said, "I just had a lot on my mind this morning. Indihar, could I hire you to manage the place for me? You know more about running the club than I do."

She stared at me for a few seconds. "Only if you give me a regular schedule," she said. "I don't want to have to come in early after staying late on night shift. Chiri made us do that all the time."

"All right, fine. You got any other ideas, let me know."

"You're gonna have to pay me what other managers make too. And I'm only gonna get up and dance if I feel like it."

I frowned, but she had me in a corner. "That's okay too. Now, who do you suggest to manage at night?"

Indihar shrugged. "I don't trust none of those sluts. Talk to Chiri. Hire her back."

"Hire *Chiri*? To work in her own club?"

"It's not her own club anymore," Yasmin pointed out.

"Yeah, right," I said. "You think she'd do it?"

Indihar laughed. "She'll make you pay her three times what any other manager on the Street gets. She'll give you hell about it too, and she'll steal you blind out of the register if you give her half a chance. But she'll still be worth it. Nobody can make money like Chiri. Without her, you'll be renting this property to some rug merchant inside of six months."

"You hurt her feelings real bad, Marîd," said Pualani.

"I know, but it wasn't my fault. Friedlander Bey organized the whole thing without talking to me about it first. He just dropped the club on me as a surprise."

"Chiri doesn't know that," said Yasmin.

I heard a car door slam behind me. I turned and saw Shaknahyi walking toward me, a big grin on his face. All I needed now was to have him join in. He was really enjoying this.

Indihar and the others hated my guts for turning cop, and the cops felt the same way because to them I was still a hustler. The Arabs say, "You take off your clothes, you get cold." That's advice against cutting yourself off from your support group. It doesn't offer any help if your friends show up in a mob and strip you naked against your will.

Shaknahyi didn't say a word to me. He went up to Indihar, bent, and whispered something in her ear. Well, a lot of the girls on the Street have this fascination with cops. I never understood it, myself. And some of the cops don't mind taking advantage of the situation. It just surprised me to find out that Indihar was one of those girls, and that Shaknahyi was one of those cops.

It didn't occur to me to add this to the list of recent unnatural coincidences: My new partner just happened to have a thing going with the new manager of the club Friedlander Bey had just given me.

"Got everything settled here, Audran?" Shaknahyi asked.

"Yeah," I said. "I got to talk to Chiriga sometime today."

"Indihar's right," said Yasmin. "Chiri's gonna give you a hard time."

I nodded. "She's entitled, I guess, but I'm still not looking forward to it."

"Let's mount up," said Shaknahyi.

"If I got time later," I said, "I'll drop in and see how y'all are doing."

"We'll be fine," said Pualani. "We know how to do *our* jobs. You just watch your ass around Chiri."

"Protect your middle," said Indihar. "If you know what I mean."

I waved and headed back to the patrol car. Shaknahyi gave Indihar a little kiss on the cheek, then followed me. He got behind the wheel. "Ready to work now?" he asked. We were still sitting at the curb.

"How long you known Indihar? I never seen you come into Chiri's club."

He gave me this wide-eyed innocent look. "I been knowing her for a long time," he said.

"Right," I said. I just left it there. It didn't sound like he wanted to talk about her.

A shrill alarm went off, and the synthesized voice of the patrol car's comp deck crackled. "Badge number 374, respond immediately to bomb threat and hostage situation, Café de la Fée Blanche, Ninth Street North."

"Gargotier's place," said Shaknahyi. "We'll take care of it." The comp deck fell silent.

And Hajjar had promised me I wouldn't have to worry about anything like this. "*Bismillah ar-Rahman ar-Raheem,*" I murmured. In the name of Allah, the Compassionate, the Merciful.

This time as we rode up the Street, Shaknahyi let the siren scream.

six

ThERE was a CROWD gathered outside the low railing of the Café de la Fée Blanche's patio. An old man sat at one of the white-painted iron tables, drinking something from a plastic tumbler. He seemed oblivious to the crisis that was occurring inside the bar. "Get him out of here," Shaknahyi growled at me. "Get these other people out of here too. I don't know what's happening in there, but we got to treat it like the guy has a real bomb. And when you got everybody moved back, go sit in the car."

"But—"

"I don't want to have to worry about you too." He ran around the corner of the café to the north, heading for the café's rear entrance.

I hesitated. I knew backup units would be getting here soon, and I decided to let them handle the crowd control. At the moment, there were more important things to worry about. I still had Complete Guardian, and I tore open the shrinkwrap with my teeth. Then I chipped the moddy in.

Audran was sitting at a table in the dimly lighted San Saberio salon in Florence, listening to a group of musicians playing a demure Schubert quartet. Across from him sat a beautiful blond woman named Costanzia. She raised a cup to her lips, and her china blue eyes looked at him over the rim. She was wearing a subtle, fascinating fragrance that made Audran think of romantic evenings and soft-spoken promises.

"This must be the best coffee in Tuscany," she murmured. Her voice was sweet and gentle. She gave him a warm smile.

"We didn't come here to drink coffee, my darling," he said. "We came here to see the season's new styles."

She waved a hand. "There is time enough for that. For now, let's just relax."

Audran smiled fondly at her and picked up his delicate cup. The coffee was the beautiful color of polished mahogany, and the wisps of steam that rose from it carried a heavenly, enticing aroma. The first taste overwhelmed Audran with its richness. As the coffee, hot and wonderfully delicious, went down his throat, he realized that Costanzia had been perfectly correct. He had never before been so satisfied by a cup of coffee.

"I'll always remember this coffee," he said.

"Let's come back here again next year, darling," said Costanzia.

Audran laughed indulgently. "For San Saberio's new fashions?"

Costanzia lifted her cup and smiled. "For the coffee," she said.

After the advertisement, there was a blackout during which Audran couldn't see a thing. He wondered briefly who Costanzia was, but he put her out of his mind. Just as he began to panic, his vision cleared. He felt a ripple of dizziness, and then it was as if he'd awakened from a dream. He was rational and cool and he had a job to do. He had become the Complete Guardian.

He couldn't see or hear anything that was happening inside. He assumed that Shaknahyi was making his way quietly through the café's back room. It was up to Audran to give his partner as much support as possible. He jumped the iron railing into the patio.

The old man at the table looked up at him. "No doubt you are eager to read my manuscripts," he said.

Audran recognized the man as Ernst Weinraub, an expatriate from some Central European country. Weinraub fancied himself a writer, but Audran had never seen him finish anything but quantities of anisette or bourbon whiskey. "Sir," he said, "you're in danger here. I'm going to have to ask you to go out into the street. For your own safety, please move away from the café."

"It's not even midnight yet," Weinraub complained. "Just let me finish my drink."

Audran didn't have time to humor the old drunk. He left the patio and walked decisively into the interior of the bar.

The scene inside didn't look very threatening. Monsieur Gargolier was standing behind the bar, beneath the huge, cracked mirror. His daughter, Maddie, was sitting at a table near the back wall. A young man sat at a table against the west wall, under Gargotier's collection of faded prints of the Mars colony. The young man's hands rested on a small box. His head swung to look at Audran. "Get the fuck out," he shouted, "or this whole place goes up in a big bright bang!"

"I'm sure he means it, monsieur," said Gargotier. He sounded terrified.

"Bet your ass I mean it!" said the young man.

Being a police officer meant sizing up dangerous situations and being able to make quick, sure judgments. Complete Guardian suggested that in dealing with a mentally disturbed individual, Audran should try to find out why he was upset and then try to calm him. Complete Guardian recommended that Audran not make fun of the individual, show anger, or dare him to carry out his threat. Audran raised his hands and spoke calmly. "I'm not going to threaten you," Audran said.

The young man just laughed. He had dirty long hair and a patchy growth of beard, and he was wearing a faded pair of blue jeans and a plaid cotton shirt with its sleeves torn off. He looked a little like Audran had, before Friedlander Bey had raised his standard of living.

"Mind if I sit and talk with you?" asked Audran.

"I can set this off any time I want," said the young man. "You got the guts, sit down. But keep your hands flat on the table."

"Sure." Audran pulled out a chair and sat down. He had his back to the barkeeper, but out of the corner of his eye he could see Maddie Gargotier. She was quietly weeping.

"You ain't gonna talk me out of this," said the young man.

Audran shrugged. "I just want to find out what this is all about. What's your name?"

"The hell's that got to do with anything?"

"My name is Marîd. I was born in Mauretania."

"You can call me Al-Muntaqim." The kid with the bomb had appropriated one of the Ninety-Nine Beautiful Names of God. It meant "The Avenger."

"You always lived in the city?" Audran asked him.

"Hell no. Misr."

"That's the local name for Cairo, isn't it?" asked Audran.

Al-Muntaqim jumped to his feet, furious. He jabbed a finger toward Gargotier behind the bar and screamed, "See? See what I mean? That's just what I'm talkin' about! Well, I'm gonna stop it once and for all!" He grabbed the box and ripped open the lid.

Audran felt a horrible pain all through his body. It was as if all his joints had been yanked and twisted until his bones pulled apart. Every muscle in his body felt torn, and the surface of his skin stung as if it had been sandpapered. The agony went on for a few seconds, and then Audran lost consciousness.

"You all right?"

No, I didn't feel all right. On the outside I felt red-hot and glowing, as if I'd been staked out under the desert sun for a couple of days. Inside, my muscles felt quivery. I had lots of uncontrollable little spasms in my arms, legs, trunk, and face. I had a splitting headache and there was a horrible, sour taste in my mouth. I was having a lot of trouble focusing my eyes, as if someone had spread a thick translucent gunk over them.

I strained to make out who was talking to me. I could barely make out the voice because my ears were ringing so loud. It turned out to be Shaknahyi, and that indicated that I was still alive. For an awful moment after I came to, I thought I might be in Allah's green room or somewhere. Not that being alive was any big thrill just then. "What—" I croaked. My throat was so dry I could barely speak.

"Here." Shaknahyi handed a glass of cold water down to me. I realized that I was lying flat on my back on the floor, and Shaknahyi and Monsieur Gargotier were standing over me, frowning and shaking their heads.

I took the water and drank it gratefully. When I finished, I tried talking again. "What happened?" I said.

"You fucked up," Shaknahyi said.

"Right," I said.

A narrow smile creased Shaknahyi's face. He reached down and offered me a hand. "Get up off the floor."

I stood up wobbly and made my way to the nearest chair. "Gin and bingara," I said to Gargotier. "Put a hit of Rose's lime in it." The barkeep grimaced, but he turned away to get my drink. I took out my pillcase and dug out maybe eight or nine Sonneine.

"I heard about you and your drugs," said Shaknahyi.

"It's all true," I said. When Gargotier brought my drink, I swallowed the opiates. I couldn't wait for them to start fixing me up. Everything would be just fine in a couple of minutes.

"You could've gotten everybody killed, trying to talk that guy down," Shaknahyi said. I was feeling bad enough already, I didn't want to listen to his little lecture right then. He went ahead with it anyway. "What the hell were you trying to do? Establish rapport or something? We don't work that way when people's lives are in danger."

"Yeah?" I said. "What *do* you do?"

He spread his hands like the answer should have been perfectly obvious. "You get around where he can't see you, and you ice the motherfucker."

"Did you ice me before or after you iced Al-Muntaqim?"

"That what he was calling himself? Hell, Audran, you got to expect a little beam diffusion with these static pistols. I'm real sorry I had to drop you too, but there's no permanent damage, *inshallah*. He jumped up with that box, and I wasn't gonna wait around for you to give me a clear shot. I had to take what I could get."

"It's all right," I said. "Where's The Avenger now?"

"The meat wagon came while you were napping. Took him off to the lock ward at the hospital."

That made me a little angry. "The mad bomber gets shipped to a nice bed in the hospital, but I got to lie around on the filthy floor of this goddamn saloon?"

Shaknahyi shrugged. "He's in a lot worse shape than you are. You only got hit by the fuzzy edge of the charge. He took it full."

It sounded like Al-Muntaqim was going to feel pretty rotten for a while. Didn't bother me none.

"No percentage in debating morality with a loon," said Shaknahyi. "You go in looking for the first opportunity to stabilize the sucker." He made a trigger-pulling motion with his right index finger.

"That's not what Complete Guardian was telling me," I said. "By the way, did you pop the moddy for me? What did you do with it?"

"Yeah," said Shaknahyi, "here it is." He took the moddy out of a shirt pocket and tossed it down on the floor beside me. Then he raised his heavy black boot and stamped the plastic module into jagged pieces. Brightly colored fragments of the webwork circuitry skittered across the floor. "Wear another one of those, I do the same to your face and then I kick the remnants out of my patrol car."

So much for Marîd Audran, Ideal Law Enforcement Officer.

I stood up feeling a lot better, and followed Shaknahyi out of the dimly lighted bar. Monsieur Gargotier and his daughter, Maddie, went with us. The bartender tried to thank us, but Shaknahyi just raised a hand and looked modest. "No thanks are necessary for performing a duty," he said.

"Come in for free drinks anytime," Gargotier said gratefully.

"Maybe we will." Shaknahyi turned to me. "Let's ride," he said. We went out through the patio gate. Old Weinraub was still sitting beneath his Cinzano umbrella, apparently oblivious to everything that had gone on.

On the way back to the car I said, "It makes me feel kind of good to be welcome somewhere again."

Shaknahyi looked at me. "Accepting free drinks is a major infraction."

"I didn't know they *had* infractions in the Budayeen," I said. Shaknahyi smiled. It seemed that things had thawed a little between us.

Before I got into the car, a muezzin from some mosque beyond the quarter chanted the afternoon call to prayer. I watched Shaknahyi go into the patrol car's backseat and come out with a rolled prayer rug. He spread the rug on the sidewalk and prayed for several minutes. For some reason it made me feel very uncomfortable. When he finished, he rolled the prayer rug again and put it back in the car, giving me an odd look, a kind of silent reproach. We both got into the patrol car, but neither of us said anything for a while.

Shaknahyi cruised back down the Street and out of the Budayeen. Curiously, I was no longer wary of being spotted in the copcar by any of my old friends. In the first place, the way they'd been treating me, I figured the hell with 'em. In the second place, I felt a little different now that I'd been fried in the line of duty. The experience at the Fée Blanche had changed my thinking. Now I appreciated the risks a cop has to take day after day.

Shaknahyi surprised me. "You want to stop somewhere for lunch?" he asked.

"Sounds good." I was still pretty weak and the sunnies had left me a little lightheaded, so I was glad to agree.

"There's a place near the station house we sometimes go to." He punched the siren and made some fast time through the traffic. About a block from the beanery, he turned off the horn and glided into an illegal parking place. "Police perks," he said, grinning at me. "There ain't many others."

When we got inside, I was pleasantly surprised. The cookshop was owned by a young Mauretanian named Meloul, and the food was pure Maghrebi. By bringing me here, Shaknahyi more than made up for the pain he'd caused me earlier. I looked at him, and suddenly he didn't seem like such a bad guy.

"Let's grab this table," he said, picking one far from the door and against a wall, where he could watch the other customers and keep an eye on what was happening outside too.

"Thanks," I said. "I don't get food from home very often."

"Meloul," he called, "I got one of your cousins here."

The proprietor came over, carrying a stainless steel pitcher and basin. Shaknahyi washed his hands carefully and dried them on a clean white towel. Then I washed my hands and dried them on a second towel. Meloul looked at me and smiled. He was about my age, but taller and darker. "I am Berber," he said. "You are Berber too, yes? You are from Oran?"

"I've got a little Berber blood in me," I said. "I was born in Sidi-bel-Abbès, but I grew up in Algiers."

He came toward me, and I stood up. We exchanged kisses on the cheek. "I live all my life in Oran," he said. "Now I live in this fine city. Sit down, be comfortable, I bring good food to you and Jirji."

"The two of you got a lot in common," said Shaknahyi.

I nodded. "Listen, Officer Shaknahyi," I said, "I want to—"

"Call me Jirji. You slapped on that goddamn moddy and followed me into Gargotier's. It was stupid, but you had guts. You been initiated, sort of."

That made me feel good. "Yeah, well, Jirji, I want to ask you something. Would you say you were very religious?"

He frowned. "I perform the duties, but I'm not gonna go out on the street and kill infidel tourists if they don't convert to Islam."

"Okay, then maybe you could tell me what this dream means."

He laughed. "What kind of dream? You and Brigitte Stahlhelm in the Tunnel of Love?"

I shook my head. "No, nothing like that at all. I dreamed I met the Holy Prophet. He had something to tell me, but I couldn't understand it." I related the rest of the vision Wise Counselor had created for me.

Shaknahyi raised his eyebrows, but he said nothing for a few moments. He played with the ends of his mustache as he thought. "Seems to me," he said finally, "it's about simple virtues. You're supposed to remember humility, as Prophet Muhammad, blessings and peace be upon him, remembered it. Now's not the time for you to make great plans. Later maybe, Allah willing. That make any sense to you?"

I kind of shivered, because as soon as he said it, I knew he was right. It was a suggestion from my backbrain that I shouldn't worry about handling my mother, Umm Saad, and Abu Adil all by myself. I should take things slowly, one thing at a time. They would all come together eventually. "Thanks, Jirji," I said.

He shrugged. "No thanks are necessary."

"I bring you good food," said Meloul cheerfully, setting a platter between Shaknahyi and me. The mounded-up couscous was fragrant with cinnamon and saffron, and it made me realize just how hungry I was. In a well in the middle of the ring of couscous, Meloul had piled bite-sized pieces of chicken and onions browned in butter and flavored with honey. He also brought a plate of bread and cups of strong black coffee. I could hardly keep myself from diving right in.

"It looks great, Meloul," said Shaknahyi.

"May it be pleasant to you." Meloul wiped his hands on a clean towel, bowed to us, and left us to our meal.

"In the name of Allah, the Compassionate, the Merciful," Shaknahyi murmured.

I offered the same brief grace, and then allowed myself to scoop up a chunk of chicken and some of the couscous. It tasted even better than it smelled.

When we'd finished, Shaknahyi called for our bill. Meloul came to the table, still smiling. "No charge. My countrymen eat for free. Policemen eat for free."

"That's kind of you, Meloul," I said, "but we're not allowed to accept—"

Shaknahyi drank the last of his coffee and put down his cup. "It's all right, Marîd," he said, "this is different. Meloul, may your table last forever."

Meloul put his hand on Shaknahyi's shoulder. "May God lengthen your life," he said. He hadn't turned a copper fiq on our patronage, but he looked pleased.

Shaknahyi and I left the cookshop well fed and comfortable. It seemed a shame to spoil the rest of the afternoon with police work.

An old woman sat begging on the sidewalk a few yards from Meloul's. She was dressed in a long black coat and black kerchief. Her sun-darkened face was deeply scored with wrinkles, and one of her sunken eyes was the color of milk. There was a large black tumor just in front of her right ear. I went up to her. "Peace be upon you, O Lady," I said.

"And upon you be peace, O Shaykh," she said. Her voice was a gritty whisper.

I remembered that I still had the envelope of money in my pocket. I took it out and opened it, then counted out a hundred kiam. It hardly made a dent in my roll. "O Lady," I said, "accept this gift with my respect."

She took the money, astonished by the number of bills. Her mouth opened, then shut. Finally she said, "By the life of my children, you are more generous than Haatim, O Shaykh! May Allah open His ways to you." Haatim is the personification of hospitality among the nomad tribesmen.

She made me feel a little self-conscious. "We thank God every hour," I said quietly, and turned away.

Shaknahyi didn't say anything to me until we were sitting in the patrol car again. "Do that a lot?" he asked.

"Do what?"

"Drop a hundred kiam on strangers."

I shrugged. "Isn't alms-giving one of the Five Pillars?"

"Yeah, but you don't pay much attention to the other four. That's odd too, because for most people, parting with cash is the toughest duty."

In fact, I was wondering myself why I'd done it. Maybe because I was feeling uncomfortable about the way I'd been treating my mother. "I just felt sorry for that old woman," I said.

"Everybody in this part of the city does. They all take care of her. That was Safiyya the Lamb Lady. She's a crazy old woman. You never see her without a pet lamb. She takes it everywhere. She lets it drink from the fountain at the Shimaal Mosque."

"I didn't see any lamb."

He laughed. "No, her latest lamb got run over by a shish kebab cart a couple of weeks ago. Right now she has an imaginary lamb. It was standing there right beside her, but only Safiyya can see it."

"Uh yeah," I said. I'd given her enough to buy herself a couple of new lambs. My little bit to alleviate the suffering of the world.

We had to skirt the Budayeen. Although the Street runs in the right direction, it comes to a dead end at the entrance to a cemetery. I knew a lot of people in there—friends and acquaintances who'd died and been dumped in the cemetery, and the still breathing who were so desperately poor that they'd taken up residence in the tombs.

Shaknahyi passed to the south of the quarter, and we drove through a neighborhood that was entirely foreign to me. At first the houses were of moderate size and not too terribly rundown; but after a couple of miles, I noticed that everything around me was getting progressively shabbier. The flat-roofed white stucco homes gave way to blocks of ugly tenements and then to burned-out, vacant lots dotted with horrible little shacks made of scrap plywood and rusting sheets of corrugated iron.

We drove on, and I saw groups of idle men leaning against walls or squatting on the bare earth sharing bowls of liquor, probably *laqbi*, a wine made from the date palm. Women screamed to each other from the windows. The air was foul with the smells of wood smoke and human excrement. Children dressed in long tattered shirts played among the garbage strewn in the gutters. Years ago in Algiers I had been like these hungry urchins, and maybe that's why the sight of them affected me so much.

Shaknahyi must have seen the expression on my face. "There are worse parts of town than Hâmidiyya," he said. "And a cop's got to be ready to go into any kind of place and deal with any kind of person."

"I was just thinking," I said slowly. "This is Abu Adil's territory. It doesn't look he does all that much for these people, so why do they stay loyal to him?"

Shaknahyi answered me with another question. "Why do you stay loyal to Friedlander Bey?"

One good reason was that Papa'd had the punishment center of my brain wired when the rest of the work was done, and that he could stimulate it any time he wanted. Instead, I said, "It's not a bad life. And I guess I'm just afraid of him."

"Same goes for these poor *fellahîn*. They live in terror of Abu Adil, and he tosses just enough their way to keep them from starving to death. I just wonder how people like Friedlander Bey and Abu Adil get that kind of power in the first place."

I watched the slums pass by beyond the windshield. "How do you think Papa makes his money?" I asked.

Shaknahyi shrugged. "He's got a thousand cheap hustlers out there, all turning over big chunks of their earnings for the right to live in peace."

I shook my head. "That's only what you see going on in the Budayeen. Probably seems like vice and corruption are Friedlander Bey's main business in life. I've lived in his house for months now, and I've learned better. The money that comes from vice is just pocket change to Papa. Counts for maybe five percent of his annual income. He's got a much bigger concern, and Reda Abu Adil is in the same business. They sell order."

"They sell *what?*"

"Order. Continuity. Government."

"How?"

"Look, half the countries in the world have split up and recombined again until it's almost impossible to know who owns what and who lives where and who owes taxes to whom."

"Like what's happening right now in Anatolia," said Shaknahyi.

"Right," I said. "The people in Anatolia, when their ancestors lived there it was called Turkey. Before that it was the Ottoman Empire, and before that it was Anatolia again. Right now it looks like Anatolia is breaking up into Galatia, Lydia, Cappadocia, Nicaea, and Asian Byzantium. One democracy, one emirate, one people's republic, one fascist dictatorship, and one constitutional monarchy. There's got to be somebody who's staying on top of it all, keeping the records straight."

"Maybe, but it sounds like a tough job."

"Yeah, but whoever does it ends up the real ruler of the place. He'll have the real power, because all the little states will need his help to keep from collapsing."

"It makes a weird kind of sense. And you're telling me that's what Friedlander Bey's racket is?"

"It's a service," I said. "An important service. And there are lots of ways for him to exploit the situation."

"Yeah, you right," he said admiringly. We turned a corner, and there was a long, high wall made of dark brown bricks. This was Reda Abu Adil's estate. It looked like it was every bit as huge as Papa's. As we stopped at the guarded gate, the luxuriousness of the main house seemed even grander contrasted to the ghastly neighborhood that surrounded it.

Shaknahyi presented our credentials to the guard. "We're here to see Shaykh Reda," he said. The guard picked up a phone and spoke to someone. After a moment, he let us continue.

"A century or more ago," Shaknahyi said thoughtfully, "crime bosses had these big illicit schemes to make money. Sometimes they also operated small legal businesses for practical reasons, like laundering their money."

"Yeah? So?" I said.

"Look at it: You say Reda Abu Adil and Friedlander Bey are two of the most powerful men in the world, as 'consultants' to foreign states. That's entirely legitimate. Their criminal connections are much less important. They just provide livelihoods for the old men's dependents and associates. Things have gotten turned around ass-backwards."

"That's progress," I said. Shaknahyi just shook his head.

We got out of the patrol car, into the warm afternoon sunshine. The grounds in front of Abu Adil's house had been carefully landscaped. The fragrance of roses was in the air, and the strong, pleasant scent of lemons. There were cages of songbirds on either side of an ancient stone fountain, and the warbling music filled the afternoon with a languorous peace. We went up the ceramic-tiled path to the mansion's geometrically carved front door. A servant had already opened it and was waiting for us to explain our business.

"I'm Officer Shaknahyi and this is Marîd Audran. We've come to see Shaykh Reda."

The servant nodded but said nothing. We followed him into the house, and he closed the heavy wooden door behind us. Sunlight streamed in from latticed windows high over our heads. From far away I heard the sound of someone playing a piano. I could smell lamb roasting and coffee brewing. The squalor only a stone's throw away had been completely shut out. The house was a self-contained little world, and I'm sure that's just as Abu Adil intended it.

We were led directly into Abu Adil's presence. I couldn't even get in to see Friedlander Bey that quickly.

Reda Abu Adil was a large, plump old man. He was like Papa in that it was impossible to guess just how old he might be. I knew for a fact that he was at least a hundred twenty-five. It wouldn't surprise me to learn that he was just as old as Friedlander Bey. He was wearing a loose white robe and no jewelry. He had a carefully trimmed white beard and mustache and thick white hair, out of which poked a dove gray moddy with two daddies snapped in. I was expert enough to notice that Abu Adil did not have a protruding plug, as I had; his hardware chipped into a corymbic socket.

Abu Adil reclined on a hospital bed that had been elevated so that he could see us comfortably as we spoke. He was covered by an expensive hand-embroidered blanket. His gnarled hands lay outside the cover, flat on either side of his body. His eyes were heavy-lidded, as if he were drugged or desperately sleepy. He grimaced and groaned frequently while we stood there. We waited for him to say something.

He did not. Instead, a younger man standing beside the hospital bed spoke up. "Shaykh Reda welcomes you to his home. My name is Umar Abdul-Qawy. You may address Shaykh Reda through me."

This Umar person was about fifty years old. He had bright, mistrustful eyes and a sour expression that looked like it never changed. He too looked well fed, and he was dressed in an impressive gold-colored robe and metallic blue caftan. He wore nothing on his head and, like his master, a moddy divided his thinning hair. I disliked him from the getgo.

It was clear to me that I was facing my opposite number. Umar Abdul-Qawy did for Abu Adil what I did for Friedlander Bey, although I'm sure he'd been at it longer and was more intimate with the inner workings of his master's empire. "If this is a bad time," I said, "we can come back again."

"This is a bad time," said Umar. "Shaykh Reda suffers the torments of terminal cancer. You see, then, that another time would not necessarily be better."

"We pray for his well-being," I said.

A tiny smile quirked the edge of Abu Adil's lips. *"Allah yisallimak,"* said Umar. "God bless you. Now, what has brought you to us this afternoon?"

This was inexcusably blunt. In the Muslim world, you don't inquire after a visitor's business. Custom further requires that the laws of hospitality be observed, if only minimally. I'd expected to be served coffee, if not offered a meal as well. I looked at Shaknahyi.

It didn't seem to bother him. "What dealings does Shaykh Reda have with Friedlander Bey?"

That seemed to startle Umar. "Why, none at all," he said, spreading his hands. Abu Adil gave a long, pain-filled moan and closed his eyes tightly. Umar didn't even turn in his direction.

"Then Shaykh Reda does not communicate at all with him?" Shaknahyi asked.

"Not at all. Friedlander Bey is a great and influential man, but his interests lie in a distant part of the city. The two shaykhs have never discussed anything of a business nature. Their concerns do not meet at any point."

"And so Friedlander Bey is no hindrance or obstacle to Shaykh Reda's plans?"

"Look at my master," said Umar. "What sort of plans do you think he has?" Indeed, Abu Adil looked entirely helpless in his agony. I wondered what had made Lieutenant Hajjar set us on this fool's errand.

"We received some information, and we had to check it out," said Shaknahyi. "We're sorry for the intrusion."

"That's quite all right. Kamal will see you to the door." Umar stared at us with a stony expression. Abu Adil, however, made an attempt to raise his hand in farewell or blessing, but it fell back limply to the blanket.

We followed the servant back to the front door. When we were alone again outside, Shaknahyi began to laugh. "That was some performance," he said.

"What performance? Did I miss something?"

"If you'd read the file all the way through, you'd know that Abu Adil doesn't have cancer. He's never had cancer."

"Then—"

Shaknahyi's mouth twisted in contempt. "You ever hear of Proxy Hell? It's a bunch of lunatics who wear bootleg, underground moddies turned out in somebody's back room. They're recordings taken from real people in horrible situations."

I was dismayed. "Is that what Abu Adil's doing? Wearing the personality module of a terminal cancer patient?"

Shaknahyi nodded as he opened the car door and got in. "He's chipped into vicarious pain and suffering. You can buy any kind of disease or condition you want on the black market. There are plenty of deranged masochists like him out there."

I joined him in the patrol car. "And I thought the girls and debs on the Street were misusing the moddies. This adds a whole new meaning to the word perversion."

Shaknahyi started up the car and drove around the fountain toward the gate. "They introduce some new technology and no matter how much good it does for most people, there's always a crazy son of a bitch who'll find something twisted to do with it."

I thought about that, and about my own bodmods, as we drove back to the station house through the wretched district that was home to Reda Abu Adil's faithful followers.

SEVEN

During the next week, I spent as much time in the patrol car as I did at my computer on the third floor of the station house. I felt good after my first experiences as a cop on patrol, although it was clear that I still had a lot to learn from Shaknahyi. We intervened in domestic squabbles and investigated robberies, but there were no more dramatic crises like Al-Muntaqim's clumsy bomb threat.

Shaknahyi had let several days pass, and now he wanted to follow up on our visit to Reda Abu Adil. He guessed that Friedlander Bey had told Lieutenant Hajjar to assign this investigation to us, but Papa was still pretending he wasn't interested in whatever it was about. Our delicate probing would be a lot more successful if someone would just tell us what we were trying to uncover.

Yet there were other concerns on my mind. One morning, after I'd dressed and Kmuzu had served me breakfast, I sat back and thought about what I wanted to accomplish that day.

"Kmuzu," I said, "would you wake my mother and see if she'll speak to me? I need to ask her something before I go to the station house."

"Of course, *yaa Sidi.*" He looked at me warily, as if I were trying to pull another fast one. "You wish to see her immediately?"

"Soon as she can make herself decent. *If* she can make herself decent." I caught Kmuzu's disapproving expression and shut up.

I drank some more coffee until he returned. "Umm Marîd will be glad to see you now," Kmuzu said.

I was surprised. "She never liked getting up much before noon."

"She was already awake and dressed when I knocked on her door."

Maybe she'd turned over a new leaf, but I hadn't been listening close enough to hear it. I grabbed my briefcase and sport coat. "I'll just drop in on her for a couple of minutes," I said. "No need for you to come with me." I should have known better by then; Kmuzu didn't say a word, but he followed me out of the apartment and into the other wing, where Angel Monroe had been given her own suite of rooms.

"This is a personal matter," I told Kmuzu when we got to her door. "Stay out here in the hall if you want." I rapped on the door and went in.

She was reclining on a divan, dressed very modestly in a shapeless black dress with long sleeves, a version of the outfit conservative Muslim women wear. She also had on a large scarf hiding her hair, although the veil over her face had been loosened on one side and hung down over her shoulder. She puffed on the mouthpiece of a *narjîlah*. There was strong tobacco in the water pipe now, but that didn't mean there hadn't been hashish there recently, or that it wouldn't be there again soon.

"Morning of well-being, O my mother," I said.

I think she was caught off-guard by my courteous greeting. "Morning of light, O Shaykh," she replied. Her brow furrowed as she studied me from across the room. She waited for me to explain why I was there.

"Are you comfortable here?" I asked.

"It's all right." She took a long pull on the mouthpiece and the *narjîlah* burbled. "You done pretty well for yourself. How'd you happen to land in this lap of luxury? Performing personal services for Papa?" She gave me a crooked leer.

"Not the services you're thinking of, O Mother. I'm Friedlander Bey's administrative assistant. He makes the business decisions and I carry them out. That's as far as it goes."

"And one of his business decisions was to make you a cop?"

"That's exactly the way it was."

She shrugged. "Uh yeah, if you say so. So why'd you decide to put me up here? Suddenly worried about your old mom's welfare?"

"It was Papa's idea."

She laughed. "You never was an attentive child, O Shaykh."

"As I recall, you weren't the doting mother, either. That's why I'm wondering why you showed up here all of a sudden."

She inhaled again on the *narjîlah*. "Algiers is boring. I lived there most of my life. After you came to see me, I knew I had to get out. I wanted to come here, see the city again."

"And see me again?"

She gave me another shrug. "Yeah, that too."

"And Abu Adil? You drop by his palace first, or haven't you been over there yet?" That's what we in the cop trade call a shot in the dark. Sometimes they pay off, sometimes they don't.

"I ain't having nothing more to do with that son of a bitch," she said. She almost snarled.

Shaknahyi would have been proud of me. I kept my emotions under control and my expression neutral. "What's Abu Adil ever done to you?"

"That sick bastard. Never mind, it's none of your business." She concentrated on her water pipe for a few moments.

"All right," I said. "I'll respect your wishes, O my mother. Anything I can do for you before I leave?"

"Everything's great. You run along and play Protector of the Innocent. Go roust some poor working girl and think of me."

I opened my mouth to make some sharp reply, but I caught myself in time. "You get hungry, or you need anything, just ask Youssef or Kmuzu. May your day be happy."

"Your day be prosperous, O Shaykh." Whenever she called me that, there was heavy irony in her voice.

I nodded to her and left the room, closing the door quietly behind me. Kmuzu was in the corridor, right where I'd left him. He was so goddamn loyal, I almost felt like scratching him behind the ears. I didn't buy that act for a minute.

"It would be well for you to greet the master of the house before we leave for the police station," he said.

"I don't need you to rehearse me on my manners, Kmuzu." He had this way of annoying me. "Are you implying that I don't know my duties?"

"I imply nothing, *yaa Sidi*. You are inferring."

"Sure." You just can't argue with a slave.

Friedlander Bey was already in his office. He sat behind his great desk, massaging his temples with one hand. Today he was wearing a pale yellow silk robe with a starched white shirt over it, buttoned to the neck and with no tie. Over the shirt he had on an expensive-looking herringbone-tweed suit jacket. It was a costume only an old and revered shaykh could get away with wearing. I thought it looked just fine. "Habib," he said. "Labib."

Habib and Labib are the Stones That Speak. The only way you can tell them apart is to call one of the names. There's an even chance one of 'em will blink. If not, it doesn't really make any difference. In fact, I couldn't swear that they blink in response to their own names. They may be doing it just for fun.

Both of the Stones That Speak were in the office, standing on either side of a straight-backed chair. In the chair, I was surprised to see, was Umm Saad's young son. The Stones each had one hand on Saad's shoulders, and the hands were kneading and crushing the boy's bones. He was being put to the question. I've had that treatment, and I can testify that it isn't a lick of fun.

Papa smiled briefly when I came into the room. He did not greet me, but looked back at Saad. "Before you came to the city," he said in a low voice, "where did you and your mother dwell?"

"Many places," Saad answered. There was fear in his voice.

Papa returned to rubbing his forehead. He stared down at his desktop, but waved a few fingers at the Stones That Speak. The two huge men tightened their grip on the boy's shoulder. The blood drained from Saad's face, and he gasped.

"Before you came to the city," Friedlander Bey repeated calmly, "where did you live?"

"Most recently in Paris, O Shaykh." Saad's voice was thin and strained.

The answer startled Papa. "Did your mother like living among the Franj?"

"I guess so."

Friedlander Bey was doing an admirable impersonation of a bored person. He picked up a silver letter opener and toyed with it. "Did you live well in Paris?"

"I guess so." Habib and Labib began to crush Saad's collarbones. He was encouraged to give more details. "We had a big apartment in the Rue de Paradis, O Shaykh. My mother likes to eat well and she likes giving parties. The months in Paris were pleasant. It surprised me when she told me we were coming here."

"And did you labor to earn money, so your mother could eat Franji food and wear Franji clothing?"

"I did no labor, O Shaykh."

Papa's eyes narrowed. "Where do you think the money came from to pay for these things?"

Saad hesitated. I could hear him moan as the Stones applied still more pressure. "She told me it came from her father," he cried.

"Her father?" said Friedlander Bey, dropping the letter opener and looking at Saad directly.

"She said from you, O Shaykh."

Papa grimaced and made a quick gesture with both hands. The Stones moved back, away from the youth. Saad slumped forward, his eyes tightly closed. His face was shiny with sweat.

"Let me tell you one thing, O clever one," said Papa. "And remember that I do not lie. I am *not* your mother's father, and I am *not* your grandfather. We share no blood. Now go."

Saad tried to stand, but collapsed back into the chair. His expression was grim and determined, and he glared at Friedlander Bey as if he were trying to memorize every detail of the old man's face. Papa had just called Umm Saad a liar, and I'm sure that at that moment the boy was entertaining some pitiful fantasy of revenge. At last he managed to stand up again, and he made his way shakily to the door. I intercepted him.

"Here," I said. I took out my pillcase and gave him two tabs of Sonneine. "You'll feel a lot better in a few minutes."

He took the tabs, looked me fiercely in the eye, and dropped the sunnies to the floor. Then he turned his back on me and left Friedlander Bey's office. I bent down and reclaimed the Sonneine. To paraphrase a local proverb: a white tablet for a black day.

After the formal greetings, Papa invited me to be comfortable. I sat in the same chair from which Saad had just escaped. I have to admit that I suppressed a little shudder. "Why was the boy here, O Shaykh?" I asked.

"He was here at my invitation. He and his mother are once again my guests."

I must have missed something. "Your graciousness is legendary, O my uncle; but whey do you permit Umm Saad to intrude on your peace? I know she upsets you."

Papa leaned back in his chair and sighed. At that moment, he showed every year of his long life. "She came to me humbly. She begged my forgiveness. She brought me a gift." He gestured to a platter of dates stuffed with nutmeats and rolled in sugar. He smiled ruefully. "I don't know where she got her information, but someone told her that these are my favorite treat. Her tone was respectful, and she made a claim upon my hospitality that I could not dismiss." He spread his hands, as if that explained it all.

Friedlander Bey observed traditions of honor and generosity that have all but disappeared in this day and age. If he wanted to welcome a viper back into his home, I had nothing to say about it. "Then your instructions concerning her have changed, O Shaykh?" I asked.

His expression did not alter. He didn't even blink. "Oh no, that's not what I mean. Please kill her as soon as it's convenient for you, but there's no hurry, my son. I find I'm getting curious about what Umm Saad hopes to accomplish."

"I will conclude the matter soon," I said. He frowned. *"Inshallah,"*

I added quickly. "Do you think she's working for someone else? An enemy?"

"Reda Abu Adil, of course," said Papa. He was very matter-of-fact about it, as if there wasn't the slightest cause for concern.

"Then it was you, after all, who ordered the investigation of Abu Adil."

He raised a plump hand in denial. "No," he insisted, "I had nothing to do with that. Speak to your Lieutenant Hajjar about it."

Lot of good that would do. "O Shaykh, may I ask you another question? There's something I don't understand about your relationship to Abu Adil."

Suddenly he looked bored again. That put me on my guard. I gave a reflexive glance over my shoulders, half expecting to see the Stones That Speak moving in close behind me. "Your wealth comes from selling updated data files to governments and heads of state, doesn't it?"

"That is greatly oversimplified, my nephew."

"And Abu Adil pursues the same business. Yet you told me you do not compete."

"Many years before you were born, before even your mother was born, Abu Adil and I came to an agreement." Papa opened a plain clothbound copy of the holy Qur'ân and glanced at the page. "We avoided competition because someday it could result in violence and harm to ourselves or those we love. On that long-ago day we divided the world, from Morocco far in the west to Indonesia far in the east, wherever the beautiful call of the muezzin awakens the faithful from sleep."

"Like Pope Alexander drawing the Line of Demarcation for Spain and Portugal," I said.

Papa looked displeased. "Since that time, Reda Abu Adil and I have had few dealings of any sort, although we live in the same city. He and I are at peace."

Yeah, you right. For some reason, he wasn't going to give me any direct help. "O Shaykh," I said, "it's time for me to go. I pray to Allah for your health and prosperity." I came forward and kissed him on the cheek.

"You will make me lonely for your presence," he replied. "Go in safety."

I left Friedlander Bey's office. In the hallway, Kmuzu tried to take my briefcase from me. "It is unseemly for you to carry this, when I am here to serve you," he said.

"You want to go through it and look for drugs," I said with some irritation. "Well, there aren't any in there. I got them in my pocket, and you'll have to wrestle me to the ground first."

"You are being absurd, *yaa Sidi*," he said.

"I don't think so. Anyway, I'm not ready to leave for the office yet."

"It is already late."

"Goddamn it, I know that! I just want to have a few words with Umm Saad, now that she's living under this roof again. Is she in the same suite?"

"Yes. This way, *yaa Sidi*."

Umm Saad, like my mother, stayed in the other wing of the mansion. While I followed Kmuzu through the carpeted halls, I opened my briefcase and took out Saied's moddy, the tough, ruthless personality. I chipped it in. The effect was remarkable. It was the opposite of the Half-Hajj's dumbing-down module, which had narrowed and blurred my senses. This one, which Saied always called Rex, seemed to focus my attention. I was filled with purpose; but more than that, I was determined to drive straight toward my goal, and I'd crush anything that tried to obstruct me.

Kmuzu knocked lightly on Umm Saad's door. There was a long pause, and I heard no one stirring inside. "Get out of the way," I said to Kmuzu. My voice was a mean growl. I stepped up to the door and rapped on it sharply. "You want to let me in?" I called. "Or you want me to let myself in?"

That got a response. The boy swung the door open and stared at me. "My mother isn't—"

"Out of the way, kid," I said. I pushed him aside.

Umm Saad was sitting at a table, watching the news on a small holoset. She looked up at me. "Welcome, O Shaykh," she said. She wasn't happy.

"Yeah, right," I said. I sat in a chair across the table from her. I reached across and tapped the holoset off. "How long you known my mother?" I asked. Another shot in the dark.

Umm Saad looked perplexed. "Your mother?"

"Goes by Angel Monroe sometimes. She's staying down the hall from you."

Umm Saad shook her head slowly. "I've only seen her once or twice. I've never spoken to her."

"You must've known her before you came to this house." I just wanted to see how big this conspiracy was.

"Sorry," she said. She gave me a wide-eyed, innocent smile that looked as out of place on her as it would have on a desert scorpion.

Okay, sometimes a shot in the dark doesn't get you anywhere. "And Abu Adil?"

"Who's that?" Her expression was all angelic and virtuous.

I started to get angry. "I just want some straight answers, lady. What I got to do, bust up your kid?"

Her face got very serious. She was doing "sincere" now. "I'm sorry, I really don't know any of those people. Am I supposed to? Did Friedlander Bey tell you that?"

I assumed she was lying about Abu Adil. I didn't know if she'd been lying about my mother. At least I could check that out later. If I could believe my mother.

I felt a heavy hand on my shoulder. "*Yaa Sidi?*" said Kmuzu. He sounded afraid that I might rip Umm Saad's head off and hand it to her.

"All right," I said, still feeling wonderfully malignant. I stood up and glared down at the woman. "You want to stay in this house, you're gonna have to learn to be more cooperative. I'm gonna talk to you again later. Think up some better answers."

"I'll be looking forward to it," said Umm Saad. She batted her heavy fake eyelashes at me. It made me want to punch her face in.

Instead, I turned and stalked out of the apartment. Kmuzu hurried behind me. "You can take the personality module out now, *yaa Sidi,*" he said nervously.

"Hell, I like it. Think I'll leave it in." Actually I *did* enjoy the feeling it gave me. There seemed to be a constant flood of angry hormones in my blood. I could see why Saied wore it all the time. Still, it wasn't the right one to wear around the station house, and Shaknahyi'd promised to annihilate any moddy I wore in his presence. I reached up reluctantly and popped it out.

I could feel the difference immediately. My body was still quivering from the leftover adrenalin, but I calmed down pretty quick. I returned the moddy to my briefcase, then grinned at Kmuzu. "I was pretty tough, huh?" I said.

Kmuzu didn't say a word, but his look let me know just how low his opinion was.

We went outside, and I waited while Kmuzu brought the car around. When Kmuzu let me out at the station house, I told him to go back home and keep Angel Monroe out of trouble. "And pay attention around Umm Saad and the boy too," I said. "Friedlander Bey is sure she's somehow connected to Reda Abu Adil, but she's playing it very cagey. Maybe you can learn something."

"I will be your eyes and ears, *yaa Sidi,*" he said.

As usual, the crowd of hungry young boys was loitering outside the copshop. They'd all begun waving and screaming when they saw my Westphalian sedan pull up to the curb. "O Master!" they cried. "O Compassionate!"

I reached for a handful of coins as I usually did, but then I remembered the Lamb Lady I'd helped the week before. I took out my wallet and dropped a five-kiam bill on each of the kids. "God open upon you," I said. I was a little embarrassed to see that Kmuzu was watching me closely.

The boys were astonished. One of the older kids took my arm and steered me away from the rest. He was about fifteen years old, and already there was a dark shadow of beard on his narrow face. "My sister would be interested to meet such a generous man," he said.

"I'm just not interested in meeting your sister."

He grinned at me. Three of his yellow teeth had been broken off in some fight or accident. "I have a brother as well," he said. I winced and went past him into the building. Behind me, the boys were yelling my praises. I was real popular with them, at least until tomorrow, when I'd have to buy their respect all over again.

Shaknahyi was waiting for me by the elevator. "Where you at?" he said. It seemed that no matter how early I got to work, Shaknahyi got there earlier.

"Aw right," I said. Actually, I was still tired and I felt mildly nauseated. I could chip in a couple of daddies that would take care of all that, but Shaknahyi had me intimidated. Around him I functioned with just my natural talents and hoped they were still enough.

It wasn't that long ago that I prided myself on having an unwired brain as smart and quick as any moddy in the city. Now I was putting all my confidence in the electronics. I'd become afraid of what might happen if I had to face a crisis without them.

"One of these days, we're gonna have to catch Abu Adil when he's not chipped in," said Shaknahyi. "We don't want to make him suspicious, but he's got some tough questions to answer."

"What questions?"

Shaknahyi shrugged. "You'll hear 'em next time we pass by there." For some reason, he wasn't confiding in me any more than Papa had.

Sergeant Catavina found us in the corridor. I didn't know much about him except he was Hajjar's right-hand man, and that meant he had to be bent one way or another. He was a short man who lugged around too much weight by about seventy pounds. He had wavy black hair parted by a moddy plug, always with at least one daddy chipped in because he didn't understand five words in Arabic. It was a total mystery to me why Catavina had come to the city. "Been lookin' for you two," he said. His voice was shrill, even filtered through the Arabic-language daddy.

"What is it?" I asked.

Catavina's predatory brown eyes flicked between me and Shaknahyi. "Just got a tip on a possible homicide." He handed Shaknahyi a slip of paper with an address on it. "Go take a look."

"In the Budayeen," said Shaknahyi.

"Yeah," said the sergeant.

"Whoever called this in, anybody recognize the voice?"

"Why should anybody recognize the voice?" asked Catavina.

Shaknahyi shrugged. "We got two or three leads like this in the last couple of months, that's all."

Catavina looked at me. "He's one of these conspiracy guys. Sees 'em everywhere." The sergeant walked away, shaking his head.

Shaknahyi glanced at the address again and jammed the slip of paper into a shirt pocket. "Back of the Budayeen, spitting distance from the graveyard," he said.

"If it isn't just a crank call," I said. "If there *is* a body in the first place."

"There will be."

I followed him down to the garage. We got into our patrol car and cut across the Boulevard il-Jameel and under the big gate. There was a lot of pedestrian traffic on the Street that morning, so Shaknahyi angled south on First Street and then west along one of the narrow, garbage-strewn alleys that wind between the flat-roofed, stucco-fronted houses and the ancient brick tenements.

Shaknahyi drove the car up onto the sidewalk. We got out and took a good look at the building. It was a pale green two-story house in terrible disrepair. The entryway and front parlor stank of urine and vomit. The wooden lattices covering the windows had all been smashed some time ago, from the look of things. Everywhere we walked, we crunched broken brick and shards of glass. The place had probably been abandoned for many months, maybe years.

It was very still, the dead hush of a house where the power is off and even the faint whir of motors is missing. As we made our way up from the ground floor to the family's rooms above, I thought I heard something small and quick scurrying through the trash ahead of us. I felt my heart pounding in my chest, and I missed the sense of calm competence I'd gotten from Complete Guardian.

Shaknahyi and I checked a large bedroom that had once belonged to the owner and his wife, and another room that had been a child's. We found nothing except more sad destruction. A corner of the house had entirely collapsed, leaving it open to the outside; weather, vermin, and vagrants had completed the ruin of the child's bedroom. At least here the fresh air had scoured out the sour, musty smell that choked the rest of the house.

We found the corpse in the next room down the hall. It was a young woman's body, a sexchange named Blanca who used to dance in Frenchy Benoit's club. I'd known her well enough to say hello, but not much better. She lay on her back; her legs bent and turned to one side, her arms thrown up above her head. Her deep blue eyes were open, staring obliquely at the water-stained ceiling above my shoulder. She was grimacing, as if there'd been something horrible with her in the room that had first terrified her and then killed her.

"This ain't bothering you, is it?" asked Shaknahyi.

"What you talking about?"

He tapped Blanca's hand with the toe of his boot. "You're not gonna throw up or nothing, are you?"

"I seen worse," I said.

"Just didn't want you throwing up or nothing." He bent down beside Blanca. "Blood from her nose and ears. Lips drawn back, fingers clutching like claws. She was juiced at close range by a good-sized static gun, I'll bet. Look at her. She hasn't been dead half an hour."

"Yeah?"

He lifted her left arm and let it fall. "No stiffness yet. And her flesh is still pink. After you're dead, gravity makes the blood settle. The medical examiner will be able to tell better."

Something struck me as kind of odd. "So the call that came into the station—"

"Bet you kiams to kitty cats the killer made the call himself." He took out his radio and his electronic log.

"Why would a murderer do that?" I asked.

Shaknahyi gazed at me, lost in thought. "The hell should I know?" he said at last. He made a call to Hajjar, asking for a team of detectives. Then he entered a brief report in his log. "Don't touch nothing," he said to me without looking up.

He didn't have to tell me that. "We done here?" I asked.

"Soon as the gold badges show up. In a hurry to travel?"

I didn't answer. I watched him pocket his electronic log. Then he took out a brown vinyl-covered notebook and a pen and made some more notations. "What's that for?" I asked.

"Just keeping some notes for myself. Like I said, there been a couple of other cases like this lately. Somebody turns up dead and it seems like the bumper himself tips us off."

By the life of my eyes, I thought, if this turns out to be a serial killer, I'm going to pack up and leave the city for good. I glanced down at Shaknahyi, who was still squatting beside Blanca's body. "You don't think it's a serial killer, do you?" I asked.

He stared through me again for a few seconds. "Nah," he said at last, "I think it's something much worse."

Eight

I remembered how much Hajjar's predecessor, Lieutenant Okking, had liked to harass me. Still, no matter how hard it had been to get along with Okking, he'd always gotten the job done. He'd been a shrewd if not brilliant cop, and he'd had a genuine concern for the victims he saw in a day's work. Hajjar was different. To him it was all a day's work, all right, but nothing more.

It didn't surprise me to learn that Hajjar was next to useless. Shaknahyi and I watched as he went about his investigation. He frowned and looked down at Blanca. "Dead, huh?" he said.

I saw Shaknahyi wince. "We got every reason to think so, Lieutenant," he said in a level voice.

"Any ideas who'd want to shade her?"

Shaknahyi looked at me for help. "Could be anybody," I said. "She was probably wearing the wrong moddy for the wrong customer."

Hajjar seemed interested. "You think so?"

"Look," I said. "Her plug's bare."

The lieutenant's eyes narrowed. "So what?"

"A moddy like Blanca never goes anywhere without *something* chipped in. It's suspicious, that's all."

Hajjar rubbed his scraggly mustache. "I guess you'd know all about that. Not much to go on, though."

"The plainclothes boys can work miracles sometimes," Shaknahyi said, sounding very sincere but winking to let me know just how little regard he had for them.

"Yeah, you right," said Hajjar.

"By the way, Lieutenant," said Shaknahyi, "I was wondering if you wanted us to keep after Abu Adil. We didn't get very far with him last week."

"You want to go out there again? To his house?"

"To his majestic palatial estate, you mean," I said.

Hajjar ignored me. "I didn't mean for you to persecute the guy. He throws a lot of weight in this town."

"Uh huh," said Shaknahyi. "Anyway, we're not doing any persecuting."

"Why do you want to bother him again in the first place?" Hajjar looked at me, but I didn't have an answer.

"I got a hunch that Abu Adil has some connection to these unsolved homicides," said Shaknahyi.

"*What* unsolved homicides?" Hajjar demanded.

I could see Shaknahyi grit his teeth. "There've been three unsolved homicides in the last couple of months. Four now, including her." He nodded toward Blanca's body, which the M.E.'s boy had covered with a sheet. "They could be related, and they could be connected to Reda Abu Adil."

"They're not unsolved homicides, for God's sake," said Hajjar angrily. "They're just open files, that's all."

"Open files," said Shaknahyi. I could tell he was really disgusted. "You need us for anything else, Lieutenant?"

"I guess not. You two can get back to work."

We left Hajjar and the detectives going over Blanca's remains and her clothes and the dust and the moldy ruins of the house. Outside on the sidewalk, Shaknahyi pulled my arm and stopped me before I got into the patrol car. "The hell was that about the bitch's missing moddy?" he asked.

I laughed. "Just hot air, but Hajjar won't know the difference. Give him something to think about, though, won't it?"

"It's good for the lieutenant to think about something now and then. His brain needs the exercise." Shaknahyi grinned at me.

We were both ready to call it a day. The sky had clouded over and a brisk, hot wind blew grit and smoke into our faces. Angry, grumbling thunder threatened from far away. Shaknahyi wanted to go back to the station house, but I had something else to take care of first. I unclipped the phone from my belt and spoke Chiri's commcode into it. I heard it ring eight or nine times before she answered it. "Talk to me," she said. She sounded irked.

"Chiri? It's Marîd."

"What do *you* want, motherfucker?"

"Look, you haven't given me any chance to explain. It's not my fault."

"You said that before." She gave a contemptuous laugh. "Famous last words, honey: 'It's not my fault.' That's what my uncle said when he sold my mama to some goddamn Arab slaver."

"I never knew—"

"Forget it, it ain't even true. You wanted a chance to explain, so explain."

Well, it was show time, but suddenly I didn't have any idea what to say to her. "I'm real sorry, Chiri," I said.

She just laughed again. It wasn't a friendly sound.

I plunged ahead. "One morning I woke up and Papa said, 'Here, now you own Chiriga's club, isn't that wonderful?' What did you expect me to say to him?"

"I know you, honey. I don't expect you to say *anything* to Papa. He didn't have to cut off your balls. You sold 'em."

I might have mentioned that Friedlander Bey had paid to have the punishment center of my brain wired, and that he could stimulate it whenever he wanted. That's how he kept me in line. But Chiri wouldn't have understood. I might have described the torment Papa could cause me anytime he touched the right keypad. None of that was important to her. All she knew was that I'd betrayed her.

"Chiri, we been friends a long time. Try to understand. Papa got this idea to buy your club and give it to me. I didn't know a thing about it in advance. I didn't want it when he gave it to me. I tried to tell him, but—"

"I'll bet. I'll just bet you told him."

I closed my eyes and took a deep breath. I think she was enjoying this a lot. "I told him about as much as anyone can tell Papa anything."

"Why *my* place, Marîd? The Budayeen's full of crummy bars. Why did he pick mine?"

I knew the answer to that: Because Friedlander Bey was prying me loose from the few remaining connections to my old life. Making me a cop had alienated most of my friends. Forcing Chiriga to sell her club had turned her against me. Next, Papa'd find a way to make Saied the Half-Hajj hate my guts too. "Just his sense of humor, Chiri," I said hopelessly. "Just Papa proving that he's always around, always watching, ready to hit us with his lightning bolts when we least expect it."

There was a long silence from her. "And you're gutless too."

My mouth opened and closed. I didn't know what she was talking about. "Huh?"

"I said you're a gutless *panya*."

She's always slinging Swahili at me. "What's a *panya,* Chiri?" I asked.

"It's like a big rat, only stupider and uglier. You didn't dare do this in person, did you, motherfucker? You'd rather whine to me over the phone. Well, you're gonna have to face me. That's all there is to it."

I squeezed my eyes shut and grimaced. "Okay, Chiri, whatever you want. Can you come by the club?"

"*The* club, you say? You mean, *my* club? The club I used to own?"

"Yeah," I said. "Your club."

She grunted. "Not on your life, you diseased jackass. I'm not setting foot in there unless things change the way I want 'em. But I'll meet you somewhere else. I'll be in Courane's place in half an hour. That's not in the Budayeen, honey, but I'm sure you can find it. Show up if you think you can handle it." There was a sharp click, and then I was listening to the burr of the dial tone.

"Dragged you through it, didn't she?" said Shaknahyi. He'd enjoyed every moment of my discomfort. I liked the guy, but he was still a bastard sometimes.

I clipped the phone back on my belt. "Ever hear of a bar called Courane's?"

He snorted. "This Christian chump shows up in the city a few years ago." He was wheeling the patrol car through Rasmiyya, a neighborhood east of the Budayeen that I'd never been in before. "Guy named Courane. Called himself a poet, but nobody ever saw much proof of that. Somehow he got to be a big hit with the European community. One day he opens what he calls a salon, see. Just a quiet, dark bar where everything's made out of wicker and glass and stainless steel. Lots of potted plastic plants. Nowadays he ain't the darling of the brunch crowd anymore, but he still pulls this melancholy expatriate routine."

"Like Weinraub on Gargotier's patio," I said.

"Yeah," said Shaknahyi, "except Courane owns his own dive. He stays in there and doesn't bother anybody. Give him that much credit, anyway. That where you're gonna meet Chiri?"

I looked at him and shrugged. "It was her choice."

He grinned at me. "Want to attract a lot of attention when you show up?"

I sighed. "Please no," I muttered. That Jirji, he was some kidder.

Twenty minutes later we were in a middle-class district of two- and three-story houses. The streets were broader than in the Budayeen, and the whitewashed buildings had strips of open land around them, planted with small bushes and flowering shrubs. Tall date palms leaned drunkenly along the verges of the pavement. The neighborhood seemed deserted, if only because there were no shouting children wrestling on the sidewalks or chasing each other around the corners of the houses. It was a very settled, very sedate part of town. It was so peaceful, it made me uncomfortable.

"Courane's is just up here," said Shaknahyi. He turned into a poorer street that was little more than an alley. One side was hemmed in by the back walls of the same flat-roofed houses. There were small balconies on the second floor, and bright lamp lit windows obscured by lattices made of narrow wooden strips. On the other side of the alley were boarded-up buildings and a few businesses: a leather-worker's shop, a bakery, a restaurant that specialized in bean dishes, a bookstall.

There was also Courane's, out of place in that constricted avenue. The proprietor had set out a few tables, but no one lingered in the white-painted wicker chairs beneath these Cinzano umbrellas. Shaknahyi tapped off the engine, and we got out of the patrol car. I supposed that Chiri hadn't arrived yet, or that she was waiting for me inside. My stomach hurt.

"Officer Shaknahyi!" A middle-aged man came toward us, a welcoming smile on his face. He was about my height, maybe fifteen or twenty pounds heavier, with receding brown hair brushed straight back. He shook hands with Shaknahyi, then turned to me.

"Sandor," said Shaknahyi, "this is my partner, Marîd Audran."

"Glad to meet you," said Courane.

"May Allah increase your honor," I said.

Courane's look was amused. "Right," he said. "Can I get you boys something to drink?"

I glanced at Shaknahyi. "Are we on duty?" I asked.

"Nah," he said. I asked for my usual, and Shaknahyi got a soft drink. We followed Courane into his establishment. It was just as I'd pictured it: shiny chrome and glass tables, white wicker chairs, a beautiful antique bar of polished dark wood, chrome ceiling fans, and, as Shaknahyi had mentioned, lots of dusty artificial plants stuck in corners and hanging in baskets from the ceiling.

Chiriga was sitting at a table near the back. "Where you at, Jirji? Marîd?" she said.

"Aw right," I said. "Can I buy you a drink?"

"Never in my life turned one down." She held up her glass. "Sandy?" Courane nodded and went to make our drinks.

I sat down beside Chiri. "Anyway," I said uncomfortably, "I want to talk to you about coming to work in the club."

"Yasmin mentioned something about that," Chiri said. "Kind of a ballsy thing for you to ask, isn't it?"

"Hey, look, I told you what the situation was. How much longer you gonna keep this up?"

Chiri gave me a little smile. "I don't know," she said. "I'm getting a big kick out of it."

I'd reached my limit. I can only feel so guilty. "Fine," I said. "Go get another job someplace else. I'm sure a big, strong *kaffir* like you won't have any trouble at all finding somebody who's interested."

Chiri looked hurt. "Okay, Marîd," she said softly, "let's stop." She opened her bag and took out a long white envelope, and pushed it across the table toward me.

"What's this?" I asked.

"Yesterday's take from your goddamn club. You're supposed to show up around closing time, you know, to count out the register and pay the girls. Or don't you care?"

"I don't really care," I said, peeking at the cash. There was a lot of money in the envelope. "That's why I want to hire you."

"To do what?"

I spread my hands. "I want you to keep the girls in line. And I need you to separate the customers from their money. You're famous for that. Just do exactly what you used to."

Her brow furrowed. "I used to go home every night with all of this." She tapped the envelope. "Now I'm just gonna get a few kiam here and there, whatever you decide to spill. I don't like that."

Courane arrived with our drinks and I paid for them. "I was gonna offer you a lot more than what the debs and changes get," I said to Chiri.

"I should hope so." She nodded her head emphatically. "Bet your ass, honey, you want me to run your club for you, you're gonna have to pay up front. Business is business, and action is action. I want 50 percent."

"Making yourself a partner?" I'd expected something like that. Chiri smiled slowly, showing those long, filed canines. She was worth more than 50 percent to me. "All right," I said.

She looked startled, as if she hadn't expected me to give in so easily. "Should've asked for more," she said bitterly. "And I don't want to dance unless I feel like it."

"Fine."

"And the name of the club stays 'Chiriga's.' "

"All right."

"And you let me do my own hiring and firing. I don't want to get stuck with Floor-Show Fanya if she tickles you into giving her a job. Bitch gets so loaded, she throws up on customers."

"You expect a hell of a lot, Chiri."

She gave me a wolfish grin. "Paybacks are a bitch, ain't they?" she said.

Chiri was wringing every last bit of advantage out of this situation. "Okay, you pick your own crew."

She paused to drink again. "By the way," she said, "that's 50 percent of the *gross* I'm getting, isn't it?"

Chiri was terrific. "Uh yeah," I said, laughing. "Why don't you let me give you a ride back to the Budayeen? You can start working this afternoon."

"I already passed by there. I left Indihar in charge." She noticed that her glass was empty again, and she held it up and waved it at Courane. "Want to play a game, Marîd?" She jerked a thumb toward the back of the bar, where Courane had a Transpex unit.

It's a game that lets two people with corymbic implants sit across from each other and chip into the machine's CPU. The first player imagines a bizarre scenario in detail, and it becomes a wholly realistic environment for the second player, who's scored on how well he adapts—or survives. Then in turn the second player does the same for the first.

It's a great game to bet money on. It scared the hell out of me at first, though, because while you're playing, you forget it's only a game. It seems absolutely real. The players exercise almost godlike power on each other. Courane's model looked old, a version whose safety features could be bypassed by a clever mechanic. There were rumors of people actually having massive strokes and coronaries while they were chipped into a jiggered Transpex.

"Go ahead, Audran," said Shaknahyi, "let's see what you got."

"All right, Chiri," I said, "let's play."

She stood up and walked back to the Transpex booth. I followed her, and both Shaknahyi and Courane came along too. "What to bet the other 50 percent of my club?" she said. Her eyes glittered over the rim of her cocktail glass.

"Can't do that. Papa wouldn't approve." I felt pretty confident, because I could read the record of the machine's previous high games. A perfect Transpex score was 1,000 points, and I averaged in the upper 800s. The top scores on this machine were in the lower 700s. Maybe the scores were low because Courane's bar didn't attract many borderline nutso types. Like me. "I'll bet what's inside this envelope, though."

That sounded good to her. "I can cover it," she said. I didn't doubt that Chiri could lay her hands on quite a lot of cash when she needed it.

Courane set fresh drinks down for all of us. Shaknahyi dragged a wicker chair near enough to watch the computer-modeled images of the illusions Chiri and I would create. I fed five kiam into the Transpex machine. "You can go first, if you want," I said.

"Yeah," said Chiri. "It's gonna be fun, making you sweat." She took one of the Transpex's moddy links and socketed it on her corymbic plug, then touched Player One on the console. I took the second link, murmured "*Bismillah,*" and chipped in Player Two.

At first there was only a kind of warm, flickering fog, veined with iridescence like shimmery mother of pearl. Audran was lost in a cloud, but he didn't feel anxious about it. It was absolutely silent and still, not even a whisper of breeze. He was aware of a mild scent surrounding him, the fragrance of fresh sea air. Then things began to change.

Now he was floating in the cloud, no longer sitting or standing, but somehow drifting through space easily and peacefully. Audran still wasn't concerned; it was a perfectly comfortable sensation. Only gradually did the fog begin to dissipate. With a shock Audran realized that he wasn't floating, but swimming in a warm, sun-dappled sea.

Below him waved long tendrils of algae that clung to hillocks of brightly colored coral. Anemones of many hues and many shapes reached their grasping tentacles toward him, but he cut smartly through the water well out of their reach.

Audran's eyesight was poor, but his other senses let him know what was happening around him. The smell of the salt air had been replaced by many subtle aromas that he couldn't name but were all achingly familiar. Sounds came to him, sibilant, rushing noises that echoed in hollow tones.

He was a fish. He felt free and strong, and he was hungry. Audran dived down close to the rolling sea bottom, near the stinging anemones where tiny fishes schooled for protection. He flashed among them, gobbling down mouthfuls of the scarlet and yellow creatures. His hunger was appeased, at least for now. The scent of others of his species wafted by him on the current, and he turned toward its source.

He swam for a long while until he realized that he'd lost the trace. Audran couldn't tell how much time had passed. It didn't matter. Nothing mattered here in the sparkling, sunny seas. He browsed over a gorgeous reef, worrying the delicate featherdusters, sending the scarlet-banded shrimps and the porcelain crabs scuttling.

Above him, the ocean darkened. A shadow passed over him, and

Audran felt a ripple of alarm. He could not look up, but compression waves told him that something huge was circling nearby. Audran remembered that he was not alone in this ocean: It was now his turn to flee. He darted down over the reef and cut a zigzag path only a few inches above the sandy floor.

The ravenous shadow trailed close behind. Audran looked for somewhere to hide, but there was nothing, no sunken wrecks or rocks or hidden caves. He made a sharp evasive turn and raced back the way he'd come. The thing that stalked him followed lazily, easily.

Suddenly it dived on him, a voracious, mad engine of murder, all dead black eyes and gleaming chrome-steel teeth. Flushed from the sea bottom, Audran knifed up through the green water toward the surface, though he knew there was no shelter there. The great beast raged close behind him. In a froth of boiling seafoam, Audran broke through the waves, into the fearfully thin air, and—flew. He glided over the white-capped water until, at last, he fell back into the welcoming element, exhausted.

And the nightmare creature was there, its ghastly mouth yawning wide to rend him. The daggered jaws closed slowly, victoriously, until for Audran there was only blackness and the knowledge of the agony to come.

"Jeez," I murmured, when the Transpex returned my consciousness.

"Some game," said Shaknahyi.

"How'd I do?" asked Chiri. She sounded exhilarated.

"Pretty good," said Courane. "623. It was a promising scenario, but you never got him to panic."

"I sure as hell tried," she said. "I want another drink." She gave me a quirky grin.

I took out my pillcase and swallowed eight Paxium with a mouthful of gin. Maybe as a fish I hadn't been paralyzed with fear, but I was feeling a strong nervous reaction now. "I want another drink too," I said. "I'll stand a round for everybody."

"Bigshot," said Shaknahyi.

Both Chiri and I waited until our heartbeats slowed down to normal. Courane brought a tray with the fresh drinks, and I watched Chiri throw hers down in two long gulps. She was fortifying herself for whatever evil things I was going to do to her mind. She was going to need it.

Chiri touched Player Two on the game's console, and I saw her eyes slowly close. She looked like she was napping placidly. That was going to end in a hell of a hurry. On the holoscreen was the same

opalescent haze I'd wandered through until Chiri'd decided it was the
ocean. I reached out and touched the Player One panel.

*Audran gazed down upon the ball of mist, like Allah in the highest
of the heavens. He concentrated on building a richly detailed illusion,
and he was pleased with his progress. Instead of letting it take on form
and reality gradually, Audran loosed an explosion of sensory information. The woman far below was stunned by the purity of color in
this world, the clarity of sound, the intensity of the tastes and textures
and smells. She cried out and her voice pealed in the cool, clean air
like a carillon. She fell to her knees, her eyes shut tightly and her hands
over her ears.*

*Audran was patient. He wanted the woman to explore his creation.
He wasn't going to hide behind a tree, jump out and frighten her. There
was time enough for terror later.*

*After a while the woman lowered her hands and stood up. She
looked around uncertainly. "Marîd?" she called. Once again the sound
of her own voice rang with unnatural sharpness. She glanced behind
her, toward the misty purple mountains in the west. Then she turned
back to the east, toward the shore of a marshy lake that reflected the
impossible azure of the sky. Audran didn't care which direction she
chose; it would all be the same in the end.*

*The woman decided to follow the swampy shoreline to the south-
east. She walked for hours, listening to the liquid trilling of songbirds
and inhaling the poignant perfume of unknown blossoms. After a while
the sun rested on the shoulders of the purple hills behind her, and then
slipped away, leaving Audran's illusion in darkness. He provided a full
moon, huge and gleaming silver like a serving platter. The woman grew
weary, and at last she decided to lie down in the sweet-smelling grass
and sleep.*

*Audran woke her in the morning with a gentle rain shower.
"Marîd?" she cried again. He would not answer her. "How long you
gonna leave me here?" She shivered.*

*The golden sun mounted higher, and while it warmed the morning,
the heat never became stifling. Just after noon, when the woman had
walked almost halfway around the lake, she came upon a pavilion
made all of crimson and sapphire blue silk. "What the hell is all this,
Marîd?" the woman shouted. "Just get it over with, all right?"*

*The woman approached the pavilion anxiously. "Hello?" she
called.*

*A moment later a young woman in a white gown came out of the
pavilion. Her feet were bare and her pale blond hair was thrown*

carelessly over one shoulder. She was smiling and carrying a wooden tray. "Hungry?" she asked in a friendly voice.

"Yes," said the woman.

"My name is Maryam. I've been waiting for you. I'm sorry, all I've got is bread and fresh milk." She poured from a silver pitcher into a silver goblet.

"Thanks." The woman ate and drank greedily.

Maryam shaded her eyes with one hand. "Are you going to the fair?"

The woman shook her head. "I don't know about any fair."

Maryam laughed. "Everybody goes to the fair. Come on, I'll take you."

The woman waited while Maryam disappeared into the pavilion again with the breakfast things. She came back out a moment later. "We're all set now," she said gaily. "We can get to know each other while we walk."

They continued around the lake until the woman saw a scattering of large peaked tents of striped canvas, all with colorful pennants snapping in the breeze. She heard many people laughing and shouting, and the sound of axes biting wood, and metal ringing on metal. She could smell bread baking, and cinnamon buns, and lamb roasting on spits turning slowly over glowing coals. Her mouth began to water, and she felt her excitement growing despite herself.

"I don't have any money to spend," she said.

"Money?" Maryam asked, laughing. "What is money?"

The woman spent the afternoon going from tent to tent, seeing the strange exhibits and miraculous entertainments. She sampled exotic foods and drank concoctions of unknown liquors. Now and then she remembered to be afraid. She looked over her shoulder, wondering when the pleasant face of this fantasy would fall away. "Marîd," she called, "what are you doing?"

"Who are you calling?" asked Maryam.

"I'm not sure," said the woman.

Maryam laughed. "Look over here," she said, pulling on the woman's sleeve, showing her a booth where a heavily muscled woman was shaping a disturbing collage from the claws, teeth, and eyes of lizards.

They listened to children playing strange music on instruments made from the carcasses of small animals, and then they watched several old women spin their own white hair into thread, and then weave it into napkins and scarves.

One of the toothless hags leered at Maryam and the woman. "Take," she said in a gravelly voice.

"Thank you, Grandmother," said Maryam. She selected a pair of human-hair handkerchiefs.

The hours wore on, and at last the sun began to set. The moon rose as full as yestereve. "Is this going to go on all night?" the woman asked.

"All night and all day tomorrow," said Maryam. "Forever."

The woman shuddered.

From that moment she couldn't shake a growing dread, a sense that she'd been lured to this place and abandoned. She remembered nothing of who she'd been before she'd awakened beside the lake, but she felt she'd been horribly tricked. She prayed to someone called Marîd. She wondered if that was God.

"Marîd," she murmured fearfully, "I wish you'd just end this already."

But Audran was not ready to end it. He watched as the woman and Maryam grew sleepy and found a large tent filled with comfortable cushions and sheets of satin and fine linen. They laid themselves down and slept.

In the morning the woman arose, dismayed to be still trapped at the eternal fair. Maryam found them a good breakfast of sausage, fried bread, broiled tomatoes, and hot tea. Maryam's enthusiasm was undiminished, and she led the woman toward still more disquieting entertainments. The woman, however, felt only a crazily mounting dread.

"You've had me here for two days, Marîd," she pleaded. "Please kill me and let me go." Audran gave her no sign, no answer.

They passed the third day examining one dismaying thing after another: teenage girls who seemed to have living roses in place of breasts; a candlemaker whose wares would not provide light in the presence of an infidel; staged combat between a blind man and two maddened dragons; a family hammering together a scale model of the fair out of iron, a project that had occupied them for generations and that might never be completed; a cage of crickets that had been taught to chirp the Shahada, the Islamic testament of faith.

The afternoon passed, and once again night began to fall. All through the fair, men jammed blazing torches into iron sconces on tall poles. Still Maryam led the woman from tent to tent, but the woman no longer enjoyed the spectacles. She was filled with a sense of impending catastrophe. She felt an urgent need to escape, but she knew she couldn't even find her way out of the infinite fairgrounds.

And then a shrill, buzzing alarm sounded. "What's that?" she asked, startled. All around her, people had begun to flee. "Yallah!" cried Maryam, her face stricken with horror. "Run! Run and save your life!"

"What is it?" the woman shouted. "Tell me what it is!"

Maryam had collapsed to the ground, weeping and moaning. "In the name of Allah, the Beneficent, the Merciful," she muttered over and over again. The woman could get nothing more sensible from her.

The woman left her there, and she followed the stream of terrified people as they ran among the tents. And then the woman saw them: two immense giants, impossibly huge, hundreds of feet tall, crushing the landscape as they came nearer. They waded among the distant mountains, and then the shocks from their jolting footsteps began to churn the water in the lake. The ground heaved as they came nearer. The woman raised a hand to her breast, then staggered backward a few steps.

One of the giants turned his head slowly and looked straight at her. He was horribly ugly, with a great scar across one empty eye socket and a mouthful of rotten, snaggled fangs. He lifted an arm and pointed to her.

"No," she said, her voice hoarse with fear, "not me!" She wanted to run but she couldn't move. The giant stooped toward her, fierce and glowering. He bent to capture her in his enormous hand.

"Marîd!" the woman screamed. "Please!" Nothing happened. The giant's fist began to close around her.

The woman tried to reach up and unplug the moddy link, but her arms were frozen. She wouldn't escape that easily. The woman shrieked as she realized she couldn't even jack out.

The disfigured giant lifted her off the ground and drew her close to his single eye. His horrid grin spread and he laughed at her terror. His stinking breath sickened the woman. She struggled again to lift her hands, to pull the moddy link free. Her arms were held fast. She screamed and screamed, and then at last she fainted.

My eyes were bleary for a moment, and I could hear Chiri panting for breath beside me. I didn't think she'd be so upset. After all, it was only a Transpex game, and it wasn't the first time she'd ever played. She knew what to expect.

"You're a sick motherfucker, Marîd," she said at last.

"Listen, Chiri, I was just—"

She waved a hand at me. "I know, I know. You won the game and the bet. I'm still just a little shook, that's all. I'll have your money for you tonight."

"Forget the money, Chiri, I—"

I shouldn't have said that. "Hey, you son of a bitch, when I lose a bet I pay up. You're gonna take the money or I'm gonna cram it down your throat. But, God, you've got some kind of twisted imagination."

"That last part," said Courane, "where she couldn't raise her hands to pop the moddy link, that was real cold." He said it approvingly.

"Hell of a sadistic thing to do," said Chiri, shivering. "Last time I ever touch a Transpex with *you*."

"A few extra points, that's all, Chiri. I didn't know what my score was. I might have needed a couple more points."

"You finished with 941," said Shaknahyi. He was looking at me oddly, as if he were impressed by my score and repelled at the same time. "We got to go." He stood up and tossed down the last slug of his soft drink.

I stood up too. "You all right now, Chiri?" I put my hand on her shoulder.

"I'm fine. I'm still shaking off the game. It was like a nightmare." She took a deep breath and let it out. "I got to get back to the club so Indihar can go home."

"Give you a ride?" asked Shaknahyi.

"Thanks," said Chiri, "but I got my own transportation."

"See you later then," I said.

"*Kwa heri*, you bastard." At least she was smiling when she called me that. I thought maybe things were okay between us again. I was real glad about that.

Outside, Shaknahyi shook his head and grinned. "She was right, you know. That was a hell of a sadistic thing. Like unnecessary torture. You *are* a sick son of a bitch."

"Maybe."

"And I got to ride around the city with you."

I was tired of talking about it. "Time to check out yet?" I asked.

"Just about. Let's pass by the station house, and then why don't you come home with me for dinner? You got plans already? You think Friedlander Bey can get along without you for one night?"

I'm not a very sociable person, and I always feel uncomfortable in other people's homes. Still, the idea of spending an evening away from Papa and his Circus of Thrills was immensely attractive. "Sure," I said.

"Let me call my wife and find out if tonight's okay."

"I didn't even know you were married, Jirji."

He just raised his eyebrows at me and spoke his commcode into the phone. He had a brief conversation with his wife, and then clipped the phone back on his belt. "She says it's okay," he said. "Now she's got to run around cleaning and cooking. She always goes crazy when I bring somebody home."

"She don't have to do that just for me," I said.

Shaknahyi shook his head. "It's not for you, believe me. She comes from this old-fashioned family, and she's all the time got to prove she's the perfect Muslim wife."

We stopped at the station house, turned the patrol car over to the guys on the night shift, and checked in briefly with Hajjar. Finally we logged out and headed back downstairs to the street. "I usually walk home unless it's pouring rain," said Shaknahyi.

"How far is it?" I asked. It was a pleasant evening, but I wasn't looking forward to a long walk.

"Maybe three, three-and-a-half miles."

"Forget it," I said. "I'll spring for a cab." There are always seven or eight taxis waiting for fares on the Boulevard il-Jameel, near the Budayeen's eastern gate. I looked for my friend Bill, but I didn't see him. We got into another cab, and Shaknahyi gave the driver his address.

It was an apartment house in the part of town called Haffe al-Khala, the Edge of the Wilderness. Shaknahyi and his family lived about as far south as you could go in the city, so near the desert that mounds of sand like infant dunes had crept up against the walls of the buildings. There were no trees or flowers on these streets. It was bare and quiet and dead, as cheerless as any place I've ever seen.

Shaknahyi must have guessed what I was thinking. "This is all I can afford," he said sourly. "Come on, though. It's better inside."

I followed him into the foyer of the apartment house, and then upstairs to his flat on the third floor. He unlocked the front door and was immediately tackled by two small children. They clung to his legs as he came into the parlor. Shaknahyi bent down laughing, and rested his hands on the boys' heads. "My sons," he said to me proudly. "This is Little Jirji, he's eight, and Hâkim, he's four. Zahra's six. She's probably getting in her mother's way in the kitchen."

Well, I don't have much patience with kids. I suppose they're fine for other people, but I've never really understood what they're *for*. I can be polite about them when I have to, though. "Your sons are very handsome," I said. "They do you honor."

"It is as Allah pleases," said Shaknahyi. He was beaming like a goddamn searchlight.

He dislodged Little Jirji and Hâkim and, to my dismay, left me alone with them while he went in to see how supper was progressing. I didn't actually bear these children any ill will, but my philosophy of raising kids is kind of extreme. I think you should keep a baby around for a few days after it's born—until the novelty wears off—and then you put it in a big cardboard box with all the best books of Eastern and Western civilization. Then you bury the box and dig it up again when the kid's eighteen.

I watched uneasily as first Little Jirji and then Hâkim realized I was sitting on the couch. Hâkim lurched toward me, a bright red toy figure in his right hand, another in his mouth. "What do I do now?" I muttered.

"How you boys getting along out here?" said Shaknahyi. I was saved. He came back into the parlor and sat beside me in an old, shabby armchair.

"Great," I said. I said a little prayer to Allah. This looked like it could be a long night.

A very pretty, very serious-faced girl came into the room, carrying a china plate of *hummus* and bread. Shaknahyi took the plate from her and kissed her on both cheeks. "This is Zahra, my little princess," he said. "Zahra, this is Uncle Marîd."

Uncle Marîd! I'd never heard anything so grotesque in my entire life.

Zahra looked up at me, blushed furiously, and ran back into the kitchen while her father laughed. I've always had that effect on women.

Shaknahyi indicated the plate of *hummus*. "Please," he said, "refresh yourself."

"May your prosperity increase, Jirji," I said.

"May God lengthen your life. I'm gonna get us some tea." He got up again and went back into the kitchen.

I wished he'd stop fussing. It made me nervous, and it left me outnumbered by the kids. I tore off some bread and dipped it in the *hummus*, keeping a careful eye on Little Jirji and Hâkim. They seemed to be playing together peacefully, apparently paying no attention to me at all; but I wasn't going to be lulled so easily.

Shaknahyi came back in a few minutes. "I think you know my wife," he said. I looked up. He was standing there with Indihar. He was grinning his damnfool grin, but she looked absolutely pissed.

I stood up, bewildered. "Indihar, how you doing?" I said. I felt like a fool. "I didn't even know you were married."

"Nobody's supposed to know," she said. She glared at her husband, then she turned and glared at me.

"It's all right, sweetheart," Shaknahyi said. "Marîd won't tell anybody, right?"

"Marîd is a—" Indihar began, but then she remembered that I was a guest in her home. She lowered her eyes modestly to the floor. "You honor our family with your visit, Marîd," she said.

I didn't know what to say. This was a major shock: Indihar as beautiful Budayeen dancer by day, demure Muslim wife by night. "Please," I said uncomfortably, "don't go to any trouble for me."

Indihar flicked her eyes at me before she led Zahra out of the room. I couldn't read what she was thinking.

"Have some tea," said Shaknahyi. "Have some more *hummus*." Hâkim had at last found the courage to look me over. He grabbed my leg and drooled on my pants.

This was going to be even worse than I'd feared.

nine

it was shaknahyi's small brown notebook, the one he'd carried in his hip pocket. The first time I'd seen it was when we'd investigated Blanca's murder. Now I stared at its vinyl cover, smeared with bloody fingerprints, and wondered about Shaknahyi's coded entries. I supposed I was going to have to find out what they all meant.

This was a week after my visit to Jirji and Indihar's apartment. The day had started off on a low note and it never improved. I looked up to see Kmuzu standing beside my bed holding a tray of orange juice, toast, and coffee. I guess he'd been waiting for my wake-up daddy to kick in. He looked so sick that I almost felt sorry for the poor sucker. "Good morning, *yaa Sidi,*" he said softly.

I felt like hell too. "Where are my clothes?"

Kmuzu winced. "I don't know, *yaa Sidi.* I don't remember what you did with them last night."

I didn't remember much either. There was nothing but sick blackness from the time I came in the front door late last night until just a moment ago. I crawled out of bed naked, my head throbbing, my stomach threatening immediate upheaval. "Help me find my jeans," I said. "My pillcase is in my jeans."

"This is why the Lord forbids drinking," said Kmuzu. I glanced at him; his eyes were closed and he was still holding the tray, but it was tilting dangerously. There was going to be coffee and orange juice all over my bed in a few seconds. That wasn't important to me right then.

My clothes weren't under the bed, which was the logical place to look. They weren't in the closet, and they weren't in the dressing room or the bathroom. I looked on the table in the dining area and in my small kitchen. No luck. I finally found my shoes and shirt rolled up in a ball in the bookcase, crammed between some paperback novels by Lutfy Gad, a Palestinian detective writer of the middle twenty-first century. My jeans had been folded neatly and hidden on my desk beneath several thick sheaves of computer printout.

I didn't even put the pants on. I just grabbed the pillcase and hurried back into the bedroom. My plan was to swallow some opiates, maybe a dozen Sonneine, with the orange juice.

Too late. Kmuzu was staring down in horror at the sticky, sweet-smelling puddle on my bedclothes. He looked up at me. "I'll clean this up," he said, gulping down a wave of nausea, "immediately." His expression said that he expected to lose his comfortable job in the Big House, and be sent out to the dusty fields with the other unskilled brutes.

"Don't worry about it right now, Kmuzu. Just hand me that cup of—"

There was a gentle scraping sound as the coffee cup and saucer slid southward and tumbled over the edge of the tray. I looked at the ruined sheets. At least you couldn't see the orange juice stain anymore.

"*Yaa Sidi—*"

"I want a glass of water, Kmuzu. Right now."

It had been a hell of a night. I'd had the bright idea to go to the Budayeen after work. "I haven't had a night out in a long time," I said to Kmuzu when he arrived to pick me up at the station house.

"The master of the house is pleased that you're concentrating on your work."

"Yeah, you right, but that don't mean I can't see my friends now and then." I gave him directions to Jo-Mama's Greek club.

"If you do this, you will not get home until late, *yaa Sidi.*"

"I know it'll be late. Would you rather I went out drinking in the morning?"

"You must be at the station house in the morning."

"That's a long time from now," I pointed out.

"The master of the house—"

"Turn left here, Kmuzu. *Now!*" I wasn't going to listen to any more argument. I guided him northwest through the twisting streets of the city. We left the car on the boulevard and walked through the gate into the Budayeen.

Jo-Mama's club was on Third Street, jammed tight against the high northern wall of the quarter. Rocky, the relief barmaid, frowned at me when I took a stool at the front bar. She was short and hefty with brushy black hair, and she didn't look glad to see me. "Ya want to see my manager's license, cop?" she said in a sour voice.

"Get a grip, Rocky. I just want a gin and bingara." I turned to Kmuzu, who was still standing behind me. "Grab a seat," I told him.

"Who's this?" said Rocky. "Your slave or something?"

I nodded. "Give him the same."

Kmuzu raised a hand. "Just some club soda, please," he said. Rocky glanced at me, and I shook my head slightly.

Jo-Mama came out of her office and grinned at me. "Marîd, where y'at? You ain't been comin' around no more."

"Been busy," I said. Rocky set a drink in front of me and an identical one in front of Kmuzu.

Jo-Mama smacked his shoulder. "You know your boss here got some guts," she said admiringly.

"I've heard the stories," said Kmuzu.

"Yeah, ain't we all?" said Rocky. Her lip curled just a little.

Kmuzu sipped his gin and bingara and grimaced. "This club soda tastes strange," he said.

"It's the lime juice," I said hastily.

"Yeah, I put some lime in it for ya," said Rocky.

"Oh," said Kmuzu. He took another taste.

Jo-Mama snorted. She's the largest woman I've ever met—big, strong, and often friendly. She has a loud, gruff voice and a remarkable memory for who owes her money and who's done her dirt. When she laughs, you see beer splash out of glasses all around the bar; and when she gets angry, you don't hang around long enough to see anything. "Your friends are at a table in the back," she said.

"Who?"

"Mahmoud and the Half-Hajj and that snotty Christian."

"*Used* to be my friends," I said. Jo-Mama shrugged. I picked up my drink and went deeper into the dark cavern of the club. Kmuzu followed me.

Mahmoud, Jacques, Saied, and Saied's adolescent American lover, Abdul-Hassan, were sitting at a table near the edge of the stage. They didn't see me at first because they were appraising the dancer, a stranger to me but clearly a real girl. I moved a couple of chairs up to their table, and Kmuzu and I sat down.

"How ya doin', Marîd?" said the Half-Hajj.

"Look who it is," said Mahmoud. "Come in to inspect the permits?"

"That's a bum line I heard already from Rocky," I said.

It didn't bother Mahmoud. Although as a girl he'd been lithe and pretty enough to dance here in Jo-Mama's club, he'd put on weight and muscle after the sexchange. I wouldn't want to fight him to see which of us was tougher.

"Why are we watching this bint?" asked Saied. Abdul-Hassan was glaring spitefully at the girl on stage. The Half-Hajj was teaching him well.

"She's not so bad," said Jacques, giving us the benefit of his militantly conventional viewpoint. "She's very pretty, don't you think?"

Saied spat on the floor. "The debs on the Street are prettier."

"The debs on the Street are constructs," said Jacques. "This girl's natural."

"Shellfish toxin is natural, if that's what you care about," said Mahmoud. "I'd rather watch somebody who's spent some time and effort making herself look good."

"Someone who's spent a fortune on bodmods, you mean," said Jacques.

"What's her name?" I asked.

They ignored my question "You hear that Blanca's dead?" Jacques said to Mahmoud.

"Probably beaten to death in a police riot," Mahmoud replied. His eyes flicked at me.

I wasn't going to put up with any more of this. I got out of my chair. "Finish your . . . club soda," I said to Kmuzu.

Saied stood up and came closer to me. "Hey, Marîd," he whispered, "don't pay any attention to 'em. They're just trying to bubble your bile."

"It's working," I said.

"They'll get tired of it soon. Everything'll go back the way it used to be."

I downed the rest of my drink. "Sure," I said, surprised by Saied's naïveté. Abdul-Hassan gave me a flirtatious look, batting his thick eyelashes. I wondered what sex he'd be when he grew up.

Jo-Mama had disappeared into her office again, and Rocky didn't bother saying goodbye. Kmuzu trailed me out of the bar. "Well," I said to him, "enjoying yourself?"

He gave me a blank stare. He didn't look pleased.

"We'll pass by Chiri's," I told him. "If anybody even looks at me cross-eyed in there, I can throw him out. It's my club." I liked the way that sounded.

I led Kmuzu south, and then turned up the Street. He came along with a solemn and disapproving look on his face. He wasn't the perfect drinking companion, but he was loyal. I knew he wouldn't abandon me if he met some hot girl somewhere.

"Why don't you loosen up?" I asked him.

"It's not my job to be loose," he said.

"You're a slave. It's your job to be what I tell you to be. Gear down a little."

I got a nice welcome when I went into the club. "Here he comes, ladies," called Chiri, "the boss man." This time she didn't sound bitter when she called me that. There were three sexchanges and two debs working with her. The real girls were all on the day shift with Indihar.

It felt great to feel at home somewhere. "How's it going, Chiri?" I asked.

She looked disgusted. "Slow night," she said. "No money."

"You always say that." I went down and took my usual seat at the far end of the bar, where it curved around toward the stage. I could sit there and look down the whole length of the bar, and see anybody coming into the club. Kmuzu sat beside me.

Chiri flipped a cork coaster toward me. I tapped the place in front of Kmuzu, and Chiri nodded. "Who is this handsome devil?" she asked.

"His name's Kmuzu," I said. "He's uncommunicative."

Chiri grinned. "I can fix that. Where you from, honey?" she asked.

He spoke to Chiri in some African language, but neither she nor I understood a word of it. "I'm Sîdi Marîd's slave," he said.

Chiri was dismayed. She was almost speechless. "Slave? Forgive me for saying it, sweetie, but being a slave's nothing to brag about. You can't really make it sound like an *achievement,* you know?"

Kmuzu shook his head. "There is a long story behind it."

"I guess so," said Chiri, looking at me for an explanation.

"If there's a story, nobody's told me," I said.

"Papa just gave him to you, right? Like he gave you the club." I nodded. Chiri put a gin and bingara on my coaster and another in front of Kmuzu. "If I was you," she said, "I'd be careful what I unwrapped under his Christmas tree from now on."

Yasmin watched me for half an hour before she came up to say hello, and then only because the other two changes were kissing on me and rubbing themselves up against me, trying to get in good with the new owner. It was working, too. "You come a long way, Marîd," Yasmin said.

I shrugged. "I feel like I'm still the same simple *noraf* I've always been."

"You know that's not true."

"Well, I owe it all to you. You're the one who bullied me into getting my skull amped, doing what Papa wanted."

Yasmin looked away. "Yeah, I guess so." She turned toward me again. "Listen, Marîd, I'm sorry if—"

I put my hand on hers. "Don't ever say you're sorry, Yasmin. We got past all that a long time ago."

She looked grateful. "Thanks, Marîd." She leaned over and kissed me on the cheek. Then she hurried back down the bar where two dark-skinned merchant seamen had taken seats.

The rest of the night passed quickly. I downed one drink after another, and I made sure that Kmuzu did the same. He still thought he was drinking club soda with some strange lime juice in it.

Somewhere along the line I began to get drunk, and Kmuzu must have been nearly helpless. I recall Chiri closing the bar about three in the morning. She counted out the register and gave me the money. I gave half the receipts back to her as per our agreement, then paid Yasmin and the other four their wages. I still ended up with another thick wad of bills for myself.

I got a very enthusiastic goodnight kiss from a change named Lily, and a slip of paper with a commcode from someone named Rani. I think Rani gave a slip of paper to Kmuzu too, just to cover her bets.

That's when I really blacked out. I don't know how Kmuzu and I got home, but we didn't bring the car with us. I guess Chiri called us a cab. The next thing I knew, I was waking up in bed and Kmuzu was about to spill orange juice and hot coffee all over me.

"Where's that water?" I called. I stumbled around my suite, holding the sunnies in one hand and my shoes in the other.

"Here, *yaa Sidi.*"

I took the glass from him and swallowed the tabs. "There's a couple left for you," I said.

He looked appalled. "I can't—"

"It's not recreational. It's medicine." Kmuzu overcame his aversion to drugs long enough to take a single Sonneine.

I was still far from sober, and the sunnies I'd taken didn't help steady me. I didn't hurt anymore, but I was only vaguely conscious. I dressed quickly without paying much attention to what I put on. Kmuzu offered me breakfast, but the whole idea turned my stomach; for once, Kmuzu didn't badger me into eating. I think he was glad not to have to cook.

We stumbled blearily downstairs. I called a taxi to take me to work, and Kmuzu came with me to pick up the sedan. In the cab, I let my head fall back against the seat, and I closed my eyes and listened to peculiar noises inside my head. My ears were thrumming like the engine room of an ancient tugboat.

"May your day be blessed," said Kmuzu, when we got to the station house.

"May I live to see lunch, you mean," I said. I got out of the cab and pushed my way through my crowd of young fans, throwing them a little money.

Sergeant Catavina gave me a jaundiced look when I got to my cubicle. "You don't look well," he said.

"I don't feel well."

Catavina clucked his tongue. "I'll tell you what I do when I get a little hung over."

"You don't show up for work," I said, dropping into my molded plastic chair. I didn't feel like conversing with him.

"That always works too," he said. He turned and left my cubicle. He didn't seem to like me, and I didn't seem to care.

Shaknahyi came by fifteen minutes later. I was still staring at my data deck, unable to dig into the mound of paperwork that waited on my desk. "Where you at?" he said. He didn't wait for an answer. "Hajjar wants to see us both right now."

"I'm not available," I said glumly.

"I'll tell him that. Come on, move your ass."

I followed him reluctantly down the corridor to Hajjar's little glass-walled office. We stood in front of his desk while he toyed with a small pile of paper clips. After a few seconds he looked up and studied us. It was a careful act. He had something difficult to tell us, and he wanted us to know that It Would Hurt Him More Than It Hurt Us. "I don't like havin' to do this," he said. He looked real sad.

"Just skip it then, Lieutenant," I said. "Come on, Jirji, let's leave him alone."

"Shut up, Audran," said Hajjar. "We got an official complaint from Reda Abu Adil. I thought I told you to lay off him." We hadn't gone out to see Abu Adil again, but we'd been talking to as many of his crummy underlings as we could corner.

"Okay," said Shaknahyi, "we'll lay off."

"The investigation is finished. We compiled all the information we need."

"Okay," said Shaknahyi.

"You both understand? Leave Abu Adil alone from now on. We ain't got a thing on him. He's not under any kind of suspicion."

"Right," said Shaknahyi.

Hajjar looked at me. "Fine," I said.

Hajjar nodded. "Okay. Now I got somethin' else I want you two to check out." He handed Shaknahyi a sheet of pale blue paper.

Shaknahyi glanced at it. "This address is right nearby," he said.

"Uh huh," said Hajjar. "There been some complaints from people in the neighborhood. Looks like another baby peddler, but this guy's got an ugly wrinkle. If this On Cheung's there, cuff him and bring him in. Don't worry about evidence; we'll make some up later if you don't find nothin'. If he ain't there, go through what you find and bring the good stuff back here."

"What do we charge him with?" I asked.

Hajjar shrugged. "Don't need to charge him with nothing. He'll hear all about it soon enough at his trial."

I looked at Shaknahyi; he shrugged. This was how the police department used to operate in the city a few years ago. Lieutenant Hajjar must have gotten nostalgic for the good old days before due process.

Shaknahyi and I left Hajjar's office and headed toward the elevator. He jammed the blue paper in his shirt pocket. "This won't take long," he said. "Then we can get something to eat." The idea of food nauseated me; I realized that I was still half-loaded. I prayed to Allah that my condition wouldn't get us into trouble on the street.

We drove about six blocks to an area of crumbling red brick tenements. Children played in the street, kicking a soccer ball back and forth and leaping on each other with loud shrieks. *"Yaa Sidi! Yaa Sidi!"* they cried when I got out of the copcar. I realized that some of them were the kids I distributed cash to every morning.

"You're becoming a celebrity in this neighborhood," Shaknahyi said with some amusement.

Groups of men were sitting in front of the tenements on battered kitchen chairs, drinking tea and arguing and watching traffic go by. Their conversation died as soon as we appeared. They watched us walk by with narrowed, hate-filled eyes. I could hear them muttering about us as we passed.

Shaknahyi consulted the blue sheet and checked the address of one of the tenements. "This is it," he said. There was a dark storefront on the ground floor, its display window obscured by flattened cardboard boxes taped in place on the inside.

"Looks abandoned," I said.

Shaknahyi nodded and walked back to where some of the men were watching us closely. "Anybody know anything about this On Cheung?" he asked.

The men looked at each other, but none of them said anything.

"Bastard's been buying kids. You seen him?"

I didn't think any of the unshaven, hungry-looking men would help us, but finally one of them stood up. "I'll talk to you," he said. The others mocked him and spat at his heels as he followed Shaknahyi and me down the sidewalk.

"What you know about it?" Shaknahyi asked.

"This On Cheung shows up a few months ago," said the man. He looked over his shoulder nervously. "Every day, women come here to his shop. They bring children, they go inside. A little while later they come out again, but they don't come out with the children."

"What does he do with the kids?" I asked.

"He breaks their legs," said the man. "He cuts off their hands or pulls out their tongues so people will feel sorry for them and give them money. Then he sells them to slavemasters who put them on the street to beg. Sometimes he sells the older girls to pimps."

"On Cheung would be dead by sundown if Friedlander Bey knew about this," I said.

Shaknahyi looked at me like I was a fool. He turned back to our informant. "How much does he pay for a kid?"

"I don't know," said the man. "Three, maybe five hundred kiam. Boys are worth more than girls. Sometimes pregnant women come to him from other parts of the city. They stay a week, a month. Then they go home and tell their family that the baby died." He shrugged.

Shaknahyi went to the storefront and tried the door. It rattled but wouldn't open. He took out his needle gun and smashed a glass panel over the lock, then reached in and opened the door. I followed him into the dark, musty storefront.

There was trash strewn everywhere, broken bottles and Styrofoam food containers, shredded newspaper and bubblewrap packing material. A strong odor of pine-scented disinfectant hung in the still air. There was a single battered table against one wall, a light fixture hanging from the ceiling, a stained porcelain sink in a back corner with one dripping faucet. There was no other furniture. Evidently On Cheung had had some warning of the police interest in his industry. We walked around the room, crunching glass and plastic underfoot. There was nothing more we could do there.

"When you're a cop," said Shaknahyi, "you spend a lot of time being frustrated."

We went outside again. The men on the kitchen chairs were shouting at our informant; none of them had any use for On Cheung, but their friend had broken some goddamn unwritten code by talking to us. He'd have to suffer for it.

We left them going at it. I was disgusted by the whole thing, and glad I hadn't seen evidence of what On Cheung had been up to. "What happens now?" I asked.

"To On Cheung? We file a report. Maybe he's moved to another part of the city, maybe he's left the city altogether. Maybe someday somebody'll catch him and cut his arms and legs off. Then he can sit on a street corner and beg, see how *he* likes it."

A woman in a long black coat and gray kerchief crossed the street. She was carrying a small baby wrapped in a red-and-white-checked *keffiya*. "*Yaa Sidi?*" she said to me. Shaknahyi raised his eyebrows and walked away.

"Can I help you, O my sister?" I said. It was highly unusual for a woman to speak to a strange man on the street. Of course, I was just a cop to her.

"The children tell me you are a kind man," she said. "The landlord demands more money because now I have another child. He says—"

I sighed. "How much do you need?"

"Two hundred fifty kiam, *yaa Sidi*."

I gave her five hundred. I took it out of last night's profits from Chiri's. There was still plenty left.

"What they say about you is true, O chosen one," she said. There were tears slipping from her eyes.

"You embarrass me," I said. "Give the landlord his rent, and buy food for yourself and your children."

"May Allah increase your strength, *yaa Sidi!*"

"May He bless you, my sister."

She hurried back across the street and into her building. "Makes you feel all warm inside, don't it?" Shaknahyi said. I couldn't tell if he was mocking me.

"I'm glad I can help out a little," I said.

"The Robin Hood of the slums."

"There are worse things to be called."

"If Indihar could see this side of you, maybe she wouldn't hate your guts so much." I stared at him, but he only laughed.

Back in the patrol car, the comp deck spoke up. "Badge number 374, respond immediately. Escaped murderer Paul Jawarski has been positively identified in Meloul's on Nûr ad-Din Street. He is desperate, well armed, and he will shoot to kill. Other units are on their way."

"We'll take care of it," said Shaknahyi. The comp deck's crackle faded away.

"Meloul's is where we ate lunch that time, right?" I said.

Shaknahyi nodded. "We'll try to ease this bastard Jawarski out of there before he puts holes in Meloul's couscous steamer."

"Holes?" I asked.

Shaknahyi turned and gave me a broad grin. "He likes old-fashioned pistols. He carries a .45 automatic. Put a dimple in you big enough to throw a leg of lamb through."

"You heard of this Jawarski?"

Shaknahyi swung into Nûr ad-Din Street. "We street cops have been seeing his picture for weeks. Claims he's killed twenty-six men. He's the boss of the Flathead Gang. There's ten thousand kiam on his head."

Evidently I was supposed to know what he was talking about. "You don't seem too concerned," I said.

Shaknahyi raised a hand. "I don't know whether the tip's genuine or just another pipe dream. We get as many fake calls as good ones in this neighborhood."

We were the first to arrive at Meloul's. Shaknahyi opened his door and got out. I did the same. "What do you want me to do?" I asked.

"Just keep the citizens out of the way," he said. "In case there's some—"

There was a volley of shots from inside the restaurant. Those projectile weapons make a respectable noise. They sure catch your attention when they go off, not like the spitting and hissing of static and seizure guns. I dropped to the sidewalk and tried to wrestle my static gun free of my pocket. There were more shots and I heard glass shattering nearby. The windshield, I guessed.

Shaknahyi had fallen back alongside the building, out of the line of fire. He was drawing his own weapon.

"Jirji," I called.

He waved to me to cut off the back of the restaurant. I got up and moved a few yards, and then I heard Jawarski run out the front door. I turned and saw Shaknahyi chasing after him, firing his needle gun down Nûr ad-Din Street. Shaknahyi shot four times, and then Jawarski turned. I was looking straight at them, and all I could think about was how big and black the mouth of Jawarski's gun looked. It seemed like it was pointed straight at my heart. He fired a few times and my blood froze until I realized I hadn't been hit.

Jawarski ran into a yard a few doors from Meloul's, and Shaknahyi went in after him. The fugitive must have realized that he couldn't cut through to the next street, because he doubled back toward Shaknahyi. I got there just as the two men stood facing each other, shooting it out. Jawarski's gun emptied and he turned and ran to the back of a two-story house.

We chased him through the yard. Shaknahyi ran up a flight of steps in the back, pushed open a door, and went inside the house. I didn't want to, but I had to follow him. As soon as I opened the back door, I saw Shaknahyi. He was leaning against a wall, shoving a fresh clip into his needle gun. He didn't seem to be aware of the large, dark stain that was spreading across his chest.

"Jirji, you're shot," I said, my mouth dry and my heart hammering. "Yeah." He took a deep breath and let it out. "Come on."

He walked slowly through the house to the front door. He went outside and stopped a civilian in a small electric car. "Too far to get the patrol car," he said to me, panting for breath. He looked at the driver. "I'm shot," he said, getting into the car.

I got in beside him. "Take us to the hospital," I ordered the mousy little man behind the wheel.

Shaknahyi swore. "Forget that. Follow him." He pointed to Jawarski, who was crossing the open space between the house he'd hidden in and the next.

Jawarski saw us and fired as he ran. The bullet went through the window of the car, but the bald-headed driver kept on going. We could see Jawarski dodging from one house to another. Between houses, he'd turn and take a few shots at us. Five more bullets spanged into the car.

Finally Jawarski got to the last house on the block, and he ran up the porch. Shaknahyi steadied his needle gun and fired. Jawarski staggered inside. "Come on," said Shaknahyi, wheezing. "I think I got him." He opened the car door and fell to the pavement. I jumped out and helped him to his feet. "Where are they?" he murmured.

I looked over my shoulder. A handful of uniformed cops were swarming up the stairs of Jawarski's hiding place, and three more patrol cars were racing up the street. "They're right here, Jirji," I said. His skin was starting to turn an awful gray color.

He leaned against the shot-up car and caught his breath. "Hurts like hell," he said quietly.

"Take it easy, Jirji. We'll get you to the hospital."

"Wasn't no accident, the call about On Cheung, then the tip on Jawarski."

"What you talking about?" I asked.

He was in a lot of pain, but he wouldn't get in the car. "The Phoenix File," he said. He looked deeply into my eyes, as if he could burn this information directly into my brain. "Hajjar let it slip about the Phoenix File. I been keeping notes ever since. They don't like it. Pay attention to who gets my parts, Audran. But play dumb or they'll take *your* bones too."

"The hell is a Phoenix File, Jirji?" I was frantic with worry.

"Take this." He gave me the vinyl-covered notebook from his hip pocket. Then his eyes closed and he slumped backward across the hood of the car. I looked at the driver. "Now you want to take him to the hospital?"

The shrimpy bald-headed man stared at me. Then he looked at Jirji. "You think you can keep that blood off my upholstery?" he asked.

I grabbed the little motherfucker by the front of his shirt and threw him out of his own car. Then I gently eased Shaknahyi into the passenger seat and drove to the hospital as fast as I've ever driven.

It didn't make any difference. I was too late.

Ten

One of khayyám's rubáiyyat kept going through my mind. Something about regret:

> Again, again, Repentance oft before
> I vowed—but was I sober when I swore?
> Again, again I failed, for younger thoughts
> my frail Repentance into tatters tore.

"Chiri, please," I said, holding up my empty glass. The club was almost empty. It was late and I was very tired. I closed my eyes and listened to the music, the same shrill, thumping hispo music Kandy played every time she got up to dance. I was getting tired of hearing the same songs over and over again.

"Why don't you go home?" Chiri asked me. "I can take care of the place by myself. What's the matter, don't you trust me with the cash?"

I opened my eyes. She'd put a fresh vodka gimlet in front of me. I was in a bottomless melancholy, the kind that doesn't get any help at all from liquor. You can drink all night and you never get loaded. You end up with a bad stomach and a pounding headache, but the relief you expect from your troubles never comes. "'S all right," I said. "I got to stay. You go ahead and close up, though. Nobody's come in for an hour at least."

"What you say, boss," said Chiri, giving me a worried look. I hadn't told her about Shaknahyi. I hadn't told anybody about him.

"Chiri, you know somebody I can trust to do a little dirty work?"

She didn't look shocked. That was one of the reasons I liked her so much. "You can't find somebody with your cop connections? You don't have enough thugs working for you at Papa's?"

I shook my head. "Somebody who knows what he's doing, somebody I can count on to keep a low profile."

Chiri grinned. "Somebody like what you used to be before your lucky number came up. What about Morgan? He's dependable and he probably won't sell you out."

"I don't know," I said. Morgan was a big blond guy, an American from Federated New England. He and I didn't travel in the same circles, but if Chiri recommended him, he was probably all right.

"What you need done?" she asked.

I rubbed my cheek. Reflected in the back mirror, my red beard was beginning to show a lot of gray. "I want him to track somebody down for me. Another American."

"See there? Morgan's a natural."

"Uh huh," I said sourly. "If they blow each other away, nobody'll miss 'em. Can you get hold of him tonight?"

She looked doubtful. "It's two o'clock in the morning."

"Tell him there's a hundred kiam in it for him. Just for showing up and talking to me."

"He'll be here," said Chiri. She dug an address book out of her bag and grabbed the bar's phone.

I gulped down half the vodka gimlet and stared at the front door. Now I was waiting for two people.

"You want to pay us?" Chiri said some time later.

I'd been staring at the door, unaware that the music had been turned off and the five dancers had gotten dressed. I shook my head to clear the fog out of it, but it didn't do much good. "How'd we do tonight?" I asked.

"Same as always," said Chiri. "Lousy."

I split the receipts with her and began counting out the dancers' money. Chiri had a list of how many drinks each girl had gotten from the customers. I figured out the commissions and added them to the wages. "Nobody better come in late tomorrow," I said.

"Yeah, right," said Kandy, snatching up her money and hurrying for the door. Lily, Rani, and Jamila were close behind her.

"You all right, Marîd?" asked Yasmin.

I looked up at her, grateful for her concern. "I'm fine," I said. "Tell you all about it later."

"Want to go out for some breakfast?"

That would have been wonderful. I hadn't gone out with Yasmin in months. I realized that it had been a very long time since I'd gone out with *anybody*. I had something else to do tonight, though. "Let me postpone that," I said. "Tomorrow, maybe."

"Sure, Marîd," she said. She turned and went out.

"There *is* something wrong, huh?" said Chiri.

I just nodded and folded up the rest of the night's cash. No matter how fast I gave it away, it just kept accumulating.

"And you don't want to talk about it."

I shook my head. "Go on home, Chiri."

"Just gonna sit here in the dark by yourself?"

I made a shooing motion with my hand. Chiri shrugged and left me alone. I finished the vodka gimlet, then went behind the bar and made myself another one. About twenty minutes later, the blond American came into the club. He nodded to me and said something in English.

I just shook my head. I opened my briefcase on the bar, took out an English-language daddy, and chipped it in. There was just a moment while my mind worked to translate what he'd said, and then the daddy kicked in and it was as if I'd always known how to speak English. "Sorry to make you come out so late, Morgan," I said.

He ran a large hand through his long blond hair. "Hey, man, what's happenin'?"

"Want a drink?"

"You can draw me a beer if it's free."

"Help yourself," I said.

He leaned across the bar and held a clean glass under one of the taps. "Chiri said something about a hundred kiam, man."

I took out my money. The size of the roll dismayed me. I was going to have to get to the bank more often, or else I'd have to let Kmuzu play bodyguard full-time. I dealt out five twenty-kiam bills and slid them down toward Morgan.

He wiped his mouth with the back of his hand and scooped up the money. He looked down at the bills, then back at me. "Now I can go, right?" he said.

"Sure," I said, "unless you want to hear how you can make a thousand more."

He adjusted his steel-rimmed spectacles and grinned again. I didn't know if the glasses were functional or just an affectation. If his eyes were bad, he could have had them reconstructed cheaply enough. "This is a lot more interesting than what I was doin', anyway," he said.

"Fine. I just want you to find somebody." I told him all about Paul Jawarski.

When I mentioned the Flathead Gang, Morgan nodded. "He's the guy that killed the cop today?" he asked.

"He got away."

"Well, hey, man, the law will bring him in sooner or later, you can bet on that."

I didn't let my expression change. "I don't want to hear about sooner or later, okay? I want to know where he's at, and I want to ask him a couple of questions before the cops get to him. He's holed up somewhere, probably been stung with a needle gun."

"You're payin' a thousand kiam just to put the finger on this guy?"

I squeezed the wedge of lime into my gimlet and drank some. "Uh huh."

"You don't want me to rough him up a little for you?"

"Just find him before Hajjar does."

"Aha," said Morgan, "I get you, man. After the lieutenant gets his hooks into him, Jawarski won't be available to talk to nobody."

"Right. And we don't want that to happen."

"I guess we don't, man. How much you gonna pay me up front?"

"Five now, five later." I cut him another five hundred kiam. "I get results tomorrow, right?"

His big hand closed on the money and he gave me his predatory grin. "Go get some sleep, man. I'll be wakin' you up with Jawarski's address and commcode."

I stood up. "Finish your beer and let's get out of here. This place is starting to break my heart."

Morgan looked around at the dark bar. "Ain't the same without the girls and the mirror balls goin', is it?" He gulped down the rest of his beer and set the glass gently on the bar.

I followed him toward the front door. "Find Jawarski," I said.

"You got it, man." He raised a hand and ambled away up the Street. I went back inside and sat in my place. My night wasn't over yet.

I drank a couple more gimlets before Indihar showed up. I knew she was going to come. I'd been waiting for her.

She'd thrown on a bulky blue coat and tied a maroon and gold scarf over her hair. Her face was pale and drawn, her lips pressed tightly together. She came to where I was sitting and looked down at me. Her eyes weren't red, though; she hadn't been crying. I couldn't imagine Indihar crying. "I want to talk to you," she said. Her voice was cold and calm.

"That's why I been sitting here," I said.

She turned away and stared at herself in the wall of mirrors behind the stage. "Sergeant Catavina said you weren't in very good shape this morning. That true?" She looked at me again. Her expression was perfectly empty.

"Is what true?" I said. "That I wasn't feeling well?"

"That you were high or hung over today when you went out with my husband."

I sighed. "I showed up at the station house with a hangover. It wasn't crippling, though."

Her hands began clenching and unclenching. I could see her jaw muscles twitch. "You think it might have slowed you down any?"

"No, Indihar," I said, "I don't think it affected me at all. You want to blame me for what happened? Is that what this is about?"

Her head turned very slowly. She stared directly into my eyes. "Yes, I want to blame you. You didn't back him up fast enough. You didn't cover him. If you'd been there for him, he wouldn't be dead."

"You can't say that, Indihar." I had a sick, hollow feeling in my belly because I'd been thinking the same thing all day. The guilt had been growing in me since I'd left Shaknahyi lying on a cot at the hospital with a bloody sheet over his face.

"My husband would be alive and my children would still have a father. They don't now, you know. I haven't told them yet. I don't know *how* to tell them. I don't know how to tell myself, if you want to know the truth. Maybe tomorrow I'll realize that Jirji's dead. Then I'll have to find a way to get through the day without him, through the week, through the rest of my life."

I felt a sudden nausea and closed my eyes. It was as if I weren't really there, as if I were just dreaming this nightmare. When I opened my eyes, though, Indihar was still looking at me. It had all happened, and she and I were going to have to play out this terrible scene. "I—"

"Don't tell me you're sorry, you son of a bitch," she said. Even then she didn't raise her voice. "I don't want to hear anybody tell me he's sorry."

I just sat there and let her say whatever she needed to say. She couldn't accuse me of anything that I hadn't already confessed to in my own mind. Maybe if I hadn't gotten so drunk last night, maybe if I hadn't taken all those sunnies this morning—

Finally she just stared at me, a look of despair on her face. She was condemning me with her presence and her silence. She knew and I knew, and that was enough. Then she turned and walked out of the club, her gait steady, her posture perfect.

I felt absolutely destroyed. I found the phone where Chiri'd left it and spoke my home commcode into it. It rang three times and then Kmuzu answered. "You want to come get me?" I said. I was slurring my words.

"Are you at Chiriga's?" he asked.

"Yeah. Come quick before I kill myself." I slapped the phone down on the bar and made myself another drink while I waited.

When he arrived, I had a little present for him. "Hold out your hand," I said.

"What is it, *yaa Sidi?*"

I emptied my pillcase into his upturned palm, then clicked the pill-case closed and put it back in my pocket. "Get rid of 'em," I said.

His expression didn't change as he closed his fist. "This is wise," he said.

"I'm way overdue." I got up from my stool and followed him back into the cool night air. I locked the front door of Chiri's and then let Kmuzu drive me home.

I took a long shower and let the hot needle spray blast my skin until I felt myself begin to relax. I dried off and went into my bedroom. Kmuzu had brought me a mug of strong hot chocolate. I sipped it gratefully.

"Will you be needing anything else tonight, *yaa Sidi?*" he asked.

"Listen," I said, "I'm not going into the station house in the morning. Let me sleep, all right? I don't want to be bothered. I don't want to answer any phone calls or deal with anybody's problems."

"Unless the master of the house requires you," said Kmuzu.

I sighed. "That goes without saying. Otherwise—"

"I will see that you're not disturbed."

I didn't chip in the wake-up daddy before I went to bed, and I got a restless night's sleep. Bad dreams woke me again and again until I fell into deep, exhausted sleep at dawn. It was close to noon when I finally got out of bed. I dressed in my old jeans and work shirt, a costume I didn't wear very often around Friedlander Bey's mansion.

"Would you like some breakfast, *yaa Sidi?*" asked Kmuzu.

"No, I'm taking a vacation from all that today."

He frowned. "There is a business matter for your attention later."

"Later," I agreed. I went to the desk where I'd thrown my briefcase the night before, and took Wise Counselor from the rack of moddies. I thought my troubled mind could use some instant therapy. I seated myself in a comfortable black leather chair and chipped the moddy in.

Once upon a time in Mauretania there was or maybe there wasn't a famous fool, trickster, and rascal named Marîd Audran. One day Audran was driving his cream-colored Westphalian sedan on his way to take care of some important business, when another car collided with his. The second car was old and broken down, and although the accident was clearly the fault of the other driver, the man jumped out of the wrecked heap and began screaming at Audran. "Look what you've done to my magnificent vehicle!" shouted the driver, who was Police Lieutenant Hajjar. Reda

Abu Adil, Hassan the Shiite, and Paul Jawarski also got out of the car. All four threatened and abused Audran, although he protested that he had done nothing wrong.

Jawarski kicked the creased fender of Hajjar's automobile. "It's useless now," he said, "and so the only fair thing is for you to give us your car."

Audran was outnumbered four to one and it was clear that they were not in a mood to be reasonable, so he agreed.

"And will you not reward us for showing you the path of honor?" asked Hajjar.

"If we hadn't insisted," said Hassan, "your actions would have put your soul in jeopardy with Allah."

"Perhaps," said Audran. "What do you wish me to pay you for this service?"

Reda Abu Adil spread his hands as if it mattered little. "It is but a token, a symbol between Muslim brothers," he said. "You may give us each a hundred kiam." So Audran handed the keys to his cream-colored Westphalian sedan to Lieutenant Hajjar, and paid each of the four a hundred kiam.

All afternoon, Audran pushed Hajjar's wrecked car back to town in the hot sun. He parked it in the middle of the souk and went to find his friend, Saied the Half-Hajj. "You must help me get even with Hajjar, Abu Adil, Hassan, and Jawarski," he said, and Saied was agreeable. Audran cut a hole in the floor of the derelict automobile, and Saied lay by the opening covered with a blanket so that none could see him, with a small bag of gold coins. Then Audran started the engine of the car and waited.

Not long after, the four villains happened by. They saw Audran sitting in the shade of the ruined automobile and laughed. "It won't drive an inch!" mocked Jawarski. "What are you warming the engine for?"

Audran glanced up. "I have my reasons," he said, and he smiled as if he had a wonderful secret.

"What reasons?" demanded Abu Adil. "Has the summer sun at last broiled your brains?"

Audran stood and stretched. "I guess I can tell you," he said lightly. "After all, I owe my good fortune to you."

"Good fortune?" asked Hajjar suspiciously.

"Come," said Audran. "Look." He led the four villains to the back of the car where the battery cap had been left open. "Piss in the battery," he said.

"You've surely gone crazy," said Jawarski.

"Then I will do it myself," said Audran, and he did, relieving him-

*self into the wreck's battery. "Now we must wait a moment. There! Did
you hear that?"*

"I heard nothing," said Hassan.

*"Listen," said Audran. And there came a gentle chink! chink! sound
from beneath the car. "Take a look," he commanded.*

*Reda Abu Adil got down on hands and knees, ignoring the dust and
the indignity, and peered under the car. "May his faith be cursed!" he
cried. "Gold!" He stretched out on the ground and reached under the
car; when he straightened up again, he held a handful of gold coins.
He showed them to his companions in amazement.*

*"Listen," said Audran. And they all heard the chink! chink! of more
gold coins falling to the ground.*

*"He pisses yellow into the car," murmured Hassan, "and yellow
gold falls from it."*

*"May Allah let you prosper if you let me have my car back!" cried
Lieutenant Hajjar.*

"I'm afraid not," said Audran.

*"Take your goddamn cream-colored Westphalian sedan and we'll
call it a fair trade," said Jawarski.*

"I'm afraid not," said Audran.

"We'll each give you a hundred kiam as well," said Abu Adil.

"I'm afraid not," said Audran.

*They begged and begged, and Audran refused. Finally they offered
to give him back his sedan plus five hundred kiam from each of them,
and he accepted. "But come back in an hour," he said. "That's still my
piss in the battery." And they agreed. Then Audran and Saied went off
and divided their profit.*

I yawned as I popped Wise Counselor out. I'd enjoyed the vision,
except for seeing Hassan the Shiite, who was dead and who could stay
dead for all I cared. I thought about what the little story might mean. It
might mean that my unconscious mind was hard at work coming up
with clever ways to outsmart my enemies. I was glad to learn this. I
already knew that I wasn't going to get anywhere by force. I didn't
have any.

I felt subtly different after that session with Wise Counselor: more
determined, maybe, but also wonderfully clear and free. I had a grim
set to my jaw now and the sense that no one at all could impose restric-
tions on me. I'd been changed by Shaknahyi's death, kicked up to a
higher energy level. I felt as if I were living in pure oxygen, bright and
clean and dangerously explosive.

"*Yaa Sidi,*" said Kmuzu softly.

"What is it?"

"The master of the house is ill today and wishes you to attend to a small business matter."

I yawned again. "Yeah, you right. What kind of business?"

"I do not know."

This liberated feeling let me forget about what Friedlander Bey might think of my clothes. That just wasn't important anymore. Papa had me under his thumb and maybe I couldn't do anything about it, but I wasn't going to be passive any longer. I intended to let him know that; but when I saw him, he looked so ill that I filed it away for later.

He lay propped up in bed with a small mountain of pillows around him and behind his back. A tray table straddled his legs, and it was stacked high with file folders, reports, multicolored memory plates, and a tiny microcomputer. He held a cup of hot aromatic tea in one hand and one of Umm Saad's stuffed dates in the other. Umm Saad must have thought she could bribe Papa with them, or that he would forget his last words to her. To be honest, Friedlander Bey's problem with Umm Saad seemed almost trivial to me now, but I did not mention her.

"I pray for your well-being," I said.

Papa raised his eyes toward me and grimaced. "It is nothing, my nephew. I feel dizzy and sick to my stomach."

I leaned forward and kissed Papa's cheek, and he muttered something I could not hear clearly.

I waited for him to explain the business matter he wanted me to take care of. "Youssef tells me there is a large, angry woman in the waiting room downstairs," he said, a frown pulling down his mouth. "Her name is Tema Akwete. She's trying to be patient because she's come a long distance to beg a favor."

"What kind of favor?" I asked.

Papa shrugged. "She represents the new government of the Songhay Republic."

"Never heard of it."

"Last month the country was called the Glorified Segu Kingdom. Before that it was the Magistracy of Timbuktu, and before that Mali, and before that it was part of French West Africa."

"And the Akwete woman is an emissary from the new regime?"

Friedlander Bey nodded. He started to say something, but his eyes closed and his head fell back against the pillows. He passed a hand across his forehead. "Forgive me, my nephew," he said, "I'm not feeling well."

"Then don't concern yourself about the woman. What is her problem?"

"Her problem is that the Segu king was very upset to find out he'd lost his job. Before he fled the palace he sacked the royal treasury, of course—that goes without saying. His gang also destroyed all the vital computer records in the capital. The Songhay Republic opened up shop without the slightest idea of how many people they rule or even where the country's boundaries are. There is no fair basis for taxation, no lists of government employees or descriptions of their duties, and no accurate information concerning the armed forces. Songhay faces immediate catastrophe."

I understood. "So they sent someone here. They want you to restore order."

"Without tax revenue, the new government cannot pay its employees or continue normal services. It's likely that Songhay will soon be paralyzed by general strikes. The army may desert, and then the country will be at the mercy of neighboring nations, if they are any better organized."

"Why is the woman angry with *you*, then?"

Papa spread his hands. "Songhay's problems are not my concern," he said. "I explained to you that Reda Abu Adil and I divided the Muslim world. This country is in his jurisdiction. I have nothing to do with the Sub-Saharan states."

"Akwete should have gone to Abu Adil in the first place."

"Exactly. Youssef gave that message to her, but she screamed and struck the poor man. She thinks we're trying to extort a higher payment from her and her government." Papa set down his teacup and searched through the disordered piles of papers on his blankets, selecting a thick envelope and passing it to me with a trembling hand. "This is the background material and the contract she offered me. Tell her to take it to Abu Adil."

I took a deep breath and let it out. It didn't sound like dealing with Akwete was going to be much fun. "I'll talk to her," I said.

Papa nodded absently. He'd disposed of one minor annoyance, and he was already turning his attention to something else. After a while I murmured a few words and left the room. He didn't even notice that I'd gone.

Kmuzu was waiting for me in the corridor leading from Papa's private apartment. I told him what Friedlander Bey and I had talked about. "I'm gonna see this woman," I said, "and then you and I are gonna take a ride out to Abu Adil's house."

"Yes, *yaa Sidi*, but it may be best if I waited for you in the car. Reda Abu Adil no doubt thinks me a traitor."

"Uh huh. Because you were hired as a bodyguard for his wife and now you look out for me?"

"Because he arranged for me to be a spy in the house of Friedlander Bey, and I no longer consider myself to be in his employ."

I had known from the beginning that Kmuzu was a spy. I'd just thought he was Papa's spy, not Abu Adil's. "You're not reporting everything back to him?"

"Back to whom, *yaa Sidi?*"

"Back to Abu Adil."

Kmuzu gave me a brief, earnest smile. "I assure you that I am not. I am, of course, reporting to the master of the house."

"Well, that's all right, then." We'd gone downstairs, and I stopped outside one of the waiting rooms. The two Stones That Speak stood on either side of the door. They glared menacingly at Kmuzu. Kmuzu glared back. I ignored all of them and went inside.

The black woman jumped to her feet as soon as I'd set foot across the threshold. "I demand an explanation!" she cried. "I warn you, as a lawful ambassador of the government of the Songhay Republic—"

I shut her up with a sharp look. "Madame Akwete," I said, "the message you received earlier was quite accurate. You've truly come to the wrong place. However, I can expedite this matter for you. I'll convey the information and the contract in this envelope to Shaykh Reda Abu Adil, who participated in establishing the Segu Kingdom. He'll be able to help you in the same way."

"And what payment will you expect as a middleman?" Akwete asked sourly.

"None whatsoever. It is a gesture of friendship from our house to a new Islamic republic."

"Our country is still young. We mistrust such friendship."

"That is your privilege," I said, shrugging. "No doubt the Segu king felt the same way." I turned and left the waiting room.

Kmuzu and I walked briskly along the hall toward the great wooden front doors. I could hear Akwete's shoes echoing behind us on the tiled floor. "Wait," she called. I thought I heard a hint of apology in her voice.

I stopped and faced her. "Yes, madame?" I said.

"This shaykh . . . can he do as you say? Or is this some elaborate swindle?"

I gave her a cold smile. "I don't see that you or your country are in any position to doubt. Your situation is hopeless now, and Abu Adil can't make it any worse. You have nothing to lose and everything to gain."

"We are not rich," said Akwete. "Not after the way King Olujimi bled our people and squandered our meager wealth. We have little gold—"

Kmuzu raised a hand. It was very unusual for him to interrupt. "Shaykh Reda is less interested in your gold than in power," he said.

"Power?" asked Akwete. "What kind of power does he want?"

"He will study your situation," said Kmuzu, "and then he will reserve certain information for himself."

I thought I saw the black woman falter. "I insist on going with you to see this man. It is my right."

Kmuzu and I looked at each other. We both knew how naive she was to think she had any rights at all in this situation. "All right," I said, "but you'll let me speak to Abu Adil first."

She looked suspicious. "Why is that?"

"Because I say so." I went outside with Kmuzu, where I waited in the warm sunlight while he went for the car. Madame Akwete followed me a moment later. She looked furious, but she said nothing more.

In the backseat of the sedan, I opened my briefcase and took Saied's tough-guy moddy from the rack and chipped it in. It filled me with the confident illusion that nobody could get in my way from now on, not Abu Adil, Hajjar, Kmuzu, or Friedlander Bey.

Akwete sat as far from me as she could, her hands clasped tightly in her lap, her head turned away from me. I wasn't concerned with her opinion of me. I looked at Shaknahyi's brown vinyl-covered notebook again. On the first page he had written *Phoenix File* in large letters. Beneath that there were several entries:

Ishaq Abdul-Hadi Bouhatta—Elwau Chami (Heart, lungs)
Andreja Svobik—Fatima Hamdan (Stomach, bowel, liver)
Abbas Karami—Nabil Abu Khalifeh (Kidneys, liver)
Blanca Mataro—

Shaknahyi had been sure that the four names on the left were somehow connected; but in Hajjar's words, they were only "open files." Under the names, Shaknahyi had written three Arabic letters: Alif, Lâm, Mîm, corresponding to the Roman letters A, L, M.

What could they mean? Were they an acronym? I could probably find a hundred organizations whose initials were A.L.M. The A and L might form the definite article, and the M might be the first letter in a name: someone called al-Mansour or al-Maghrebi. Or were the letters

Shaknahyi's shorthand, an abbreviation referring to a German *(almâni)* or a diamond *(almâs)* or something else? I wondered if I could ever discover what the three letters meant, without Shaknahyi to explain his code.

I slipped an audio chip into the car's holosystem, then put the notebook and Tema Akwete's envelope in the briefcase and locked it. While Umm Khalthoum, The Lady of the twentieth century, sang her laments, I pretended she was mourning Jirji Shaknahyi, crying for Indihar and their children. Akwete still stared out her window, ignoring me. Meanwhile, Kmuzu steered the car through the narrow, twisting streets of Hâmidiyya, the slums that guarded the approach to Reda Abu Adil's mansion.

After a ride of nearly half an hour, we turned into the estate. Kmuzu remained in the car, pretending to doze. Akwete and I got out and went up the ceramic-tiled path to the house. When Shaknahyi and I had been here before, I'd been impressed by the luxurious gardens and the beautiful house. I noticed none of that today. I rapped on the carved wooden door and a servant answered my summons immediately, giving me an insolent look but saying nothing.

"We have business with Shaykh Reda," I said, pushing by him. "I come from Friedlander Bey."

Thanks to Saied's moddy, my manner was rude and brusque, but the servant didn't seem to be upset. He shut the door after Tema Akwete and hurried ahead of me, going down a high-ceilinged corridor, expecting us to follow. We followed. He stopped before a closed door at the end of a long, cool passage. The fragrance of roses was in the air, the smell I'd come to identify with Abu Adil's mansion. The servant hadn't said another word. He paused to give me another insolent look, then walked away.

"You wait here," I said, turning to Akwete.

She started to argue, then thought better of it. "I don't like this at all," she said.

"Too bad." I didn't know what was on the other side of the door, but I wasn't going to get anywhere standing in the hallway with her, so I grabbed the doorknob and went through.

Neither Reda Abu Adil nor his secretary, Umar Abdul-Qawy, heard me come into the office. Abu Adil was in his hospital bed, as he was the previous time I'd seen him. Umar was leaning over him. I couldn't tell what he was doing.

"Allah grant you health," I said gruffly.

Umar jerked upright and faced me. "How did you get in here?" he demanded.

"Your servant brought me to the door."

Umar nodded. "Kamal. I will have to speak to him." He looked at me more closely. "I'm sorry," he said, "I don't recall your name."

"Marîd Audran. I work for Friedlander Bey."

"Ah yes," said Umar. His expression softened just a little. "The last time, you came as a policeman."

"I'm not actually a cop. I look after Friedlander Bey's interests with the police."

A little smile curled Umar's lips. "As you wish. Are you looking after them today?"

"His interests and yours also."

Abu Adil raised a feeble hand and touched Umar's sleeve. Umar bent to hear the old man's whispered words, then straightened up again. "Shaykh Reda invites you to make yourself comfortable," said Umar. "We would have prepared suitable refreshments if you'd let us know you were coming."

I looked around for a chair and seated myself. "A very upset woman came to Friedlander Bey's house today," I said. "She represents a revolutionary government that's just socialized the Glorified Segu Kingdom." I opened my briefcase, took out the envelope from the Songhay Republic, and tossed it to Umar.

Umar looked amused. "Already? I really thought Olujimi would last longer. I suppose once you've transferred all the wealth there is in a country to a foreign bank, there's really no point in being king anymore."

"I didn't come here to talk about that." The Half-Hajj's moddy was making it difficult for me to be civil to Umar. "By the terms of your agreement with Friedlander Bey, this country is under your authority. You'll find all the relevant information in that packet. I left the woman fuming outside in the hallway. She seems like a cutthroat bitch. I'm glad you have to deal with her, and not me."

Umar shook his head. "They always try to order and reorganize our lives for us. They forget how much we can do for their cause if we're in the right mood."

I watched him play with the envelope, turning it around and around on the desk. A weak, drawn-out groan came from Abu Adil, but I'd seen too much real pain in the world to pity the suffering of a Proxy Hell maggot. I looked back at Umar. "If you can do something to make your master more alert," I said, "Madame Akwete needs to speak with him. She seems to think the fate of the Islamic world rests on her shoulders alone."

Umar gave me an ironic smile. "The Songhay Republic," he said, shaking his head in disbelief. "Tomorrow it will be a kingdom again or a conquered province or a fascist dictatorship. And no one will care."

"Madame Akwete will care."

That amused him even more. "Madame Akwete will be one of the first to go in the new wave of purges. But we've talked enough about her. Now we must discuss the matter of your compensation."

I looked at him closely. "I didn't have any thought of payment," I said.

"Of course not. You were fulfilling the agreement, the compact between your employer and mine. Nevertheless, it's always wise to express gratitude to our friends. After all, someone who has helped you in the past is more likely to help you again. Perhaps there is some small service I may do for you in return."

This was the whole purpose behind my little jaunt into Abu Adil's part of town. I spread my hands and tried to look casual. "No, I can't think of anything," I said. "Unless . . ."

"Unless what, my friend?"

I pretended to examine my boot's rundown heel. "Unless you're willing to tell me why you've installed Umm Saad in our household."

Umar pretended to be just as casual. "You must know by now that Umm Saad is a very intelligent woman, but she is by no means as clever as she believes. We wished her only to keep us apprised of Friedlander Bey's plans. We said nothing to her about confronting him directly or abusing his hospitality. She's antagonized your master, and that has made her worthless to us. You may dispose of her as you wish."

"It's only as I suspected," I said. "Friedlander Bey doesn't hold you or Shaykh Reda responsible for her actions."

Umar raised one hand in a rueful gesture. "Allah gives us tools to use as best we can," he said. "Sometimes a tool breaks and we must discard it."

"Allah be praised," I murmured.

"Praise Allah," said Umar. We seemed to be getting along just fine now.

"One other thing," I said. "The policeman who was with me the last time, Officer Shaknahyi, was shot and killed yesterday."

Umar didn't stop smiling, but his brow furrowed. "We heard the news. Our hearts go out to his widow and children. May Allah grant them peace."

"Yeah. In any event, I greatly desire to have the man who killed him. His name is Paul Jawarski."

I looked at Abu Adil, who writhed restlessly on his hospital bed. The plump old man made a few low, unintelligible sounds, but Umar wasn't paying any attention to him. "Certainly," he said. "We'll be glad to put our resources at your disposal. If any of our associates know anything about this Jawarski, you'll be informed immediately."

I didn't like the way Umar said that. It was too glib, and he looked too unhappy. I just thanked him and stood up to go.

"A moment, Shaykh Marîd," he said in a quiet voice. He stood up and took my arm, guiding me to another exit. "I'd like to have a private word with you. Would you mind stepping into the library?"

I felt a peculiar chill. I knew this invitation was coming from Umar Abdul-Qawy, acting independently, not Umar Abdul-Qawy, the secretary of Shaykh Reda Abu Adil. "Fine," I said.

He reached up and popped the moddy he was wearing. He hadn't spared so much as a glance at Abu Adil.

Umar held the door for me, and I went through into the library. I seated myself at a large oblong table of glossy dark wood. Umar didn't sit, however. He paced in front of a high wall lined with bookshelves, idly tossing the moddy in one hand. "I think I understand your position," he said at last.

"Which position is that?"

He waved irritably. "You know what I mean. How much longer will you be content to be Friedlander Bey's trained dog, running and fetching for a madman who doesn't have the wit to realize he's already dead?"

"You mean Papa, or Shaykh Reda?" I asked.

Umar stopped pacing and frowned at me. "I'm speaking of both of them, and I'm sure you goddamn well know it."

I watched Umar for a moment, listening to the trilling of some of the songbirds that were caged all through Abu Adil's house and grounds. It gave the afternoon a false sense of peace and hopefulness. The air in the library was musty and stale. I began to feel caged myself. Maybe it had been a mistake coming here today. "What are you suggesting, Umar?" I asked.

"I'm suggesting that we begin thinking of the future. Someday, not long from now, the old men's empires will be in our hands. Hell, I run Shaykh Reda's business for him right now. He spends the whole day chipped in to . . . to—"

"I know what he's got chipped in," I said.

Umar nodded. "All right, then. This moddy that I use is a recent recording of his mind. He gave it to me because his only sexual kick is jamming himself, or an accurate facsimile of himself. Does that disgust you?"

"You're kidding." I'd heard much worse in my time.

"Forget that, then. He doesn't realize that with his moddy, I'm his equal as far as tending to business is concerned. I *am* Abu Adil, but I have the added advantage of my own native skills. He is Shaykh Reda, a great man; but with this moddy, I am Shaykh Reda and Umar Abdul-Qawy together. Why do I need him?"

I found this all terrifically amusing. "Are you proposing the elimination of Abu Adil and Friedlander Bey?"

Umar looked around himself nervously. "I propose no such thing," he said in a quiet voice. "There are too many other people depending on their judgment and vision. Yet there may come a day when the old men themselves are a hindrance to their own enterprises."

"When the time comes to push them aside," I said, "the right people will know it. And Friedlander Bey, at least, will not begrudge them."

"What if the time is now?" Umar asked hoarsely.

"You may be ready, but I'm not prepared to take over Papa's affairs."

"Even that problem could be solved," insisted Umar.

"Possibly," I said. I didn't let any expression cross my face. I had no idea if we were being watched and recorded, and yet I didn't want to antagonize Umar. I knew now that he was a very dangerous man.

"You will learn that I am right," he said. He tossed the moddy in his hand some more, his brow furrowed again in thought. "Go back to Friedlander Bey now and think about what I've said. We'll talk again soon. If you do not share my enthusiasm, I may need to push you aside along with both our masters." I started to rise from my chair. He raised a hand to stop me. "That is not a threat, my friend," he said calmly. "It is only how I see the future."

"Allah alone sees the future."

He laughed cynically. "If you think that pious talk has any real meaning, I may end up with more power than Shaykh Reda ever dreamed of." He indicated another door on the south side of the library. "You may go out that way. Follow the corridor to the left, and it will lead you to the front entrance. I must go back and discuss this Songhay Republic business with the woman. You needn't worry about her. I'll send her back to her hotel with my driver."

"Thank you for your kindness," I said.

"May you go in peace and safety," he said.

I left the library and followed Umar's directions. Kamal, the servant, met me along the way and showed me out. Again he kept silent as we walked. I went down the steps toward the car, and then I turned to look back. Kamal stood in the doorway, staring after me as if I might be concealing stolen silverware in my clothing.

I got into the sedan. Kmuzu started the engine and swung the car around and out through the main gate. I thought about what Umar had said, what he'd offered me. Abu Adil had exercised his power for almost two centuries. Surely in all that time there had been many young men who'd filled the position Umar now held. Surely some of them had had the same ambitious ideas. Abu Adil still remained, but what had happened to those young men? Maybe Umar had never considered that question. Maybe Umar was nowhere near as smart as he thought he was.

ELEVEN

Jirji shaknahyi had been killed on Tuesday, and it wasn't until Friday that I was able to go into the station house again. It was, of course, the Sabbath, and I toyed with the idea of passing by a mosque on the way, but I felt hypocritical about that. I figured I was such a crummy person that no amount of worshiping could make me acceptable to Allah. I know that's all hollow rationalization—it's the sinners, after all, who need the benefits of prayer most, and not the saints—but I just felt too soiled and guilty to enter the House of God. Besides, Shaknahyi had set an example of true faith, and I'd failed him. I had to redeem myself in my own eyes first, before I could expect to do the same in the eyes of Allah.

My life has been like a rolling ocean, with waves of comfort and ease followed by waves of adversity. No matter how peaceful things get, I know more trouble will soon sweep over me. I've always told everyone how much I preferred being on my own, a solitary agent answerable only to myself. I wished I meant it half as much as I pretended.

I needed every bit of the inner strength and confidence I'd achieved to deal with the obstinate forces around me. I was getting no help at all from Lieutenant Hajjar, Friedlander Bey, or anyone else. No one at the station house seemed particularly interested in talking with me on Friday morning. There were a lot of part-time office workers there, Christians who filled in for the religious Muslims on the Sabbath. Lieutenant Hajjar was there, of course, because on his list of favorite pastimes, religion finished down somewhere between oral surgery and paying taxes. I went immediately to his square, glass-walled office.

Eventually he looked up to see who was looming beside his desk. "What now, Audran?" he snapped. He hadn't seen me in three days, but he made it sound as if I'd been badgering him nonstop all that time.

"Just wanted to know what your plans for me were."

Hajjar looked up from his data deck. He stared at me for a long moment, his mouth twisted as if he'd just chewed a rotten date. "You're flatterin' yourself," he said in a quiet voice. "You don't enter into my plans at all."

"I was just volunteering to help in the investigation of Jirji Shaknahyi's death."

Hajjar raised his eyebrows. He leaned back in his chair. "What investigation?" he asked incredulously. "He was shot by Paul Jawarski. That's all we need to know."

I waited until I could speak without shouting at him. "We have Jawarski in custody?"

"*We?*" demanded Hajjar. "Who's *we?* You mean, does the police department have Jawarski? Not yet. But don't worry, Audran, he won't slip away. We're closin' in on him."

"How do you expect to find him? This is a big city. You think he's just sitting in a room somewhere, waiting for you to show up with a warrant? He's probably back in America by now."

"Good police work's how we'll find him, Audran. You never have much faith in good police work. I know he ain't left town. He's here somewhere, and we're tightenin' the net around him. Just a matter of time."

I didn't like the sound of that. "Tell that to his widow," I said. "She'll be heartened by your confidence."

Hajjar stood up. I'd made him angry. "You accusin' me of somethin', Audran?" he asked, jabbing a stiff forefinger into my chest. "You hintin' that maybe I'm not pushin' this investigation hard enough?"

"I never said nothing, Hajjar. I just wanted to find out what your plans are."

He gave me an evil grin. "What, you think I got nothin' better to do than sit around and worry about how to utilize your special talents? Hell, Audran, we were gettin' along fine without you the last few days. But I suppose now you're here, there must be somethin' for you to do." He sat down again at his desk and riffled through a stack of papers. "Uh yeah, here we go. I want you to go on with that investigation you and Shaknahyi started."

I wasn't happy about that. I wanted to be directly involved in tracking down Jawarski. "I thought you said we were supposed to lay off Abu Adil."

Hajjar's eyes narrowed. "I didn't say anything about Abu Adil, did I? You'd *better* lay off him. I'm talkin' about this dink, On Cheung. The baby seller. Can't afford to let his trail get cold."

I felt a cold chill pass through me. "Anybody can follow up on On Cheung," I said. "I got a special interest in finding Paul Jawarski."

"Marîd Audran, Man on a Mission, huh? Well, forget it. We don't need you roarin' around the city workin' off your grudge. Anyway, you ain't shown me yet that you know what you're doin'. So I'm assignin' you a new partner, somebody with a lot of experience. This ain't some ladies' volunteer club, Audran. You do what I tell you. Or don't you think puttin' On Cheung out of commission is worth your time?"

I gritted my teeth. I didn't like the assignment, but Hajjar was right about it being just as important as collaring Jawarski. "Whatever you say, Lieutenant."

He gave me that same grin. I wanted to whack it off his face. "You'll be ridin' around with Sergeant Catavina from now on. He ought to teach you plenty."

My heart sank. Of all the cops in that station house, Catavina was the man I least wanted to spend time with. He was a bully and a lazy son of a bitch. I knew that if we ever did catch up to On Cheung, it wouldn't be because of Catavina's contributions.

The lieutenant must have read my reaction from my expression. "Any problem with that, Audran?" he asked.

"If I had a problem, is there any chance it would change your mind?"

"None whatsoever," said Hajjar.

"Didn't think so."

Hajjar looked back at the screen of his data deck. "Report to Catavina. I want to hear some good news real soon. You cut the legs out from under this dink, there may be commendations for the two of you."

"I'll get right on it, Lieutenant," I said. I was impressed with Hajjar's cleverness. He'd skillfully maneuvered me away from both Abu Adil and Jawarski by throwing me into a time-consuming but perfectly valid investigation. I was going to have to find a way to accomplish both my official assignment and my own personal goals.

Hajjar paid no further attention to me, so I left his office. I went to find Sergeant Catavina. I'd rather proceed without him, but that wasn't going to be possible.

Catavina wasn't that excited about being paired with me, either. "I already got the word from Hajjar," he told me. We were walking down to the garage, to pick up Catavina's patrol car. Catavina was trying to give me the benefit of all his years' experience in one disjointed lecture. "You ain't a good cop, Audran," he said in a grim voice. "You may never be a good cop. I don't want you fucking up with me like you fucked up Shaknahyi."

"What's that mean, Catavina?" I asked.

He turned and looked at me, his eyes wide. "Figure it out. If you'd known what you was doing, Shaknahyi'd still be alive and I wouldn't have to be holding your hand. Just stay out of my way and do what I tell you."

I was mad as hell, but I didn't say anything. I planned to stay out of his way, all right. I figured I'd have to lose Catavina if I wanted to make any progress.

We got into the patrol car, and he had nothing more to say to me for a long while. That was okay with me. I thought he might drive back to the neighborhood where On Cheung was last known to have operated. Maybe we could learn something useful by interviewing those people again, even though they'd been so uncooperative before.

That wasn't his plan, however. He headed west, in the opposite direction. We drove about a mile and half through an area of narrow, twisting streets and alleys. At last, Catavina pulled up in front of a crumbling apartment building, the tallest building on the block. The windows on the ground floor had been covered over with plywood, and the front door into the foyer had been taken off its hinges. The walls inside and out were covered with spray-painted names and slogans. The lobby reeked; it had been used as a toilet for a long time. As we crossed to the elevator, we crunched broken glass beneath our boots. There was a thick layer of dust and grit over everything.

"What are we doing here?" I asked.

"You'll see," said Catavina. He punched the button for the elevator. When it arrived, I was hesitant about getting in. The condition of the building didn't give me any confidence that the cables would hold our weight. When the elevator asked what floor we wanted, Catavina muttered "Eight." We looked away from each other as the door slid closed. We rode in silence, the only noise coming from the elevator as it creaked its way upward.

We got out on the eighth floor, and Catavina led the way down the dark hallway to room 814. He took a key out of his pocket and unlocked the front door.

"What's this?" I asked, following him into the seedy apartment.

"Police officers' lounge," said Catavina.

There was a large living room, a small kitchen, and a bathroom. There wasn't much furniture—a cheap card table and six chairs in the living room, along with a torn black vinyl couch, a small holoset, and

four folding cots. There were uniformed cops asleep on two of the cots.
I recognized them but didn't know their names. Catavina dropped
heavily onto the couch and stared at me across the bare floor. "Want a
drink?" he asked.

"No," I said.

"Bring me some whiskey then. There's ice in the kitchen."

I went into the kitchen and found a good collection of liquor bottles. I tossed a few ice cubes into a glass and poured in three fingers of
raw Japanese liquor. "So what are we doing here," I called, thinking of
the department's motto, "protecting or serving?" I carried the drink
back into the living room and handed it to Catavina.

"You're serving," he said, grunting. "I'm protecting."

I sat down in one of the folding chairs and stared at him, watching
him down half the Japanese whiskey in one long gulp. "Protecting
what?" I asked.

Catavina smiled contemptuously. "Protecting my ass, that's what.
It ain't gonna get shot up while I'm here, that's for damn sure."

I glanced at the two sleeping cops. "Gonna stay here long?"

"Till the shift's over," he said.

"Mind if I take the car and get some work done in the meantime?"

The sergeant looked at me over the rim of his whiskey glass. "Why
the hell you want to do that?" he asked.

I shrugged. "Shaknahyi never let me drive."

Catavina looked at me like I was crazy. "Sure, just don't smash it
up." He dug in his pocket and fished out the car keys, then tossed them
to me. "You better come back and pick me up by five o'clock."

"Right, Sergeant," I said. I left him staring at the holoset, which
wasn't even turned on. I rode the elevator back down to the filthy
lobby, wondering what I was going to do next. I felt an obligation to
find something that might lead me to On Cheung, but instead it was
Jirji Shaknahyi who occupied my mind.

His funeral had been the day before, and for a while I thought I'd
just stay home. For one thing, I didn't know if I was emotionally settled enough to handle it; for another, I still felt partly responsible for
his death, and it didn't seem right for me to attend. I didn't want to face
Indihar and the children under those circumstances. Nevertheless, on
Thursday morning I went to the small mosque near the station house
where the memorial was being held.

Only men were permitted to participate in the worship service. I
removed my shoes and performed the ritual ablutions, then entered the
mosque and took a place near the back. A lot of the other cops in the
congregation seemed to be looking at me with vengeful expressions. I

was still an outsider to them, and in their eyes I might as well have pulled the trigger that killed Shaknahyi.

We prayed, and then an elderly, gray-bearded imam delivered a sermon and a eulogy, going through some weary truisms about duty and service and bravery. None of it made me feel any better. I was truly sorry that I'd talked myself into attending the service.

Then we all got up and filed out of the mosque. Except for some birds singing and a dog barking, it was almost supernaturally quiet. The sun burned down from a high, cloudless sky. A faint, tremulous breeze rippled the dusty leaves in the trees, but the air was almost too hot to breathe. The odor of spoiled milk hung like a sour mist over the cobblestone alleys. The day was just too oppressive to draw the business out much longer. I'm sure Shaknahyi'd had many friends, but right now they all just wanted to get to the graveyard and get him planted.

Indihar led the procession from the mosque to the cemetery. She was dressed in a black dress with her face veiled and her hair covered with a black kerchief. She must have been stifling. Her three children walked beside her, their expressions bewildered and frightened. Chiri had told me that Indihar hadn't had enough money to pay for a tomb in the cemetery in Haffe al-Khala where Shaknahyi's parents were buried, and she wouldn't accept a loan from us. Instead, Shaknahyi was laid to rest in what amounted to a pauper's grave in the cemetery on the western edge of the Budayeen. I followed far behind her as Indihar crossed the Boulevard il-Jameel and passed through the eastern gate. People who lived in the quarter as well as foreign tourists came out and stood on the sidewalks as the funeral party made its way up the Street. I could see many people weeping and murmuring prayers. There was no way to tell if those people even knew who the deceased was. It probably didn't make any difference to them.

All of Shaknahyi's former comrades wanted to help carry the particleboard coffin through the streets, so instead of six pallbearers there was a pushing, shoving mob of uniformed men all straining to reach the flimsy box. The ones who couldn't get near enough to touch it marched alongside and in a long parade to the rear, beating their chests with their fists and shouting testaments of their faith. There was a lot of chanting and fingering of Muslim rosaries. I found myself moving my lips along with the others, reciting ancient prayers that had been inscribed in my memory as a young child. After a while, I too was caught up in the odd mixture of despair and celebration. I found myself praising Allah for visiting so much injustice and horror on our helpless souls.

In the cemetery, I kept my distance again as the unadorned coffin was lowered into the ground. Several of Shaknahyi's closest friends on the police force took turns shoveling in dirt. The mourners offered more prayers in unison, although the imam had declined to accompany the funeral to its conclusion. Indihar stood bravely by, clutching the hands of Hâkim and Zahra, and eight-year-old Little Jirji held tightly to Hâkim's other hand. Some representative of the city went up to Indihar and murmured something, and she nodded gravely. Then all of the uniformed police officers filed past and offered her their individual condolences. That's when I saw Indihar's shoulders begin to slump; I could tell that she had begun to weep. Meanwhile, Little Jirji looked out over the crumbling tombs and overgrown grave markers, his expression perfectly blank.

When the funeral was over, everyone left but me. The police department had provided a small spread of food at the station house, because Indihar didn't have the money for that, either. I saw how humiliating the whole situation was for her. Besides grieving for her husband, Indihar also suffered the pain of having her poverty revealed to all her friends and acquaintances. To many Muslims, an unworthy funeral is as much a calamity for the survivors as the death of the loved one itself.

I chose not to attend the reception at the station house. I stayed behind, staring down at Jirji's unmarked grave, my mind confused and troubled. I said a few prayers alone and recited some passages from the Qur'ân. "I promise you, Jirji," I murmured, "Jawarski won't get away with this." I didn't have any illusions that making Jawarski pay would let Shaknahyi rest any easier, or make Indihar's grief any less, or ease the hardships for Little Jirji, Hâkim, and Zahra. I just didn't know what else to say. Finally I turned away from the grave. I blamed myself for my hesitancy, and prayed that it wouldn't lead to anyone else getting hurt ever again.

The funeral was on my mind as I drove from Catavina's secret coop back to the station house. I heard the rolling rumble of thunder, and it surprised me because we don't get many thunderstorms in the city. I glanced through the windshield up at the sky, but there were no clouds at all in sight. I felt an odd chill, thinking that maybe the thunder had been a humbling sign from God, underscoring my memories of Shaknahyi's burial. For the first time since his death, I felt a deep emotional loss.

I also began to think that my idea of vengeance would not be adequate. Finding Paul Jawarski and bringing him to justice would neither restore Shaknahyi nor free me from the intrigue in which Jawarski,

Reda Abu Adil, Friedlander Bey, and Lieutenant Hajjar were somehow
involved. In a sudden realization, I knew that it was time to stop thinking of the puzzle as one large problem with one simple solution. None
of the individual players knew the entire story, I was certain of that. I'd
have to pursue them separately and assemble what clues I could find,
hoping that in the end it would all add up to something indictable. If
Shaknahyi's hunches were wrong and I was heading off on a fool's
errand, I would end up worse than disgraced. I would surely end up
dead.

I parked the copcar in the garage and went up to my cubicle on the
third floor of the station house. Hajjar rarely left his glass booth, so I
didn't think there'd be much chance that he'd catch me. Catch me!
Hell, all I was doing was getting some work done.

It had been a couple of weeks since I'd done any serious work at
my data deck. I sat down at my desk and put a new cobalt-alloy cell-
memory plate in one of the computer's adit ports. "Create file," I said.

"File name," prompted the data deck's indifferent voice.

"Phoenix File," I said. I didn't have a lot of actual information to
enter. First I read in the names from Shaknahyi's notebook. Then I
stared at the monitor screen. Maybe it was time to follow up on Shaknahyi's research.

All of the satellite decks in the station house were connected to
the central police database. The problem was that Lieutenant Hajjar
had never entirely trusted me, and so I'd been given only the lowest
security clearance. With my password, I could only obtain information that was also available to any civilian who came in the front door
of the station house and inquired at the information desk. However, in
the months I'd worked at the copshop, I'd casually nosed out all the
codes from other paper-pushers with higher ratings. There was a great
and active underground involved with circulating classified information among the nonuniformed staff. This was technically highly illegal, of course, but in actual fact it was the only way any of us could
get our jobs done.

"Search," I said.

"Enter string to be searched," muttered the Annamese deck in its
peculiar American accent.

"Bouhatta." Ishaq Abdul-Hadi Bouhatta was the first entry in
Shaknahyi's notebook, a murder victim whose killer had not yet been
caught.

"Enter password," said the computer.

I had the list of security codes scribbled on a torn sheet of paper
that I'd hidden in a tech manual. I'd memorized the top-level password

long ago, however. It was a twenty-four-character mix of alphanumerics and Arabic Standard Code for Information Interchange symbols. I had to key those in manually.

"Accepted," said the data deck. "Searching."

In about thirty seconds, Bouhatta's complete file appeared on my monitor. I skipped through the personal biography and the details of his death—except to note that he'd been killed at close range by a charge from a static pistol, the same as Blanca. What I wanted to know was where his body had been taken. I found that information in the medical examiner's report, which formed the last page of the file. There'd been no autopsy; instead, Bouhatta's corpse had been delivered to Abu Emir Hospital in Al-Islam Square.

"Search again?" asked the deck.

"No," I said. "Import data."

"Database?"

"Abu Emir Hospital," I said.

The computer thought about that for a moment. "Current security code is sufficient," it decided. There was a long pause while it accessed the computer records of the hospital.

When I saw the hospital's main menu on my screen, I ordered a search of Bouhatta's records. It didn't take long, and I found what I needed. Just as Shaknahyi's notes suggested, Bouhatta's heart and lungs had been removed almost immediately after his death and transplanted into the body of Elwau Chami. I supposed then that Shaknahyi's other information was correct, concerning the victims of the other unsolved murders.

Now I wanted to take his research one important step further. "Search again?" the hospital's database inquired.

"Yes," I said.

"Enter string to be searched."

"Chami." A few seconds later, I saw a list of five names, from Chami, Ali Masoud to Chami, Zayd.

"Select entry," said the deck.

"Chami, Elwau." When the file came up on the screen, I read through it carefully. Chami was a faceless man, not as poor as some, not as rich as others. He was married and had seven children, five sons and two daughters. He lived in a middle-class neighborhood northeast of the Budayeen. The medical records said nothing about any run-ins with the law, of course, but there was one important fact buried in the redundant forms and reports: Elwau Chami operated a small shop in the Budayeen, on Eleventh Street north of the Street. It was a shop I knew well enough. Chami sold cheap Oriental rugs in the front, and he leased the rear of the establishment to an old Pakistani married couple who sold brass ornaments to tourists. The interesting fact was that I knew Friedlander Bey owned the building; Chami probably also worked as gatekeeper for the high-stakes gambling parlor upstairs.

Next I researched Blanca Mataro, the sexchange whose corpse I'd discovered with Jirji Shaknahyi. Her body had been taken to another hospital, and it had provided urgently needed kidneys and liver to a seriously ill young woman she'd never met. This in itself wasn't unusual; many people signed up to donate organs in case of sudden or accidental death. I just found it rather coincidental that the recipient happened to be the niece of Umar Abdul-Qawy.

I spent an hour and a half tracking down files on all the other names in Shaknahyi's notebook. Besides Chami, two of the murder victims— Blanca and Andreja Svobik—had ties to Papa. I was able to prove to my satisfaction that of the other four names, two had rather obvious connections to Reda Abu Adil. I was willing to bet a large sum of money that the rest did too, but I didn't need to pursue the matter any further. None of this was ever going to have to stand up in court. Neither Abu Adil nor Friedlander Bey would ever be dragged in front of a judge.

So what had I learned, after all? One: There had been at least four unsolved murders in the city in the last several weeks. Two: All four victims had been killed in the same way, with a shot at close range, from a static pistol. Three: Healthy organs were taken from all four victims after death, because all four were listed in the city's charity file of voluntary donors. Four: All four victims and all four recipients had direct ties to either Abu Adil or Papa.

I had proved Shaknahyi's suspicion beyond the possibility of coincidence, but I knew that Hajjar would still deny that the murders were related. I could point out that the killers had used a static pistol so that none of the internal organs would be damaged, but Hajjar'd shrug that off too. I was pretty damn certain that Hajjar knew about all this already, which was why I'd been put to pasture investigating On Cheung, instead of looking into Shaknahyi's death. There were a lot of powerful men allied against me. It was a good thing I had God on my side.

"Search again?" asked my data deck.

I hesitated. I did have one more name to check, but I really didn't want to know the details. After he'd been shot, Shaknahyi had told me to find out where his parts went. I thought I already knew, although I didn't have an exact name. I was sure that some of Jirji Shaknahyi still lived on in the body of some low-level employee of Abu Adil or Friedlander Bey, or one of their friends or relatives. I was completely disgusted, so I just said "Quit." I looked at the monitor's dark screen and thought about what I needed to do next.

I was just fighting down the urge to find somebody in the station house who might sell me a few sunnies when the phone on my belt rang. I unclipped it and leaned back in my padded chair. "Hello," I said.

"*Marhaba,*" said Morgan's gruff voice.

That was about all the Arabic that he knew. I leaned over and grabbed my English-language daddy from the rack, then reached up and chipped it in.

"Where y'at, man?" he said.

"All right, praise be to God. What's up?"

"Remember how I promised to let you know Wednesday where this Jawarski guy's hidin' out?"

"Yeah, I was wondering when you'd check in."

"Well, turns out I was maybe a little optimistic." He sounded rueful.

"Had a feeling Jawarski'd cover his tracks pretty well."

"Got a feelin' he's had help, man."

I sat up straight. "What do you mean?"

There was a pause before Morgan spoke again. "There's a lot of talk on the street about Shaknahyi's shooting. Most people couldn't care less that a cop got dusted, but I can't find nobody with a personal grudge against Shaknahyi himself. And Jawarski's crazy as a bedbug, so nobody I know would lift a finger to help him get clear."

I closed my eyes and massaged my forehead. "Then why haven't you or I located him yet?" I asked.

"I'm comin' to that. What it comes down to is it looks like the cops are hidin' the son of a bitch."

"Where? Why?" Chiri vouched for Morgan's dependability, but this story of his was a little too incredible.

"Ask your Lieutenant Hajjar. He and Jawarski had some drinks together in the Silver Palm a couple weeks ago."

In the words of the great Christian humorist, Mark Twain, this was too various for me. "Why would Hajjar, a high-ranking police official, set up one of his own officers for a lunatic escaped killer?"

I could almost hear Morgan shrug. "You think maybe Hajjar's involved with somethin' crooked, man?"

I laughed sourly, and Morgan laughed too. "It's not funny, though," I said. "I guessed all along that Hajjar was mixed up with something, but I didn't see him passing orders to Jawarski. Still, it answers some of my own questions."

"What's it all about, then?"

"It's about something called the Phoenix File. I don't know yet what the hell that means. Just keep trying to pin down Jawarski, okay? You learn anything useful about him yet?"

"Some," said Morgan. "He was waitin' around in a jail cell in Khartoum, supposed to be executed. Some guy smuggled a gun in to him. One afternoon Jawarski walks down a corridor and meets two unarmed guards. He shoots the guys, then walks into the jail office and starts firin' all around like a maniac till somebody hands over the keys. Then he unlocks the big main doors and walks out calmly into the street. There's a crowd of people out there 'cause of the gunshots, and he pushes his way through 'em and goes half a block to a waitin' car. Jawarski drives away and there's no sign of him again till he shows up here in the city."

"When was that?" I asked.

"Been here a month, maybe six weeks. Pulled a couple of robberies, killed another couple of people. Then the other day somebody recognized Jawarski in Meloul's and called the cops. Hajjar sent Shaknahyi and you. You know the rest."

"I wonder," I said. "I wonder if somebody really recognized him in the cookshop. Shaknahyi thought that Hajjar had fingered us, putting Jawarski in Meloul's and sending Jirji and me over there to get taken down."

"Could be, man. We'll have to ask Jawarski when we collar him."

"Yeah, you right," I said grimly. "Thanks, Morgan. You keep nosing around."

"You got it, man. I want to earn the rest of that money. Take care of yourself."

"You bet," I said, clipping the phone to my belt again.

It helped that I knew more than my enemies did. I had the advantage of having my eyes open. I still couldn't see where it all was leading me, but at least I understood the extent of the conspiracy I was trying to uncover. I wouldn't be so foolish as to trust anyone entirely. Anyone at all.

When the shift was over, I drove the patrol car back to the "police officers' lounge" and picked up Sergeant Catavina, who had gotten very drunk. I dropped him off at the station house, turned the car over to the night shift, and waited for Kmuzu to arrive. The workday was done, but I still had plenty of investigating to do before I could go to sleep.

twelve

Fuad il-manhous was not the brightest person I knew. One look at Fuad and you said to yourself, "This guy is a *fool*." He looked like the character in a fairy tale who would get three wishes from a *djinn* and blow the first on a plate of beans, the second on a spoon, and the third on cleaning the dish and spoon when he was done eating.

He was tall, but so thin and starved-looking he might have been a refugee from the Benghazi death camps. I once saw my friend Jacques circle Fuad's arm above the elbow with his thumb and forefinger. And Fuad's joints were huge, swollen as if from some horrible bone disease or vitamin deficiency. He had long, dirty brown hair that he combed into a high pompadour, and he wore thick eyeglasses in heavy plastic frames. I don't suppose Fuad had ever had enough cash to afford new eyes, not even the cheap Guatemalan ones with the counterfeit Nikon lenses. His expression was permanently bewildered and hurt, because Fuad was always a beat and a half behind the rest of the band.

"*Il manhous*" means something like "the permanently hapless," yet Fuad didn't seem to mind the nickname. In fact, he seemed happy to be recognized at all. And he played the part of fool better than anyone I'd ever known. He had a certain genius for it, as a matter of fact.

I was sitting at a table in Chiriga's with Kmuzu, near the back. We were talking about what my mother had been up to lately. Fuad il-Manhous came and stood beside me, holding a cardboard box. "Indihar lets me come in here in the daytime, Marîd," he said in his raspy, twangy voice.

"I got no problem with that," I said. He'd made me forget what I'd been about to say. I looked up at him, and he grinned down and shook the cardboard box. Something inside made a rattling sound. "What's in the box?" I asked.

Fuad took that as an invitation to sit down. He dragged a chair over from another table, making the legs shriek on the flooring. "Indihar said as long as nobody complained, it was all right with her."

"*What's* all right?" I demanded impatiently. I hate having to pry information out of people. "The hell you got in there?"

Fuad ran a gnarled hand through his greasy hair and shot Kmuzu a mistrustful look. Then he hunched forward over the table, set the box down, and lifted the lid. There were maybe a dozen cheap gold-filled chains inside. Fuad reached in with a long forefinger and poked them around. "See?" he said.

"Uh huh," I said. I looked up and caught Kmuzu's eye. He was finishing a glass of iced tea—I felt bad about tricking him into drinking so much liquor that time, and since then I'd respected his feelings. He set his glass down carefully on the cocktail napkin. He was keeping his face free of any expression, but I could tell that he didn't approve of Fuad at all. Kmuzu didn't approve of anything he saw in Chiri's.

"Where'd you get them, Fuad?" I said.

"Take a look." He grinned. His teeth were bad too.

I fished one of the chains out of the box and tried to examine it closely, but the light was too dim in the club. I turned the price tag around. It said two hundred and fifty kiam. "Sure, Fuad," I said dubiously. "The tourists and locals we get in here complain about paying eight kiam for a drink. I think you're gonna have some sales resistance."

"Well, I'm not selling them for that much."

"How much *are* you selling them for?"

Il-Manhous closed his eyes, pretending to concentrate. Then he looked at me as if he were begging a favor. "Fifty kiam?"

I looked back into the box and pushed the chains around myself. Then I shook my head.

"Okay," said Fuad, "ten kiam, but *yaa lateef!* I won't make any profit that way."

"Maybe you could sell them for ten," I admitted. "The price tags are from some of the best shops in town."

Fuad grabbed the box away from me. "So they're worth more than ten, huh?"

I laughed. "See," I said to Kmuzu, "the chains are cheap plated metal. Probably not worth fifty fîqs. Fuad here goes into some exclusive boutique and steals some tags with the shop's classy name on

them and a price in three figures. Then he ties the tags to his junk jewelry and hawks it to drunken tourists. He figures they might not notice
what they're buying, especially out of the bright sunlight."

"That's why I wanted to ask you if it'd be okay to come in during
the night shift," said Fuad. "It's even darker in here at night. I'd probably do a whole lot better."

"Nah," I said. "If Indihar wants to let you hustle tourists during the
day, that's up to her. I'd rather not have you doing it at night when I
might be here."

"Beyond the Budayeen, *yaa Sidi*, "Kmuzu pronounced ominously,
"they'd cut his hands off if they caught him doing that."

Fuad looked horrified. "You wouldn't let them do anything like
that to me, would you, Marîd?"

I shrugged. " 'As for the thief, both male and female, cut off their
hands. It is the reward of their own deeds, an exemplary punishment
from Allah. Allah is Mighty, Wise.' That's right from the blessed
Qur'ân. You could look it up."

Fuad clutched the box to his sunken chest. "You wait till you need
something from me, Marîd!" he cried. Then he stumbled toward the
door, knocking over a chair and bumping into Pualani on the way.

"He'll get over it," I said to Kmuzu. "He'll be back in here tomorrow. Won't even remember what you told him."

"That's too bad," said Kmuzu gravely. "Someday he'll try to sell
one of those chains to the wrong person. He may regret it for the rest of
his life."

"Yeah, but that's what makes him Fuad. Anyway, I need to talk to
Indihar before the shift changes. You mind if I leave you alone for a
couple of minutes?"

"Not at all, *yaa Sidi*." He stared at me blankly for a moment. It
always unsettled me when he did that.

"I'll have somebody bring you another iced tea," I said. Then I got
up and went to the bar.

Indihar was rinsing glasses. I'd told her that she didn't have to
come into work until she felt better, but she said she'd rather work than
sit home with her kids and feel bad. She needed to make money to pay
the babysitter, and she still had a lot of expenses from the funeral. All
the girls were tiptoeing around her, not knowing what to say to her or
how to act. It made for a pretty glum ambience in the club.

"Need something, Marîd?" she said. Her eyes were red and sunken.
She looked away from me, back at the glasses in the sink.

"Another iced tea for Kmuzu, that's all," I said.

"All right." She bent to the refrigerator under the bar and brought up a pitcher of iced tea. She poured a glassful and continued to pay no attention to me.

I looked down the bar. There were three new girls working the day shift. I could only remember one of their names. "Brandi," I said, "take this to that tall guy in the back."

"You mean that *kaffir?*" she said. She was short, with fat arms and plump thighs, with large breast implants and brushy hair whose blondness had been artificially encouraged. She had tattoos on both arms, above her right breast, on her left shoulder blade, peeking out of her G-string, on both ankles, and on her ass. I think she was embarrassed by them, because she always wore a fringy black shawl when she sat with customers at the bar, and when she danced she wore bright red platform shoes and high white socks. "Want me to collect from him?"

I shook my head. "He's my driver. He drinks for free."

Brandi nodded and carried the iced tea away. I stayed at the bar, idly spinning one of the round cork coasters. "Indihar," I said at last.

She gave me a weary look. "I said I didn't want to hear you say you were sorry."

I raised a hand. "I'm not gonna say that. I just think you should accept some help now. For your kids' sake, if not your own. I would've been happy to pay for a tomb in your in-laws' cemetery. Chiri'd be glad to lend you all the money—"

Indihar let out an exasperated breath and wiped her hands on a bar towel. "That's something else I don't want to hear. Jirji and I never borrowed money. I'm not gonna start now."

"Sure, okay, but the situation is different. How much pension are you getting from the police department?"

She threw the towel down disgustedly. "A third of Jirji's salary. That's all. And they're giving me some kind of song and dance about a delay. They don't think I can start collecting the pension for at least six months. We were barely keeping our noses above water before. I don't know how I'll make it now. I guess I'll have to look for someplace cheaper to live."

My first thought was that any place cheaper than the apartment in Haffe al-Khala wouldn't be fit to raise children in. "Maybe," I said. "Look, Indihar, I think you've earned a paid vacation. Why don't you just let me pay you for two or three weeks in advance, and you can stay home with Zahra and Hâkim and Little Jirji. Or you could use the time to make some extra money, maybe—"

Brandi came back to the bar and plopped down beside me with a contemptuous look on her face. "Motherfucker didn't give me a tip," she said.

I looked at her. She probably wasn't any smarter than Fuad. "I told you, Kmuzu drinks for free. I don't want you hustling him."

"Who is he, your special friend?" Brandi asked with a crooked smile.

I looked at Indihar. "How badly you want this bitch to keep working here?" I said.

Brandi hopped off the stool and headed toward the dressing room. "All right, all right," she said, "forget I said anything."

"Marîd," said Indihar in a low, carefully controlled voice, "leave me alone. No loans, no deals, no presents. Okay? Just have enough respect for me to let me work everything out my own way."

I couldn't argue with her anymore. "Whatever you want," I said. I turned away and went back to Kmuzu's table. I truly wished Indihar had let me help her somehow. I'd gained a tremendous amount of admiration for her. She was a fine, intelligent woman, and kind of on the beautiful side too.

I had a couple of drinks and killed some time, and then it was eight o'clock. Chiri and the night crew came in, and I watched Indihar count out the register, pay the day shift girls, and leave without saying another word to anyone. I went to the bar to say hello to Chiri. "I think Indihar's trying too hard to be brave," I told her.

She sat on her stool behind the bar and surveyed the seven or eight customers. "Yesterday she was telling me about her twelfth birthday," Chiri said in a distant voice. "She said she'd known Jirji all her life. They both grew up in the same little village. She always liked Jirji, and when her parents told her that they'd arranged with the Shaknahyis for the two kids to be married, Indihar was happy."

Chiri leaned down and brought out her private bottle of *tende*. She poured herself half a glassful and tasted it. "Indihar had a traditional childhood," she said. "Her folks were very old-fashioned and superstitious. She grew up in Egypt, where there's this old wives' tale that girls who drink the water of the Nile grow up too passionate. They exhaust their poor husbands. So it's the custom for the girls to be circumcised before their weddings."

"Lots of country Muslims still do that," I said.

Chiri nodded. "The village midwife cut Indihar and put onions and salt on the wound. Indihar stayed in bed for seven days afterward, and her mother fed her lots of chicken and pomegranates. When she finally got up again, her mother gave her a new dress she'd just finished making. Indihar's clitoris was sewn up in the lining. Together the two of them took the dress and threw it into the river."

I shuddered. "Why you telling me all this?"

Chiri swallowed some more *tende*. "So you'll understand how much Jirji meant to Indihar. She told me the circumcision was very painful, but she was glad to have it done. It meant she was finally a grown woman, and she could marry Jirji with the blessings of her family and friends."

"I suppose it's none of my business," I said.

"I'll tell you what's none of your business: badgering her about her financial situation. Leave her alone, Marîd. Your intentions are good, and it was right to offer help after Jirji was killed. But Indihar's said she doesn't want our money, and you're making her feel worse by bringing it up all the time."

I let my shoulders sag. "I guess I didn't realize it," I said. "All right, thanks for letting me know."

"She'll be fine. And if she runs into trouble, she'll let us know. Now, I want you to put in a good word with Kmuzu. I like the way that honey looks."

I raised my eyebrows at her. "You just trying to make me jealous? Kmuzu? He's not a party kind of guy, you know. You'd eat him alive."

"I'd sure like to give it a shot," she said with her best file-toothed grin.

Time for another shot in the dark. "Chiri," I said, "What do the letters A.L.M. mean to you?"

She thought about that for a little while. "The Association of Lesbian Mothers," she said. "This girl Hanina, used to dance by Frenchy's. She used to get their newsletter. Why?"

I chewed my lip. "That can't be right. If you think of something else A.L.M. might mean, let me know."

"Okay, honey. What is it, some kind of puzzle?"

"Yeah, a puzzle."

"Well, I'll think about it." She drank a little *tende* and stared over my head at the mirrored wall behind me. "So what's this I hear about you flushing all your recreational drugs? Never thought I'd see the day. We gonna have to find a new chemical champion?"

"I guess so. I emptied my pillcase right after Jirji died."

Chiri's expression became serious. "Uh yeah."

There was an uncomfortable silence for a few seconds. "I'll tell you, though," I said at last, "I've had these strong cravings. It's been pretty hard on me, but I'm keeping away from the drugs."

"Cutting back is one thing, but quitting altogether seems kind of extreme. I suppose it's for the best, but I've always believed in moderation in all things, and that goes for abstinence too."

I smiled. "I appreciate your concern," I said, "but I know what I'm doing."

Chiri shook her head sadly. "I hope so. I hope you're not just kidding yourself. You don't have much experience handling yourself sober. You could get hurt."

"I'll be fine, Chiri."

"Maybe you should pass by Laila's shop in the morning. She's got these moddies that make you feel like you've taken a handful of pills. She's got the whole line: sunnies, beauties, tri-phets, RPM, whatever you want. You chip the moddy in and if you need to use your brain for something later, you pop it out and you're straight again."

"I don't know. Sounds dumb to me."

Chiri spread her hands. "It's up to you."

"Make me a gin and bingara?" I didn't want to talk about drugs anymore. I was beginning to feel the craving again.

I watched Yasmin dance on stage while Chiri built my drink. Yasmin was still the prettiest collection of XY chromosomes I've ever known. Since we'd gotten friendly again, she told me she was sorry she'd cut her long black hair. She was letting it grow back. As she moved sensuously to the music, she kept glancing down at me. Every time she caught my eye, she smiled. I smiled back.

"Here you go, boss," said Chiri, setting the drink on a coaster in front of me.

"Thanks," I said. I picked it up, threw a sizzling look toward Yasmin, and went back to sit with Kmuzu. "Say," I said, "you've got a secret admirer. You know that?"

Kmuzu looked perplexed. "What do you mean, *yaa Sidi?*"

I grinned at him. "I think Chiriga would like to elevate your pulse rate."

"That is not possible," he said. He looked very disturbed.

"Don't you like her? She's really a very nice person. Don't be scared off by that headhunter routine of hers."

"It's not that, *yaa Sidi.* I do not plan to marry until I am no longer a slave."

I laughed. "That fits in fine with Chiri's plans. I don't think she wants to get married, either."

"I told you when we first met that I am a Christian."

Chiri came over to the table and joined us before I could say anything more. "Kmuzu, how you doin'?" she said.

"I am well, Miss Chiriga," he said. His tone was almost icy.

"Well, I was wondering if you'd ever made it with anybody who was wearing Honey Pílar's latest. *Slow, Slow Burn.* It's my favorite of all of hers. Leaves me so weak I can barely get up out of bed."

"Miss Chiriga—"

"You can call me Chiri, honey."

"—I wish you'd stop making sexual advances to me."

Chiri looked at me and raised her eyebrows. "Am I making sexual advances? I was just asking if he'd ever made it—"

"Did I hear that Honey Pílar's getting divorced again?" said Rani, one of the night-shift debs who'd wandered over to our table. Evidently none of the customers were tipping or buying anybody cocktails. I knew it was a slow night when Kmuzu and I were the most interesting thing happening in the club.

Chiri looked aggravated. "Somebody get up on the goddamn stage and dance!" she shouted. Then she stood up and went back behind the bar. Lily, the pretty Belgian sexchange, took off her blouse and went to play her music.

"I think I've had about enough of all this excitement," I said, yawning. "Kmuzu, come on. Let's go home."

Yasmin came up and put her hand on my arm. "Will you come in tomorrow?" she asked. "I need to talk to you about something personal."

"You want to talk right now?"

She looked away, embarrassed. "No," she said. "Some other time. But I wanted to give you this." She held out her pocket *I Ching* calculator. She swore by the *I Ching,* and she still believed that it had accurately foretold all the terrible events of several months ago. "Maybe you need it again."

"I don't think so," I said. "Why don't you keep it?"

She put it in my hand and closed my fingers over it. Then she kissed me. It was a gentle, unhurried kiss on the lips. I was surprised to find that it left me trembling.

I said goodnight to Chiri and the debs and changes, and Kmuzu followed me out into the warm, raucous night on the Street. We walked back down to the gate and found the car. All the way home, Kmuzu explained to me that he found Chiri too brazen and shameless.

"But you think she's sexy?" I asked him.

"That's beside the point, *yaa Sidi,*" he said. From then on, he just concentrated on his driving.

After we got back to Friedlander Bey's estate, I went to my suite and tried to relax. I took a notebook and stretched out on my bed, trying to order my thoughts. I looked at Yasmin's electronic *I Ching* and laughed softly. For no particular reason, I pressed the white button marked H. The little device played its tinkling tune, and a synthesized woman's voice spoke up. "Hexagram Six. Sung. Conflict. Changes in the first, second, and sixth lines."

I listened to the judgment and the commentary, and then I pressed

L for the lines. What it all amounted to was a warning that I was in a difficult period, and that if I tried to force my way toward my goal, I'd encounter a lot of conflict. I didn't need a pocket computer to tell me that.

The image was "Heaven above the waters," and I was advised to stay close to home. The problem was that it was just a little too late for that. "If you determine to confront the difficulties," the mechanical woman cautioned, "you'll make minor progress that will soon be reversed, leaving you in a worse situation than before. Sidestep this trouble by tending your garden and ignoring your powerful adversaries."

Well, hell, I would have loved to do just that. I could have forgotten all about Abu Adil and all about Jawarski, just written Shaknahyi off as a painful tragedy, and let Papa deal with Umm Saad by ordering the Stones That Speak to twist her devious head off. I could have left my mother a fat envelope of cash, kissed Chiriga's club goodbye, and caught the next bus out of the city.

Unfortunately, none of that was possible. I stared at the toy *I Ching* ruefully, then remembered that the changing lines gave me a second hexagram that might indicate where events were leading. I pressed CH.

"Hexagram Seventeen. Sui. Following. Thunder in the lake." Whatever that meant. I was told that I was coming into very positive circumstances. All I had to do was attune my actions into harmony with the personalities of the people I had to deal with. I just had to adapt my own desires to the needs of the times.

"Okay," I said, "that's just what I'll do. I just need someone to tell me what 'the needs of the times' are."

"Such fortune telling is blasphemous," said Kmuzu. "Every orthodox religion in the world forbids it." I hadn't heard him come into my room.

"The idea of synchronicity makes a certain logical sense," I said. Actually, I felt pretty much about the *I Ching* as he did, but I felt it was my job to bait him as much as possible. Maybe something would get him to loosen up a little.

"You are dealing with dangerous people, *yaa Sidi*," he said. "Surely your actions must be governed by reason, not by this child's plaything."

I tossed Yasmin's gimmick to him. "You're right, Kmuzu. Something like that could be dangerous, in the hands of a gullible fool."

"I'll return it to Miss Yasmin tomorrow."

"Fine," I said.

"Will you need anything more tonight?"

"No, Kmuzu, I'm just gonna make some notes to myself, and then I'll get some sleep."

"Then goodnight, *yaa Sidi*."

"Goodnight, Kmuzu." He closed the door to my bedroom behind him.

I got up and undressed, then pulled back the covers on my bed and laid down again. I began listing names in my notebook: Friedlander Bey, Reda Abu Adil and Umar Abdul-Qawy, Paul Jawarski, Umm Saad, Lieutenant Hajjar. The bad guys. Then I made a list of the good guys: me.

I remembered a proverb I'd heard as a child in Algiers. "Fleeing when it is not necessary is better than not fleeing when it *is* necessary." A quick trip to Shanghai or Venice seemed like the only reasonable response to this situation.

I suppose I fell asleep thinking about stuffing a bag full of clothes and money and running off into the honeysuckle-scented night. I was having a bizarre dream about Chiriga's. Lieutenant Hajjar seemed to be running the place, and I went in looking for somebody who might have been Yasmin or possibly Fayza, one of my adolescent loves. There was some kind of argument with my mother about whether or not I'd brought in a case of bottled sherbet, and then I was in school without any clothes on, and I hadn't studied for some important exam.

Someone was shaking me and shouting. "Wake up, *yaa Sidi!*"

"What is it, Kmuzu?" I said blearily. "What's the matter?"

"The house is on fire!" he said. He pulled on my arm until I got out of bed.

"I don't see any fire." I could smell the smoke, though.

"This whole floor is burning. We don't have much time. We've got to get out."

I was completely awake now. I could see a heavy layer of smoke hanging in the bright moonlight that slanted in through the lattice-covered windows. "I'm all right, Kmuzu," I said. "I'll wake Friedlander Bey. Do you think the whole house is on fire, or just this wing?"

"I'm not sure, *yaa Sidi*."

"Then run over to the east wing and wake my mother. Make sure she gets out all right."

"And Umm Saad as well."

"Yeah, you right." He hurried out of my room. Before I went out into the hall, I stopped to find the telephone on my desk. I punched the city's emergency number, but the line was busy. I muttered a curse and tried again. Still the line was busy. I kept calling and calling; it seemed like hours went by before a woman's voice answered.

"Fire," I cried. I was frantic by that time. "The Friedlander Bey estate near the Christian Quarter."

"Thank you, sir," said the woman. "The fire brigade is on its way."

The air had gotten very bad, and the acrid smoke burned my nose and throat as I bent lower trying to breathe. I paused at the entrance to the suite, and then ran back to find my jeans. I know you're supposed to get out of a burning building as quickly as possible, but I still hadn't seen any actual flames and I didn't feel as if I were in any immediate danger. It turned out that I was wrong; while I stopped to pull on my jeans, I was already being burned by the hot ash in the air. I didn't feel it at the time, but I was getting second-degree burns on my head, neck, and shoulders, which were bare. My hair was badly singed, but my beard protected my face. I've since promised myself that I'm never going to shave it off again.

I first saw flames in the corridor. The heat was intense I ran with my arms around my head, trying to shield my face and eyes. The soles of my feet were badly scorched within ten feet of my apartment. I pounded on Papa's door, sure that I was going to die right there, bravely but foolishly attempting to rescue an old man who was likely already dead. A stray thought lodged in my consciousness, the memory of Friedlander Bey asking me if I had the courage to fill my lungs again with fire.

There was no response. I knocked louder. The fire was blistering the skin on my back and arms, and I'd begun to choke. I took a step back, raised my right leg, and kicked the door as hard as I could. Nothing happened. It was locked, and the bolt had probably expanded in the heat. I kicked again, and this time the wooden frame around the lock splintered. One more kick and the door sprang back, slamming in against the wall of Papa's parlor.

"O Shaykh!" I shouted. The smoke billowed even more densely here. There was the sharp smell of burning plastic in the air, and I knew that I had to get Papa out quickly, before he and I were overcome by poisonous fumes. That made me even less hopeful of finding Friedlander Bey alive. His bedroom was back and to the left, and that door was closed and locked too. I kicked it in, paying no attention to the stabbing pain that shot through my ankle and shin. I'd have time to nurse my injuries later—if I lived.

Papa was awake, lying on his back in bed, his hands clutching the sheet that covered him. I ran to him, and his eyes followed my every movement. He opened his mouth to speak, but no sound came out. He raised one hand feebly. I didn't have time for whatever he was trying to communicate. I just threw back the covers and scooped him up as if he'd been a child. He was not a tall man, but he'd put on a moderate amount of weight since the days of his athletic prime. It didn't matter; I carried him out of the bedroom with a maniac strength that I knew wouldn't last very long. "Fire!" I shouted as I crossed the parlor again. "Fire! Fire!" The Stones That Speak had their rooms adjoining Papa's. I didn't dare set him down to rouse the Stones. I had to keep fighting my way through the flames toward safety.

Just as I reached the far end of the corridor, the two huge men came up behind me. Neither said a word. They were both as naked as the day they'd been born, but that didn't seem to bother them. One of them took Friedlander Bey from me. The other picked me up and carried me the rest of the way, down the stairs and out into the clean, fresh air.

The Stone must have realized how badly I was hurt, how exhausted I was, and how close to collapse I'd come. I was terrifically grateful to him, but I didn't have the strength to thank him. I promised myself that I'd do something for the Stones as soon as I was able—maybe buy them a few infidels to torture. I mean, what do you get the Gog and Magog who have everything?

The firemen were already setting up their equipment when Kmuzu came to see how I was. "Your mother is safe," he said. "There was no fire in the east wing."

"Thank you, Kmuzu," I said. The inside of my nose was raw and painful, and my throat hurt.

One of the firemen rinsed me with sterile water, then wrapped me in a sheet and rinsed me again. "Here," he said, handing me a glass of water. "This'll make your mouth and throat feel better. You're gonna have to go to the hospital."

"Why?" I asked. I hadn't yet realized how badly I was burned.

"I will go with you, *yaa Sidi*," said Kmuzu.

"Papa?" I said.

"He also needs immediate medical attention," said Kmuzu.

"We'll go together then," I said.

The firemen led me to an ambulance. Friedlander Bey had already been put on a stretcher and lifted inside. Kmuzu helped me up into the vehicle. He beckoned toward me, and I leaned down toward him. "While you're recuperating in the hospital," he said softly, "I will see if I can learn who set this fire."

I looked at him for a moment, trying to collect my thoughts. I blinked and realized that all my eyelashes had been burned off. "You think it's arson?" I said.

The ambulance driver closed one of the rear doors. "I have proof," said Kmuzu. Then the driver closed the second door. A moment later, Papa and I were speeding through the constricted streets, siren screaming. Papa didn't move on his stretcher. He looked pitifully frail. I didn't feel so well myself. I suppose it was my punishment for laughing at Hexagram Six.

Thirteen

my mother had brought me pistachio nuts and fresh figs, but I was still having some trouble swallowing. "Then have some of this," she said. "I even brought a spoon." She took the lid from a plastic bowl and set it on the hospital tray table. She was very self-conscious about this visit.

I was sedated, but not as sedated as I could have been. Still, a mild dose of Sonneine from a perfusor is better than a poke in the eye with a sharp stick. Of course, I own an experimental daddy that blocks pain, and I could have chipped it in and stayed completely clearheaded and lucid. I just didn't want to use it. I hadn't told my doctors and nurses about it, because I'd rather have the drug. Hospitals are too tedious to endure sober.

I lifted my head from the pillow. "What is it?" I asked in a hoarse voice. I leaned forward and took the plastic bowl.

"Curdled camel's milk," said my mother. "You used to love that when you were sick. When you were little." I thought I detected an uncharacteristic softness in her voice.

Curdled camel's milk doesn't sound like something that could get you to jump out of bed with glee. It isn't, and I didn't. I picked up the spoon, however, and made a show of enjoying it just to please her. Maybe if I ate some of the stuff, she'd be satisfied and leave. Then I could call for another shot of Sonneine and take a nice nap. That's what was worst about being in the hospital: reassuring all the visitors and listening to the histories of their own illnesses and accidents, which were always of far more traumatic proportions than yours.

"You were really worried about me, Marîd?" she asked.

"Course I was," I said, letting my head fall back to the pillow. "That's why I sent Kmuzu to make sure you were safe."

She smiled sadly and shook her head. "Maybe you'd be happier if I'd burned up in the fire. Then you wouldn't be embarrassed about me no more."

"Don't worry about it, Mom."

"Okay, honey," she said. She looked at me in silence for a long moment. "How are your burns?"

I shrugged, and that made me wince. "They still hurt. The nurses come in and slather this white gunk on me a couple of times a day."

"Well, I suppose it's good for you. You just let 'em do what they want."

"Right, Mom."

There was another awkward silence. "I suppose there's things I ought to tell you," she said at last. "I ain't been completely honest with you."

"Oh?" This wasn't any surprise, but I thought I'd swallow the sarcastic comments that came to mind, and let her tell her story her own way.

She stared down at her hands, which were twisting a frayed linen handkerchief in her lap. "I know a lot more about Friedlander Bey and Reda Abu Adil than I told you."

"Ah," I said.

She glanced up at me. "I known both of 'em from before. From even before you was born, when I was a young girl. I was a lot better looking in those days. I wanted to get out of Sidi-bel-Abbès, maybe go someplace like Cairo or Jerusalem, be a holoshow star. Maybe get wired and make some moddies, not sex moddies like Honey Pílar, but something classy and respectable."

"So did Papa or Abu Adil promise to make you a star?"

She looked back down at her hands. "I came here, to the city. I didn't have no money when I got here, and I went hungry for a while. Then I met somebody who took care of me for a while, and he introduced me to Abu Adil."

"And what did Abu Adil do for you?"

Again she looked up, but now tears were slipping down her cheeks. "What do you think?" she said in a bitter voice.

"He promise to marry you?"

She just shook her head.

"He get you pregnant?"

"No. In the end, he just laughed at me and handed me this bus ticket back to Sidi-bel-Abbès." Her expression grew fierce. "I hate him, Marîd."

I nodded. I was sorry now that she'd begun this confession. "So you're not telling me that Abu Adil is my father, right? What about Friedlander Bey?"

"Papa was always good to me when I first came to the city. That's why even though I was so mad at you for finding me in Algiers, I was glad to hear that Papa was taking care of you."

"Some people hate him, you know," I said.

She stared at me, then shrugged. "I went back to Sidi-bel-Abbès, after all, and then after a few years I met your father. It was like my life was passing so fast. You were born, and then you got older and left Algiers. Then more years went by. Finally, right after you came to see me, I got a message from Abu Adil. He said he'd been thinking about me and wanted to see me again."

She had gotten agitated, and now she paused until she calmed down a little. "I believed him," she said. "I don't know why. Maybe I thought I could have a second chance to live my life, get back all those years I lost, fix all the mistakes. Anyway, goddamn if I didn't fuck up all over again."

I shut my eyes and rubbed them. Then I looked at my mother's anguished face. "What did you do?"

"I moved in with Abu Adil again. In that big place he's got in the slums. That's how I know all about him, and about Umm Saad. You got to watch out for her, baby. She works for Abu Adil, and she's planning to ruin Papa."

"I know."

My mother looked bewildered. "You know already? How?"

I smiled. "Abu Adil's little fuck-buddy told me. They've pretty much written off Umm Saad. She's not part of their plans anymore."

"Still," said my mother, raising a warning finger, "you got to watch out for her. She's got her own schemes in the fire."

"Yeah, I guess so."

"You know about Abu Adil's moddy? The one he's made of himself?"

"Uh huh. That son of a bitch Umar told me all about it. I'd like to get my hands on it for a few minutes."

She chewed her lip thoughtfully. "Maybe I could think of a way."

Yipe. That's all I needed. "It's not that important, Mom," I told her.

She began to weep again. "I'm so sorry, Marîd. I'm so sorry for everything I done, for not being the kind of mother you needed."

Jeez, I really wasn't feeling well enough to deal with her attack of conscience. "I'm sorry too, Mom," I said, and I was surprised to realize that I truly meant it. "I never showed you the respect—"

"I never *earned* no respect—"

I raised both hands. "Why don't we stop before we're fighting over who's hurt who the most? Let's call a truce or something."

"Maybe we could start over again?" Her voice had a peculiar shyness to it.

I had a lot of doubt about all of this. I didn't know if it was possible to start over again, especially after all that had happened between us, but I thought I could give her a chance. "That's fine with me," I said. "I got no love for the past."

She smiled crookedly. "I like living in Papa's house with you, baby. It makes me think I won't have to go back to Algiers and . . . you know."

I took a deep breath and let it out. "I promise you, Mom," I said, "you'll never have to go back to that life again. Just let me take care of you from now on."

She got up and came toward my bed, her arms outstretched, but I wasn't quite ready for an exchange of mother-son affection. I have a little trouble expressing my feelings, I guess, and I've never been a very demonstrative person. I let her bend down and kiss my cheek and give me a hug, and she murmured something that I couldn't make out. I kind of patted her on the back. It was the best I could manage. Then she went back to her chair.

She sighed. "You made me very happy, Marîd. Happier than I got a right to be. All I ever wanted was a chance for a normal life."

Well, what the hell, what did it cost me? "What do you want to do, Mom?" I asked.

She frowned. "I don't really know. Something useful. Something real."

I had a ludicrous image of Angel Monroe as a candystriper in the hospital. I dismissed the notion immediately. "Abu Adil brought you to the city to spy on Papa, right?"

"Yeah, and I was a sucker to think he really wanted me."

"And on what kind of terms did you leave him? Would you be willing to spy on him for us?"

She looked doubtful. "I really let him know I didn't like being used," she said. "If I went back there, I don't know if he'd believe I was sorry. But maybe he would. He's got a big ego, you know. Men like that, they always think their women'd walk through fire for 'em. I suppose I could make him buy it." She gave me a wry grin. "I was always a good actress. Khalid used to tell me I was the best."

Khalid, I remembered, had been her pimp. "Let me think about it, Mom. I wouldn't get you into anything dangerous, but I'd like to have a secret weapon Abu Adil didn't know anything about."

"Well, anyway, I feel like I owe Papa something. For letting Abu Adil use me like that, and for all Papa's done for me since I came to live in his house."

I wasn't crazy about letting my mother get involved any further with the intrigue, but I was aware that she might be a wonderful source of information. "Mom," I said casually, "what do the letters A.L.M. mean to you?"

"A.L.M.? I don't know. Nothing, really. The Alliance of Lingerie Models? That's a hooker's trade union, but I don't even know if they got a local in this city."

"Never mind. How about the Phoenix File? That ring a bell?"

I saw her flinch just a little. "No," she said slowly, "I never heard of that at all." There was something about the way she said it, though, that persuaded me she was lying. I wondered what she was hiding now. It took the optimistic edge off our previous conversation, making me doubt how much I could trust her. It wasn't the right time to pursue the matter, but there'd be a moment of truth when I got out of the hospital again.

"Mom," I said, yawning, "I'm getting kind of sleepy."

"Oh, baby, I'll go then." She got up and fussed with my covers. "I'll leave the curdled camel's milk with you."

"Great, Mom."

She bent and kissed me again. "I'll be back tomorrow. I'm gonna see how Papa's doing now."

"Give him my regards and tell him that I pray to Allah for his well-being." She went to the door, turned, and waved to me. Then she was gone.

The door had barely shut before a thought struck me: The only person who knew that I'd gone to visit my mother in Algiers had been Saied the Half-Hajj. He must have located Mom for Reda Abu Adil. It must have been Saied who'd brought her to the city to spy on Papa and me. Saied had to be working for Abu Adil. He'd sold me out.

I promised myself still another moment of truth, one that the Half-Hajj would never forget.

Whatever the goal of the conspiracy, whatever the significance of the Phoenix File, it must be tremendously urgent to Abu Adil. In the past few months, he'd set Saied, Kmuzu, and Umm Saad to pry into our affairs. I wondered how many others there were that I hadn't identified yet.

Later that afternoon, just before suppertime, Kmuzu came to visit. He was dressed in a white shirt, no tie, and a black suit. He looked like an undertaker. His expression was solemn, as if one of the nurses outside had just told him that my situation was hopeless. Maybe my burned hair would never grow back, or I'd have to live with that awful, cold white gunk on my skin for the rest of my life.

"How are you feeling, *yaa Sidi?*" he asked.

"I'm suffering from Delayed Post-Fire Stress Syndrome," I said. "I'm just realizing how close I came to not making it. If you hadn't been there to wake me up—"

"You would have been roused by the fire if you hadn't been using the sleep add-on."

I hadn't thought of that. "I suppose," I said. "Still, I owe you my life."

"You rescued the master of the house, *yaa Sidi.* He shelters me and protects me from Reda Abu Adil. You and I are even."

"I still feel I'm in your debt." How much was my life worth to me? Could I give him something of equivalent value? "How would you like your freedom?" I asked.

Kmuzu's brows drew together. "You know that liberty is what I desire most. You also know it's in the hands of the master of the house. It's up to him."

I shrugged. "I have a certain amount of influence with Papa. I'll see what I can do."

"I would be most grateful, *yaa Sidi.*" Kmuzu's expression had become noncommittal, but I knew he wasn't as cool as he was pretending.

We talked for a few minutes more, and then he got up to go. He reassured me that my mother and our servants would be safe enough, *inshallah.* We had two dozen armed guards. Of course, they hadn't prevented someone from entering the grounds and torching the west wing. Collusion, espionage, arson, attempted murder—it had been a long while since Papa's enemies had so noisily expressed their displeasure.

After Kmuzu left, I got bored very quickly. I turned on the holoset fixed to the furniture across from my bed. It wasn't a very good unit and the projection coordinates were off by a considerable margin. The vertical variable needed adjusting; the actors in some contemporary Central European drama struggled along knee-deep in the dresser. The elaborate production was subtitled, but unfortunately the captions were lost, out of sight with the actors' legs in my sock drawer. Whenever there was a close-up, I'd see the person only from the top of his head to the bottom of his nose.

I didn't think I'd care, because at home I don't watch much holo. In the hospital, however, where the order of the day was boredom, I

found myself turning it on again and again all day long. I browsed through
a hundred channels from around the world, and I never found anything
worth watching. That might have been due to my semistoned state and
my lack of concentration; or it might have been the fault of the little
amputated figures wading around on the dresser, speaking a dozen different languages.

So I bailed out of the Thuringian tragedy and told the holoset to
turn itself off. Then I got out of bed and put on my robe. That was kind
of uncomfortable because of my burns and also because of the white
gunk; I hated the way it felt, stuck to my hospital gown. I stuck my
feet into the green paper slippers the hospital provided, and headed for
the door.

An orderly was coming in just as I was going out, carrying a tray
with my lunch. I was pretty hungry and my mouth began to water, even
before I found out what was on the plates. I decided to stay in the room
until after I ate. "What do we have?" I asked.

The orderly set it down on my tray table. "You got tasty fried
liver," he said. His tone let me know it wasn't anything to look forward to.

"I'll eat it later." I left my room and walked slowly down the corridor. I spoke my name to the elevator, and in a few seconds the car
arrived. I didn't know how much freedom of movement I had.

When the elevator asked me what floor I wanted, I asked for Friedlander Bey's room number. "VIP Suite One," it told me.

"What floor is that on?" I asked.

"Twenty." That was as high as you could go. This hospital was one
of only three in the city with VIP suites. It was the same hospital where
I'd had my brainwork done, less than a year before. I liked having a
private room, but I didn't really need a suite. I didn't really feel like
entertaining.

"Do you wish the twentieth floor?" the elevator asked.

"You bet."

"Do you wish the twentieth floor?"

"Yes," I said. It was a stupid elevator. I stood hunched over while it
traveled slowly from the fifteenth floor to the twentieth. I was looking
for a posture that didn't feel sticky and squishy, and I wasn't having
any luck. I was also starting to get very sick of the white gunk's intense
peppermint smell.

I got off on Twenty, and the first thing I saw was a beefy, thick-
necked woman in a white uniform sitting in the middle of a circular
nurse's station. There was a muscular man nearby too, dressed in a
Eur-Am style security guard outfit. He had a huge seizure cannon

holstered on his hip, and he looked at me as if he were deciding whether or not to let me live.

"You're a patient in this hospital," said the nurse. Well, she was at least as bright as the elevator.

"Room 1540," I said.

"This is the twentieth floor. What are you doing here?"

"I want to visit Friedlander Bey."

"Just a moment." She frowned and consulted her computer terminal. From her tone of voice, it was obvious she didn't think anyone as scruffy as me could possibly be on her list of approved visitors. "Your name?"

"Marîd Audran."

"Well, here you are." She glanced up at me. I thought maybe when she found my name on the list, she'd show a little grudging respect. No such luck. "Zain, show Mr. Audran to Suite One," she told the guard.

Zain nodded. "Right this way, sir," he said. I followed him down a lushly carpeted hallway, turned into a cross corridor, and stopped outside the door to Suite One.

I wasn't surprised to see one of the Stones standing sentry duty. "Habib?" I said. I thought I saw his expression flicker just a bit. I pushed by him, half-expecting him to reach out his brawny arm to stop me, but he let me pass. I think both Stones accepted me now as Friedlander Bey's deputy.

Inside the suite, the lights were turned off and the shades drawn on the windows. There were flowers everywhere, jammed into vases and growing from elaborate pots. The sweet fragrance was almost sickening; if it had been my room, I would have told a nurse to give some of the flowers to other sick people in the hospital.

Papa lay motionless in his bed. He didn't look well. I knew he'd been burned as badly as I'd been, and his face and arms had been smeared with the same white gunk. His hair was neatly combed, but he hadn't been shaved in a few days, probably because his skin was still too painful. He was awake, but his eyelids drooped. The Sonneine was knocking him out; he didn't have my tolerance.

There was a second room adjoining, and I could see Youssef, Papa's butler, and Tariq, his valet, sitting at a table playing cards. They started to get up, but I signaled that they should go on with their game. I sat in a chair beside Papa's bed. "How do you feel, O Shaykh?" I said.

He opened his eyes, but I could see that it was difficult for him to stay awake. "I am being well cared for, my nephew," he said.

That wasn't what I'd asked, but I let it pass. "I pray every hour for your return to health."

He attempted a weak smile. "It is good that you pray." He paused to take a deep breath. "You risked your life to save me."

I spread my hands. "I did what I had to."

"And you suffered pain and injury on my account."

"It is of small consequence. The important thing is that you are alive."

"I owe you a great debt," said the old man wearily.

I shook my head. "It was only what Allah decreed. I was but His servant."

He frowned. Despite the Sonneine, he was still in discomfort. "When I am well, and we are both again at home, you must allow me to find a gift equal to your deed."

Oh no, I thought, not another gift from Papa. "In the meantime," I said, "how may I serve you?"

"Tell me: How did the fire start?"

"It was clumsily done, O Shaykh," I said. "Immediately after we escaped, Kmuzu found matches and half-burnt rags soaked in some flammable fluid."

Papa's expression was grim, almost murderous. "I feared as much. Do you have any other clues? Whom do you suspect, O my nephew?"

"I know nothing more, but I will investigate the matter tirelessly when I leave the hospital."

He seemed satisfied for the moment. "You must promise me one thing," he said.

"What do you wish, O Shaykh?"

"When you learn the identity of the arsonist, he must die. We cannot appear weak to our enemies."

Somehow I just knew he was going to say that. I was going to have to get a little pocket notebook just to keep track of everybody I was supposed to murder for him. "Yes," I said, "he will die." I didn't promise that I, personally, would kill the son of a bitch. I mean, *everybody* dies. I thought I might turn the matter over to the Stones That Speak. They were like pet leopards; you had to take them off their leashes now and then and let them run around to catch their own meal.

"Good," said Friedlander Bey. He let his eyes close.

"There are two more matters, O Shaykh," I said hesitantly.

He looked at me again. His expression was agonized. "I am sorry, my nephew. I do not feel well. Even before the fire, I was suffering from some illness. The pain in my head and belly has grown worse."

"Have the doctors here explained it?"

"No, they are fools. They tell me they can find nothing wrong.

There are always more tests they wish to run. I am plagued by incompetence and tortured with indignity."

"You must put yourself in their hands, my uncle," I said. "I was treated very well in this hospital."

"Yes, but you were not a frail old man, clinging hopelessly to life. Every one of their barbarous procedures robs me of another year of life."

I smiled. "It's not as bad as that, O Shaykh. Let them discover the cause of your ailment and cure it, and then soon you will be as strong as ever."

Papa waved a hand impatiently, indicating that he didn't want to talk about it anymore. "What are these other worries you will inflict on me?"

I had to approach both of them correctly. They were very sensitive matters. "The first concerns my servant, Kmuzu," I said. "Even as I rescued you from the fire, Kmuzu rescued me. I promised him that I would ask you to reward him."

"Why, of course, my son. He surely has earned a good reward."

"I thought you might give him his freedom."

Papa looked at me in silence, his expression empty. "No," he said slowly, "it is not yet time. I will consider the circumstances, and decide on some other appropriate compensation."

"But—" He stopped me with a single gesture. Even weakened as he was, the force of his personality would not permit me to press him further when he'd already made up his mind. "Yes, O Shaykh," I said humbly. "The second matter concerns the widow and children of Jirji Shaknahyi, the police officer who was my partner. They are in desperate financial straits, and I wish to do more than merely offer them cash. I seek your permission to move them into our house, perhaps for only a little while."

Papa's expression told me that he did not want to talk any longer. "You are my darling," he said weakly. "Your decisions are my decisions. It is good."

I bowed to him. "I will leave you to rest now. May Allah grant you peace and well-being."

"I will miss your presence, O my son."

I got up from my chair and glanced into the other room. Youssef and Tariq appeared to be engrossed in their card game, but I was sure they'd noted every word that had passed between Papa and me. As I headed for the door, Friedlander Bey began to snore. I tried to make no noise as I left the suite.

I went down in the elevator to my room, and climbed back into bed. I was glad to see that the liver lunch had been taken away. I'd just turned on the holoset again when Dr. Yeniknani came in to visit me. Dr. Yeniknani had assisted the neurosurgeon who'd amped my skull. He was a dark, fierce-looking Turk who was actually a student of Sufi mysticism. I'd gotten to know him pretty well during my last stay here, and I was glad to see him again. I looked up at the holoset and said "Off."

"How are you feeling, Mr. Audran?" said Dr. Yeniknani. He came up next to my bed and smiled down at me. His strong teeth looked very white against his swarthy skin and his big, black mustache. "May I sit down?"

"Please, make yourself comfortable," I said. "So, are you here to tell me that the fire baked my brain, or is this just a friendly call?"

"Your reputation suggests that you don't have much brain left to bake," he said. "No, I just wanted to see how you were feeling, and if there's anything I can do for you."

"I'm grateful. No, I don't think I need anything. I'd just like to get out of here already."

"Everyone says that. You'd think we tortured people in here."

"I've had nicer holidays."

"I have an offer for you, Mr. Audran," said Dr. Yeniknani. "How would you like to hold off some of the effects of the aging process? Prevent the degeneration of your mind, the slow deterioration of your memory?"

"Uh oh," I said. "There's some kind of horrible catch coming, I can tell."

"No catch. Dr. Lisân is experimenting with a technique that promises to do everything I just mentioned. Imagine never having to worry about your mental faculties wearing out as you get older. Your thought processes will be as sharp and quick when you're two hundred as they are today."

"Sounds great, Dr. Yeniknani. But you're not talking about vitamin supplements here, are you?"

He gave me a rueful grin. "Well, no, not exactly. Dr. Lisân is working with plexiform cortical augmentation. He's wrapping the cerebral cortex of the brain in a mesh of microscopic wire reticulations. The mesh is made of incredibly fine gold filaments to which are bonded the same organic nemes that link your corymbic implant to your central nervous system."

"Uh huh." It sounded like mad scientist stuff to me.

"The organic strands pass your brain's electrical impulses from your cerebral cortex to the gold mesh, and back in the opposite direction. The mesh serves as an artificial storage mechanism. Our early results show that it can triple or quadruple the number of neuronal connections in your brain."

"Like adding extra memory to a computer," I said.

"That's too easy an analogy," said Dr. Yeniknani. I could tell that he was getting excited, explaining his research to me. "The nature of memory is holographic, you know, so we're not just offering you a vast number of empty slots in which to file thoughts and recollections. It goes beyond that—we're supplying you with a better redundancy system. Your brain already stores each memory in many locations, but as brain cells wear out and die, some of these memories and learned activities disappear. With cortical augmentation, however, there is a capability for multiply storing information on a level many times higher than normal. Your mind will be safe, protected against gradual failure, except of course in the case of traumatic injury."

"All I have to do," I said dubiously, "is let you and Dr. Lisân plop my brain into a string bag, like a cabbage head at the market."

"That's all. You'll never feel a thing." Dr. Yeniknani grinned. "And I think I can promise, in addition, that the augmentation will speed up the processing in your brain. You'll have the reflexes of a superman. You'll—"

"How many people have you done this to, and how do they feel about it?"

He studied his long, tapered fingers. "We haven't actually performed the operation on a human subject," he said. "But our work with laboratory rats shows a lot of promise."

I felt relieved. "I really thought you were trying to sell me on this," I said.

"Just keep it in mind, Mr. Audran," he said. "In a couple of years we'll be looking for some brave volunteers to help us push back the frontiers of medicine."

I reached up and tapped my two corymbic implants. "Not me. I've already done my part."

Dr. Yeniknani shrugged. He leaned back in his chair and gazed at me thoughtfully. "I understand that you saved the life of your patron," he said. "I once told you that death is desirable as our passage to paradise, and that you should not fear it. It is also true that life is even more desirable as our means of reconciliation with Allah, if we choose to follow the Straight Path. You are a courageous man."

"I don't think I really did anything brave," I said. "I wasn't really thinking about that at the time."

"You do not strictly follow the commands of the Messenger of

God," said Dr. Yeniknani, "but you are a worshipful man in your own way. Two hundred years ago, a man said that the religions of the world are like a lantern with many different colored glass panels, but that God was the single flame within." He shook my hand and stood up. "With your permission."

It seemed that every time I spoke with Dr. Yeniknani, he gave me some Sufi wisdom to think about. "Peace be upon you," I said.

"And upon you be peace," he said. Then he turned and left my room.

I ate supper later, a kind of baked lamb, chick-pea, and bean casserole with onions and tomatoes, which would have been pretty good if only someone would tell the kitchen staff about the existence of salt and maybe a little lemon juice. Then I was bored all over again, and I turned on the holoset, turned it off, stared at the walls, and turned it on again. Finally, to my great relief, the telephone beside my bed warbled. I answered it and said, "Praise Allah."

I heard Morgan's voice on the other end. I didn't have an English-language daddy with me, and Morgan can't even find the bathroom in Arabic, so the only words I understood were "Jawarski" and "Abu Adil." I told him I'd talk to him when I got out of the hospital; I knew he didn't understand any more of what I said than I'd understood of him, so I hung up.

I lay back on my pillow and stared up at the ceiling. I wasn't really surprised to learn there might be a connection between Abu Adil and the crazy American killer. The way things were starting to shape up, I wouldn't be surprised to hear that Jawarski was really my own long-lost brother.

fourteen

i spent almost a week in the hospital. I watched the holoset and got a lot of reading done, and despite my wishes a few people came to see me—Lily, the sexchange who had a crush on me, Chiri, Yasmin. There were two surprises: the first was a basket of fruit from Umar Abdul-Qawy; the second was a visit from six total strangers, people who lived in the Budayeen and the neighborhood around the copshop. Among them I recognized the young woman with the baby to whom I'd given some money, that day Shaknahyi and I had been sent to look for On Cheung.

She seemed just as shy and embarrassed as she had when she'd approached me in the street. "O Shaykh," she said in a trembling voice, setting a cloth-covered basket on my tray table, "we all beseech Allah for your recovery."

"Must be working," I said, smiling, "because the doctor says I'll be out of here today."

"Praise God," said the woman. She turned to the others who'd come with her. "These people are the parents of children, the children who call to you in the streets and at the police station house. They are grateful for your generosity."

These men and women lived in the kind of poverty I'd known most of my life. The odd thing was that they didn't show any petulance toward me. It may seem ungrateful, but sometimes you resent your benefactors. When I was young, I'd learned how humiliating it can be to take charity, especially when you're so desperate that you can't afford the luxury of pride.

It all depends on the attitude of the givers. I'll never forget how much I hated Christmas as a kid in Algiers. Christians in the neighborhood used to put together baskets of food for my mother, my baby brother, and me. Then they'd come by our shabby apartment and stand around beaming at us, proud of their good deeds. They'd look from my mother to Hussain to me, waiting until we'd acted appropriately grateful. How many times I wished that we weren't so hungry, that we could just throw those goddamn canned goods back in their faces!

I was afraid these parents might feel the same way about me. I wanted them to know that they didn't have to go through any forelock-tugging acts of appreciation for my benefit.

"I'm glad to help, my friends," I said. "But, really, I got my own selfish motives. In the noble Qur'ân it says 'That which you spend for good must go to parents and near kindred and orphans and the needy and the wayfarer. And whatever good ye do, lo! Allah is aware of it.' So maybe if I kick a few kiam to a worthy cause, it'll make up for the night I stayed up partying with the blond twins from Hamburg."

I saw a couple of my visitors smile. That let me relax a little. "Even so," said the young mother, "we thank you."

"Less than a year ago, I wasn't doing so well myself. Sometimes I was eating only every other day. There were times when I didn't have a home to go to, and I slept in parks and abandoned buildings. I been lucky since, and I'm just returning a favor. I remember how much kindness everyone showed me when I was broke." Actually, practically none of that was true, but it sure was gracious as all hell.

"We'll leave you now, O Shaykh," said the woman. "You probably need your rest. We just wanted to let you know, if there's anything we can do for you, it would give us much happiness."

I studied her closely, wondering if she meant what she said. "As it happens, I'm looking for two guys," I said. "On Cheung the baby seller, and this killer, Paul Jawarski. If anyone's got any information, I'd be very grateful."

I saw them exchange uneasy glances. No one said anything. It was just as I expected. "Allah grant you peace and well-being, Shaykh Marîd al-Amîn," murmured the woman, backing toward the door.

I'd earned an epithet! She'd called me Marîd the Trustworthy. "*Allah yisallimak*," I replied. I was glad when they left.

About an hour later, a nurse came in and told me that my doctor had signed my release from the hospital. That was fine with me. I called Kmuzu, and he brought me some clean clothes. My skin was still very tender and it hurt to get dressed, but I was just glad to be going home.

"The American, Morgan, wishes to see you, *yaa Sidi*," said Kmuzu. "He says he has something to tell you."

"Sounds like good news," I said. I got into the electric sedan, and Kmuzu closed the passenger door. Then he went around and got in behind the steering wheel.

"You also have some business matters to take care of. There is a considerable amount of money on your desk."

"Uh yeah, I guess so." There should be two fat pay envelopes from Friendlander Bey, plus my share of the take from Chiri's.

Kmuzu let his glance slide over to me. "Do you have any plans for that money, *yaa Sidi?*" he asked.

I smiled at him. "What, you got a horse you want me to back?"

Kmuzu frowned. No sense of humor, I recalled. "Your wealth has grown large. With the money that came while you were in the hospital, you have more than a hundred thousand kiam, *yaa Sidi.* Much good could be done with that great a sum."

"Didn't know you were keeping such close tabs on my bank balance, Kmuzu." He was such a friend sometimes, I tended to forget that he was really only a spy. "I had some ideas about putting the money to good use. A free clinic in the Budayeen, maybe, or a soup kitchen."

I'd really startled him. "That's wonderful and unexpected!" he said. "I heartily approve."

"I'm so glad," I said sourly. I really had been thinking along those lines, but I didn't know how to begin. "How'd you like to study the feasibility? All my time is taken up with this Abu Adil-Jawarski thing."

"I would be more than happy. I don't think you have enough to fund a clinic, *yaa Sidi,* but providing hot meals to the poor, that is a worthy gesture."

"I hope it's more than just a gesture. Let me know when you have some plans and figures for me to look at." The nice part of all this was that it would keep Kmuzu busy and out of my hair for a while.

When I went into the house, Youssef grinned and gave me a bow. "Welcome home, O Shaykh!" he said. He insisted on wrestling my suitcase away from Kmuzu. The two of them followed me down the corridor.

"Your apartment is still being rebuilt, *yaa Sidi,*" said Kmuzu. "I've made us comfortable in a suite in the east wing. On the first floor, away from your mother and Umm Saad."

"Thank you, Kmuzu." I was already thinking about the work I had to do. I couldn't take any more time off to recuperate. "Is Morgan here now, or do I have to call him?"

"He's in the antechamber of the office," said Youssef. "Is that all right?"

"Fine. Youssef, why don't you give that suitcase back to Kmuzu.

He can carry it to our temporary apartment. I want you to let me into Friedlander Bey's inner office. You don't think he'd mind if I used it while he's in the hospital, do you?"

Youssef thought about that for a moment. "No," he said slowly, "I don't see any problem."

I smiled. "Good. I'm gonna have to take care of his business until he's healthy again."

"Then I'll leave you, *yaa Sidi*," said Kmuzu. "May I begin working on our charity project?"

"As soon as possible," I said. "Go in safety."

"God be with you," said Kmuzu. He turned toward the servants' wing. I went on with Youssef to Papa's private office.

Youssef paused at the threshold. "Shall I send the American in?" he asked.

"No," I said, "let him wait a couple of minutes. I need my English-language add-on, or I won't understand a word he says. Would you mind fetching it?" I told him where to find it. "Then when you come back, you can show Morgan in."

"Of course, O Shaykh." Youssef hurried away to do my bidding.

I felt an unpleasant thrill when I sat in Friedlander Bey's chair, as if I'd occupied a place of unholy strength. I didn't like the feeling at all. For one thing, I had no desire to step into the role of Junior Crime Lord, or even the more legitimate office of International Power Broker. I was at Papa's feet now; but if, Allah forbid, something terminal were to happen to him, I wouldn't hang around to be anointed as his successor. I had other plans for my future.

I glanced through the papers on Papa's desk for a few minutes, finding nothing racy or incriminating. I was about to start rummaging through the drawers when Youssef returned. "I've brought the entire rack, *yaa Side*," he said.

"Thank you, Youssef. Please show Morgan in now."

"Yes, O Shaykh." I was getting to like all this subservience, but that was a bad sign.

I chipped in the English daddy just as the big, blond American came in. "Where y'at, man?" he said, grinning. "I never been here before. You got a nice place."

"Friedlander Bey's got a nice place," I said, indicating that Morgan should make himself comfortable. "I'm just his errand boy."

"Whatever you say. Now, you want to hear what I got?"

I leaned back in the chair. "Where's Jawarski?" I said.

Morgan's grin disappeared. "Still don't know, man. I got the word out to everybody, but I haven't heard a clue. I don't think he's left the city. He's here somewhere, but he's done a damn good job of evaporating."

"Yeah, you right. So what's the good news?"

He rubbed his stubbly chin. "I know somebody who knows somebody who works for some business front that's owned by Reda Abu Adil. It's a shady package delivery service. Anyway, this guy my friend knows says he heard somebody else say that this Paul Jawarski wanted his money. Seems like your friend Abu Adil arranged to make it easy for Jawarski to blast his way out of the pokey."

"A couple of guards died on account of it, but I don't suppose that bothers Abu Adil none."

"I suppose not. So Abu Adil hired Jawarski through this delivery company to come to the city. I don't know what Abu Adil wanted, but you know what Jawarski's specialty is. This friend of mine calls it the Jawarski Finishing School."

"And now Abu Adil is making sure Jawarski stays unstumbled on, right?"

"The way I figure it."

I closed my eyes and thought about it. It made perfect sense. I didn't have hard evidence that Abu Adil had hired Jawarski to kill Shaknahyi, but in my heart I knew it was true. I also knew Jawarski had killed Blanca and the others in Shaknahyi's notebook. And because Lieutenant Hajjar was two-timing both Friedlander Bey and the halls of justice, I was pretty confident that the police were never going to dig Jawarski up. Even if they did, Jawarski would never be prosecuted.

I opened my eyes and stared at Morgan. "Just keep looking, buddy," I said, "because I don't think anybody else is."

"Money?"

I blinked at him. "What?"

"You got any money for me?"

I stood up angrily. "No, I ain't got money for you! I told you I'd pay you another five hundred when you found Jawarski. That's the deal."

Morgan stood up. "All right, man, just take it easy, okay?"

I was embarrassed by my outburst. "I'm sorry, Morgan," I said. "I'm not mad at you. This whole business is making me crazy."

"Uh yeah. I know you were good friends with Shaknahyi. All right, I'll keep at it."

"Thanks, Morgan." I followed him out of the office and showed him to the front door. "We're not gonna let them get away with it."

"Crime don't pay, right, man?" Morgan grinned and slapped my burned shoulder. The pain made me wince.

"Yeah, you right." I walked with him down the curving gravel driveway. I wanted to get away from the house, and if I left right now, I could escape without Kmuzu tagging along. "Like a ride to the Budayeen?" I asked.

"No, that's all right. I got some other stuff to do, man. See you later."

I turned back toward the house and got the car out of the garage. I thought I'd drop in on my club and see if it was still in one piece.

The day shift was still on, and there were only five or six customers. Indihar frowned and looked away when I caught her eye. I decided to sit at a table, rather than at my usual place at the bar. Pualani came up to say hello. "Want a White Death?" she asked.

"White Death? What's that?"

She shrugged her slender shoulders. "Oh, that's what Chiri calls that awful gin and bingara thing you drink." She grimaced.

"Yeah, bring me a White Death." It wasn't a bad name.

Brandi was on stage, dancing to the Sikh propaganda music that had suddenly become wildly popular. I hated it a lot. I didn't want to listen to political rantings, even if it had a great beat and a catchy two-bar figure.

"Here you go, boss," said Pualani, dropping a cocktail napkin in front of me and pinning it in place with a highball glass. "Mind if I sit down?"

"Huh? Oh, sure."

"Want to ask you about something. I'm thinkin' of, you know, havin' my brain wired so I can use moddies?" She cocked her head to the side and peered at me, as if I might not comprehend what she was telling me. She didn't say anything more.

"Yeah," I said at last. You had to respond like that with Pualani or you could spend the rest of your life trapped in the same conversation.

"Well, everybody says you know more'n anybody about it. I was wonderin' if you could, like, recommend somebody?"

"A surgeon?"

"Uh huh."

"Well, there's plenty of doctors around who'll do it for you. Most of 'em are pretty reliable."

Pualani gave me a pretty frown. "Well, I was wonderin' if I could go to your doctor and use your name."

"Dr. Lisân doesn't have a private practice. But his assistant, Dr. Yeniknani, is a good man."

Pualani squinted at me. "Would you write his name down for me?"

"Sure." I scribbled the name and commcode on the cocktail napkin.

"And also," she said, "does he do tits?"

"I don't think so, honey." Now Pualani had already spent a small fortune modifying her body. She had a cute ass that had been rounded with silicone, and cheekbones accentuated with silicone, and her chin and nose reshaped, and she'd already had breast implants. She had a devastating figure, and I thought it was a mistake to blow up her bust any more; but I'd learned a long time ago that you can't reason with dancers when it comes to breast size.

"Oh, okay," she said, obviously disappointed. I took a sip of my White Death. Pualani showed no sign of going away. I waited for her to continue. "You know Indihar?" she said.

"Sure."

"Well, she's havin' a lot of trouble. She's really broke."

"I tried giving her a loan, but she wouldn't take it."

Pualani shook her head. "No, she won't take a loan. But maybe you could help her out some other way." Then she got up and wandered toward the front of the club, and sat down next to a couple of Oriental men wearing sailor's caps.

Sometimes I just wished real life would leave me alone. I gulped a little more of my drink, then stood up and went to the bar. Indihar noticed me and came over. "Get you something, Marîd?" she asked.

"Jirji's pension ain't gonna help you very much, right?"

She gave me an annoyed look and turned away. She headed for the other end of the bar. "Don't want your money," she said.

I followed her. "I'm not offering money. How would you like a low-hassle job where you can live free and watch your kids all day? You wouldn't have to pay a babysitter."

She turned around. "What's this all about?" Her expression was mistrustful.

I smiled. "I mean bringing Little Jirji, Zahra, and Hâkim and moving into one of the empty apartments in Papa's house. Save you a lot of money every month, Indihar."

She considered that. "Maybe. Why would you want me in Papa's house?"

I had to come up with some phony but real-sounding reason. "It's my mother. I need someone to keep an eye on her. I'd be willing to pay you whatever you wanted."

Indihar patted the bar with one hand. "Already got a job, remember?"

"Hey," I said, "if that's the problem, you're fired."

Her face lost its color. "The hell you talking about?"

"Think about it, Indihar. I'm offering you a nice home, free rent and meals, plus good money every week for a part-time job making sure my mom doesn't do anything crazy. Your kids'll be taken care of and you won't have to come into this bar every day. You won't have to take your clothes off and dance, and you won't have to deal with the drunk jerks and the lazy-ass girls like Brandi."

She raised her eyebrows. "I'll let you know, Marîd," she said. "Soon as I figure out what kind of hustle you're trying to pull. Sounds too good to be straight, sweetheart. I mean, you're not wearing a Santa Claus moddy or nothing."

"Yeah, you think about it. Talk it over with Chiri. You trust her. See what she thinks."

Indihar nodded. She was still watching me uncertainly. "Even if I say yes," she said, "I'm not gonna fuck you."

I sighed. "Yeah, you right." I went back to my table. A minute after I sat down again, Fuad il-Manhous let himself drop into the other chair. "I woke up the other day," he said in his high-pitched, nasal voice, "and my mama says to me, 'Fuad, we don't have no money, go out and take one of the chickens and sell it.' "

He was starting one of his dumb fables. He was so desperate for attention that he'd make himself look like a total fool just to make me laugh. The sad thing was that even his most fantastic stories were based on Fuad's actual fuck-ups.

He looked at me closely, to make sure I understood him so far. "So I did. I went out to my mama's chicken coop and I chased those chickens around and around till I caught one. Then I carried it down the hill and up the hill and over the bridge and through the streets till I came to the Souk of the Poultry Dressers. Well, I never took a chicken to market before, so I didn't know what to do. I stood there in the middle of the square all day, until I saw the merchants locking their money up in boxes and loading their leftover stuff onto their carts. I'd already heard the sunset call to prayer, so I knew I didn't have much time.

"I took my chicken to one of the men and told him I wanted to sell it, and he looked at it and shook his head. 'This chicken has lost all it's teeth,' he says.

"So I looked at it, and by Allah, he was right. That chicken didn't have a tooth in its head. So I says, 'What will you give me for it?' And the man gave me a handful of copper fîqs.

"Then I walked home with one hand in my pocket and my other hand holding the copper fîqs. Just when I was crossing the bridge over the drainage canal, there was this fierce swarm of gnats. I started waving my hands and swatting them, and then I ran the rest of the way across the bridge. When I got to the other side, I looked and I saw that I didn't have the money anymore. I'd dropped all the coins into the canal."

Fuad coughed quietly. "Can I have a glass of beer, Marîd?" he asked. "I'm getting real thirsty."

I signaled to Indihar to draw one. "You paying for this, Fuad?" I said. His long face fell further. He looked like a puppy about to get a beating. "Just kidding," I said. "The beer's on the house. I want to hear how this story comes out."

Indihar set a mug in front of him, then stood around to hear the rest of the story. "*Bismillah*," murmured Fuad, and he took a long gulp. Then he set the beer down, gave me a quick, thankful grimace, and started again. "Anyway," he said, "when I got home, my mama was real mad. I didn't have no chicken and I didn't have no money. 'Next time,' she says, 'put it in your pocket.'

" 'Ah,' I go, 'I should have thought of that.' So the next morning, my mama wakes me up and tells me to take another chicken to the souk. Well, I got dressed and went out and chased them around some more and caught one and carried it down the hill and up the hill and across the bridge and through the streets to the souk. And this time I didn't stand in the hot sun all morning and all afternoon. I went right up to the merchant and showed him the second chicken.

" 'This one looks as bad as the one you brought yesterday,' he says. 'And besides, I'll have to provide space for it here in my stall all day. But I'll tell you what I'll do. I'll give you a big jug of honey in trade. It's very fine honey.' "

"Well, it was a good trade because my mama had four other chickens, but she didn't have no honey. So I took the jug of honey from him and started home. I'd just crossed the bridge when I remembered what my mama told me. I opened the jug and poured the honey in my pocket. By the time I climbed the last hill, it was all gone.

"So my mama was real mad again. 'Next time,' she says, 'balance it on your head.'

" 'Ah,' I go, 'I should have thought of that.' On the third morning, I got up and caught another chicken, and carried it to the souk and brought it to the merchant.

" 'Are all your chickens in such bad shape?' he says. 'Well, in the name of Allah, I will give you my supper for this bird.' And the merchant gave me a mess of curds and whey.

"Well, I remembered what my mama told me, and I balanced it on my head. I went through the streets and across the bridge and down the hill and up the hill. When I got home, my mama asked me what I got for the chicken. 'Enough curds and whey for our evening meal,' I go.

" 'Then where is it?' she says.

" 'On my head,' I go. She took one look and dragged me to the washstand. She poured a whole pitcher of cold water over my head and scrubbed my hair with a stiff brush. All the time she was shouting and blaming me for losing the curds and whey.

" 'Next time, carry it carefully in your hands,' she says.

" 'Ah,' I go, 'I should have thought of that.' So the next morning, very early before the sun came up, I went out to the chicken coop and chose the nicest, fattest chicken that was left. I left the house before my mama woke up, and I carried the chicken down the hill and through the streets to the Souk of the Poultry Dressers.

" 'Good morning, my friend,' says the merchant. 'I see you have another aged, toothless chicken.'

" 'This is a very nice chicken,' I go, 'and I want what it's worth and nothing less.'

"The merchant looked at the chicken closely and mumbled to himself. 'You know,' he says at last, 'these feathers are stuck on very tight.'

" 'Isn't that how they're supposed to be?' I go.

"He pointed to a row of dead chickens with their heads cut off. 'See any feathers on these?'

" 'No,' I go.

" 'Ever eat a roast chicken with feathers?'

" 'No,' I go.

" 'Then I'm sorry. It will cost me much time and labor to unstick all these feathers. I can only offer you this big fierce tomcat.'

"I thought that was a good trade, because the tomcat would catch the mice and rats that crept into the coop and stole the chicken feed. I remembered what my mama had told me, and I tried to carry the tomcat carefully in my hands. Just after I went down the hill and before I went up the hill, the tomcat snarled and spit and squirmed and scratched until I couldn't hold him any longer. He jumped out of my hands and ran away.

"I knew my mama was gonna be mad again. 'Next time,' she says, 'tie him with a string and pull him behind you.'

" 'Ah,' I go, 'I should have thought of that.' Now, there's only two chickens left, so it took me longer to catch one the next morning, even though I didn't even care which one it was. When I got to the souk, the merchant was very glad to see me.

" 'Praise Allah that we are both well this morning,' he says, smiling at me. 'I see you have a chicken.'

" 'Yeah, you right,' I go. I laid the chicken on the warped board he used for a counter.

"The merchant picked up the chicken and weighed it in his hands, and thumped it with his finger like you'd thump a melon. 'This chicken doesn't lay eggs, does it?' he asks.

" 'Sure, it lays eggs! It's the best egg-laying hen my mama ever had.'

"The man shook his head and frowned. 'You see,' he says, 'that's a problem. Every egg this chicken lays, that's less meat on its bones. This might've been a nice heavy chicken if it hadn't laid no eggs. It's a good thing you brought it to me now, before it shrunk away to nothing.'

" 'All the eggs ought to be worth something,' I go.

" 'I don't see no eggs. I'll tell you what I'll do. I'll trade you this killed, cleaned chicken ready to eat for your egg-laying chicken. You won't find a better deal than that from any of these other poultry dressers. Once they hear this chicken is such a good egg-layer, they won't give you two copper fiqs.'

"I was just glad this man had taken a liking to me, because he was telling me things none of the other merchants would've told me. So I traded my worthless egg-layer for his dressed chicken, even though to me it looked a little scrawny and smelled funny and was kind of the wrong color. I remembered what my mama told me, so I tied a string around it and pulled it along behind me as I walked home.

"You should've heard my mama yelling at me when I got home! That poor plucked chicken was completely ruined. 'By the life of my eyes!' she shouted. 'You are the biggest fool in all the lands of Islam! Next time, carry it on your shoulder!'

" 'Ah,' I go, 'I should have thought of that.'

"So there was one chicken left, and I promised myself that I was gonna get the better of the deal the next day. Again I didn't wait for my mama to wake me. I rose early, scrubbed my face and hands, put on my best suit of clothes, and went out to the coop. It took me an hour to catch that last chicken, which had always been my mama's favorite. It's name was Mouna. Finally I got my hands on its thrashing, flapping body. I carried it out of the chicken coop, down the hill, up the hill, across the bridge, through the streets to the souk.

"But this morning the poultry dresser was not in his stall. I stood there for several minutes, wondering where my friend could be. Finally, a girl came up to me. She was dressed as a modest Muslim woman should be dressed, and I couldn't see her face because of the veil; but when she spoke, I knew from her voice that she probably was the most beautiful girl I'd ever met."

"You can get yourself in a lot of trouble that way," I told Fuad. "I've made the mistake of falling in love over the telephone. More than once."

He frowned at the interruption and went on. "She was probably the most beautiful girl I'd ever met. Anyway, she says, 'Are you the gentleman who has been trading his chickens with my father every morning?'

"I go, 'I'm not sure. I don't know who your father is. Is this his poultry stall?' She says it is. I go, 'Then I'm that gentleman, and I have our last chicken right here. Where's your father this morning?'

"Big bright tears collect in the corners of her eyes. She looks up at me with a pitiful expression on her face, at least the part of it I can see. 'My father is desperately ill,' she says. 'The doctor doesn't expect him to live through the day.'

"Well, I was shocked by the news. 'May Allah have mercy on your father, and grant him health. If he dies, I'll have to sell my chicken to someone else today.'

"The girl didn't say anything for a moment. I don't think she really cared what happened to my chicken. At last she said, 'My father sent me here this morning to find you. His conscience is troubling him. He says that he traded unfairly with you, and he wishes to make up for it before he is called to the bosom of Allah. He begs that you accept his donkey, the very donkey that faithfully pulled my father's cart for ten years.'

"I was a little suspicious about this offer. After all, I didn't know this girl as well as I knew her father. 'Let me get this straight,' I go. 'You want to trade your fine donkey for this chicken?'

"'Yes,' she says.

"'I'll have to think it over. It's our last chicken, you know.' I thought about it and thought about it, but I couldn't see anything that would make my mama mad. I was sure that finally she'd be happy about one of my trades. 'All right,' I go, and I grabbed the donkey's rope halter. 'Take the chicken, and tell your father that I will pray for his well-being. May he return tomorrow to his stall in this souk, *inshallah.*'

"'*Inshallah,*' the girl says, and she lowered her eyes to the ground. She went away with my mama's last chicken, and I never saw her again. I think about her a lot, though, because she's probably the only woman I'll ever love."

"Yeah, you right," I said, laughing. Fuad has this thing for mean hookers, the kind who carry straight razors. You can find him every night over at the Red Light Lounge, Fatima and Nassir's place. Nobody else I know even has the guts to go in there alone. Fuad spends a lot of time in there, falling in love and getting ripped off.

"Anyway," he said, "I started leading the donkey home, when I remembered what my mama told me. So I strained and pushed and lifted until I got that donkey to my shoulders. I got to admit, I really didn't know why my mama wanted me to carry it that way, when it could walk by itself just as well as I could. Still, I didn't want her mad at me anymore.

"I staggered toward home with the donkey across my back, and as I climbed down the hill, I passed the beautiful walled palace of Shaykh Salman Mubarak. Now, you know Shaykh Salman lived in that great mansion with his beautiful daughter, who was sixteen years old and had never laughed from the time she'd been born. She had never even smiled. She could talk all right, but she just didn't. Nobody, not even her wealthy father, had ever heard her say a single word since the shaykh's wife, the girl's mother, had died when the girl was three years old. The doctors said that if anyone could make her laugh, she'd be able to speak again; or if anyone could make her speak, she'd then laugh as any normal person might. Shaykh Salman had made the usual offers of riches and his daughter's hand in marriage, but suitor after suitor had tried and failed. The girl just sat glumly by the window, watching the world pass by below.

"That's when I happened to walk by carrying the donkey. It must have looked pretty weird, upside down on my back with its hooves waving in the air. I was told later that the shaykh's beautiful daughter stared at me and the donkey for a few seconds, and then burst out into a helpless fit of laughter. She recovered her speech then too, because she called loudly for her father to come look. The shaykh was so grateful, he ran out into the road to meet me."

"Did he give you his daughter?" asked Indihar.

"You bet," said Fuad.

"How romantic," she said.

"And when I married her, I became the richest man in the city after the shaykh himself. And my mother was quite pleased, and didn't mind that she had no chickens left at all. She came to live with my wife and me in the shaykh's palace."

I sighed. "How much of that was true, Fuad?" I asked.

"Oh," he said, "I forgot a part. It turns out that the shaykh was really the poultry dresser, who went to the souk every morning. I don't remember the reason why. And so the veiled girl was just as beautiful as I thought she'd be."

Indihar reached over and grabbed Fuad's half-full mug of beer. She raised it to her lips and finished it off. "I thought the poultry dresser was dying," she said.

Fuad frowned in serious thought. "Yeah, well, he was, see, but when he heard his daughter laughing and calling his name, he was miraculously healed."

"All praise to Allah, Fount of blessings," I said.

"I made up that part about Shaykh Salman and his beautiful daughter," said Fuad.

"Uh huh," said Indihar. "You and your mama really raise chickens?"

"Oh sure," he said eagerly, "but we don't got any right at the moment."

"Because you traded them?"

"I told my mama we should start again with younger chickens that still got their teeth."

"Thank God, I have to go mop up the spilled beer," said Indihar. She went back behind the bar.

I drained the last of my White Death. After Fuad's story, I wanted three or four more drinks. "Another beer?" I asked him.

He stood up. "Thanks, Marîd, but I got to make some money. I want to buy a gold chain for this girl."

"Why don't you give her one of the ones you try selling to the tourists?"

He looked horrified. "She'd scratch my eyes out!" he said. It sounded like he'd found another hot-blooded sweetheart. "By the way, the Half-Hajj said I should show you this." He pulled something out of his pocket and dropped it in front of me.

I picked it up. It was heavy, shiny, and made of steel, about six inches long. I'd never held one in my hand before, but I knew what it was: an empty clip from an automatic pistol.

Not many people used the old projectile weapons anymore, but Paul Jawarski used a .45 caliber gun. That's what this came from.

"Where'd you get this, Fuad?" I asked casually, turning the clip over in my hands.

"Oh, in the alley behind Gay Che's. Sometimes you can find money there, it falls out of their pockets when they go out into the alley. I showed it to Saied first, and he said you'd like to see it."

"Uh huh. I never heard of Gay Che's."

"You wouldn't like it. It's a tough place. I don't ever go in there. I just hang around in the alley."

"Sounds smart. Where is it?"

Fuad closed one eye and looked thoughtful. "Hâmidiyya. On Aknouli Street."

Hâmidiyya. Reda Abu Adil's little kingdom. "Now, why did Saied think I'd want to know about this?" I asked.

Fuad shrugged. "He didn't tell me. Did you? Want to see it, I mean?"

"Yeah, thanks, Fuad. I owe you one."

"Really? Then maybe—"

"Another time, Fuad." I made a distracted, dismissing motion with my hand. I guess he took the hint, because in a little while I noticed he was gone. I had a lot to think about: Was this a clue? Was Paul Jawarski hiding out in one of Abu Adil's crummier enterprises? Or was it some kind of a trap baited by Saied the Half-Hajj, who couldn't know that I no longer trusted him?

I didn't have any choice. Trap or not, I was going to follow it up. But not just yet.

fifteen

Ī waīteᴅ until the next morning before I followed up on Fuad's information. I had the disconcerting feeling that I was being set up, but at the same time I felt I might as well live dangerously. I sure wasn't getting any closer to finding Jawarski using more conventional methods. Maybe sticking my head on the block would tempt the executioner to make an appearance.

And then maybe the clip didn't belong to Jawarski, after all, and there wasn't anything at Gay Che's but a lot of guys in exquisitely tailored caftans.

I thought about this as I walked back on the Street, past Frenchy Benoit's club to the cemetery. I had a sense that events were moving quickly to their conclusion, although I couldn't yet tell if that ending would be tragic or happy for me. I wished I had Shaknahyi to advise me, and I wished I had made better use of his experience while he was still alive. It was his grave I wanted to visit first.

There were several people at the entrance to the cemetery, sitting or squatting on the uneven, broken slabs of concrete. They all jumped to their feet when they saw me, the old men selling Coca-Cola and Sharâb from battered coolers on tricycles, the toothless old women grinning and shoving bundles of dead, drooping flowers in my face, the children crying "O Generous! O Compassionate!" and blocking my way. Sometimes I don't respond well to organized, clamorous begging. I lose a lot of my sympathy. I pushed through the crowd, stopping only to trade a couple of kiam for a wilted bouquet. Then I passed beneath the brick arch, into the cemetery.

Shaknahyi's grave was across the way, near the wall on the western side. The dirt was still bare, although a little grass had begun to poke through. I bent down and placed the meager bouquet at the grave's head, which in accordance with Muslim tradition pointed toward Mecca.

I stood up and looked back toward Sixteenth Street, over the many graves thrown haphazardly together. The Muslim tombs were each marked with a crescent and star, but there were also a few Christian crosses, a few Stars of David, and many unmarked at all. Shaknahyi's final resting place had only an upended flat rock with his name and the date of his death scratched on. Someday soon that rock would topple over, and no doubt it would be stolen by another mourner too poor to afford a proper marker. Shaknahyi's name would be removed with a little sandpaper or steel wool, and the rock would serve as someone else's headstone until it was stolen again. I made a mental note to pay for a permanent grave marker. He deserved that much, at least.

A young boy in a robe and turban tugged on my sleeve. "O Father of sadness," he said in a high-pitched voice, "I can recite."

This was one of the young shaykhs who'd committed the entire Qur'ân to memory. He probably supported his family by reciting verses in the cemetery. "I will give you ten kiam to pray for my friend," I said. He'd caught me in a weak moment.

"Ten kiam, effendi! Do you want me to recite the whole Book?"

I put my hand on his bony shoulder. "No. Just something comforting about God and Heaven."

The boy frowned. "There's much more about Hell and the eternal flames," he said.

"I know. I don't want to hear that."

"All right, effendi." And he began murmuring the ancient phrases in a singsong voice. I left him beside Shaknahyi's grave and wandered back toward the entrance.

My friend and occasional lover, Nikki, had been laid to rest in a low whitewashed tomb that was already falling into disrepair. Nikki's family certainly could have afforded to bring her body home for burial, but they'd preferred to leave her here. Nikki had been a sexchange, and her family probably didn't want to be embarrassed. Anyway, this lonely tomb seemed to be in keeping with Nikki's hard, loveless life. On my desk in the police station, I still kept a small brass scarab that had belonged to her. A week didn't go by when I didn't think of Nikki.

I passed by the graves of Tamiko, Devi, and Selima, the Black Widow Sisters, and of Hassan the Shiite, the son of a bitch who'd almost killed me. I found myself maundering gloomily along the narrow brick paths, and I decided that wasn't how I wanted to spend the rest of the afternoon. I shook off the growing depression and headed back toward the Street. When I glanced over my shoulder, the young shaykh was still standing beside Shaknahyi's grave, reciting the holy words. I felt sure that he'd stay there ten kiams' worth, even after I was gone.

I had to force my way through the mob of beggars again, but this time I threw a handful of coins to them. When they scrambled for the money, it made it easier to escape. I unclipped my phone from my belt and spoke Saied the Half-Hajj's commcode. I waited a few rings, and I was about to give up when he answered. "*Marhaba*," he said.

"It's Marîd. How you doin'?"

"Aw right. What's happening?"

"Oh, nothing much. I got out of the hospital."

"Ah! Glad to hear it."

"Yeah, I get tired of that place. Anyway, you with Jacques and Mahmoud?"

"Uh yeah. We're all sitting in Courane's getting drunk. Why don't you come on by?"

"I think I will. I need you to do me a favor."

"Yeah?"

"Tell you about it later. See you in maybe half an hour. *Ma'assalaama.*"

"*Allah yisallimak.*"

I clipped the phone back on my belt. I'd walked all the way back to Chiriga's, and suddenly I had a terrific urge to go in and see if Indihar or any of the girls had a few sunnies or tri-phets they could spare. It wasn't withdrawal I was feeling; it was a hunger that had been growing for many days. It took a lot of willpower to fight off the craving. It would have been so much easier to admit my true nature and give in. I might have, except I knew that later I'd need my brains unaddled.

I kept on walking until I got to Fifth Street, when I was stopped by one of the most unusual sights I've ever seen. Laila, the old black hag who owned the modshop, was standing in the middle of the Street, screaming shrill curses at Safiyya the Lamb Lady, who was standing a block away and yelling her head off too. They looked like two gunfighters from an American holoshow, screeching and snarling and threatening each other. I saw some tourists coming up the street; they stopped and watched the old women nervously, then backed away again toward the eastern gate. I felt the same way. I didn't want to get in between those two witches. You could almost see the green rays shooting out of their eyes.

I couldn't actually understand what they were saying. Their voices were strained and hoarse, and they may not have been screaming in

Arabic. I didn't know if the Lamb Lady'd had her skull amped, but Laila never went anywhere without a moddy and a handful of daddies. She could have been ranting in ancient Etruscan for all I knew. After a little while they both got tired of it. Safiyya left first, making an obscene gesture in Laila's direction and heading back down the Street toward the Boulevard il-Jameel. Laila stared after her, throwing a few final unpleasantries her way. Then, muttering to herself, she turned down Fourth Street. I followed her. I thought I might find a useful moddy in her shop.

When I got there, Laila was behind her cash register, humming to herself and sorting a stack of invoices. When I came in, she looked up and smiled. "Marîd," she said sadly, "do you know how *boring* it is to be the wife of a country doctor?"

"To be honest, Laila, no, I don't." Evidently, she'd chipped in another moddy as soon as she got back to her shop, and now it was as if she hadn't seen the Lamb Lady at all.

"Well," she said slyly, giving me a wicked smile, "if you did know, you wouldn't blame me at all if I considered taking a lover."

"Madame Bovary?" I asked.

She just winked. The effect was moderately hideous.

I began browsing in her dusty bins. I didn't exactly know what I was looking for. "Laila," I called over my shoulder, "do the letters A.L.M. mean anything to you?"

"L'Association des Larves Maboules?"

That meant the Association of Crazy Wimps. "Who are they?" I asked.

"You know. People like Fuad."

"Never heard of it," I said.

"I just made it up, *chéri.*"

"Uh huh." I picked up a moddy package that caught my eye. It was an anthology of fictional types, mostly Eur-Am defenders of the meek, although there was an ancient Chinese poet-king, a Bantu demigod, and a Nordic trickster. The only name I recognized was Mike Hammer. I still owned a Nero Wolfe moddy, although the companion hardware, Archie Goodwin, had died horribly under the heel of Saied the Half-Hajj.

I decided to get the anthology. I figured it gave me a wide sampling of skills and personalities. I took it over to Laila. "Just this one today," I said.

"There's a special on—"

"Wrap it, Laila." I handed her a ten-kiam bill. She took my money and looked hurt. I thought about what I'd chip in to visit Gay Che's. I still had Rex, Saied's badass moddy. I decided I'd wear that, and carry this new one in reserve.

"Your change, Marîd."

I took my package, but let the old woman keep the change. "Buy yourself something pretty, Laila," I told her.

She smiled again. "And you know, I expect Leon will bring me a romantic surprise this evening."

"Yeah, you right." I left the shop feeling as creepy as I always did around her.

I took three steps toward the Street, and then I heard blaam! blaam! blaam! A flying chip of concrete cut my face just under my right eye. I threw myself into the doorway of the gambling den next to Laila's. Blaam! blaam! blaam! I heard bricks shatter and saw puffs of red dust drift from the edge of the doorway. I pressed myself in as far as I could. Blaam! blaam! Two more: Someone had just taken eight shots at me with a high-powered pistol.

Nobody came running. Nobody was curious enough to see if I was all right, or maybe needed medical attention. I waited, wondering how long before it was safe to stick my head out again. Was Jawarski still hiding somewhere across the street, a fresh clip in his .45? Or was this only a warning? Surely, if he truly wanted to kill me, he could have done a better job of it.

I got tired of being scared after a few minutes and left the safety of the doorway. I have to admit that I had a peculiar vulnerable feeling between my shoulder blades as I hurried down to the corner. I decided that this had been Jawarski's way of sending me an invitation. I had no intention of declining; I just wanted to be prepared.

Yet even so, I still had other business to finish before I could turn my full attention to the American. I went to my car and threw the new moddy into the backseat, where I'd left my briefcase. I drove slowly and calmly through the Rasmiyya neighborhood to Courane's. When I got there, I parked the car in the narrow street and took Saied's moddy out of the briefcase. I looked at it thoughtfully for a moment and chipped it in, along with the daddies that blocked pain and fatigue. Then I got out of the car and went into Courane's dim bar.

"Monsieur Audran!" said the expatriate, coming toward me with both hands outstretched. "Your friends told me you'd be coming. It's good to see you again."

"Yeah," I said. I could see the Half-Hajj, Mahmoud, and Jacques at a table near the back.

Courane followed me, speaking in a low voice. "Wasn't that just terrible about Officer Shaknahyi?"

I turned to look at him. "That's what it was, Courane. Terrible."

"I was truly upset." He nodded to let me know how sincere he was.

"Vodka gimlet," I said. That made him go away.

I dragged over a chair and sat at the table with the others. I looked at them but didn't say anything. The last time I'd been with this group, I hadn't been very popular. I wondered if anything had changed.

Jacques was the Christian who was always patronizing me about how he had more European blood than I did. This afternoon he just closed one eye and nodded his head. "I hear you pulled Papa out of a burning building."

Courane arrived with my drink. Instead of answering, I lifted the glass and sipped.

"I was in a fire once," said the Half-Hajj. "Well, actually, I was in a building that burned down about an hour after I left. I could've been killed."

Mahmoud, the male sexchange, snorted, "So, Marîd," he said, "I'm impressed."

"Yeah," I said, "I really just wanted to impress you bastards." I squeezed the wedge of lime into the gimlet. Vitamin C, you know.

"No, really," Mahmoud went on, "everybody's talking about it. It was pretty gutsy."

Jacques shrugged. "Especially if you think that you could've ended up with all of Friedlander Bey's lightspeed clout for yourself. Just by letting the old fucker fry."

"Did you think about that?" asked Mahmoud. "While it was all happening, I mean?"

It was time to take a long swallow of vodka, because I was getting really mad. When I set my glass down again, I looked from one to the other. "You know Indihar, right? Well, since Jirji's been dead, she's having a tough time paying her bills. She won't take a loan from me or Chiri, and she can't make enough tending bar in the club."

Mahmoud's eyebrows went up. "She want to come work for me? She's got a nice ass. I could get her good money."

I shook my head. "She's not interested in that," I said. "She wants me to find a new home for one of her kids. She's got two boys and a girl. I told her she could spare one of the boys."

That shut 'em up for a little while. "Maybe," said Jacques at last. "I can ask around, anyway."

"Do it," I said. "Indihar said she might even be willing to part with the girl too. If they both go together, and if the price is right."

"When do you need to know?" said Mahmoud.

"Soon as you can find out. Now, I got to go. Saied, you mind taking a ride with me?"

The Half-Hajj looked first at Mahmoud, then at Jacques, but neither of them had anything to say. "Guess not," he said.

I took twenty kiam out of my pocket and dropped it on the table. "Drinks are on me," I said.

Mahmoud gave me a judicious look. "We been kind of hard on you lately," he said.

"I hadn't noticed."

"Well, we're glad things are straightened out between us. No reason things can't be like they were before."

"Sure," I said, "right."

I gave Saied's shoulder a little shove, and we headed back out into the sunlight. I stopped him before he got into the car. "I need you to tell me how to find Gay Che's," I said.

His face went suddenly pale. "Why the hell you want to go there?"

"I heard about it, that's all."

"Well, I don't want to go. I'm not even sure I can give you directions."

"Sure you can, pal," I said, my voice grim and threatening. "You know all about it."

Saied didn't like being pushed around. He stood up straight, trying to give himself a little height advantage. "Think you can *make* me go with you?"

I just stared at him, my face empty of emotion. Then very slowly I raised my right hand up to my lips. I opened my mouth and bit myself savagely. I ripped a small gobbet of flesh loose from the inside of my wrist and spat it at the Half-Hajj. My own blood trickled down the corners of my mouth. "Look, mother-fucker," I growled hoarsely, "that's what I do to *me*. Wait till you see what I do to *you!*"

Saied shuddered and backed away from me on the sidewalk. "You're crazy, Marîd," he said. "You gone fuckin' crazy."

"In the car."

He hesitated. "You're wearing Rex, ain't you? You shouldn't wear that moddy. I don't like what it does to you."

I threw back my head and laughed. I was only behaving the way *he* acted when *he* wore the same moddy. And he wore it often. I could understand why—I was beginning to like it a lot.

I waited until he slid into the passenger seat, then I went around and got behind the wheel. "Which way?" I asked.

"South." His voice was tired and hopeless.

I drove for a while, letting him worry about how much I knew. "So," I said finally, "what kind of place is it?"

"Nothing much." The Half-Hajj was sullen. "A hangout for this jackboot gang, the *Jaish*."

"Yeah?" From the name, I'd pictured the clientele of Gay Che's like that guy I'd seen in Chiri's a few weeks before, the one in the vinyl pants with his hand chained behind his back.

"The Citizen's Army. They wear these gray uniforms and have parades and pass out a lot of leaflets. I think they want to get rid of the foreigners in the city. Down with the heathen Franj. You know that routine."

"Uh huh. I get the idea from il-Manhous that you spend some time there."

Saied didn't like this conversation at all. "Look, Marîd," he began, but then he fell silent. "Anyway, you gonna believe everything you hear from Fuad?"

I laughed. "What you think he told me?"

"I don't know." He slid farther away from me, up against the passenger door. I almost felt sorry for him. He didn't speak again except to give me directions.

When we got there, I reached under my seat where my weapons were hidden. I had the small seizure gun I'd gotten so long ago from Lieutenant Okking, and the static pistol Shaknahyi'd given me. I looked at the guns thoughtfully. "This a setup, Saied? You supposed to bring me here so Abu Adil's thugs could ice me?"

The Half-Hajj looked frightened. "What's this all about, Marîd?"

"Just tell me why the hell you told Fuad to show me that .45 caliber clip."

He sagged unhappily in his seat. "I went to Shaykh Reda because I was confused, Marîd, that's all. Maybe it's too late now, but I'm real sorry. I just didn't like standing around while you got to be the big hero, when you got to be Friedlander Bey's favorite. I felt left out."

My lip curled. "You mean you set me up to be killed because you were fucking *jealous?*"

"I never meant for anything like that."

I took the empty clip from my pocket and held it in front of his eyes. "An hour ago, Jawarski emptied another one of these at me, in broad daylight on Fourth Street."

Saied rubbed his eyes and muttered something. "I didn't think this would happen," he said softly.

"What *did* you think would happen?"

"I thought Abu Adil would treat me the way Papa's treating you."

I stared at him in amazement. "You really hired yourself out to Abu Adil, didn't you? I thought you just told him about my mother. But you're one of his tools, right?"

"I told you I was sorry," he said in an anguished voice. "I'll make it up to you."

"Goddamn right you will." I handed him the seizure gun. "Take this. We're going in there and we're gonna find Jawarski."

The Half-Hajj took the weapon hesitantly. "I wish I had Rex," he said sadly.

"No, I don't trust you with Rex. I'm gonna keep wearing it." I got out of the car and waited for Saied. "Put your gun away. Keep it out of sight unless you need it. Now, is there any kind of password or anything?"

"No, you just got to remember nobody in there's very fond of foreigners."

"Uh huh. Come on, then." I led the way into the bar. It was crowded and noisy and all I saw were men, most of them dressed in what I guessed was the gray uniform of this right-wing Citizen's Army. It wasn't dimly lighted and there wasn't music playing: Gay Che's wasn't that kind of bar. This was a meeting place for the kind of men who liked dressing up as brave soldiers and marching through the streets and not actually having shots fired at them. What these jokers reminded me of was Hitler's SA, whose main attributes had been perversion and pointless brutality.

Saied and I pushed our way through the mob of men to the bar. "Yeah?" said the surly bartender.

I had to shout to make myself heard. "Two beers," I said. This didn't look like a place to order fancy drinks.

"Right."

"And we're looking for a guy."

The bartender glanced up from his tap. "Won't find him here."

"Oh yeah?" He set the beers in front of the Half-Hajj and me, and I paid. "An American, might still be recovering—"

The bartender grabbed the ten-kiam bill I'd laid down. He didn't offer any change. "Look, cap, I don't answer questions, I pour beer. And if some American came in here, these guys'd probably tear him apart."

I took a gulp of the cold beer and looked around the room. Maybe Jawarski hadn't been in this bar. Maybe he was hiding out upstairs in the building, or in a nearby building. "Okay," I said, turning back to the bartender, "he ain't been in here. But you seen any Americans around this neighborhood lately?"

"Didn't you hear me? No questions."

Time to bring out the hidden persuader. I took a hundred-kiam bill from my pocket and waved it in the bartender's face. I didn't need to say a word.

He looked into my eyes. It was clear that he was torn by indecision. Finally he said, "Let me have the money."

I gave him a tight smile. "Look at it a little longer. Maybe improve your memory."

"Well, stop flashing it around, cap. You'll get us both roughed up." I put the money on the bar and covered it with my hand. I waited. The bartender went away for a moment. When he came back, he slid a torn piece of cardboard toward me.

I picked it up. There was an address written on it. I showed the cardboard to Saied. "Know where this is?" I asked.

"Yeah," he said in an unhappy voice, "it's about two blocks from Abu Adil's place."

"Sounds right." I handed the hundred kiam to the bartender, who made it disappear. I took out the static pistol and let him see it. "If you've fucked me over," I said, "I'm coming back and using this on you. Understand?"

"He's there," said the bartender. "Just get out of here and don't come back."

I put the gun away and shoved my way toward the door. When we were on the sidewalk again, I looked at the Half-Hajj. "See now?" I said. "That wasn't so bad."

He gave me a hopeless look. "You want me to go with you to find Jawarski, right?"

I shrugged. "No," I said, "I already paid somebody else to do that. I don't want to have to come near Jawarski if I can help it."

Saied was furious. "You mean you put me through all that grief and dragged me into that place for nothing?"

I opened the car door. "Hey, it wasn't for nothing," I said, smiling. "Allah probably agrees it was good for your soul."

sixteen

The westphalian sedan was headed north, away from Hâmidiyya. I had my English daddy chipped in and I was speaking on the phone to Morgan. "I found him," I said.

"Great, man." The American sounded disappointed. "That mean I don't get the rest of the money?"

"Tell you what I'll do. I'll give you the other five hundred if you baby-sit Jawarski for a few hours. You got a gun?"

"Yeah. You want me to use it?"

The idea was very tempting. "No. I just want you to keep an eye on him." I read off the address on the piece of cardboard. "Don't let him go anywhere. Hold him till I get there."

"Sure, man," said Morgan, "but don't take all day. I'm not crazy about hangin' around all day with a guy who's killed twenty-some people."

"I got faith in you. Talk to you later." I hung up the phone.

"What you gonna do?" asked Saied.

I didn't want to tell him, because despite his earnest confession and apology, I still didn't trust him. "I'm taking you back to Courane's," I said. "Or you rather I drop you off somewhere in the Budayeen?"

"Can't I go with you?"

I laughed coldly. "I'm gonna visit your favorite kingpin, Abu Adil. You still on good terms with him?"

"I don't know," said the Half-Hajj nervously. "But maybe I ought to go back to Courane's. I thought of something I got to tell Jacques and Mahmoud."

"I'll bet."

"Besides, I don't need to run into that bastard Umar ever again."

Saied pronounced the name "Himmar," by changing the vowel just a little and aspirating it. It was an Arabic pun. The word *Himmar* means donkey, and Arabs consider the donkey one of the filthiest animals on earth. This was a clever way of insulting Umar, and when he was wearing Rex, the Half-Hajj may even have said it to Abdul-Qawy's face. That may be one of the reasons Saied wasn't popular around Hâmidiyya anymore.

He was quiet for a little while. "Marîd," he said at last, "I meant what I said. I made a bad mistake, turning my coat like that. But I never had no contract with Friedlander Bey or nothing. I didn't think I was hurting anybody."

"I almost died twice, pal. First the fire, then Jawarski."

I pulled the car to the curb outside Courane's. Saied was miserable. "What you want me to say?" he pleaded.

"You got nothing to say. I'll see you you later."

He nodded and got out of the car. I watched him walk into Courane's bar, then I popped the tough-guy moddy. I drove west and north, to Papa's house. Before I confronted Abu Adil, I had two or three other things to take care of.

I found Kmuzu in our temporary apartment, working at my Chhindwara data deck. He looked up when he heard me come into the room. "Ah, *yaa Sidi!*" he said, as pleased as I'd ever seen him. "I have good news. It will cost less to organize charity food distribution than I thought. I hope you'll forgive me for examining your financial situation, but I've learned that you have more than twice what we need."

"That a hint, Kmuzu? I'm only going to open one soup kitchen, not two. You got an operating budget worked out?"

"We can run the food center for a full week on the money you get from Chiriga's on a single night."

"Great, glad to hear it. I was just wondering why you're so excited about this project. How come it means so much to you?"

Kmuzu's expression turned solidly neutral. "I just feel responsible for your Christian moral education," he said.

"I don't buy it," I said.

He looked away. "There is a long story, *yaa Sidi*," he said. "I do not wish to tell it now."

"All right, Kmuzu. Another time."

He turned to me again. "I have information about the fire. I told you I'd found proof it was deliberately set. That night in the corridor between your apartment and that of the master of the house, I discovered rags that had been soaked in some flammable fluid." He opened a desk drawer and took out some badly scorched cloth remnants. They'd

been burned in the fire, but hadn't been totally destroyed. I could still
see a decorative pattern of eight-pointed stars in pale pink and brown.

Kmuzu held up another cloth. "Today I found this. It's obviously
the cloth from which those rags were torn."

I examined the larger cloth, part of an old robe or sheet. There
wasn't any doubt that it was the same material. "Where'd you find
this?" I asked.

Kmuzu put the rags back in the desk drawer. "In the room of young
Saad ben Salah," he said.

"What were you doing poking around in there?" I asked with some
amusement.

Kmuzu shrugged. "Looking for evidence, *yaa Sidi*. And I believe
I've found enough to be certain of the arsonist's identity."

"The kid? Not Umm Saad herself?"

"I'm sure she directed her son to set the fire."

I wouldn't put it past her, but it didn't quite fit. "Why would she do
that, though? Her whole scheme has been to get Friedlander Bey to
admit that Saad is his grandson. She wants her son to be heir to Papa's
estate. Killing the old man off now would leave her out in the cold."

"Who can say what her reasoning was, *yaa Sidi?* Perhaps she gave
up her plan, and now she's seeking revenge."

Jeez, in that case, who knew what she'd try next? "You're keeping
an eye on her already, aren't you?" I asked.

"Yes, *yaa Sidi*."

"Well, be extra watchful." I turned to go, then faced him once
more. "Kmuzu," I said, "do the letters A.L.M. mean anything to you?"

He gave it a moment's thought. "Only the African Liberation
Movement," he said.

"Maybe," I said dubiously. "What about the Phoenix File?"

"Oh, yes, *yaa Sidi,* I heard about it when I worked in Shaykh Reda's
house."

I'd run into so many dead ends that I'd almost given up hope. I'd
begun to think the Phoenix File was something Jirji Shaknahyi had
invented, and that the meaning of the words had died with him. "Why
did Abu Adil discuss it with you?" I asked.

Kmuzu shook his head. "Abu Adil never discussed anything with
me, *yaa Sidi*. I was only a bodyguard. But bodyguards are often over-
looked or forgotten. They become like the furniture in a room. Several
times I overheard Shaykh Reda and Umar talk about whom they
wished to add to the Phoenix File."

"So what is the damn thing?" I demanded.

"A list," said Kmuzu. "A compilation of the names of everyone who works for Shaykh Reda or Friedlander Bey, either directly or indirectly. And of anyone who owes either of them a great favor."

"Like rosters," I said, puzzled. "But why should the file be so important? I'm sure the police could put together the same list anytime they wanted. Why did Jirji Shaknahyi risk his life investigating it?"

"Each person on the list has a coded entry that describes his physical condition, his tissue-matching profile, and his record of organ transplants and other modifications."

"So both Abu Adil and Papa keep up with their people's health. That's great. I didn't think they'd bother with details like that."

Kmuzu frowned. "You don't understand, *yaa Sidi*. The file is not a list of who might need to receive a transplant. It is a list of available donors."

"Available donors? But these people aren't dead, they're still—" My eyes opened wider and I just stared at him.

Kmuzu's expression let me know that my horrified realization was correct. "Everyone on the list is ranked," he said, "from the lowest underling to Umar and yourself. If a person on the list is injured or becomes ill and needs an organ transplant, Abu Adil or Friedlander Bey may choose to sacrifice someone with a lower rating. This is not always done, but the higher one's rating, the more likely it is that a suitable donor will be chosen."

"May their houses be destroyed! The sons of thieves!" I said softly. This explained the notations in Shaknahyi's notebook—the names on the left side were people who'd been prematurely relaxed to provide spare parts for people on the right side. Blanca had been too far down on the list for her own good; she'd been just another expendable slut.

"Perhaps everyone you know is listed in the Phoenix File," said Kmuzu. "You yourself, your friends, your mother. My name is there as well."

I felt fury growing in me. "Where does he keep it, Kmuzu? I'm gonna shove this file down Abu Adil's throat."

Kmuzu raised a hand. "Remember, *yaa Sidi,* that Shaykh Reda is not alone in this terrible enterprise. He cooperates with our master. They share information, and they share the lives of their associates. A heart from one of Shaykh Reda's minions may be put in the chest of Friedlander Bey's lieutenant. The two men are great competitors, but in this they are cordial partners."

"How long has this been going on?" I asked.

"For many years. The two shaykhs began it to make certain they themselves would never die for lack of compatible organs."

I slammed my fist on the desk. "That's how they've both lived to such doddering old age. They're fucking fossils!"

"And they are insane, *yaa Sidi*," said Kmuzu.

"You didn't tell me where to find it. Where is the Phoenix File?"

Kmuzu shook his head. "I don't know. Shaykh Reda keeps it hidden."

Well, I thought, I'd planned to take a ride out to that neighborhood that afternoon anyway. "Thanks, Kmuzu. You've been a lot of help."

"*Yaa Sidi*, you aren't going to confront Shaykh Reda with this, are you?" He looked very troubled.

"No, of course not," I said. "I know better than to take on both of the old men together. You just keep working on our soup kitchen. I think it's time the House of Friedlander Bey began giving back something to the poor people."

"That is good."

I left Kmuzu working at the data deck. I went back out to the car, revising my schedule for the day in light of the blockbuster that had just gone off at my feet. I drove to the Budayeen, parked the car, and started up the Street to Chiri's.

My phone rang. "*Marhaba*," I said.

"It's me, man. Morgan." I was glad I was still wearing the English daddy. "Jawarski's here, all right. He's holed up in a crummy apartment in a real slum. I'm hangin' out in the stairwell, watchin' the door. You want me to drop in on the man?"

"No," I said, "just make sure he doesn't leave. I want to know that he'll be there when I come by later. If he tries to go somewhere, though, stop him. Use your gun and back him up into the apartment. Do whatever you got to, but keep him under wraps."

"You got it, man. But don't take too long. This isn't as much fun as I thought it'd be."

I clipped the phone back on my belt and went into the club. Chiri's was pretty crowded for late afternoon. A new black girl named Mouna was on stage. I recalled suddenly that Mouna had been the name of the pet chicken in Fuad's long story. That meant he was probably adoring this girl, and that meant she was probably trouble. I'd have to keep my eyes open.

The other girls were sitting with customers, and love was in bloom all along the bar. It was fucking heartwarming.

I went down to my usual place and waited for Indihar to come over. "White Death?" she asked.

"Not right now. You thought any about what we talked about?"

"About me moving into Friedlander Bey's little cottage? If it wasn't for the kids, I wouldn't give it a second thought. I don't want to owe him nothing. I don't want to be one of Papa's little wenches."

I'd felt that way myself, not so long ago. and now that I'd learned the significance of the Phoenix File, I knew she had even more reason to distrust Papa. "You're right about that, Indihar," I said, "but I promise you that won't happen. Papa's not doing this for you; *I* am."

"Is there a difference?"

"Yes. A big one. Now, what's your answer?"

She sighed. "Okay, Marîd, but I'm not going to be one of *your* wenches, either. You know what I mean?"

"You're not going to fuck me. You already made that clear."

Indihar nodded. "Just so you understand. I'm mourning my husband. I may go on mourning him forever."

"Take as long as you need. You got a lot of life left to live, honey," I said. "Someday you'll find someone else."

"I don't even want to think about it."

It was past time to change the subject. "You can start moving in any time you want, but finish out the shift for me," I said. "This means I got to find a new daytime barmaid."

Indihar looked left and right, then leaned closer. "If I was you," she said in a low voice, "I'd hire somebody from outside. I wouldn't trust any of these girls to run this place. They'd rob you blind, especially that Brandi. And Pualani's not bright enough to put the napkin down, *then* the drink."

"What do you think I should do?"

She chewed her lip for a moment. "I'd hire Dalia away from Frenchy Benoit. That's what I'd do. Or Heidi from the Silver Palm."

"Maybe," I said. "Call me if you need anything." It was just something else I had to worry about. Right now, though, my thoughts were centered mainly on the blighted neighborhood on the western side of town. I walked back out into the late afternoon sun. It had begun to rain, and there was a good, wet smell coming from the warm sidewalks.

A few minutes later, I was back in the modshop on Fourth Street. Twice in one day was enough of Laila to last anybody a year. I overheard her discussing a module with a customer. The man needed something to let him do armadontia. That's the science of converting human teeth into high-tech weapons. Laila was still Emma: Madame Bovary, Dentist of Tomorrow.

When the customer left—yes, Laila'd found just what he was looking for—I tried to tell her what I wanted without getting into a conversation. "Got any Proxy Hell moddies?" I asked.

She'd already opened her mouth to greet me with some second-hand Flaubertian sentiment, but I'd shocked her. "You don't want that, Marîd," she said in her whiny voice.

"Not for me. It's for a friend."

"None of your friends do that, either."

I stopped myself before I grabbed her by the throat. "It's not for a friend, then. It's for a goddamn enemy."

Laila smiled. "Then you want something *really* bad, right?"

"The worst," I said.

She bustled out from behind her counter and went to the locked door in the rear of the shop. "I don't keep merchandise like that out," she explained as she dug in a pocket for her keys. Actually, they were on a long, green plastic necklace around her neck. "I don't sell Proxy Hell moddies to kids."

"Keys are around your neck."

"Oh thanks, dear." She unlocked the door and turned to look at me. "Be right back." She was gone a minute or two, and she returned with a small brown cardboard box.

There were three moddies in the box, all plain, gray plastic, all without manufacturer's labels. These were bootleg modules, dangerous to wear. Regular commercial moddies were carefully recorded or programmed, and all extraneous signals were removed. You gambled when you wore an underground moddy. Sometimes bootlegs were "rough," and when you popped them out, you found they'd caused major brain damage.

Laila had stuck handwritten labels on the moddies in the box. "How about infectious granuloma?" she asked.

I considered it for a moment, but decided that it was too much like what Abu Adil had been wearing when I'd first met him. "No," I said.

"Okay," said Laila, pushing the moddies around with her long, crooked forefinger. "Cholecystitis?"

"What's that?"

"Don't have any idea."

"What's the third one?"

Laila held it up and read the label. "D Syndrome."

I shivered. I'd heard about that. It's some kind of awful nerve degeneration, a disease caused by slow viruses. The patient first suffers gaps in both long- and short-term memories. The viruses continue to eat away at the nervous system until the patient collapses, staring and stupid, bedridden and in terrible agony. Finally, in the last stages, he dies when his body forgets how to breathe or keep its heart beating. "How much for this?" I asked.

"Fifty kiam," she said. She looked up slowly into my eyes and grinned. The few teeth she still had were black stumps, and the effect was grotesquely ugly. "You pay extra 'cause it's a hard-to-get item."

"All right," I said. I paid her and stuffed the D Syndrome moddy in my pocket. Then I tried to get out of Laila's shop.

"You know," she said, putting her clawlike hand on my arm, "my lover is taking me to the opera tonight. All of Rouen will see us together!"

I pulled myself away and hurried out the door. "In the name of Allah, the Beneficent, the Merciful," I muttered.

During the long drive out to Abu Adil's estate, I thought about recent events. If Kmuzu were right, then the fire had been started by Umm Saad's son. I didn't think that young Saad had acted on his own. Yet Umar had assured me that neither he nor Abu Adil still employed Umm Saad. He had flatly invited me to dispose of her, if I found her too irritating. Then if Umm Saad wasn't getting her orders direct from Abu Adil, why had she decided suddenly to take things into her own hands?

And Jawarski. Had he taken a few potshots at me because he didn't like my looks, or because Hajjar had let Abu Adil know that I was nosing around after the Phoenix File? Or were there even more sinister connections that I hadn't yet discovered? At this point, I didn't dare trust Saied or even Kmuzu. Morgan was the only other person who had my confidence, and I had to admit that there really wasn't any good reason to trust him, either. He just reminded me of the way I used to be, before I'd gone to work changing a corrupt system from within.

That, by the way, was my current rationalization for what I was doing, the easy life I was leading. I suppose the bitter truth was that I didn't have the guts to face Friedlander Bey's wrath, or the heart to turn my back on his money. I told myself that I was using my position deep in the pits of dishonor to help the less fortunate. It didn't really shut up my guilty conscience.

As I drove, the guilt and loneliness amounted almost to desperation, and are probably to blame for the tactical error that came next. Maybe I *should* have had more faith in Saied or Kmuzu. I could at least have brought one of the Stones That Speak with me. Instead, I was counting on my own cleverness to see me through a confrontation with Abu Adil. After all, I did have two separate plans: First, I thought I might try bribing him with the D Syndrome moddy; and second, if he didn't take to buttering up, my fallback position consisted of hitting him between the eyes with my full knowledge of what he was up to.

Well, hell, it sounded like a great idea at the time.

The guard at Abu Adil's gate recognized me and passed me through, although Kamal, the butler, demanded to know what I wanted. "I've brought a gift for Shaykh Reda," I said. "It's urgent that I talk with him."

He wouldn't let me leave the foyer. "Wait here," he said with a sneer. "I will see if it is permitted."

"The passive voice should be avoided," I said. He didn't get it.

He went all the way down to Abu Adil's office, and came all the way back with the same contemptuous look on his face. "I'm to bring you to my master," he said. It sounded like it broke his heart to accommodate me.

He led me into one of Abu Adil's offices, not the same one I'd seen on my first visit with Shaknahyi. A sweet smell, maybe incense, filled the air. There were framed prints of European art masterpieces on the walls, and I heard a recording of Umm Khalthoum playing softly.

The great man himself was sitting in a comfortable armchair, with a beautifully embroidered blanket over his legs. His head lolled back against the back of the chair, and his eyes were closed. His hands were laid flat on his knees, and they trembled.

Umar Abdul-Qawy was there, of course, and he didn't look happy to see me. He nodded to me and put one finger to his lips. I guessed this was a signal not to mention any of the things he'd discussed with me concerning his plans to unseat Abu Adil and rule the old shaykh's empire in his place. That wasn't why I was here. I had more important things to worry about than Umar's half-assed power struggle.

"I have the honor to wish Shaykh Reda good afternoon," I said.

"May Allah make the afternoon prosperous to you," said Umar.

We'll see, I thought. "I beg to present the noble shaykh with this small gift."

Umar made a small gesture, the little flick of the hand a lordly king uses to command a peasant to approach. I wanted to stuff the moddy down his fat throat. "What is it?" he asked.

I said nothing. I just gave it to him. Umar turned it over in his hand a few times. Then he looked up at me. "You are more clever than I gave you credit," he said. "My master will be greatly pleased."

"I hope he doesn't already have this module."

"No, no." He placed it on Abu Adil's lap, but the old man made no move to examine it. Umar studied me thoughtfully. "I would offer you something in return, although I'm certain you would be courteous enough to refuse."

"Try me," I said. "I'd like a little information."

Umar frowned. "Your manners—"

"They're terrible, I know, but what can I say? I'm just an ignorant beaneater from the Maghreb. Now, I seem to have uncovered all kinds of incriminating information about you and Shaykh Reda—about Friedlander Bey too, to be honest. I'm talking about this goddamn Phoenix File of yours." I waited to see Umar's reaction.

It wasn't long in coming. "I'm afraid, Monsieur Audran, that I don't know what you're talking about. I suggest that your master may be engaged in highly illegal activities, and has attempted to shift the blame—"

"Be silent." Umar and I both turned to stare at Reda Abu Adil, who had popped the Proxy Hell moddy he'd been wearing. Umar was badly shaken. This was the first time Abu Adil had seen fit to participate in a conversation. It seemed he wasn't just a senile, helpless figurehead. Without the cancer moddy chipped in, his face lost its slackness, and his eyes gained an intelligent fierceness.

Abu Adil threw off the blanket and stood up from the chair. "Hasn't Friedlander Bey explained to you about the Phoenix File?" he demanded.

"No, O Shaykh," I said. "It's something I learned of only today. He has kept the thing hidden from me."

"But you delved into matters that don't concern you." I was frightened by Abu Adil's intensity. Umar had never shown such passion or such strength of will. It was as if I were seeing Shaykh Reda's *baraka*, a different kind of personal magic than Papa's. The moddy of Abu Adil that Umar wore did not hint at the depth of the man. I supposed that no electronic device could hope to capture the nature of *baraka*. This answered Umar's claim that with the moddy he was the equal of Abu Adil. That was just self-delusion.

"I think they concern me," I said. "Isn't my name in that file?"

"Yes, I'm sure it is," said Abu Adil. "But you are placed highly enough that you stand only to benefit."

"I'm thinking of my friends, who aren't so lucky."

Umar laughed humorlessly. "You show your weakness again," he said. "Now you bleed for the dirt beneath your feet."

"Every sun has its setting," I told him. "Maybe someday you'll find yourself slipping down in the Phoenix File ratings. Then you'll wish you'd never heard of it."

"O Master," said Umar angrily, "have you not heard enough of this?"

Abu Adil raised a weary hand. "Yes, Umar. I have no great love for Friedlander Bey, and even less for his creatures. Take him into the studio."

Umar came toward me, a needle gun in his hand, and I backed away. I didn't know what he had in mind, but it wasn't going to be pleasant. "This way," he said. Under the circumstances, I did what he wanted.

We left the office and walked down a connecting hallway, then climbed a stairway to the second floor. There was always an air of peace in this house. The light was filtered through wooden lattices over high windows, and sounds were muffled by thick rugs on the floors. I knew this serenity was an illusion. I knew I'd soon see Abu Adil's true nature.

"In here," he said, opening a thick metal door. He had a strange, expectant expression on his face. I didn't like it at all.

I went past him into a large soundproofed room. There was a bed, a chair, and a cart with some electronic equipment on it. The far wall was a single sheet of glass, and beyond it was a small control booth with banks of dials and readouts and switches. I knew what it was. Reda Abu Adil had a personality module recording studio in his home. It was like the hobbyist's ultimate dream.

"Give me the gun," said Abu Adil.

Umar passed the needle gun to his master, then left the sound-proofed room. "I suppose you want to add me to your collection," I said. "I don't see why. My second-degree burns won't be all that enter-taining." Abu Adil just stared at me with that fixed grin on his face. He made my skin crawl.

A little while later, Umar returned. He had a long, thin metal rod, a pair of handcuffs, and a rope with a hook at one end. "Oh jeez," I said. I was starting to feel sick to my stomach. I was truly afraid that they wanted to record more than just that.

"Stand up straight," said Umar, walking around and around me. He reached out and removed the moddy and daddies I was wearing. "And whatever you do, don't duck your head. That's for your own good."

"Thanks for your concern," I said. "I appreciate—" Umar raised the metal rod and brought it down across my right collarbone. I felt a knife-edge of pain shoot through me, and I cried out. He hit me on the other side, across the other collarbone. I heard the abrupt snapping of bone, and I fell to my knees.

"This may hurt a little," said Abu Adil in the voice of a kindly old doctor.

Umar began beating me on the back with the rod, once, twice, three times. I screamed. He struck me a few more times. "Try to stand up," he urged.

"You're crazy," I gasped.

"If you don't stand up, I'll use this on your face."

I struggled to my feet again. My left arm hung uselessly. My back was a bleeding ruin. I realized I was breathing in shallow sobs.

Umar paused and walked around me again, evaluating me. "His legs," said Abu Adil.

"Yes, O Shaykh." The son of a bitch whipped the rod across my thighs, and I fell to the floor again. "Up," grunted Umar. "Up."

He hit me where I lay, on my thighs and calves until they were dripping with blood too. "I'll get you," I said in a voice hoarse with agony. "I swear by the blessed Prophet, I'll get you."

The beatings went on for a long time, until Umar had slowly and carefully worked over every part of me—except my head. Abu Adil had instructed him to spare my head, because he didn't want anything to interfere with the quality of the recording. When the old man decided that I'd had enough, he told Umar to stop. "Connect him," he said.

I lifted my head and watched. It was almost like being in someone else, far away. My muscles jumped in anguished spasms, and my wounds sent sharp signals of torment through every part of me. Yet the pain had become a barrier between my mind and body. I knew that I still hurt terribly, but I'd taken enough punishment to send my body into shock. I muttered curses and pleas to my two captors, threatening and begging them to give me back the pain-blocking daddy.

Umar only laughed. He went over to the cart and did something with the equipment there. Then he carried a large, shiny moddy link over to me. It looked a lot like the one we used with the Transpex game. Umar knelt beside me and showed it to me. "I'm going to chip this in for you," he said. "It will allow us to record exactly what you're feeling."

I was having a difficult time breathing. "Motherfuckers," I said, my voice a shallow wheeze.

Umar snapped the chrome-steel moddy link onto my anterior corymbic plug. "Now, this is a completely painless procedure," he said.

"You're gonna die," I muttered. "You're gonna fuckin' die."

Abu Adil was still holding the needle gun on me, but I couldn't have done anything heroic anyway. Umar knelt down and fastened my hands behind me with the handcuffs. I felt like I was going to pass out, and I kept shaking my head to stay conscious. I didn't want to black out and be completely at their mercy, though that was probably already true.

After he got my wrists bound, Umar caught the handcuffs with the hook and pulled on the rope until I staggered to my feet. Then he threw the end of the rope over a bar mounted on the wall high over my head. I saw what he was going to do. "*Yallah*," I cried. He pulled on the rope until I was hoisted up on tiptoes with my arms raised behind my back. Then he pulled some more until my feet no longer touched the floor. I was hanging from the rope, the full weight of my body slowly pulling my arms from their sockets.

It was so excruciating, I could only take panting little breaths. I tried to shut out the horrible pain; I prayed first for mercy, then for death.

"Put the moddy in now," said Abu Adil. His voice seemed to come from another world, from high on a mountaintop or far below the ocean.

"I take refuge with the Lord of the Dawn," I murmured. I kept repeating that phrase like a magic charm.

Umar stood on the chair with the gray moddy in his hand, the D Syndrome moddy I'd brought. He chipped it onto my posterior plug.

He was hanging from the ceiling, but he couldn't remember why. He was in terrible agony. "In the name of Allah, help me!" he cried. He realized that shouting just made the pain worse. Why was he here? He couldn't remember. Who had done this to him?

He couldn't remember. He couldn't remember anything.

Time went by, and he might have been unconscious. He had the same feeling one has on waking from a particularly vivid dream, when the waking world and the dream are superimposed for a moment, when aspects of one distort images of the other, and one must make an effort to sort them and decide which shall have precedence.

How could he explain being alone and bound like this? He wasn't afraid of the hurting, but he was afraid he wasn't equal to the task of understanding his situation. There was the low hum of a fan above his head, and a faint spicy smell in the air. His body twisted a little on the rope, and he felt another slash of pain. He was bothered more by the notion that he appeared to be involved in a terrible drama and had no sense at all of its significance.

"Praise be to Allah, Lord of the Worlds," he whispered, "the Beneficent, the Merciful. Owner of the Day of Judgment. Thee alone we worship. Thee alone we ask for help."

Time passed. The suffering grew. Finally, he did not remember enough even to wince or writhe. Sights and sounds played through his numbed senses upon his drowsing mind. He was beyond evaluating or reacting, but he was not yet quite dead. Someone spoke to him, but he did not respond.

"How's that?"

Let me tell you, it was horrible. All of a sudden, understanding poured back into my consciousness. Every bit of pain that had been held at bay suddenly returned with a vengeance. I must have whimpered, because he kept saying "It's all right, it's all right."

I looked up. It was Saied. "Hey," I said. It was all I could manage.

"It's all right," he told me again. I didn't know if I should believe him. He looked pretty worried.

I was lying in an alley between some rundown, abandoned tenement buildings. I didn't know how I'd gotten there. At the moment, I didn't care.

"These yours?" he said. He was folding a small handful of daddies and three moddies.

One of them was Rex and one was the gray D Syndrome moddy. I almost wept when I recognized the pain-blocker daddy. "Gimme," I said. My hands shook as I reached up and chipped it in. Almost instantly I felt great again, although I knew I still had terrible lacerations and at least a broken collarbone. The daddy worked faster than even a ton of Sonneine. "You got to tell me what you're doing here," I said. I sat up, filled with the illusion of health and well-being.

"I came after you. Wanted to make sure you didn't get into any trouble or anything. The guard at the gate knows me, and so does Kamal. I went into the house and saw what they were doing to you, then I waited till they dragged you out. They must've thought you were dead, or else they don't care if you recover or not. I grabbed up the hardware and followed. They dumped you in this stinking alley, and I hid around the corner till they left."

I put my hand on his shoulders. "Thanks," I said.

"Hey," said the Half-Hajj with a loopy grin, "no thanks are needed. Muslim brothers and all that, right?"

I didn't want to argue with him. I picked up the third moddy he'd found. "What's this?" I asked.

"You don't know? It's not one of yours?"

I shook my head. Saied took the moddy from me, reached up, and chipped it in. A moment later his expression changed. He looked awed. "May my father's balls burn in Hell!" he said. "It's Abu Adil."

Seventeen

The half-hajj insisted on going with me to find the building where Paul Jawarski was hiding out. "You're a wreck," he told me, shaking his head. "You pop that daddy, you'll realize what bad shape you're in. You should go to the hospital."

"I just got out of the hospital," I said.

"Well, obviously it didn't take. You got to go back again."

"Fine, I'll go when this business with Jawarski's all over. I'll keep the daddy in till then. And I'll probably need Rex."

Saied squinted at me. "You need a lot more than Rex. You need half a dozen of your cop buddies."

I laughed bitterly. "I don't think they'd show up. I don't think Hajjar would even send them."

We were making our way slowly along Hâmidiyya's main north-south avenue. "What do you mean?" asked Saied. "You think Hajjar wants to pull off Jawarski's capture himself? Get himself a commendation and a medal?"

We turned down a narrow trash-choked alley and found the rear of the building we were looking for. "Shaknahyi had the idea that he'd been set up," I said. "He thought maybe Jawarski was working for Hajjar."

"I thought Jawarski was working for Shaykh Reda."

I shrugged. Without the pain-blocker, that would have been excruciatingly painful. "Everybody we know moonlights. Why should Jawarski be any different?"

"No reason, I guess," said the Half-Hajj. "Now, you want me to go in with you?"

"No thanks, Saied. I want you to stay down here and guard this back entrance. I'm going upstairs and talk with Morgan. I want to be alone with Jawarski. I'm gonna send Morgan down to watch the front."

Saied looked worried. "I don't think that's smart, Maghrebi. Jawarski's a clever guy, and he don't mind killing people. You're not in any condition to wrestle with him."

"I won't have to." I reached up and chipped in Rex. I took my static pistol out of my pocket.

"Well, what you gonna do? If Hajjar's just gonna let Jawarski go free—"

"I'm going over Hajjar's head," I said. I was determined that Jawarski wasn't going to escape justice. "I'm gonna call the captain and the police superintendent and the news media. They can't all be crooked."

"I don't see why not," said the Half-Hajj. "But you're probably right. Remember, we'll be right down here if you need help. Jawarski won't get away this time."

I grinned at him. "Bet your ass he won't." I moved past him into the tenement building. I was in a cool, dark hallway that led to a flight of stairs. There was the usual dank, musty smell of an abandoned building. My feet scattered bits of rubble as I climbed up to the third floor. "Morgan?" I called. He probably had a gun in his hand, and I didn't want to surprise him.

"Is that you, man? You sure took long enough getting here."

I arrived at the landing where he was sitting. "Sorry," I said, "I ran into a little trouble."

His eyes got big when he saw how torn and hurt I was. "Looks like you already ran into as much as you can handle today, man."

"I'm fine, Morgan." I took five hundred kiam out of my jeans and paid him the rest of his money. "Now, go keep an eye on the street entrance. I'll call if I need help."

The blond American started downstairs. "You need help," he said dubiously, "it'll be too late by the time you shout."

The daddy had me feeling no pain, and Rex made me think I was equal to any challenge Jawarski might present. I checked the charge in my static pistol, then rapped on the apartment door. "Jawarski," I shouted, "this is Marîd Audran. Jirji Shaknahyi was my partner. I'm here to take you in for his murder."

I didn't have to wait long. Jawarski opened the door, laughing. He was holding a black .45 caliber automatic pistol. "*Stupid* son of a bitch, ain't you?" he said. He stood back so I could get by.

I made sure he saw my weapon as I went past him, but he was so sure of himself that he didn't act the least bit concerned. I sat down on a torn couch opposite the door. Jawarski dropped into an armchair covered in bloodstained floral material. I was shocked by how young he was. I was surprised to see that he was at least five years younger than me.

"Ever hear what Islamic law does to murderers?" I asked him. We were holding our guns on each other, but Jawarski seemed almost nonchalant.

"Nah, it don't make much difference," he said. "I don't care if I die." Jawarski had a peculiar way of talking out of one side of his mouth, as if he thought it made him look tough and fierce. He obviously had some serious psychological problems, but he wasn't going to live long enough to clear them up. "So who told you I was here? I always bumped off squealers. Tell me who it was, so I can fog the bastard."

"You won't get the chance, pal. You can't have the whole city bought off."

"Let's make this quick," he said, trying to upset me. "I'm supposed to collect my money and leave town tonight." He didn't seem to be bothered at all by my static pistol.

He was staring to my right. I let my eyes drift in that direction, toward a small wooden table not far from the couch, covered with newspaper. There were three clips of ammunition lying there. "Was it Hajjar who told you to kill Shaknahyi?" I asked. "Or Umar, Abu Adil's punk?"

"I ain't a squawker," he said. He gave me a twisted grin.

"And the others—Blanca Mataro, the rest of them. You didn't use that .45. How come?"

Jawarski shrugged. "They told me not to. They didn't want any of the parts damaged, I guess. They told me who to put away and I done it with a little static gun. I always called in the tip to the cops myself, so the cripple cart'd get there fast. I guess they didn't want the meat to spoil." He gave a grunting chuckle that set my teeth on edge.

I glanced at the table, thinking that Jawarski might not have bothered to put a clip into his pistol before he let me into the room. He looked like he enjoyed bluffing. "How many have you killed?" I asked.

"You mean altogether?" Jawarski looked up at the ceiling. "Oh, I've got twenty-six anyway. That's all I ever kept track of. Pretty near one for every year. And my birthday's comin' up soon. How'd you like to be number twenty-seven?"

I felt a rush of fury. "You're real close, Jawarski," I said through clenched teeth.

"Go ahead, you got a girl's gun, lay me out if you got the guts." He was enjoying this, mocking me and goading me. "Look, here's a clipping," he said. " 'Jawarski Bad Man, Legendary Figure,' it says. How 'bout that?"

"Ever think about the people you shoot?" I asked.

"I remember that cop. I turned and let him have it in the chest. He didn't even wobble, but he shot back at me. I wasn't hit, though, and I beat it around behind the house. When I got to the other side, I peeked around the corner and saw the cop I shot coming after me. I let fly at him again, and ran behind another house. When I looked again he was still following me. There was blood running all over the front of his coat then, but he was still following me. God, that guy was a real man."

"Ever think about his family? Shaknahyi had a wife, you know. He had three kids."

Jawarski stared at me, and another crazy grin spread slowly across his face. "Fuck 'em," he said.

I stood up and took three steps. Jawarski raised his eyebrows at me, inviting me to come closer. As he stood, I tossed him the static gun. He fumbled it against his chest with his left hand, and I pulled my fist back and cracked him in the corner of his mouth. Then I grabbed his right wrist tightly and turned outward, prepared to break the bones if I had to. He grunted and dropped the automatic. "I'm not Hajjar," I snarled. "I'm not that goddamn Catavina. You're not gonna buy me off, and right now I'm in no mood to worry about protecting your civil rights. Understand?" I bent and scooped up his gun. I'd been wrong. It *was* loaded.

Jawarski put a hand to his lips. When he pulled it away, his fingers were bloody. "You been watching those holoshows again, buddy," he said. He grinned, still not terribly worried. "You're no better'n Hajjar. You're no better'n me, you want to know the truth. You'd put a round right through me, if you thought you could get away with it."

"You're right about that," I said.

"But you think there's too many like Hajjar already. And it ain't even that Hajjar's a rotten cop. He ain't. He's just acting the way they all act, the way everybody expects him to act, the way he's *supposed* to act. It ain't wrong if everybody knows about it ahead of time. I'll tell you a secret: You're gonna end up just like Shaknahyi. You're gonna help little old ladies across the street until you're old enough to retire, and then some young son of a bitch like me is gonna plant you in the ground." He reached his little finger into his ear and jiggled it a few times. "And then," he said thoughtfully, "after you're gone, the young son of a bitch is gonna jam your wife."

My face felt hard and tense, frozen into a cold stare. I raised the pistol calmly and held it steadily, pointed between Jawarski's eyes. "Watch it," he said scornfully. "That ain't a toy."

I grabbed back the static pistol and put it in my pocket. I motioned for Jawarski to sit down, and I returned to my seat on the couch. We looked at each other for a few seconds. I was breathing hard; Jawarski looked like he was enjoying himself.

"I'll bet you're doing everything you can to comfort Shaknahyi's widow," he said. "You jammed her yet?"

I felt rage and frustration growing in me again. I hated hearing his lies, his justifications for crime and corruption. The worst part was that he was telling me Shaknahyi had died stupidly, for no good reason. I wasn't going to let him say that. "Shut up," I said in a strained voice. I found myself waving the automatic pistol at Jawarski.

"See? You can't shoot. It'd be smart to shoot. I'll get away clean otherwise, 'cause no matter who locks me up, I'll be sprung. Shaykh Reda will make sure I get sprung. I'll never be brought to trial in this town."

"No, you wouldn't be," I said, knowing it was probably true. I fired once. The explosion was tremendous, and the booming crack rumbled on forever, like thunder. Jawarski fell backward in slow motion, half of his face blasted away. There was blood everywhere. I dropped the pistol to the floor. I'd never shot anyone with a projectile weapon before. I backed away and fell against the couch, unable to catch my breath.

When I'd come through the door, I hadn't planned to kill this man, but I had done it. It had been a conscious decision. I had taken the responsibility for seeing justice done, because I'd become certain it would be done no other way. I looked at the blood on my hands and arms.

The door crashed loudly into the room. Morgan ran in first, followed by Saied. They stopped just inside the threshold and took in the scene. "Aw right," said the Half-Hajj quietly. "That's one loose end tied up tight."

"Listen, man," said Morgan, "I got to go. You don't need me for anything more, do you?"

I just stared at them. I wondered why they weren't horrified too.

"Let's go, man," said Morgan. "Somebody might've heard that."

"Oh, somebody heard it, all right," Saied said. "But in this neighborhood, nobody's dumb enough to check on it."

I reached up and popped the tough-guy moddy. I'd had enough of Rex for a while. We left the apartment and went down the stairs. Morgan turned one way on the sidewalk, and the Half-Hajj and I turned the other.

"What now?" asked Saied.

"We got to go get the car," I said. I didn't like the idea at all. The sedan was still back at Abu Adil's. I really didn't feel like going back there so soon after the bastard mind-raped me. I *was* going back there; I had that score to settle. But not just yet, not just now.

Saied must have guessed my feelings from the tone of my voice. "Tell you what," he said. "I'll go get the car, you sit here and wait. Won't take long."

"Fine," I said, and I gave him the keys. I was immensely grateful that he'd come looking for me, and that I could count on him for help. I had no trouble trusting him again. That was good, because even with the pain-override daddy chipped in, my body was near collapse. I needed to get to a doctor soon.

I didn't want to sit down on a step, because I thought I'd have a hard time standing again. Instead, I leaned against the white stucco front of a small, tottery house. Overhead, I heard the shrill peenting cries of nighhawks as they swooped over the rooftops hunting for insects. I stared across the street at another apartment building, and I saw wild, healthy ferns growing from horizontal surfaces up and down the wall, weeds that had found favorable conditions in the most unlikely place. Cooking smells drifted from open windows: cabbage boiling, meat roasting, bread baking.

I was immersed in life here, yet I could not forget that I'd shed a murderer's blood. I was still holding the automatic pistol. I didn't know how I was going to dispose of it. My mind wasn't thinking clearly.

After a while, I saw the cream-colored sedan stop beside me at the curb. Saied got out and helped me around to the passenger side. I slid into the seat, and he closed the door. "Where to?" he asked.

"Goddamn hospital," I said.

"Good idea."

I closed my eyes and felt the car thrumming through the streets. I dozed a little. Saied woke me when we got there. I shoved my static pistol and the .45 under the seat, and we got out of the car.

"Listen," I said, "I'm just going into the emergency room and get patched up. After that, I got a few people to see. Why don't you get going?"

The Half-Hajj's brows narrowed. "What's the matter? Still don't trust me?"

I shook my head. "It's not that, Saied. I've gotten over all that. It's just sometimes I work better without an audience, okay?"

"Sure. A busted collarbone ain't enough for you. You won't be happy till we got to bury you in five separate containers."

"Saied."

He raised both hands. "All right, all right. You want to storm back in on Shaykh Reda and Himmar, that's your business."

"I'm not gonna face them again," I said. "I mean, not yet."

"Uh yeah, well, let me know when you do."

"You bet," I said. I gave him twenty kiam. "You can get a cab here, can't you?"

"Uh huh. Give me a call later." He gave me back the keys to my car.

I nodded and went up the curving drive to the emergency room entrance. Saied had brought me to the same hospital I'd been in twice before. I was beginning to feel comfortable there.

I filled out their damn forms and waited half an hour until one of the residents could see me. He pumped something under the skin of my shoulder with a perfusor, then went about manipulating the broken bones. "This is probably gonna hurt," he said.

Well, he didn't know that I had software chipped in that took care of that. I was probably the only person in the world who had that add-on, but I wasn't a well-known celebrity. I made some appropriate grunts and grimaces, but on the whole I acted brave. He immobilized my left arm with a kind of superstiff shrinkwrap. "You're handling this real well," he said.

"I've had esoteric training," I said. "The control of pain is all in the mind." That was true enough; it was plugged into the mind on the end of a long, plastic-sheathed silver wire.

"Whatever," said the doctor. When he finished with my collarbone, he treated the cuts and scrapes. Then he scribbled something on a prescription pad. "Still, I'm gonna give you this for pain. You may find that you need it. If you don't, great." He ripped the page loose and handed it to me.

I glanced at it. He'd written me for twenty Nofeqs, painkillers so feeble that in the Budayeen you couldn't trade ten of them for a single Sonneine. "Thanks," I said bluntly.

"No sense being a hero and toughing it out when medical science is there to help." He glanced around and decided that he was finished with me. "You'll be all right in about six weeks, Mr. Audran. I advise you to see your own physician in a few days."

"Thanks," I said again. He gave me some papers and I took them to a window and paid cash. Then I went out into the main lobby of the hospital and took the elevator up to the twentieth floor. There was a different nurse on duty, but Zain, the security guard, recognized me. I went down the hall to Suite One.

A doctor and a nurse stood beside Papa's bed. They turned to look at me as I came in, their faces grim. "Is something wrong?" I asked, frightened.

The doctor rubbed his gray beard with one hand. "He's in serious trouble," he said.

"What the hell happened?" I demanded.

"He'd been complaining of weakness, headaches, and abdominal pain. For a long while we couldn't find anything to explain it."

"Yes," I said, "he'd been getting ill at home, before the fire. He was too sick to escape by himself."

"We ran more sensitive tests," said the doctor, "and finally something turned up positive. He's been given a rather sophisticated neurotoxin, apparently over a period of weeks."

I felt cold. Someone had been poisoning Friedlander Bey, probably someone in the house. He certainly had enough enemies, and my recent experience with the Half-Hajj proved that I couldn't dismiss anyone as a suspect. Then, suddenly, my eyes fell on something resting on Papa's tray table. It was a round metal tin, its cover lying beside it. In the tin was a layer of dates stuffed with nutmeats and rolled in sugar.

"Umm Saad," I murmured. She'd been feeding those dates to him since she'd come to live in his house. I went to the tray table. "If you analyze these," I told the doctor, "I'll bet you'll find the source."

"But who—"

"Don't worry about who," I said. "Just make him well." This was all because I'd been so caught up in my own vendetta against Jawarski that I hadn't given proper attention to Umm Saad. As I headed for the door I thought, didn't Augustus Caesar's wife poison him with figs from his own tree, to get rid of him so her son could be emperor? I excused myself for overlooking the similarity before; there's so goddamn much history, it just can't help repeating itself.

I went down and bailed my car out of the parking lot, then drove to the station house. I had myself completely under control by the time the elevator brought me up to the third floor. I headed toward Hajjar's office; Sergeant Catavina tried to stop me, but I just shoved him up against a painted plasterboard wall and kept walking. I flung open Hajjar's door. "Hajjar," I said. All the anger and disgust I felt toward him were in those two syllables.

He glanced up from some paperwork. His expression turned fearful when he saw the look on my face. "Audran," he said. "What is it?"

I lofted the .45 onto his desk in front of him. "Remember that American we were looking for? The guy who killed Jirji? Well, they found him lying on the floor of some rattrap. Somebody shot him with his own gun."

Hajjar stared unhappily at the automatic. "Somebody shot him, huh? Any idea who?"

"Unfortunately, no." I gave him an evil grin. "I don't have a microscope or nothing, but it looks to me like whoever did it also wiped his fingerprints right off the weapon. We may never solve this murder, either."

Hajjar sat back in his reclining chair. "Probably not. Well, at least the citizens will be glad to hear that Jawarski's been neutralized. Good police work, Audran."

"Yeah," I said. "Sure." I turned to leave, and I got as far as the door. Then I faced him again. "That's one down, know what I mean? And two to go."

"The hell you talking about?"

"I mean Umm Saad and Abu Adil are next. And something else: I know who you are and I know what you're doing. Watch your ass. The guy who blew Jawarski away is out there, and he may have you in his sights next." I had the pleasure of seeing Hajjar's superior grin vanish. When I left his office, he was muttering to himself and reaching for his phone.

Catavina was waiting in the corridor by the elevator. "What'd you say?" he asked worriedly. "What'd you tell him?"

"Don't worry, Sarge," I said, "your afternoon nap is safe, at least for a while. But I wouldn't be surprised if suddenly there's a call to reform the police department. You might have to start acting like a real cop for a change." I pushed the button for the elevator. "And lose some weight while you're at it."

My mood was a little better as I rode back down to the ground floor. When I walked back into the early evening sunlight, I felt almost normal.

Almost. I was still a prisoner of my own guilt. I'd planned to go home and find out more details about Kmuzu's relationship to Abu Adil, but I found myself heading in the other direction. When I heard the evening call to prayer, I left the car on Souk el-Khemis Street. There was a small mosque there, and I paused in the courtyard to remove my shoes and make the ablution. Then I went into the mosque and prayed. It was the first time I'd done that seriously in years.

Joining in worship with the others who came to this neighborhood mosque didn't cleanse me of my doubts and bad feelings. I hadn't expected that they would. I did feel a warmth, however, a sense of belonging that had been missing from my life since childhood. For the first time since coming to the city, I could approach Allah in all humility, and with sincere repentance my prayers might be accepted.

After the prayer service, I spoke with an elder of the mosque. We talked for some time, and he told me that I had been right to come and pray. I was grateful that he didn't lecture me, that he made me comfortable and welcome.

"There is one more thing, O Respected One," I said.

"Yes?"

"Today I killed a man."

He did not seem terribly shocked. He stroked his long beard for several seconds. "Tell me why you did this," he said at last.

I told him everything I knew about Jawarski, about his record of violent crimes before he'd come to the city, about his shooting of Shaknahyi. "He was a bad man," I said, "but, even so, I feel like a criminal myself."

The elder put one hand on my shoulder. "In the Sûrah of The Cow," he said, "it is written that retaliation is prescribed in the matter of murder. What you did is no crime in the eyes of Allah, all praise to Him."

I looked deeply into the old man's eyes. He wasn't merely trying to make me feel better. He wasn't just putting my conscience at ease. He was reciting the law as the Messenger of God had revealed it. I knew the passage of the Qur'ân he'd mentioned, but I needed to hear it from someone whose authority I respected. I felt wholly absolved. I almost wept with gratitude.

I left the mosque in a strange mixture of moods: I was filled with unrequited rage toward Abu Adil and Umm Saad, but at the same time I felt a well-being and gladness I could not describe. I decided to make another stop before I went home.

Chiri was taking over the night shift when I came into the club. I sat on my usual stool at the bend of the bar. "White Death?" she asked.

"No," I said, "I can't stay long. Chiri, you got any Sonneine?"

She stared at me for a few seconds. "I don't think so. How'd you hurt your arm?"

"Any Paxium then? Or beauties?"

She rested her chin in her hand. "Honey, I thought you'd sworn off drugs. I thought you were being clean from now on."

"Aw hell, Chiri," I said, "don't give me a hard time."

She just reached under the counter and came up with her little black pillcase. "Take what you want, Marîd," she said. "I guess you know what you're doing."

"I sure do," I said, and I helped myself to half a dozen caps and tabs. I got some water and swallowed them, and I didn't even pay much attention to what they were.

Eighteen

I didn't do anything strenuous for a week or so, but my mind raced like a frantic greyhound. I plotted revenge against Abu Adil and Umar a hundred different ways: I scalded their flesh in boiling vats of noxious fluids; I let loose hideous plague organisms that would make their Proxy Hell moddies seem like summer colds; I hired teams of sadistic ninjas to creep into the great house and slaughter them slowly with subtle knife wounds. In the meantime, my body began to recover its strength, although all the superluminal brain augmentation in the world couldn't speed up the knitting of broken bones.

The delay was almost more than I could stand, but I had a wonderful nurse. Yasmin had taken pity on me. Saied had been responsible for distributing the story of my heroics. Now everyone in the Budayeen knew how I'd faced down Jawarski single-handed. They'd also heard that he'd been so shamed by my moral example that he embraced Islam on the spot, and that while we prayed together Abu Adil and Umar tried to tiptoe in and kill me, but Jawarski leaped between us and died saving the life of his new Muslim brother.

Then there was the sequel, in which Umar and Abu Adil captured me and took me back to their evil castle, where they tortured me, mind-raped me, and forced me to sign blank checks and deceptive home repairs contracts until Saied the Half-Hajj burst in to my rescue. What the hell. I didn't see that embellishing the facts a little hurt him or me.

In any event, Yasmin was so attentive and solicitous, I think Kmuzu was a little jealous. I didn't see why. Many of the attentions I received from Yasmin weren't in Kmuzu's job description at all. I awoke one morning to find her straddling me, rubbing my chest. She didn't have a stitch of clothing on.

"Well," I said sleepily, "in the hospital, the nurses rarely take their uniforms off."

"They've had more training," said Yasmin. "I'm a beginner at this, I'm still not entirely sure what I'm doing."

"You know what you're doing, all right," I said. Her massaging moved slowly south. I was waking up fast.

"Now, you're not supposed to do anything too strenuous, so let me do all the work."

"Fine," I said. I looked up at her and remembered how much I loved her. I also remembered how crazy she could make me in bed. Before I got completely carried away, I said, "What if Kmuzu comes in?"

"He's gone to church. Besides," she said wickedly, "even Christians must learn about sex sooner or later. Otherwise, where do new Christians come from?"

"Missionaries convert them from people who are minding their own business," I said.

But Yasmin really didn't intend to get into a religious discussion. She raised up and slid herself down on top of me. She let out a happy sigh. "It's been a long time," she said.

"Yeah," I said. It was all I could think to say; my concentration was elsewhere.

"When my hair gets long again, I'll be able to tickle you with it like I used to."

"You know," I said, beginning to breathe heavily, "I've always had this fantasy—"

Yasmin's eyes opened wide. "Not with my hair, you won't!" she said. Well, we all have our inhibitions. I just didn't think I'd ever suggest anything kinky enough to shock Yasmin.

I'm not going to claim that we jammed all morning until we heard Kmuzu enter the living room. First of all, I hadn't jammed anyone at all in weeks; second, being together again made both of us frantic. It was a short bout, but very intense. Afterward, we held each other and didn't say anything for a while. I could have fallen back to sleep, but Yasmin doesn't like that.

"You ever wish I was a tall, willowy, blond woman?" she asked.

"I've never gotten along very well with real women."

"You like Indihar, I know you do. I've seen you looking at her."

"You're crazy. She's just not as bad as the other girls."

I felt Yasmin shrug. "But do you ever wish I was tall and blond?"

"You could've been. When you were still a boy, you could've asked the surgeons for that."

She buried her face against my neck. "They told me I didn't have the skeleton," she said, her voice muffled.

"I think you're perfect just the way you are." I waited a beat. "Except you've got the biggest feet I've ever seen in my life."

Yasmin sat up quickly. She wasn't amused. "You want your other collarbone broken, *baheem?*"

It took me half an hour and a long hot shower together to restore peace. I got dressed and watched Yasmin get herself ready to go out. For once, she wasn't running late. She didn't have to go to work until eight o'clock that evening. "Coming by the club later?" she asked, looking at my reflection in the mirror over my dresser.

"Sure," I said. "I've got to make my presence felt, or all you employees will get the idea I'm running a resort."

Yasmin grinned. "You ain't running nothing, honey," she said. "Chiri runs that club, like she always has."

"I know." I'd come to enjoy owning the place. I'd originally planned to turn the club back to Chiri as soon as possible, but now I'd decided to hang on to it for a while. It made me feel great to get special treatment from Brandi, Kandy, Pualani and the others. I liked being Mr. Boss.

After Yasmin left, I went to my desk and sat down. My original apartment had been repaired and painted, and I was living again on the second floor of the west wing. Staying just down the hall from my mother had been nerve-wracking, even for only a few days, even after our surprise reconciliation. I felt recovered enough to turn my attention back to the unfinished business of Umm Saad and Abu Adil.

When I finally decided that I couldn't put it off any longer, I picked up the tan-colored moddy, the recording of Abu Adil. "*Bismillah,*" I murmured, and then hesitantly I reached up and chipped it in.

Madness, by the life of the Prophet!

Audran felt as if he were peering through a narrow tunnel, seeing the world with Abu Adil's mean, self-centered outlook. Things were only good for Abu Adil or bad for Abu Adil; if they were neither, they did not exist.

The next thing Audran noticed was that he was in a state of sexual arousal. Of course; Abu Adil's only sexual pleasure came from jamming himself, or a facsimile of himself. That's what Umar was—a frame on which to hang this electronic duplicate. And Umar was too stupid to realize that's all he was, that he had no other qualifications that made him valuable. When he displeased Abu Adil, or began to bore

him, Umar would be replaced immediately, as so many others had been
disposed of over the years.

What about the Phoenix File? What did A.L.M. mean?

Of course, the memory was right there . . . Alif. Lâm. Mîm.

They weren't initials at all. They weren't some unknown acronym.
They came from the Qur'ân. Many of the sûrahs in the Qur'ân began
with letters of the alphabet. No one knew what they meant. Indications
of some mystical phrase, perhaps, or the initials of a scribe. Their significance had been lost through the centuries.

There was more than one sûrah that began with Alif. Lâm, Mîm,
but Audran knew immediately which one was special. It was Sûrah
Thirty, called The Romans; the important line read "Allah is He Who
created you and then sustained you, then causeth you to die, then
giveth life to you again." It was obvious that, just like Friedlander Bey,
Shaykh Reda also pictured his own face when he spoke the name of
God.

And suddenly Audran knew that the Phoenix File, with its lists of
unsuspecting people who might be murdered for organs, was recorded
on a cobalt-alloy memory plate hidden in Abu Adil's private bedroom.

And other things became clear to Audran as well. When he thought
of Umm Saad, Abu Adil's memory related that she was not, in fact, any
relation to Friedlander Bey, but that she had agreed to spy on him.
Umm Saad's reward would be the removal of her name and that of her
son from the Phoenix File. She would never have to worry that someday someone she did not even know might have greater need of her
heart or her liver or her lungs.

Audran learned that it had been Umm Saad who'd hired Paul
Jawarski, and Abu Adil had extended his protection to the American
killer. Umm Saad had brought Jawarski to the city and passed along
the assignments from Shaykh Reda to kill certain people listed on the
Phoenix File. Umm Saad was partly responsible for those deaths, and
for the fire and the poisoning of Friedlander Bey.

Audran was sickened, and the horrible, floating feeling of insanity
was threatening to overwhelm him. He reached up and grabbed the
moddy and pulled it free.

Yipe. That was the first time I'd ever used a moddy recorded from
a living person. It had been a disgusting experience. It had been like
being immersed in slime, except that you could wash slime away; having your mind fouled was more intimate and more terrible. From now
on, I promised myself, I'd stick with fictional characters and moddy
constructs.

Abu Adil was even more brainsick than I'd imagined. Still, I'd learned a few things—or, at least, my suspicions had been confirmed. Surprisingly, I could understand Umm Saad's motivations. If I'd known about the Phoenix File, I'd have done anything to get my name off it too.

I wanted to talk some of this over with Kmuzu, but he wasn't back from his Sabbath service yet. I thought I'd see if my mother had anything more to tell me.

I crossed the courtyard to the east wing. There was a little pause when I knocked on her door. "Coming," she called. I heard glass clinking, then the sound of a drawer opening and shutting. "Coming." When she opened the door to me, I could smell the Irish whiskey. She'd been very circumspect during her stay in Papa's house. I'm sure she drank and took drugs as much as ever, but at least she had the self-control not to parade herself around when she was smashed.

"Peace be on you, O Mother," I said.

"And on you be peace," she said. She leaned against the door a little unsteadily. "Do you want to come in, O Shaykh?"

"Yes, I need to talk to you." I waited until she'd opened the door wider and stepped back. I came in and took a seat on the couch. She faced me in a comfortable armchair.

"I'm sorry," she said, "I got nothin' to offer you."

"Uh yeah, that's okay." She looked well. She had abandoned the outlandish makeup and clothing, and now she rather resembled my former mental image of her: Her hair was brushed, she was suitably dressed, and she was modestly seated with her hands folded in her lap. I recalled Kmuzu's comment that I judged my mother more harshly than I judged myself, and forgave her the drunkenness. She wasn't hurting anybody.

"O Mother," I said, "you said that when you came back to the city, you made the mistake of trusting Abu Adil again. I know that it was my friend Saied who brought you here."

"You know that?" she said. She seemed wary.

"And I know about the Phoenix File. Now, why were you willing to spy on Friedlander Bey?"

Her expression was amazed. "Hey," she said, "if somebody offered to cross you off that goddamn list, wouldn't you do just about anything? I mean, hell, I told myself I wouldn't give Abu Adil nothin' he could really use against Papa. I didn't think I was hurtin' nobody."

That's just what I'd hoped to hear. Abu Adil had squeezed Umm Saad and my mother in the same vise. Umm Saad had responded by trying to kill everyone in our house. My mother had reacted differently; she'd fled to Friedlander Bey's protection.

I pretended that the matter wasn't important enough to discuss further. "You also said that you wished to do something useful with your life. You still feel that way?"

"Sure, I suppose," she said suspiciously. She looked uncomfortable, as if she were waiting for me to condemn her to some horrible fate of civic consciousness.

"I've put away some money," I said, "and I've given Kmuzu the job of starting up a kind of charity kitchen in the Budayeen. I was wondering if you'd like to help with the project."

"Oh sure," she said, frowning, "whatever you want." She couldn't have been less enthusiastic if I'd asked her to cut out her own tongue.

"What's wrong?" I asked.

I was startled to see tears slipping down her pale cheek. "You know, I didn't think I'd come to this. I'm still good lookin', ain't I? I mean, your father thought I was beautiful. He used to tell me that all the time, and that wasn't so long ago. I think if I had some decent clothes—not that stuff I brought with me from Algiers—I could still turn a few heads. No reason I got to be lonely the rest of my life, is there?"

I didn't want to get into that. "You're still attractive, Mother."

"You bet your ass," she said, smiling again. "I'm gonna get me a short skirt and some boots. Don't look at me that way, I mean a *tasteful* short skirt. Fifty-seven years old ain't so bad these days. Look at Papa."

Yeah, well, Papa was lying helpless in a hospital bed, too weak to pull his own sheet up under his chin.

"And you know what I want?" she asked with a dreamy expression.

I was afraid to ask. "No, what?"

"I saw this picture of Umm Khalthoum in the souk. Made out of thousands of flat-head nails. This guy pounded 'em all into this big board, then painted each nail head a different color. You can't see what it is close up, but when you step back, it's this gorgeous picture of The Lady."

"Yeah, you right," I said. I could just see it hanging on the wall over Friedlander Bey's expensive and tasteful furniture.

"Well, hell, I got some money put away too." I must have looked surprised, because she said, "I got some secrets of my own, you know. I been around, I seen things. I got my own friends and I got my own cash. So don't think you can order my life for me just 'cause you set me up here. I can pick up and leave anytime I want."

"Mother," I said, "I really don't want to tell you how to act or what to do. I just thought you might like helping out in the Budayeen. There's a lot of people there as poor as we used to be."

She wasn't listening closely. "We used to be poor, Marîd," she said, drifting off to a fantasy recollection of what those times had been like, "but we was always happy. Those were the *good* days." Then her expression turned sad, and she looked at me again. "And look at me now."

"Got to go," I said. I stood up and headed for the door. "May your vigor continue, O Mother. By your leave."

"Go in peace," she said, coming with me to the door. "Remember what I told you."

I didn't know what she meant. Even under the best conditions, conversations with my mother were filled with little information and much static. With her, it was always one step forward and two steps back. I was glad to see that she didn't seem to have any thoughts of returning to Algiers, or going into her old line of work here. At least, that's what I thought she'd meant. She'd said something about "turning some heads," but I hoped she meant purely in a noncommercial way. I thought about these things as I went back to my suite in the west wing.

Kmuzu had returned, and was gathering up our dirty laundry. "A call came for you, *Yaa Sidi,*" he said.

"Here?" I wondered why it hadn't come on my personal line, on the phone I wore on my belt.

"Yes. There was no message, but you are supposed to call Mahmoud. I left the number on your desk."

This could be good news. I'd planned to tackle the second of my three targets next—Umm Saad; but she might have to wait. I went to the desk and spoke Mahmoud's commcode into the phone. He answered immediately. "*Allô,*" he said.

"Where y'at, Mahmoud. It's Marîd."

"Good. I have some business to discuss with you."

"Let me get comfortable." I pulled out a chair and sat down. I couldn't help a grin from spreading over my face. "Okay, what you got?"

There was a slight pause. "As you know, I was greatly saddened by the death of Jirji Shaknahyi, may the blessings of Allah be on him."

I knew nothing of the kind. If I hadn't known Indihar was married, I doubted if Mahmoud or Jacques or anybody else knew either. Maybe Chiriga. Chiri always knew these things. "It was a tragedy to the entire city," I said. I was staying noncommittal.

"It was a tragedy to our Indihar. She must be helpless with grief. And to have no money now, that must make her situation even harder. I'm sorry that I suggested she work for me. That was callous. I spoke quickly before I considered what I was saying."

"Indihar is a devout Muslim," I said coldly. "She's not about to turn tricks for you or for anyone."

"I know that, Marîd. No need for you to be so defensive on her behalf. But she's realized that she can't support all her children. You mentioned that she'd be willing to place one of them in a good foster home, and perhaps earn enough that way to feed and clothe the others in a proper manner."

I hated what I was doing. "You may not know it," I said, "but my own mother was forced to sell my little brother when we were children."

"Now, now Maghrebi," said Mahmoud, "don't think of it as 'selling.' No one's got the right to sell a child. We can't continue this conversation if you maintain that attitude."

"Fine. Whatever you say. It's not selling; call it whatever you want. The point is, have you found someone who might be interested in adopting?"

Mahmoud paused. "Not exactly," he said at last. "But I know a man who frequently acts as go-between, arranging these matters. I've dealt with him before, and I can vouch for his honesty and delicacy. You can see that these transactions require a great amount of sympathy and tact."

"Sure," I said. "That's important. Indihar is in enough pain as it is."

"Exactly. That's why this man is so highly recommended. He's able to place a child in a loving home immediately, and he's able to present the natural parent with a cash gift in such a way as to prevent any guilt or recriminations. It's just his way. I think Mr. On is the perfect solution to Indihar's problem."

"Mr. On?"

"His name is On Cheung. He's a businessman from Kansu China. I've had the privilege of acting as his agent before."

"Uh yeah." I squeezed my eyes shut and listened to the blood roaring in my head. "This is leading us into the topic of money. How much will this Mr. On pay, and do you get a cut of it?"

"For the elder son, five hundred kiam. For the younger son, three hundred kiam. For the daughter, two hundred fifty. There are also bonuses: an extra two hundred kiam for two children, and five hundred if Indihar relinquishes all three. I, of course, take 10 percent. If you have arranged with her for a fee, that must come from the remainder."

"Sounds fair enough. That's better than Indihar had hoped, to be truthful."

"I told you that Mr. On was a generous man."

"Now what? Do we meet somewhere or what?"

Mahmoud's voice was growing excited. "Of course, both Mr. On and I will need to examine the children, to be sure they're fit and healthy. Can you have them at 7 Rafi ben Garcia Street in half an hour?"

"Sure, Mahmoud. See you then. Tell On Cheung to bring his money." I hung up the phone. "Kmuzu," I called, "forget about the laundry. We're going out."

"Yes, *yaa Sidi*. Shall I bring the car around?"

"Uh huh." I got up and threw a *gallebeya* over my jeans. Then I stuffed my static pistol in the pocket. I didn't trust either Mahmoud or the baby seller.

The address was in the Jewish Quarter, and it turned out to be another storefront covered with newspaper, very much like the place Shaknahyi and I had investigated in vain. "Stay here," I told Kmuzu. Then I got out of the car and went to the front door. I rapped on the glass, and after a little while Mahmoud opened the door an inch or two.

"Marîd," he said in his husky voice. "Where's Indihar and the children?"

"I told 'em to stay in the car. I want to check this out first. Let me in."

"Sure." He swung the door wider, and I pushed past him. "Marîd, this is Mr. On."

The baby seller was a small man with brown skin and brown teeth. He was sitting on a battered metal folding chair at a card table. There was a metal box at his elbow. He looked at me through a pair of wire-rimmed spectacles. No Nikon eyes for him, either.

I stepped across the filthy floor and held out my hand to him. On Cheung peered up at me and made no move to shake hands. After a few seconds, feeling like a fool, I dropped my hand.

"Okay?" asked Mahmoud. "Satisfied?"

"Tell him to open the box," I said.

"I don't tell Mr. On to do anything," said Mahmoud. "He's a very—"

"Everything okay," said On Cheung. "You look." He flipped open the top of the metal box. There was a stack of hundred-kiam bills in there that could have bought every child in the Budayeen.

"Great," I said. I reached into my pocket and brought out the pistol. "Hands on heads," I said.

"You son of a bitch," shouted Mahmoud. "What's this, a robbery? You're not gonna get away with it. Mr. On will make you sorry. That money's not going to do you a damn bit of good. You'll be dead before you spend a fîq of it."

"I'm still a cop, Mahmoud," I said sadly. I closed the metal box and handed it to him. I couldn't carry it with my one good arm and still point the static pistol. "Hajjar's been looking for On Cheung for a long time. Even a crooked cop like him has to bust somebody for real now and then. I guess it's just your turn."

I led them out to the car. I kept the gun on them while Kmuzu drove to the station house. All four of us went up to the third floor. Hajjar was startled as our little parade entered his glass-walled office. "Lieutenant," I said, "this is On Cheung, the baby seller. Mahmoud, drop the box of money. It's supposed to be evidence, but I don't expect anybody'll ever see it again after today."

"You never cease to amaze me," said Hajjar. He pushed a button on his desk, calling cops from the outer office.

"This one's for free," I said. Hajjar looked puzzled. "I told you I still had two to go. That's Umm Saad and Abu Adil. These stiffs are kind of a bonus."

"Right, thanks a lot. Mahmoud, you can go." The lieutenant looked up at me and shrugged his shoulders. "You really think Papa'd let me hold him?" he said. I thought about that for a moment and realized he was right.

Mahmoud looked relieved. "Won't forget this, Maghrebi," he muttered as he shoved by me. His threat didn't worry me.

"By the way," I said, "I quit. You want anybody to file traffic reports or enter logbook records from now on, you get somebody else. You need somebody to waste his time on wild-goose chases, get somebody else. You need help covering up your own crimes or incompetence, check with somebody else. I don't work here anymore."

Hajjar smiled cynically. "Yeah, some cops react that way when they face real pressure. But I thought you'd last longer, Audran."

I slapped him twice, quickly and loudly. He just stared at me, his own hand coming up slowly to touch his stinging cheeks. I turned and walked out of the office, followed by Kmuzu. Cops were coming from all around, and they'd seen what I'd done to Hajjar. Everybody was grinning. Even me.

nineteen

kmuzu," I said as he drove the sedan back to the house, "would you invite Umm Saad to have dinner with us?"

He looked across at me. He probably thought I was a complete fool, but he was great at keeping his opinions to himself. "Of course, *yaa Sidi*," he said. "In the small dining room?"

"Uh huh." I watched the streets of the Christian Quarter go by, wondering if I knew what I was doing.

"I hope you're not underestimating the woman," said Kmuzu.

"I don't think so. I think I've got a healthy regard for what she's capable of. I also think she's basically sane. When I tell her I know about the Phoenix File, and about her reasons for insinuating herself in our house, she'll realize the game is over."

Kmuzu tapped the steering wheel with his index fingers. "If you need help, *yaa Sidi,* I'll be there. You won't have to face her alone, as you faced Shaykh Reda."

I smiled. "Thanks, Kmuzu, but I don't think Umm Saad is as loony or as powerful as Abu Adil. She and I will just be sitting down to a meal. I intend to stay in control, *inshallah.*"

Kmuzu gave me one more thoughtful glance, then turned his attention back to driving.

When we arrived at Friedlander Bey's mansion, I went upstairs and changed my clothes. I put on a white robe and a white caftan, into which I transferred my static pistol. I also popped the pain-blocking daddy. I didn't really need it all the time anymore, and I was carrying plenty of sunnies just in case. I felt a flood of annoying aches and pains, all of which had been blocked by the daddy. The worst of all was the throbbing discomfort in my shoulder. I decided there was no point in suffering bravely, and I went right for my pillcase.

While I waited for Umm Saad's response to my invitation, I heard the sunset call to prayer from Papa's muezzin. Since my talk with the elder of the mosque in Souk el-Khemis Street, I'd been worshiping more or less regularly. Maybe I didn't manage to hit all five daily prayers, but I was doing decidedly better than ever before. Now I went downstairs to Papa's office. He kept his prayer rug there, and he had a special *mihrab* built into one wall. The *mihrab* is the shallow semicircular alcove you find in every mosque, indicating the precise direction of Mecca. After I washed my face, hands, and feet, I unrolled the prayer mat, cleared my mind of uncertainty, and addressed myself to Allah.

When I'd finished praying, Kmuzu murmured, "Umm Saad waits for you in the small dining room."

"Thank you." I rolled up Papa's prayer rug and put it away. I felt determined and strong. I used to believe that this was a temporary illusion caused by worship, but now I thought that doubt was the illusion. The assurance was real.

"It is good that you've regained your faith, *yaa Sidi,*" said Kmuzu. "Sometime you must let me tell you of the miracle of Jesus Christ."

"Jesus is no stranger to Muslims," I replied, "and his miracles are no secret to the faith."

We went into the dining room, and I saw Umm Saad and her young son sitting in their places. The boy hadn't been invited, but his presence wouldn't stop me from what I planned to say. "Welcome," I said, "and may Allah make this meal wholesome to you."

"Thank you, O Shaykh," said Umm Saad. "How is your health?"

"Fine, all praise be to Allah." I sat down, and Kmuzu stood behind my chair. I noticed that Habib had come into the room as well—or maybe it was Labib, whichever of the Stones wasn't guarding Papa in the hospital. Umm Saad and I exchanged more pleasantries until a serving woman brought in a platter of *tahini* and salt fish.

"Your cook is excellent," said Umm Saad. "I have relished each meal here."

"I am pleased," I said. More appetizers were brought out: cold stuffed grape leaves, stewed artichoke hearts, and eggplant slices stuffed with cream cheese. I indicated that my guests should serve themselves.

Umm Saad piled generous portions of each dish on her son's plate. She looked back at me. "May I pour coffee for you, O Shaykh?" she asked.

"In a moment," I said. "I'm sorry that Saad ben Salah is here to hear what I've got to say. It's time to confront you with what I've learned. I know all about your work for Shaykh Reda, and how you've attempted to murder Friedlander Bey. I know that you ordered your son to set the fire, and I know about the poisoned stuffed dates."

Umm Saad's face went pale with horror. She had just taken a bite of a stuffed grape leaf, and she spat it out and dropped the remainder on her plate. "What have you done?" she said hoarsely.

I picked up another stuffed grape leaf and put it in my mouth. When I finished chewing, I said, "I've done nothing as terrible as you're thinking."

Saad ben Salah stood up and moved toward me. His young face was twisted in an expression of rage and hate. "By the beard of the Prophet," he said, "I won't allow you to speak that way to my mother!"

"I only speak the truth," I said. "Isn't that so, Umm Saad?"

The boy glared at me. "My mother had nothing to do with the fire. That was my own idea. I hate you, and I hate Friedlander Bey. He's my grandfather, yet he denies me. He leaves his own daughter to suffer in poverty and misery. He deserves to die."

I sipped some coffee calmly. "I don't believe it," I said. "It's commendable of you to shoulder the blame, Saad, but it's your mother who's guilty, not you."

"You're a liar!" cried the woman.

The boy leaped toward me, but Kmuzu put himself between us. He was more than strong enough to restrain Saad.

I turned again to Umm Saad. "What I don't understand," I said, "is why you've tried to kill Papa. I don't see that his death would benefit you at all."

"Then you don't know as much as you think," she said. She seemed to relax a little. Her eyes flicked from me to Kmuzu, who still held her son in an unbreakable grip. "Shaykh Reda promised me that if I discovered Friedlander Bey's plans, or eliminated him so that Shaykh Reda would have no further obstacle, he would back my claim to be mistress of this house. I would take over Friedlander Bey's estate and his business ventures, and I would then turn over all matters of political influence to Shaykh Reda."

"Sure," I said, "and all you'd have to do is trust Abu Adil. How long do you think you'd last before he eliminated you the way you eliminated Papa? Then he could unite the two most powerful houses in the city."

"You're just inventing stories!" She got to her feet, turning to look at Kmuzu again. "Let my son go."

Kmuzu looked at me. I shook my head.

Umm Saad took a small needle gun from her bag. "I said, let my son go!"

"My lady," I said, holding up both hands to show that she had nothing to fear from me, "you've failed. Put down the gun. If you go on, not even the resources of Shaykh Reda will protect you from the vengeance of Friedlander Bey. I'm sure Abu Adil's interest in your affairs has come to an end. At this point, you're only deluding yourself."

She fired two or three flechettes into the ceiling to let me know she was willing to use the weapon. "Release my boy," she said hoarsely. "Let us go."

"I don't know if I can do that," I said. "I'm sure Friedlander Bey would want to—"

I heard a sound like *thitt! thitt!* and realized that Umm Saad had fired at me. I sucked in a deep breath, waiting to feel the bite of pain that would tell me where I'd been wounded, but it didn't happen. Her agitation had spoiled her aim even at this close range.

She swung the needle gun toward Kmuzu, who remained motionless, still shielded by Saad's body. Then she turned back toward me. In the meantime, however, the Stone That Speaks had crossed the few feet between us. He raised one hand and chopped down on Umm Saad's wrist, and she dropped the needle gun. Then the Stone raised his other hand, clenched into a huge fist.

"No," I shouted, but it was too late to stop him. With a powerful backhand clout, he knocked Umm Saad to the floor. I saw a bright trail of blood on her face below her split lip. She lay on her back with her head twisted at a grotesque angle. I knew the Stone had killed her with one blow. "That's two," I whispered. Now I could give my complete attention to Abu Adil. And Umar, the old man's deluded plaything.

"Son of a dog!" screamed the boy. He struggled a moment, and then Kmuzu permitted him to go to her. He bent and cradled his mother's corpse. "O Mother, Mother," he murmured, weeping.

Kmuzu and I let him mourn her for a short while. "Saad, get up," I said finally.

He looked up at me. I don't think I've ever seen so much malignity in a person's face. "I'll kill you," he said. "I promise you that. All of you."

"Get up, Saad," I said. I wished this hadn't happened, but it was too late for regrets.

Kmuzu put his hand on Saad's shoulder, but the boy shrugged it off. "You must listen to my master," said Kmuzu.

"No," said Saad. Then his hand flashed out quickly for his mother's needle gun. The Stone stamped down on the boy's forearm. Saad collapsed beside his mother, holding his arm and whimpering.

Kmuzu knelt and took the needle gun. He stood up again and gave the weapon to me. "What do you wish to do, *yaa Sidi?*" he asked.

"About the boy?" I looked at Saad thoughtfully. I knew that he bore me nothing but malice, but I only pitied him. He had been only a pawn in his mother's bargain with Abu Adil, a dupe in her vicious scheme to usurp Friedlander Bey's power. I didn't expect that Saad could understand that, of course. To him, Umm Saad would always be a martyr and a victim of cruel injustice.

"What is to be done?" Kmuzu said, breaking in on my thoughts.

"Oh, just let him go. He's certainly suffered enough." Kmuzu stood aside, and Saad got to his feet, holding his bruised forearm close to his chest. "I'll make all the proper preparations for your mother's funeral," I said.

Once again, his expression twisted in loathing. "You will not touch her!" he cried. "I will bury my mother." He backed away from me and stumbled toward the door. When he reached the exit, he turned to face me. "If there are such things as curses in this world," he uttered in a feverish voice, "I call them all down on you and your house. I will make you pay a hundred times for what you've done. I swear this three times, on the life of the Prophet Muhammad!" Then he fled the dining room.

"You have made a bitter enemy, *yaa Sidi,*" said Kmuzu.

"I know," I said, "but I can't worry about it." I just shook my head sadly.

A telephone on the sideboard warbled, and the Stone answered it. "Yes?" he said. He listened for a moment, then held it out to me.

I took it from him. "Hello?" I said.

There was just one word from the caller, "Come." It had been the other Stone.

I felt chilled. "We've got to get to the hospital," I said. I glanced down at Umm Saad's body, undecided what to do.

Kmuzu understood my problem. "Youssef can make the arrangements, *yaa Sidi,* if that's what you wish."

"Yes," I said. "I may need both of you."

Kmuzu nodded, and we left the dining room with Labib or Habib right behind me. We went outside, and Kmuzu drove the sedan around to the front of the house. I got in the back. I thought the Stone would have an easier time cramming himself into the passenger seat.

Kmuzu raced through the streets almost as wildly as Bill the taxi driver. We arrived at Suite One just as a male nurse was leaving Papa's room.

"How is Friedlander Bey?" I asked fearfully.

"He's still alive," said the nurse. "He's conscious, but you can't stay long. He's going into surgery shortly. The doctor is with him now."

"Thank you," I said. I turned to Kmuzu and the Stone. "Wait outside."

"Yes, *yaa Sidi*," said Kmuzu. The Stone didn't even grunt. He just cast a quick, hostile glance at Kmuzu.

I went into the suite. I saw another male nurse shaving Papa's skull, evidently prepping it for surgery. Tariq, his valet, stood by looking very worried. Dr. Yeniknani and another doctor sat at the card table, discussing something in low voices.

"Praise God you're here," said the valet. "Our master has been asking for you."

"What is it, Tariq?" I asked.

He frowned. He looked almost on the point of tears. "I don't understand. The doctors can explain. But now you must let our master know that you're here."

I went to Papa's bedside and looked down at him. He seemed to be dozing, his breath light and fluttery. His skin was an unhealthy gray color, and his lips and eyelids were unnaturally dark. The nurse finished shaving his head, and that just accentuated Papa's bizarre, deathlike appearance.

He opened his eyes as I stood there. "You have made us lonely, my nephew," he said. His voice was faint, like words carried on the wind.

"May God never make you lonely, O Shaykh," I said. I bent and kissed him on the cheek.

"You must tell me," he began. His breath wheezed and he couldn't finish his sentence.

"All goes well, praise Allah," I said. "Umm Saad is no more. I have yet to instruct Abu Adil on the folly of plotting against you."

The corners of his mouth quirked. "You will be rewarded. How did you defeat the woman?"

I wished he would stop thinking in terms of debts and rewards. "I have a personality module of Shaykh Reda," I said. "When I chipped it in, I learned many things that have been useful."

He caught his breath and looked unhappy. "Then you know—"

"I know of the Phoenix File, O Shaykh. I know that you protect that evil thing in cooperation with Abu Adil."

"Yes. And you know also that I am your mother's grandfather. That you are my great-grandson. But do you understand why we kept that knowledge a secret?"

Well, no, I hadn't known that until just that moment, although if

I'd been wearing Abu Adil's moddy and stopped to think about myself or my mother, the information might have popped into my consciousness.

So all that stuff about Papa possibly being my father was just Mom being cute and clever. I guess she'd known the truth all along. And that's why Papa'd been so upset when I'd kicked her out of the house when she first came to the city. That's why Umm Saad had caused him so much grief: Because everybody but me understood that she was trying to squeeze out the natural heirs, with Abu Adil's assistance. And Umm Saad was using the Phoenix File to blackmail Papa. Now I saw why he allowed her to remain in the house so long, and why he preferred that I dispose of her.

And ever since Friedlander Bey's divine finger first descended from the clouds to tap me so long ago, I'd been aimed toward lofty ends. Had I been cut out to be merely Papa's indispensable, reluctant assistant? Or had I been groomed all along to inherit the power and the wealth, every bit of it, along with the terrible life-and-death decisions Papa made every day?

How naive I'd been, to think that I might find a way to escape! I was more than just under Friedlander Bey's thumb; he owned me, and his indelible mark was written in my genetic material. My shoulders sagged as I realized that I would never be free, and that any hope of liberty had always been empty illusion.

"Why did you and my mother keep this secret from me?" I asked.

"You are not alone, my . . . son. As a young man, I fathered many children. When my own eldest son died, he was older than you are now, and he has been dead more than a century. I have dozens of grandchildren, one of whom is your mother. In your generation, I do not know how many descendants I can claim. It would not have been appropriate for you to feel unique, to use your relationship with me to further selfish ends. I needed to be sure that you were worthy, before I acknowledged you as my chosen one."

I wasn't as thrilled by that speech as he probably thought I should be. He sounded like a lunatic pretending to be God, passing on his blessing like a birthday present. Papa didn't want me to use my connection for selfish ends! Jeez, if that wasn't the height of irony!

"Yes, O Shaykh," I said. It didn't cost me anything to sound docile. Hell, he was going to have his skull carved in a few minutes. Still, I made no promises.

"Remember," he said softly, "there are many others who would take away your privileged position. You have scores of cousins who may someday do you harm."

Great. Something else to look forward to. "Then the computer records I searched—"

"Have been changed and changed again many times over the years." He smiled faintly. "You must learn not to put your faith in truth that has only electronic existence. Is it not our business, after all, to supply versions of that truth to the nations of the world? Have you not learned how supple truth can be?"

More questions occurred to me every second. "Then my father was truly Bernard Audran?"

"The Provençal sailor, yes."

I was relieved that I knew one thing for certain.

"Forgive my, my darling," murmured Papa. "I did not wish to reveal the Phoenix File to you, and that made it more difficult for you to deal with Umm Saad and Abu Adil."

I held his hand; it trembled in my grasp. "Don't worry, O Shaykh. It's almost over."

"Mr. Audran." I felt Dr. Yeniknani's large-knuckled hand on my shoulder. "We'll be taking your patron down to surgery now."

"What's wrong? What are you going to do?"

It was obvious that there wasn't time to go into a long explanation. "You were right about the tainted dates. Someone had been feeding him the poison for some time. It has severely impaired his medulla, the part of the brain that controls respiration, heartbeat, and wakefulness. It's been damaged to such an extent that, unless something is done very soon, he will fall into an irreversible coma."

My mouth was dry, and my heart was racing. "What are you going to do?" I asked.

Dr. Yeniknani looked down at his hands. "Dr. Lisân believes the only hope is a partial medullar transplant. We have been waiting for healthy tissue from a compatible donor."

"And today you've found it?" I wondered who on that goddamn Phoenix File had been sacrificed for this.

"I can't promise success, Mr. Audran. The operation has only been tried three or four times before, and never in this part of the world. But you must know that if any surgeon can offer you hope, it's Dr. Lisân. And of course, I will be attending. Your patron will have all the skill at our disposal, and all the prayers of his faithful friends."

I nodded dumbly. I looked up to see two male nurses lifting Friedlander Bey from his hospital bed onto a wheeled cart. I went to grasp his hand once more.

"Two things," he said in a husky whisper. "You have moved the policeman's widow into our home. When the four months of proper mourning are over, you must marry her."

"Marry her!" I was so startled, I forgot to be properly respectful.

"And when I recover from this illness—" He yawned, almost unable to keep his eyes open against the medication the nurses had given him. I lowered my head to catch his words. "When I am again well, we will go to Mecca."

That wasn't what I expected, either. I guess I groaned. "Mecca," I said.

"The pilgrimage." He opened his eyes. He looked frightened, not of the surgery but of his unfulfilled obligation to Allah. "It is past time," he said, and then they wheeled him away.

Twenty

I decided the wise thing was to wait until my arm was unwrapped before I faced down Abu Adil. After all, the great Salah ad-Dîn didn't reconquer Jerusalem and drive out the Franj Crusaders by riding down into battle with half his army. Not that I planned to get into a fistfight with Shaykh Reda or Umar, but I'd taken enough nicks and scrapes lately to learn a little prudence.

Things had quieted down considerably. For a time, we worried and prayed to Allah for Friedlander Bey's recovery. He'd survived the surgery and Dr. Lisân had pronounced it a success; but Papa slept almost around the clock, day after day. He roused occasionally and talked with us, although he was terribly confused about who we all were and what century it was.

With Umm Saad and her son gone, the atmosphere in the house was more cheerful. I concerned myself with Papa's business matters, acting in his place to settle disputes among the city's caterers of the ungodly. I let Mahmoud know that I would be tough but fair as Friedlander Bey's deputy, and he seemed to accept that. At least, he dropped his resentment. That may have been just an act. You can never accurately read Mahmoud.

I also had to handle a major foreign crisis, when the new tyrant of Eritrea came to me demanding to know what was going on in his own country. I took care of that mess, thanks to Papa's impeccable record keeping and Tariq and Youssef's knowledge of where everything was.

My mother continued to alternate between modestly mature and brazenly foolish. Sometimes when we talked, we were sorry for the way we'd punished each other in the past. Other times, we wanted to slit each other's throats. Kmuzu told me that this kind of relationship is not unusual between parent and child, particularly after both have reached a certain age. I accepted that, and I didn't worry about it anymore.

Chiriga's continued to make lots of money, and both Chiri and I were satisfied. I guess she would've been more satisfied if I'd sold the club back to her, but I enjoyed owning it too much. I decided to hang on to it a little while longer, the way I decided to hang on to Kmuzu.

When the muezzin's call to prayer came, I answered it a large percentage of the time, and went to the mosque on a Friday or two. I was becoming known as a kind and generous man, not just in the Budayeen but all through the city. Wherever I went, people called me Shaykh Marîd al-Amîn. I didn't completely stop taking drugs, however, because I was still injured and I saw no reason to take the chance of enduring unnecessary agony.

All in all, the month after I'd kissed off the police department was a welcome experiment with peace and quiet. It all came to an end one Tuesday, just before lunch, when I answered the phone. "*Marhaba*," I said.

"Praise be to God. This is Umar Abdul-Qawy."

I didn't say anything for a few seconds. "The hell do you want?" I said.

"My master is concerned for the health of Friedlander Bey. I'm calling to inquire as to his condition."

I was coming to a quick boil. I didn't really know what to say to Umar. "He's fine. He's resting."

"Then he's able to take care of his duties?" There was a smugness in his voice that I hated a lot.

"I said he's fine, all right? Now, I got work to do."

"Just a second, Monsieur Audran." And then his voice got positively sanctimonious. "We believe you may have something that properly belongs to Shaykh Reda."

I knew what he was talking about, and it made me smile. I liked being the screwer rather than the screwee. "I don't know what you mean, Himmar." I don't know, something made me say it. I knew it would pluck his beard.

"The moddy," he said. "The goddman moddy."

I paused to savor what I heard in his voice. "Well, hell," I said, "you got it all wrong. As I recall, *you* have the goddamn moddy. Remember? *Himmar?* You cuffed my hands behind my back, and then you beat me bloody, and then you jacked me into a moddy link and read off my brain. You guys done with it yet?"

There was silence. I think Umar hoped I wouldn't remember that moddy. That's not what he wanted to talk about. I didn't care, I had the floor. "How's it work, you son of a bitch?" I said. "You wear my brain while that sick bastard jams you? Or the other way around? How am I, Umar? Any competition for Honey Pílar?"

I heard him trying to get himself under control. "Perhaps we could arrange an exchange," he said at last. "Shaykh Reda truly wishes to make amends. He wants his personality module returned. I'm sure he would agree to give you the recording we made of you plus a suitable cash settlement."

"Cash," I said. "How much?"

"I can't say for certain, but I'm sure Shaykh Reda would be very generous. He realizes that he's put you through a great deal of discomfort."

"Yeah, you right. But business is business, and action is action. How much?"

"Ten thousand kiam," said Umar.

I knew that if I balked, he'd name a higher figure; but I wasn't interested in their money. "Ten thousand?" I said, trying to sound impressed.

"Yes." Umar's voice got smug again. He was going to pay for that. "Shall we meet here, in an hour? Shaykh Reda instructed me to say that our staff is preparing a special midday meal in your honor. We hope you'll let our past differences go, Shaykh Marîd. Shaykh Reda and Friedlander Bey must join together now. You and I must be partners in harmony. Don't you agree?"

"I do testify that there is no god but Allah," I declared solemnly.

"By the Lord of the Kaaba," swore Umar, "this will be a memorable day for both our houses."

I hung up the phone. "Damn straight about that," I said. I sat back in my chair. I didn't know who would have the upper hand when the afternoon was over, but the days of the false peace had come to an end.

I'm not a total fool, so I didn't go to Abu Adil's palace alone. I took one of the Stones That Speak with me, as well as Kmuzu and Saied. Now, the latter two had been exploited by Shaykh Reda, and they both felt they had scores to settle with him. When I asked if they'd like to join me in my devious charade, they eagerly agreed.

"I want a chance to make up for selling you out to Shaykh Reda," said the Half-Hajj.

I was checking my two weapons, and I looked up. "But you've already done that. When you pulled me out of that alley."

"Nah," he said, "I still feel like I owe you at least one more."

"You have an Arabic proverb," said Kmuzu thoughtfully. "'When he promised, he fulfilled his promise. When he threatened, he did not fulfill his threat, but he forgave.' It is equivalent to the Christian idea of turning the other cheek."

"That's right," I said. "But people who live their lives by proverbs waste their time doing lots of stupid things. 'Getting even is the best revenge' is my motto."

"I wasn't counseling retreat, *yaa Sidi.* I was only making a philological observation."

Saied gave Kmuzu an irritated look. "And this big bald guy is something else you got to pay back Abu Adil for," he said.

The ride out to Abu Adil's palace in Hâmidiyya was strangely pleasant. We laughed and talked as if we were on some enjoyable picnic or outing. I didn't feel afraid, even though I wasn't wearing a moddy or any daddies. Saied talked almost nonstop in the scatterbrained way that had given him his nickname. Kmuzu kept his eyes straight ahead as he drove, but even he put in a lighthearted comment now and then. Habib or Labib—whichever he was—sat beside Saied in the backseat and did his silent sandstone giant routine.

Abu Adil's guard passed us immediately through the gate, and we drove up through the beautifully landscaped grounds. "Let's wait a minute," I said, as Kamal, the butler, opened the house's massive, carved front door. I checked my static pistol again and passed the small seizure gun to the Half-Hajj; Kmuzu had the needle gun that had formerly belonged to Umm Saad. The Stone didn't need any weapon beyond his own bare hands.

I clucked my tongue impatiently. "What is it, *yaa Sidi?*" asked Kmuzu.

"I'm deciding what to wear." I browsed through my rack of moddies and daddies. I finally decided that I'd wear Rex and carry the Abu Adil moddy. I also chipped in the daddies that blocked pain and fear.

"When this is over," Saied said wistfully, "can I have Rex back? I really miss wearing him."

"Sure," I said, even though I enjoyed wearing the badass moddy myself. Saied just wasn't the same without it. For now, I let him have the anthology. I was hoping to see Mike Hammer put his fist in Abu Adil's face.

"We must be careful," said Kmuzu. "We cannot be lulled, because treachery runs in Shaykh Reda's blood like the bilharzia worm."

"Thanks," I said, "but I'm not likely to forget it."

Then the four of us got out of the car and walked up the ceramic-tiled path to the door. It was a warm, pleasant day, and the sun felt good on my face. I was dressed in a white *gallebeya* and my head was covered with a knitted Algerian skullcap. It was a simple costume, and it made me look humble.

We followed Kamal to a meeting room on the second floor. I felt myself tense as we passed Abu Adil's recording studio. I took a few deep breaths, and by the time the butler bowed us into his master's presence, I was relaxed again.

Abu Adil and Umar were sitting on large pillows spread in a semicircle in the center of the room. There was a raised platform in the midst of the arrangement, and already several large bowls of food had been set there, along with pots of coffee and tea.

Our hosts rose to greet us. I noticed immediately that neither of them had any hardware chipped in. Abu Adil came to me, smiling broadly. He embraced me and said, "*Ahlan wa sahlan!*" in a cheerful voice. "Welcome, and be refreshed!"

"I am glad to see you again, O Shaykh. May Allah open His ways to you."

Abu Adil was happy to see how subdued I was behaving. He wasn't happy, however, that I'd brought Kmuzu, Saied, and the Stone. "Come, rinse the dust from your hands," he said. "Let me pour water for you. Of course, your slaves are welcome too."

"Watch it, chum," growled Saied, wearing the Mike Hammer moddy. "I'm no slave."

"Exactly, of course," said Abu Adil, never losing his good humor.

We made ourselves comfortable on the cushions and exchanged still more of the obligatory compliments. Umar poured me a cup of coffee, and I said, "May your table last forever."

"May God lengthen your life," said Umar. He wasn't nearly so happy as his boss.

We sampled the food and chatted amiably for a while. The only sour note was struck by the Half-Hajj, who spat out an olive pit and said, "this all you got?" Shaykh Reda's face froze. I had a hard time not laughing out loud.

"Now," said Abu Adil after a proper amount of time had passed, "will you object if I bring up the matter of business?"

"No, O Shaykh," I said, "I am eager to conclude this matter."

"Then give me the personality module you took from this house." Umar handed him a small vinyl satchel, which Abu Adil opened. There were banded stacks of fresh ten-kiam bills in it.

"I ask something more in trade," I said.

Umar's face darkened. "You are a fool if you think you can change our bargain now. The agreement was ten thousand kiam."

I ignored him. I turned to Abu Adil. "I want you to destroy the Phoenix File."

Abu Adil laughed delightedly. "Ah, you are a remarkable man. But I know that from wearing this." He held up the moddy he'd made the day he'd mind-raped me. "The Phoenix File is life to me. Because of it, I have lived to this advanced age. I will no doubt need it again. With the file, I may live another hundred years."

"I'm sorry, Shaykh Reda," I said, taking out my static pistol, "but I'm very determined." I glanced at my friends. They too held their weapons on Abu Adil and Umar.

"No more of this foolishness," said Umar. "You came here to exchange moddies. Let's complete the transaction, and then whatever happens in the future is in the hands of Allah."

I kept my gun pointed at Abu Adil, but I took a sip from my cup of coffee. "The refreshments are most excellent, O Shaykh," I said. I set my cup down again. "I want you to destroy the Phoenix File. I've worn your moddy, I know where it is. Kmuzu and Saied can hold you here while I go get it."

Abu Adil didn't seem the least bit upset. "You're bluffing," he said, spreading his hands. "If you've worn my moddy, then you know that I have copies. The moddy will tell you where one or two duplicate files are, but Umar has still others, and you won't learn where they are."

"Hell," said the Half-Hajj, "I bet I can make him talk."

"Never mind, Saied," I said. I realized that Abu Adil was right; we were at an impasse. Destroying a bubble plate here and a printout there would accomplish nothing. I couldn't destroy the *concept* of the Phoenix File, and at this point Abu Adil would never agree to abandon it.

Kmuzu leaned nearer. "You must persuade him to give it up, *yaa Sidi.*"

"Any ideas?"

"Unfortunately, no."

I had one last trump to play, but I hated to use it. If it failed, Abu Adil would win, and I'd never be able to protect myself or Friedlander Bey's interests against him. Still, there was no other choice. "Shaykh Reda," I said slowly, "there are many other things recorded on your moddy. I learned astonishing things about what you've done and what you plan to do."

Abu Adil's expression grew worried for the first time. "What are you talking about?" he asked.

I tried to look unconcerned. "You know, of course, that the strict religious leaders disapprove of brain implants. I couldn't find an imam who'd had one, so none of them could chip in your moddy and experience it directly. But I did speak with Shaykh Al-Hajj Muhammad ibn Abdurrahman, who leads prayers at the Shimaal Mosque."

Abu Adil stared at me, his eyes wide. The Shimaal Mosque was the largest and most powerful congregation in the city. The pronouncements of its clergy often had the force of law.

I was bluffing, of course. I'd never set foot inside the Shimaal Mosque. And I'd just invented that imam's name.

Shaykh Reda's voice faltered. "What did you discuss with him?"

I grinned. "Why, I gave him a detailed description of all your past sins and your intended crimes. Now, there's a fascinating technical point that hasn't been cleared up yet. I mean, the religious elders haven't ruled on whether or not a personality module recorded from a living person is admissible as evidence in a court of Islamic law. You know and I know that such a moddy is wholly reliable, much more so than any sort of mechanical lie detector. But the imams, bless their righteous hearts, are debating the matter back and forth. It may be a long while before they pass a ruling, but then again, you may already be in very serious trouble."

I paused to let what I'd said sink in. I'd just made up this religious-legal wrangle on the fly, but it was entirely plausible. It was a question that Islam would have to come to grips with, just as the faith had had to deal with every other technological advance. It was only a matter of judging how the science of neuroaugmentation related to the teachings of Prophet Muhammad, may the blessings of Allah be on him and peace.

Abu Adil moved restlessly on his cushion. He was obviously wrestling with two unpleasant options: destroying the Phoenix File, or being turned over to the notoriously unforgiving representatives of the Messenger of God. Finally, he gave a great sigh. "Hear my decision," he said. "I offer you Umar Abdul-Qawy in my place."

I laughed. There was a horrified squeal from Umar. "The hell do we want with *him?*" asked the Half-Hajj.

"I'm sure you learned from the moddy that Umar originated many of my less honorable business practices," said Abu Adil. "His guilt is nearly as great as my own. I, however, have power and influence. Maybe not enough to hold off the wrath of the city's entire Islamic community, but certainly enough to deflect it."

I appeared to consider this point. "Yes," I said slowly, "it would be very difficult to convict you."

"But not difficult at all to convict Umar." Shaykh Reda looked at his assistant. "I'm sorry, my boy, but you've brought this on yourself. I know all about your shabby plottings. When I wore Shaykh Marîd's moddy, didn't I find out about your conversation with him? The one in which he turned down your invitation to dispose of me and Friedlander Bey?"

Umar's face had gone deathly pale. "But I never intended—"

Abu Adil did not seem angry, only very sad. "Did you think you were the first to have that notion? Where are your predecessors, Umar? Where are all the ambitious young men who've held your position that last century and a half? Almost every one of them plotted against me, sooner or later. And they are all gone now and forgotten. Just as you will be."

"Face it, Himmar," taunted Saied, "you have to wear the shirt you sewed. Paybacks are a bitch, ain't they?"

Abu Adil shook his head. "I will be sorry to lose you, Umar. I couldn't have cared for you more if I'd been your true father."

I was amused, and glad that events were turning out as I planned. A line of American fiction occurred to me: "If you lose a son it's possible to get another—but there's only one Maltese falcon."

Umar, though, had other ideas. He jumped up and screamed at Abu Adil. "I'll see you dead first! All of you!"

Saied fired the seizure gun before Umar even drew his own weapon. Umar collapsed to the floor, writhing in convulsions, his face twisted in an ugly grimace. At last, he was still. He'd be unconscious for a few hours but he'd recover, and he'd feel like hell for a long time afterward.

"Well," said the Half-Hajj, "he folds up real nice."

Abu Adil let out a sigh. "This is not how I intended for this afternoon to go."

"Really?" I said.

"I must admit, I've underestimated you. Do you wish to take him with you?"

I didn't really want to be saddled with Umar because, after all, I hadn't actually spoken to the imam. "No," I said, "I think I'll leave him in your hands."

"You can be assured there will be justice," said Shaykh Reda. The look he turned on his scheming assistant was chilling. I was almost sorry for Umar.

"Justice," I said, using an old Arab saying, "is that you should restore things to their places. I would like my moddy now."

"Yes, of course." He leaned across the still form of Umar Abdul-Qawy and put the moddy in my hand. "And take the money," he said.

"No, I don't think so," I said. "But I'll keep the moddy I have of you. To guarantee your cooperation."

"If you must," he said unhappily. "You understand that I have not agreed to abandon the Phoenix File."

"I understand." Then I was struck by a sudden thought. "I have one last request, however."

"Yes?" He looked suspicious.

"I wish to have my name removed from the file, and the names of my friends and relatives."

"Of course," said Abu Adil, glad that my last demand was so easy to fulfill. "I would be pleased to oblige. Merely send me a complete list at your convenience."

Later, as we walked back to the car, Kmuzu and Saied congratulated me. "That was a complete victory," said the Half-Hajj.

"No," I said, "I wish it were. Abu Adil and Papa still have that goddamn Phoenix File, even if some of our names will be taken off. I feel like I'm trading the lives of my friends for the lives of other innocent people. I told Shaykh Reda, 'Go ahead, kill those other guys, I don't care.'"

"You accomplished as much as was possible, *yaa Sidi*," said Kmuzu. "You should be grateful to God."

"I suppose." I popped Rex and gave the moddy to Saied, who grinned to have it back. We rode back to the house; Kmuzu and Saied discussed what had happened at great length, but I just rode in silence, wrapped in gloomy thoughts. For some reason, I felt like a failure. I felt as if I'd made an evil compromise. I also felt uncomfortably sure that it wouldn't be my last.

Late that night, I was awakened by someone opening the door to my bedroom. I lifted my head and saw a woman enter, dressed in a short, clinging negligee.

The woman lifted the covers and slipped into bed beside me. She put one hand on my cheek and kissed me. It was a great kiss. I woke up completely. "I bribed Kmuzu to let me in," she whispered. I was surprised to realize it was Indihar.

"Yeah? How do you bribe Kmuzu?"

"I told him I'd take your mind off your pain."

"He knows I got pills and software to do that." I rolled over on my side to face her. "Indihar, what are you doing here?" I asked. "You said you weren't going to sleep with me."

"Well, I changed my mind," she said. She didn't sound very enthusiastic. "Here I am. I've been thinking about how I acted when . . . after Jirji died."

"May the mercy of Allah be on him," I murmured. I put my arm around her. Despite her attempt to be brave, I could feel warm tears on her face.

"You've done a lot for me, and for the kids."

Yipe. "That's why you're here? Because you're grateful?"

"Well," she said, "yes. I'm in your debt."

"You don't love me, do you, Indihar?"

"Marîd," she said, "don't get me wrong. I like you, but—"

"But that's all there is. Listen, I really don't think being here together is a great idea. You told me you weren't going to sleep with me, and I respected that."

"Papa wants us to be married," she said. Her voice took on an angry edge.

"He thinks it shames his house for us to be living together otherwise. Even if we aren't, you know, sleeping together."

"Even though my children need a father, and they like you, I won't marry you, Marîd. I don't care what Papa says."

Actually, marriage was something I thought happened only to other people, like fatal traffic accidents. I still felt an obligation to take care of Shaknahyi's widow and children, and if I had to marry someone, I could do worse than Indihar. But still . . .

"I think Papa may forget all about it by the time he gets out of the hospital."

"Just so you understand," said Indihar. She gave me another kiss—this one chastely on the cheek—and then she quietly got out of my bed and went back to her own room.

I felt like such a noble son of a bitch. I'd made her feel better, but deep down I had no confidence at all that Friedlander Bey would forget his decree. All I could think about was Yasmin, and if she'd still go out with me after I was married to Indihar.

I couldn't get back to sleep. I just turned from one side to the other, twisting the sheets up into a tangled mess. Finally I gave up and got out of bed and went into the study. I sat in the comfortable leather armchair and picked up the Wise Counselor moddy. I looked at it for a few seconds, wondering if it could possibly make sense out of recent events. *"Bismillah,"* I murmured. Then I reached up and chipped it in.

Audran seemed to be in a deserted city. He wandered through narrow, congested alleys—hungry, thirsty, and very tired. After a while he turned a corner and came into a great market square. The booths and stalls were deserted, empty of merchandise. Still, Audran recognized where he was. He was back in Algeria. "Hello?" he shouted. There was no answer. He remembered an old saying: "I came to the place of my birth, and cried, 'The friends of my youth, where are they?' An echo answered, 'Where are they?'

He began to weep with sadness. Then a man spoke, and Audran turned. He recognized the man as the Messenger of God. "Shaykh Marîd," said the Prophet, may blessings be on him and peace, "don't you consider me the friend of your youth?"

And Audran smiled. "Yaa Hazrat, does not everyone in the world desire your friendship? But my love for Allah so completely fills my heart that there is no room there for love or hate for anyone."

"If that is true," said Prophet Muhammad, "then you are blessed. Remember, though, that this verse was revealed: 'Thou shalt never reach the broad door of piety until thou givest away what thou lovest best.' What do you love best, O Shaykh?"

I awoke, but this time I didn't have Jirji Shaknahyi to explain the vision. I wondered what the answer to the Prophet's question might be: comfort, pleasure, freedom? I hated the idea of giving up any of those, but I might as well get used to the idea. My life with Friedlander Bey rarely entailed the notions of ease or liberty.

But my life needn't begin again until morning. In the meantime, I had the problem of getting through the night. I went to search for my pillcase.

The Exile Kiss

To the science fiction community of the South Central region, which has given me so much support and encouragement over the years. My thanks to ArmadilloCon in Austin, SwampCon in Baton Rouge, the New Orleans Science Fiction and Fantasy Festival, and CoastCon in Biloxi.

And special thanks to Fred Duarte and Karen Meschke for hospitality above and beyond the call of duty, while my car was in a near-fatal coma during the writing of this book.

Though it rain gold and silver in a foreign land and daggers and spears at home, yet it is better to be at home.

—Malay Proverb

O! a kiss
Long as my exile, sweet as my revenge!

—William Shakespeare
Coriolanus
Act 5, scene 3

ONE

It never occurred to me that I might be kidnapped. There was no reason why it should. The day had certainly begun innocently enough. I'd snapped wide awake just before dawn, thanks to an experimental add-on I wear on my anterior brain implant. That plug is the one that gives me powers and abilities far beyond those of mortal men. As far as I know, I'm the only person around with two implants.

One of these special daddies blasts me into full consciousness at any hour I choose. I've learned to use it along with another daddy that supercharges my body to remove alcohol and drugs from my system at better than the normal rate. That way I don't wake up still drunk or damaged. Others have suffered in the past because of my hangovers, and I've sworn never to let that happen again.

I took a shower, trimmed my red beard, and dressed in an expensive, sand-colored *gallebeya*, with the white knit skullcap of my Algerian homeland on my head. I was hungry, and my slave, Kmuzu, normally prepared my meals, but I had a breakfast appointment with Friedlander Bey. That would be after the morning call to prayer, so I had about thirty minutes free. I crossed from the west wing of Friedlander Bey's great house to the east, and rapped on the door to my wife's apartment.

Indihar answered it wearing a white satin dressing gown I'd given her, her chestnut hair coiled tightly on the back of her head. Indihar's large, dark eyes narrowed. "I wish you good morning, husband," she said. She was not terrifically pleased to see me.

Indihar's youngest child, four-year-old Hâkim, clung to her and cried. I could hear Jirji and Zahra screaming at each other from another room. Senalda, the Valencian maid I'd hired, was nowhere in evidence. I'd accepted the responsibility of supporting the family because I felt partly to blame for the death of Indihar's husband. Papa—Friedlander Bey—had decided that in order to accomplish such a worthy goal without causing gossip, I also had to marry Indihar and formally adopt the three children. I couldn't remember another instance when Papa had cared at all about gossip.

Nevertheless, despite Indihar's outrage and my flat refusal, the two of us now found ourselves man and wife. Papa *always* got his way. Some time ago, Friedlander Bey had grabbed me by the scruff of the neck and shaken the dust off me and turned me from a small-time hustler into a heavy hitter in the city's underworld.

So Hâkim was now legally . . . my son, as queasy as that concept made me. I'd never been around kids before and I didn't know how to act with them. Believe me, they could tell. I hoisted the boy up and smiled in his jelly-smeared face. "Well, why are you crying, O Clever One?" I said. Hâkim stopped just long enough to suck in a huge breath, then started wailing even louder.

Indihar gave an impatient grunt. "Please, husband," she said, "don't try being a big brother. Jirji is his big brother." She lifted Hâkim out of my arms and dropped him back to the floor.

"I'm not trying to be a big brother."

"Then don't try being a pal, either. He doesn't need a pal. He needs a father."

"Right," I said. "You just tell me what a father does, and I'll do it." I'd been trying my best for weeks, but Indihar had only given me a hard time. I was getting very tired of it.

She laughed humorlessly and shooed Hâkim toward the rear of the apartment. "Is there some actual point to this visit, husband?" she asked.

"Indihar, if you could just stop resenting me a little, maybe we could make the best of this situation. I mean, how awful could it be for you here?"

"Why don't you ask Kmuzu how *he* feels?" she said. She still hadn't invited me into the suite.

I'd had enough of standing in the hall, and I pushed by her into the parlor. I sat down on a couch. Indihar glared at me for a few seconds, then sighed and sat on a chair facing me. "I've explained it all before," I said. "Papa has been giving me things. Gifts I didn't want, like my implants and Chiriga's bar and Kmuzu."

"And me," she said.

"Yes, and you. He's trying to strip me of all my friends. He doesn't want me to keep any of my old attachments."

"You could simply refuse, husband. Did you ever think of that?"

How I wished it were that easy! "When I had my skull amped," I said, "Friedlander Bey paid the doctors to wire the punishment center of my brain."

"The punishment center? Not the pleasure center?"

I grinned ruefully. "If he'd had the pleasure center wired, I'd probably already be dead. That's what happens to those wireheads. It wouldn't have taken me long, either."

Indihar frowned. "Well, then, I don't understand. Why the punishment center? Why would you want—"

I raised a hand and cut her off. "Hey, *I* didn't want it! Papa had it done without my knowledge. He's got lots of little electronic gimmicks that can remotely stimulate my pain centers. That's how he keeps me in line." Learning recently that he was truly my mother's grandfather had not disposed me more favorably toward him. Not as long as he refused to discuss the matter of my liberty.

I saw her shudder. "I didn't know that, husband."

"I haven't told many people about it. But Papa's always there looking over my shoulder, ready to jam his thumb on the agony button if I do something he doesn't like."

"So you're a prisoner, too," said Indihar. "You're his slave, as much as the rest of us."

I didn't see any need to reply. The situation was a trifle different in my case, because I shared Friedlander Bey's blood, and I felt obliged to try to love him. I hadn't actually succeeded in that yet. I had a difficult time dealing with that emotion in the first place, and Papa wasn't making it easy for me.

Indihar reached out her hand to me, and I took it. It was the first time since we'd been married that she'd relented any at all. I saw that her palm and fingers were still stained a faint yellow-orange, from the henna her friends had applied the morning of our wedding. It had been a very unusual ceremony, because Papa had declared that it wouldn't be appropriate for me to marry anyone but a maiden. Indihar was, of course, a widow with three children, so he had her declared an honorary virgin. Nobody laughed.

The wedding itself was a mixture of customs observed in the city as well as those from Indihar's native Egyptian village. It pretended to be the joining of a young virgin and a Maghrebi youth of promising fortune. Friedlander Bey announced that it wasn't necessary to fetch Indihar's family to the celebration, that her friends from the Budayeen could stand in for them.

"We'll pass over the ritual certification, of course," Indihar had said.

"What's that?" I asked. I was afraid that at the last minute, I was going to be required to take some kind of written test that I should've been studying for ever since puberty.

"In some backward Muslim lands," explained Friedlander Bey, "on the wedding night, the bride is taken into a bedroom, away from all the other guests. The women of both families hold her down on the bed. The husband wraps a white cloth around his forefinger, and inserts it to prove the girl's virginity. If the cloth comes out stained with blood, the husband passes it out to the bride's father, who then marches around waving it on a stick for all to see."

"But this is the seventeenth century of the Hegira!" I said, astonished.

Indihar shrugged. "It's a moment of great pride for the bride's parents. It proves they've raised a chaste and worthy daughter. When I was first married, I wept at the indignity until I heard the cheers and joy of the guests. Then I knew that my marriage had been blessed, and that I'd become a woman in the eyes of the village."

"As you say, my daughter," said Friedlander Bey, "in this instance such a certification will not be required." Papa could be reasonable if he didn't stand to lose anything by it.

I'd bought Indihar a fine gold wedding band, as well as the traditional second piece of jewelry. Chiri, my not-so-silent partner, helped me select the gift in one of the expensive boutiques east of the Boulevard il-Jameel, where the Europeans shopped. It was a brooch, an emerald-encrusted lizard made of gold, with two rubies for eyes. It had cost me twelve thousand kiam, and it was the most expensive single item I'd ever purchased. I gave it to Indihar the morning of the wedding. She opened the satin-lined box, looked at the emerald lizard for a few seconds, and then said, "Thank you, Marîd." She never mentioned it again, and I never saw her wear it.

Indihar had not been well-off, even before her husband was killed. She brought to our marriage only a modest assortment of household furnishings and her meager personal belongings. Her contribution wasn't materially important, because I'd become wealthy through my association with Papa. In fact, the amount specified as her bride-price in our marriage contract was more than Indihar had ever seen in her lifetime. I gave two thirds of it to her in cash. The final third would go to her in the event of our divorce.

I merely dressed in my best white *gallebeya* and robe, but Indihar had to endure much more. Chiri, her best friend, helped her prepare for the ceremony. Early in the day, they removed the hair from Indihar's arms and legs by covering her skin with a mixture of sugar and lemon juice. When the paste hardened, Chiri peeled it off. I'll never forget how wonderfully fresh and sweet-smelling Indihar was that evening. Sometimes I still find myself getting aroused by the fragrance of lemons.

When Indihar finished dressing and applying a modest amount of makeup, she and I sat for our official wedding holos. Neither of us looked especially happy. We both knew that it was a marriage in name only, and would last only as long as Friedlander Bey lived. The holographer kept making lewd jokes about wedding nights and honeymoons, but Indihar and I just watched the clock, counting the hours until this entire ordeal would be finished.

The ceremony itself took place in Papa's grand hall. There were hundreds of guests; some were friends of ours, and some were sinister, silent men who stood watchfully at the edges of the crowd. My best man was Saied the Half-Hajj, who in honor of the occasion was wearing no moddy at all, something remarkable in its own right. Most of the other club owners in the Budayeen were there, as well as the girls, sexchanges, and debs we knew, and such Budayeen characters as Laila, Fuad, and Bill the cab driver. It could have been a truly joyous occasion, if Indihar and I had loved each other and wanted to get married in the first place.

We sat face to face before a blue-turbaned shaykh who performed the Muslim marriage ceremony. Indihar was lovely in a beautiful white satin dress and white veil, with a bouquet of fragrant blossoms. First the shaykh invoked the blessings of Allah, and read from the first sûrah of the noble Qur'ân. Then he asked Indihar if she consented to the marriage. There was a brief pause, when I thought I saw her eyes fill with regret. "Yes," she said in a quiet voice.

We joined our right hands, and the shaykh covered them with a white handkerchief. Indihar repeated the words of the shaykh, stating that she married me of her own free will, for a bride-price of seventy-five thousand kiam.

"Repeat after me, Marîd Audran," said the shaykh. "I accept from thee your betrothal to myself, and take thee under my care, and bind myself to afford thee any protection. Ye who are present bear witness of this." I had to say it three times to make it work.

The shaykh finished it off by reading some more from the holy Qur'ân. He blessed us and our marriage. There was an instant of peace in the hall, and then from the throats of all the women came the shrill, trilling sound of the *zagareet*.

There was a party afterward, of course, and I drank and pretended to be happy. There was plenty to eat, and the guests gave us gifts and money. Indihar left early with the excuse that she had to put her children to bed, although Senalda was there to do just that. I left the celebration not long afterward. I went back to my apartment, swallowed seven or eight tabs of Sonneine, and lay on my bed with my eyes closed.

I was married. I was a husband. As the opiates began to take effect, I thought about how beautiful Indihar had looked. I wished that I had at least kissed her.

Those were my memories of our wedding. Now, as I sat in her parlor, I wondered what my real responsibilities were. "You've treated me and my children well," Indihar said. "You've been very generous, and I should be grateful. Forgive me for my behavior, husband."

"You have nothing to be sorry for, Indihar," I said. I stood up. The mention of the children reminded me that they could run squawking and drooling into the parlor at any moment. I wanted to get out of there while I still could. "If there's anything you need, just ask Kmuzu or Tariq."

"We're well provided for." She looked up into my eyes, then turned away. I couldn't tell what she was feeling.

I began to feel awkward myself. "Then I'll leave you. I wish you a good morning."

"May your day be pleasant, husband."

I went to the door and turned to look at her again before I left. She seemed so sad and alone. "Allah bring you peace," I murmured. Then I closed the door behind me.

I had enough time to get back to the smaller dining room near Friedlander Bey's office, where we had breakfast whenever he wanted to discuss business matters with me. He was already seated in his place when I arrived. The two taciturn giants, Habib and Labib, stood behind him, one on either side. They still eyed me suspiciously, as if even after all this time, I might still draw a naked blade and leap for Papa's throat.

"Good morning, my nephew," said Friedlander Bey solemnly. "How is your health?"

"I thank God every hour," I replied. I seated myself across the table from him and began helping myself from the breakfast platters.

Papa was wearing a pale blue long-sleeved shirt and brown woolen trousers, with a red felt *tarboosh* on his head. He hadn't shaved in two or three days, and his face was covered with gray stubble. He'd been hospitalized recently, and he'd lost a lot of weight. His cheeks were sunken and his hands trembled. Still, the sharpness of his mind hadn't been affected.

"Do you have someone in mind to help you with our datalink project, my darling?" he asked me, cutting short the pleasantries and getting right to business.

"I believe so, O Shaykh. My friend, Jacques Dévaux."

"The Moroccan boy? The Christian?"

"Yes," I said, "although I'm not sure that I completely trust him."

Papa nodded. "It's good that you think so. It's not wise to trust any man until he's been tested. We will talk about this more after I hear the estimates from the datalink companies."

"Yes, O Shaykh."

I watched him carefully pare an apple with a silver knife. "You were told of the gathering this evening, my nephew?" he said.

We'd been invited to a reception at the palace of Shaykh Mahali, the amir of the city. "I'm startled to learn that I've come to the prince's attention," I said.

Papa gave me a brief smile. "There is more to it than joy over your recent marriage. The amir has said that he cannot permit a feud to exist between myself and Shaykh Reda Abu Adil."

"Ah, I see. And tonight's celebration will be the amir's attempt to reconcile you?"

"His *futile* attempt to reconcile us." Friedlander Bey frowned at the apple, then stabbed it fiercely with the knife and put it aside. "There will be no peace between Shaykh Reda and myself. That is quite simply impossible. But I can see that the amir is in a difficult position: when kings do battle, it is the peasants who die."

I smiled. "Are you saying that you and Shaykh Reda are the kings in this case, and the prince of the city is the peasant?"

"He certainly cannot match our power, can he? His influence extends over the city, while we control entire nations."

I sat back in my chair and gazed at him. "Do you expect another attack tonight, my grandfather?"

Friedlander Bey rubbed his upper lip thoughtfully. "No," he said slowly, "not tonight, while we're under the protection of the prince. Shaykh Reda is certainly not that foolish. But soon, my nephew. Very soon."

"I'll be on my guard," I said, standing and taking my leave of the old man. The last thing in the world I wanted to hear was that we were being drawn into another intrigue.

During the afternoon I received a delegation from Cappadocia, which wanted Friedlander Bey's help in declaring independence from Anatolia and setting up a people's republic. Most people thought that Papa and Abu Adil made their fortunes by peddling vice, but that was not entirely true. It was a fact that they were responsible for almost all the illicit activities in the city, but that existed primarily as employment for their countless relatives, friends, and associates.

The true source of Papa's wealth was in keeping track of the ever-shifting national lineup in our part of the world. In a time when the average lifespan of a new country was shorter than a single generation of its citizens, someone had to preserve order amid the political chaos. That was the expensive service that Friedlander Bey and Shaykh Reda provided. From one regime to the next, they remembered where the boundaries were, who the taxpayers were, and where the bodies were buried, literally and figuratively. Whenever one government gave way to its successor, Papa or Shaykh Reda stepped in to smooth the transition—and to cut themselves a larger chunk of the action with each change.

I found all of this fascinating, and I was glad that Papa had put me to work in this area, rather than overseeing the lucrative but basically boring criminal enterprises. My great-grandfather tutored me with endless patience, and he'd directed Tariq and Youssef to give me whatever help I needed. When I'd first come to Friedlander Bey's house, I'd thought they were only Papa's valet and butler; but now I realized they knew more about the high-level goings-on throughout the Islamic world than anyone else, except Friedlander Bey himself.

When at last the Cappadocians excused themselves, I saw that I had little more than an hour before Papa and I were expected at the amir's palace. Kmuzu helped me select an appropriate outfit. It had been some time since I'd last put on my old jeans and boots and work shirt, and I was getting used to wearing a more traditional Arab costume. Some of the men in the city still wore Euram-style business suits, but I'd never felt comfortable in one. I'd taken to wearing the *gallebeya* around Papa's house, because I knew he preferred it. Besides, it was easier to hide my static pistol under a loose robe, and a *keffiya*, the Arab headdress, hid my implants, which offended some conservative Muslims.

So when I'd finished dressing, I was wearing a spotless white *gallebeya* suitable for a bridegroom, beneath a royal blue robe trimmed in gold. I had comfortable sandals on my feet, a ceremonial dagger belted around my waist, and a plain white *keffiya* held by a black rope *akal*.

"You look very handsome, *yaa Sidi*," said Kmuzu.

"I hope so," I said. "I've never gone to meet a prince before."

"You've proven your worth, and your reputation must already be known to the amir. You have no reason to be intimidated by him."

That was easy for Kmuzu to say. I took a final glance at my reflection and wasn't particularly impressed by what I saw. "Marîd Audran, Defender of the Downtrodden," I said dubiously. "Yeah, you right." Then we went downstairs to meet Friedlander Bey.

Tariq drove Papa's limousine, and we arrived at the amir's palace on time. We were shown into the ballroom, and I was invited to recline on some cushions at the place of honor, at Shaykh Mahali's right hand. Friedlander Bey and the other guests made themselves comfortable, and I was introduced to many of the city's wealthy and influential men.

"Please, refresh yourself," said the amir. A servant offered a tray laden with small cups of thick coffee spiced with cardamom and cinnamon, and tall glasses of chilled fruit juices. There were no alcoholic beverages because Shaykh Mahali was a deeply religious man.

"May your table last forever," I said. "Your hospitality is famous in the city, O Shaykh."

"Rejoicings and celebrations!" he replied, pleased by my flattery. We conversed for about half an hour before the servants began bringing in platters of vegetables and roasted meats. The amir had ordered enough food to stuff a company five times our size. He used an elegant, jeweled knife to offer me the choicest morsels. I've had a lifelong distrust of the rich and powerful, but despite that, I rather liked the prince.

He poured a cup of coffee for himself and offered me another. "We live in a mongrel city," he told me, "and there are so many factions and parties that my judgment is always being tested. I study the methods of the great Muslim rulers of the past. Just today I read a wonderful story about Ibn Saud, who governed a united Arabia that for a time bore his family's name. He, too, had to devise swift and clever solutions to difficult problems.

"One day when Ibn Saud was visiting the camp of a tribe of nomads, a shrieking woman ran to him and clasped his feet. She demanded that the murderer of her husband be put to death.

" 'How was your husband killed?' asked the king.

"The woman said, 'The murderer climbed high up on a date palm to pick the fruit. My husband was minding his own business, sitting beneath the tree in the shade. The murderer lost his grip in the tree and fell on him, breaking my husband's neck. Now he is dead and I am a poor widow with no way to support my orphaned children!'

"Ibn Saud rubbed his chin thoughtfully. 'Do you think the man fell on your husband intentionally?' he asked.

" 'What difference does it make? My husband is dead all the same!'

" 'Well, will you take an honest compensation, or do you truly demand the death of this man?'

" 'According to the Straight Path, the murderer's life belongs to me.'

"Ibn Saud shrugged. There was very little he could do with such an obstinate woman, but he said this to her, 'Then he will die, and the manner of his death must be the same as the way he took your husband's life. I command that this man be tied firmly to the trunk of the date palm. You must climb forty feet to the top of the tree, and from there you shall fall down upon the neck of the man and kill him.' The king paused to look at the woman's family and neighbors gathered around. 'Or will you accept the honest compensation, after all?'

"The woman hesitated a moment, accepted the money, and went away."

I laughed out loud, and the other guests applauded Shaykh Mahali's anecdote. In a short time I'd completely forgotten that he was the amir of the city and I was, well, only who I am.

The pleasant edge was taken off the evening by the grand entrance of Reda Abu Adil. He came in noisily, and he greeted the other guests as if he and not the amir were the host of the party. He was dressed very much as I was, including a *keffiya*, which I knew was hiding his own corymbic implant. Behind Abu Adil trailed a young man, probably his new administrative assistant and lover. The young man had short blond hair, wire-rimmed spectacles, and thin, bloodless lips. He was wearing an ankle-length white cotton shift with an expensively tailored silk sport coat over it, and blue felt slippers on his feet. He glanced around the room and turned a look of distaste on everyone in turn.

Abu Adil's expression turned to joy when he saw Friedlander Bey and me. "My old friends!" he cried, crossing the ballroom and pulling Papa to his feet. They embraced, although Papa said nothing at all. Then Shaykh Reda turned to me. "And here is the lucky bridegroom!"

I didn't stand up, which was a blatant insult, but Abu Adil pretended not to notice. "I've brought you a fine gift!" he said, looking around to be certain that everyone was paying attention. "Kenneth, give the young man his gift."

The blond kid stared at me for a brief moment, sizing me up. Then he reached into his jacket's inner pocket and took out an envelope. He held it out toward me between two fingers, but he wasn't going to come close enough for me to take it. Apparently he thought this was some kind of contest.

Personally, I didn't give a damn. I went to him and grabbed the envelope. He gave me a little quirk of the lips and raised his eyebrows, as if to say "We'll sort out where we stand later." I wanted to throw the envelope in the fool's face.

I remembered where I was and who was watching, so I tore open the envelope and took out a folded sheet of paper. I read Abu Adil's gift, but I couldn't make any sense of it. I read it again, and it wasn't any clearer the second time. "I don't know what to say," I said.

Shaykh Reda laughed. "I knew you'd be pleased!" Then he turned slowly, so that his words would be heard easily by the others. "I have used my influence with the *Jaish* to obtain a commission for Marîd Audran. He's now an officer in the Citizen's Army!"

The *Jaish* was this unofficial right-wing outfit that I'd run into before. They liked to dress up in gray uniforms and parade through the streets. Originally their mission was to rid the city of foreigners. As time passed, and as more of the paramilitary group's funding came from people such as Reda Abu Adil—who himself had come to the city at a young age—the aim of the *Jaish* changed. Now it seemed that its mission was to harass Abu Adil's enemies, foreigner and native alike.

"I don't know what to say," I said again. It was a pretty bizarre thing for Shaykh Reda to have done, and for the life of me, I couldn't figure what his motive had been. Knowing him, however, it would all become painfully clear soon enough.

"All our past disagreements have been settled," said Abu Adil cheerfully. "We'll be friends and allies from now on. We must work together to better the lives of the poor *fellahîn* who depend on us."

The assembled guests liked that sentiment and applauded. I glanced at Friedlander Bey, who only gave me a slight shrug. It was obvious to us both that Abu Adil had some new scheme unfolding before our eyes.

"Then I toast the bridegroom," said Shaykh Mahali, rising. "And I toast the ending of conflict between Friedlander Bey and Reda Abu Adil. I am known among my people as an honest man, and I have tried to rule this city with wisdom and justice. This peace between your houses will make my own task simpler." He lifted his cup of coffee, and everyone else stood and followed suit. To all but Papa and me, it must have seemed a hopeful time of reconciliation. I felt nothing but a growing knot of dread deep in my belly.

The remainder of the evening was pleasant enough, I guess. After a while I was quite full of food and coffee, and I'd had enough conversation with wealthy strangers to last me many days. Abu Adil did not go out of his way to cross our paths again that night, but I couldn't help noticing that his blond pal, Kenneth, kept glancing at me and shaking his head.

I suffered through the party for a little while longer, but then I was driven outside by boredom. I enjoyed Shaykh Mahali's elaborate gardens, taking deep breaths of the flower-scented air and sipping an iced glass of Sharâb. The party was still going strong inside the amir's official residence, but I'd had enough of the other guests, who came in two varieties: men I'd never met before and with whom I had little in common, and men I did know and whom I just wanted to avoid.

There were no female guests at this affair, so even though it was nominally a celebration of my marriage, my wife Indihar was not present. I'd come with Kmuzu, Friedlander Bey, his driver, Tariq, and his two giant bodyguards, Habib and Labib. Tariq, Kmuzu, and the Stones That Speak were enjoying their refreshments with the other servants in a separate building that also served as the amir's garage and stables.

"If you wish to return home, my nephew," said Friedlander Bey, "we may take leave of our host." Papa had always called me "nephew," although he must have known of our true relationship since before our first meeting.

"I've had my fill of this amusement, O Shaykh," I said. Actually, for the last quarter hour I'd been watching a meteor shower in the cloudless sky.

"It is just as well. I've grown very tired. Here, let me lean on your arm."

"Certainly, O Shaykh." He'd always been a bull of a man, but he was old, nearing his two-hundredth birthday. And not many months before, someone had tried to murder him, and he'd required a lot of sophisticated neurosurgery to repair the damage. He'd not yet completely recovered from that experience, and he was still weak and rather unsteady.

Together we made our way up from the beautiful formal gardens and back along the cloistered walk to the softly lighted ballroom. When he saw us approaching, the amir rose and came forward, extending his arms to embrace Friedlander Bey. "You have done my house great honor, O Excellent One!" he said.

I stood aside and let Papa take care of the formalities. I had the sense that the reception had been some kind of meeting between those two powerful men, that the celebration of my marriage had been entirely irrelevant to whatever subtle discussions they had conducted. "May your table last forever, O Prince!" said Papa.

"I thank you, O Wise One," said Shaykh Mahali. "Are you leaving us now?"

"It is after midnight, and I'm an old man. After I depart, you young men may get on with the serious revelry."

The amir laughed. "You take our love with you, O Shaykh." He leaned forward and kissed Friedlander Bey on both cheeks. "Go in safety."

"May Allah lengthen your life," said Papa.

Shaykh Mahali turned to me. *"Kif oo basat!"* he said. That means "Good spirits and cheer!" and it kind of sums up the city's attitude toward life.

"We thank you for your hospitality," I said, "and for the honor you've done us."

The amir seemed pleased with me. "May the blessings of Allah be on you, young man," he said.

"Peace be with you, O Prince." And we backed away a few steps, then turned and walked out into the night.

I had been given a veritable hillock of gifts by the amir and by many of the other guests. These were still on display in the ballroom, and would be gathered up and delivered to Friedlander Bey's house the next day. As Papa and I emerged into the warm night air, I felt well fed and content. We passed through the gardens again, and I admired the carefully tended flowering trees and their shimmering images in the reflecting pool. Faintly over the water came the sound of laughter, and I heard the liquid trickle of fountains, but otherwise the night was still.

Papa's limousine was sheltered in Shaykh Mahali's garage. We'd begun to cross the grassy courtyard toward it, when its headlights flashed on. The ancient car—one of the few internal combustion vehicles still operating in the city—rolled slowly toward us. The driver's window slid silently down, and I was surprised to see not Tariq but Hajjar, the crooked police lieutenant who supervised the affairs of the Budayeen.

"Get in the car," he said. "Both of you."

I looked at Friedlander Bey, who only shrugged. We got in the car. Hajjar probably thought he was in control, but Papa didn't seem the least bit worried, even though there was a big guy with a needle gun in his hand facing us on the jump seat.

"The hell's this all about, Hajjar?" I said.

"I'm placing both of you under arrest," said the cop. He pressed a control, and the glass panel slid up between him and the passenger compartment. Papa and I were alone with Hajjar's goon, and the goon didn't seem interested in making conversation.

"Just stay calm," said Papa.

"This is Abu Adil's doing, isn't it?" I said.

"Possibly." He shrugged. "It will all be made clear according to the will of Allah."

I couldn't help fretting. I hate being helpless. I watched Friedlander Bey, a prisoner in his own limousine, in the hands of a cop who'd taken the pay of both Papa and his chief rival, Reda Abu Adil. For a few minutes, my stomach churned and I rehearsed several clever and heroic things I'd do when Hajjar let us out of the car again. Then, as we drove through the twisting, narrow back streets of the city, my mind began searching for some clue as to what was happening to us now.

Soon the pain in my belly really began to gripe me, and I wished I'd brought my pillcase with me. Papa had warned me that it would be a serious breach of etiquette to carry my cache of pharmaceuticals into the amir's house. This was what I got for turning into such a respectful guy. I got kidnapped, and I had to suffer through every little physical discomfort that came my way.

I had a small selection of daddies on a rack in the pocket of my *gallebeya*. One of them did a great job of blocking pain, but I didn't want to find out what the goon would do if I tried to reach inside my robe. It wouldn't have cheered me up to hear that things would soon get a lot worse before they got better.

After what seemed like an hour of driving, the limousine came to a stop. I didn't know where we were. I looked at Hajjar's goon and said, "What's going on?"

"Shut up," the goon informed me.

Hajjar got out of the car and held the door open for Papa. I climbed out after him. We were standing beside some buildings made of corrugated metal, looking at a private suborbital shuttle across a broad concrete apron, its running lights flashing but its three giant thrusters cool and quiet. If this was the main airfield, then we were about thirty miles north of the city. I'd never been there before.

I was getting worried, but Papa still had a calm look on his face. Hajjar pulled me aside. "Got your phone on you, Audran?" he said quietly.

"Yeah," I said. I always wear it on my belt.

"Let me use it a minute, okay?"

I unclipped my phone and handed it to Hajjar. He grinned at me, dropped the phone to the pavement, and stomped it into tiny broken pieces. "Thanks," he said.

"The fuck is going on?" I shouted, grabbing him by the arm.

Hajjar just looked at me, amused. Then his goon grabbed me and pinned both of my arms behind my back. "We're going to get on that shuttle," he said. "There's a qadi who has something to tell the both of you."

We were taken aboard the suborbital and made to take seats in an otherwise empty front cabin. Hajjar sat beside me, and his goon sat beside Friedlander Bey. "We have a right to know where you're taking us," I said.

Hajjar examined his fingernails, pretending indifference. "Tell you the truth," he said, gazing out the window, "I don't actually know where you're going. The qadi may tell you that when he reads you the verdict."

"Verdict?" I cried. "What verdict?"

"Oh," said Hajjar with an evil grin, "haven't you figured it out? You and Papa are on trial. The qadi will decide you're guilty while you're being deported. Doing it this way saves the legal system a lot of time and money. I should've let you kiss the ground good-bye, Audran, because you're never going to see the city again!"

two

honey pílar is the most desirable woman in the world. Ask any-body. Ask the ancient, wrinkled imam of the Shimaal Mosque, and he'll tell you "Honey Pílar, no question about it." She has long, pale hair, liquid green eyes, and the most awe-inspiring body known to anthropological science. Fortunately, she's attainable. What she does for a living is record personality modules of herself during sex play. There are Brigitte Stahlhelm and other stars in the sex-moddy industry, but none of them come close to delivering the super-light-speed eroti-cism of Honey Pílar.

A few times, just for variety, I told Yasmin that I wanted to wear one of Honey's moddies. Yasmin would grin and take over the active role, and I'd lie back and experience what it felt like to be a hungry, furiously responsive woman. If nothing else, the moddy trade has helped a lot of people get some insight into what makes the eight oppo-site sexes tick.

After we'd finished jamming, I'd keep Honey's moddy chipped in for a while. Honey's afterglow was just as phenomenal as her orgasms. Without the moddy, I might have rolled over and drifted off to sleep. With it, I curled up close to Yasmin, closed my eyes, and just bathed in physical and emotional well-being. The only other thing I can compare it to is a nice shot of morphine. The way the morphine makes you feel after you're done throwing up, I mean.

That's just how I felt when I opened my eyes. I didn't have any memory of supersonic sex, so I assumed that somewhere along the line I'd run into a friendly pharmaceutical or two. My eyelids seemed stuck together, and when I tried to rub the gunk out of them, my arm wouldn't work. It felt like a phony arm made out of Styrofoam or something, and it didn't want to do anything but flop around on the sand next to me.

Okay, I thought, I'm going to have to sort all this out in a minute or two. I forgot about my eyes and sunk back into delicious lethargy. Someday I wanted to meet the guy who invented lethargy, because I now believed he hadn't gotten enough credit from the world at large. This was exactly how I wanted to spend the rest of my life, and until somebody came up with a reason why I couldn't, I was just going to lie there in the dark and play with my floppy arm.

I was lying with my back on the earth, and my mind was floating in Heaven somewhere, and the dividing line seemed to run right through my body. Right through the part that hurt so much. I could feel the ragged pain thrumming down there, beneath the opiate haze. As soon as I realized what kind of agony I'd feel when the drug wore off, I began to get very afraid. Fortunately, I couldn't keep my mind on it for more than a few seconds, and then I was grinning and murmuring to myself again.

I suppose I fell asleep, although in that state it was very hard to tell the difference between consciousness and dreams. I remember trying again to open my eyes, and this time I could move my hand to my chin and kind of walk the fingers across my lips and nose to my eyelids. I wiped my eyes clean, but I was so tired from that exertion that I couldn't move my hand back down. I had to rest for a minute or so with my fingers blocking my vision. Finally I tried to focus on my surroundings.

I couldn't see much. It was still too much trouble to raise my head, so all I could make out was what was directly in front of me. There was a bright triangle with a narrow base on the ground, rising up to a sharp point a few feet high. All the rest was blackness. I asked myself if I'd ever been put in mortal danger by a bright triangle. The answer was slow in coming: no. Good, I thought, then I can forget about it. I went back to sleep.

The next time I woke up, things were different. Not pleasantly different. I had a tremendous, throbbing misery in my head, and my throat felt as if a tiny little man in goggles had crawled down there and sandblasted it. My chest ached as if I'd inhaled a couple of pounds of mud and then had to cough it all up again. Every joint in my body shrieked with soreness whenever I made the slightest movement. My arms and legs were in particular agony, so I decided never to move them again.

Cataloguing all the discomfort occupied me for a few minutes, but when I got to the end of the list—when I realized that most of my skin surface was sizzling with pain, proof that I'd been flayed alive by some madman before he got around to cracking my bones—there were only a few choices: I could lie there and appreciate the totality of my suffering, I could try cataloguing again to see if I'd missed anything, or I could attempt to make myself feel better.

I opted for number three. I decided to get out my pillcase, even though that act would probably cost me a lot in terms of further distress. I remembered what my doctors told me in times like this: "Now," they always said, "this might sting a little." Uh huh.

I gently moved my right hand down across my belly, until it was resting flat beside me. Then I sort of worm-walked my fingers down my *gallebeya* toward the pocket where I kept my drugs. I made three rapid observations. The first was that I wasn't wearing my *gallebeya*. The second was that I was wearing a long, filthy shirt with no pockets. The third was that there was no pillcase.

I've been confronted by maniacs whose immediate concern was ending my life on the spot. Even in those most desperate hours, I never experienced the sheer, cold emptiness I felt now. I wonder what it says about me, that I'd prefer to risk death than endure pain. I suppose, deep down, I'm not a brave man. I'm probably motivated by a fear that other people might learn the truth about me.

I almost began to weep when I couldn't find my pillcase. I'd counted on it being there, and on the tabs of Sonneine inside to take away all this horrible pain, at least for a while. I tried to call out. My lips were as crusted over as my eyelids had been. It took a little effort even to open my mouth, and then my throat was too hoarse and dry for me to speak. At last, after much effort, I managed to croak "Help." Uttering the single syllable made the back of my throat feel as if someone had hacked my neck open with a dull knife. I doubted that anyone could have heard me.

I don't know how much time passed. I grew aware that in addition to my other discomforts, I was also suffering from great hunger and thirst. The longer I lay there, the more I began to worry that I'd finally gotten myself into trouble I wouldn't survive. I hadn't yet begun to speculate on where I was or how I'd got there.

I noticed after a while that the bright triangle was getting dimmer. Sometimes I thought the triangle seemed obscured, as if someone or something was passing in front of it. At last, the triangle almost completely disappeared. I realized that I missed it very much. It had been the only actual thing in my world besides myself, even though I didn't really know what it was.

A spot of yellow light appeared in the gloom where the bright triangle had been. I blinked my eyes hard a few times, trying to make them focus more clearly. I saw that the yellow light was coming from a small oil lamp, in the hand of a small person swathed almost completely in black. The black-clothed person came toward me through the triangle, which I now guessed must be the opening of a tent. A truly evil-smelling tent, I realized.

My visitor held the lamp up to let the light fall upon my face. *"Yaa Allah!"* she murmured when she saw that I was conscious. Her other hand quickly grasped the edge of her head cloth and pulled it across her face. I had seen her only briefly, but I knew that she was a solemn, pretty, but very dirty girl, probably in her late teens.

I took as deep a breath as I could with the pain in my chest and lungs, and I croaked out another "Help." She stood there, blinking down at me for a few moments. Then she knelt, placed the lamp on the level sand beyond my reach, stood up again, and ran from the tent. I have that effect on women sometimes.

Now I began to worry. Where exactly was I, and how did I get here? Was I in the hands of friends or enemies? I knew I must be among desert nomads, but which desert? There are quite a number of sand seas throughout the geographic expanse of the Islamic world. I could be anywhere from the western edge of the Sahara in Morocco to the fringes of the Gobi in Mongolia. I might have been only a few miles south of the city, for that matter.

While I was turning these thoughts over in my troubled mind, the dark-shrouded girl returned. She stood beside me and asked me questions. I could tell they were questions by the inflections. The trouble was that I could make out only about one word in ten. She was speaking some rough dialect of Arabic, but she might as well have been jabbering in Japanese for all I could tell.

I shook my head, once slightly to the left, once to the right. "I hurt," I said in my dead voice.

She just stared at me. It didn't seem that she'd understood me. She was still holding her head cloth modestly across her face, just below her nose, but I thought her expression—that part of it that was visible—was very kind and concerned. At least, I chose to believe that for the moment.

She tried speaking to me again, but I still couldn't understand what she was saying. I managed to get out "Who are you?" and she nodded and said "Noora." In Arabic, that means "light," but I guessed it was also her name. From the moment she'd come into the tent with her lamp, she'd been the only light in my darkness.

The front flap was thrown roughly aside and someone else entered, carrying a leather bag and another lamp. This was not a large tent, maybe twelve feet in diameter and six feet high, so it was getting kind of crowded. Noora moved back against the black wall, and the man squatted beside me and studied me for a moment. He had a stern, lean face dominated by a huge hooked nose. His skin was lined and weathered, and it was difficult for me to guess his age. He wore a long shirt and he had a *keffiya* on his head, but it wasn't bound with a black rope *akal*, merely twisted around with its ends stuffed in somehow. In the dancing shadows he looked like a murderous savage.

Matters weren't made any better when he asked me a few questions in the same dialect Noora had used. I think one of them had to do with where I'd come from. All I could do was tell him about the city. He may have then asked me where the city was, but I couldn't be sure that's what he said.

"I hurt," I croaked.

He nodded and opened his leather bag. I was surprised when he pulled out an old-fashioned disposable syringe and a vial of some fluid. He loaded the needle and jammed it into my hip. I gasped in pain, and he patted my wrist. He clucked something, and even ignorant of his dialect I could tell it was "There, there."

He stood up and regarded me thoughtfully for a while longer. Then he signaled to Noora and they left me alone. In a few minutes, the injection had taken effect. My expertise in these matters told me that I'd been given a healthy dose of Sonneine; the injectable variety was much more effective than the tabs I bought in the Budayeen. I was tearfully grateful. If that rough-skinned man had come back into the tent just then, I would have given him anything he asked.

I surrendered myself to the powerful drug and floated, knowing all the while that the relief from pain would soon end. In the illusory moments of well-being, I tried to do some serious thinking. I knew that something was terribly wrong, and that as soon as I was better I'd need to set things right again. The Sonneine let me believe that nothing was beyond my power.

My drug-deluded mind told me that I was in a state of grace. Everything was fine. I'd achieved a separate peace with the world and with every individual in it. I felt as if I had immense stores of physical and intellectual energy to draw upon. There were problems, yes, but they were eminently solvable. The future looked like one golden vista of victory after another: Heaven on Earth.

It was while I was congratulating myself on my good fortune that the hawk-faced man returned, this time without Noora. I was sort of sad about that. Anyway, the man squatted down beside me, resting his haunches on his heels. I could never get the hang of sitting like that for very long; I've always been a city boy.

This time when he spoke to me, I could understand him perfectly. "Who are you, O Shaykh?" he asked.

"Ma—" I began. My throat tightened up. I pointed to my lips. The man understood me and passed me a goatskin bag filled with brackish water. The bag stunk and the water was the most foul-tasting I'd ever encountered. "*Bismillah,*" I murmured: in the name of God. Then I drank that horrible water greedily until he put a hand on my arm and stopped me.

"Marîd," I said, answering his question.

He took back the water bag. "I am Hassanein. Your beard is red. I've never seen a red beard before."

"Common," I said, able to speak a little better now that I'd had some water. "In Mauretania."

"Mauretania?" He shook his head.

"Used to be Algeria. In the Maghreb." Again he shook his head. I wondered how far I'd wandered, that I'd met an Arab who had never heard of the Maghreb, the name given to the western Muslim lands of North Africa.

"What race are you?" Hassanein asked.

I looked at him in surprise. "An Arab," I said.

"No," he said, "*I* am an Arab. You are something else." He was firm in his statement, although I could tell that it was made without malice. He was truly curious about me.

Calling myself an Arab was inaccurate, because I am half Berber, half French, or so my mother always told me. In my adopted city, anyone born in the Muslim world and who spoke the Arabic language was an Arab. Here in Hassanein's tent that relaxed definition would not do. "I am Berber," I told him.

"I do not know Berbers. We are Bani Salim."

"Badawi?" I asked.

"Bedu," he corrected me. It turned out that the word I'd always used for the Arabian nomads, Badawi or Bedouin, was an inelegant plural of a plural. The nomads themselves preferred Bedu, which derives from the word for desert.

"You treated me?" I said.

Hassanein nodded. He reached out his hand. In the flickering lamplight, I could see the dusting of sand on the hairs of his arm, like sugar on a lemon cake. He lightly touched my corymbic implants. "You are cursed," he said.

I didn't reply. Apparently he was a strict Muslim who felt that I was going to hell because I'd had my brain wired.

"You are doubly cursed," he said. Even here, my second implant was a topic of conversation. I wondered where my rack of moddies and daddies was.

"Hungry," I said.

He nodded. "Tomorrow, you may eat, *inshallah*." If God wills. It was hard for me to imagine that Allah had brought me through whatever trials I'd endured, just to keep me from having breakfast in the morning.

He picked up the lamp and held it close to my face. With a grimy thumb he pulled down my eyelid and examined my eye. He had me open my mouth, and he looked at my tongue and the back of my throat. He bent forward and put his ear on my chest, then had me cough. He poked and prodded me expertly. "School," I said, pointing at him. "University."

He laughed and shook his head. He slowly bent my legs up and then tickled the soles of my feet. He pressed on my fingernails and watched to see how long it took for the color to return.

"Doctor?" I asked.

He shook his head again. Then he looked at me and came to some decision. He grabbed his *keffiya* and pulled it loose. I was astonished to see that he had his own moddy plug on the crown of his skull. Then he carefully wrapped the *keffiya* around his head again.

I looked at him questioningly. "Cursed," I said.

"Yes," he said. He wore a stoic expression. "I am the shaykh of the Bani Salim. It is my responsibility. I must wear the mark of the *shaitan*."

"How many moddies?" I asked.

He didn't understand the word "moddies." I rephrased the question, and found out that he'd had his skull amped so that he could use just two modules: the doctor moddy, and one that made him the equivalent of a learned religious leader. Those were all he owned. In the arid wilderness that was home to the Bani Salim, Hassanein was the wise elder who had, in his own eyes, damned his soul for the sake of his tribe.

I realized that we were understanding each other thanks to grammar and vocabulary built into the doctor moddy. When he took it out, we'd have as much trouble communicating as we'd had before. I was getting too weary to keep up this conversation any further, though. Any more would have to wait until tomorrow.

He gave me a capsule to help me sleep through the night. I swallowed it with more of the water from the goatskin. "May you arise in the morning in well-being, O Shaykh," he said.

"God bless you, O Wise One," I murmured. He left the lamp burning on the sand floor beside me, and stood up. He went out into the darkness, and I heard him drop the tent flap behind him. I still didn't know where I was, and I didn't know a damn thing about the Bani Salim, but for some reason I felt perfectly safe. I fell asleep quickly and woke up only once during the night, to see Noora sitting crosslegged against the black wall of the tent, asleep.

When I woke again in the morning, I could see more clearly. I raised my head a little and stared out through the bright triangle. Now I could see a landscape of golden sand and, not far away, two hobbled camels. In the tent, Noora still watched over me. She had awakened before me, and when she saw me move my head, she came closer. She still self-consciously drew the edge of her head scarf across her face, which was a shame because she was very pretty.

"Thought we were friends," I said. I didn't have so much trouble talking this morning.

Her brows drew together and she shook her head. I wasn't having trouble talking, but I was still having trouble being understood. I tried again, speaking more slowly and using both hands to amplify my words.

"We . . . are . . . friends," she said. Each word was strangely accented, but I could decipher the dialect if she gave me a little time. "You . . . guest . . . of . . . Bani Salim."

Ah, the legendary hospitality of the Bedu! "Hassanein is your father?" I asked. She shook her head; I didn't know if she was denying the relationship or if she just hadn't understood my question. I repeated it more slowly.

"Shaykh . . . Hassanein . . . father's . . . brother," she said.

After that, we both got used to speaking simply and putting space between our words. It wasn't long before we weren't having any trouble following each other, even at normal conversational speed.

"Where are we?" I asked. I had to find where I was in relation to the city, and how far from the nearest outpost of civilization.

Noora's brow wrinkled again as she considered her geography. She poked a forefinger into the sand in front of her. "Here is Bir Balagh. The Bani Salim have camped here two weeks." She poked another hole in the sand, about three inches from the first. "Here is Khaba well, three days south." She reached across the much greater distance between us and made another hole with her finger. "Here is Mughshin. Mughshin is *hauta*."

"What's *hauta*?" I asked.

"A holy place, Shaykh Marîd. The Bani Salim will meet other tribes there, and sell their camel herd."

Fine, I thought, we were all headed for Mughshin. I'd never heard of Mughshin, and I imagined it was probably just a little patch of palm trees and a well, stuck in the middle of the awful desert. It most likely didn't have a suborbital shuttle field nearby. I knew I was lost somewhere in the kingdoms and unmarked tribal turfs of Arabia. "How far from Riyadh?" I asked.

"I don't know Riyadh," said Noora. Riyadh was the former capital of her country, when it had been united under the House of Saud. It was still a great city.

"Mecca?"

"Makkah," she corrected me. She thought for a few seconds, then pointed confidently across my body.

"That way," I said. "Good. How far?" Noora only shrugged. I hadn't learned very much.

"I'm sorry," she said. "The old shaykh asked the same questions. Maybe Uncle Hassanein knows more."

The old shaykh! I'd been so wrapped up in my own misery that I'd forgotten about Papa. "The old shaykh is alive?"

"Yes, thanks to you, and thanks to the wisdom of Uncle Hassanein. When Hilal and bin Turki found the two of you on the dunes, they thought you were both dead. They came back to our camp, and if they hadn't told Uncle Hassanein about you later that evening, you surely *would* be dead."

I stared at her for a moment. "Hilal and bin Turki just left us out there?"

She shrugged. "They thought you were dead."

I shivered. "Glad it crossed their minds to mention us while they were sitting comfortably around the communal fire."

Noora didn't catch my bitterness. "Uncle Hassanein brought you back to camp. This is his tent. The old shaykh is in the tent of bin Musaid." Her eyes lowered when she mentioned his name.

"Then where are your uncle and bin Musaid sleeping?" I asked.

"They sleep with the others who have no tents. On the sand by the fire."

That naturally made me feel a little guilty, because I knew the desert got very cold at night. "How is the old shaykh?" I asked.

"He is getting stronger every day. He suffered greatly from exposure and thirst, but not as greatly as you. It was your sacrifice that kept him alive, Shaykh Marîd."

I didn't remember any sacrifice. I didn't remember anything about what we'd been through. Noora must have seen my confusion, because she reached out and almost touched my implants. "These," she said.

"You abused them and now you suffer, but it saved the life of the old shaykh. He wants very much to speak with you. Uncle Hassanein told him that tomorrow you may have visitors."

I was relieved to hear that Friedlander Bey was in better shape than I was. I hoped that he might be able to fill in some of the gaps in my recollection. "How long have I been here?"

She did some mental figuring, then replied, "Twelve days. The Bani Salim planned to remain in Bir Balagh only three days, but Uncle Hassanein decided to stay until you and the old shaykh were fit to travel. Some of the tribe are angry about that, especially bin Musaid."

"You mentioned him before. Who is this bin Musaid?"

Noora lowered her eyes and spoke in a low voice. "He desires to marry me," she said.

"Uh huh. And how do you feel about him?"

She looked into my face. I could see anger in her eyes, although I couldn't tell if it was directed at me or her suitor. She stood up and walked out of the tent without saying another word.

I wished she hadn't done that. I'd meant to ask her for something to eat, and to pass the word to her uncle that I'd like another jolt of Sonneine. Instead, I just tried to find a comfortable position to lie in, and I thought about what Noora had told me.

Papa and I had almost died in this wilderness, but I didn't yet know whom to blame that on. I wouldn't be surprised if it was all connected to Lieutenant Hajjar, and through him to Reda Abu Adil. The last thing I remembered was sitting on that suborbital shuttle, waiting for it to take off. Everything that came after—the flight itself, the arrival at the destination, and whatever events had led me into the middle of the desert—was still missing from my memory. I hoped it would all come back as I got stronger, or that Papa had a clearer idea of what had happened.

I decided to focus my rage on Abu Adil. I knew that although I felt peaceful enough now, I was still in deadly peril. For one thing, even if the Bani Salim permitted us to accompany them to Mughshin— wherever the hell *that* was—it would be very difficult to arrange our travel back to the city. We couldn't just show up again without risking arrest. We'd have to avoid Papa's mansion, and it would be very dangerous for me to set foot in the Budayeen.

All that was in the future, however. We had more immediate things to worry about. I had no real assurance that the Bani Salim would remain friendly. I guessed that Bedu hospitality required them to nurse Papa and me back to health. After that, all bets were off. When we were able to fend for ourselves again, the tribe might even capture us and turn us over to our enemies. There might be reward money in it for them. It would be a mistake to let our guard down too far.

I knew one thing for certain: if Hajjar and Abu Adil were responsible for what happened to us after we left the shuttle, they would pay dearly for it. I would swear an oath to that effect.

My grim thoughts were interrupted by Hassanein, who gave me a cheerful greeting. "Here, O Shaykh," he said, "you may eat." He gave me a round, flat piece of unleavened bread and a bowl of some ghastly white fluid. I looked up at him. "Camel's milk," he said. I'd been afraid he was going to say that.

"Bismillah," I murmured. I broke a piece of bread and ate it, then sipped from the bowl. The camel's milk wasn't bad, actually. It was certainly much easier to get down than the water in the goatskin bag.

Shaykh Hassanein squatted on his heels beside me. "Some of the Bani Salim are restless," he said, "and they say that if we wait here too long, we won't get as much money for our camels in Mughshin. Also, we must find somewhere else to graze the animals. You must be ready to travel in two days."

"Sure, be ready when you are." Ha ha, I thought. I was just putting up a noble front.

He nodded. "Eat some more bread. Later, Noora will bring you some dates and tea. Tonight, if you wish, you may have a little roasted goat."

I was so hungry that I'd have gnawed an uncooked carcass. There was sand in the bread and grit in the milk, but I didn't care.

"Have you used this time to ponder the meaning of what has happened to you?" asked Hassanein.

"Yes, indeed, O Wise One," I said. "My mind is empty of the details, but I've thought long and hard about why I came so near to death. I've looked ahead, too. There will come a harvesting."

The leader of the Bani Salim nodded. I wondered if he knew what I was thinking. I wondered if he would recognize the name of Reda Abu Adil. "That is well," he said in a carefully neutral voice. He stood up to leave.

"O Wise One," I said, "will you give me something for the pain?"

His eyes narrowed as he looked down at me. "Are you truly still in such pain?"

"Yes. I'm stronger now, all praise be to Allah, but my body still suffers from the abuse."

He muttered something under his breath, but he opened his leather bag and prepared another injection. "This will be the last," he told me. Then he jabbed me in the hip.

It occurred to me that he probably didn't have a vast store of medical supplies. Hassanein had to tend to all the accidents and illnesses that struck the Bani Salim, and I had probably already consumed much of his pain-relieving medication. I wished I hadn't selfishly taken this last shot. I sighed as I waited for the Sonneine to take effect.

Hassanein left the tent, and Noora entered again.

"Anyone ever told you you're very beautiful, my sister?" I said. I wouldn't have been so bold if the opiate hadn't chosen that instant to bloom in my brain.

I could see that I'd made Noora very uncomfortable. She covered her face with her head scarf and took her position against the wall of the tent. She did not speak to me.

"Forgive me, Noora," I said, my words slurring together.

She looked away from me, and I cursed my stupidity. Then, just before I drifted off into warm, wonderful sleep, she whispered, "Am I truly so beautiful?" I grinned at her crookedly, and then my mind spun away out of this world.

Three

When my memory began to come back, I recalled that I'd been sitting next to Hajjar on the suborbital ship, and facing us had been Friedlander Bey and Hajjar's goon. The crooked cop had derived a lot of enjoyment from looking at me, shaking his head, and making little snotty chuckling noises. I found myself wondering how hard I'd have to twist his scrawny neck before his head would pop off.

Papa had maintained his air of calm. He simply wasn't going to give Hajjar the satisfaction of troubling him. After a while, I just tried to pretend that Hajjar and the goon didn't exist. I passed the time imagining them suffering all sorts of tragic accidents.

About forty minutes into the flight, when the shuttle had boosted to the top of its parabola and was coasting down toward its destination, a tall man with a thin face and a huge black mustache jerked aside the curtains to the rear cabin. This was the qadi, I imagined, the civil judge who had reached a decision in whatever case Papa and I were involved in. It did my mood no good to see that the qadi was dressed in the gray uniform and leather boots of an officer in Reda Abu Adil's *Jaish*.

He glanced down at a sheaf of papers in his hand. "Friedlander Bey?" he asked. "Marîd Audran?"

"Him and him," said Lieutenant Hajjar, jerking his thumb at us in turn.

The qadi nodded. He was still standing beside us in the aisle. "This is a most serious charge," he said. "It would have gone better for you if you'd pleaded guilty and begged for mercy."

"Listen, pal," I said, "I haven't even heard the charge yet! I don't even know what we're supposed to have done! How could we have pleaded guilty? We weren't given a chance to enter a plea at all!"

"Say, your honor?" said Hajjar. "I took the liberty of entering their pleas for them. In the interest of saving the city time and money."

"Most irregular," muttered the qadi, shuffling through his papers. "But as you entered both pleas of innocent, I see no further problem."

I slammed my fist on my seat's armrest. "But you just said it would have gone better for us if—"

"Peace, my nephew," said Papa in his imperturbable voice. He turned to the qadi. "Please, your honor, what *is* the charge against us?"

"Oh, murder," said the distracted judge. "Murder in the first degree. Now, as I have all the—"

"Murder!" I cried. I heard Hajjar laugh, and I turned and gave him a deadly look. He raised his hands to protect himself. The goon reached across and slapped my face, hard. I turned toward him, raging, but he just waved the barrel of his needle gun under my nose. I subsided a little.

"Whom were we supposed to have killed?" asked Papa.

"Just a moment, I have it here somewhere," said the qadi. "Yes, a police officer named Khalid Maxwell. The crime was discovered by an associate of Shaykh Reda Abu Adil."

"I knew Abu Adil's name would come into this," I growled.

"Khalid Maxwell," said Papa. "I've never had any contact at all with anyone by that name."

"I haven't either," I said. "I've never even heard of the guy."

"One of my most trusted subordinates," said Hajjar. "The city and the force have suffered a great loss."

"We didn't do it, Hajjar!" I shouted. "And you know it!"

The qadi looked at me sternly. "It's much too late for denials," he said. His dark face didn't seem sturdy enough to support either his bulbous nose or the bushy growth attached to it. "I've already reached my verdict."

Papa began to look a trifle upset. "You've already made your decision, without letting us present our side of the story?"

The qadi slapped his handful of paper. "All the facts are here. There are eyewitness accounts and reports from Lieutenant Hajjar's investigation. There's too much documented evidence to allow for even the slightest doubt. What is your side of the story? That you deny committing this foul crime? Of course, that's what you'd have said to me. I didn't need to waste my time listening to it. I have all this!" Again he slapped the papers.

"Then you've reached a verdict," said Papa, "and you've found us guilty."

"Precisely," said the qadi. "Guilty as charged. Guilty in the eyes of

Allah and your fellow man. However, the death penalty will be set aside because of an earnest petition from one of the city's most respected citizens."

"Shaykh Reda?" I said. My stomach was starting to bother me again.

"Yes," said the qadi. "Shaykh Reda appealed to me on your behalf. Out of respect for him, you will not be beheaded in the courtyard of the Shimaal Mosque as you deserve. Rather, your sentence is banishment. You're forbidden ever to return to the city, under pain of arrest and summary execution."

"Well," I said sourly, "that's a relief. Where are you taking us?"

"This shuttle's destination is the kingdom of Asir," said the qadi.

I looked across at Friedlander Bey. He was doing his serene old wise man routine again. I felt a little better, too. I didn't know anything about Asir other than it bordered the Red Sea south of Mecca. Asir was better than some places they could have shipped us, and from there we could begin drawing on our resources to prepare our return to the city. It would take time and a lot of money passed under a lot of tables, but we'd come home eventually. I was already looking forward to my reunion with Hajjar.

The qadi glanced from me to Papa, then nodded and retired again to the rear cabin. Hajjar waited for him to leave, then let loose a loud guffaw. "Hey!" he cried. "What you think of that?"

I grabbed his throat before he could duck out of the way. The goon rose out of his seat and threatened me with the needle gun. "Don't shoot!" I said with feigned terror, all the while squeezing Hajjar's larynx tighter. "Please, don't shoot me!"

Hajjar tried to say something, but I had his windpipe shut off. His face was turning the color of the wine of Paradise.

"Release him, my nephew," said Friedlander Bey after a moment.

"Now, O Shaykh?" I asked. I still hadn't let go.

"Now."

I flung Hajjar away from me, and the back of his head bounced off the bulkhead behind him. He gasped and choked as he tried to force air into his lungs. The goon lowered his needle gun and sat down again. I got the impression that he was no longer personally concerned with how Hajjar was feeling. I took that to mean that he didn't have a much higher opinion of the lieutenant than I did, and as long as I didn't kill Hajjar outright, I could pretty much do whatever I wanted to him without the goon interfering.

Hajjar glared at me hatefully. "You're gonna be sorry you did that," he said in a hoarse voice.

"I don't think so, Hajjar," I said. "I think the memory of your red, pop-eyed face will sustain me through all the difficulties to come."

"Sit in your seat and shut up, Audran," Hajjar uttered through clenched teeth. "Make a move or a sound, and I'll have your friend over there break your face."

I was getting bored, anyway. I put my head back and closed my eyes, thinking that when we arrived in Asir, I might need my strength. I could feel the maneuvering engines roar to life, and the pilot began turning the giant shuttlecraft in a long, slow arc toward the west. We descended rapidly, spiraling down through the night sky.

The shuttle began to tremble, and there was a long booming noise and a high-pitched wail. Hajjar's goon looked frightened. "Landing gear locking into place," I said. He gave me a brief nod.

And then the shuttle was down and screaming across a concrete field. There were no lights outside that I could see, but I was sure we must have been surrounded by a great airfield. After a while, when the pilot had braked the shuttle to what seemed like a crawl, I could see the outlines of hangars, sheds, and other buildings. Then the shuttle came to a complete stop, although we hadn't arrived at a terminal building.

"Stay in your seats," said Hajjar.

We sat there, listening to the air-conditioning whining above our heads. Finally, the qadi reappeared from the rear cabin. He still clutched his sheaf of papers. He held up one page and read from it:

" 'Witness, that regarding the acts of members of the community, which acts are certain crimes and affronts to Allah and all brothers in Islam, those in custody identified as Friedlander Bey and Marîd Audran are herein found guilty, and their punishment shall be exile from the community which they so grievously offended. This is a mercy shown unto them, and they should count the remainder of their days a blessing, and spend them in seeking the nearness of God and the forgiveness of men.' "

Then the qadi leaned against the bulkhead and put his signature to the paper, and signed a duplicate copy so that Papa could have one and I could have the other. "Now, let's go," he said.

"Come on, Audran," said Hajjar. I got up and moved into the aisle behind the qadi. The goon followed me with Papa behind him. Hajjar brought up the rear. I turned to look back at him, and his expression was oddly mournful. He must have thought that soon we'd be out of his hands, and so his fun was almost over.

We climbed down the gangway to the concrete apron. Papa and I stretched and yawned. I was very tired and getting hungry again, despite all the food I'd eaten at the amir's celebration. I looked around the airfield, trying to learn something of value. I saw a big hand-painted sign that said *Najran* on one of the low, dark buildings.

"Najran mean anything to you, O Shaykh?" I asked Friedlander Bey.

"Shut up, Audran," said Hajjar. He turned to his goon. "Make sure they don't talk or do anything funny. I'm holding you responsible." The goon nodded. Hajjar and the qadi went off together toward the building.

"Najran is the capital city of Asir," said Papa. He completely ignored the goon's presence. For his part, the goon no longer showed much interest in what we did, as long as we didn't try streaking across the landing field toward freedom.

"We have friends here?" I asked.

Papa nodded. "We have friends almost everywhere, my nephew. The problem is getting in touch with them."

I didn't understand what he meant. "Well, Hajjar and the qadi will be getting back aboard the shuttle in a little while, right? After that, I guess we're on our own. Then we can contact these friends and get some nice, soft beds to spend the rest of the night in."

Papa gave me a sad smile. "Do you truly think our troubles end here?"

My confidence faltered. "Uh, they don't?" I said.

As if to justify Papa's concern, Hajjar and the qadi came out of the building, accompanied now by a burly guy in a cop-like uniform, carrying a rifle slung under his arm. He didn't look like a particularly intelligent cop or a well-disciplined cop, but with his rifle he was probably more than Papa and I could handle.

"We must speak soon of revenge," Papa whispered to me before Hajjar reached us.

"Against Shaykh Reda," I replied.

"No. Against whoever signed our deportation order. The amir or the imam of the Shimaal Mosque."

That gave me something else to think about. I'd never learned why Friedlander Bey so scrupulously avoided harming Reda Abu Adil, whatever the provocation. And I wondered how I'd respond if Papa ordered me to kill Shaykh Mahali, the amir. Surely the prince couldn't have received us so hospitably tonight, knowing that when we left his reception we'd be kidnapped and driven into exile. I preferred to believe that Shaykh Mahali knew nothing of what was happening to us now.

"Here are your prisoners, Sergeant," Hajjar said to the fat-assed local cop.

The sergeant nodded. He looked us over and frowned. He wore a nameplate that told me his name was al-Bishah. He had a gigantic belly that was pushing its way to freedom from between the buttons of his sweat-stained shirt. There were four or five days of black stubble on his face, and his teeth were broken and stained dark brown. His eyelids drooped, and at first I thought it was because he'd been awakened in the middle of the night; but his clothes smelled strongly of hashish, and I knew that this cop passed the lonely nights on duty with his *narjîlah*.

"Lemme guess," said the sergeant. "The young guy pulled the trigger, and this raggedy-looking old fool in the red *tarboosh* is the brains of the operation." He threw his head back and roared with laughter. It must have been the hashish, because not even Hajjar cracked a smile.

"Pretty much," said the lieutenant. "They're all yours now." Hajjar turned to me. "One last thing before we say good-bye forever, Audran. Know what the first thing is I'm gonna do tomorrow?"

His grin was about the most vicious and ugly one I'd ever seen. "No, what?" I said.

"I'm gonna close down that club of yours. And you know what's the second thing?" He waited, but I refused to play along. "Okay, I'll tell you. I'm gonna bust your Yasmin for prostitution, and when I got her in my special, deep-down hole, I'm gonna see what she's got that you like so much."

I was very proud of myself. A year or two ago, I'd have smashed his teeth in, goon or no goon. I was more mature now, so I just stood there, looking impassively into his wild eyes. I repeated this to myself: the next time you see this man, you will kill him. The next time you see this man, you will kill him. That kept me from doing anything stupid while I had two weapons trained on me.

"Dream about it, Audran!" Hajjar shouted, as he and the qadi climbed back up the gangway. I didn't even turn to watch him.

"You were wise, my nephew," said Friedlander Bey. I looked at him, and I could tell from his expression that he had been favorably impressed by my behavior.

"I've learned much from you, my grandfather," I said. That seemed to please him, too.

"Aw right," said the local sergeant, "come on. Don't wanna be out here when they get that sucker movin'." He jerked the barrel of his rifle in the direction of the dark building, and Papa and I preceded him across the runway.

It was pitch black inside, but Sergeant al-Bishah didn't turn on any lights. "Just follow the wall," he said. I felt my way along a narrow corridor until it turned a corner. There was a small office there with a battered desk, a phone, a mechanical fan, and a small, beat-up holo system.

There was a chair behind the desk, and the sergeant dropped heavily into it. There was another chair in a corner, and I let Papa have it. I stood leaning against a filthy plasterboard wall.

"Now," said the cop, "we come to the matter of what I do with you. You're in Najran now, not some flea-bitten village where you got influence. You're nobody in Najran, but I'm somebody. We gonna see what you can do for me, and if you can't do nothin', you gonna go to jail."

"How much money do you have, my nephew?" Papa asked me.

"Not much." I hadn't brought a great deal with me, because I didn't think I'd need it at the amir's house. I usually carried my money divided between the pockets in my *gallebeya*, just for situations like this. I counted what I had in the left pocket; it came to a little over a hundred and eighty kiam. I wasn't about to let the dog of a sergeant know I had more in the other pocket.

"Ain't even real money, is it?" complained al-Bishah. He shoved it all into his desk drawer anyway. "What about the old guy?"

"I have no money at all," said Papa.

"Now, that's too bad." The sergeant used a lighter to fire up the hashish in his *narjîlah*. He leaned over and took the mouthpiece between his teeth. I could hear the burbling of the water pipe and smell the tang of the black hashish. He exhaled the smoke and smiled. "You can pick your cells, I got two. Or you got somethin' else I might want?"

I thought of my ceremonial dagger. "How about this?" I said, laying it in front of him on the desk.

He shook his head. "Cash," he said, shoving the dagger back toward me. I thought he'd made a bad mistake, because the dagger had a lot of gold and jewels stuck on it. Maybe he didn't have anywhere to fence an item like that. "Or credit," he added. "Got a bank you can call?"

"Yes," said Friedlander Bey. "It will be an expensive call, but you can have my bank's computer transfer funds to your account."

Al-Bishah let the mouthpiece fall from his lips. He sat up very straight. "Now, that's what I like to hear! Only, *you* pay for the call. Charge it to your home, right?"

The fat cop handed him the desk phone, and Papa spoke a long series of numbers into it. "Now," said Papa to the sergeant, "how much do you want?"

"A good, stiff bribe," he said. "Enough so I *feel* bribed. Not enough, you go to the cell. You could stay there forever. Who's gonna know you're here? Who's gonna pay for your freedom? Now's your best chance, my brother."

Friedlander Bey regarded the man with unconcealed disgust. "Five thousand kiam," he said.

"Lemme think, what's that in real money?" A few seconds passed in silence. "No, better make it ten thousand." I'm sure Papa would have paid a hundred thousand, but the cop didn't have the imagination to ask for it.

Papa waited a moment, then nodded. "Yes, ten thousand." He spoke into the phone again, then handed it to the sergeant.

"What?" asked al-Bishah.

"Tell the computer your account number," said Papa.

"Oh. Right." When the transaction was completed, the fat fool made another call. I couldn't hear what it was all about, but when he hung up, he said, "Fixed up some transportation for you. I don't want you here, don't want you in Najran. Can't let you go back where you come from, either, not from this shuttle field."

"All right," I said. "Where we going, then?"

Al-Bishah gave me a clear view of his stumpy, rotted teeth. "Let it be a surprise."

We had no choice. We waited in his reeking office until a call came that our transportation had arrived. The sergeant stood up from behind his desk, grabbed his rifle and slung it under his arm, and signaled us that we were to lead the way back out to the airfield. I was just glad to get out of that narrow room with him.

Outside under the clear, moonless night sky, I saw that Hajjar's suborbital shuttle had taken off. In its place was a small supersonic chopper with military markings. The air was filled with the shriek of its jet engines, and a strong breeze brought me the acrid fumes of fuel spilled on the concrete apron. I glanced at Papa, who gave me only the slightest shrug. There was nothing we could do but go where the man with the rifle wanted us to go.

We had to cross about thirty yards of empty airfield to the chopper, and we weren't making any kind of resistance. Still, al-Bishah came up behind me and clubbed me in the back of the head with the butt of his rifle. I fell to my knees, and bright points of color swam before my eyes. My head throbbed with pain. I felt for a moment as if I were about to vomit.

I heard a drawn-out groan nearby, and when I turned my head I saw that Friedlander Bey sprawled helplessly on the ground beside me. That the fat cop had beaten Papa angered me more than that he'd slugged me. I got unsteadily to my feet and helped Papa up. His face had gone gray, and his eyes weren't focused. I hoped he hadn't suffered a concussion. Slowly I led the old man to the open hatch of the chopper.

Al-Bishah watched us climb into the transport. I didn't turn around and look at him, but over the roar of the aircraft's motors I heard him call to us. "Ever come to Najran again, you're dead."

I pointed down at him. "Enjoy it while it lasts, motherfucker," I shouted, "because it won't last long." He just grinned up at me. Then the chopper's co-pilot slammed the hatch, and I tried to make myself comfortable beside Friedlander Bey on the hard plastic bench.

I put my hand under the *keffiya* and gingerly touched the back of my head. My fingers came away bloody. I turned to Papa and was glad to see that the color had come back into his face. "Are you all right, O Shaykh?" I asked.

"I thank Allah," he said, wincing a little. We couldn't say anything more because our words were drowned out as the chopper prepared for takeoff. I sat back and waited for whatever would happen next. I entertained myself by entering Sergeant al-Bishah on my list, right after Lieutenant Hajjar.

The chopper circled around the airfield and then shot off toward its mysterious destination. We flew for a long time without changing course in the slightest. I sat with my head in my hands, keeping time by the excruciating, rhythmic stabs in the back of my skull. Then I remembered that I had my rack of neural software. I joyfully pulled it out, removed my *keffiya*, and chipped in the daddy that blocked pain. Instantly, I felt a hundred percent better, and without the adverse effects of chemical painkillers. I couldn't leave it in for very long, though. If I did, sooner or later there'd be a heavy debt to repay to my central nervous system.

There was nothing I could do to make Papa feel better. I could only let him suffer in silence, while I pressed my face to the plastic port in the hatch. For a long time I hadn't seen any lights down there, not a city, not a village, not even a single lonely house stuck far away from civilization. I assumed we were flying over water.

I found out how wrong I was when the sun began to come up, ahead of us and a little to starboard. We'd been flying northeast the entire time. According to my inaccurate mental map, that meant that we'd been heading out over the heart of Arabia. I hadn't realized how unpopulated that part of the world was.

I decided to remove the pain daddy about half an hour after I chipped it in. I popped it, expecting to feel a wave of renewed agony wash over me, but I was pleasantly surprised. The throbbing had settled down to a normal, manageable headache. I replaced my *keffiya*. Then I got up from the plastic bench and made my way forward to the cockpit.

"Morning," I said to the pilot and co-pilot.

The co-pilot turned around and looked at me. He took a long look at my princely outfit, but he stifled his curiosity. "You got to go back and sit down," he said. "Can't be bothering us while we're trying to fly this thing."

I shrugged. "Seems like we could've been on autopilot the whole way. How much actual flying are you guys doing?"

The co-pilot didn't like that. "Go back and sit down," he said, "or I'll take you back and cuff you to the bench."

"I don't mean any trouble," I said. "Nobody's told us a thing. Don't we have a right to know where we're going?"

The co-pilot turned his back on me. "Look," he said, "you and the old guy murdered some poor son of a bitch. You ain't got any rights anymore."

"Terrific," I muttered. I went back to the bench. Papa looked at me, and I just shook my head. He was disheveled and streaked with grime, and he'd lost his *tarboosh* when al-Bishah bashed him in the back of the head. He'd regained a lot of his composure during the flight, however, and he seemed to be pretty much his old self again. I had the feeling that soon we'd both need all our wits about us.

Fifteen minutes later, I felt the chopper slowing down. I looked out through the port and saw that we'd stopped moving forward, hovering now over reddish-brown sand dunes that stretched to the horizon in all directions. There was a long buzzing note, and then a green light went on over the hatch. Papa touched my arm and I turned to him, but I couldn't tell him what was going on.

The co-pilot unbuckled himself and eased out of his seat in the cockpit. He stepped carefully through the cargo area to our bench. "We're here," he said.

"What do you mean, 'we're here'? Nothing down there but sand. Not so much as a tree or a bush."

The co-pilot wasn't concerned. "Look, all I know is we're supposed to turn you over to the Bayt Tabiti here."

"What's the Bayt Tabiti?"

The co-pilot gave me a sly grin. "Tribe of Badawi," he said. "The other tribes call 'em the leopards of the desert."

Yeah, you right, I thought. "What are these Bayt Tabiti going to do with us?"

"Well, don't expect 'em to greet you like long-lost brothers. My advice is, try to get on their good side real fast."

I didn't like any of this, but what could I do about it? "So you're just going to set this chopper down and kick us out into the desert?"

The co-pilot shook his head. "Naw," he said, "we ain't gonna set it down. Chopper ain't got desert sand filters." He pulled up on a release lever and slid the hatch aside.

I looked down at the ground. "We're twenty feet in the air!" I cried.

"Not for long," said the co-pilot. He raised his foot and shoved me out. I fell to the warm sand, trying to roll as I hit. I was fortunate that I didn't break my legs. The chopper was kicking up a heavy wind, which blew the stinging sand into my face. I could barely breathe. I thought about using my *keffiya* the way it was meant to be used, to protect my nose and mouth from the artificial sandstorm. Before I could adjust it, I saw the co-pilot push Friedlander Bey from the hatch opening. I did my best to break Papa's fall, and he wasn't too badly hurt, either.

"This is murder!" I shouted up at the chopper. "We can't survive out here!"

The co-pilot spread his hands. "The Bayt Tabiti are coming. Here, this'll last you till they get here." He tossed out a pair of large canteens. Then, his duty to us at an end, he slammed the hatch shut. A moment later, the jet chopper swung up and around and headed back the way it had come.

Papa and I were alone and lost in the middle of the Arabian Desert. I picked up both canteens and shook them. They gurgled reassuringly. I wondered how many days of life they held. Then I went to Friedlander Bey. He sat in the hot morning sunlight and rubbed his shoulder. "I can walk, my nephew," he said, anticipating my concern.

"Guess we'll have to, O Shaykh," I said. I didn't have the faintest idea what to do next. I didn't know where we were or in which direction to start traveling.

"Let us first pray to Allah for guidance," he said. I didn't see any reason not to. Papa decided that this was definitely an emergency, so we didn't have to use our precious water to cleanse ourselves before worship. In such a situation, it's permissible to use clean sand. We had plenty of that. He removed his shoes and I took off my sandals, and we prepared ourselves for seeking the nearness of God as prescribed by the noble Qur'ân.

He took his direction from the rising sun and turned to face Mecca. I stood beside him, and we repeated the familiar poetry of prayer. When we finished, Papa recited an additional portion of the Qur'ân, a verse from the second sûrah that includes the line "And one who attacketh you, attack him in like manner as he attacked you."

"Praise be to Allah, Lord of the Worlds," I murmured.

"God is Most Great," said Papa.

And then it was time to see if we could save our lives. "I suppose we should reason this out," I said.

"Reason does not apply in the wilderness," said Papa. "We cannot reason ourselves food or water or protection."

"We have water," I said. I handed him one of the canteens.

He opened it and swallowed a mouthful, then closed the canteen and slung it across his shoulder. "We have *some* water. It remains to be seen if we have *enough* water."

"I've heard there's water underground in even the driest deserts." I think I was just talking to keep his spirits up—or my own.

Papa laughed. "You remember your mother's fairy tales about the brave prince lost among the dunes, and the spring of sweet water that gushed forth from the base of the mountain of sand. It doesn't happen that way in life, my darling, and your innocent faith will not lead us from this place."

I knew he was right. I wondered if he'd had any experience in desert survival as a younger man. There were entire decades of his early life that he never discussed. I decided it would be best to defer to his wisdom, in any case. I figured that if I shut up for a while, I might not die. I also might learn something. That was okay, too.

"What must we do, then, O Shaykh?" I asked.

He wiped the sweat from his forehead with his sleeve and looked around himself. "We're lost in the very southeastern portion of the Arabian Desert," he said. "The Rub al-Khali."

The Empty Quarter. That didn't sound promising at all.

"What is the nearest town?" I asked.

Papa gave me a brief smile. "There are no towns in the Rub al-Khali, not in a quarter million square miles of sand and waste. There are certainly small groups of nomads crossing the dunes, but they travel only from well to well, searching for grazing for their camels and goats. If we hope to find a well, our luck must lead us to one of these Bedu clans."

"And if we don't?"

Papa sloshed his canteen. "There's a gallon of water for each of us. If we do no walking at all in the daylight hours, manage our drinking carefully, and cover the greatest possible distance in the cool of the night, we may live four days."

That was worse than even my most pessimistic estimate. I sat down heavily on the sand. I'd read about this place years ago, when I was a boy in Algiers. I thought the description must have been pure exaggeration. For one thing, it made the Rub al-Khali sound harsher than the

Sahara, which was our local desert, and I couldn't believe that any-place on Earth could be more desolate than the Sahara. Apparently, I was wrong. I also remembered what a Western traveler had once called the Rub al-Khali in his memoirs:

The Great Wrong Place.

four

according to some geographers, the Arabian Desert is an extension of the Sahara. Most of the Arabian peninsula is uninhabited waste, with the populated areas situated near the Mediterranean, Red, and Arabian seas, beside the Arabian Gulf—which is our name for what others call the Persian Gulf—and in the fertile crescent of old Mesopotamia.

The Sahara is greater in area, but there is more sand in the Arabian Desert. As a boy, I carried in my mind the image of the Sahara as a burning, endless, empty sandscape; but that is not very accurate. Most of the Sahara is made up of rocky plateaus, dry gravel plains, and ranges of windswept mountains. Expanses of sand account for only 10 percent of the desert's area. The portion of the Arabian Desert called the Rub al-Khali tops that with 30 percent. It might as well have been nothing but sand from one end to the other, as far as I was concerned.

What the hell difference did it make?

I squinted my eyes nearly shut and looked up into the painfully bright sky. One of the minor advantages of being stranded in such a deadly place was that it was too deadly even for vultures. I was spared the unnerving sight of carrion birds circling patiently, waiting for me to have the courtesy to die.

I was pretty determined *not* to die. I hadn't talked it over with Friedlander Bey, but I was confident he felt the same way. We were sitting on the leeward side of a high, wind-shaped dune. I guessed that the temperature was already a hundred degrees Fahrenheit or more. The sun had climbed up the sky, but it was not yet noon—the day would get even hotter.

"Drink your water when you're thirsty, my nephew," Papa told me. "I've seen men dehydrate and die because they were too stingy with their canteens. Not drinking enough water is like spilling it on the ground. You need about a gallon a day in this heat. Two or three quarts won't keep you alive."

"We only have one gallon each, O Shaykh," I said.

"When it's gone, we'll have to find more. We may stumble across a trail, *inshallah*. There are trails even in the heart of the Rub al-Khali, and they lead from water hole to water hole. If not, we must pray that rain has fallen here not long ago. Sometimes there is damp sand in the hollow beneath the steep side of a dune."

I was in no hurry to try out my Desert Scout skills. All the talk of water had made me thirstier, so I unscrewed the cap of my canteen. "In the name of Allah, the Compassionate, the Merciful," I said, and drank a generous quantity. I'd seen holograms of Arab nomads sitting on the sand, using sticks to make tents of their *keffiyas* for shade. There weren't even sticks in this landscape, however.

The wind changed direction, blowing a fine curtain of grit into our faces. I followed Friedlander Bey's example and rested on my side, with my back to the wind. After a few minutes, I sat up and took off my *keffiya* and gave it to him. He accepted it wordlessly, but I saw gratitude in his red-rimmed eyes. He put on the head cloth, covered his face, and lay back to wait out the sandstorm.

I'd never felt so exposed to the elements before in my life. I kept telling myself, "Maybe it's all a dream." Maybe I'd wake up in my own bed, and my slave, Kmuzu, would be there with a nice mug of hot chocolate. But the broiling sun on my head felt too authentic, and the sand that worked its way into my ears and eyes, into my nostrils, and between my lips didn't feel at all dreamlike.

I was distracted from these annoyances by the bloodcurdling cries of a small band of men coming over the shoulder of the dune. They dismounted from their camels and ran down on us, waving their rifles and knives. They were the scruffiest, most villainous-looking louts I'd ever seen. They made the worst scum of the Budayeen look like scholars and gentlemen by comparison.

These, I assumed, were the Bayt Tabiti. The leopards of the desert. Their leader was a tall, scrawny man with long stringy hair. He brandished his rifle and screamed at us, and I could see that he had two snaggled teeth on the right side of his upper jaw, and two broken teeth on the left side of his lower jaw. He probably hadn't celebrated occlusion in years. He hadn't taken a bath in that long, either.

He was also the one we were supposed to trust with our lives. I glanced at Friedlander Bey and shook my head slightly. Just in case the Bayt Tabiti felt like murdering us where we sat instead of leading us to water, I got to my feet and drew my ceremonial dagger. I didn't really think that weapon was of much value against the Bedu's rifles, but it was all I had.

The leader came toward me, reached out, and fingered my expensive robe. He turned back to his companions and said something, and all six of them broke up with laughter. I just waited.

The leader looked into my face and frowned. He slapped his chest. "Muhammad Musallim bin Ali bin as-Sultan," he announced. As if I was supposed to recognize his name.

I pretended to be impressed. I slapped my own chest. "Marîd al-Amîn," I said, using the epithet I'd been given by the poor *fellahîn* of the city. It meant "the Trustworthy."

Muhammad's eyes grew wide. He turned to his buddies again. "Al-Amîn," he said in a reverent tone. Then he doubled over with laughter again.

A second Bayt Tabiti went over to Friedlander Bey and stood looking down at the old man. *"Ash-shaykh,"* I said, letting the stinking nomads know that Papa was a man of importance. Muhammad flicked his eyes from me to Papa, then back again. He spoke some rapid words in their puzzling dialect, and the second man left Papa alone and went back to his camel.

Muhammad and I spent some time trying to get answers to our questions, but their rough Arabic slowed down our communication. After a while, though, we could understand each other well enough. It turned out that the Bayt Tabiti had received orders from their tribal shaykh to come find us. Muhammad didn't know how his shaykh knew about us in the first place, but we were where they expected us to be, and they'd seen and heard the military chopper from a long way off.

I watched as two of the filthy rogues pulled Friedlander Bey roughly to his feet and led him to one of the camels. The camel's owner prodded the knees of the beast's forelegs with a stick, and made a sound like "khirr, khirr!" The camel roared its displeasure and didn't seem willing to kneel down. Papa said something to the Bayt Tabiti, who grabbed the animal's head rope and pulled it down. Papa placed a foot on the camel's neck, and it lifted him up where he could scramble into the saddle.

It was obvious that he'd done this before. I, on the other hand, had never ridden a camel in my life, and I didn't feel the need to start now. "I'll walk," I said.

"Please, young shaykh," said Muhammad, grinning through his sparse dentition, "Allah will think we are being inhospitable."

I didn't think Allah had any misconceptions at all about the Bayt Tabiti. "I'll walk," I said again.

Muhammad shrugged and mounted his own camel. Everyone started off around the dune, with me and the Bedu who'd given his camel to Papa walking alongside.

"Come with us!" cried the leader of the party. "We have food, we have water! We take you to our camp!"

I had no doubt that they were heading back to their camp, but I had serious misgivings that Papa and I would arrive there alive.

The man walking beside me must have sensed my thoughts, because he turned to me and winked slowly. "Trust us," he said with a cunning expression. "You are safe now."

You bet, I thought. There was nothing to do but go along with them. What would happen to us after we arrived at the main camp of the Bayt Tabiti was in the hands of God.

We traveled in a southerly direction for several hours. Finally, as I was reaching exhaustion—and about the time my canteen ran out of water—Muhammad called a halt. "We sleep here tonight," he said, indicating a narrow gap between two linked chains of sand dunes.

I was glad that the day's exertions were over; but as I sat beside Papa and watched the Bedu tend to their animals, it occurred to me that it was strange they didn't push on to rejoin the rest of their tribe before dark. Their shaykh had sent them out to find us, and they arrived only a few hours after we'd been dumped out of the chopper. Surely, the main camp of the Bayt Tabiti couldn't have been far away.

They went about their chores, whispering to each other and pointing at us when they thought we weren't watching. I started toward them, offering to help unload their camels. "No, no," said Muhammad, blocking me off from the animals, "please, just rest! We can see to the packs ourselves." Something was wrong here. And Friedlander Bey sensed it, too.

"I do not like these men," he said to me in a low voice. We were watching one of the Bedu put handfuls of dates in wooden bowls. Another man was boiling water for coffee. Muhammad and the rest were hobbling the camels.

"They haven't shown any outward signs of hostility," I said. "At least, not since they first ran down on us, yelling and screaming and waving their weapons."

Papa gave a humorless laugh. "Don't be fooled into thinking that we've won their grudging admiration. Look at that man dividing the dates. You know the packs on the camels are loaded with far better food than that. These Bayt Tabiti are too greedy to share it with us. They will pretend they have nothing better to eat than old, stonehard dates. Later, after we're gone, they'll prepare themselves a better meal."

"After we're gone?" I said.

"I don't believe there is a larger camp within a day's journey from here. And I don't believe the Bayt Tabiti are willing to offer us their hospitality much longer."

I shivered, even though the sun had not yet set, and the heat of the day had not yet dissipated. "Are you afraid, O Shaykh?"

He pursed his lips and shook his head. "I'm not afraid of these creatures, my nephew. I'm wary—I think it would be wise to know what they're up to at every moment. These are not clever men, but their advantages are that they are more than we, and that they know this terrain."

Further discussion was interrupted when the Bedu we'd been watching came to us and offered us each a bowl of rancid-smelling dates and a dirty china cup filled with weak coffee. "These poor provisions are all we have," said the man in a flat voice, "but we'd be honored if you'd share them with us."

"Your generosity is a blessing from Allah," said Friedlander Bey. He took a bowl of dates and a cup of coffee.

"I am quite unable to express my thanks," I said, taking my own supper.

The Bedu grinned, and I saw that his teeth were just as bad as Muhammad's. "No thanks are needed, O Shaykh," he replied. "Hospitality is a duty. You must travel with us and learn our ways. As the proverb says, 'Who lives with a tribe forty days becomes one of them.' "

That was a nightmarish thought, traveling with the Bayt Tabiti and becoming one of them!

"*Salaam alaykum,*" said Papa.

"*Alaykum as-salaam,*" the man responded. Then he carried bowls of dates to his fellows.

"In the name of Allah, the Compassionate, the Merciful," I murmured. Then I put one of the dates in my mouth. It didn't stay there long. First, it was completely coated with sand. Second, it was almost hard enough to crack my teeth; I wondered if these dates had been the downfall of the Bayt Tabiti's dental work. Third, the piece of fruit smelled as if it had been left to decay under a dead camel for a few weeks. I gagged as I spat it out, and I had to wash away the taste with the gritty coffee.

Friedlander Bey put one of the dates in his mouth, and I watched him struggle to maintain a straight face as he chewed it. "Food is food, my nephew," he said. "In the Empty Quarter, you can't afford to be fastidious."

I knew he was right. I rubbed as much sand as I could from another date, and then I ate it. After a few of them, I got used to how rotten they tasted. I thought only about keeping my strength up.

When the sun slipped behind the ridge of a western dune, Friedlander Bey removed his shoes and got slowly to his feet. He used my *keffiya* to sweep the sand in front of him. I realized he was preparing to pray. Papa opened his canteen and moistened his hands. Because I didn't have any more water in my own canteen, I stood beside him and extended my hands, palms up.

"*Allah yisallimak*, my nephew," said Papa. God bless you.

As I executed the ablutions, I repeated the ritual formula: "I perform the Washing in order to cleanse myself from impurity and to make myself eligible for seeking the nearness to Allah."

Once again, Papa led me in prayer. When we finished, the sun had completely disappeared and the sudden night of the desert had fallen. I imagined that I could already feel the heat leaching out of the sand. It would be a cold night, and we had no blankets.

I decided to see how far I could push the false hospitality of the Bayt Tabiti. I went over to their small fire of dried camel dung, where the six bandits were sitting and talking. "You pray to Allah," said Muhammad with a sarcastic grin. "You're good men. We mean to pray, but sometimes we forget." His tribesmen cackled at his wit.

I didn't pay any attention to that. "We'll need water for tomorrow's journey, O Shaykh," I said. I suppose I could've phrased that more politely.

Muhammad thought about it for a moment. He couldn't very well refuse, but he wasn't happy about parting with any of his own supply. He leaned over and muttered something to one of the others. The second Bedu got up and fetched a goatskin bag of water and brought it to me. "Here, my brother," he said with a blank expression. "May it be pleasant to you."

"We're obliged," I said. "We'll just fill our canteens, and return the rest of the water to you."

The man nodded, then reached out and touched one of my corymbic implants. "My cousin wants to know what these are," he said.

I shrugged. "Tell your cousin that I like to listen to music on the radio."

"Ah," said the Bayt Tabiti. I don't know if he believed me. He came with me while I filled my canteen and Papa's. Then the Bedu took the goatskin bag and returned to his friends.

"The sons of bitches didn't invite us to join them by the fire," I said, sitting down on the sand beside Papa.

He only turned one hand over. "It means nothing, my nephew," he said. "Now, I must sleep. It would be well if you remained awake and watchful."

"Of course, O Shaykh." Papa made himself as comfortable as he could on the hard-packed sand of the desert floor. I sat for a little while longer, lost in thought. I remembered what Papa had said about revenge, and from the pocket of my *gallebeya* I took the paper the qadi had given me. It was a copy of the charges against Friedlander Bey and me, the verdict, and the order for our deportation. It was signed by Dr. Sadiq Abd ar-Razzaq, imam of the Shimaal Mosque and adviser to the amir on the interpretation of *shari'a*, or religious law. I was happy to see that Shaykh Mahali had apparently played no part in our kidnapping.

Finally, I decided to lie down and pretend to be asleep, because I realized that the Bayt Tabiti were watching me, and that they wouldn't retire for the night until I did. I stretched out not far from Friedlander Bey, but I didn't close my eyes. I was sleepy, but I didn't dare drift off. If I did, I might never awaken again.

I could see the top of a gracefully curved dune about a hundred yards away. This particular sand hill must have been two hundred feet high, and the wind had blown it into a delicate, sinuous fold. I thought I could see a stately cedar tree growing from the very crest of the dune. I knew the mirage was a product of my fatigue, or perhaps I was already dreaming.

I wondered how the cedar tree could live in this waterless place, and I told myself that the only answer was that someone must be cultivating it. Someone had planned for that cedar to be there, and had worked very hard to make it grow.

I opened my eyes and realized that there was no cedar tree on that dune. Maybe it had been a vision from Allah. Maybe God was telling me that I had to make plans, and work very hard and persevere. There was no time now for rest.

I lifted my head a little, and saw that the Bayt Tabiti had thrown themselves on the ground near their fire, which had died down to pale, weakly glowing embers. One of the Bedu had been ordered to keep watch, but he sat against a wall of sand with his head thrown back and his mouth open. His rifle lay discarded beside him on the ground.

I believed all six of them were sound asleep, but I did not stir. I did nothing for another hour but stare at the seconds as they flicked by in the window of my watch. When I was certain that all the Bayt Tabiti were in deep slumber, I sat up quietly and touched Friedlander Bey on the shoulder. He came awake quickly. Neither of us said a word. We picked up our canteens and rose as silently as we could. I agonized for a few moments about trying to steal food and rifles, but at last I knew it would be suicidal to approach the camels or the sleeping Bedu. Instead, Papa and I just slipped away into the night.

We marched westward for a long time before either of us spoke. "Will they follow us when they find we're missing?" I asked.

Papa frowned. "I can't say, my nephew. Perhaps they'll just let us go. They're sure we'll die in the desert anyway."

There wasn't much I could say to that. From then on, we just concentrated on putting as much distance between us and them as we could, heading off at a right angle to the direction we'd traveled with them during the day. I prayed that if we crossed a desert track in the night we'd see it. It was our only hope of finding a well.

We had the stars as guides, and we trudged westward for two hours, until Papa announced that he had to stop and rest. We'd been traveling against the dunes, which ran from west to east, due to the prevailing winds. The westward slope of each dune was smooth and gradual, but the east side, which we'd have to climb, was usually high and steep. Consequently, we were making long detours as we tried to cross each hill at one of its low shoulders. It was slow, tiring, zigzag progress, and we couldn't have covered more than a mile or two as the sand grouse flies.

We sat panting beside each other at the base of yet another monstrous cliff of sand. I opened my canteen and gulped down a mouthful before I realized how brackish and alkaline it was. "Praise Allah," I groaned, "we'll be lucky if this water doesn't kill us before the sun does."

Papa had drunk his fill, too. "It is not sweet water, my nephew," he said, "but there is very little sweet water in the desert. This is the water the Bedu drink almost every day of their lives."

I'd known that the nomads lived harsh, desperate lives, but I was beginning to learn that I'd undervalued their skill at forcing a living from this most inclement environment. "Why don't they just go somewhere else?" I asked, capping my canteen again.

Papa smiled. "They are proud people. They get satisfaction in their ability to exist here, in a place that means death for any outsider. They scorn the softness and luxury of villages and towns."

"Yeah, you right. Luxuries like fresh water and actual food."

We stood up and started walking again. It was now about midnight. The path across the dunes didn't get any easier, and in a little while I could hear Papa's heavy breathing. I worried about the old man's condition. My own body was beginning to protest this unaccustomed exercise.

The stars turned slowly overhead, and when I looked at my watch again, it was half past one. Maybe we'd come another mile.

Papa estimated that the Rub al-Khali was about seven hundred and fifty miles west to east, and three hundred miles north to south. I figured it was likely that the military chopper had dropped us smack in the middle, so figuring a generous mile per hour, walking eight hours a night, we could get out of the Empty Quarter in, oh, just under forty-seven days. If we could also have a gigantic caravan of support equipment and supplies trailing along behind us.

We rested again, drank some more of the bitter water, and headed off on the last leg of the night's journey. We were both too tired to talk. I lowered my head against the wind, which was constantly flinging sand into our faces. I just kept putting one foot in front of the other. I told myself that if Friedlander Bey had the resolve to keep moving, so did I.

We reached our limit about four o'clock, and collapsed in utter exhaustion. The sun wouldn't rise for another hour or so, but the idea of going any farther that night was out of the question. We stopped beneath the vertical face of a gigantic dune, which would give us some protection from the wind. There we drank as much water as we could hold, and then prepared to sleep. I removed my beautiful royal blue robe and covered Papa with it. Then I huddled in a fetal position within my *gallebeya* and fell into cold, restless sleep.

I kept waking and falling back to sleep, and I was troubled by confused, anxious dreams. I was aware after a while that the sun had risen, and I knew the best thing would be to stay asleep as long as possible during the hot day. I pulled the *gallebeya* up over my head, to protect my face and scalp from burning. Then I pretended that everything was just fine, and closed my eyes.

It was about ten o'clock when I realized that I wasn't going to be able to sleep any later. The sun was beating down on me, and I could feel the exposed areas of skin burning. Friedlander Bey woke up then, too, and he didn't look as if he'd rested any better than I had.

"Now we must pray," he said. His voice sounded peculiar and hoarse. He struck the sand in front of him with his palms, and rubbed the sand on his face and hands. I did the same. Together we prayed, thanking Allah for giving us His protection, and asking that if it was His will, we might survive this ordeal.

Each time I joined in worship with Papa, I was filled with peace and hope. Somehow, being lost in this wilderness had made the meaning of our religion clear to me. I wish it hadn't taken such a drastic demonstration to make me understand my relationship to Allah.

When we'd finished, we drank as much water as we could hold. There wasn't much left in our canteens, but we didn't see any reason to discuss that fact. "My nephew," the old man said, "I think it would be wise to bury ourselves in the sand until evening."

That sounded crazy to me. "Why?" I asked. "Won't we bake ourselves like a lamb pie?"

"The deeper sand will be cooler than the surface," he said. "It will keep our skin from burning any further, and it will help reduce our loss of water through perspiration."

Once again, I shut up and learned something. We dug shallow pits and covered ourselves over with the sand. At one point, I noted to myself how very like graves they were. I was surprised to find that my body seemed to enjoy the experience. The warm sand soothed my aching muscles, and I was able to relax for the first time since we'd been snatched at the amir's celebration. In fact, after a while, listening to the murmurous buzzing of insects, I dozed off into a light sleep.

The day passed slowly. I had my *gallebeya* pulled up over my head again, so I couldn't see anything. There was nothing to do but lie there in the sand and think and plan and indulge in fantasies.

After a few hours, I was startled to hear a low vibrating hum. I couldn't imagine what it could be, and at first I thought it was only a ringing noise in my ears. It didn't go away, however, and if anything it got louder. "Do you hear that, O Shaykh?" I called.

"Yes, my nephew. It is nothing."

By now I was convinced that it was the warning whine of an approaching aircraft. I didn't know if that was good news or bad. The sound grew louder, until it was almost a shriek. I couldn't stand not being able to see, so I pushed my hands up out of the sand and pulled down the neck of my *gallebeya*.

There was nothing there. The buzzing had increased in volume until the aircraft should have been visible above our heads, but the sky was empty and blue. Then suddenly, as the wind shifted direction, everything fell silent again. The loud noise did not fade away but disappeared abruptly. "What was that?" I asked, bewildered.

"That, O Clever One, was the famous 'singing sands.' It is a very rare privilege to hear it."

"The sand made that sound? It was like the roaring of an engine!"

"They say it is made by one layer of sand slipping over another, nothing more."

Now I felt dumb for getting so upset over a little humming noise created by a sand dune. Papa, however, was not one to laugh or mock me, and I was grateful for that. I covered myself in the sand again and told myself not to be such a fool.

About five o'clock, we emerged from our sandy beds and prepared for the night's exertions. We prayed and drank the brackish water, and then headed off toward the west again. After we'd walked for half an hour, I had a brilliant idea. I took out my rack of neuralware and chipped in the special daddy that blocked thirst. Immediately, I felt refreshed. This was a dangerous illusion, because although I didn't feel thirsty—and wouldn't again, as long as I had that daddy chipped in— my body was still dehydrating at the same rate. Still, I felt that I could go on without water longer now, and so I gave my canteen to Papa.

"I can't take this from you, my nephew," he said.

"Sure you can, O Shaykh," I said. "This add-on will keep me from suffering for as long as our canteens do the same for you. Look, if we don't find more water soon, we'll both die anyway."

"That's true, my darling, but—"

"Let's walk, my grandfather," I said.

The sun began to set and the air began to get cooler. We took a rest stop some time later, and we prayed. Papa finished all the water in one of the canteens. Then we pushed on.

I was beginning to feel very hungry, and I realized that except for the crummy dates of the Bayt Tabiti, the last meal I'd eaten had been almost forty-eight hours ago, at the amir's palace. I was lucky, because I had a daddy that blocked hunger, too. I chipped it in, and the hollow pangs in my belly disappeared. I knew that Papa must be ravenous, but there was nothing I could do about that. I put everything out of my mind except making tracks across the remainder of the Empty Quarter.

Once, when we'd topped the crest of a high dune, I turned to look back. I saw what I thought was a smudge of dust rising in the pale moonlight from behind a distant dune. I prayed to Allah that it wasn't the Bayt Tabiti coming after us. When I tried to point it out to Friedlander Bey, I couldn't find the dust cloud again. Maybe I'd imagined it. The vast desert was good for that kind of hallucination.

After the second hour, we had to rest. Papa's face was drawn and haggard. He opened his other canteen and drained it dry. All our water was now gone. We looked at each other wordlessly for a moment. "I testify that there is no god but God," said Papa in a quiet voice.

"I testify that Muhammad is the Prophet of God," I added. We got up and continued our march.

After a while, Papa fell to his knees and began retching. He had nothing in his belly to vomit, but his spasms were long and violent. I hoped he wasn't losing much water. I knew that nausea was one of the first signs of severe dehydration. After a few minutes, he waved a hand weakly to let me know he wanted to keep going. From then on, I was more frightened than ever. I had no more illusions that we'd be able to save ourselves without a miracle.

I began to experience severe muscle cramps, and for the third time I turned to my moddy rack. I chipped in the pain-blocking daddy, knowing that I was going to be in pretty terrible shape if I ever lived to pop it out again. As my friend Chiriga likes to say, "Paybacks are a bitch."

About midnight, after another rest period, I noticed that Papa had begun to stagger. I went up to him and touched his shoulder. He faced me, but his eyes seemed unfocused. "What is it, my son?" he said. His voice was thick and his words indistinct.

"How are you feeling, O Shaykh?"

"I feel . . . strange. I'm not hungry anymore, which is a blessing, but I have a terrible headache. There are many little bright spots in front of my eyes; I can barely see in front of me. And there is the most annoying tingling in my arms and legs. Unfortunate symptoms."

"Yes, O Shaykh."

He looked up at me. For the first time in all the time I'd known him, he had genuine sadness in his eyes. "I do not wish to walk anymore."

"Yes, O Shaykh," I said. "Then I will carry you."

He protested, but he didn't do a very good job of it. I begged his forgiveness, then picked him up and slung him over my shoulder. I wouldn't have been able to haul him fifty yards without the daddies, which were damping out every last unpleasant signal my body was sending to my brain. I went on with a blithe, completely false sense of well-being. I wasn't hungry, I wasn't thirsty, I wasn't tired, and I didn't even ache. I even had another daddy I could use if I started to feel afraid.

In a little while, I realized that Papa was muttering deliriously. It was up to me to get us both out of this mess. I just gritted my teeth and went on. My amped brain was ridiculously confident that I'd emerge victorious against the most murderous desert in the world.

The night passed. I plodded my way through the swirling sand like a robot. All the while, my body was suffering the same debilitating effects of dehydration that had struck down Papa, and fatigue poisons were building up in my muscles.

The sun came up behind me, and I felt the heat grow on the back of my head and neck. I trudged on through the morning. Papa was no longer making any sounds at all. Once, about 8 A.M., my arms and legs just gave out. I dropped Papa heavily to the ground and fell down beside him. I let myself rest there for a little while. I knew I'd been abusing my body. I thought perhaps lying there motionless for a few minutes would be helpful.

I suppose I was unconscious, because the next time I checked my watch, two hours had passed. I got to my feet and picked up Papa and put him across my other shoulder. Then I walked some more.

I kept going until I collapsed again. This became a pattern, and soon I lost all track of time. The sun rose in the sky, the sun went away. The sun rose, the sun went away. I have no idea how far I managed to get. I have a vague memory of sitting on the side of a large dune, patting Friedlander Bey's hand and weeping. I sat there for a long time, and then I thought I heard a voice calling my name. I picked up Papa and stumbled on, in the direction of the voice.

This time, I didn't get far. I crossed two, maybe three great dunes, and then my muscles quit on me again. I could only lie on the ground, my face half-pressed into the hot, red sand. I could see Papa's leg from the corner of my eye. I was pretty sure that I was never going to get up again. "I take refuge . . ." I murmured. I didn't have enough saliva to finish. "I take refuge with the Lord of the Worlds," I said in my mind.

I passed out again. The next thing I knew, it was night. I was probably still alive. A man with a stern, lean face dominated by a huge hooked nose was bending over me. I didn't know who he was, or even if he was really there. He said something to me, but I couldn't understand his words. He wet my lips with water, and I tried to grab the goatskin bag out of his hands, but I couldn't seem to work my arms. He said something more to me. Then he reached forward and touched my implants.

With horror, I realized what he was trying to do. "No!" I cried in my cracked voice. "Please, for the love of Allah, no!"

He pulled his hand back and studied me for another few seconds. Then he opened a leather bag, removed an old-fashioned disposable syringe and a vial of some fluid, and gave me an injection.

What I really wanted was about a quart of clean, fresh water. But the shot of Sonneine was okay, too.

five

ī was now clear on the events between the kidnapping and our rescue by the Bani Salim. The days after that, however, were probably lost forever in a fog of delirium. Shaykh Hassanein had sedated me, and then pulled free the daddies. My mind and body had immediately been overwhelmed by a ravaging flood of agony. I was grateful to Hassanein for keeping me knocked out with Sonneine until I'd begun to recover.

Noora was awake and watchful when I sat up and stretched in the morning. It took me a few seconds to recall where I was. The front and back flaps of the goat-hair tent had been thrown open, and a fresh, warm breeze passed through. I bowed my head and prayed, "Oh, that this day may be fortunate; give Thou that we see not the evil!"

"Blessings of Allah be on you, O Shaykh," said Noora. She came nearer, carrying a bowl of camel's milk and a plate of bread and *hummus*, a paste made of chick-peas and olive oil.

"*Bismillah*," I murmured, tearing off a piece of bread. "May your day be pleasant, Noora." I began wolfing down the breakfast.

"It's good to see that your appetite is back. Would you like some more?"

My mouth was crammed full, so I just nodded. Noora went out of the tent to fetch a second helping. I took a few deep breaths and experimented with moving my limbs. There was still a deep soreness in my muscles, but I felt that I could get up soon. I remembered what Hassanein had told me, that the Bani Salim would need to find new grazing for their animals very soon. I wasn't thrilled by the prospect of walking a couple of hundred miles with them, so it was probably time that I learned how to ride a camel.

Noora returned with another plate of bread and *hummus*, and I attacked it hungrily. "The old shaykh will visit you when you're fin- ished eating," she said.

I was glad to hear that. I wanted to see how well Friedlander Bey had survived our ordeal. It wasn't over by any means, though. We still had a long distance to travel, and the conditions would be just as harsh. The lifesaving difference was that we'd be traveling with the Bani Salim, and they knew where all the wells were. "Papa and I have much to talk over," I said.

"You must plan your vengeance."

"What do you know of that?" I asked.

She smiled. I realized that she was no longer holding her head scarf over her face. "You've told me many times about the amir and the qadi and the imam and Shaykh Reda. Most of the time, you just bab- bled; but I understood enough of what you were saying, and the old shaykh told me much the same story."

I raised my eyebrows and mopped up the last dollop of *hummus* with a chunk of bread. "What do you think we should do?"

Her expression turned solemn. "The Bedu insist on revenge. We practically make it a necessary part of our religion. If you didn't return to your city and slay those who plotted against you, the Bani Salim wouldn't be your friends when you returned to us."

I almost laughed when I heard her speak of my returning to the Rub al-Khali. "Even though the man responsible is a revered imam? Even though he's beloved by the *fellahîn* of the city? Even though he's known for his goodness and generosity?"

"Then he is an imam of two faces," said Noora. "To some, he may be wise in the worship of Allah, and kind to his brothers in Islam. Yet he did this evil to you, so his true nature is corrupt. He takes the coins of your enemy, and unjustly sentences innocent men to an exile that is almost surely death. The second face renders the first false, and is an abomination in the eyes of God. It's your duty to repay his treachery with the penalty accorded by tradition."

I was startled by her vehemence. I wondered why this matter between Papa and me, on the one side, and Dr. Abd ar-Razzaq, on the other, disturbed her so much. She saw me studying her, and she blushed and covered her face with her head cloth.

"The tradition of the Bedu may not be legal in the city," I said.

Her eyes flashed. "What is 'legal'? There's only right and wrong. There's a story the Bedu women tell their children, about the evil imam in the well."

"Noora, if it had been an accountant who'd done us harm, this story would be about the evil accountant in the well, right?"

"I don't even know what an accountant is," she said. "Listen, then. Maybe there was, and maybe there wasn't an evil imam of Ash-Shâm, which you call Damascus, when Ash-Shâm was the only city in the world. The Bedu have no need of imams, because every member of the tribe prays to God as an equal and defers to no other. The weak city folk needed an imam to help them, because they'd forgotten what it was to find their own water and make their own food, and they'd come to depend on other people to supply these things. So, too, had they come to depend on an imam to lead the way to Allah.

"Now, many of the people of Ash-Shâm still thought the evil imam was wise and good, because he made sure everyone who heard him preach gave money to their needy brothers. The imam himself never gave any of his own money, because he'd grown very fond of it. He loved gold so much that he sold his influence to one of Ash-Shâm's most corrupt and ambitious citizens.

"When Allah realized that the imam's heart had turned black, He sent one of His angels down to earth. The angel's instructions were to take the imam away into the desert, and imprison him so that he might never lead any of the people of Ash-Shâm astray. The angel found the imam in his secret treasury, stacking up his piles of gold and silver coins, and cast a spell over the imam that made him fall into a deep sleep.

"The angel picked up the evil imam and carried him in the palm of his hand, and brought him to the very heart of the Rub al-Khali. The imam knew nothing of this, because he was still fast asleep. The angel built a deep, deep well, and put the imam down at the very bottom, where there was only the most bitter and foul water. Then the angel caused the imam to awaken.

" 'Yaa Allah!' cried the evil imam. 'Where am I, and how did I come to this place?'

" 'It is too late to call on God, O Son of Adam,' said the angel. His stern voice cracked like thunder in the air, and the walls of the well shook around the imam.

" 'Let me out,' said the imam fearfully, 'and I promise to change my ways! Have mercy on me!'

"The angel shook his head, and his eyes loosed terrible flashes of lightning. 'It is for me neither to judge nor to have mercy. The One Judge has already condemned you to this place. Think on your deeds and repair your soul, for you have still to meet your God on the Last Day.' Then the angel departed, and left the evil imam all alone.

"A day came when the evil imam's successor, whose name was Salim and who was the founder of our tribe, came upon the well in his travels. Salim had never known the evil imam, and he was as different from him as the sun and the moon. This young man was truly kind and generous, and well beloved of all the people of Ash-Shâm, who had appointed him to be their imam in recognition of his virtues.

"As Salim bent forward to peer into the well, he was startled to see that a number of creatures had fallen into it and were trapped with the evil imam. The animals begged him to release them from the deep well. Salim felt so sorry for the animals that he unwound his *keffiya* and lowered it into the dark hole.

"The first animal to climb up the cloth ladder to freedom was a lizard, the one the Bedu call 'Abu Qurush,' or Father of Coins, because the end of this lizard's tail is flat and round. Abu Qurush was so grateful to be rescued that he shed a piece of his skin and gave it to Salim, saying, 'If ever you need help in a desperate situation, burn this piece of skin and I will come to you.' He began to run away across the hot sands, but he called back to Salim, 'Beware the Son of Adam who is in the well! He is an evil man, and you should leave him down there!'

"The next creature Salim pulled out was a she-wolf. The wolf was just as overjoyed as the lizard had been. She pulled out two of her whiskers and gave them to Salim, saying, 'If you should be in such a difficult place as that from which you rescued me, burn these and I will come to you.' She bounded away, but she too called back to him, 'Know, O Man, that the Son of Adam in the well is most evil.'

"Salim finished pulling out all the rest of the animals, and he listened to their warnings. Then he began to wrap his *keffiya* around his head once more. His countryman, the evil imam, shouted up to him in a heartbreaking voice. 'How can you save all those creatures, yet leave me to face my death in this pit of darkness? Are we not brothers according to the holy words of the Prophet, may the blessings of Allah be on him and peace?'

"Salim was torn between the warnings of the animals and his own good nature. He decided that he shared a bond of humanity with the unseen prisoner, and he once again lowered his *keffiya* down into the well. When he'd freed the evil imam, he took up his journey again, and many weeks later returned to Ash-Shâm."

"This is a great story, Noora," I said, yawning, "but it sounds like it's going to go on forever, and I remember your uncle telling me that the Bani Salim needed to move on to the next well soon. Surely, you don't want your camels and goats to die of starvation while you spin out this wonderful Bedu folklore for me."

Noora sighed. "I will finish it quickly," she said. I could see that she really loved telling stories. Maybe it was unkind of me to cut her off, but I had the feeling she was trying to make some special point. If she had some wisdom to impart, she could do it just as well in fifty words as five thousand.

I knew, of course, that in the story Salim represented me, and the evil imam must be Dr. Abd ar-Razzaq. I thought I could guess what was going to happen. "So Salim gets in some kind of trouble, and it's the evil imam's fault, and he calls the lizard and the wolf."

"Actually," she said, trying to stay ahead of me, "Salim didn't get into trouble at first. He burned the lizard's skin, and Abu Qurush appeared before him before the last lick of gray smoke faded in the air. 'What do you wish?' asked the lizard.

" 'I'd like to be as rich as a king,' said Salim.

" 'The solution to that is simple. You must do as I tell you. Take the basket your servant uses to fetch bread, and leave it outside the city gates tonight. Then you must get up before the sun and bring it home again.' Salim did just as he was instructed, and he left the empty basket against the walls of the king's palace, and when he went to get it in the morning, it was filled with gold."

"Is that how Salim gets in trouble?" I asked.

Noora patted the air impatiently. "Wait, wait. So for a few days, Salim lived well. He ate the best food in the city, he bought himself a new wardrobe, he enjoyed all the pleasures of Ash-Shâm that Allah did not forbid. After a time, however, the king noticed that a part of his treasury was missing. He was outraged and furious, and he put out a decree: 'Whoever finds the robber of the king's gold shall have the king's beautiful daughter in marriage, and half the kingdom besides!'

"With that reward being offered, many wise and clever men came to examine the king's vaults. All were bewildered, and without exception they told the king that no man could have entered the treasury and stolen the gold. Finally, the cleverest of all asked that many armloads of dry palm fronds be put in the treasury. The king asked no questions, but did as the clever man said. Then the clever man set fire to the palm fronds and led the king and his courtiers outside the building. In a few minutes, all could see a black ribbon of smoke rising from a slender breach in the foundation of the palace wall. The clever man stepped closer and examined the ground itself, where he saw tiny footprints in the dust. 'Behold, your majesty!' he said. 'The thief was no man, but a lizard!'

"The king, who had little patience with clever men, thought this one was trying to make a fool of him, and so he ordered the clever man to be taken away and beheaded. And that was the end of the clever man."

"Is there supposed to be a moral in that for me?" I asked.

Noora smiled. "No, the story isn't even finished. The clever man wasn't important at all. I didn't even give him a name. Anyway, word of all this ran through the city of Ash-Shâm, until it reached the ears of the evil imam. The evil imam realized that the hand of the king's daughter and half the kingdom could be his, because he'd heard the words of Abu Qurush at the well. He ran to the king's audience chamber and cried, 'Your thief is your own imam, Salim!'

"Well, the king doubted this was true, but he sent his soldiers to Salim's house, where they found the rest of the gold. They arrested Salim and brought him in chains to the king's deepest, foulest dungeon. Salim knew who'd betrayed him, and he cursed his foolishness in ignoring the warnings of the animals and setting the evil imam free.

"Salim languished in his gloomy cell for a day and a night, and a day and a night, and then he remembered the words of the she-wolf. He took out the wolf's whiskers and burned them. In the blink of an eye, the she-wolf stood before him. 'What do you want of me?' she asked.

"'Only for you to get me out of this dreadful prison, just as I released you from the well,' said Salim.

"'Tonight you will be free,' said the wolf, and she squeezed beneath the door of his cell and was gone.

"Many hours passed, until it was the darkest watch of the night. Suddenly, there came screams of terror from the bedchamber of the king's young son and heir. The king ran into the room and saw the wolf with the boy's head gripped between her long, sharp teeth. Whenever the king or one of his soldiers or advisers tried to approach, the wolf let loose a loud, fierce growl. No one could do anything to save the young prince.

"Eventually, the news spread throughout the palace. The dungeon guards discussed it loudly, and Salim overheard them. 'Take me to the king,' he called, 'and I will save the life of the prince.'

"The guards laughed at him, saying the bravest of their number could do nothing, so what could this mere preacher hope to accomplish? At last, Salim persuaded the guards to bring him before the king. They hurried up to the prince's chamber. As soon as Salim entered, the wolf began wagging her tail and making sounds like a dog pleased to see its master. 'The she-wolf will depart without harming the boy,' said Salim, 'but only if you offer it the heart of the former imam of Ash-Shâm.'

"The king commanded his soldiers to hurry, and they ran out into the city and found the evil imam. They arrested him and dragged him back to the palace and cut off his head. Then they hacked open his chest, cut out his heart, and put it in a golden bowl. Salim placed the golden bowl before the she-wolf. The animal licked his hand, took the heart of the evil imam in her mouth, and ran from the palace to freedom.

"The king was so pleased that he pardoned Salim, and then gave him his daughter's hand in marriage!"

I waited a moment to be sure the story was finally over. "I'm supposed to cut Dr. Sadiq Abd ar-Razzaq's heart out?" I said.

"Yes, and feed it to a dog," said Noora fiercely.

"Even though we don't do that kind of thing in the city anymore? I mean, we're talking about a theologian here. Not Hitler or Xarghis Khan."

Noora looked at me blankly. "Who are they?" she asked.

I smiled at her. "Never mind."

She took the empty plate and bowl from me and went out of the tent. Friedlander Bey entered almost immediately. He sat down beside me on the sand and clasped my hand. "How are you feeling, my darling?" he asked.

I was glad to see him. "It is as Allah pleases, O Shaykh," I said.

He nodded. "But look, your face is badly burned by the sun and the wind. And your hands and arms, from carrying me!" He shook his head. "I came to see you every day, even when you were unconscious. I saw the pain you suffered."

I let out a deep breath. "It was necessary, my grandfather."

Again he nodded. "I suppose I'm trying to express my gratitude. It's always—"

I raised my free hand. "Please, O Shaykh, don't make us both uncomfortable. Don't thank me. I did what I could to save our lives. Anyone would have done the same."

"Yet you pushed yourself beyond endurance, and you damaged your body and mind for my sake. I gave you those cursed implants, and I made you my weapon. Now you've repaid me with boundless courage. I feel shame."

I closed my eyes for a few seconds. If this went on much longer, it would be as unendurable as the walk in the desert had been. "I don't wish to talk about that anymore," I said. "We don't have time to indulge our emotions. The only hope we have of living through this trouble and returning to the city, and then restoring ourselves to our proper place, is to keep our minds focused clearly on a plan of action."

Papa rubbed his cheek, where his gray stubble was turning into a patchy beard. I watched him chew his lip as he thought. Evidently, he arrived at a decision, because from then on he was the old Friedlander Bey we all knew and feared back in the Budayeen. "We are in no danger from the Bani Salim," he said.

"Good," I said, "I didn't know where they stood."

"They've accepted responsibility for our well-being until we get to Mughshin. We'll be treated as honored guests and receive every courtesy. We must be careful not to abuse their hospitality, because they'll give us their food even if it means they themselves must go hungry. I don't want that to happen."

"Neither do I, O Shaykh."

"Now, I've never heard of Mughshin before, and I suppose it's just a community of huts and tents around a large well, somewhere to the south. We were wrong in thinking the sergeant in Najran arranged to have us dropped in the center of the Empty Quarter. The chopper traveled much farther than we thought, and we were thrown out in the northeastern part of the Sands." I frowned. "That's what the Bedu call this huge desert," Papa explained, "simply the Sands. They've never heard of the Rub al-Khali."

"Where we were didn't make any difference to us," I said. "If the Bani Salim hadn't found us, we'd have died long ago."

"We should have walked in the opposite direction, to the east. We're closer to Oman than we are to the western edge."

"We couldn't have made it to Oman, either. But we're still going to travel south with the Bani Salim?"

"Yes, my nephew. We can trust them. That counts for more in our situation than time or distance."

I drew up my knees experimentally, just to see if they still worked. They did, and I was happy about it, although they felt very weak after two weeks of enforced rest. "Have you planned our future after we reach Mughshin?"

He looked up, over my head, as if gazing into the distance toward the Budayeen and our enemies. "I do not know where Mughshin is, and even the shaykh, Hassanein, cannot show me. There are no maps or books among the Bani Salim. Several of the Bedu have assured me that beyond Mughshin, it is not a difficult journey across the mountains to a coastal town called Salala." Papa smiled briefly. "They speak of Salala as if it were the most wonderful place on earth, with every kind of luxury and pleasure."

"Mountains," I said unhappily.

"Yes, but not great mountains. Also, Hassanein promised to find us trustworthy guides in Mughshin to take us onward."

"And then?"

Papa shrugged. "Once we reach the coast, then we travel by ship to a city with a suborbital shuttle field. We must be extremely careful when we return home, because there will be spies—"

Noora returned, this time carrying some folded garments. "These are for you, Shaykh Marîd," she said. "Would you like to put on clean clothes, and take a walk with me?"

I wasn't in a hurry to put my aching muscles to work, but I couldn't refuse. Papa stood up and went outside the tent. Noora followed him and dropped the flaps in the front and the back, so I could dress in privacy.

I stood up slowly, ready to quit for the day in case I experienced any severe stabs of pain. I shook out the clean garments. First, there was a threadbare loincloth that I wrapped around myself. I wasn't exactly sure how the Bani Salim men wore them, and I wasn't about to find out. Over that I pulled a long, white smock, which the Bedu called a *thobe*. The poor men of the city wore something very similar, and I knew that Friedlander Bey often dressed in one, betraying his origins. On top of the *thobe* I wore a long, white shirt that was open all the way down the front, with wide, long sleeves. For my head there was a clean cotton *keffiya*, but my *akal* had been lost somewhere; I wound the head cloth around and tucked it in as these southern Bedu wore it. Then I drew on my now-tattered and travel-stained blue robe, which the Bayt Tabiti had so admired. There were no sandals with the rest of the clothes; I figured I could go barefoot.

It felt good again to be up and dressed and ready for action. When I stepped outside the tent, I was a little self-conscious because my outfit made me look like a wealthy shaykh from the decadent, feeble world beyond the Rub al-Khali. I was aware that the eyes of everyone in the camp were on me.

Waiting for me were Friedlander Bey, Noora, and her uncle Hassanein. The shaykh of the Bani Salim greeted me with a broad smile. "Here," he said, "I have your belongings. I took these for safekeeping. I feared that a few of our younger men might have been tempted to borrow them." He handed me my sandals, my ceremonial dagger, and my rack of moddies and daddies. I was extremely glad to get all these things back.

"Please, O Shaykh," I said to Hassanein, "I would be most honored if you would accept this gift. It can only begin to repay the great debt we owe." I presented him with the gorgeous jeweled dagger.

He took it in his hands and stared at it. He did not speak for a few moments. "By the life of my eyes," he said at last, "this is not for me! This is for some noble prince, or a king."

"My friend," said Papa, "you are as noble as any prince in the land. Accept it. This dagger has a long history, and it will do you honor."

Hassanein did not stammer out effusive thanks. He just nodded to me and tied the woven belt around his waist. In the Bedu manner, he wore the dagger directly in front, over his stomach. He said nothing more about it, but I could see that the gift had greatly pleased him.

We walked slowly among the black goat-hair tents. I could see the faces of the men turn to follow us. Even the women peeked at us as we passed, while they tended to the day's work. Not far away, the young boys herded the camels and goats toward the low, scrubby salt-bushes. This wasn't the best food for the animals, but in this desolate place it would have to do. I understood immediately what Hassanein had meant about moving on. There was little sustenance here for the animals.

The camp consisted of a dozen tents. The terrain around Bir Bal-agh was the same as that Papa and I had traveled through. There were no shade trees here, no date palms, no real oasis at all. All that recom-mended this low, flat stretch in a hollow between two chains of dunes was a single wide hole in the ground—the well. Whenever a traveler came upon one of these wells, he sometimes had to spend hours dig-ging it out, because it didn't take the shifting sands long to fill it in.

I realized how helpless Papa and I would've been, even if we'd stumbled across such a muddy hole. The water was often ten feet or more below the surface, and there were no buckets or ropes. Each wan-dering Bedu band carried its own rope for the purpose of drawing out the life-giving water. Even if Allah had granted us the good fortune to find one of these brackish trickles, we might easily have died of thirst only ten vertical feet from the water.

That thought made me shudder, and I murmured a prayer of thanks. Then the four of us continued our walk. In one of the nearby tents, a few men were relaxing and drinking coffee from small cups lit-tle bigger than thimbles. This was the normal occupation of Bedu males in the camp. One of the men saw me and said something, throw-ing his coffee cup to the ground. A commotion arose among his friends, and he leaped to his feet and rushed toward me, yelling and gesturing madly.

"What is this?" I asked Hassanein.

The shaykh moved to intercept the angry young man. "These are our guests," said Hassanein. "Be silent, or you will dishonor us all."

"There's the one who brings dishonor!" cried the furious Bedu. He pointed one long, bony finger at me. "He's doing it right beneath your nose! He's trying to spoil her! He's seducing her with his unholy city ways! He's no true Muslim, may his father's infidel religion be cursed! He cares nothing for her, and he'll ruin her and leave her to go back to his *hareem* of unclean women!"

Hassanein was having no success restraining the young man, who kept shouting and waving his fist at me. I tried to ignore him, but soon the entire tribe had gathered around us. The whole thing was rapidly getting out of hand.

Noora's face grew pale. I caught her eye, and she looked away. I was afraid she would break out into tears. "Don't tell me," I said to her, "that's bin Musaid, your secret admirer, right?"

She looked into my face helplessly. "Yes," she said softly. "And now he's decided to kill you."

I thought how much better things would've been if I'd declined Shaykh Mahali's invitation, and just gone out and gotten drunk instead.

six

i watched the Bani Salim pack up their camp. It didn't take them long. Each person in the tribe had his particular task, and he went about it quickly and efficiently. Even the sullen Ibrahim bin Musaid, who'd been restrained and persuaded not to murder me where I stood, was busy rounding up the pack camels.

He was a dark, brooding young man about twenty years old, with a long, narrow face. Like some of the younger Bani Salim, he didn't wear a *keffiya*, and his head was framed by his wild, stringy hair. His upper jaw thrust forward, giving him an unfortunate foolish expression, but his black eyes glared at the world beneath knotted brows.

The situation between him and Noora was more complicated than I'd thought. It wasn't just a matter of unrequited love, which in the closed community of a Bedu tribe would be bad enough. Hassanein told me that bin Musaid was the son of one of the shaykh's two brothers, and Noora was the daughter of the other. Among the Bani Salim, a girl is betrothed at birth to her first cousin, and cannot marry anyone else unless he releases her. Bin Musaid had no intention of doing that, even though Noora had made it clear that she wanted to marry another young man named Suleiman bin Sharif.

I'd made everything worse, because bin Musaid had focused all his jealousy on me. I guess I was an easier target than bin Sharif, because I was an outsider and a civilized weakling. Bin Musaid made it abundantly clear that he resented the hours Noora had spent with me, particularly those long nights while I was recuperating. It didn't make any difference to him that I'd been unconscious most of that time. He still hinted at all kinds of unseemly behavior.

This morning, though, there wasn't time for more accusations. The camels lay couched on the ground, while the men of the Bani Salim stacked the folded tents and packs of belongings and supplies nearby. The air was filled with the loud grunting and roaring of the camels, who were aware of what was going on and were unanimous in their displeasure. Some turned their heads and snapped at their owners, who were trying to adjust the loads, and the Bedu had to be quick to dance out of the way.

When everything was divided and properly stowed, we were ready to travel. Bin Sharif, Noora's boyfriend, brought a small female camel named Fatma to me. The tribe had a few dozen camels in its herd, but only two or three were bulls. Bin Sharif explained to me that they sold or ate the rest of the bulls, because they didn't believe in giving food and water to an animal that wouldn't return milk.

I saw one of the men mounting a camel that was already on the move. He did this by climbing up one of the animal's forelegs, gripping it above the knee with his toes, and then pulling himself up over the camel's neck and into the saddle. I wasn't ready to display that kind of nonchalance, and I waited until bin Sharif couched Fatma by tapping behind her front knees with a stick, and making the same "khirr, khirr!" noise I'd heard the Bayt Tabiti use. Then I dragged myself awkwardly into the sheepskin-covered wooden saddle. Bin Sharif got the animal to her feet and handed me the head rope and a riding stick. I saw that Friedlander Bey had been helped onto another small camel.

"In the name of Allah, the Compassionate, the Merciful!" cried Shaykh Hassanein, leading the Bani Salim south from Bir Balagh.

"*Allahu akbar!* God is Most Great!" shouted his tribesmen. And then we were off on the three-day journey to Khaba, the next well.

Papa maneuvered his camel alongside me on the left, and Hilal, one of the two Bani Salim who'd found us in the desert, rode on my right. I was not enjoying the experience, and I couldn't imagine staying in that saddle for the three days to Khaba, let alone the two weeks it would take to reach Mughshin.

"How do you feel, my nephew?" asked Papa.

I groaned. "I hate this," I said.

"These saddles aren't as comfortable as those of the northern Bedu. Our muscles will hurt tonight."

"Look," said Hilal, "we don't sit in our saddles like city people. We kneel." He was, in fact, kneeling on the back of the camel. I was having enough trouble maintaining my balance, wedged into the wooden saddle and hanging on for dear life. If I'd tried to kneel like Hilal, I would've rolled off and fallen the ten feet to the ground with the camel's next lurching step. Then I would've had a broken neck to go along with my aching back.

"Maybe I'll just get off and walk," I said.

Hilal grinned and showed me his strong white teeth. "Be cheerful, my brother!" he said. "You're alive, and you're with friends!"

Actually, I've never been among such horribly cheerful people as the Bedu. They chanted and sang the whole way from Bir Balagh to Khaba. I suppose there was little else to pass the time. Now and then, one of the young men would ride up to one of his cousins; they'd have a wrestling match atop their camels, each trying to topple the other to the ground. The possibility of broken bones didn't seem to daunt them.

After about an hour and a half, my back, neck, and legs began to complain. I couldn't stretch adequately, and I realized it was only going to get worse. Then I remembered my daddies. At first, I hesitated to chip in the pain blocker again, but my argument was that it was only the abuse of drugs and daddies that was dangerous. I took out the daddy and chipped it in, promising myself that I wasn't going to leave it in any longer than necessary. From then on, the camel ride was less of a strain on my cramped muscles. It never got any less boring, though.

For the remainder of the day, I felt pretty good. As a matter of fact, I felt almost invincible. We'd survived being abandoned in the Rub al-Khali—with the help of the Bani Salim, of course—and we were on our way back to punish Reda Abu Adil and his tame imam. Once more, I'd shown Friedlander Bey that I was a man of honor and courage; I doubted that he'd ever again resort to blasting my brain's punishment center to get my cooperation. Even if at the moment all wasn't right with the world, I was confident that it soon would be.

I felt as if a strong current of dynamic force was flowing into me from some mystic source. As I sat uneasily astride Fatma, I imagined Allah inspiring our allies and creating confusion for our foes. Our goals were honest and praiseworthy, and I assumed God was on our side. Even before the abduction, I'd become more serious about my religious obligations. Now when the Bani Salim paused for prayer at each of the five prescribed times, I joined in with sincere devotion.

When we came into a valley between two parallel ridges of sand, Hassanein called a halt for the evening. The men couched the camels and unloaded them. Then the boys herded the beasts toward some low, dead-looking shrubs. "Do you see the *haram*, the salt-bush?" said Suleiman bin Sharif. He and Ibrahim bin Musaid had unloaded Fatma and Papa's camel.

"Yes," I said. The *haram* had dead-looking reddish-green leaves, and was as unhappy as any plant I'd ever seen.

"It's not dead, although it looks like dry sticks poking up out of the sand. No water has fallen in almost two years in this part of the Sands, but if it rained tomorrow, the *haram* would flower in a week, and then it could stay alive another two years."

"The Bani Salim are like the *haram*," said bin Musaid, looking at me with a contemptuous expression. "We aren't like the weak city-dwellers, who can't live without their Christian ornaments." "Christian" seemed to be the worst insult he could think of.

I had a response to that, something to the effect that bin Musaid did indeed remind me of the *haram*, but I couldn't imagine him all covered with flowers because he'd need to bathe first. I decided not to say it aloud, because I could just picture the headlines: BUDAYEEN CLUB OWNER DIES IN SALT-BUSH MASSACRE.

The women put up the goat-hair tents for the night, and Hassanein generously offered to let Papa and me use his. "Thank you, O Shaykh," I said, "but I'm well enough now to sleep by the fire."

"Are you sure?" asked Hassanein. "It reflects badly on my hospitality for you to sleep under God's sky tonight. I'd truly be honored—"

"I accept your most kind invitation, Shaykh Hassanein," said Friedlander Bey. "My grandson wants to experience the life of the Bedu. He still entertains romantic notions of the nomadic existence, no doubt put in his mind by Omar Khayyám. A night by the fire will be good for him."

Hassanein laughed, and went to tell his wife to make room in their tent for Papa. As for me, I hoped it wouldn't get too cold that night. At least I'd have my robe to help keep me warm.

We shared a simple supper of dried goat meat, rice porridge, bread, coffee, and dates. I'd gotten plenty hungry during the day, and this food was as satisfying as any meal I could remember. Some of the enjoyment came from the company. The Bani Salim had unanimously welcomed Papa and me, and it was as if we'd been born among them.

Well, the acceptance was *almost* unanimous. The lone dissenter, of course, was Ibrahim bin Musaid. Noora's cousin didn't have any problem with Friedlander Bey, but he still gave me the fishy eye and muttered under his breath whenever he caught me looking at him. I was under the protection of Shaykh Hassanein, however, and therefore completely safe from his nephew. And bin Musaid was bright enough to realize that if he just waited long enough, I'd go away again.

After I finished eating, I popped out the pain daddy. Except for some soreness in my neck and back, I felt pretty good. I watched some of the men get up to make sure the boys had hobbled the camels properly for the night. There were still five or six of us at the fire, and a good-humored story-telling session began, concerning the men who had wives to prepare their meals and tents to sleep in. One man told some gossip about bin Shahira who, like many of the Bani Salim, had been named after his mother rather than his father. "Bearing his mother's name has made him crazy all his life," said the narrator. "All the years we were boys together, he complained about what a strict tyrant his mother was. So who does he marry? Old Wadood Ali's daughter. Badia the Boss we used to call her. Now he's the most henpecked man who ever rode a camel. Tonight at prayers, I think I heard him ask Allah to let the Bayt Tabiti raid us and carry her off. Just her and nothing else!"

"Min ghayr sharr," said one of the other men, who wasn't amused. That was a superstitious formula to avoid the evil bin Shahira had wished for.

No one was safe from the loose tongues of the Bani Salim, except of course the other men who sat by the campfire. Even Shaykh Hassanein came in for some sarcastic comments about how he was handling his hot-headed nephew, bin Musaid, and his beautiful niece, Noora. It was clear that bin Musaid and bin Sharif weren't the only men of the tribe who had their eyes on Noora, but because bin Musaid was her first cousin, he had an unshakable claim on her.

The talk drifted in one direction and then another. One of the older men began a recitation of some long-ago battle in which he'd distinguished himself. The younger men complained that they'd heard the story a hundred times before, but that didn't dismay the speaker. Hilal and bin Turki got up from their places and came to sit beside me.

"Do you remember us, O Shaykh?" asked Hilal, who'd ridden beside me most of the day.

"Yes, of course," I said. "You're the clever young men who found us in the desert."

Hilal and bin Turki grinned at each other. "My cousin would like to ask you a question," said Hilal.

"Sure," I said.

Bin Turki was a handsome, shy youth. Even by the firelight I could see that he was blushing furiously. "O Shaykh," he said, "when you return to your city, will you be far from China?"

I wondered what he meant. "Very far, bin Turki," I said. "Why?"

"Ten days' march?" he asked. "Twenty?"

I stopped to do some quick calculation. The camels made a steady three miles an hour, and the Bani Salim put in about twelve hours of travel per day. Call it thirty-six miles, then. Now, the distance from the city to China . . . "Hundreds of days, O my friend, across deserts and seas and great mountains."

Bin Turki just blinked at me a few times. "O Shaykh," he said in a quavering voice, "even Allah's world is not so big."

He thought I was lying to him, but he couldn't bring himself to accuse a guest of his tribe. "Indeed it is so big. The Sands are only a portion of Arabia, and all of Arabia is to the world as . . . as one she-camel to the entire herd."

"*Wallâhi!*" murmured Hilal, which means "By Almighty God," and is one of the Bani Salim's strongest oaths. I rarely heard them resort to obscenity.

"What is your curiosity about China, bin Turki?" I asked. These were people who had never heard of England, Nuevo Tejas, or even the western lands of the Muslim world.

"Does not the Prophet—may the blessings of Allah be on him and peace—say, 'Seek knowledge even unto China'? I thought maybe I could return with you to your city, and then go from there to China."

Hilal laughed. "Bin Turki's hungry for knowledge," he said in a teasing voice. "He's already eaten all the knowledge there is to be had in the Sands."

"You don't have to go to China," I said. "If you're serious about learning, maybe you could travel with us after we reach Mughshin. Would you like that?"

I could see that bin Turki was trembling. "Yes, O Shaykh," he said softly.

"Is there any reason why you couldn't come with us? Do the Bani Salim need you? Might Shaykh Hassanein forbid you to go away for a few months?"

"I haven't yet discussed this with the shaykh," said bin Turki.

"The Bani Salim won't need you," said Hilal. "You never do anything useful anyway. It will be one less belly to fill with water from the wells of the Sands. Seriously, my brother, Shaykh Hassanein will let you go with his blessing."

There were a few moments of quiet while bin Turki thought over the consequences of what he wanted to do. We listened to dead limbs of the mimosa-like *ghaf* trees spit and crackle in the fire. Then the young man worked up his courage. "If Shaykh Hassanein gives his permission," he asked, "would I be welcome to join you?"

I smiled at the young man. "Do you know the way across the mountains from Mughshin to that coastal town?"

"To Salala?" said bin Turki. "Yes, I've been there many times. Two or three times, anyway."

"Well, then, we'd be glad of your company. Talk it over with

Shaykh Hassanein and see what he has to say. It's a big, strange world out there, and you may wish you never left the Bani Salim."

"If that happens, I will come back to the Sands, *inshallah*."

Hilal looked from bin Turki to me, realizing that his friend might soon be leaving their community for the unimaginable life beyond the desert. *"La illah ill'Allah,"* he said in astonishment. "There is no god but God."

Bin Musaid came to the fire and stared down at me for a few seconds. "You don't have to sleep here on the sand tonight," he said. "You're welcome to share my tent."

His sour expression belied the generosity of his offer. I wondered why he was making this overture. Maybe Hassanein had had a little talk with him. "May Allah reward you, bin Musaid," I said, "but tonight I wish to sleep under the stars."

"Good," he said. He wasn't going to try to talk me out of it. One of the others passed him a goatskin of camel's milk, and he squatted down to drink. It's considered shameful for a Bedu to drink standing up. Don't ask me why.

Noora joined us, but she didn't even glance at bin Musaid. "My uncle wishes to know if there's anything you need," she said.

There was a time not long ago when I would have weakened and asked the shaykh for some medication. "Tell Hassanein that I feel very well," I said.

"Noora," said Hilal, "tell us about the time Abu Zayd was rescued by the Bayt Tabiti!"

"There *is* no story about Abu Zayd and the Bayt Tabiti," said one of the other men.

"Give Noora a minute or two and there will be," said bin Turki.

Bin Musaid grunted in disgust, got up, and stalked away into the deepening darkness.

"He better be hung like a bull camel," said Hilal, "because his wife won't get any happiness from him any other way." There was an uncomfortable silence, while we all tried hard not to look at Noora.

"Well, does anybody want to hear about Abu Zayd?" she said at last.

"Yes!" came several voices. Abu Zayd is a popular hero of Arabian folklore. His mythical tribe is responsible for everything from the Roman ruins in North Africa to the mysterious petroglyphs in the Rub al-Khali.

"All you who love the Prophet," Noora began, "say, 'May Allah be pleased with him and grant him salvation.' Now, one day Abu Zayd found himself lost in a part of the Sands he had never traveled before. There were no familiar landmarks, and he did not know that he was on the edge of the terrible gypsum flat called Abu Khawf, or Father of Fear. He led his faithful camel, Wafaa, down onto the flat, which stretched ahead of him for eight days' journey. After three days, Abu Zayd had drunk all of his water. By the end of the next day, when he'd reached the very middle of Abu Khawf, he was suffering from thirst, and even Wafaa, his camel, was beginning to stumble.

"Another day passed, and Abu Zayd was afraid for his life. He prayed to God, saying that if it was the will of Allah, he'd much prefer getting out of Abu Khawf alive. Just then, he heard a loud voice. Coming toward him, leading two camels loaded with bulging goatskin bags, was a man of the Bayt Tabiti. '*Salaam alaykum*, my brother!' cried the stranger. 'I am Abduh bin Abduh, and I will give you water!'

"'*Alaykum as-salaam*,' said Abu Zayd, overcome with relief. He watched as the Bayt Tabiti took several bags of water and slung them on Wafaa. Then Abduh bin Abduh gave him a bag of camel's milk, from which Abu Zayd drank greedily. 'You've done me a great service,' he said. 'You've kept me from dying in this miserable gypsum flat. No man has ever shown me greater hospitality and generosity. I insist that you turn your camels around and return with me to the nearest oasis. There I will give you a suitable reward.'

"'Of course,' said Abduh bin Abduh, 'I had no thought at all of reward. Still, if you insist.' And he did turn his camels around, and together the two men made their away across the remainder of Abu Khawf, the Father of Fear. Two days later, they arrived at Bir Shaghir, a settlement around a well of the sweetest water in all the Sands. Abu Zayd made good on his promise, buying a huge load of flour, butter, dates, coffee, rice, and dried meat, and giving it all to Abduh bin Abduh. Afterward, the two men expressed gratitude and good wishes to each other, and then they parted, going their separate ways.

"A year later to the very day, Abu Zayd again found himself lost in the Sands, and this time he stumbled into Abu Khawf from a different direction. After three days passed, he realized that fate had led him into the very same situation he'd endured the year before. He prayed for God, saying, '*Yaa Allah*, how like a woven web of spider silk is Your will. All glory be to God!'

"And on the fifth day, when Abu Zayd and his camel, Wafaa, were growing weak without water, who should come toward them across the gypsum flat but the very same Bayt Tabiti! 'God bless you!' cried Abduh bin Abduh. 'All year, I've told my friends of your generosity. I hoped we'd meet again, so you could know that your name is legendary for gratitude among my people.'

"Abu Zayd was amazed, but once again he persuaded Abduh bin Abduh to turn his camels and go back with him to Bir Shaghir. This time he bought the Bayt Tabiti so much flour, butter, dates, coffee, rice, and dried meat that he also needed to buy the man a third camel to help carry it all. Then they swore undying friendship to each other and went off in opposite directions.

"Before Abduh bin Abduh disappeared from view, however, Abu Zayd turned and shouted after him. 'Go with safety, my brother,' he called, 'and enjoy my gifts to you, because for a second time you saved my life. I will never forget what you've done, and as long as my sons and my sons' sons draw breath, they will sing your praises. But listen, O fortunate one: I am not a rich man. If you come upon me next year in Abu Khawf, pass me by and let me die of thirst! I can't afford to thank you one more time!' "

All the men at the campfire laughed loudly, and Noora stood up, smiling and looking pleased. "Good night, my brothers," she said. "May you arise in the morning in health."

"And you are the daughter of well-being," said bin Sharif. That's a Bedu idiom, possibly even an exclusively Bani Salim idiom. Noora raised a hand, and then crossed the open area of the camp to her father's tent.

Morning would come early, and the unmarried men soon settled in for the night. I wrapped myself in my cloak and tried to relax, knowing that there would be another long day of travel tomorrow. Before I fell asleep, I entertained myself with stories of what would happen when I got back to the city. I imagined that Indihar and Chiri and Yasmin ran to me, tears of joy streaming down their faces, praising Allah that I was alive and well. Imagined that Reda Abu Adil sat in his lonely palace, gnashing his teeth in fear of the retribution that would soon come. I imagined that Friedlander Bey rewarded me with tons of money, and told me that he was hiring an outside contractor to deal with Dr. Sadiq Abd ar-Razzaq, and that I needn't concern myself with him.

Breakfast in the morning was rice porridge, dates, and coffee. It wasn't very appetizing, and there wasn't enough of it. There was still plenty of water from Bir Balagh; but it had started out brackish, and after a day in the goatskin bags, it had begun to taste like, well, goatskin. I was already looking forward to getting to Khaba well, which the Bani Salim all talked about as the last sweet well before the long haul to Mughshin.

Friedlander Bey rode beside me again on the second day. "I've been thinking of the future, my nephew," he said, yawning. I'm sure it had been years since he'd had to sleep on the ground and share such meager rations, yet I hadn't heard him complain.

"The future," I said. "Imam ar-Razzaq first, and then Abu Adil? Or maybe the other way around?"

Papa didn't say anything for a little while. "Haven't I made it clear that you are not to harm Shaykh Reda under any circumstances?" he said. "Neither him nor his sons, if he has sons."

I nodded. "Yes, I know all that. How do you mean 'harm'? Do you mean physically? Then we won't raise a hand against him. Surely you won't mind if we destroy his business and influence in the city. He deserves that much at least."

"He deserves that much, Allah knows it. We can't destroy his influence. We don't have the means."

I laughed without humor. "Do I have your permission to try?"

Papa waved a hand, dismissing the entire subject. "When I spoke of the future, I meant our pilgrimage."

This wasn't the first time he'd brought up the trip to Mecca. I pretended I didn't know what he was talking about. "Pilgrimage, O Shaykh?" I said.

"You're a young man, and you have decades yet to fulfill that duty. I do not. The Apostle of God, may the blessings of Allah be on him and peace, laid upon us all the obligation to travel to Mecca at least once during our lifetime. I've put off that holy journey year after year, until now I'm afraid that I have very few years left. I'd planned to go this year, but when the month of the pilgrimage came, I was too ill. I strongly desire that we make definite plans to do it next year."

"Yes, O Shaykh, of course." My immediate concern was returning to the city and reestablishing ourselves; Friedlander Bey had thought past all that, and was already making plans for when life got back to normal. That was an outlook I wished I could learn from him.

The second day's march was much like the first. We pressed on over the high dune walls, stopping only to pray at the required times. The Bani Salim took no lunch breaks. The rocking gait of Fatma, my camel, had a lulling effect, and sometimes I dozed off into uneasy sleep. Every now and then, out of the blue, one of the men would shout "There is no god but God!" Others would join in, and then they'd all fall silent again, absorbed in their own thoughts.

When the tribe stopped for the second evening, the valley between the dunes looked identical to our camp of the previous night. I wondered how these people actually found their way from place to place in this huge desert. I felt a quick thrill of fear: what if they really couldn't? What if they only *pretended* they knew where they were going? What would happen when the water in the goatskins gave out?

I forgot my foolishness as I waited for Suleiman bin Sharif to couch Fatma. I slipped down her bulging side and stretched my aching muscles. I'd ridden the whole day without the aid of my daddy, and I was proud of myself. I went to Papa and helped him off his mount. Then the two of us pitched in to help the Bani Salim set up the camp.

It was another peaceful, lovely night in the desert. The first disturbing moment came when Ibrahim bin Musaid came up to me and put his nose about an inch from mine. "I watch you, city man!" he shouted. "I see you looking at Noora. I see her looking shamelessly at you. I swear by the life of my honor and by Almighty God that I'll kill her, rather than let you mock the Bani Salim!"

I'd had just about all I could take from bin Musaid. What I really wanted to do was knock the son of a bitch down, but I'd learned that the Bedu take physical violence very seriously. A crummy punch in the nose would be enough of a provocation for bin Musaid to kill me, and he'd have the sympathy of all the other Bani Salim. I grabbed my beard, which is how the Bedu swear their oaths, and said, "I haven't dishonored Noora, and I haven't dishonored the Bani Salim. I doubt anyone could dishonor you, because you have no honor to speak of."

There was a loud murmur on all sides, and I wondered if I'd gone a little too far. I have a tendency to do that sometimes. Anyway, bin Musaid's face darkened, but he said nothing more. As he stormed away, I knew I had a lifelong enemy in him. He paused and turned to face me again, raising his thin arm and pointing a finger at me, shaking in rage. "I'll kill her!" he cried.

I turned to Hilal and bin Turki, but they just shrugged. Bin Musaid was my problem, not theirs.

It wasn't long before another loud altercation broke out. I looked across the fire to the far side of the camp. There were five people involved in a shouting match that was getting louder and more violent by the moment. I saw bin Musaid and Noora waving their arms wildly at each other. Then bin Sharif, the young man Noora wished to marry, came to her defense, and I thought the two young men would begin strangling each other right there. An older woman joined them, and she began firing accusations at Noora, too.

"That's Umm Rashid," said Hilal. "She has a temper like a fennec fox."

"I can't make out what she's saying," I said.

Bin Turki laughed. "She's accusing Noora of sleeping with her husband. Her husband is too old to sleep with anybody, and all the

Bani Salim know it, but Umm Rashid is blaming her husband's inattention on Noora."

"I don't understand. Noora is a good, sweet child. She's done nothing to deserve all this."

"Being good and sweet in this life is enough to attract evil," said Hilal, frowning. "I seek refuge with the Lord of the Worlds."

Umm Rashid screeched at Noora and flapped her arms like a crazed chicken. Bin Musaid joined in, practically accusing Noora of seducing the old woman's husband. Bin Sharif tried to defend her, but he could barely get a word in edgewise.

Then Noora's father, Nasheeb, was finally stirred to action. He came out of his tent, yawning and scratching his belly. "What's this all about?" he said.

That got Umm Rashid yelling in one of his ears, and bin Musaid in the other. Noora's father smiled lazily and waved his hands back and forth. "No, no," he said, "it can't be. My Noora is a good girl."

"Your Noora is a slut and a whore!" cried Umm Rashid. That's when Noora felt she'd had enough. She ran—not into her father's tent, but into her uncle Hassanein's.

"I won't let you call her that," said bin Sharif angrily.

"Ah, and here's her pimp!" said the old woman, putting her hands on her hips and cocking her head sideways. "I warn you, if you don't keep that bitch away from my husband, you'll wish you had. The Qur'ân allows me that. The Straight Path permits me to kill her if she threatens to break up my household."

"It does not," said bin Sharif. "It doesn't say that anywhere."

Umm Rashid paid him no attention. "If you know what's good for her," she said, turning back to Nasheeb, "you'll keep her away from my husband."

Noora's father just smiled. "She's a good girl," he said. "She's pure, a virgin."

"I hold you responsible, my uncle," said bin Musaid. "I'd rather see her dead than spoiled by the likes of that infidel from the city."

"*What* infidel from the city?" asked Nasheeb in confusion.

"You know," said Hilal thoughtfully, "for someone as good and kind as Noora, there sure are an awful lot of people ready to hurt her."

I nodded. The next morning, I remembered what he said when I discovered Noora's lifeless body.

SEVEN

The bani Salim were standing crowded together in the hollow of a horseshoe-shaped dune near their camp, grouped in a semicircle around Noora's corpse. She lay on her back with her right arm up on the hill of sand as if reaching toward Heaven. Her eyes were wide open, staring up at the cloudless sky. The girl's throat had been slashed from ear to ear, and the golden sand was darkly stained with her blood. "Like an animal," murmured bin Turki. "She's been butchered like a goat or a camel."

The Bedu had gathered into several groups of people. Friedlander Bey and I stood with Hilal and bin Turki. On one side were Nasheeb and his wife, who were on their knees and shrieking their grief. Nasheeb looked dazed and kept repeating "There is no god but God. There is no god but God." Not far from them stood Ibrahim bin Musaid and Suleiman bin Sharif, who were engaged in a fierce argument. I saw bin Sharif point sharply toward Noora's body, and bin Musaid raised both his hands as if to ward off a blow. Shaykh Hassanein stood aside with a grim expression, nodding as his brother, Abu Ibrahim, spoke to him. Everyone else contributed to the noise and confusion, all loudly speculating, debating, and praying.

There was a lot of scriptural citation going on, too. " 'He who is wrongfully slain,' " quoted Hilal, " 'We have given license to his heir, but let him not revenge himself in too great a measure. Behold! he will be helped.' "

"All praise be to Allah," said bin Turki, "but what heir did Noora have to settle this blood-debt?"

Hilal shook his head. "Only Nasheeb, her father, but I don't think he'll do very much. He doesn't have the temperament for vengeance."

"Perhaps her uncles," I said.

"If not them, then *we* will take up this matter," said Friedlander Bey. "This is a needless tragedy. I liked the young woman a great deal. She was very kind to me while I recovered."

I nodded. I felt the flame of rage burning in me, the same hot, frightening feeling I've gotten whenever I've witnessed the scene of a murder. Those other times, however, were back home. In the Budayeen, crime and violent death are daily occurrences; they barely raise an eyebrow among my hardened friends.

This was different. This was a killing among close-knit people, a tribe that depended on each member for the continued well-being of all. I knew that the justice of the desert people was more sure and swift than the justice of the city, and I was glad. Vengeance would not bring Noora back, but it helped a little to know that her murderer's hours were numbered.

It wasn't immediately clear who her killer was, however. The two likely candidates, based on their loudly publicized threats the previous evening, were bin Musaid and Umm Rashid.

Shaykh Hassanein raised his arms and called for attention. "This girl must be buried by sundown," he said. "And her murderer must be identified and punished."

"And the blood-price paid!" cried the grief-stricken Nasheeb.

"All will be done in accordance with the Book," Hassanein assured him. "Abu Ibrahim, help me carry our niece back to the camp. Hilal, you and bin Turki must begin digging a grave."

"May God have mercy on her!" someone said, as Hassanein and his brother wrapped Noora in a cloak and lifted her up. We made a slow procession from the horseshoe dune through a narrow gully to the campsite. The shaykh chose a spot for Noora's final resting place, and Hilal and bin Turki fetched two folding shovels and began digging down through the hard belly of the desert.

Meanwhile, Hassanein disappeared into his tent for a few minutes. When he returned, his *keffiya* was arranged more carefully on his head. I guessed that he'd also chipped in one of his two moddies, probably the one that loaned him the wisdom of a Sunni Muslim religious leader.

The Bani Salim were still upset and angry, and there were many loud discussions going on, trying to make sense of the killing. The only one who wasn't involved was bin Musaid. He seemed to be holding himself apart. I looked at him, and he stared back at me across the open space. Finally he turned his back on me, slowly and insultingly.

"Shaykh Marîd," said Hassanein, "I'd like to speak with you."

"Hm? Sure, of course." He led me into his shady tent. He invited me to sit down, and I did.

"Please forgive me," he said, "but I must ask you some questions. If you don't mind, we'll do without the preliminary coffee and conversation. Right now, I'm only interested in learning how Noora died. Tell me all about how you found her this morning."

I felt a lot of anxiety, although Hassanein probably didn't consider me a prime suspect. I was one of those kids who, when the teacher came in and asked who'd written the dirty word on the blackboard, even though I hadn't done it, I'd blush and look guilty. All I had to do now, I told myself, was take a deep breath and tell the shaykh just what had happened.

I took the deep breath. "I must've gotten up a little before dawn," I said. "I had to relieve myself, and I remember wondering how long it would be before old Hamad bin Mubarak woke us with his Call to Prayer. The moon was low on the horizon, but the sky was so bright I didn't have any trouble following the little alleys among the dunes east of camp. When I finished, I stumbled back toward the fire. I must've taken a different path, because I hadn't seen Noora before. She was stretched out in front of me, just as you saw her. The pale moonlight made her drained face look ghastly. I knew immediately that she was dead. That's when I decided to come straight to your tent. I didn't want to disturb the others until I told you."

Hassanein just regarded me for a few seconds. With the imam moddy in, his behavior and speech were more deliberate. "Did you see signs of anyone else? Were there footprints? The weapon, perhaps?"

"Yes," I said, "there was footprints. I can't read footprints in sand as well as footprints in mud, O Shaykh. I imagine they were Noora's footprints and her killer's."

"Did you see long tracks, as if she'd been dragged to the place?"

I thought back to that moonlit scene. "No," I said, "I definitely didn't see tracks. She must've walked there and met the other person. Or maybe she was carried. She was alive when she got there, because there was no trail of blood leading back to camp."

"After you told me about Noora," he said, "did you tell anyone else?"

"Forgive me, O Shaykh, but when I got back to the fire, bin Turki was awake and asked me if I was all right. I told him about Noora. He was very upset, and our talking roused Hilal, and then in a little while everyone had heard the news."

"All is as Allah wills," said Hassanein, holding up his hands with his palms out. "Thank you for your truthfulness. Would you do me the honor of helping me question some of the others?"

"I'll do whatever I can," I said. I was surprised that he asked for my help. Maybe he thought city Arabs were more accustomed to this sort of thing. Well, at least in my case he was right.

"Then fetch in my brother, Nasheeb."

I went back outside. Hilal and bin Turki were still digging the grave, but were making slow progress. I went to Nasheeb and his wife, who were kneeling on the ground beside the cloak-wrapped body of their daughter. I bent down and touched the old man on his shoulder. He looked up at me with a vacant expression. I was afraid he was in shock. "Come," I said, "the shaykh wishes to speak to you."

Noora's father nodded and got slowly to his feet. He helped his wife get up, too. She was shrieking and beating her chest with her fist. I couldn't even understand what she was crying. I led them into Hassanein's tent.

"The peace of Allah be upon you," said the shaykh. "Nasheeb, my brother, I'm with you in your grief."

"There is no god but God," muttered Nasheeb.

"Who did this?" his wife shouted. "Who took my baby from me?"

I felt like an intruder witnessing their anguish, and it made me uncomfortable that there wasn't anything I could do to help them. I just sat quietly for about ten minutes, while Hassanein murmured soothing things and tried to get the couple into a frame of mind to answer some questions.

"There will come a Day of Resurrection," said Hassanein, "and on that day Noora's face will be bright, looking on her Lord. And the face of her murderer will be full of fear."

"Praise be to Allah, the Lord of the Worlds," prayed Umm Noora. "The Compassionate, the Merciful. Owner of the Day of Judgment."

"Nasheeb—" said Hassanein.

"There is no god but God," said the shaykh's brother, hardly aware of where he was.

"Nasheeb, who do you think killed your daughter?"

Nasheeb blinked once, twice, and then sat up straight. He ran his long fingers through his gray beard. "My daughter?" he whispered. "It was Umm Rashid. That crazy woman said she'd kill her, and now she has. And you must make her pay." He looked straight into his brother's eyes. "You must make her pay, Hassanein, swear it on the grave of our father!"

"No!" cried his wife. "It wasn't her! It was bin Musaid, that jealous, evil-minded murderer! It was him!"

Hassanein shot me a pain-filled glance. I didn't envy him his responsibility. He spent another few minutes calming Noora's parents, and then I led them out of the tent again.

Hassanein next wanted to speak to Suleiman bin Sharif. The young man entered the shaykh's tent and sat down on the sandy floor. I could tell that he was barely keeping himself under control. His eyes darted from one side to the other, and his fists clenched and unclenched in his lap.

"*Salaam alaykum*, O good one," said Hassanein. His eyes narrowed, and I saw that he was observing bin Sharif carefully.

"*Alaykum as-salaam*, O Shaykh," said the boy.

Hassanein paused for a long moment before he said anything more. "What do you know of this?" he asked at last.

Bin Sharif sat up straight, as if he'd been pricked. "What do *I* know of it?" he cried. "How should I come to know anything of this terrible thing?"

"That is what I must find out. How did you feel toward Noora bint Nasheeb?"

Bin Sharif looked from Hassanein to me and back again. "I loved her," he said flatly. "I suppose all the Bani Salim knew that."

"Yes, it was common knowledge. And do you think she returned your affection?"

He didn't hesitate. "Yes," he said. "I know it."

"But your marriage was impossible. Ibrahim bin Musaid would never allow it."

"God blacken the dog's face!" shouted bin Sharif. "God destroy his house!"

Hassanein held up a hand and waited until the young man calmed down again. "Did you kill her? Did you murder Noora bint Nasheeb, rather than see her belong to bin Musaid?"

Bin Sharif tried to answer, but no sound emerged. He took a breath and tried again. "No, O Shaykh, I did not kill her. I swear this upon the life of the Prophet, may the blessings of Allah be on him and peace."

Hassanein stood up and put a hand on bin Sharif's shoulder. "I believe you," he said. "I wish I could do something to lessen your grief."

Bin Sharif looked up at him with tormented eyes. "When you discover the murderer," he said in a low voice, "you must let me be the instrument of his destruction."

"I'm sorry, my son. That hard duty must be mine alone." It didn't look like Hassanein was looking forward to that responsibility, either.

Bin Sharif and I went back outside. Now it was Umm Rashid's turn. I went to her, but as I approached, she cowered away from me.

"Peace be with you, O lady," I said. "The shaykh wishes to speak with you."

She stared at me in horror, as if I were an *afrit*. She backed away across the open ground. "Don't come near me!" she shrieked. "Don't talk to me! You're not of the Bani Salim, and you're nothing to me!"

"Please, O lady. Shaykh Hassanein wishes—"

She fell to her knees and began praying. "O my Lord! My trials and tribulations are great, and my sorrows and sufferings are deep, and my good deeds are few, and my faults lie heavily upon me. Therefore, my Lord, I implore Thee in the name of Thy greatness—"

I tried to raise her up, but she began screaming at me again and pummeling me with her fists. I turned helplessly to Hassanein, who saw my difficulty and came out of his tent. I stepped back, and Umm Rashid fell to her knees again.

The shaykh stooped and murmured to her. I could see her shake her head vigorously. He spoke to her again, gesturing with one hand. His expression was mild and his voice was pitched too low for me to hear his words. Again the woman shook her head. At last, Hassanein put his hand beneath her elbow and helped her to her feet. She began to weep, and he escorted her to her husband's tent.

He returned to his own tent and began gathering his coffee-brewing equipment. "Whom do you wish to speak to next?" I asked.

"Sit down, Shaykh Marîd," he said. "I'll make coffee."

"The only other real suspect is Ibrahim bin Musaid."

Hassanein acted as if he hadn't heard me. He poured a large handful of coffee beans into a small iron pan with a long handle. This he set on the glowing coals of the cooking fire his wife had built that morning. "If we get a good start in the morning," he said, "we should reach Khaba well by evening prayers tomorrow, *inshallah*."

I looked out at the camp, but I didn't see Friedlander Bey. The two young men were still digging the dead girl's grave. Some of the Bani Salim were standing nearby, arguing every aspect of the situation, but the rest had already returned to their tents or were seeing to the animals. Bin Musaid stood all by himself to one side, with his back still turned toward us, as if none of this affected him at all.

When the coffee beans had been roasted to Hassanein's satisfaction, he let them cool. He stood up and got a small goatskin bag and brought it back to the cook fire. "Here," he said, "my wife makes fresh *laban* for me every morning, no matter what happens." This was curdled camel's milk, sort of like yogurt.

I took the goatskin bag and murmured *"Bismillah."* Then I drank some, thinking how odd it was that everyone from my mother to

Shaykh Hassanein tried to push curdled camel's milk on me. I really didn't like it very much, but I pretended to enjoy it out of respect for his hospitality.

I gave him back the bag, and he swallowed a little *laban*. By then, the coffee beans had cooled, and he put them in a brass mortar and crushed them with a stone pestle. He had two coffeepots; one was bright brass, shiny and polished, and the other was black with soot. He opened the sooty pot, which contained the leftovers of the morning's coffee, and dumped in the freshly ground beans. He added some water from another goatskin bag, and a pinch of powdered cardamom. Then he put the blackened pot in the fire, and carefully stirred the coffee until it boiled.

"Let us give thanks to Allah for coffee!" said Hassanein. He poured it from the black pot into the shiny pot, back into the black pot, and then into the shiny pot again. This let most of the coffee grounds settle and stay behind. Finally, he jammed a piece of hemp into the spout of the bright coffeepot to act as a filter.

"*Il hamdu lillah!*" he said. Praise be to God. He set out three small coffee cups.

I took one of the cups. "May your table last forever, O Shaykh," I said.

He filled my cup, then looked up. "Ibrahim bin Musaid," he called. "Come! There is coffee!"

Bin Musaid turned and regarded us. His expression said that he didn't understand what the shaykh was doing. He walked slowly toward us. "O Shaykh," he said suspiciously, "don't you have more important duties?"

Hassanein shrugged. "There is time for everything. The Bani Salim have plenty of time. Now is the time for coffee. Be refreshed!" He gave one of the cups to the young man.

We drank a cup of coffee, and then another. Hassanein chatted idly about his favorite camel, whose feet had grown tender and probably wouldn't be able to carry him across the gravel plains to the south.

It's customary to drink three small cups of coffee, and then signal by waggling the empty cup that you've had enough. After the third cup, Hassanein sat back and looked at bin Musaid. The silence became thick and threatening. Finally, bin Musaid laughed out loud. "This is some trick, O Shaykh. You hope to shame me with your coffee and your hospitality. You think I'll clasp your knees and beg forgiveness of Allah. You think I murdered Noora."

He got to his feet and angrily threw the china coffee cup to the ground, where it shattered into scattered fragments. I saw Hassanein wince. "I've mentioned nothing to you about that," he said.

"Look elsewhere for your murderer, O Shaykh," said bin Musaid fiercely. "Look to your guest here, the infidel from the city. Maybe only he and Allah know the truth." He turned and strode off across the camp, disappearing into his own black tent.

I waited for Hassanein to speak. Several minutes passed, and he just sat outside his tent with a sour expression, as if he'd just tasted something rotten. Then, when my patience was about ended, he let out his breath in a heavy sigh. "We've learned nothing," he said sadly. "Nothing at all. We must begin again."

He got slowly to his feet, and I joined him. We crossed to where Hilal and bin Turki were digging in the ground. "A little deeper yet, O excellent ones," said Hassanein. "But when you've dug the grave, don't lay the poor girl in it."

"We should bury her soon," said bin Turki, looking up and shading his eyes with his hand. "The noble Qur'ân—"

Hassanein nodded. "She'll be laid to rest before sunset, as the Wise Mention of God prescribes. But do not lower her into the ground until I tell you."

"Yes, O Shaykh," said Hilal. He glanced at bin Turki, who just shrugged. None of us had any idea what Hassanein had in mind.

"In the Hadhramaut, which is the shaykhdom in the heel of the boot of Arabia," said Hassanein, "a murderer is sometimes made to undergo a trial by fire. Of course, that's all superstition, and the value of such an ordeal is only as great as the belief in its power."

I saw that he was leading me out of the camp, toward the herd of camels. Young boys had scrambled up into the *ghaf* trees that grew in the narrow valleys between the dunes. They'd cut loose the tops of the trees, and the camels were grazing contentedly on the vegetation.

Hassanein continued with his story of justice in the Hadhramaut. "The ceremony always takes place in the morning, after the dawn prayers. The master of ordeals assembles the accused killer, the witnesses, the victim's family, and anyone else who has an interest in the matter. The master uses a knife blade which has been heated in a fire. When he decides that the knife is sufficiently hot, he makes the accused man open his mouth and stick out his tongue. The master wraps his own hand in his *keffiya*, and grasps the accused man's tongue. With his other hand, he takes hold of the fiery knife and strikes the man's tongue, first with one flat side and then the other."

"What's the point of that?" I asked.

Hassanein went to his favorite camel and patted her neck. "If the man is innocent, he'll be able to spit right then and there. The master usually gives him a couple of hours' grace, though. Then the accused man's tongue is examined. If it looks badly burned, then he's judged guilty. He'll be executed immediately, unless the victim's family accepts a reasonable blood-price. If there's no sign of burns, or only minor discoloration, the man is declared innocent and given his freedom."

I wondered what the shaykh was up to. He'd couched the camel and had begun saddling her. "And that's not the custom among the Bani Salim?"

Hassanein laughed. "We're not superstitious like the wild men of the Hadhramaut."

I thought the Bani Salim were plenty superstitious, but I didn't think it was wise to say anything. "Are you going on a journey?" I asked.

"No," said Hassanein. He threw two palm-fiber pads on the camel's back behind the hump, and then laid the wooden frame of his saddle over them. He tied the frame securely in place over the beast's withers, in front of the hump. Next he put a thick palm-fiber pad over the wooden frame, fitting it behind the hump and tying it with a string. This pad rose up high in the rear, and made a kind of uncomfortable backrest. Next, Hassanein draped a blanket over the pad, and then a heavy sheepskin over the blanket. He used stout woolen cords to hold everything firmly in place.

"Good," he said, stepping back and examining his handiwork. He grasped the camel's head rope, got her to stand up, and led her back into the middle of the camp.

"Do you know who the murderer is?" I asked.

"Not yet, but soon," he said. "I once listened to a man in Salala talk about how criminals are caught and punished in other countries." He shook his head ruefully. "I didn't think I'd ever need to try one of those methods."

"You're going to use this camel?"

He nodded. "You know, the Arabs aren't the only shrewd and clever people in the world. Sometimes I think our pride gets in the way of adopting ideas that might truly help us."

He brought the camel right up to the edge of the grave, where Hilal and bin Turki were scrambling up out of the hole. "I need the help of all three of you," said the shaykh, couching the camel again. He indicated the cloak-covered body of Noora.

"You want to put her in the saddle?" asked Hilal.

"Yes," said Hassanein. The three of us looked at one another, and then at the shaykh, but we bent and helped him lift the dead girl into place. He used some more cords to tie her securely, so that she wouldn't fall to the ground when the camel stood up. I didn't know what he was up to, but I thought it was pretty bizarre.

"Get up, Ata Allah," Hassanein murmured. His camel's name was "God's Gift." He gave her a little more urging and she complained, but slowly she rocked to her feet. The shaykh pulled on her head rope and began leading her around the broad circumference of the camp, beyond all the tents.

Hilal, bin Turki, and I watched in astonishment as Hassanein led the camel away. "Is this some custom of the Bani Salim?" I asked. "Like a moving wake, where the relatives stay in one place and the corpse does the traveling?"

"No," said bin Turki, frowning, "I've never seen the shaykh behave like this. Maybe he's been driven mad by the murder of his niece."

"Are there a lot of murders among the Bedu?" I asked.

The two young men looked at each other and shrugged. "As common as anywhere else, I guess," said bin Turki. "One tribe raids another, and men die. Blood must be avenged, and feuds begin. Sometimes the feuds last for years, decades, even generations."

"But there's rarely murder within a tribe, like this," said Hilal. "This is unnatural."

Hassanein called back over his shoulder. "Come, Shaykh Marîd, walk with me!"

"I don't understand what he's doing," said Hilal.

"I think he expects to figure out who the murderer is this way," I said. "I can't imagine how." I hurried after Ata Allah and her macabre burden.

By now, many of the Bani Salim were standing outside their tents, pointing at Hassanein and the camel. "My baby! My child!" shrieked Noora's mother. The woman flung herself away from her husband's grasp and ran stumbling in the path of the camel. She shouted prayers and accusations until she collapsed in tears to the ground. Nasheeb went to her and tried to help her to her feet, but she would not be comforted. Noora's father stared down dumbly at his wife, then up at the bundled figure of his daughter. He didn't seem to know exactly what was going on.

Suleiman bin Sharif cut across the camp and intercepted us. "What are you doing? This is disgraceful!" he said.

"Please, O excellent one," said Hassanein, "you must trust me."

"Tell me what you're doing," bin Sharif demanded.

"I'm making sure everyone knows what happened to Noora, the light of our days."

"But there isn't anyone in the tribe who hasn't heard the news," said bin Sharif.

"Hearing the news is one thing. Seeing the truth is another."

Bin Sharif threw his hands up in disgust, and let the shaykh lead the camel on around the circle.

We came abreast of Umm Rashid's tent, and the old woman just shook her head. Her husband, who was indeed far too old to be dallying with any woman, poked his head out of the tent and whined to be fed. Umm Rashid mouthed a prayer in Noora's direction, then went inside.

When we'd gotten three-quarters of the way around, I saw that Ibrahim bin Musaid was watching us with an expression of absolute hatred. He stood like a statue carved from sandstone, turning only his head a little as we drew nearer. He said nothing as we passed him and came again to the grave Hilal and bin Turki had carved into the desert floor.

"Is it time to bury her now, O Shaykh?" I asked.

"Watch and learn," said Hassanein.

Instead of stopping, he led Ata Allah past the grave and started a second perambulation of the camp. A loud sigh went up from the Bani Salim who were watching us, who were just as bewildered as I was.

Noora's mother stood beside our path and shouted curses at us. "Son of a dog!" she cried, hurling handfuls of sand at Hassanein. "May your house be destroyed! Why won't you let my daughter have peace?"

I felt sorry for her, but Hassanein just went on, his face empty of expression. I didn't know what his reasoning was, but it seemed to me that he was being unnecessarily cruel. Nasheeb still stood silently beside his wife. He seemed to be more aware now of what was happening around him.

Bin Sharif had had a while to think about what Hassanein was doing. He'd lost some of the edge of his anger. "You're a wise man, O Shaykh," he said. "You've proved that over the years, leading the Bani Salim with a sure and equitable hand. I defer to your knowledge and experience, but I still think what you are doing is an affront to the dead."

Hassanein stopped and went to bin Sharif. He put a hand on the young man's shoulder. "Perhaps someday you'll be shaykh of this tribe," he said. "Then you'll understand the agony of leadership. You're right, though. What I'm doing is an unkindness to my sweet niece, but it must be done. *Ham kitab*." That meant "It is written." It didn't really explain anything, but it cut off bin Sharif's argument.

Bin Sharif looked into the shaykh's eyes, and finally his gaze turned down to the ground. As we took up our progress again, I saw that the young man had begun walking back to his tent with a thoughtful expression on his face. I hadn't had much opportunity to talk with him, but I'd gotten the impression that he was an intelligent, serious young man. If Hassanein were correct and bin Sharif would someday succeed him, I guessed that the Bani Salim would remain in very capable hands.

I just stared ahead, a little unhappy about being part of this strange procession. It was another typical day in the Empty Quarter, and the hot wind blew sand into my face until I was grumbling under my breath. I'd had just about enough of all this; and despite what Friedlander Bey thought, I didn't find the Bedu way of life romantic in the least. It was hard and dirty and entirely without pleasure, as far as I was concerned, and they were welcome to it. I prayed that Allah would let me get back to the city soon, because it had become very obvious to me that I would never make a very good nomad.

Along the last part of the loop, bin Musaid was still watching us with hooded eyes. He stood in the same place as before, his arms folded across his chest. He hadn't said a word and he hadn't moved an inch. I could almost see him trembling with the effort to keep himself under control. He looked as if he were ready to explode. I didn't want to be near him when he did.

"Enough, O Shaykh?" said bin Turki as we drew abreast of the grave. Already it was beginning to fill in with fine sand blown across the desert floor.

Hassanein shook his head. "Another circle," he said. My heart sank.

"Will you explain what you're doing, O Shaykh?" I said.

Hassanein looked toward me, but his gaze was over my head, into the distance. "There were people on the back of the world," he said in a tired voice. "People as poor as we, who also led lives of wandering and hardship. When one of their tribe was killed, the elders carried the corpse around their camp five or six times. The first time, everyone in the tribe stopped whatever they were doing to watch, and they joined together in mourning the unfortunate victim. The second time, half the tribe watched. The third time, only a few people were still interested. By the fifth or sixth time, there was only one person who was still paying close attention to the progress of the body, and that was the killer himself."

I looked around the camp area, and I saw that almost everyone had gone back to his chores. Even though a popular young woman had died that morning, there was still hard work that had to be done, or there would be no food or water for the Bani Salim or for their animals.

We led Ata Allah slowly around the circle, with only bin Musaid and a few others observing our progress. Noora's father looked around for his wife, but she'd gone into their tent much earlier. Nasheeb leaned against a taut rope and stared at us with vacant eyes.

As we drew near bin Musaid, he blocked our way. "May Allah blight your lives for this," he growled, his face dark with fury. Then he went to his tent.

When we came up to the two young men this time, Hassanein gave them instructions. "You must look for the murder weapon," he told them. "A knife. Hilal, you look for it where Shaykh Marîd discovered Noora's body. Bin Turki, you must search around the tent of her parents." We went by the grave and started our final circuit. As Hassanein had predicted, there was only one person watching us now: Nasheeb, his brother, Noora's father.

Before we reached him, Hilal ran up to us. "I found it!" he cried. "I found the knife!"

Hassanein took it and examined it briefly. He showed it to me. "See?" he said. "This is Nasheeb's mark."

"Her own father?" I was surprised. I would've bet that the killer was bin Musaid.

Hassanein nodded. "I suspect he'd begun to worry that the loose talk and gossip might have some basis in truth. If Noora had been ruined, he'd never get her bride-price. He probably killed her, thinking that someone else would be blamed—my nephew Ibrahim, or old Umm Rashid—and at least he'd collect the blood money."

I looked at Nasheeb, who was still standing blank-faced beside his tent. I was horrified that the man could kill his own daughter for such a foolish reason.

The Bedu system of justice is simple and direct. Shaykh Hassanein had all he needed to be convinced of the murderer's identity, yet he gave Nasheeb a chance to deny the evidence. When we stopped beside him, the rest of the Bani Salim realized that we'd found the killer, and they came out of their tents and stood nearby, to witness what would happen next.

"Nasheeb, my father's son," said Hassanein, "you've murdered your own daughter, the flesh of your blood and the spirit of your spirit. 'Slay not your children, fearing a fall into poverty,' it says in the noble Qur'ân, 'we shall provide for them and for you. Lo! the slaying of them is great sin.'"

Nasheeb listened to him with his head bowed. He seemed to be only vaguely aware of what was happening. His wife had collapsed on the ground, weeping and calling on Allah, and some of the other women in the tribe were tending to her. Bin Musaid had turned away, and his shoulders shook. Bin Sharif just stared at Nasheeb in bewilderment.

"Do you deny this accusation?" asked Hassanein. "If you wish, you may swear your innocence on the great shrine of Shaykh Ismail bin Nasr. Remember that it was only a year and a year ago that Ali bin Sahib swore falsely on that holy shrine, and within a week he was dead of a snakebite." This was the same Shaykh Hassanein who'd assured me earlier that the Bani Salim weren't superstitious. I wondered how much he believed in the swearing-on-shrines stuff, and how much was purely for Nasheeb's benefit.

The murderer, Noora's own father, spoke in a voice so low that only Hassanein and I could hear. "I will swear no oath," he said. That was his admission of guilt.

Hassanein nodded. "Then let us prepare Noora for her rest unto the Day of Judgment," he said. "Tomorrow at sunrise, Nasheeb, you'll be allowed to pray for your soul. And then I will do what I must do, *inshallah*."

Nasheeb only closed his eyes. I've never seen such pitiful anguish on a man's face before. I thought he might faint on the spot.

We brought Noora back to the grave site. Two of the women fetched a white sheet to use as a shroud, and they wrapped the girl in it and wept and prayed over her. Hassanein and Abu Ibrahim, Noora's uncles, lowered her into the grave, and the shaykh prayed for her. Then there was nothing to do but cover her over and mark the place with a few stones.

Hassanein and I watched Hilal and bin Turki finish that work, and neither of us spoke. I don't know what the shaykh was thinking, but I was asking myself why it is that so many people seem to think that murder can be a solution to their problems. In the crowded city or here in the empty desert, can life really become so unbearable that someone else's death will make it better? Or is it that deep down inside, we never truly believe that anyone else's life is worth quite as much as our own?

As the two young men completed their sad task, Friedlander Bey joined us. "May the blessings of Allah be on her and peace," he said. "Shaykh Hassanein, your brother has fled."

Hassanein shrugged, as if he knew it would happen. "He seeks his own death in the desert, rather than from my sword." He stretched and sighed. "Yet we must track him and fetch him back, if God wills. This tragedy is not yet over."

Eight

Well, as much as I hated the idea, my time among the Bani Salim had changed my life. I was almost sure of it. As I drowsed aboard Fatma, I daydreamed what things might be like when I got back to the city. I especially liked the fantasy of bursting in on Reda Abu Adil and giving him the big kiss, the one that Sicilian crime lords knew as the mark of death. Then I reminded myself that Abu Adil was off-limits, and I turned my attention elsewhere.

Whose neck would I most like to wring? Hajjar's? That went without saying, but dusting Hajjar wouldn't give me the true satisfaction I was looking for. I'm sure Friedlander Bey would expect me to aim higher.

A fly landed on my face, and I gave it an annoyed swipe. I opened my eyes to see if anything had changed, but it hadn't. We were still slowly rocking and rolling across the sand mountains called the Uruq ash-Shaiba. These were indeed mountains, not just hills. I'd had no idea that dunes could rise so high. The sand peaks of the Uruq ash-Shaiba towered six hundred feet, and they stretched on and on toward the eastern horizon like waves of frozen sunlight.

It was sometimes very difficult for us to get the camels up the backs of those dunes. We often had to dismount and lead the animals by their head ropes. The camels complained constantly, and sometimes we even had to lighten their loads and carry the stuff ourselves. The sand on the slopes was soft, compared with the firm, packed sand on the desert floor, and even the surefooted camels had trouble struggling up to the crest of the high dunes. Then, on the leeward side, which of course was much steeper, the beasts were in danger of tumbling and seriously injuring themselves. If that happened, it might cost us our lives.

There were six of us in the chase party. I rode beside Hassanein, who was our unspoken leader. His brother, Abu Ibrahim, rode with bin Musaid, and Suleiman bin Sharif rode with Hilal. When we stopped next to rest, the shaykh squatted and drew a rough map in the sand.

"Here is the track from Bir Balagh to Khaba well to Mugh0shin," he said, drawing a crooked line from north to south. He drew another line parallel to it, about a foot to the right. "Here is Oman. Perhaps Nasheeb thinks he can beg the safety of the king there, but if so, he's badly mistaken. The king of Oman is weak, under the thumb of the amir of Muscat, who is a fierce defender of Islamic justice. Nasheeb would live no longer there than if he returned to the Bani Salim."

I indicated the space between the desert track and the Omani border. "What is this?" I asked.

"We've just entered this area," said Hassanein. He patted the honey-colored sand. "This is the Uruq ash-Shaiba, these high dune peaks. Beyond it, though, is something worse." Now he ran his thumbnail in the sand along the border with Oman. "The Umm as-Samim."

That meant "Mother of poison." "What kind of a place is it?" I asked.

Hassanein looked up at me and blinked. "Umm as-Samim," he said, as if just repeating the name explained everything. "Nasheeb is my brother, and I think I know his plans. I believe he's heading there, because he'd rather choose his own way to die."

I nodded. "So you're not really anxious to catch up to him?"

"If he intends to die in the wilderness, I'll allow it. But just the same, we should be prepared to head him off if he tries to escape, instead." He turned to his brother. "Musaid, take your son and ride to the northern limits of the Umm as-Samim. Bin Sharif, you and Hilal ride to the south. This noble city man and I will follow Nasheeb to the edge of the quicksands."

So we split up, making plans to meet again with the rest of the Bani Salim at Mughshin. We didn't have a lot of extra time, because there were no wells in the Uruq ash-Shaiba. We had only the water in our goatskin bags to last us until we caught up with Nasheeb.

As the day wore on, I was left alone again with my thoughts. Hassanein was not a talkative man, and there was very little that needed discussion. I'd learned quite a lot from him. It seemed to me that in the city, I sometimes paralyzed myself, worrying over right and wrong and all the gray shades in-between. That was a kind of weakness.

Here in the Sands, decisions were clearer. It could be fatal to delay too long, debating all the sides of a course of action. I promised myself that when I got back to the city, I'd try to maintain the Bedu way of

thinking. I'd reward good and punish evil. Life was too short for exten-
uating circumstances.

Just then, Fatma stumbled and recovered her footing. The interruption in the rhythmically swaying ride jolted me from my introspection
and reminded me that I had more immediate matters to think about.
Still, I couldn't help feeling that it was the will of Allah that I should
have this lesson. It was as if Noora's murder had been arranged to
teach me something important.

Why Noora had to die for it, I couldn't begin to understand. If I'd
asked the deeply religious Friedlander Bey about it, he'd only have
shrugged and said, "It's what pleases God." That was an unsatisfactory
answer, but it was the only one I'd get from anyone. The discussion of
such matters always devolved into late-adolescent speculation about
why Allah permitted evil in the world.

Praise Allah the Unknowable!

We rode until sundown, then Shaykh Hassanein and I stopped and
made camp in a small flat area between two immense dunes. I'd always
heard it was wiser to travel by night and sleep during the hot afternoon,
but the Bani Salim felt it was safer to reverse the conventional wisdom.
After all, Fatma had enough trouble with her balance in the daytime,
where she could see where she was going. In the dark, we'd be court-
ing disaster.

I unloaded Fatma and staked her down with a long chain that let
her find her own spare dinner. We needed to travel light, so our own
meal wasn't much better. We each chewed two or three strips of dried
goat meat while Hassanein prepared hot mint tea over a small fire.

"How much farther?" I asked, staring into the flickering fire.

He shook his head. "That's hard to say, without knowing Nasheeb's
plans. If, indeed, he's attempting a crossing of the Umm as-Samim,
then our task will be completed by noon tomorrow. If he tries to elude
us—which he cannot do, since his life depends on finding water
soon—we'll have to close in on him from three sides, and there may be
a violent confrontation. I trust that my brother will do the honorable
thing, after all."

There was something I didn't understand, "O Shaykh," I said, "you
called the Umm as-Samim 'quicksands.' I thought they existed only in
holoshows, and then usually along some unlikely jungle trail."

Hassanein gave one short, barking laugh. "I've never seen a
holoshow," he said.

"Well, the quicksand usually looks like thick mud. Seems to me
that if you can tread water, you ought to be able to stay above the surface in an even denser medium. You aren't sucked down immediately."

"Sucked down?" asked the shaykh. He frowned. "Many men have died in the Umm as-Samim, but none of them were sucked down. 'Fall through' is a better choice of words. The quicksands consist of a swampy lake of undrinkable water, over which is a crust of alkaline crystals washed by streams from the hills along the Omani border. In some places, the crust can bear the weight of a man. The crust is hidden from observation, however, by the desert sands that have drifted over it. From a distance, the Umm as-Samim looks like a quiet, safe floor at the edge of the desert."

"But if Nasheeb tries to travel across it—"

Hassanein shook his head. "May Allah have mercy on his soul," he said.

That reminded us that we'd delayed our sunset prayers, although only for a few minutes. We each cleared a small area of desert bottom, and performed the ritual ablutions with clean sand. We prayed, and I added a prayer asking for a blessing on Noora's soul, and guidance for all the rest of us. Then it was time to sleep. I was exhausted.

I had strange dreams all through the restless night. I can still recall one—something to do with a strong father figure giving me stern lectures about going to the mosque on Friday. In fact, the father figure wouldn't permit me to choose any old mosque; it had to be the one he attended, and he wouldn't tell me which one that was. It wasn't until I awoke that I realized he wasn't even my father, he was Jirji Shaknahyi, who had been my partner during the brief time I worked for the city's police department.

I was deeply troubled by that dream for two reasons: now and then, I still blamed myself for Shaknahyi's death, and I wondered how he came to represent strict and harsh behavior in my dreams. He hadn't been like that at all. Why was he troubling my rest now, instead of, say, a dream Friedlander Bey?

We had another meal of dried goat meat and tea before we loaded the camels and went off in pursuit of Nasheeb. Normally, breakfast was only rice porridge and dates. "Eat what you will," said Hassanein. "This will be a day filled with happenings that will not be pleasant. Eat and drink your fill, because we will not stop again until my brother is dead."

Yipe, I thought. How can he speak so calmly about such a thing? I'd thought that *I* was hard, yet this desert chieftain was showing me what real strength and toughness were.

I threw the elaborate saddle over Fatma's back, and she made her obligatory, halfhearted objections. I hung half of our supplies from the saddle, and then I got the camel to her feet. This was no simple task, believe me. More than once I'd wished that the Bani Salim had turned out to be one of those desert clans who speed across the landscape on beautiful horses. Instead, I got this balky, foul-smelling beast instead. Oh well, it was as Allah pleased.

We urged our camels on toward the east, toward the Umm as-Samim. Hassanein was right: this was going to be an unpleasant day. Yet at the end of it, there'd be a resolution that would prove cathartic for the shaykh, *inshallah*.

Neither of us spoke. We were each wrapped in dark thoughts as we sat on our camels, rocking slowly toward our appointment with Nasheeb. A few hours passed this way, until I heard an exclamation from the shaykh. *"Allahu Akbar!"* he said fiercely. "There he is!"

I looked up at once. I guess I'd been dozing, because I hadn't before noticed the broad, sparkling plain ahead of us. Standing at the western edge was a man, unloading his camel as if he planned to camp there.

"Well," I said, "at least he isn't going to take the poor animal with him."

Hassanein turned to glare at me. All his usual good humor had been burned away. His expression was hard and perhaps a little vindictive.

We urged our camels to their highest speed, and rode down out of the high dunes like a Bedu raiding party. When we were only fifty yards from Nasheeb, he turned to look at us. His face held no fear or anger, but only a kind of immense sadness. He raised an arm and gestured toward us. I didn't know what it meant. Then he turned and ran toward the bright crust of Umm as-Samim.

"Nasheeb!" cried Hassanein in despair. "Wait! Return with us to the Bani Salim, where at least you may be forgiven before I must execute you! Isn't it better to die in the bosom of your tribe, than out here in this desolate place, all alone?"

Nasheeb didn't acknowledge his brother's words. We'd almost caught up with him as he took his first hesitant step onto the sand-covered crust.

"Nasheeb!" shouted Hassanein. This time the murderer did turn around. He touched his chest above the heartbeat, brought his fingers to his lips and kissed them, then touched his forehead.

Finally, after what seemed like the longest moment in the history of the world, he turned again and took a few more steps across the crusted alkaline surface.

"Maybe he'll—" My words were silenced by Nasheeb's cry of utter hopelessness, as his next step broke through the crust, and he fell helplessly into the marshy lake below. His head reappeared briefly, but he was thrashing about helplessly. Knowing how to swim is not high in the list of the Bani Salim's necessary survival skills.

"In the name of Allah, the Beneficent, the Merciful," wailed Hassanein. "May the blessings of Allah be on him and peace."

"I testify that there is no god but God," I said, almost as shaken as my companion. I closed my eyes, even though there was nothing to see now but the small hole Nasheeb had broken in the salt crust. There was never any other sign of him. He'd died very quickly.

There was nothing else to do here, and the harshness of the environment dictated that we had to find the rest of the tribe at Mughshin as quickly as possible. Hassanein understood that truth better than I did, and so without speaking another word he dismounted and took the head rope of Nasheeb's camel, leading it across the whistling sand to his own mount. If there was grieving to be done, the shaykh would do it quietly, as we lurched our way to the southwest.

I don't recall sharing a single word with Hassanein during the remainder of that day. He pushed our little party to the utmost, and we rode for an hour or two after night fell, stopping only to pray at sunset. The shaykh explained the situation tersely. "The southern part of the Sands is hungry now," he said. "There is little water and little grazing for the camels. This part of the desert is going through a drought."

Well, hell, I was about to ask him how a place as dry as the Empty Quarter could have a drought. I mean, how could you tell? You could probably hold the entire annual rainfall for the region in a ten-ounce tumbler. I could see that Hassanein was not yet in a mood for talking, so I kept my peace.

About two hours after we'd made camp, eaten our meager dinner, and spread our blankets near the fire, we were joined by Hilal and bin Sharif. I was cheered to see them, although the recent events hung over this small reunion like the fear of God.

The two newcomers prepared their places near the fire. "We could see you and Nasheeb from a long way," said Hilal. "As soon as we saw you leave the edge of Umm as-Samim, we realized that Nasheeb must have killed himself. Then we angled across the Sands to intercept you. We would've met you sooner, but you must have kept up an exhausting pace."

"I don't wish to spend any more time here than necessary," said Hassanein in a grim voice. "Our food and water—"

"Is sufficient, I think," said bin Sharif. "You just want to leave what happened behind."

The shaykh stared at him for a long moment. "Are you judging me, Suleiman bin Sharif?" he asked in the fiercest of voices.

"*Yaa salaam*, I wouldn't dare," said the young man.

"Then spread your blanket and get some sleep. We have a long way to travel in the morning."

"As you say, O Shaykh," said Hilal. In a few minutes, we were all dreaming beneath the cold, black sky of the Rub al-Khali.

The next morning, we broke camp and started off across the desert, with no track to guide us but Hassanein's memory. We traveled for days like that, no one but Hassanein speaking, and he wouldn't utter a word unless it was necessary: "Time to pray!" or "Stop here!" or "Enough for today!" Otherwise, I had plenty of time for introspection, and believe me, I used it all. I'd come to the conclusion that not only had my time among the Bani Salim changed me, but when I got back— not *if* I got back—to the city, some drastic changes in my behavior were in order. I'd always been fiercely independent, yet somehow I'd come to desire the approval of this rough clan and its taciturn leader.

Finally, we'd traveled so far, over so many days, that thoughts of the city faded from my mind. I thought only of getting safely to another town, another Bedu village on the southern edge of the Sands. And therefore I was immensely happy when Hassanein stopped us and pointed to the horizon, slightly south of southwest. "The mountains," he announced.

I looked. I didn't see any mountains.

"These are the last miles of the Sands. We are in Ghanim now."

Sure, O Shaykh, if you think so. Nothing looked any different at all to me. But we turned a little to the south, and soon we found the centuries-old path worn from Khaba well to Mughshin on the far side of the Qarra Mountains. Mughshin was our goal, where we'd meet the rest of the tribe. The Bani Salim talked about Mughshin as if it were a treasure house of wonders, as if it were Singapore or Edo or New York. I'd already told myself that I'd withhold judgment until I had a chance to wander its alleys myself.

In another two or three days' travel the terrain began to rise, and I no longer doubted that the shaykh knew where he was going. At the base of the mountains that separated us from the seacoast was Mughshin. I'd imagined the place completely, from the stories of my companions, so I wasn't prepared for the shock of the truth. Mughshin consisted of fifty or sixty tents—commercial, European-made tents— strewn across a broad plain so that each occupant had sufficient privacy. A strong, gritty wind blew across the village, and no one was in sight.

Bin Sharif and Hilal were overjoyed to see the village come into view, and they stood on the backs of their camels, waved their rifles, and shouted the conventional pious phrases. "Go," said Hassanein, "and see if our tribe is there. Our usual camping ground looks empty."

"We may well have beaten them here," said bin Sharif. "We can travel faster than the slow procession of the Bani Salim."

The shaykh nodded. "And then we'll abide here until they arrive."

Hilal knelt in his saddle and shouted something I didn't understand. Then he prodded his camel into high gear, followed closely by bin Sharif.

Hassanein pointed toward the village. "Is your city greater than even this?" he asked.

That startled me. I stared at the handful of green and gray tents. "In some ways, yes," I said. "In some ways, definitely no."

The shaykh grunted. The time for talking had ended. He kicked up his camel, and I followed at a moderate pace. I began to feel a great sense of victory, in that I'd survived in this extremely low-tech environment. My skull-amping had been of very little use since my rescue by the Bani Salim; I'd even tried to stop using the pain, hunger, and thirst blockers, because I wanted to prove to myself that I could bear everything that the unmodified Bedu could.

Of course, I wasn't nearly as disciplined as they were. Whenever the pain, hunger, or thirst grew too great, I retreated thankfully behind the numb shield of my intracranial software. There was no point in overdoing anything, especially if only pride was at stake. Pride seemed too expensive in the Sands.

It was true that the Bani Salim had not yet arrived. Shaykh Hassanein led us to the tribe's usual stopping place, and we pitched a temporary, shelterless camp. How I stared longingly at the permanent tents! I'd have given a lot of money to rent one for myself, because the wind was chill and it carried a full weight of sand in its teeth. An earlier version of Marîd Audran would've said, "To hell with this!" and gone to rest within one of the tents. Now it was only my pride, my expensive pride, that kept me from abandoning Hassanein and the two young men. I was more concerned with what they'd think of me than with my own comfort. That was something new.

The next day I was very bored. We had nothing to do until the Bani Salim caught up with us. I explored the village, an accomplishment that took little time. I did discover a small *souk* where the more ambitious of the Mughshin merchants had spread blankets on the ground covered with various items. There was fresh meat and semifresh meat, vegetables, dates and other fruits, and the staples of the Bedu diet: rice and coffee and dried meat and cabbage, carrots, and other vegetables.

I was rather surprised to see one old man who had just seven little squares of plastic on his blanket: daddies brought across the mountains from Salala, imported from who-knows-where. I examined them with great curiosity, wondering what subjects this canny old fellow thought might sell to the few blazebrains who wandered the Rub al-Khali.

There were two Holy Imam daddies, probably the same as that owned by Hassanein; two medical daddies; a daddy programmed with various Arabic dialects spoken in the southern part of Arabia; an outlaw sex manual; and a compendium of *shari'a*, or religious law. I thought the latter might make a good gift for the shaykh. I asked the old man how much it cost.

"Two hundred fifty riyals," he said, his voice faint and quavery.

"I have no riyals," I admitted, "only kiam." I had almost four hundred kiam that I'd kept hidden from Sergeant al-Bishah in Najran.

The old man gave me a long, shrewd look. "Kiam, eh? All right, one hundred kiam."

It was my turn to stare. "That's ten times what it's worth!" I said.

He just shrugged. "Someday, someone will think it's worth a hundred, and I'll sell it for a hundred. No, no. Because you're a guest in our village, I'll give it to you for ninety."

"I'll give you fifteen for it," I said.

"Go then, see to your companions. I don't need your money. The Almighty Lord will provide for me in my state of want, *inshallah*. Eighty kiam."

I spread my hands. "I cannot afford such a steep price. I'll give you twenty-five, but that's as high as I can go. Just because I'm a stranger, that doesn't mean I'm rich, you know."

"Seventy-five," he said, without blinking an eye. His bargaining routine was more of a social custom than a true attempt to extort money from me.

This went on for a few more minutes, until I finally bought the legal-advice daddy for forty kiam. The old man bowed to me as if I were some grand shaykh. Of course, from his point of view, I was.

I took the daddy and headed back toward our campsite. Before I'd walked twenty yards, one of the other villagers intercepted me. "*Salaam*," he said.

"*Alaykum as-salaam*," I replied.

"Would you be interested, O Excellent One, in trying out some particularly fine and rare personality modules?"

"Well," I said, curious, "maybe."

"We've got some so . . . . unusual that you won't find their like anywhere, not in Najran or across the mountains in Salala."

I gave him a patient smile. I didn't come from some near-barbarous town like Najran or Salala. I thought I'd tested out some of the strangest and most perverted moddies in the world. Still, I was interested in seeing what this tall, thin camel jockey had by way of merchandise. "Yes," I said, "show them to me."

The man was very nervous, as if he were afraid someone might overhear us. "I could have my hand cut off for showing you the kind of moddies we sell. However, if you go in without any money, it will protect us both."

I didn't quite understand. "What do I do with my money?"

"The merchant who sold you the daddy has some metal cash boxes, O Shaykh. Give him your money, and he'll put it away safely, give you a receipt, and a key to the cash box. Then you go inside my tent, experiment with our moddies as long as you like. When you've decided to buy or not to buy, we come back and get your money. This way, if someone in authority interrupts the demonstration, we can prove you had no intention of buying, and I had no intention of selling, because you won't have any money on your exalted person."

"How often are your 'demonstrations' interrupted?" I asked.

The Bedu hustler looked at me and blinked a couple of times. "Now and then," he said, "now and then, O Shaykh. It's a hazard of this industry."

"Yes, I know. I know very well."

"Then, O Excellent One, come with me and deliver your money to Ali Muhammad, the old merchant."

I was a little suspicious of the younger man, but the old merchant had struck me as honest in an old-fashioned way.

We walked to his blanket. The younger man said, "Ali Muhammad, this lord desired to inspect our stock of number-one moddies. He's prepared to deposit his money with you."

Ali Muhammad squinted at me. "He's not the police or some other kind of troublemaker?"

"Just in speaking to this noble shaykh," the nervous man said, "I've come to trust him completely. I promise you on the shrines of all the imams that he will make no trouble."

"Eh, well, we'll see," said Ali Muhammad grumpily. "How much cash does he have."

"I know not, O Wise One," said my new friend.

I hesitated a moment, then brought out most of my roll. I didn't want to give him all of it, but both men seemed to know I'd do that.

"You must keep none in your pocket," said Ali Muhammad. "Ten riyals would be enough to earn severe chastisement for all three of us."

I nodded. "Here, then," I said, giving him the remainder of the money. In for a penny, in for a pound, I told myself. Except I was in for a few hundred kiam.

The old merchant disappeared inside a nearby tent. He was gone only two or three minutes. When he returned, he handed me a key and a written receipt. We thanked each other in the conventional manner, and then my fidgety guide led me toward another tent.

Before we'd covered half the distance, he said, "Oh, did you pay the five-kiam deposit on the key, O Shaykh?"

"I don't know," I said. "What deposit? You didn't mention the deposit before."

"I'm truly sorry, my lord, but we can't let you see the moddies unless you've paid the deposit. Just five kiam."

A warning chill settled into my belly. I let the skinny weasel read my receipt. "Here," I said.

"There's nothing about the deposit here, O Shaykh," he said. "But it's just five kiam more, and then you can play all day with the moddies of your choice."

I'd been too easily seduced by the idea of X-classification moddies. "Right," I said angrily, "you witnessed me giving every damn kiam I had to your old man. I don't have another five kiam."

"Well, that worries me, O Wise One. I can't show you the moddies without the deposit."

I knew right then I'd been had, that there probably were no moddies. "Right," I said fiercely. "Let's go back and get my money."

"Yes, O Shaykh, if that's what you wish."

I turned and headed back to Ali Muhammad's blanket. He was gone. There was no sign of him. Guarding the entrance to the tent that housed the cash boxes was a gigantic man with a dark, glowering face. I went to him and showed my receipt, and asked to be let in to retrieve my money.

"I cannot let you in unless you pay the five-kiam deposit," he said. He growled more than a human being should, I thought.

I tried threatening, pleading, and promises of a large stipend when Friedlander Bey arrived with the rest of the Bani Salim. Nothing worked. Finally, acknowledging that I'd been out-scammed, I turned to my nervous guide. He was gone, too.

So I was left holding a worthless receipt, a key—which probably holds the world record for Most Expensive Worthless Key—and the knowledge that I'd just been given a lesson in pride. It was a very costly lesson, but a lesson nonetheless. I knew that Ali Muhammad and his young confederate were probably halfway across the Qarra Mountains already, and as soon as I turned my back on Mr. Bedu Muscles, he'd vanish, too. I began to laugh. This was an anecdote I'd never tell Friedlander Bey. I could claim that someone robbed me one night while I slept. It was virtually the truth.

I just walked away, mocking myself and my lost superiority. Dr. Sadiq Abd ar-Razzaq, who'd condemned us to this horrible place, had actually done me a favor. More than one, as I was stripped of many illusions about myself. I'd come out of the desert a vastly different man from the one I was when I dropped in.

In four or five days the Bani Salim arrived, and there were many loud celebrations and reunions. I confirmed that Friedlander Bey was none the worse for the trek, and he seemed happier and healthier than ever. At one of the celebrations, Shaykh Hassanein embraced me as he would a family member, and formally adopted Friedlander Bey and myself into his clan. We were now full-fledged Bani Salim. I wondered if that would ever come in handy. I gave Hassanein the *shari'a* daddy, and he was greatly pleased.

The next day, we prepared for our departure. Bin Turki was coming with us, and would guide us across the mountains to the coastal town of Salala. From there we'd book passage aboard the first ship bound for Qishn, about two hundred miles to the west, the nearest city with a suborbital-class airfield.

We were going home.

nine

aboard the suborbital craft *Imam Muhammad al-Baqir*, the amenities were hardly superior to those on the ship that had flown us to Najran, into exile. We weren't prisoners now, but our fare didn't include a meal or even free drinks. "That's what we get for being stranded at the ends of the Earth," I said. "Next time, we should work to be stranded in a more comfortable place."

Friedlander Bey only nodded; he saw no joke in my statement, as if he foresaw many such kidnappings and strandings to come. His lack of humor was something of a trademark with him. It had raised him from a penniless immigrant to one of the two most influential men in the city. It had also left him with an exaggerated sense of caution. He trusted no one, even after testing people again and again over a period of years. I still wasn't entirely sure that he trusted me.

Bin Turki said hardly a word. He sat with his face pressed against the port, occasionally making excited comments or stifled exclamations. It was good to have him with us, because he reminded me of what it was like before I'd become so jaded with modern life. All of this was new to bin Turki, who'd stuck out like a hayseed hick in the poor crossroads town of Salala. I shuddered to think what might happen to him when he got home. I didn't know whether to corrupt him as quickly as possible—so he'd have defenses against the wolves of the Budayeen—or protect his lovely innocence.

"Flight time from Qishn to Damascus will be forty minutes," the captain of the suborbital announced. "Everyone on board should make his connections with plenty of time to spare."

That was good news. Although we wouldn't have the leisure time to explore a bit of Damascus, the world's oldest continually inhabited city, I was glad that travel time back to our city would be at a minimum. We'd have a layover in Damascus of about thirty-five minutes. Then we'd catch another suborbital direct to the city. We'd be home. We'd be powerless to move around in complete freedom, but at least it would be home.

Friedlander Bey stared out of his port for a long while after takeoff, thinking about matters I could only guess at. Finally, he said, "We must decide where we're going when the ship from Damascus to the city touches down."

"Why don't we just go to the house?" I asked.

He regarded me with a blank expression for a few seconds. "Because we're still criminals in the eyes of the law. We're fugitives from what passes for 'justice' there."

I'd forgotten all about that. "They don't know the meaning of the word."

Papa waved impatiently. "In the city, as soon as we showed our faces, your Lieutenant Hajjar would arrest us and put us on trial for that unexplained murder."

"Does everyone in the city speak that mutilated Arabic gibberish?" asked bin Turki. "I can't even make out what you're saying!"

"I'm afraid so," I told him. "But you'll get the hang of the local dialect quickly." I turned back to Papa. His sobering insight had made me realize that our troubles were far from over. "What do you suggest, O my uncle?" I asked.

"We must think of someone trustworthy, who'd be willing to house us for a week or so."

I couldn't follow his idea. "A week? What will happen in a week?"

Friedlander Bey turned the full power of his terrifying cold smile on me. "By then," he said, "we'll have arranged for an interview with Shaykh Mahali. We'll make him see that we've been cheated of our final legal recourse, that we're entitled to an appeal, and that we strongly urge the amir to protect our rights because in doing so he'll uncover official corruption under his very nose."

I shuddered, and then I thanked Allah that I wasn't going to be the target of the investigation—at least, not long enough to get nervous about. I wondered how well Lieutenant Hajjar slept, and Dr. Abd ar-Razzaq. I wondered if they foresaw events closing in on them. I got a delicious thrill while I imagined their imminent doom.

I must've drifted off to sleep because I was awakened some time later by one of the ship's stewards, who wanted bin Turki and me to make sure that our seat belts were securely fastened prior to landing. Bin Turki studied his and figured out how to work the catch. I cooper-

ated because it seemed to please the steward so much. Now he
wouldn't have to worry about my various separated limbs flying toward
the cockpit, in case the pilot planted the aircraft up to its shoulders in
the sand dunes beyond the city's gates.

"I think it's an excellent opportunity, O Shaykh," I said.

"What do you mean?" said Papa.

"We're supposed to be dead already," I explained. "We've got an
advantage then. It might be some time before Hajjar, Shaykh Reda, and
Dr. Abd ar-Razzaq realize that their two abandoned corpses are poking
around in matters they don't want brought to light. Maybe we should
proceed slowly, to delay our eventual discovery as long as possible. If
we go charging into the city with banners and bugles, all our sources
will dry up immediately."

"Yes, very good, my nephew," said Friedlander Bey. "You are
learning the wisdom of reason. Combat rarely ever succeeds without
logic to guide the attack."

"Still, I also learned from the Bani Salim the dangers of hesitancy."

"The Bani Salim would not sit in the dark and hatch plans," said
bin Turki. "The Bani Salim would ride down upon their enemies and
let their rifles speak. Then they'd let their camels trample the bodies in
the dust."

"Well," I said, "we don't have any camels to trample with. Still, I
like the Bani Salim's approach to the problem."

"You have indeed been changed by our experiences in the desert,"
said Papa. "Yet we won't be hesitating. We'll go forward slowly but
firmly, and if it becomes necessary to dispatch one of the key players,
we must be ready to commit that deed without regret."

"Unless, of course, the player is Shaykh Reda Abu Adil," I said.

"Yes, of course."

"I wish I knew the whole story. Why is Shaykh Reda spared when
better men—I'm thinking of his pet imam—may be sacrificed to our
honor?"

A long sigh came from Papa. "There was a woman," he said, turning his head and gazing out the port again.

"Say no more," I said. "I don't need to hear the details. A woman,
well, that alone explains so much."

"A woman and an oath. It appears that Shaykh Reda has forgotten
the oath we took, but I have not. After I am dead, you will be released
from that oath, but not before."

I let my breath out heavily. "Must've been *some* woman," I said.
This was the most he'd ever discussed the mysterious ground rules of
his lifelong conflict with his rival, Abu Adil.

Friedlander Bey did not deign to respond to that. He just stared out at the blackness of the sky and the darkness of the planet we were hurrying to meet.

An announcement came over the PA system instructing us to remain seated until the suborbital came to a complete stop and then underwent the quarter-hour cooling-down procedure. It was frustrating in a way, because I'd always wanted to visit Damascus, and we'd be there but I wouldn't get a chance to see anything but the terminal building.

The *Imam Muhammad al-Baqir* slipped into its landing configuration, and in a few more minutes we'd be on the ground. I shuddered a little in relief. I always do. It's not that I'm afraid of being shot into the sky in a rocket; it's just that when I'm aboard, suddenly I lose all my faith in modern physics and suborbital-craft design. I always fall back on a frightened child's thought, that they'll never be able to get so many tons of steel into the air, and even if they do, they'll never be able to keep it there. Actually, the time I'm most worried is during takeoff. If the ship doesn't explode in glittering smithereens, I figure we've got it licked and I relax. But for a few minutes, I keep waiting to hear the pilot say something like "Ground Control has decided to abort this flight once we're far enough downrange. It's been a real pleas—"

We came to a nice, smooth landing in Damascus, and then stared out the ports for fifteen minutes while the suborbital shrunk back to its IAA-approved tolerances. Papa and I had only three small bags between us, and we carried them across the tarmac to the terminal. It didn't take us long to figure out where we had to go to catch the suborbital that would take us home.

I went to the small souvenir shop, thinking to buy something for myself and maybe something for Indihar and something for Chiri. I was disappointed to discover that nearly all the souvenirs had "Made in the Western Reserve" or "Made in Occupied Panama" stickers on them. I contented myself with a few holocards.

I began writing one out to Indihar, but I stopped. No doubt the phones in Papa's palace were now tapped, and the mail was probably scrutinized by unfriendly eyes as well. I could blow our cover by sending a holocard announcing our triumphant return.

No doubt weeks ago Indihar and all my friends had reconciled themselves to my tragic demise. What would we find when we got back to the city? I guessed I'd learn a lot about how people felt toward me. Youssef and Tariq were probably maintaining Friedlander Bey's estate, but Kmuzu must have seen his liberation in my death, and would be long gone.

I felt a thrill as I climbed aboard the second suborbital. Knowing that the *Nasrullah* would ferry us back to the city made me tingle with anticipation. In under an hour, we'd be back. The uneasy alliances and conspiracies that had tried to kill us would be shaken, perhaps shaken to death, as soon as we got down to work. I looked forward eagerly to our vengeance. The Bani Salim had taught me that.

It turned out to be the shortest long flight I'd ever taken. My nose was pressed right up against the port, as if by concentrating with all my might, I could help steer the *Nasrullah* and give it a little extra acceleration. It seemed that we'd just passed through Max Q when the steward came by to tell us to buckle up for landing. I wondered if, say, we should plummet back to Earth and plow a crater a hundred feet deep, would the seat belt provide enough protection so that we could walk away unharmed, through the fireball?

The three of us didn't spend much time in the terminal, because Friedlander Bey was too well known to go long without being recognized, and then the word would get back to Abu Adil, and then . . . Sand Dune City again. Or maybe one shot through four cerebral lobes.

"What now, O Shaykh?" I asked Papa.

"Let us walk a bit," he said. I followed him out of the terminal, to a cab stand. Bin Turki, anxious to make himself useful, carried the bags.

Papa was about to get into the first cab in line, but I stopped him. "These drivers have pretty good memories," I said. "And they're probably bribable. There's a driver I use who's perfectly suited to our needs."

"Ah," said the old man, "You have something on him? Something that he doesn't want to come to light?"

"Better than that, O Shaykh. He is physically unable to remember anything from one hour to the next."

"I don't understand. Does he suffer from some sort of brain injury?"

"You could say that, my uncle." Then I told him all about Bill, the crazy American. Bill had come to the city long before I did. He had no use for cosmetic bodmods—appearances meant nothing to Bill. Or for skull-wiring, either. Instead, he'd done a truly insane thing: he'd paid one of the medical hustlers on the Street to remove one of Bill's lungs and replace it with a sac that dripped a constant, measured dose of lightspeed RPM into his bloodstream.

RPM is to any other hallucinogen as a spoonful of crushed saccharin is to a single granule of sugar. I deeply regret the few times I ever tried it. Its technical name is *l*-ribopropylmethionine, but nowadays I hear people on the street calling it "hell." The first time I took it, my reaction was so fiercely horrible that I had to take it again because I couldn't believe anything could be *that* bad. It was an insult to my self-image as the Conqueror of All Substances.

There isn't enough money in the world to get me to try it again.

And this was the stuff Bill had dripping into his arteries day and night, day and night. Needless to say, Bill's completely and permanently fried. He doesn't look so much like a cab driver as he does a possessed astrologer who'll probably seduce the entire royal family and end up being assassinated in an icy river at midnight.

Riding with Bill was a lunatic's job, too, because he was always swerving to avoid things in the road only he could see. And he was positive that demons—the *afrit*—sat beside him in the front, distracting him and tempting him and being just enough of a nuisance that it took all his concentration to keep from dying in a fiery crash on the highway. I always found Bill and his muttered commentaries fascinating. He was an anti-role model for me. I told myself, "You could end up like him if you don't stop swallowing pills all the time."

"And yet you recommend this driver?" said Friedlander Bey dubiously.

"Yes," I said, "because Bill's total concentration could pass through the eye of a needle and leave enough room for a five-tier flea pyramid to slide by above. He has no mind. He won't remember us the next day. He may not even remember us as soon as we get out of the cab. Sometimes he zooms off before you can even pay him."

Papa stroked his white beard, which was desperately in need of trimming. "I see. So he truly wouldn't be bribable, not because he's so honest, but because he won't remember."

I nodded. I was already looking for a public phone. I went to one, dropped in a few coins, and spoke Bill's commcode into the receiver. It took fifteen rings, but at last Bill answered. He was sitting at his customary place, just beyond the Budayeen's eastern gate, on the Boulevard il-Jameel. It took a couple of minutes for Bill to recall who I was, despite the fact that we'd known each other for years. He said he'd come to the airfield to pick us up.

"Now," said Friedlander Bey, "we must decide carefully on our destination."

I chewed a fingernail while I thought. "No doubt Chiri's is being watched."

Chiri's was a nightclub on the Street. Papa had forced Chiriga to sell it to him, and then he'd presented it to me. Chiri had been one of my best friends, but after the buyout she could barely bring herself to speak to me. I had persuaded her that it had been all Papa's idea, and then I'd sold her a half-interest in the club. We were pals again.

"We dare not contact any of your usual friends," he said. "Perhaps I have the answer." He went to the phone and spoke quietly for a short while. When he hung up, he gave me a brief smile and said, "I think I have the solution. Ferrari has a couple of spare rooms above his night-club, and I've let him know that I need help tonight. I also reminded him of a few favors I've done for him over the years."

"Ferrari?" I said. "The Blue Parrot? I never go in there. The place is too classy for me." The Blue Parrot was one of those high-toned, for-mal attire, champagne-serving, little Latin band clubs. Signor Ferrari glided among the tables, murmuring pleasantries while the ceiling fans turned lazily overhead. Not a single undraped bosom to be seen. The place gave me the creeps.

"Just that much better. We'll have your driver friend take us around to the back of Ferrari's place. The door will be unlocked. We're to make ourselves comfortable in the rooms upstairs, and our host will join us when he closes his nightclub at 2 A.M., *inshallah*. As for young bin Turki, I think it would be better and safer if we sent him ahead to our house. Write out a brief note on one of your holocards and sign it without using your name. That will be enough for Youssef and Tariq."

I understood what he wanted. I scribbled a quick message on the back of one of the Damascene holocards—"Youssef and Tariq: This is our friend bin Turki. Treat him well until we return. See you soon. [signed] The Maghrebi." I gave the card to bin Turki.

"Thank you, O Shaykh," he said. He was still quivering with excitement. "You've already done more than I can ever repay."

I shrugged. "Don't worry about repaying anything, my friend," I said. "We'll find a way to put you to work." Then I turned to Friedlan-der Bey. "I'll trust your judgment concerning Ferrari, O Shaykh, because I personally don't know how honest he is."

That brought another smile to Papa's lips. "Honest? I don't trust honest men. There's always the first time for betrayal, as you have learned. Rather, Signor Ferrari is fearful, and that is something I can depend on. As for his honesty, he's no more honest than anyone else in the Budayeen."

That wasn't very honest. Papa had a point, though. I thought about how I'd pass the time in Ferrari's rooms, and my own agenda began to take shape. Before I could discuss it with Friedlander Bey, however, Bill arrived.

Bill glared out of his cab with insane eyes that almost seemed to sizzle. "Yeah?" he said.

Papa murmured, "In the name of Allah, the Beneficent, the Mer-ciful."

"In the name of Christy Mathewson, the dead, the buried," growled Bill in return.

I looked at Papa. "Who is Christy Mathewson?" I asked.

Friedlander Bey just gave me a slight shrug. I was curious, but I knew it was wrong to start a conversational thread with Bill. He would either blow up in a rage and leave, or he'd start talking unstoppably and we'd never get to the Blue Parrot before dawn.

"Yeah?" said Bill in a threatening voice.

"Let's get in the cab," said Friedlander Bey calmly. We climbed in. "The Blue Parrot in the Budayeen. Go to the rear entrance."

"Yeah?" said Bill. "The Street's not open to vehicular traffic, which is what we are, or soon will be, as soon as I start moving. Actually, we'll all start moving, because we're—"

"Don't worry about the city ordinance," said Papa. "I'm giving you permission."

"Yeah? Even though we're transporting fire demons?"

"Don't worry about that, either," I said. "We have a Special Pass." I just made that part up.

"Yeah?" snarled Bill.

"*Bismillah,*" prayed Papa.

Bill tromped the accelerator and we shot out of the airport lot, zooming and rocketing and careening around corners. Bill always sped up when he came to a turn, as if he couldn't wait to see what was around the corner. Someday it's going to be a big delivery wagon. Blammo.

"*Yaa Allah!*" cried bin Turki, terrified. "*Yaa Allah!*" His cries died away to a constant fearful moan through the duration of the journey.

Actually, our ride was fairly uneventful—at least for me. I was used to Bill's driving. Papa pushed himself deep into the seat, closed his eyes, and repeated "*bismallah, bismallah*" the whole time. And Bill kept up a nonsensical monologue about how baseball players complained about scuffed balls, you should have to hit against an *afrit* once, see how hard *that* is, trying to connect with a ball of fire, even if you do, it won't go out of the infield, just break up in a shower of red and yellow sparks, try *that* sometime, maybe people would understand . . . and so forth.

We turned off the beautiful Boulevard il-Jameel and passed through the Budayeen's eastern gate. Even Bill realized that the pedestrian traffic on the Street was too dense for his customary recklessness, and so we made our way slowly to the Blue Parrot, then drove around the block to the rear entrance. When Papa and I got out of the cab, Friedlander Bey paid the fare and gave Bill a moderate tip.

Bill waved one sunburned arm. "It was nice meeting you," he said.

"Right, Bill," I said. "Who is Christy Mathewson?"

"One of the best players in the history of the game. 'The Big Six,' they called him. Maybe two hundred, two hundred fifty years ago."

"Two hundred fifty years!" I said, astonished.

"Yeah?" said Bill angrily. "What's it to ya?"

I shook my head. "You know where Friedlander Bey's house is?"

"Sure," said Bill. "What's the matter? You guys forget where you put it? It just didn't get up and *walk* away."

"Here's an extra ten kiam. Drive my young friend to Friedlander Bey's house, and make sure he gets there safely."

"Sure thing," said the cab driver.

I peered into the back seat, where bin Turki looked horrified that he'd have to ride with Bill, all alone and lost in the big city. "We'll see you in a day or two," I told him. "In the meantime, Youssef and Tariq will take care of you. Have a good time!"

Bin Turki just stared at me with wide eyes, gulping but not actually forming any coherent words. I turned on my heel and followed Papa to the unlocked door at the rear of the Blue Parrot. I was sure that Bill would forget the entire conversation soon after he delivered bin Turki to the mansion.

We went up a stairway made of fine polished hardwood. It twisted around in a complete circle, and we found ourselves on a landing, faced by two doors. The door to the left was locked, probably Ferrari's private apartment. The door to the right opened into a spacious parlor, decorated in a European style with lots of dark wood paneling and potted palms and a piano in one corner. The furniture was very tasteful and modern, however. Leading off from the parlor were a kitchen and two bedrooms, each with its own bathroom.

"I imagine we can be comfortable here," I said.

Papa grunted and headed for a bedroom. He was almost two hundred years old, and it had been a long and tiring day for him. He shut the bedroom door behind him, and I stayed in the parlor, softly knuckling bits of music at the piano.

In about ten or fifteen minutes, Signor Ferrari came upstairs. "I heard movement up here," he explained in an apologetic manner, "and I wanted to be sure it was you. Did Signor Bey find everything to his liking?"

"Yes, indeed, and we both want to thank you for your hospitality."

"It's nothing, nothing at all." Ferrari was a grossly fat man stuffed inside a plain white linen suit. He wore a red felt fez with a tassel on his head, and he rubbed his hands together anxiously, belying the suave, almost oily tone of his voice.

"Still," I said, "I'm sure Friedlander Bey will find some way to reward your kindness."

"If that is his wish," said Ferrari, his little pig eyes squinting at me, "then I would be honored to accept."

"I'm sure."

"Now, I must get back to my patrons. If there's anything you need, just pick up the phone and call 111. My staff has orders to bring you anything you desire."

"Excellent, Signor Ferrari. If you'll wait a moment, I'd like to write a note. Would one of your staff deliver it for me?"

"Well . . ."

"Just to Chiriga's, on the Street."

"Certainly," he said.

I wrote out a quick message to Chiri, telling her that I was, in fact, still alive, but that she had to keep the news secret until we cleared our names. I told her to call Ferrari's number and get extension 777 if she wanted to talk to me about anything, but she shouldn't use the phone in the club because it might be tapped. I folded the note and gave it to Ferrari, who promised that it would be delivered within fifteen minutes.

"Thank you for everything, signor," I said, yawning.

"I will leave you now," said Ferrari. "You no doubt need to rest."

I grunted and shut the door behind him. Then I went to the second guest room and stretched out on the bed. I expected the phone to ring soon.

It didn't take long. I answered the phone with a curt "Where y'at?"

It was Chiri, of course. For a few seconds, all I could hear was gibberish. Then I slowly began to separate words from the hysterical flow. "You're really alive? This isn't some kind of trick?"

I laughed. "Yeah, you right, Chiri, I set this all up before I died. You're talking to a recording. Hey, *of course* I'm alive! Did you really believe—"

"Hajjar brought me the news that you'd been picked up on a murder rap, both you and Papa, and that you'd been flown into exile from which you couldn't possibly return."

"Well, Chiri, here I am."

"Hell, we all went through a terrible time when we thought you were dead. The grieving was all for nothing, is that what you're telling me?"

"People grieved?" I have to admit the notion gave me a perverse sort of pleasure.

"Well, I sure as hell grieved, and a couple of the girls, and . . . and Indihar. She thought she'd been widowed a second time."

I chewed my lip for a few seconds. "Okay, you can tell Indihar, but no one else. Got that? Not Saied the Half-Hajj or any of my other friends. They're all still under suspicion. Where you calling from?"

"The pay phone in the back of Vast Foods." That was a lunch counter kind of place. The food wasn't really vast. That was a sign painter's error that they never bothered to correct.

"Fine, Chiri. Remember what I said."

"How 'bout if I give you a visit tomorrow?"

I thought that over, and finally I decided that there was little risk, and I really wanted to see Chiri's cannibal grin again. "All right. You know where we are?"

"Above the Blue Parrot?"

"Uh huh."

"This black girl happy-happy, see you tomorrow, Bwana."

"Yeah, you right," I said, and I hung up the phone.

My mind was crammed with thoughts and half-formed plans. I tried to go to sleep, but I just lay there for an hour or so. Finally, I heard Friedlander Bey stirring in the kitchen. I got up and joined him.

"Isn't there a teapot around here?" Papa grumbled.

I glanced at my watch. It was a quarter after two in the morning. "Why don't we go downstairs?" I said. "Ferrari will be closing up the place now."

He considered the idea. "I'd like that," he said. "I'd like to sit and relax with a glass or two of tea."

We went downstairs. I carefully checked to make sure all the patrons had left the Blue Parrot, and then Papa took a seat at one of the tables. One of Ferrari's flunkies brought him a pot of tea, and after the first glass, you'd never have known that Papa had just returned from a grim and dangerous exile. He closed his eyes and savored every drop of tea. "Civilized tea," he called it, longing for it every time he'd had to swallow the thin, alkaline tea of the Bani Salim.

I stayed by the door, watching the sidewalk outside. I flinched two or three times as police patrol cars rattled by on the stone-paved street.

Finally, the fatigue caught up with us, and we bid Signor Ferrari good night once more. Then we climbed the stairs to our hiding place. I was asleep within a few minutes of undressing and climbing into Ferrari's comfortable guest bed.

I slept about ten hours. It was the most refreshing, luxurious night's sleep I could remember. It had been a long while since I'd enjoyed clean sheets. Again, I was jolted awake by the phone. I picked up the extension beside my bed. "Yeah?" I said.

"Signor Audran," said Ferrari's voice, "there are two young women to see you. Shall I send them up?"

"Please," I said, running my hand sleepily through my rumpled hair. I hung up the phone and dressed hurriedly.

I could hear Chiri's voice calling from the stairwell, "Marîd? Which door? Where are you, Marîd?"

I hadn't had time to shower or shave, but I didn't care, and I didn't think Chiri would, either. I answered the door and was surprised to see Indihar, too. "Come on in," I said in a low voice. "We'll have to keep it down, because Papa's still asleep."

"All right," murmured Chiri, coming into the parlor. "Nice place Ferrari has up here."

"Oh, these are just his guest rooms. I can only imagine what his own suite is like."

Indihar was wearing widow's black. She came up to me and touched my face. "I am glad to see that you're well, husband," she said, and then she turned away, weeping.

"One thing I gotta know," said Chiri, dropping heavily into an antique wing chair. "Did you or did you not kill that policeman?"

"I did not kill a cop," I said fiercely. "Papa and I were framed for that, and we were tried *in absentia*, and cast out into the Empty Quarter. Now that we're back—and you can be damn sure that somebody never expected us to get back—we have to solve that crime to clear our names. When we do, heads will roll. Quite literally."

"I believe you, husband," said Indihar, who sat beside me on an expensive couch that matched Chiri's wing chair. "My . . . my late husband and I were good friends with the murdered patrolman. His name was Khalid Maxwell, and he was a kind, generous man. I don't want his killer to get away unpunished."

"I promise you, my wife, that won't happen. He'll pay dearly."

There was an awkward silence for a moment. I looked uncomfortably at Indihar and she stared down at her hands, folded in her lap. Chiri came to our rescue. She coughed politely and said, "Brought something for you, Mr. Boss." I looked toward her; she was grinning, her tattooed face wrinkled up in delight. She held out a plastic moddy rack.

"My moddies!" I said happily. "It looks like all of them."

"You've got enough weirdo stuff there to keep you occupied while you're laying low," said Chiri.

"And here is something else, husband." Indihar was offering me a tan plastic item on the palm of her hand.

"My pillcase!" I was more happy to see it than the moddy rack. I took it and opened it, and saw that it was crammed full of beauties, sunnies, Paxium, everything a working fugitive needed to keep sane in a hostile world. "Although," I said, clearing my throat self-consciously, "I am trying to cut down."

"That's good, husband," said Indihar. The unspoken text was that she still blamed me and my substance abuse for the death of her first husband. She was making a large gesture by giving me the pillcase.

"Where did you get these things?" I asked.

"From Kmuzu," said Chiri. "I just sweet-talked that pretty boy until he didn't know which direction was up."

"I'll bet," I said. "So now Kmuzu knows I'm back, too."

"Hey, it's just Kmuzu," said Chiri. "You can trust him."

Yes, I did trust Kmuzu. More than just about anyone else. I changed the subject. "Wife, how are my step-children?"

"They're all fine," she said, smiling for the first time. "They all want to know where you've gone. I think little Zahra has a crush on you."

I laughed, although I was a little uneasy about that bit of news.

"Well," said Chiri, "we should be going. The Maghrebi here has to get to work on his plans of vengeance. Right, Marîd?"

"Well, sort of. Thanks so much for coming by. And thanks for bringing the moddies and the pillcase. That was very thoughtful."

"Not at all, husband," said Indihar. "I will pray to Allah, thanking Him for returning you." She came to me and gave me a chaste kiss on the cheek.

I walked them to the door. "And the club?" I asked.

Chiri shrugged. "Same old story. Business is dead, the girls are still trying to rob us blind, you know the rest."

Indihar laughed. "The rest is that the club's probably making money like crazy, and your share will need a tractor-trailer to haul it to the bank."

In other words, all was right with the world. Except in the area of personal freedom for myself and Friedlander Bey. I had some ideas on how to improve things along those lines, however. I just needed to make a few important phone calls.

"*Salaamtak,*" said Indihar, bowing before me.

"*Allah yisallimak,*" I replied. Then the two women left, and I closed the door.

Almost immediately, I went to the kitchen and swallowed a few sunnies with a glass of water. I promised myself that I wouldn't get back into my old habits, but that I could afford to reward my recent heroic behavior. Then I'd put the pillcase away and save it for emergencies.

Out of curiosity, I browsed through my rack of moddies and dad-dies, and discovered that Chiriga had left me a little gift—a new sex-moddy. I examined it. The label said it was *Inferno in the Night*, one of Honey Pílar's early moddies, but it was recorded from her partner's point of view.

I went into the bedroom, undressed, and lay down on the bed. Then I reached up, murmured *"Bismillah,"* and chipped the moddy in.

The first *thing Audran noticed was that he was much younger, much stronger, and filled with an anticipation that bordered on desper-ation. He felt wonderful, and he laughed as he took off his clothes.*

The woman in the bedroom with him was Honey Pílar. Audran had loved her with a consuming passion ever since he met her, two hours ago. He thought it was a great privilege to be allowed to gaze at her and compose clumsy poems in her honor. That he and she might jam was more than he could've hoped for.

She stripped slowly and enticingly, then joined Audran on the bed. Her hair was pale blond, her eyes a remarkable green like clean, cool waves in the ocean. "Yes?" she said. "You are much hurt?" Her voice was languid and musical.

Inferno in the Night was one of Honey's earliest sex-moddies, and it had a vestigial story line. Audran realized that he was a wounded hero of the Catalonian struggle for independence, and Honey was playing the courageous daughter of the evil Valencian duke.

"I'm fine," said Audran.

"You need bad massage," she murmured, moving her fingertips gently across his chest and stopping just at the top of his pubic hair. She waited, looking at him for permission.

"Oh, please go ahead," Audran said.

"For the revolution," she said.

"Sure."

And then she caressed his prick until he could stand it no more. He ran his fingers through her fragrant hair, then grabbed her and turned her on her back.

"Your wounds!" she cried.

"You've miraculously healed me."

"Oh good!" she said, sighing as Audran entered her. They jammed slowly at first, then faster and faster until Audran burst with exquisite pleasure.

After a while, Honey Pílar sat up. "I must go," she said sadly. "There are others wounded."

"I understand," Audran said. He reached up and popped the moddy out.

"JEEZ," I muttered. It had been a long time since I'd last spent any time with Honey Pílar. I was beginning to think I was getting too old for this stuff. I mean, I wasn't a kid anymore. As I lay panting on the bed, I realized I'd come dangerously close to pulling a hamstring. Maybe they had sex-moddies recorded by couples who'd been married twenty years. That was more my speed.

There was a knock on my room's door. "My nephew," called Friedlander Bey, "are you all right?"

"Yes, O Shaykh," I answered.

"I ask only because I heard you exclaim."

Yipe. "A nightmare, that's all. Let me take a quick shower, and then I'll join you."

"Very good, O Excellent One."

I got off the bed, ran a quick shower, dressed, and went out into the parlor. "I'd like to get some clean clothes," I said. "I've been wearing this same outfit since we were kidnapped, and I think it's finally dead."

Papa nodded. "I've taken care of that already. I've sent a message to Tariq and Youssef, and they will be here momentarily with fresh clothing and a supply of money."

I sat in the wing chair, and Papa sat on the couch. "I suppose your businesses have been purring along just fine with them at the wheel."

"I trust Tariq and Youssef with my life and more: I trust them with my holdings."

"It will be good to see them again."

"You had visitors earlier. Who were they?"

I gulped. I suddenly realized that he might interpret the visit from Indihar and Chiri as a serious breach in security. Worse than that, he might see it as a punishable stupidity. "My wife and my partner, Chiriga," I said. My mouth went suddenly dry.

But Papa only nodded. "They are both well, I pray?" he said.

"Yes, praise Allah, they are."

"I am glad to hear it. Now—" He was interrupted by a knock on the front door of the apartment. "My nephew," he said quietly, "see who's there. If it's not Tariq and Youssef, do not let them in, even if it's one of your friends."

"I understand, O Shaykh." I went to the door and peered through the small peephole. It was indeed Tariq and Youssef, Papa's valet and butler, and the managers of his estate.

I opened the door and they were enthusiastic in their greetings. "Welcome home!" cried Youssef. "Allah be thanked for your safe return! Not that we believed for an instant that story that you both had died in some distant desert."

Tariq carried a couple of hard-sided suitcases into the parlor and set them down. *"As-salaam alaykum, yaa Shaykh,"* he said to me. He turned to Papa and said the same.

"Alaykum as-salaam," said Friedlander Bey. "Tell me what I must know."

They had indeed been keeping business matters up to date. Most of what they discussed with Papa I knew nothing about, but there were two situations in which I'd become involved. The first was the Cappadocian attempt to win independence from Anatolia. I'd met with the Cappadocian representatives—how long ago? It seemed like many months, but it couldn't have been more than a few weeks.

Youssef spoke up. "We've decided that the Cappadocians have a good chance of overthrowing the Anatolian government in their province. With our aid, it would be a certainty. And it would not cost us very much, relatively speaking, to keep them in power long enough."

Long enough? Long enough for what? I wondered. There was still so much I had to learn.

When all the geopolitical issues had been discussed and commented on, I asked, "What about the datalink project?"

"That seems to be stalled, Shaykh Marîd," said Tariq.

"Unstall it," said Papa.

"We need someone who is not in our household to accept an executive position," said Tariq. "Of course, the executive position will have no real power or influence—that will remain in the household—but we need a, uh, a—"

"Fall guy," I said.

Tariq just blinked. "Yes," he said, "precisely."

"You're working on that, aren't you, my nephew?" asked Papa.

I nodded. "I'm developing someone for that position, yes."

"Very well," said Friedlander Bey, standing. "Everything seems to be in order. I expected no less. Still, you will be rewarded."

Youssef and Tariq bowed and murmured their thanks. Papa placed his left hand on Tariq's head, and his right on Youssef's. He looked like a saint blessing his followers.

"O Shaykh," I said, "isn't there one more thing?"

"Hmm?" he said, glancing at me.

"Concerning Shaykh Mahali," I said.

"Ah yes, O Excellent One. Thank you for reminding me. Youssef, I

want you to make an appointment for my grandson and me to meet
with the amir. Tell him that we realize that we're fugitives, but also
remind him that we were denied our lawful chance to appeal the verdict of our contrived trials. We think we can persuade him that we're
innocent, and beg only for an opportunity to plead our case."

"Yes," said Youssef, "I understand. It will be done as you wish."

"As Allah wishes, rather," said Papa.

"As Allah wishes," Youssef murmured.

"Did the boy arrive safely?" I asked.

"Bin Turki?" said Tariq. "Yes, we've installed him in an empty
suite of rooms, and he's rather overawed by everything he's seen. He
has struck up a friendship with Umm Jirji, your wife."

My mouth twisted. "Wonderful," I said.

"One more thing," said Friedlander Bey, the ruler of half the city.
"I want one round-trip suborbital ticket to the town of Najran, in the
kingdom of Asir."

That made my blood run cold, let me tell you.

ten

It seemed as if a year had passed since the first time I visited the prince's palace. In fact, it couldn't have been more than a few weeks. I, however, had changed somewhat in that time. I felt that my vision was clearer and that I'd been stripped of my intellectual objections to direct action. Whether that would be a help or a hindrance in my future in the city was yet to be seen.

The amir's estate was even more beautiful in the daylight than it had been on the evening of my wedding reception. The air was clean and the breeze was cool and refreshing. The liquid gurgling of the fountains relaxed me as I walked through Shaykh Mahali's gardens. When we got to the house, a servant opened the door.

"We have an appointment with the amir," said Friedlander Bey.

The servant looked at us carefully, decided we weren't madmen or assassins, and nodded. We followed him down a long gallery that bordered an inner courtyard. He opened the door to a small audience chamber, and we entered and took seats and waited for the shaykh to arrive. I felt very uncomfortable, as if I'd been caught cheating on a test and was now waiting for the principal to come in and punish me. The difference was that I hadn't been caught cheating; the charge was murder of a police officer. And the penalty wouldn't be just ten swats, it would be death.

I decided to let Papa handle the defense. He'd had a century and a half more practice at verbal tap dancing than I had.

We sat there in anxious silence for about a quarter hour. Then, with more bustle than ceremony, Shaykh Mahali and three other men entered. The shaykh was handsome in white *gallebeya* and *keffiya*, and two of his attendants wore European-style dark gray business suits.

The third man wore the robes and dark turban of a scholar of the noble Qur'ân; he was evidently Shaykh Mahali's vizier.

The prince took his seat on a handsomely carved chair, and turned toward us. "What is this matter?" he asked quietly.

"O Prince," said Friedlander Bey, stepping forward, "we were wrongfully accused of the death of a police officer, Khalid Maxwell. Then, without benefit of public trial, or even an opportunity to confront our accusers and present a de-fense, we were kidnapped—right from Your Highness's own grounds, after the wedding reception you gave for my great-grandson. We were forced aboard a suborbital ship, and presented with the news that we'd already been tried. When we landed in Najran, we were taken aboard a helicopter, and then pushed out into the Arabian Desert, in the southern, most dreadful portion known as the Rub al-Khali. We were most fortunate to survive, and it took great courage and sacrifice on the part of my beloved great-grandson to keep us alive until we were rescued by a nomadic tribe of Bedu, may the blessings of Allah be on them. It is only now that we've been able to make our way back to the city. We beg your attention on this matter, because we believe we have the right to ask for an appeal, and a chance to clear our names."

The amir consulted quietly with his adviser. Then he turned back to us. "I knew nothing of this," he said simply.

"Nor I," said the vizier, "and your file should have crossed my desk before your trial. In any case, such a verdict and sentence cannot be legal without the concurrence of Shyakh Mahali."

Friedlander Bey stepped forward and gave the vizier the copy of the charges and verdict that he'd gotten from the qadi. "This was all we were allowed to see. It bears the signatures of the qadi and Dr. Sadiq Abd ar-Razzaq."

The vizier studied the paper for a few moments, then passed it on to the prince. The prince glanced at it and said, "There is neither my signature upon this warrant, nor that of my vizier. It is not a valid order. You will have your appeal, one month from today. At that time, I will assemble Lieutenant Hajjar, Dr. Abd ar-Razzaq, and this qadi, who is unknown to me. In the meantime, I will investigate why this matter was passed along without our knowledge."

"We thank you for your generosity, O Prince," said Friedlander Bey humbly.

The amir waved a hand. "No thanks are necessary, my friend. I am only performing my duty. Now, tell me: did either or both of you have anything to do with the death of this police officer?"

Friedlander Bey took a step nearer and looked the prince in the eye. "I swear upon my head, upon the life of the Prophet—may the blessings of Allah be on him and peace—that we had nothing to do with Officer Maxwell's death. Neither of us even knew the man."

Shaykh Mahali rubbed his carefully trimmed beard thoughtfully. "We shall see. Now return to your home, because your month's grace is already beginning to slip away."

We bowed low and backed out of the audience chamber. Outside, I released the deep breath I'd been holding. "We can go home now!" I said.

Papa looked very happy. "Yes, my nephew," he said. "And against our resources, and a month's time to prepare, Hajjar and the imam cannot hope to prevail."

I didn't know exactly what he had in mind, but I intended to dive back into my normal existence as soon as possible. I was hungry for a quiet life, familiar little problems, and no threats greater than a mouse in the ladies' room of my nightclub. However, as a great Franji poet of the dim, dark past once wrote, "The best-laid plans of mice and men often get jammed all to hell."

It would happen in its own time, I knew it instinctively. It always did. That's why I avoided making plans of any kind now. I could wait for Allah in His infinite benevolence to waft His intentions my way.

Sometimes, though, it takes a few days for the Lord of the Worlds to get around to you. In the meantime I just relaxed in Chiri's, comfortable in my usual seat at the curve of the bar. About four or five nights later, long after midnight, I watched Chiriga, my partner and night barmaid, scoop a meager tip from a customer. She gave him a dismaying look at her filed teeth and drifted down to my end of the bar. "Cheap bastard," she said, stuffing the money into a pocket of her tight jeans.

I didn't say anything for a while. I was in a melancholy mood. Three o'clock in the morning and many drinks always do that to me. "You know," I said at last, staring up at Yasmin on stage, "when I was a kid, and I imagined what it would be like to be grown up, this wasn't it. This wasn't it at all."

Chiri's beautiful black face relaxed in one of her rare smiles. "Me, too. I never thought I'd end up in this city. And when I did, I didn't plan to get stuck in the Budayeen. I was aiming at a higher-class neighborhood."

"Yet here we are."

Chiriga's smile faded. "Here *I* am, Marîd, probably forever. You got great expectations." She took my empty glass, threw a few fresh ice cubes into it, and mixed me another White Death. That's what Chiri had named my favorite drink, gin and bingara with a slug of Rose's lime juice. I didn't need another drink, but I wanted one.

She set it in front of me on an old, ragged cork coaster, then headed back up the bar toward the front of the club. A customer had come in and sat down near the door. Chiri shrugged at him and pointed toward me. The customer got up and moved slowly down the narrow aisle between the bar and the booths. When he got a little closer, I saw it was Jacques.

Jacques is very proud of being a Christian in a Muslim city, and conceited about being three-quarters European where most people are Arab. That makes Jacques dumb, and it also makes him a target. He's one of my three old buddies: Saied the Half-Hajj is my friend; I can't stand Mahmoud; and Jacques is in the middle. I don't give a phony fîq about what he does or says, and neither does anyone else I know.

"Where you at, Marîd?" he said, sitting beside me. "You had us all worried for a few weeks."

"All right, Jacques," I said. "Want something to drink?" Yasmin had danced her third song, and was grabbing up her clothes and hurrying off the stage, to wring tips from the few morose customers we still had.

Jacques frowned. "I don't have much money with me tonight. That's what I want to talk to you about."

"Uh huh," I said. In the months that I'd owned the club, I'd heard it all. I signaled to Chiri to draw a beer for my old pal, Jacques.

We watched her fill a tall glass and bring it down the bar. She put it in front of Jacques but said nothing to him. Chiri can't stand him. Jacques is the kind of guy, if his house was burning in the night, most people in the Budayeen would write him a postcard and drop it in the mail to warn him.

Yasmin came up to us, dressed now in a short leather skirt and a black, lacy brassiere. "Tip me for my dancing, Jacques?" she said with a sweet smile. I think she's the sexiest dancer on the Street, but because Jacques is strictly heterosexual and Yasmin wasn't quite born a girl, I didn't think she'd have any luck with him.

"I don't have much money—" he began.

"Tip her," I said in a cold voice.

Jacques gave me a quick glance, but dug in his pocket and pulled out a one-kiam bill.

"Thanks," said Yasmin. She moved on to the next lonely customer.

"You gonna keep ignoring me, Yasmin?" I said.

"How's your *wife*, Marîd?" she called, without turning around.

"Yeah," said Jacques, smirking, "honeymoon over already? You hanging out here all night?"

"I own this place, you know."

Jacques shrugged. "Yeah, but Chiri could run it just fine without you. She used to, if I remember right."

I squeezed the little wedge of lime into my drink and gulped it down. "So you just felt like dropping in this late for a free beer, or what?"

Jacques gave me a weak grin. "I do have something I want to ask you," he said.

"I figured." I waved my empty glass back and forth at Chiri. She just raised her eyebrows; she thought I'd been drinking too much lately, and that was her way of letting me know.

I wasn't in the mood for her disapproval. Chiri was usually a non-interventionist, meaning that she believed every person was entitled to his own flaming stupidity. I signaled again, more sharply this time, and she finally nodded and put together another White Death in a fresh glass. She marched down to my end of the bar, dropped it heavily in front of me, and marched away again without saying a word. I couldn't see what she was so upset about.

Jacques sipped slowly at his beer, then put his glass down in the very center of the coaster. "Marîd," he said, his eyes on a pretty sex-change named Lily who was tiredly doing her bit on stage, "would you go out of your way to help Fuad?"

What can I say about Fuad? His nickname on the Street was il-Manhous, which means "The Permanently Fucked," or words to that effect. Fuad was a tall, skinny guy with a big mop of hair that he wore in a greasy pompadour. He'd suffered some kind of degenerative disease as a kid, because his arms were as thin and frail-looking as dry sticks, with huge, swollen joints. He meant well, I suppose, but he had this pitiful puppy-dog quality. He was so desperate to be liked and so anxious to please that he sometimes got obnoxious about it. Some of the dancers in the clubs exploited him, sending him off to fetch food and run other errands, for which they neither paid nor thanked him. If I thought about him at all—which I didn't do very often—I tended to feel a little sorry for the guy.

"Fuad's not very bright," I said. "He still hasn't learned that those hookers he falls in love with always rob him blind at the first opportunity."

Jacques nodded. "I'm not talking about his intelligence, though. I mean, would you help him out if money was involved?"

"Well, I think he's kind of a sad person, but I can't remember him ever doing anything to hurt someone else. I don't think he's smart enough. Yeah, I guess I'd help him. It depends."

Jacques took a deep breath and let it out slowly. "Well, listen," he said, "he wants me to do him a big favor. Tell me what you think."

"It's about that time, Marîd," called Chiri from the other end of the bar.

I glanced at my watch and saw that it was almost half past three. There were only two other customers in the club now, and they'd been sitting there for almost an hour. No one but Jacques had come in during that time. We weren't going to do any more business tonight. "Okay," I announced to the dancers, "you ladies can get dressed now."

"Yay!" shouted Pualani. She and the four others hurried to the dressing room to put on their street clothes. Chiri began counting out the register. The two customers, who had been having deep, meaningful conversations with Kandy and Windy just a moment before, stared at each other in bewilderment.

I got up and tapped on the overhead lights, then sat down again beside Jacques. I've always thought that there is no lonelier place in the city than a bar in the Budayeen at closing time. "What's this that Fuad wants you to do?" I said wearily.

"It's a long story," said Jacques.

"Terrific. Why didn't you come in eight hours ago, when I felt more like hearing long stories?"

"Just listen. Fuad comes up to me this afternoon with this long, mournful look on his face. You know the look I mean. You'd think the world was coming to an end and he'd just found out he hadn't been invited. Anyway, I was having a little lunch at the Solace with Mahmoud and the Half-Hajj. Fuad comes up and drags a chair over and sits down. Starts eating off my plate, too."

"Yeah, sounds like our boy, all right," I said. I prayed to Allah that Jacques would get to the point in less time than it had taken Fuad.

"I slapped his hand and told him to go away, because we were having an important discussion. We weren't, really, but I wasn't in the mood to put up with him. So he says he needed somebody to help him get his money back. Saied says, 'Fuad, you let another one of those working girls steal your money again?' And Fuad says no, it wasn't anything like that.

"Then he takes out this official-looking paper and hands it to Saied, who glanced at it and handed it to me, and I looked at it and passed it on to Mahmoud. 'What's this?' Mahmoud says.

" 'It's a cashier's check for twenty-four hundred kiam,' says Fuad.

" 'How'd you get it?' I ask.

" 'It's a long story,' he says."

I closed my eyes and held the ice-cold glass against my throbbing forehead. I could've chipped in my pain-blocking daddy, but it was sitting in a rack in my briefcase on my desk in my suite in Friedlander Bey's mansion.

"Jacques," I said in a low, dangerous voice, "you said this is a long story, and now *Fuad's* said this is a long story, and I don't want to listen to a long story. Okay? Can you just kind of go over the high points from here on?"

"Sure, Marîd, take it easy. What he said was that he'd been saving up his money for months, that he wanted to buy a used electric van from some guy in Rasmiyya. He said he could live in the van cheaper than renting an apartment, and he also planned to go on a trip to visit his folks in Tripoli."

"That where Faud's from? I didn't know that."

Jacques shrugged. "Anyway, he said the guy in Rasmiyya quoted him a price of twenty-four hundred kiam for this van. Fuad swears it was in great shape and only needed a little work here and there, and he'd gotten all of his money together and had a bank check drawn up in the other guy's name. That afternoon, he walked all the way from the Budayeen to Rasmiyya, and the guy had sold the van to somebody else, after promising he'd hold it for Fuad."

I shook my head. "Fuad, all right. What a hopeless son of a bitch."

"So Fuad trudges all the way back through the eastern gate, and finds us at the Café Solace and tells us his tale of woe. Mahmoud just laughed in his face, and Saied was wearing Rex, his ass-kicker moddy, so Fuad was totally beneath his notice. I kind of felt sorry for him, though."

"Uh huh," I said. I had trouble believing that Jacques felt sorry for Fuad. If that were true, the heavens would have split open or something, and I didn't think they had. "What did Fuad want you to do?"

Jacques squirmed uneasily on his bar stool. "Well, apparently Fuad has never had his own bank account. He keeps his money in cash in an old cigar box or something. That's why he had to have a bank check drawn up. So here he was, stuck with a cashier's check made out to somebody else, and no way to get his twenty-four hundred kiam back."

"Ah," I said. I began to see the predicament.

"He wants me to cash it for him," said Jacques.

"So do it."

"I don't know," said Jacques. "It's a lot of money."

"So *don't* do it."

"Yeah, but—"

I looked at him in exasperation. "Well, Jacques, what the hell do you want *me* to do?"

He stared down into his empty beer glass for a few seconds. He was more uncomfortable than I'd ever seen him. Over the years, he's derived a lot of fierce glee by reminding me that I was half-French and half-Berber, while he was superior to the tune of one whole European grandparent. It must have cost him a lot of self-esteem to come to me for advice.

"Maghrebi," he said, "you're getting quite a reputation lately as someone who can fix things. You know, solve problems and stuff."

Sure, I was. Since I became Friedlander Bey's reluctant avenger, I've had to deal directly and violently with some vicious bad-guy types. Now many of my friends looked at me differently. I imagined they were whispering to one another, "Be careful of Marîd—these days, he can arrange to have your legs broken."

I was becoming a force to be reckoned with in the Budayeen—and beyond it as well, in the rest of the city. Occasionally I had misgivings about that. As interested as I was in the tasks Papa gave me, despite the glamorous power I could now wield, there were still many days when all I really wanted was to run my little club in peace.

"What do you want me to do, Jacques? Strong-arm the guy who screwed Fuad? Grab him by the throat and shake him until he sells the van to him?"

"Well, no, Marîd, that's silly. The guy doesn't even have the van anymore."

I'd come to the end of my patience. "Then *what*, goddamn it?"

Jacques looked at me and then immediately looked away. "I took the cashier's check from Fuad and I don't know what to do with it. Just tell me what you'd do."

"Jeez, Jacques, I'd deposit it. I'd put it in my account and wait for it to clear. When the twenty-four hundred kiam showed up on my balance, I'd withdraw it and give it to Fuad. But not before. Wait for the check to clear first."

Jacques's face widened in a shaky smile. "Thanks, Marîd. You know they call you Al-Amîn on the Street now? 'The Trustworthy.' You're a big man in the Budayeen these days."

Some of my poorer neighbors had begun referring to me as Shaykh Marîd the Trustworthy, just because I'd loaned them a little money and opened a few soup kitchens. No big deal. After all, the holy Qur'ân requires us to look after the welfare of others.

"Yeah," I said sourly, "Shaykh Marîd. That's me, all right."

Jacques chewed his lip and then came to a decision. "Then why don't you do it?" he said. He pulled the pale green check from his shirt pocket and put it down in front of me. "Why don't you go ahead and deposit it for Fuad? I really don't have the time."

I laughed. "You don't have the *time*?"

"I got some other things to worry about. Besides, there are reasons why I don't want the twenty-four hundred kiam showing up on my bank balance."

I stared at him for a moment. This was just so typical. "Your problem, Jacques, is that tonight you came *real close* to doing someone a good deed, but you're catching yourself in the nick of time. No, I don't see any reason why I should."

"I'm asking you as a friend, Marîd."

"I'll do this much," I said. "I'll stand up for Fuad. If you're so afraid of being stiffed, I'll guarantee the check. Got something to write with?" Jacques handed me a pen and I turned the check over and endorsed it, first with the name of the guy who'd broken Fuad's heart, then with my own signature. Then I pushed the check back toward him with my fingertips.

"I appreciate it, Marîd," he said.

"You know, Jacques, you should've paid more attention to fairy stories when you were young. You're acting like one of the bad princes who pass by the old woman in distress on the road. Bad princes always end up getting eaten by a *djinn*, you know. Or are you mostly European types immune to folk wisdom?"

"I don't need the moral lecture," said Jacques with a scowl.

"Listen, I expect something from you in return."

He gave me a weak smile. "Sure, Marîd. Business is business."

"And action is action. That's how things work around here. I want you to take a little job for me, *mon ami*. For the last few months now, Friedlander Bey has been talking about getting involved with the datalink industry. He told me to watch out for a bright-eyed, hardworking person to represent his new enterprise. How would you like to get in on the ground floor?"

Jacques's good humor disappeared. "I don't know if I have the time," he said. His voice was very worried.

"You'll love it. You'll be making so much money, *inshallah*, you'll forget all about your other activities." This was one of those cases when the will of God was synonymous with Friedlander Bey.

His eyes shifted back and forth like a small animal in a trap. "I really don't want—"

"I think you *do* want to, Jacques. But don't worry about it for now.

We'll discuss it over lunch in a day or two. Now I'm glad you came to me with your problem. I think this will work out very nicely for both of us."

"Got to deposit this in the bank machine," he said. He got up from his stool, muttered something under his breath, and went back out into the night. I was willing to bet that he deeply regretted passing by Chiri's tonight. I almost laughed at the look on his face when he left.

Not much later, a tall, strong black man with a shaven head and a grim expression came into the club. It was my slave, Kmuzu. He stood just inside the door, waiting for me to pay Chiri and the dancers and lock up the bar. Kmuzu was there to drive me home. He was also there to spy on me for Friedlander Bey.

Chiri was always glad to see him. "Kmuzu, honey, sit down and have a drink!" she said. It was the first time she'd sounded cheerful in at least six hours. She wouldn't have much luck with him, though. Chiri was seriously hungry for Kmuzu's body, but he didn't seem to return her interest. I think Chiri'd begun to regret the ritual scars and tattoos on her face, because they seemed to disturb him. Still, every night she offered him a drink, and he replied that he was a devout Christian and didn't consume alcohol; he let her pour him a glass of orange juice instead. And he told her that he wouldn't consider a normal relationship with a woman until he'd won his freedom.

He understands that I *intend* to free him, but not just yet. For one thing, Papa—Friedlander Bey—had given Kmuzu to me, and he wouldn't permit me to announce any free-lance emancipations. For another, well, as much as I hate to admit it, I liked having Kmuzu around in that capacity.

"Here you go, Mr. Boss," said Chiri. She'd taken the day's receipts, pocketed half off the top according to our agreement, and now slapped a still-healthy stack of kiam on the bar in front of me. It had taken me quite a while to overcome my guilt at banking so much money every day without actually working, but in the end I'd succeeded. I was no longer bothered by it, because of the good works I sponsored, which cost me about 5 percent of my weekly income.

"Come get your money," I called. I wouldn't have to call twice. The assortment of real girls, sexchanges, and pre-operation debs who worked on Chiri's nightshift lined up to get their wages and the commissions on the drinks they'd hustled. Windy, Kandy, and Pualani took their money and hurried out into the night without a word. Lily, who'd harbored a crush on me for months, kissed me on the cheek and whispered an invitation to go out drinking with her. I just patted her cute little ass and turned to Yasmin.

She flipped her beautiful black hair over her shoulder. "Does Indihar wait up for you?" she said. "Or do you still go to bed alone?" She grabbed the cash from my hand and followed Lily out of the club. She'd never forgiven me for getting married.

"Want me to straighten her out, Marîd?" asked Chiri.

"No, but thanks anyway." I was grateful for her concern. Except for a few brief periods of unfortunate misunderstanding, Chiri had long been my best friend in the city.

"Everything okay with Indihar?" she asked.

"Everything's just fine. I hardly ever see her. She has an apartment for herself and the kids in the other wing of Papa's mansion. Yasmin was right about me going to bed alone."

"Uh huh," said Chiri. "That won't last long. I saw the way you used to stare at Indihar."

"It's just a marriage of convenience."

"Uh huh. Well, I got my money, so I'm going home. Though I don't know why I bother, there's nobody waiting there for me, either. I got every sex-moddy Honey Pílar ever made, but nobody to jam with. Guess I'll just pull my old shawl around my shoulders and sit in my rocking chair with my memories, and rock and rock until I fall asleep. Such a waste of my sexual prime, though." She kept looking at Kmuzu with her eyes all big and round, and trying real hard to stifle her grin but not having much success. Finally, she just scooped up her zipper bag, downed a shot of *tende* from her private stock, and left Kmuzu and me alone in the club.

"You're not really needed here every night, *yaa Sidi*," said Kmuzu. "The woman, Chiriga, is fully able to keep order. It would be better for you to remain at home and tend to your more pressing concerns."

"Which concerns are those, Kmuzu?" I asked, tapping off all the lights and following him out onto the sidewalk. I locked up the club and began walking down the Street toward the great eastern gate, beyond which lay the Boulevard il-Jameel and my car.

"You have important work to do for the master of the house."

He meant Papa. "Papa can get along without me for a little longer," I said. "I'm still recuperating from my ordeal."

I did not in any way want to be a heavy hitter. I did not want to be Shaykh Marîd Audran al-Amîn. I desperately wanted to go back to scrabbling for a living, maybe missing a meal now and then but having the satisfaction of being my own man, and not being marked for doom by all the other heavy hitters in the game.

You just couldn't explain that kind of thing to Friedlander Bey. He had an answer for everything; sometimes the answer was bribes and rewards, and sometimes it was physical torture. It was like complaining to God about sand fleas. He has more important things on His mind.

A warm breeze offered conflicting fragrances: roasting meat from the cookshops, spilled beer, the scent of gardenias, the stink of vomit. Down the block, a starved-looking man in a long white shirt and white cotton trousers was using a green plastic hose to wash the night's trash from the sidewalk into the gutter. He grinned toothlessly at us as we approached, turning the stream of water to the side as we passed. "Shaykh Marîd," he said in a hoarse voice. I nodded to him, sure that I'd never seen him before.

Even with Kmuzu beside me, I felt terribly forlorn. The Budayeen did that to me sometimes, very late at night. Even the Street, which was never completely quiet, was mostly deserted, and our footsteps echoed on the bricks and flat paving stones. Music came from another club a block away, the raucous noise worn to a mournful smoothness by the distance. I carried the dregs of my last White Death in a plastic go-cup, and I swallowed it, tasting only ice water and lime and a hint of gin. I wasn't ready for the night to be ending.

As we walked nearer to the arched gate at the eastern end of the walled quarter, I felt a great, expectant hush settle over me. I shuddered. I wasn't sure if what I felt was some mysterious signal from my unconscious mind, or merely the result of too many drinks and too much tiredness.

I stopped in my tracks on the sidewalk at the corner of Third Street. Kmuzu stopped, too, and gave me a questioning look. Bright blood red neon zigzags framed a holo display for one of the inexpensive Kafiristani bodmod clinics on the Street. I glanced at the holo for a moment, watching a plump, slack-featured boy metamorphose into a slender, voluptuous girl. Hurray for the miracles of time-lapse holography and elective surgery.

I turned my face up to the sky. I suddenly understood that my few days of respite were coming to an end, that I'd have to move along to the next stage of my development. Of course, I've had this sensation before. Many times, as a matter of fact, but this was different. Tonight I had no illicit drugs in my system at all.

"Jeez," I muttered, feeling a chill in that desert summer night, and leaning against the clinic's plate-glass front.

"What is it, *yaa Sidi*?" asked Kmuzu.

I looked at him for a moment, grateful for his presence. I told him what had just passed through my dazzled mind.

"That was no message from the stars, *yaa Sidi*. That was what the master of the house told you this morning. You'd taken an unfortunate number of Sonneine tablets, so perhaps you don't remember. The master of the house said he had decided what the next step of his vengeance should be."

"That's what I was afraid of, Kmuzu. Any idea what he means?" I liked it better when I thought the crazy notion had come from outer space.

"He does not share all his thoughts with me, *yaa Sidi*."

I heard a low rustling sound and I turned, suddenly afraid. It was only the wind. As we walked the rest of the way down the Street, the wind grew stronger and louder, until it was whipping scraps of paper and fallen leaves in fierce whirling gusts. The wind began to drag sullen clouds across the night sky, covering the stars, hiding the fat yellow moon.

And then the wind died, just as we emerged from the Budayeen onto the boulevard beyond the wall. Suddenly everything was quiet and calm again. The sky was still overcast, and the moon was a pale glow behind a silver cloud.

I turned to look back at the eastern gate. I don't believe in prescience or premonitions, but I do recall the disquiet I felt as Kmuzu and I headed toward my cream-colored Westphalian sedan parked nearby. Whatever it was, I said nothing of it to Kmuzu. He is in every situation almost repellently rational.

"I want to get home quickly, Kmuzu," I said, waiting for him to unlock the passenger door.

"Yes, *yaa Sidi*." I got into the car and waited for him to walk around and get behind the wheel. He tapped in the ignition code and steered the electric car north on the broad, divided street.

"I'm feeling pretty strange tonight," I complained, leaning my head back against the seat and closing my eyes.

"You say that almost every night."

"I mean it this time. I'm starting to feel very uncomfortable. Everything seems different to me now. I look at these tenements and I see they're like human ant farms. I hear a scrap of music, and suddenly I'm listening to somebody's cry of anguish lost in the void. I'm not in the mood for mystical revelations, Kmuzu. How do I make them stop?"

He uttered a low-pitched laugh. "You could sober up, *yaa Sidi*."

"I told you, it's not that. I am sober."

"Yes, of course, *yaa Sidi*."

I watched the city slide by beyond my window. I wasn't up to arguing with him any further. I did feel sober and wide-awake. I felt filled with energy, which at four o'clock in the morning is something I hate a lot. It's the wrong time of day for enthusiasm. The solution to that was simple, of course: a largish dose of butaqualide HCL when I got home. The beauties would give me a few minutes of delicious confusion, and then I'd fall out for a good night's sleep. In the morning, I wouldn't even remember this unpleasant interlude of clarity.

We rode in silence for a while, and gradually the weird mood left me. Kmuzu wheeled the car toward Friedlander Bey's palace, which lay just beyond the city's Christian quarter. It would be good to get home, stand under a hot shower for a few minutes, and then read a little before going to sleep. One of the reasons I'd been staying in Chiri's until closing time every night was that I wanted to avoid running into anyone at the house. At four o'clock, they'd all be sound asleep. I wouldn't have to face them until morning.

"Yaa Sidi," said Kmuzu, "there was an important call for you this evening."

"I'll listen to my messages before breakfast."

"I think you ought to hear about it now."

I didn't like the sound of that, although I couldn't imagine what the trouble could be. I used to hate answering my phone, because I owed money to so many people. Nowadays, though, other people owed *me* money. "It's not my long-lost brother, is it? He hasn't shown up expecting me to share my good fortune with him, has he?"

"No, it wasn't your brother, *yaa Sidi*. And even if it were, why wouldn't you be glad to—"

"I wasn't serious, Kmuzu." Kmuzu's a very intelligent guy, and I've come to depend on him quite a lot, but he has this huge blind spot where other people have a sense of humor. "What was the message, then?"

He turned from the street into the gate to Papa's mansion. We paused long enough at the guard's post to be identified, then rolled slowly up the curving driveway. "You've been invited to a celebratory dinner," he said. "In honor of your return."

"Uh huh," I said. I'd already endured two or three of those in recent days. Evidently, most of Friedlander Bey's minions in the Budayeen felt obliged to fete us, or risk having their livelihoods stripped away. Well, I'd gotten some free meals and some decent gifts out of it, but I thought all that had come to an end. "Who is it this time? Frenchy?" He owned the club where Yasmin used to work.

"A man of much greater significance. Shaykh Reda Abu Adil."

I just stared in disbelief. "I've been invited to have dinner with our worst enemy?"

"Yes, *yaa Sidi*."

"When is this dinner, then?" I asked.

"After evening prayers tonight, *yaa Sidi*. Shaykh Reda has a busy schedule, and tonight was the only possible time."

I let out a deep breath. Kmuzu had stopped the car at the foot of the wide marble stairs leading up to the mahogany front door. "I wonder if Papa would mind if I slept late this morning, then," I said.

"The master of the house gave me specific instructions to make certain you attended him at breakfast."

"I'm definitely not looking forward to this, Kmuzu."

"To breakfast? Then eat lightly, if your stomach is still upset."

"No," I said with some exasperation, "to this dinner party with Shaykh Reda. I hate being off-balance. I don't have any idea what the purpose of this meeting is, and it's fifty-fifty that Papa won't see fit to tell me about it."

Kmuzu shrugged. "Your judgment will see you through, *yaa Sidi*. And I will be there with you."

"Thank you, Kmuzu," I said, getting out of the car. Actually, I felt better about having him around than I did about my judgment. But I couldn't very well tell *him* that.

ELEVEN

I'll always remember it as "The Day of Three Meals."

Actually, the meals themselves were not memorable—in fact, I can't remember much about what I actually ate that day. The significance comes from what happened and what was said across the three tables.

The day began with Kmuzu shaking me awake a full half hour earlier than I'd planned to get up. My alarm-clock daddy was set for half past seven, but Friedlander Bey had moved up the breakfast hour by thirty minutes. I hate getting up, whether it's bright-eyed, high-stepping, and resentful thanks to the chip, or sluggish, yawning, and resentful thanks to Kmuzu. I figured if Allah had wanted us up that early, He wouldn't have invented noon.

I also hate breakfast. Lately, however, I'd been sharing an early morning meal with Friedlander Bey about four times a week. I imagined that things would only get worse, as Papa loaded me with more and more responsibility.

I always wore conservative Arab dress to those meetings. I spent more time in a *gallebeya* than I did in blue jeans, work shirt, and boots. My former standard of dress hung on a hook in the closet, and silently reproached me every time I glanced that way.

The jeans were a constant reminder of what I'd given up since Papa'd tapped me with his magic finger. I'd traded away much of what I formerly called "freedom"; the ironic thing was that every one of my friends would pay that much and more to have the luxuries I now enjoyed. At first, I hated Papa for the loss of my liberty. Now, although I sometimes still had twinges of regret in the dark night, I realized that Friedlander Bey had given me a great opportunity. My horizons had expanded far beyond anything I might have imagined in the old days. Nevertheless, I was acutely aware that I could decline neither the luxuries nor the new responsibilities. In some ways, I was the proverbial bird in the proverbial gilded cage.

The money was nice, though.

So I showered and trimmed my red beard, and dressed in the robe and *keffiya* that Kmuzu had chosen for me. Then we went downstairs to the small dining room.

Friedlander Bey was already there, of course, tended by Tariq, his valet. Kmuzu seated me at my usual place, and then stood behind my chair. "Good morning to you, my nephew," said Papa. "I trust you arose this morning in well-being."

"Il-hamdu lillah," I said. Praise be to God.

For breakfast there was a bowl of steamed wheat cereal with orange peel and nuts; a platter of eggs; a platter of breakfast meats; and, of course, coffee. Papa let Tariq serve him some eggs and roast lamb. "I've given you several days to relax, O Excellent One," he said. "But now the time for rest is over. I wish to know what you've done to advance the datalink project."

"I believe I've got an excellent agent in my friend, Jacques. I did a favor for him, and now I think he's willing to do a small favor for me in return."

Papa beamed at me as if I were a prize pupil. "Very good, my son!" he said. "I'm delighted that you're learning the ways of power so readily. Now let me show you the datalink terminal you'll be using—rather, that your friend will be using." Tariq left the room and returned shortly with what appeared to be a hard-sided briefcase. He placed it on the table, snapped its latches, and raised the lid.

"Wow," I said, impressed by the compact design of the terminal, "that's a little beauty."

"Indeed," said Friedlander Bey. "It has its commlink built-in, as well as the conventional datalink printer. To save on cost, this model doesn't accept voice commands. Everything must be keyed in manually. I expect, however, that the datalink project will earn out its set-up expenses within six months to a year, and then we can begin replacing these terminals with voice-activated models."

I nodded. "And it's up to me to sell the owners of every bar, nightclub, and restaurant in the Budayeen on the idea of renting one of them from me. I don't get it. I don't see why people will pay twenty-five fîqs for an information service that's now provided free by the city."

"We've been contracted by the city," Tariq explained. "The amir's special commission decided that it couldn't afford to run Info any longer. Within weeks, all the free Info terminals will be replaced by our machines, *inshallah*."

"I know that," I said. "What I meant was what do I do if the bar owners flat-out refuse?"

Friedlander Bey flashed a cold smile. "Don't worry about that," he said. "We have specialized technicians who will persuade those reluctant proprietors."

"Specialized technicians." I loved the euphemism. All of Papa's technicians have names like Guido and Tiny and Igor.

Papa went on. "It would be best if you and your friend worked as a team for a few days, before you send him off on his own. When we have the whole Budayeen covered, we can begin to exercise even closer control. We can tell who is using the service, and what questions they're asking. Because they have to use an official identification card to log on, we can monitor the dispensing of information. We could even prevent certain information from getting to some individuals."

"But surely we won't do that," I said.

Papa was silent for a second or two. "Of course not," he said at last. "That would be contrary to the principles of the holy Prophet."

"May the blessings of Allah be on him and peace," I responded automatically.

Tariq laid a booklet in front of me. "Here is the complete set of commands," he said, "and in the back of the book is a pocket with a special ID card, so that you won't have to pay for calls."

"Thank you," I said. "I'll familiarize myself with these commands today, and tomorrow I'll go with Jacques to talk to the club owners on the Street."

"Excellent, my nephew," said Papa. "Now, as to our vengeance. It would be best if it combined the discovery of the real murderer of Khalid Maxwell, as well as the disposition of those who plotted against us. I will accept only the most elegant solution."

"What if Dr. Sadiq Abd ar-Razzaq wasn't actually involved?" I asked. I was referring to the imam who'd given permission for Hajjar and his goons to kidnap us.

Papa flew into a rage. "Don't talk to me about that son of a diseased camel!" he cried. I'd never seen him show so much emotion. His face turned blood red, and his fists shook as his fury carried him away.

"O Shaykh—"

"The people of the Budayeen are crazy with worry!" he said, pounding the table. "All they can think about is what might happen if we're kidnapped again, and if this time we don't return. There are ugly rumors going around that we've lost control, that our associates no longer enjoy protection. The last few days, all I've done is calm and soothe my troubled friends. Well, I swear on the life of my children that I will not be weakened, nor will I be pushed aside! I have a plan, my nephew. Wait and see if that cursed imam can separate me again from the people who love me. If he is not involved, then *make* him involved."

"Yes, O Shaykh," I said.

Jeez. That's the way things worked around *that* breakfast table. Punishments and rewards were handed out with a blithe disregard for appropriateness. Sometimes Friedlander Bey reminded me of the whimsical Greek gods in the works of Homer—whimsical in that they often disturbed entire human nations because of some imagined slight, or out of boredom, or for no particular reason at all.

Even while Papa spoke about the datalink project, I could see that he was now controlled by hate, and it would continue until he could strike a deadly blow against those who'd conspired against us. Friedlander Bey's motto was "Getting even is the best revenge." Nothing else would do, no forgiveness for the sake of moral superiority, no intensely ironic symbolic acts.

It wasn't only the Bani Salim who demanded proper retaliation. That concept was stated explicitly in the noble Qur'ân, and it was part of the Muslim point of view, something the Western world had learned the hard way on numerous occasions. Someone would die—Hajjar, Shaykh Mahali, Dr. Abd ar-Razzaq, the actual murderer of Khalid Maxwell—and it seemed to be up to me to choose whom.

Friedlander Bey frowned in concentration. "There's another stone in my shoe," he said at last. "I'm speaking of Police Lieutenant Hajjar. Fortunately, it's very simple to rid oneself of such an irritation."

"Didn't he work for you, once upon a time?" I asked.

Papa turned his head and pretended to spit on the floor. "He's a traitor. He goes with whoever offers the most money at the time. He had no honor, no loyalty. I'm glad he works for Shaykh Reda now and not for me. I couldn't trust him when he was my man. Now I know where he is, and I suspect that I could buy him back at any time, if I wished. I may do that; and then when I have him, I can empty my shoe of him at my leisure."

He was talking murder here. Once upon a time I might have been appalled at the casual way Papa discussed terminating someone, but no longer. I looked at the situation as one of the Bedu might, and I knew Papa was entirely correct. It was just a matter of planning. All the details had yet to be worked out, but that was not difficult. I was only concerned that first Papa talked about eliminating the imam, and now

Lieutenant Hajjar. I didn't think we ought to get into depopulating the city in our rightful wrath.

A few minutes later I was in my office, tapping trial commands into the data deck. I found that I could learn just about anything about anybody in the city with that little machine. With my special, confidential commands, I had free access to information the average citizen didn't even know had been recorded. I got a dizzying sense of power as I pried into the private lives of both friends and enemies. I felt like a high-tech snoop, and the feeling was delicious.

When I'd gotten proficient with the datalink terminal, I was able to get a list of all of Dr. Abd ar-Razzaq's phone calls for the last two months, incoming and outgoing. The incoming calls were identified by their commcodes only. Then I did the same for Lieutenant Hajjar's commcode at the police station. I found that Hajjar and the imam had spoken together eleven times during those eight weeks. There were probably other calls from other phones, but I didn't need to track them all down. This evidence would never have to be admitted in a court of law.

About half an hour before I planned to have lunch, Kmuzu announced that I had visitors. They were Indihar and bin Turki, the Bani Salim youth.

"Morning of well-being," I said to them.

"Morning of light, husband," said Indihar. "I hope we're not interrupting your work."

I indicated that they could get comfortable on my couch. "No, not at all. It gives me pleasure to see you. And I was going to knock off for lunch in a little while, anyway. Is there something you need?"

"I bring you words of greeting from your mother," said Indihar. "She wonders why you've only visited her once since your return."

Well, the truth was that she still made me uncomfortable. She'd arrived in the city several months ago, looking brassy and blowsy. She'd been a hooker for most of her life, but I'd taken her in and given her a suite of rooms in the eastern wing, and she'd worked hard to tone down her style and be acceptable in Friedlander Bey's house. We'd talked at great length and finally reconciled, but she still embarrassed me. I understood that was my problem, not hers, and I'd tried to overcome my feelings. I wasn't all the way there yet, despite the good works my mother was doing in the city, using my money to establish and run soup kitchens and shelters. Her behavior was certainly laudable, but I couldn't erase the memory of how shocked I was to see her after a long time.

"Tell Umm Marîd that I've been very busy trying to catch up with all that happened while I was gone. Tell her that I'll come to see her very soon. Give her my love and ask her forgiveness for my inattention."

"Yes, husband," said Indihar. I don't think she was satisfied by my response, but she said nothing more.

Bin Turki cleared his throat. "I have much to be thankful for, O Shaykh," he said. "Every day brings wonder upon wonder. I see things that my brothers would not believe, even if I told them myself. Yet I wish to be free to explore your world as I wish. I have no money, and because of that I have no liberty. We Bani Salim are not used to imprisonment, even under such pleasant conditions as these."

I chewed my lip in thought. "You really think you're ready to step outside these walls? You've learned enough already to protect yourself against the well-dressed wolves of the city?"

The young man shrugged. "Perhaps I don't know how to keep out of trouble, but I claim the right to learn for myself."

Then I had a sudden inspiration. "You will need money, as you say. Would you consider doing some work for me, for which I'll see that you're rewarded with a moderate weekly salary?"

Bin Turki's eyes opened wider. "Certainly, O Shaykh," he said, his voice trembling. "I thank you for the opportunity."

"You don't know what I want yet," I said grimly. "Do you recall the story of our kidnapping and transporting to the Rub al-Khali?"

"Yes, O Shaykh."

"Do you remember how I spoke of the unnecessarily cruel sergeant in the town of Najran? How he beat the old shaykh for no reason?"

"Yes, O Shaykh."

I opened my desk drawer and took out the suborbital ticket. I pushed it across the desk. "Here, then," I said. "His name was Sergeant al-Bishah. You can leave tomorrow morning." That was all.

Indihar's hand went to her mouth. "Marîd!" she exclaimed. She'd guessed what sort of mission I was sending the young man on, and she was clearly shocked.

Bin Turki hesitated a moment, then accepted the ticket.

"Good," I said. "When you get back, there will be five thousand kiam for you, and a weekly allowance of two hundred kiam. With that you'll be able to rent a house or an apartment and lead your own life as you wish, but you'll always have the gratitude of Friedlander Bey and myself."

"That is worth more to me than any amount of money," murmured bin Turki.

"Indihar," I said, "would you mind taking our young friend under your wing? Help him find a place to live, and give him advice to keep him and his money safe?"

"I'd be happy to, husband," she said. Her expression was troubled. She hadn't seen the new me before.

"I thank both of you," I said. "Now, I have work to do."

"Good day to you, then, husband," said Indihar, rising.

"Yes, thank you, O Shaykh," said bin Turki. I pretended to be engrossed in some papers, and they left quietly. I was shaking like a newborn lamb. I hadn't seen the new me yet, either.

I waited for five minutes, for ten minutes. I was waiting for my sense of moral outrage to make itself heard, but it never happened. One part of my mind sat aloof, judging me, and what it discovered was unsettling. Apparently, I had no moral qualms at all about dispatching people on grim assignments. I tried to work up some sense of sadness, but it was impossible. I felt nothing. It wasn't something to be proud of, and I decided it was not something I could tell anyone about. Like Friedlander Bey, I had learned to live with what I had to do.

I told my data deck to quit, and when the screen of the monitor went dark, I began to make plans for lunch. I'd seen Jacques since I'd been home, but I hadn't run into Mahmoud or Saied. I knew they'd probably be sitting on the patio of the Café Solace, playing cards and gossiping. Suddenly that seemed like just what I needed. I called Kmuzu, and told him that I wanted to be driven to the Budayeen. He nodded wordlessly and went to get the Westphalian sedan.

We parked on the Boulevard il-Jameel, and walked through the eastern gate. The Street was filled with daytime tourists who would soon regret the fact that they'd ignored their hotel manager's advice that they should avoid the walled quarter. If they didn't leave soon, they'd be hustled for every loose kiam in their pockets and purses.

Kmuzu and I walked to the Solace, and just as I suspected, I saw my three friends sitting at a table near the patio's iron railing. I went through the small gate and joined them.

"Hullo, Marîd," said Jacques in a dull voice. "Hullo, Kmuzu."

"Where y'at, Marîd?" said Mahmoud.

"I been wondering what happened to you," said Saied the Half-Hajj. He'd been my best friend at one time, but he'd betrayed me to Shaykh Reda Abu Adil, and since then I'd kept a close eye on him.

"I'm fine," I said. "I suppose you've all heard the story."

"Yeah, we heard it," said Mahmoud, "but we haven't heard it from you. You were snatched, right? Out of the amir's palace? I thought Papa had more on the ball than that."

"Papa's pretty shrewd," said the Half-Hajj. "It's just that Shaykh Reda is shrewder than they gave him credit for."

"I have to admit that's true," I said.

"Kmuzu, sit down," said Jacques. "You don't have to play slave with us. We like you. Have a drink or something."

"Thank you," said Kmuzu in a flat voice. "I prefer to remain standing."

"We insist," grumbled Mahmoud. "You're making us nervous." Kmuzu nodded, then got a chair from another table and sat behind me.

Old Ibrahim came to take my order, and I just had a plate of *hummus* and bread, and a gin and bingara to wash it all down.

"Bleah," said Mahmoud.

I turned to respond, but I was interrupted by a man who came to the iron railing. "Shaykh Marîd," he said in an urgent voice, "do you remember me?"

I looked at him for a moment, but although I knew I'd seen him before, I couldn't place precisely where. "I'm sorry," I said.

"My name is Nikos Kouklis. A few months ago, you lent me the money to open my own gyro-souvlaki shop on Ninth Street. Since then, I've done better than I'd ever dreamed. My shop is successful, my wife is happy, my children are well fed and well dressed. Here. It gives me great pleasure to return to you your investment, and my wife made a pan of baklava for you. Please accept it, with my undying gratitude."

I was taken aback. I'd loaned lots of people a little money here and there, but this was the first time one of them had made a big deal out of paying me back. Indeed, it made me a little uncomfortable. "You keep that money," I said. "Save it for your wife and children."

"I'm sorry, O Shaykh," said Kouklis, "but I insist on repaying you."

I understood the man's pride, and I took the money with a courteous nod. I also accepted the plate of baklava. "May your success continue," I said. "May your fortunes increase."

"I owe everything to you," said the Greek restaurant owner. "I will be in your debt forever."

"Perhaps someday there will come a chance to discharge it," I said.

"Anything," said Kouklis. "Anytime." He bowed to the four of us and backed away.

"Oh, Mr. Bigshot," said Mahmoud mockingly.

"Yeah," I said, "that's right. What have *you* ever done for anybody?"

"Well—" Mahmoud began.

I cut him off. I'd known Mahmoud since he'd been a slim-hipped girl named Misty, working for Jo-Mama. I knew that I couldn't trust him as far as I could throw him. Nowadays, with the weight he'd put on after his sexchange, that was about a foot and a half.

Instead, I turned to Jacques and said, "You still up to helping us out?"

"Of course." Jacques looked a little frightened. As with most of the people of the Budayeen, he preferred to accept the protection of the house of Friedlander Bey, but he was scared out of his mind when it came time to repay that generosity.

"Then call me tomorrow, about noon," I said. "You have my number at Papa's mansion, don't you?"

"Uh huh," said Jacques nervously.

"Oh," said Mahmoud, "have you sold out now, too?"

"Look who's talking," said Jacques. "Mr. Lackey of Shaykh Reda himself finds room to criticize."

"I'm no one's lackey," said Mahmoud, half-rising from his seat.

"Oh no, of course not," said Saied.

I ignored their childish debate. "I've got the hardware, Jacques," I said, "and I've been playing around with it, and it definitely looks like a good deal for us as well as for the club owners who subscribe. You don't have to worry about doing anything illicit—we have a complete set of permits from the city, and everything's legal and aboveboard."

"Then why is Friedlander Bey interested?" said Mahmoud. "I didn't think he cared about anything that wasn't at least a little bit bent."

The Half-Hajj leaned back in his chair and regarded Mahmoud for a few seconds. "You know, my friend," he said at last, "someday somebody's going to take care of that mouth of yours. You're going to wish you'd never changed sexes and joined the big boys."

Mahmoud only laughed disdainfully. "Any time you think you're man enough, Saied," he said.

The bickering was interrupted by the arrival of Yasmin. "How y'all are?" she asked.

"Fine," said the Half-Hajj. "We're just sitting here in the sun, drinking and eating baklava and listening to ourselves claw at each other's throats. Have some?"

Yasmin was tempted by the honey pastry, but she exercised more restraint than I gave her credit for. "No," she said, smiling, "can't do it. Hips are just right the way they are."

"I'll second that," said Jacques.

"You bad boy," said Yasmin.

"Listen, Yasmin," I said.

"The hell do *you* want, married man?" she said bitterly.

"I was only wondering when you were going to drop this jealousy thing."

"*What* jealousy thing?" she asked haughtily. "You think I even think about such midges and mites as you and Indihar? I have more important things on my mind."

I shook my head. "As I see it," I said, "Islam gives me the option of marrying up to four wives, if I can support them all equally. That means that I can still date, even though I'm married to Indihar. And I'm married to her in name only."

"Ha!" cried Saied. "I knew it! You've never consummated that wedding, have you!"

I glared at him for a few seconds. "Yasmin," I said, "give me a break, all right? Let me buy you dinner sometime. I think we need to talk."

She frowned at me, giving me no encouragement at all. "We'll talk," she said. "We'll talk at the club tonight, if Indihar gives you permission to go out." Then she grabbed a piece of baklava, turned on her heel, and headed off down the Street.

Not long after she left, I got up and bid my friends good day. Then I had Kmuzu drive me back to Papa's estate. I still had paperwork to attend to.

The third meal of the day, of course, was *chez* Shaykh Reda. When I returned home after my lunch break, I tried to get a little work done. It was very difficult. I knew Friedlander Bey was counting on my contribution to both the datalink project and the on-going business of stabilizing or destabilizing the Muslim nations who came to us for help. Still, on this particular day, I couldn't help worrying a little about what was in Abu Adil's mind. Why had he invited us to dinner? To finish what he'd started when he'd had us kidnapped several weeks ago?

That's why I wore a small needle gun on my belt, turned around so that it rested in the small of my back. I chose the needle gun because it was constructed entirely of plastic, and wouldn't show up on an X-ray. It was loaded with razor flechettes, unpoisoned. Half a clip of those suckers would rip away enough flesh to be memorable, if the target survived.

I'd worn my best outfit to the wedding reception Shaykh Mahali had thrown, and so it had been destroyed by the rigors of our desert travels. I'd also given the valuable ceremonial dagger to Shaykh Hassanein. Tonight I wore my best remaining outfit, a long white *gallebeya* decorated with hand-embroidered flowers in a cream-colored silk thread. It was a beautiful *gallebeya*, and I was very proud of it. It had been a gift from a family in the Budayeen I'd given a little help to.

I wore sandals and a black-and-white checked *keffiya*. I also carried a sheathed dagger in the manner of the Bedu, front and center against my belly. When I put it on my belt, I decided to ask Friedlander Bey if we could bring bin Turki with us to the dinner. We'd already planned to bring Tariq and Youssef. We didn't want to offer ourselves up within Shaykh Reda's stronghold without a small army of our own.

Papa agreed that bin Turki might be useful, so he accompanied the four of us to Shaykh Reda's mansion in the city's western district, Hâmidiyya. Abu Adil squatted like a toad in the center of one of the worst parts of town. His own estate was rivaled in the city only by Papa's and Shaykh Mahali's, but Shaykh Reda was surrounded by the burned-out, abandoned, fallen-in tenements of Hâmidiyya. It always reminded me of Satan sitting at the center of his hellish realm.

We drove through a gate in the high, brown brick wall that enclosed the mansion and stopped to identify ourselves to a guard. Then we parked the car and the five of us went to the front door. This time we wouldn't permit our party to be separated.

We had no trouble with the man who answered the doorbell. He led us to a small dining hall where places for ten had been set. Our group took seats at one end of the table, and we waited for Abu Adil to make his entrance.

And that's just what he did. A hefty bodyguard type entered first, followed by Shaykh Reda in a wheelchair, which was pushed by his little Kenneth. Following them came two more bruisers. I have no doubt that the shaykh watched our arrival from somewhere and made up a guest list of his employees equal to our number. Five against five.

"I'm happy you've chosen to honor my house," said Abu Adil. "We should do this sort of thing more often. Perhaps then there'd be less tension between us."

"We thank you for the invitation, O Shaykh," I said warily.

Kenneth was looking at me appraisingly. Then he gave a quiet laugh and shook his head. He had nothing but contempt for me, and I didn't know why. Maybe if I broke his fingers and toes for him, he'd lose that smirk. It was a harmless fantasy, I thought.

Servants brought in platters of couscous, kefta kabobs, roast lamb, and vegetables in wonderful, succulent sauces. "In the name of Allah, the Beneficent, the Merciful, may it be pleasant to you!" said Shaykh Reda.

"May your table last forever, O Father of Generosity," said Friedlander Bey.

Papa and I ate sparingly, watching for any sign of treachery from Abu Adil or his musclemen. Bin Turki ate as if he'd never seen food before. I'm sure he'd never seen such a banquet.

I whispered to him, "Shaykh Reda is probably trying to seduce you away from our household." I didn't really mean it. It was a joke.

Bin Turki turned white. "You don't think my loyalty is for sale, do you?" His hands began to tremble with suppressed emotion.

"I was just kidding, my friend," I said.

"Ah," he said, "good. Your city humor is sometimes incomprehensible to me. In fact, I don't even know what's happening here tonight."

"You're not the only one," I told him.

Abu Adil's goons said nothing, as usual. Kenneth said nothing, either, although he rarely turned his gaze away from me. We ate in silence, as if we were waiting for some dreadful trap to spring shut around us. Finally, when the meal was almost at an end, Shaykh Reda stood and began to speak.

"Once again," he said, "it's my great pleasure to present a little gift to Marîd Audran. Let us give thanks to Allah that he and Friedlander Bey have returned safely from their ordeal."

There was a chorus of "Allah be praised!" around the table.

Abu Adil reached down and got a gray cardboard box. "This," he said, opening it, "is the uniform that befits your rank of lieutenant in the *Jaish*. You command three platoons of loyal patriots, and lately they've grown restive, wondering why you do not attend our rallies and exercises. One reason, I thought, was that you didn't have a proper outfit. Well, you no longer have that excuse. Shaykh Marîd, wear this in good health!"

I was struck speechless. This was even more ludicrous than the original commission. I didn't know what to say, so I just stammered a few words of thanks and accepted the boxed uniform. A lieutenant's insignia had already been added to it.

Shortly thereafter, when none of us could eat another thing, Shaykh Reda excused himself and wheeled out of the dining room, followed by Kenneth and his three goons.

Bin Turki bent toward me and whispered, "What was wrong with him? Why is he in a wheelchair? Surely he's wealthy enough to afford any sort of medical aid. Even in the Rub al-Khali, we heard marvelous tales of the miracles that are wrought by civilized physicians."

I spread my hands. "He's not really an invalid," I explained in a low voice. "His 'hobby' is collecting personality modules recorded from actual sufferers from all sorts of fatal illnesses. It's a perversion called Proxy Hell. He can enjoy—if that's the right word—the worst pain and disablement, and pop the moddy out whenever it gets to be too much. I suppose he's got an unusual tolerance for pain, though."

"That's contemptible," whispered bin Turki, frowning.

"That's Shaykh Reda Abu Adil," I said.

In two or three minutes, we were all walking back to our car. "How about that," exclaimed Tariq. "The one time we're ready for him and come into his house armed to the teeth, he just serves us a dandy meal and drops a uniform on Shaykh Marîd."

"What do you think that means?" asked Youssef.

"I trust we'll find out eventually," said Papa. I knew his words were true. There had to be something devious happening at that meal, but I couldn't imagine what.

And did it all mean that we were now obliged to have *them* over sometime? If this kept going, sooner or later the two houses would end up going to movies and watching prizefights on the holoset and drinking beer together. I couldn't face that.

Twelve

I waited for Yasmin so that we could have our talk, but she never came into work that night. I went home about two o'clock in the morning, and let Chiri close up. There was no breakfast meeting with Papa the next day, so I told Kmuzu I wanted to sleep a little later. He gave me permission.

When I awoke, I eased into the morning. I took a long, hot bath and reread one of my favorite Lutfy Gad murder mysteries. Gad was the greatest Palestinian writer of the last century, and I guess now and then I unconsciously imitate his great detective, al-Qaddani. Sometimes I fall into that clipped, ironic way al-Qaddani spoke. None of my friends ever noticed, though, because as a group they're not terribly well read.

When I emerged from the tub, I dressed and skipped the well-balanced breakfast Kmuzu'd prepared for me. He gave me a grim look, but he'd learned over many months that if I didn't feel like eating, I wouldn't eat. Unless Papa demanded it.

Kmuzu silently handed me an envelope. Inside was a letter from Friedlander Bey addressed to Lieutenant Hajjar, requiring that I be reinstated on the city's police force for the duration of my investigation of Khalid Maxwell's death. I read it through and nodded. Papa had an uncanny ability to anticipate that sort of thing. He also knew that he could "require" something of the police and it would be done.

I put the letter in my pocket and relaxed in a comfortable black leather chair. I decided it was time to check in with Wise Counselor. The Counselor was a personality module that gauged my current emotional state, and offered a super-realistic fantasy that expressed my problems and offered a symbolic—sometimes indecipherable—solution. *"Bis-millah,"* I murmured, and reached up to chip the moddy in.

ḪUḐꞦꜲꞂ ꞶꜲꙄ *transformed into the great Persian poet, Hafiz. He'd led a life of luxury, and his poems also contained imagery that stricter Muslims objected to. Over the years, Audran had made a large number of enemies, so that when he died, the strict Muslims argued that his body should be denied the blessing of the traditional funeral prayer. Their reasoning condemned Audran with his own words.*

"Has the poet not written about unholy practices such as imbibing alcoholic beverages and indulging in promiscuous sex?" they asked. "Listen to his poetry:

> *"Come here, come here, cup-bearer!*
> *Pass around and give the cup,*
> *For love looked free and easy at first,*
> *But too many troubles have come up."*

This fueled a long debate between Audran's enemies and his admirers. Finally, it was decided that the correct course of action should be dictated by a random reference to his own poems. To that end, a large selection of Audran's verses were written out on slips of paper and thrown into an urn. An innocent child was asked to reach into the urn and pick one verse. This is the couplet that the child drew:

> *In the funeral of Audran gladly take part,*
> *For sinful as he was, for Heaven doth he start.*

The verdict was acknowledged by both sides, and so Audran was given a funeral with all proper ceremonies. When the story came to its end, Audran reached up and popped the moddy out.

ꙇ ꙅꞡꞷꙂꙂꝗꞂꙆꙄ. Those fantasies that showed me dead and hovering over my own funeral always gave me the creeps. Now I had to decide what it meant, how it related to me. I hadn't written a poem in fifteen years. I filed the vision away as something to discuss Real Soon Now with Kmuzu.

It was time to start digging up information about Khalid Maxwell and his violent death. The first step, I decided, was to go to the copshop that oversaw the activities in the Budayeen, where Lieutenant Hajjar was in charge. I didn't hate Hajjar, he just made my skin crawl. He wasn't the sort of person who derived pleasure from pulling the wings from flies—he was the sort of person who'd go into the next room and watch someone else do it, through a secret peephole.

Kmuzu drove me in the cream-colored Westphalian sedan to the precinct house on Walid al-Akbar Street. As usual, there was a crowd of boys on the sidewalk, and I waded through them flinging coins left and right. Still they begged, chanting, "Open to us, O Generous One!" I liked the kids. It wasn't so long ago that I myself haunted the edges of crowds, pleading for money to feed myself. Somewhere along the line the roles were reversed, and now I was the big rich guy. I was rich, all right, but I never forgot my origins. I didn't begrudge the kids their *baksheesh.*

I entered the police station and headed toward the computer room on the second floor. I was braced a couple of times by uniformed men, but I said nothing, just showing them the letter with Friedlander Bey's signature. The cops all melted aside like phantoms.

I remembered very well how to operate the computers. I even recalled the secret backdoor password, *Miramar.* The staff in this station house had rather relaxed standards, and I was confident they hadn't gotten around to changing that password in months. I guess the risk of an outsider getting into the police files was preferable to making the entire force memorize a new word.

I sat down at the beat-up old Annamese data deck and began murmuring commands. The female sergeant who acted as the data librarian saw me and hurried over. "I'm sorry, sir," she said in a voice that wasn't sorry at all, "but these decks are not accessible to the public."

"You don't remember me, do you?" I asked.

She squinted one eye and considered. "No, so you'll have to leave."

I took out Papa's letter and showed it to her. "I've just got a few minutes' work to do here," I said.

"I'll have to check on this," she said, folding the letter again and giving it back to me. "No one's spoken to me about any of this. I'll call the lieutenant. In the meantime, leave that data deck alone."

I nodded, knowing that I'd have to wait for her to work her way up through the chain of command. It didn't take long. In a few minutes, Lieutenant Hajjar himself came huffing into the data library. "What do you think you're doing, Audran?" he shouted. His expression was a black scowl.

I held out Papa's letter. I wasn't about to stand up or try to explain myself. The letter could speak for me, and I felt like exerting a little dominance. Hajjar needed to be put in his place every once in a while.

He snatched the paper from my hand and read through it once and then again. "What's this?" he said harshly.

"It's a letter. From you know who, you've already read it."

He glared at me and crumpled the sheet of paper into a ball. "This letter don't cut it with me, Audran. Not at all. And what are you doing at large? You were formally exiled. I should take you into custody right now."

I shook my finger at him and smiled. "Nuh uh, Hajjar. The amir's granted us an appeal, and you know it."

"Still," he said.

"Still," I said, taking the crumpled paper and holding it against his temple. "You really don't think this letter cuts it, huh?"

"No way." He sounded much less sure this time.

"Well," I said calmly, "Papa has plenty of people who *could* cut you."

Hajjar licked his lips. "Well, what the hell do you want, then?"

I smiled in a completely phony friendly way. "I just want to use this data deck for a minute or two."

"I suppose that could be arranged. What are you trying to dig up?"

I spread my hands. "I want to clear our names, of course. I want to find out what you know about Khalid Maxwell."

A look of fear came and went in his eyes. "I can't allow that," he said. Now his voice shook noticeably. "It's classified police business."

I laughed. "I'm classified police," I said. "At least for the moment."

"No," he said, "I won't allow it. That case is closed."

"I'm reopening it." I shook the crumpled paper at him.

"Right," he said, "go ahead. But there are going to be repercussions from this. I'm warning you."

"I'm *hoping* for repercussions, Hajjar. I advise you to get out of the way of them."

He stared at me for a few seconds. Then he said, "*Yallah*, your mother must've been a syphilitic camel, Audran, and your father was a Christian bastard."

"Close," I said, and I turned my back on him and continued to murmur commands to the data deck. I suppose Hajjar stalked away.

The first thing I did was call up the file on Khalid Maxwell. I didn't learn much. Evidently, the file had been tampered with and edited until there was very little information left. I did find out that Maxwell had been with the police force for four years, that he'd earned a commendation for bravery, and that he'd been killed while off-duty. According to the cop computer, he died while interceding in a violent argument between Friedlander Bey and myself in front of Maxwell's house at 23 Shams Alley.

That was nonsense, of course. I didn't even know where Shams Alley was; I was sure it wasn't in the Budayeen. Maxwell was the second police officer from Hajjar's precinct to be killed during the year. That didn't look good for Hajjar, but of course it looked even worse for poor Maxwell.

I had the data deck print out the file, and then I passed a little time by poking into other files. Lieutenant Hajjar's dossier gave even less information than it had the last time I looked. All mention of his own difficulties with the force's Internal Affairs Department had been erased. There wasn't much left but his name, age, and address.

My own file listed me as the killer of Khalid Maxwell (released pending appeal). That reminded me that the clock was running, and there were only a few weeks left of my freedom. It would be very hard to prove my innocence—and Papa's—from inside a prison cell or with my head on the chopping block. I decided to stir things up a little and see what happened.

When I left the station house, I found Kmuzu sitting in the car a little farther up Walid al-Akbar Street. I got into the back seat and told him to drive me to the Budayeen's eastern gate. When we got there, I sent him home because I didn't know how long my business would take. When Kmuzu objected, I told him I could get a cab to come home. He frowned and said he'd rather wait for me, but I just told him in a firm voice to do what I said.

I took with me the portable datalink unit Friedlander Bey and I were marketing, and as I walked up the Street toward the Café Solace, my phone rang. I unclipped it from my belt and said, "Hello."

"Audran?" asked a nasal voice that sounded fat with disgust.

"Yeah," I said, "who is this?"

"Kenneth. Calling on behalf of Shaykh Reda Abu Adil."

That explained the disgust; the feeling was definitely mutual. "Yeah, Kenny, what do you want."

There was a brief pause. "My name is Kenneth, not Kenny. I'd appreciate it if you'd keep that in mind."

I grinned. "Sure, pal. Now what's behind this call?"

"Shaykh Reda has just heard that you're digging around in the Khalid Maxwell case. Don't."

The news sure had traveled fast. "Don't?"

"Right," said Kenneth. "Just don't. Shaykh Reda is concerned for your safety, as you are an officer in the *Jaish*, and he fears what might happen to you if you continue this investigation."

I laughed without humor. "I'll tell you what will happen if I *don't* continue the investigation: Papa and I will lose our appeal and we'll be put to death."

"We understand that, Audran. If you want to save your necks, there are two ways to proceed, the right way and the wrong way. The right way is to establish a bullet-proof alibi for yourselves the night of the murder. The wrong way is to go on doing what you're doing."

"That's great, Ken, but to tell the truth, I can't even remember what I did on the night in question."

"It's *Kenneth*," he growled, just before he hung up. I grinned again and put my phone back on my belt.

I found Jacques and Mahmoud playing dominoes at the Café Solace. I pulled up a chair to their table and watched for a while. Finally, old Ibrahim came and asked if I wanted anything. I ordered a White Death, and Mahmoud looked at me curiously. "How long you been here, Marîd?" he asked. "We been playing dominoes and I never saw you come up."

"Not long," I told him. I turned to my other friend. "Jacques," I said, "you ready to start pushing data this afternoon?"

He gave me a look which said he regretted ever agreeing to help me out. "Don't you have more important things to do?" he said. "I mean, like clearing your name and reputation."

I nodded. "Don't worry, I've started taking care of that, too."

"We heard," said Mahmoud.

"The rumor on the Street is that you're looking for someone to pin Maxwell's murder on," said Jacques.

"Instead of proving where you were the night of the crime," said Mahmoud. "You're going about it all wrong. You're trying to do it the hard way."

"That's just what Abu Adil's current Bendable Benny told me," I said slowly. "What a coincidence."

"Kenneth told you that?" said Mahmoud. "Well, see, he's probably right."

I didn't have any specific questions to ask them, so I changed the subject. "Ready to go, Jacques?" I said.

"Well, Marîd, to tell the truth, my stomach hurts today. How 'bout tomorrow afternoon?"

"Oh, you'll be on your own tomorrow," I said, smiling, "but you're also going with me today."

I waited patiently until Mahmoud won the domino game, and then as Jacques settled up his wager. "It's not starting out to be a good day for me," said Jacques. He was well dressed, as usual, but he wore that miffy Christian look that all his friends hated so much. He looked as if he wanted to go somewhere and start a new life under another name.

I looked at him from the corner of my eye and stifled a smile. He was so upset. "What's wrong, Jacques?" I asked.

His upper lip pulled back in disdain. "I'll tell you one thing, Marîd," he said. "This job is beneath me. It's not appropriate for me to act like a . . . a common salesman."

I couldn't help laughing. "Don't think of yourself as a salesman, if that's your problem. Truthfully, you're not. You're much more than that. Try to see the whole picture, O Excellent One."

Jacques didn't look convinced. "I *am* looking at the big picture. I see myself going into a bar or a club, taking out my wares, and trying to wangle money out of the proprietor. That's retail sales. It's demeaning to someone of my blood. Have I ever told you that I'm three-quarters European?"

I sighed. He'd told us nearly every day for the last seven years. "Haven't you ever wondered who works retail sales in Europe?"

"Americans," said Jacques, shrugging.

I rubbed my aching forehead. "Forget sales. You won't be a salesman. You'll be a Data Placement Specialist. And when you get rolling, you'll be promoted to Information Retrieval Engineer. With a suitable increase in your commission percentage."

Jacques glared. "You can't trick me, Marîd," he said.

"That's the great part! I don't *have* to trick you. I've got enough power these days to twist your arm and make you delighted to help me."

Jacques gave a short, humorless laugh. "My arm is untwistable, O Shaykh. You're still street scum, just like the rest of us."

I shrugged. "That may well be true, my Christian friend, but I'm street scum with Habib and Labib at my command."

"Who are they?"

"The Stones That Speak," I said calmly. I saw the color go out of Jacques's face. Everyone in the Budayeen knew about Papa's huge bodyguards, but I was one of the few privileged to know their individual names. Of course, I still couldn't tell which one was which, but that was all right because they always traveled together.

Jacques spat on the ground in front of me. "It's true what they say about power corrupting," he said bitterly.

"You're wrong, Jacques," I said in a quiet voice. "I wouldn't threaten one of my friends. I don't need that power. I'm only counting on you to return a favor. Didn't I cover Fuad's check for you? Didn't you agree to help me?"

He winced. "Yes, well, if it's a matter of honor, well then, of course I'm happy to return the favor."

I clapped him on the back. "I knew I could count on you."

"Anytime, Marîd." But the look on his face told me his stomach still bothered him.

We arrived at Frenchy's club, which was across the Street and up a block from my own. Frenchy was a huge, burly, black-bearded guy who looked like he ought to be rolling barrels into a warehouse in some sunny French seaport. He was as tough a joker as I've ever met. Disturbances didn't last long in Frenchy's place.

"Where y'at, Marîd?" called Dalia, Frenchy's barmaid.

"Just fine, Dalia. Frenchy around?"

"He's in back. I'll go get him." She tossed her bar towel down and disappeared into the back office. There weren't very many customers, but it was still early in the day.

"Can I buy you a drink?" I asked Jacques while we waited.

"The Lord doesn't approve of liquor," he said. "You should know that."

"I do," I said. "I do know that God disapproves. But He's never said anything directly to me about it."

"Oh no? What do you call vomiting all over yourself? What do you call blackouts? What do you call getting your face smashed in because you were so drunk you said the wrong thing to the wrong person? And you shouldn't be blasphemous."

I couldn't take him seriously. "I've seen you drink your share, too."

Jacques nodded vigorously. "Yes, my friend, but then I go to confession and do my penance and then everything's all right again."

I was saved from further religious exegesis by Frenchy, who showed up in the nick of time. "What's happening?" he said, taking the bar stool to my right.

"Well, Frenchy," I said, "it's nice to see you, and I'm glad I'm still welcome in your club, but we don't really have time to sit here and chat. I want to sell you something."

"You want to sell me something, *noraf*," he said in his gruff voice. "Wait a minute. I'm impossible to scam when I'm sober."

"I thought you stopped drinking," I said, "On account of your stomach."

"Well, I started again," said Frenchy. He signaled to his barmaid, and Dalia brought him an unopened bottle of Johnnie Walker. I don't know what it is, but most of these ex-seamen won't drink anything but

Johnnie Walker. I first noticed it over in Jo-Mama's club among the Greek merchant sailors, and the two Filipino bars on Seventh Street. Frenchy twisted open the bottle and filled a tumbler half full. "Gonna give you a fair chance," said Frenchy, gulping down the whiskey and refilling the tumbler.

"Let me have a gin and bingara," I told the barmaid.

"Want some lime juice in that?" Dalia asked.

I smiled at her. "You never forget."

She shuddered in disgust. "How could I?" she muttered. "What about you, Jacques?"

"You've got that Ecuadorian beer on draft? I'll have one." Dalia nodded and drew Jacques his beer.

Frenchy threw down a second glass of whiskey and belched. "*Eh bien*, Marîd," he said, rubbing his thick beard, "what's in the suitcase?"

I put it up on the bar between us and snapped open the latches. "You're going to love this," I said.

"Not yet," said Frenchy, "but maybe in a few minutes." He downed a third tumbler of Johnnie Walker.

"Whatcha got, Marîd?" said Dalia, resting her elbows on the bar.

Frenchy glared at her, and his head wobbled a little. "Go wipe off some tables," he told her. He was beginning to feel the liquor. That was good.

I opened the lid of the suitcase and let Frenchy look at the datalink. It was a state-of-the-art terminal with just enough memory so that it wouldn't forget its own job. It was useless unless it was connected to a mainframe somewhere. Friedlander Bey had contracted with an electronics firm in Bosnia to supply the datalinks at a price well below the fair market standard. That was because the Bosnian corporation was owned by an industrial conglomerate with its headquarters in Bahrain; both the chief executive officer and the vice president for sales owed their current positions of power, wealth, and comfort to Papa's intervention in local political affairs some ten years before.

I reached over and poured Frenchy a fourth drink. *"Merde alors,"* he murmured.

"Friedlander Bey wants you to be the first in the Budayeen," I told him.

The big Frenchman was sipping his whiskey now, not gulping. "First for what, and will I live through it?" he asked.

I smiled. "You're gonna get the chance to be the first on the Street to have one of these datalinks. You can set it up right down there on the end of the bar, right where people can see it when they first come into the club."

"Uh huh," said Frenchy. "The fuck do I want one?"

I glanced at Jacques to see if he was paying attention. "These units will access more than the city's Info service," I said. "Your customers will be able to tap into a global data network that will provide almost unlimited information."

Frenchy shook his head. "How much is it gonna cost 'em?"

"One kiam. Just one kiam per data request."

"*Minute, papillon!* The city's Info service is free. All you got to do is pick up a phone."

I smiled again. "Not for long, Frenchy. Nobody knows this yet, so don't go spreading it around. Friedlander Bey's bought the Info service from the city."

Frenchy laughed. "What did he do, bribe the amir?"

I shrugged. "He persuaded the amir. It doesn't make any difference how. The amir has just come to believe that Papa will administer the service better than the previous Public Service Commission. Of course, Papa's also explained that in order to give the people the service they deserve, there will have to be a small fee for each transaction."

Frenchy nodded. "So the free Info service is being phased out. And these datalink units will take its place. And you and Papa are gonna be in charge, doling out bits of information. What happens if someone wants the scoop on Papa's personal life?"

I turned away and casually drank half my White Death. "Oh," I said calmly, "we're unfortunately going to limit the free access of certain people to certain data."

Frenchy slammed his fist down on the bar and laughed. Actually, it was more like a bellow. "He is magnificent!" he cried. "He's throttled the exchange of information, and he'll decide who may or may not benefit! Wait until Abu Adil finds out!"

Jacques leaned closer. "I didn't know about any of this, Marîd," he said softly. "You didn't mention any of this to me, and I think that dissolves our agreement."

I indicated that he should drink up his beer. "That's why I came along with you today," I said. "I want you to be clear about all the ramifications. It's the dawn of an exciting age."

"But I don't think I like it. What am I getting into?"

I spread my hands. "One of the greatest commercial enterprises in history," I said.

A customer came into the club just then, a tall man dressed in a European-style business suit. He had gray hair that had been expensively cut and styled, and at his neck he wore a silver brooch set with many diamonds and a cluster of large emeralds in the center. He carried a briefcase not much smaller than my own, and he stood in the doorway letting his eyes adjust to the darkness in Frenchy's bar.

One of Frenchy's dancers went to him and invited him in. I didn't know the girl. She may have been new to the Budayeen, but if she stayed around any time at all I'd eventually learn more than I wanted to know about her. She was wearing a long gown of very sheer material, so that her small breasts and her dark pubic triangle were visible, even in that dim light. "Would you like a drink?" she asked.

The elegantly dressed man squinted at her. "Is your name Theoni?" he asked.

The dancer's shoulders slumped. "No," she said, "but she's over there. Theoni, this is one of yours."

Theoni was one of the sweetest girls on the Street, completely out of place in Frenchy's club. She'd never worked for me; but I'd be overjoyed if she ever came into Chiriga's looking for a job. She was small and lithe and graceful, and she'd had only a moderate amount of surgery. Her bodmods accentuated her natural prettiness without making her into the kind of caricature we saw too often around there. Unlike most of the dancers, she'd never had her brain wired at all, and when she wasn't entertaining a customer, she sat by herself near the back of Frenchy's, drinking Sharâb and reading paperback books. I think it was her reading that I found most attractive about her.

She emerged from the dark rear of the bar and greeted the customer, leading him to a table right behind where Frenchy, Jacques, and I were sitting. Dalia came over to take his order, and he got a beer for himself and a champagne cocktail for Theoni.

Frenchy poured himself another healthy round of Johnnie Walker. "Dalia," he said, "gimme a glass of mineral water." He turned to me. "She's the best barmaid on the Street, you know that? You think Chiri's a good barmaid, I wouldn't trade Dalia for Chiri if you threw in Yasmin as well. Jeez, how do you put up with her? Yasmin, I mean. Always late. She's pretty for a boy and she makes money, but she's got a temper—"

"Frenchy," I said, cutting off his drunken monologue, "believe me, I know all about Yasmin's temper."

"I suppose you would. How does she take working for you now that you're married?" He laughed again, a low rumbling sound from deep within his chest.

"Let's talk about the terminal, Frenchy," I said, trying again to steer the conversation back on course. "You're gonna want one, because everyone else on the Street is gonna have one, and without one you'll lose business. Like not having a phone or a bathroom."

"Bathroom only works on Tuesdays and Thursdays anyway," muttered Frenchy. "What's in it for me?"

I took that to mean what was in it for him if he accepted the terminal. "Well, my friend, we're prepared to loan you some money if you'll do us the favor of letting us install our first datalink here in your club. One thousand kiam in cash, right here and now, and you don't have to do a thing for it. Just sign the order form, and tomorrow a wirecutter will come in and set up the unit on the end of your bar. You won't have to lift a finger."

"A thousand kiam?" he said. He leaned close to me and stared into my eyes. He was breathing heavily in my face, and it wasn't a pleasant experience.

"A thousand. Cash. Right now. And the beauty part, Frenchy, is that we won't ask you to repay it. We're gonna split the take from the datalink with you sixty-five to thirty-five. We'll collect the loan payments out of your thirty-five percent. You won't even miss the money. And when it's all paid back, we'll loan you another thousand, in cash, up front, to do with as you will."

He rubbed his beard some more and squinted his eyes, trying to see what the catch was. "You're going to split the take with me every month?" he said.

"Thirty-five percent is yours," I said.

"So these loans are more—"

"They're more like a gift!" said Jacques. I turned to look at him.

There was silence in the club for a few moments. From the corner of my eye, I saw Theoni sitting very close to the customer with the jeweled brooch. She slipped her hand along his thigh, and he looked very uncomfortable. "Where are you from, then, honey?" she said, sipping her cocktail.

"Achaea," he said. He lifted her hand out of his lap.

Frenchy heaved his huge body up and grabbed two glasses from across the bar. He poured them half full of whiskey, and set one in front of Jacques and the other in front of me. Then he took Jacques's bottle of beer and sniffed it. *"Pipi de chat,"* he said scornfully. "Drink with me."

I shrugged and picked up the glass of whiskey. Frenchy and I tinked glasses and I downed it. Jacques was having more trouble with his. He wasn't much of a drinker.

"Marîd," said Frenchy, suddenly serious, "what happens to me and my bar if I decline your generous offer? What if I refuse? This is my club, after all, and I say what goes and what doesn't go in here. I don't want a datalink. What is Papa gonna think about that?"

I frowned and shook my head. "How long we known each other, Frenchy?"

He just stared at me.

"Take the datalink," I said in a calm voice.

He was big enough to break me in half, but he knew this was a critical moment. He knew that throwing me out of his club was not the appropriate response. With a long, sad sigh he stood up. "All right, Marîd," he said at last, "sign me up. But don't think I don't know what this means."

I grinned at him. "It's not so bad, Frenchy. Here. Here's your thousand kiam." I reached into the pocket of my *gallebeya* and took out a sealed envelope.

Frenchy snatched it from me and turned away. He stalked back toward his office without saying another word. "This afternoon," I told Jacques, "you can offer the same thousand kiam to Big Al and the others, but they get theirs when the datalink terminal is actually installed. All right?"

Jacques nodded. He shoved the unfinished glass of whiskey away from him. "And I get a commission on each terminal?"

"One hundred kiam," I said. I was sure that Jacques would do a fine job selling the project to our friends and neighbors, especially with the inducement of a hundred-kiam commission per sale, and with the weighty endorsement of Friedlander Bey. Papa's influence would make Jacques's job that much easier.

"I'll do my best, Marîd," he said. He sounded a little more confident now. He slowly drank the rest of the Ecuadorian beer in his bottle.

A little while later, the customer from Achaea stood up and opened his briefcase. He took out a slender, wrapped package. "This is for you," he told Theoni. "Don't open it until after I'm gone." He bent and kissed her on the cheek, then went back outside into the warm sunshine.

Theoni began to tear the wrapping paper. She opened the package and found a leather-bound book. As she flipped it open, my belt phone rang. I unclipped it and said hello.

"Is this Marîd Audran speaking?" said a hoarse voice.

"It is," I said.

"This is Dr. Sadiq Abd ar-Razzaq." It was the imam who'd signed our death warrants. I was startled.

Theoni jumped to her feet and pointed after the gentleman from Achaea. "Do you know who that *was*?" she cried, tears streaming down her face. "That was my *father*!"

Dalia, Jacques, and I glanced over at Theoni. Things like that happened all the time in the Budayeen. It was nothing to get excited about.

"I would like to discuss how you intend to clear your name," said Abd ar-Razzaq. "I will not stand for the breaking of any Muslim law. I will grant you a hearing tomorrow at two o'clock." He hung up before I could respond.

I slid the sample datalink terminal in the suitcase down to Jacques, and he closed the lid and went on his way. "Well," I told Dalia, "I've talked with everybody I can think of who might be involved in the Khalid Maxwell case. So I've made the first circuit around the village."

She looked at me and cleaned off the counter with a bar rag. She didn't have any idea what I was talking about.

Thirteen

I lay in bed reading another Lutfy Gad novel until it was about three o'clock in the morning. My stomach was upset, there was a loud ringing in my ears, and I realized after a while that I was sweating so much that the bedclothes were soaked. I was in the opening round of a full-fledged anxiety attack.

Well, heroes aren't supposed to go to pieces. Look at al-Qaddani, Gad's unstoppable detective. He never worried himself into helplessness. He never stayed up all night wishing he could run away somewhere and start over again. After a couple of hours of nervous trembling, I decided to get my life back in order, and immediately. I slid out of the drenched bed and crossed my bedroom, where I found my tan plastic pillcase.

It was crammed full of helpful medications, and I had to think for a few seconds about my selection. Tranquilizers, I decided at last. I was trying to end my old habits of recreational drug use, but this was a situation where my favorite pills and caps were legitimately indicated. I went with Paxium, taking twelve of the lavender pills and four of the yellow ones. That should take the edge off my anxiety, I told myself.

I went back to bed, flopped the pillows over, and read another couple of chapters. I waited for the Paxium to hit, and I admit that after half an hour or so, I did feel just the tiniest, most insignificant hint of euphoria. It was laid on top of my mental distress like the sugar frosting on a petit four. Underneath it, I was still eating my guts out with apprehension.

I got up again and padded barefoot to the closet. I opened the pillcase and dug out eight tabs of Sonneine, my favorite painkiller. I wasn't actually in severe pain, but I figured the opiate warmth would blot out the remainder of my anxiety. I swallowed the chalky tablets with a gulp of warm mineral water.

By the time al-Qaddani had been captured by the Israeli villain and received his obligatory once-per-novel beating, I was feeling much better. The anxiety was only an abstract memory, and I was filled with a wonderful confidence that later that day I'd be able to overpower Dr. Sadiq Abd ar-Razzaq with the force of my personality.

I felt so good, in fact, that I wanted to share my joy with someone. Not Kmuzu, however, who would certainly report my late night binge to Friedlander Bey. No, instead I dressed myself quickly and slipped out of my apartment. I went quietly through the dark corridors from the west wing of Papa's palace to the east wing. I stood outside Indihar's door and rapped softly a few times. I didn't want to wake the kids.

I waited a minute, then knocked more loudly. Finally I heard movement, and the door was opened by Senalda, the Valencian maid I'd hired to help Indihar. "Señor Audran," she said sleepily. She rubbed her eyes and glared at me. She wasn't happy about being awakened so early in the morning.

"I'm sorry, Senalda," I said, "but it's urgent that I speak to my wife."

The maid stared at me for a couple of seconds but didn't say anything. She turned and went back into the dark apartment. I waited by the door. In a little while, Indihar came, wrapped in a satin robe. Her expression was grim. "Husband," she said.

I yawned. "I need to talk with you, Indihar. I'm sorry about the hour, but it's very important."

She ran a hand through her hair and nodded. "It better be, Maghrebi. The children will be awake in a couple of hours, and I won't have time to take a nap after that." She stepped aside, allowing me to brush by her, into the parlor.

By now, I felt terrific. I felt invincible. Fifteen minutes before, I decided to go to Indihar and have her say I was brave and true and strong, because I needed to hear that from someone. Now, though, the Sonneine was telling me everything I needed to know, and I only wanted to discuss my misgivings concerning strategy. I knew I could trust Indihar. I wasn't even concerned that she'd be angry with me for getting her out of her nice, warm bed.

I sat down on one of the couches, and waited for her to sit opposite me. She spent a few seconds rubbing her face with her long, delicate fingers. "Indihar," I said, "you're my wife."

She stopped massaging her forehead and glanced up at me. "I told you before," she said through clenched teeth, "I won't jam with you. If you woke me up in the middle of the night in some drunken—"

"No, that's not it at all. I need to get your honest opinion about something."

She stared at me without saying anything. She didn't look mollified.

"You may have noticed," I said, "that lately Papa has been putting more and more responsibility on my shoulders. And that I've had to use some of his methods, even though I personally deplore them."

Indihar shook her head. "I saw the way you sent bin Turki back to Najran on his . . . assignment. It didn't seem to me that you had any problem at all ordering some stranger's death. Not so long ago, you would have been appalled, and you would've left it to Youssef or Tariq to take care of that loose end."

I shrugged. "It was necessary. We have hundreds of friends and associates who depend on us, and we can't let anyone get away with attacking us. If we did, we'd lose our influence and power, and our friends would lose our protection."

"Us. We. You've subconsciously begun to identify with Friedlander Bey. He's won you over completely now, hasn't he? Whatever happened to your outrage?"

I was starting to get depressed, despite the Sonneine. That meant that I needed to take more Sonneine, but I couldn't. Not in front of Indihar. "I'm going to have to find out who actually murdered Khalid Maxwell, and then I'm going to have to see that he's dealt with the same way as that sergeant in Najran."

Indihar smiled without warmth. "You've also adopted a cute way of speaking around the truth. He'll have to be 'dealt with,' instead of 'killed.' It's like you have your conscience on a goddamn daddy, and you just never chip it in."

I stood up and let out a deep breath. "Thanks, Indihar. I'm glad we had this talk. You can go back to sleep now." I turned and left her apartment, closing the door behind me. I felt bad.

I walked silently down the corridor past my mother's apartment. I turned into the gloomy passageway in the main part of the house, and a dark figure slipped from the shadows and came up to me. At first I was frightened—it was always possible that a very clever assassin might defeat the human guards and electronic alarms—but then I saw that it was Youssef, Papa's butler and assistant.

"Good evening, Shaykh Marîd," he said.

"Youssef," I said warily.

"I just happened to be awake, and I heard you moving about. Is there something you need?"

We continued walking toward the west wing. "No, not really, Youssef. Thank you. You just happened to be awake?"

He looked at me solemnly. "I'm a very light sleeper," he said.

"Ah. Well, I just had something I wanted to discuss with my wife."

"And did Umm Jirji satisfy you with her reply?"

I grunted. "Not exactly."

"Well then, maybe I could be of some help."

I started to decline his offer, but then I thought that maybe Youssef was the perfect person to talk to about my feelings. "Indihar mentioned that I've changed quite a bit in the last year or so."

"She is quite correct, Shaykh Marîd."

"She is not altogether happy about what I seem to have become."

Youssef shrugged in the dim light. "I would not expect her to understand," he said. "It is a very complex situation, one that only persons in administrative roles can understand. That is, Friedlander Bey, you, Tariq, and myself. To everyone else, we are monsters."

"I am a monster in my own mind, Youssef," I said sadly. "I want my old liberty back. I don't want to play an administrative role. I want to be young and poor and free and happy."

"That will never happen, my friend, so you must stop teasing your imagination with the possibility. You've been given the honor of caring for many people, and you owe them all your best efforts. That means concentration unbroken by self-doubt."

I shook my head. Youssef wasn't quite grasping my point. "I have a lot of power now," I said slowly. "How can I know if I'm using that power properly? For instance, I dispatched a young man to terminate a ruffian who brutalized Friedlander Bey in Najran. Now, the holy Qur'ân provides for revenge, but only at the same level as the original injury. The sergeant could be severely beaten without feelings of guilt, but to end his life—"

Youssef raised a hand and cut me off. "Ah," he said, smiling, "you misunderstand both The Wise Mention of God and your own position. What you say about revenge is certainly true, for the average man who has only his own life and the lives of his immediate family to worry about. But just as they say that with privilege comes responsibility, the opposite is also true. That is, with increased responsibility comes increased privilege. So we here in this house are above certain plain interpretations of Allah's commands. In order to maintain the peace of the Budayeen and the city, we must often act quickly and surely. If we are brutalized, as you put it, we don't have to wait for a death to occur before we end the threat against us. We maintain the well-being of our friends and associates by prompt action, and we may go on from there secure in the knowledge that we have not transgressed the *intent* of the teachings of the Holy Prophet."

"May the blessings of Allah be on him and peace," I said. I kept my expression studiously blank, but I was howling on the inside. I hadn't heard such a ridiculous piece of sophistry since the days when the old shaykh who lived in a box in our alley in Algiers tried to prove that the entire Earth was flat because the city of Mecca was flat. Which it isn't.

"I'm concerned that you're still showing such reluctance, Shaykh Marîd," said Youssef.

I waved my hand. "It's nothing. I've always dithered a little before doing what had to be done. But you and Friedlander Bey well know that I've always completed my tasks. Is it necessary that I relish them?"

Youssef gave a short laugh. "No, indeed. As a matter of fact, it is good that you don't. If you did, you'd run the risk of ending up like Shaykh Reda."

"Allah forbid," I murmured. We'd come to my door, and I left Youssef to seek out his own bed once again. I went inside, but I didn't feel like going to sleep. My mind was still unsettled. I paused only long enough to take another four Sonneine and a couple of tri-phets for energy. Then I slowly opened my door again, careful not to wake Kmuzu, and peered into the hall. I didn't see Youssef anywhere. I slipped out again, made my way downstairs, and sat behind the wheel of my electric sedan.

I needed a drink with a lot of laughing people around it. I drove myself to the Budayeen, indulging myself in the peculiar and pleasant loneliness you feel so early in the morning, with no one else on the road. Don't talk to me about driving under the influence—I know, it's stupid and I should be caught and made an example of. I just figured that with all the really terrible things hanging over my head, something like a traffic accident wouldn't dare happen to me. That was the artificial confidence of the drugs again.

Anyway, I arrived outside the eastern gate without incident, and parked my car near the cab stand on the Boulevard il-Jameel. My club was closed—had been for an hour or more—and many of the others were likewise dark. But there were plenty of after-hours bars and twenty-four-hour cafés. A lot of the dancers went over to the Brig when they got off work. You'd think that after drinking with customers for eight hours, they'd have had enough, but that wasn't the way it worked. They liked to sit together at the bar, throw back shots of schnapps, and talk about the idiot guys they'd had to talk to all night.

The Brig was a dark, cool bar hard by the southern wall of the Budayeen on Seventh Street. I headed there. In the back of my mind was the faint hope that I'd run into someone. Someone like Yasmin.

It was smoky and loud in the Brig, and they'd covered the lights with blue gels, so everyone looked dead. There wasn't an open stool along the bar, so I sat in a booth against the opposite wall. Kamal ibn ash-Shaalan, the owner, who also worked behind the bar, saw me and came over. He made a couple of feeble swipes at the tabletop with a rag soaked in stale beer. "Where y'at tonight, Marîd?" he said in his hoarse voice.

"Aw right," I said. "Gin and bingara with a little Rose's lime juice in it, okay?"

"You bet. You lookin' for company this evening?"

"I'll find it for myself, Kamal." He shrugged and walked away to make my drink.

Maybe ten seconds later, a drunk pre-op deb sat down across from me. The name she'd chosen for herself was Tansy, but at work everyone was supposed to call her Nafka. Nobody wanted to tell her what "nafka" meant in Yiddish. "Buy me a drink, mister?" she said. "I could come sit beside you and start your day off with a bang."

She didn't remember who I was. She thought I was just any old mark. "Not tonight, honey," I said. "I'm waiting for someone."

She smiled crookedly, her eyelids half-closed. "You'd be surprised what I could accomplish, While-U-Wait."

"No, I don't think I'd be surprised. I'm just not interested. Sorry."

Tansy stood up and wobbled a little. She closed one eye in a slow wink. "I know what *your* problem is, mister." She giggled to herself and headed back to the bar.

Well, no, she didn't know what my problem was. I didn't have much time to think about it, though, because I saw Yasmin stagger out of the ladies' room in the dark recesses of the club. She looked like she'd downed plenty of drinks at work, and then had a few here, too. I stood up and called her name. Her head swung around in slow motion, like an apatosaurus searching for another clump of weeds to munch.

"Whozat?" she said. She lurched toward me.

"It's Marîd."

"Marîd!" She grinned sloppily and dropped into the booth like a sack of onions. She reached under the table and fiddled under my *galle-beya*. "I've missed you, Marîd! You still got that thing under there?"

"Yasmin, listen—"

"I'm real tired tonight, Marîd. Would you take me back to my apartment? I'm kind of drunk."

"I noticed. Look, I really just wanted to talk with you about—"

She got up again and stood beside me, bending down to wrap her arms around my neck. She started tickling my ear with her tongue. "You used to like this, Marîd, remember?"

"I never liked that. You're thinking of someone else."

Yasmin slid her hand down my chest. "C'mon, Marîd, I want to go home. I live back on Fourteenth Street now."

"All right," I said. When Yasmin got drunk and got an idea in her head, there was no way you could talk your way out of doing what she wanted. I got up, put my arm around her shoulders, made sure she had her purse, and half-led, half-dragged her out of the Brig. It took us half an hour to walk the seven blocks back on the Street.

We finally reached her building and I found her keys in her purse. I opened her front door and led her over to her bed. "Thanks, Marîd," she said in a singsong voice. I took her shoes off for her and then turned to go. "Marîd?"

"What is it?" I was getting sleepy again. I wanted to get home and sneak back into my apartment before Youssef or Tariq or Kmuzu found out I was gone, and informed Friedlander Bey.

Yasmin called me again. "Rub my neck a little?"

I sighed. "All right, but just a little." Well, I started rubbing her neck, and while I was doing that she was slipping down her short black skirt. Then she reached up and tried to throw my *gallebeya* over my head. "Yasmin, you're drunk," I said.

"Do it to me, will ya?" she said. "I don't get a hangover that way." It wasn't the most sensual invitation I'd ever had. She kissed me deep and long, and she hadn't lost any speed in that department. And she knew what to do with her hands, too. In a little while, we were jamming hard and hungry. I think she was asleep before I finished. Then I had a weary climax and crashed right beside her.

How do I describe the beginning of the new day? I slept fitfully, half on and half off Yasmin's bare mattress. I dreamed vivid, crazy dreams as the remainders of the opiates and the speed disappeared from my bloodstream. I woke up once about ten o'clock in the morning, a foul taste in my mouth, a dull throbbing behind my forehead. I couldn't remember where I was, and I gazed around Yasmin's apartment, hopeful of finding a clue. Finally, I examined her graceful back, slender waist, and luscious hips. What was I doing in bed with Yasmin? She hated me. Then I recalled the end of the night before. I yawned and turned away from her, and was almost instantly asleep again.

I dreamed that my mother was shouting at me. I dream that a lot. On the surface, my mom and I have patched up all our differences, and the guilts and resentments have been put away forever. The dreams told me that most of that progress had been only cosmetic, and that deep within, I still had awkward, unsettled emotions where my mother was concerned.

My mother's voice rose in both pitch and volume, but I couldn't quite make out what she was mad about this time. I saw her face turn red and ugly, and she shook her fist at me. With her harsh words echoing painfully in my ears, I ducked as she began beating my head and shoulders.

I woke up. It was Yasmin who was screaming, and who was also punching me in my sleep. Yasmin had started out as a rather large and well-built young man, so that even after her sexchange operation, she was still a formidable opponent. In addition, she had the element of surprise on her side.

"Get out of here! Get out of here!" she cried.

I rolled off the mattress onto the cold floor. I glanced at my watch: it was now about noon. I didn't understand what Yasmin's problem was.

"You're slime, Audran!" she shouted. "You're slug vomit, taking advantage of me in the shape I was in!"

Despite all the many times we'd made love in the past, however long we'd actually lived together, I felt embarrassed to be naked in her presence. I dodged out of range of her fists, then stood kind of hunched over, trying to hide my nude vulnerability. "I didn't take advantage of you, Yasmin," I said. The throbbing behind my forehead started up again, but worse this time. "I ran into you a few hours ago at the Brig. You begged me to make sure you got home all right. I was trying to leave when you started begging me to jam you. You climbed all over me. You wouldn't let me leave."

She held her forehead and winced. "I don't remember anything like that at all."

I shrugged, grabbing my underwear and *gallebeya*. "What can I say? I'm not responsible for what you can or can't remember."

"How do I know you didn't bring me home passed out, and then raped me when I was at your mercy?"

I pulled the *gallebeya* over my head. "Yasmin," I said sadly, "don't you know me better than that? Have I ever done anything that would make you think I was capable of rape?"

"You've killed people," she said, but the steam had gone out of her argument.

I balanced on one foot and slipped on a sandal. "I didn't rape you, Yasmin," I said.

She relaxed a little more. "Yeah?" she said. "How was it?"

I tugged on the other sandal. "It was great, Yasmin. We've always been great together. I've missed you."

"Yeah? Really, Marîd?"

I knelt beside the mattress. "Look," I said, staring into her dark eyes, "just because I'm married to Indihar—"

"I won't let you cheat on her with me, Marîd. Indihar and I been friends for a long time."

I closed my eyes and rubbed them. Then I gazed back at Yasmin. "Even Prophet Muhammad—"

"May the blessings of Allah be on him and peace," she murmured.

"Even the Prophet had more than one wife. I'm entitled to four, if I can support them all equally and treat them all with fairness."

Yasmin's eyes grew larger. "What are you telling me, Marîd?"

I shrugged. "I don't know, honey. Indihar and I are married in name only. We're good friends, but I think she resents me a little. And I really meant what I said about missing you."

"Would you really marry me? And what would Indihar say about that? And how—"

I raised a hand. "I've got a lot to work out in my mind," I said. "And we'd all have to get together and talk about this. And Papa might not approve. Anyway, I have an appointment with the imam of the Shimaal Mosque in two hours. I've got to go get cleaned up."

Yasmin nodded, but she stared at me with her head tilted to one side. I made sure I had my keys and everything else I'd come in with— particularly my essential pill case. I went to her front door.

"Marîd?" she called.

I turned and looked at her.

"I wouldn't be just your Number Two wife. I won't be a servant to Indihar and her kids. I'd expect to be treated equally, just like the noble Qur'ân says."

I nodded. "We've got plenty of time," I said. I crossed the room and knelt to kiss her good-bye. It was a soft, lingering kiss, and I was sorry to end it. Then I stood up, sighed, and closed her door behind me. *Yaa Allah*, what had those drugs gotten me into *this* time?

Outside on the street, it was a gray and drizzly morning. It fit my mood perfectly, but that didn't make it any more enjoyable. I had a long walk along the Street from Fourteenth to the eastern gate. I lowered my head and strode along close to the storefronts, hoping no one would recognize me. I wasn't in the mood for a reunion with Saied the Half-Hajj or Jacques or any of my other old pals. Besides, I barely had time to get home and shower and change clothes for my appointment with Abd ar-Razzaq.

Of course, as usual, what I wanted didn't seem to matter to the cosmos. I'd gone only about a block and a half, when a high-pitched voice called out "Al-Amîn! O Great One!"

I shuddered and looked behind me. There was a scrawny boy about fifteen years old, taller than me, dressed in a torn, dirty white shirt and white trousers. His filthy feet looked as if they'd never seen shoes or sandals. He had a purple and white checked *keffiya* knotted around his grimy neck. "Morning of light, O Shaykh," he said happily.

"Right," I said. "How much do you need?" I reached into my pocket and pulled out a roll of bills.

He looked astonished, then glanced around in all directions. "I didn't mean to ask you for money, Shaykh Marîd," he said. "I wanted to tell you something. You're being followed."

"What?" I was honestly startled by the news, and very unhappy. I wondered who'd set the tail on me, Hajjar or Abd ar-Razzaq or Abu Adil.

"It's true, O Shaykh," said the boy. "Let's walk together. On the other side of the Street, about a block behind us, is a fat *kaffir* in a sky-blue *gallebeya*. Don't look for him."

I nodded. "I wonder if he sat outside Yasmin's apartment all night, waiting for me."

The boy laughed. "My friends told me he did."

I was astonished. "How did you—they—know where I was last night?"

"Buy me something to eat, O Father of Generosity?" he asked. It sounded good to me. We turned around and walked back to Kiyoshi's, a better-than-average Japanese cookshop on South Fourteenth Street. I got a good look at the big man who was trying desperately to be inconspicuous. He didn't appear dangerous, but that didn't mean anything.

We sat in a booth, watching the holographic rock band that appeared between us. The cookshop owner also fancied himself a musician, and his band entertained at every table, whether you wanted it to or not. The boy and I split a double order of hibachi chicken. It seemed safe enough to talk.

"You are our protector, *yaa Amîn*," said the boy between greedy gulps of food. "Whenever you come to the Budayeen, we watch over you from the moment you step through the eastern gate. We have a system of signals, so we always know where you are. If you needed our help, we'd be at your side in a moment."

I laughed. "I knew nothing of this," I said.

"You've been good to us, with your shelters and soup kitchens. So this morning, my friends sat up while you visited that sexchange,

Yasmin. They noticed the *kaffir* doing the same. When I awoke this morning, they told me all the news. Listen: whenever you hear this tune"—and he whistled a familiar children's song well known to all the youngsters in the city "—you'll know that we're there, and that we're telling you to be careful. You may be being followed, or possibly the police are looking for you. When you hear that tune, it would be good to become invisible for a while."

I sat back, taking in his words. So I had an army of children guarding my back. It made me feel great. "I am unable to express my thanks," I said.

The boy spread his hands. "There is no need," he said. "We wish we could do more. Now my family, of course, is in greater want than some of the others, and that means that I can't devote as much time to—"

I understood immediately. I took out my roll again and dealt out a hundred kiam. I shoved the money across the table. "Here," I said. "For the ease of your blessed parents."

The boy picked up the hundred kiam and stared at it in wonder. "You are even nobler than the stories say," he murmured. He quickly tucked the money away out of sight.

Well, I didn't feel noble. I gave the kid a few bucks out of self-interest, and a hundred kiam doesn't hurt my bankroll very much. "Here," I said, standing up, "you finish the food. I've got to get going. I'll keep an eye out. What's your name?"

He looked me directly in the eye. "I am Ghazi, O Shaykh. When you hear two quick low notes followed by a long high note, that means that one boy is passing responsibility for you to the next boy. Be careful, Al-Amîn. We in the Budayeen depend on you."

I put my hand on his long, dirty hair. "Don't worry, Ghazi. I'm too selfish to die. There are too many beautiful things in God's world that I haven't yet experienced. I have a few important things holding me here."

"Like making money, drinking, playing cards, and Yasmin?" he asked, grinning.

"Hey," I said, feigning shock, "you know too much about me!"

"Oh," said the boy airily, "everyone in the Budayeen knows all about that."

"Terrific," I muttered. I walked by the fat black man, who'd been lingering across the way from the Japanese cookshop, and headed east along the Street. Behind me and high overhead I heard someone whistle the children's tune. The whole time I walked with my shoulders slightly hunched, as if at any moment I might be struck from behind by the butt of a pistol. Nevertheless, I made it all the way to the other end of the walled quarter without being jumped. I got into my car, and I saw my tail dive for a taxi. I didn't care if he followed me further; I was just going home.

I didn't want to run into anyone as I slunk upstairs to my apartment, but once again luck was against me. First Youssef and then Tariq crossed my path. Neither of them said anything to me, but their expressions were grave and disapproving. I felt like the useless, drunken sot of a son wasting the resources of a great family. When I got to my rooms, Kmuzu was waiting in the doorway. "The master of the house is very angry, *yaa Sidi*," he said.

I nodded. I expected as much. "What did you tell him?"

"I said that you'd risen early and gone out. I told the master of the house that I didn't know where you'd gone."

I sighed with relief. "Well, if you speak to Papa again, tell him that I went out with Jacques, to see how well he was coming along with the datalink project."

"That would be a lie, *yaa Sidi*. I know where you've been."

I wondered how he knew. Maybe the fat black man who'd followed me wasn't working for the bad guys, after all. "Can't you bring yourself to tell one little falsehood, Kmuzu? For my sake?"

He gave me a stern look. "I am a Christian, *yaa Sidi*," was all he said.

"Thanks anyway," I said, and pushed past him to the bathroom. I took a long, hot shower, letting the hard spray pound my aching back and shoulders. I washed my hair, shaved, and trimmed my beard. I was starting to feel better, even though I'd had only a few hours of sleep. I stared into my closet for a long while, deciding what to wear to my appointment with the imam. Feeling a little perverse, I chose a conservative blue business suit. I almost never wore Western-style clothing anymore, and even when I did, I steered away from business suits. I had to have Kmuzu tie my necktie; not only did I not know how, I obstinately refused to learn.

"Would you care for something to eat, *yaa Sidi?*" he asked.

I glanced at my watch. "Thanks, Kmuzu, but I barely have time to get there. Would you be so kind as to drive me?"

"Of course, *yaa Sidi*."

For some reason, I felt no anxiety at all about facing Dr. Sadiq Abd ar-Razzaq, the imam of the greatest mosque in the city and one of our leading religious thinkers. That was good, because it meant that I didn't feel the need to pop a few tabs and caps in preparation for the meeting. Sober, and with my wits about me, I might come away from the appointment with my head still attached to my shoulders.

Kmuzu double-parked the car on the street outside the mosque's western wall, and I hurried through the rain and up the well-worn granite steps. I slipped off my shoes and made my way deeper through the shadowy spaces and chambers that formed an asymmetric network beneath high, vaulted ceilings. In some of the columned areas, robed teachers taught religious lessons to groups of serious-faced boys. In others, individuals or small congregations prayed. I followed a long, cool colonnade to the rear of the mosque, where the imam had his offices.

I spoke first to a secretary, who told me that Dr. Abd ar-Razzaq was running a bit late that afternoon. He invited me to sit in a small waiting room to the side. There was one window looking out over the inner courtyard, but the glass was so grimy that I could barely see through it. The waiting room reminded me of the visits I'd made to Friedlander Bey, in the time before I came to live in his mansion. I'd always had to cool my heels in a waiting room very much like this one. I wondered if it was a common psychological ploy of the rich and powerful.

After about half an hour, the secretary opened the door and said the imam would see me now. I stood up, took a deep breath, pressed my suit jacket with my hands and followed the secretary. He held open a heavy, wonderfully carved wooden door, and I went in.

Dr. Sadiq Abd ar-Razzaq had placed his large desk in the darkest corner of the room, and as he sat in his padded leather chair, I could barely make out his features. He had a green-shaded lamp providing light on the desk, but when I took the seat he indicated, his face sank once again into the indistinguishable shadows.

I waited for him to speak first. I squirmed a little in the armchair, turning my head a little from side to side, seeing only shelves of books reaching up out of sight toward the ceiling. There was a peculiar odor in the room, compounded of old, yellowing paper, cigar smoke, and pine-scented cleaning solutions.

He sat observing me for some time. Then he leaned forward, bringing the lower part of his face into the light from the lamp. "Monsieur Audran," he said in an old, cracked voice.

"Yes, O Wise One."

"You dispute the evidence that has been gathered, evidence that clearly proves you and Friedlander Bey murdered Officer Khalid Maxwell." He tapped a blue cardboard folder.

"Yes, I dispute it, O Wise One. I never even met the murdered patrolman. Neither I nor Friedlander Bey have any connection to this case."

The imam sighed and leaned back out of the light. "There is a strong case against you, you must know that. We have an eyewitness who has come forward."

I hadn't heard that before. "Yes? Who is this eyewitness, and how do you know he's reliable?"

"Because, Monsieur Audran, the witness is a lieutenant of police. Lieutenant Hajjar, as a matter of fact."

"Son of an ass!" I cried. Then I caught myself. "I apologize, O Wise One."

He waved a hand in dismissal. "It comes down to this: your word against that of a high-ranking police official. I must make my judgments according to Islamic law, according to proper civil procedure, and using my somewhat limited faculties to sort truth from lies. I must warn you that unless you can provide conclusive proof of your innocence, the case will no doubt be judged against you."

"So I understand, Imam Abd ar-Razzaq. We have avenues of investigation yet to explore. We're hopeful of presenting sufficient evidence to change your mind."

The old man coughed hoarsely a few times. "For your sakes, I hope you do. But be assured that my primary motive will be to see that justice is done."

"Yes, O Wise One."

"To that end, I wish to know what your immediate plans are, as far as investigating this sad event."

This was it. If the imam was too shocked by my intention, he could very well veto it, and then I'd be up the proverbial dune without a sunshade. "O Wise One," I began slowly, "it has come to our attention that no proper autopsy was performed on the corpse of Khalid Maxwell. I wish your permission to exhume the body, and have a thorough study done by the city's coroner."

I could not see the man's expression, but I could hear his sharp intake of breath. "You know that it is a commandment from Allah that burial follow death immediately."

I nodded.

"And exhumation is permitted only in the most extreme and urgent situations."

I shrugged. "May I remind you, O Wise One, that my life and the life of Friedlander Bey may depend on the results of an autopsy. And I'm sure that Shaykh Mahali would agree, even if you don't."

The imam slammed his wrinkled hand down on the desk. "Watch your words, boy!" he whispered. "You threaten to go over my head on this matter? Well, there is no need. I will grant permission for the exhumation. But in return, I will say that your proof must be gathered in two weeks, not the month you were given previously. The people of the city cannot tolerate a longer delay for justice to be done." He bent over his desk and found a clean sheet of paper. I watched him write out a short paragraph and sign it.

Abd ar-Razzaq was making it almost impossible for us to clear our names. Two weeks! I didn't like that at all. We could have used twelve. I merely stood, bowed my head slightly, and said, "Then if you will excuse me, O Wise One, I will go directly to the coroner's office in the Budayeen. I do not wish to take up any more of your time."

I could not see him, and he said nothing more to me. He just handed me the sheet of paper. I glanced at it; it was an official order for Khalid Maxwell's autopsy, to be performed within the next two weeks.

I stood there in his darkened office for a few seconds, feeling more and more uncomfortable. Finally, I thought to myself, "Fuck him," and turned around. I hurried back through the sprawling mosque, regained my shoes, and got back in the car behind Kmuzu.

"Do you wish to go home now, *yaa Sidi?*" he asked.

"No," I said. "I need to go to the Budayeen."

He nodded and started the car. I sat back in the seat and thought about what I'd learned. Hajjar was claiming to be an eyewitness, huh? Well, I suspected I could shake his testimony. All in all, I wasn't feeling too bad. I was even congratulating myself for the way I'd handled myself with Abd ar-Razzaq.

Then I got two phone calls that tracked mud across my nice, fresh mood.

The first one was about money. My phone rang and I unclipped it. "Hello," I said.

"Mr. Marîd Audran? This is Kirk Adwan from the Bank of the Dunes."

That's the bank where I kept my own accounts. "Yes?" I said warily.

"We have a check here made out to a Farouk Hussein in the amount of twenty-four hundred kiam. It has your endorsement on the back, as well as Mr. Hussein's in what appears to be your handwriting."

Uh huh. The check that poor Fuad had given to Jacques. Jacques had waited for the check to clear, then he'd withdrawn the twenty-four hundred kiam and given it to Fuad.

"Yes?" I said.

"Mr. Audran, Mr. Hussein has reported that check as stolen. Now, we're not eager to prosecute, but unless you can cover the twenty-four hundred kiam by five o'clock tomorrow, we'll be forced to call the police on this matter. You can visit any of our branches for your convenience."

"Uh, just a minute—" Too late. Adwan had hung up.

I closed my eyes and cursed silently. What was this, some kind of sting? Fuad was too dumb to pull off anything this complicated. Was Jacques in it, too? I didn't care. I was going to get to the bottom of it, and whoever was responsible was going to be sorry. He'd better get used to breathing fine yellow sand.

I was furious. The situation even had me muttering to myself. Maybe an hour passed. Kmuzu and I were getting something to eat at the Café Solace when the phone rang again. "Yeah?" I said impatiently.

"Yeah, yourself, Audran." It was Lieutenant Hajjar, the expert eyewitness himself.

"I got something I need to go over with you, Hajjar," I said gruffly.

"Take your turn, *noraf*. Tell me, didn't you have an appointment to see Imam Sadiq Abd ar-Razzaq this afternoon?"

My eyes narrowed. "How did you know that?"

Hajjar snorted. "I know lots. Anyway, I was wondering if you could tell me how, less than an hour after your visit, the next time his secretary went in to see him, the holy man ended up dead, sprawled all over his floor with half a dozen poisoned needle-gun flechettes in his chest?"

I just stared at Kmuzu's face.

"Hello?" said Hajjar sweetly. "Mr. Suspect? Would you mind dropping by the office here at your earliest convenience?"

I just clipped the phone back on my belt. Now that I had only two weeks instead of a month to establish our innocence, I had more trouble to take care of than ever. I reached into my suit jacket for my pillcase—after all, this was another one of those moments when illicit drugs were definitely indicated—but I had left it behind in my *gallebeya*.

I asked myself, *What would Shaykh Hassanein do in a situation like this?* Unfortunately, the only answer was *Hightail it back into the untrackable wastes of the Rub al-Khali.*

Say, maybe that wasn't such a bad idea. . . .

fourteen

i took care of both the major problems that very afternoon, which is further proof of how much I've matured. In the olden days, I would've hidden in my bedroom, deep within a fog of Sonneine, and put off thinking about my troubles for a day or two, until the matters became critical. I'd since learned that it was much easier to deal with hassles while they're still in the yellow-alert stage.

I had to decide, first of all, which crisis was the more pressing. Was it more important to save my life, or my credit rating? Well, I've always been on good terms with my banker—especially since I'd become Papa's junior executive, and the beneficiary of frequent fat envelopes stuffed with money. I supposed that the Bank of the Dunes could wait an hour or two, but that Lieutenant Hajjar might not have the same patience.

It was still raining as Kmuzu drove me to the police station on Walid al-Akbar Street. As usual, I had to pass through a crowd of dirty-faced young boys, all of whom were pressing against me and loudly clamoring for *baksheesh*. I wondered why the kids hung out here at the copshop, instead of, say, the Hotel Palazzo di Marco Aurelio, where the rich tourists were. Maybe they thought people going in and out of the police station had other things on their minds, and might be more generous. I don't know; I just flung a few kiam down the block, and they all chased after the money. As I climbed the stairs, I heard one boy whistle the familiar children's tune.

I found my way upstairs to Lieutenant Hajjar's glassed-in office in the middle of the detective division. He was on the phone, so I just let myself in and sat in an uncomfortable wooden chair beside his desk. I picked up a stack of Hajjar's mail and began sorting through it, until he grabbed it back with an angry scowl. Then he barked a few words into the phone and slammed it down. "Audran," he said in a loud, greedy voice.

"Lieutenant," I said. "What's happening?"

He stood up and paced a little. "I know you're gonna get shortened by one head-length even sooner than you thought."

I shrugged. "You mean because Abd ar-Razzaq cut two weeks off the time we had to clear our names."

Hajjar stopped pacing, turned to face me, and let his face widen slowly in an evil grin. "No, you stupid motherfucker," he said, "the whole city's gonna come after you and hang you by your heels for the murder of the holy man. With blazing torches, they'll drag you out of bed and separate you into little piles of internal organs. You and Friedlander Bey both. And it's about time, too."

I closed my eyes and sighed wearily. "I didn't kill the imam, Hajjar."

He sat down again behind his desk. "Let's look at this scientifically. You had an appointment with the imam at two o'clock. The secretary said you went in to see him about quarter past the hour. You were in Abd ar-Razzaq's office a little more than fifteen minutes. There were no more appointments until half past three. When the secretary looked in on the imam at three-thirty, Dr. Abd ar-Razzaq was dead."

"There's a solid hour there when someone else could've gotten by the secretary and killed the son of a bitch," I said calmly.

Hajjar shook his head. "It's an open-and-shut case," he said. "You won't live long enough to find out anything about Khalid Maxwell."

I was starting to get annoyed. Not frightened or worried—just annoyed. "Did you ask the secretary if he left his desk anytime during that hour? Did you ask him if he saw anyone else during that time?"

Hajjar shook his head. "No need," he said. "Open-and-shut case."

I stood up. "What you're telling me is that I have to prove myself innocent of *two* murders now."

"In a hell of a hurry, too. We're not going to release the news about the imam until morning, because the amir wants us to get ready for the riots and demonstrations first. There *are* going to be terrible riots and demonstrations, you know. You're going to get to witness them from the very middle, from inside an iron cage, is my prediction. If Friedlander Bey wants to clear his name as far as Maxwell is concerned, he's gonna have to do it without you. You're gonna be a stiff in a few days, unless you skip town. And believe me, you're gonna have a tough time doing that, 'cause we're watching you every minute."

"I know," I said. "The fat black guy."

Hajjar looked embarrassed. "Well," he said, "he's not one of my best."

I headed for the door. These visits with Hajjar were never very rewarding. "See you later," I called over my shoulder.

"I wouldn't be in your shoes for nothin'. Been waiting a long time for this, Audran. Where you going now?"

I turned and faced him. "Oh, I was planning to drop by the medical examiner's office in the Budayeen. I got permission from the imam to have Khalid Maxwell exhumed."

He turned red and blew up like a balloon. "What?" he cried. "No such thing! Not in my jurisdiction! I won't allow it!"

I smiled. "Life is hard, Lieutenant," I said, letting him look at the official okay I'd gotten from Abd ar-Razzaq. I didn't trust Hajjar enough to let him touch it, though. "This is all I need. If worse comes to worst, I can get Shaykh Mahali to hold your leash if I have to."

"Maxwell? Exhumed? What the hell for?" shouted Hajjar.

"They say a murder victim keeps an imprint of his murderer's face on his retinas, even after death. Ever hear that before? Maybe I'll find out who killed the patrolman. *Inshallah.*"

Hajjar slammed his fist on his desk. "That's just superstition!"

I shrugged. "I don't know. I thought it was worth a peek. See ya." I escaped from the lieutenant's office, leaving him fuming and sucking in air and blowing it out.

I climbed into the car, and Kmuzu turned to look at me. "Are you all right, *yaa Sidi*?" he asked.

"More trouble," I grunted. "There's a branch of the Bank of the Dunes around the corner on the boulevard, about ten blocks down. I need to see someone there."

"Yes, *yaa Sidi.*"

As we made our way through the congested traffic, I wondered if Hajjar really could pin the imam's murder on me. After all, I did have the opportunity, as well as a kind of bent motive. Was that enough to build a legal case? Just the fact that, except for the murderer himself, I was probably the last to see Dr. Sadiq Abd ar-Razzaq alive?

My next thought was sobering. Hajjar didn't *need* to build a tight legal case. Starting tomorrow, there were going to be two hundred thousand anguished Muslims mourning the brutal murder of their religious leader. All somebody had to do was whisper in enough ears that I was responsible, and I'd pay for the crime without ever standing before an Islamic judge. And I wouldn't even be given a chance to speak in my own defense.

I'd stopped caring about the rain. With this latest development of

Hajjar's, I'd even stopped caring about the twenty-four hundred kiam. I stepped into the bank and looked around. There was soft music playing, and the faint fragrance of roses on the air. The lobby of the bank was all glass and stainless steel. To the far right was a row of human tellers, and then a row of automatic teller machines. Across from me were the desks of several bank officers. I went to the receptionist and waited for her to acknowledge my presence.

"Can I help you, sir?" she said in a bored tone of voice.

"I got a call earlier today from a Mr. Kirk Adwan—"

"Mr. Adwan's with a customer right now. Take a seat and he'll be right with you."

"Uh huh," I said. I slouched on a sofa and rested my chin on my chest. I wished again that I had my pillcase with me, or my rack of moddies. It would've been good to escape into somebody else's personality for a while.

Finally, the customer with Adwan got up and left, and I stood and crossed the carpet. Adwan was busy signing papers. "I'll be right with you," he said. "Take a seat."

I sat. I just wanted to get this stupid business over with.

Adwan finished his busywork, looked up blankly, let my face register for a split second, then flashed me his official smile. "Now," he said in a charming voice, "how may I help you?"

"You called me earlier today. My name is Marîd Audran. Some confusion over a twenty-four-hundred-kiam check."

Adwan's smile vanished. "Yes, I remember," he said. His voice was very cold. Mr. Adwan didn't like me, I'm afraid. "Mr. Farouk Hussein reported the cashier's check stolen. When it came through the bank, there was only his name on the front, and yours on the back."

"I didn't steal the check, Mr. Adwan. I didn't deposit it."

He nodded. "Certainly, sir. If you say so. Nevertheless, as I mentioned on the phone, if you're unwilling to repay the money, we'll have to turn this matter over for prosecution. I'm afraid that in the city, this sort of grand theft is punished harshly. Very harshly."

"I fully intend to repay the bank," I said. I reached inside my suit coat and took out my wallet. I had about five thousand kiam in cash with me. I sorted out twenty-four hundred and slid the money across the desk.

Adwan scooped it up, counted it, and excused himself. He got up and went through a door marked No Admittance.

I waited. I wondered what was going to happen next. Would Adwan come back with a troop of armed bank guards? Would he strip me of my ATM and credit cards? Would he lead all the other bank employees in a chorus of public denunciation? I didn't fuckin' care.

When Adwan did return to his desk, he sat down and folded his hands in front of him. "There," he said, "we're glad you chose to take care of this matter promptly."

There was an awkward silence for a moment. "Say," I said, "how do I know that there was ever a stolen check? I mean, you called me up, you told me the check was stolen, I came in here and handed you twenty-four hundred kiam, you got up and disappeared, and when you came back the money was gone. How do I know you just didn't deposit it in your own account?"

He blinked at me for a few seconds. Then he opened a desk drawer, removed a thin file in a cardboard cover, and glanced through it. He looked me straight in the eye and murmured a commcode into his telephone. "Here," he said. "Talk to Hussein yourself."

I waited until the man answered. "Hello?" I said.

"Hello. Who is this?"

"My name is . . . well, never mind. I'm sitting here in a branch of the Bank of the Dunes. Somehow, a check with your name on it ended up in my possession."

"You stole it," said Hussein gruffly.

"I wasn't the one who stole it," I said. "One of my business associates was trying to do a favor for a friend, and asked me to endorse the check and cover it."

"You're not even lying good, mister."

I was getting annoyed again. "Listen, pal," I said in a patient voice, "I've got this friend named Fuad. He said he wanted to buy a van from you, but you sold it to—"

"Fuad?" Hussein said suspiciously. And then he described Fuad il-Manhous from the greasy hair down to the worn-out shoes.

"How do you know him?" I asked, astonished.

"He's my brother-in-law," said Hussein. "Sometimes he stays by me and his sister. I must've left that check laying around, and Fuad thought he could get away with something. I'll break his fuckin' arms, the scrawny bastard."

"Huh," I said, still amazed that Fuad could come up with such a plausible story. It was a better scam than I thought he was capable of. "It looks like he tried to swindle both of us."

"Well, I'm getting my money back from the bank. Did you cover the check?"

I knew what was coming. "Yeah," I said.

Hussein laughed. "Then good luck trying to recover your money from Fuad. He never has two kiam to rub together. If he's blown that twenty-four hundred, you can just sing in the moonlight for it. And he's probably left town already."

"Yeah, you right. I'm glad we got this all sorted out." I hung up the phone. Later, when I'd cleared up all my major troubles, Fuad would have to pay.

Although, in a way, I half-ass admired him for pulling it off. He used my own prejudice against me—me and Jacques both. We trusted him because we thought he was too stupid to pull a fast one. Weeks ago, I'd been taken by Bedu con men, and now by Fuad. I still had plenty to be humble about.

"Sir?" said Adwan.

I gave him back his phone. "All right, I understand it all now," I told him. "Mr. Hussein and I have a mutual friend who tried to play both ends against the middle."

"Yes, sir," said Adwan. "The bank only cared that it was properly repaid."

I stood up. "Fuck the bank," I said. I even toyed with the idea of withdrawing all my money from the Bank of the Dunes. The only thing was, they were just too convenient. I would've liked to have slugged that snotty Kirk Adwan just once, too.

It had been a very long day, and I hadn't gotten much sleep at Yasmin's apartment. I was beginning to run down. As I got into the car again, I told myself that I was going to make one more little visit, and then I was going to sit on the end of the bar in my club and watch naked female-shaped creatures wiggle to the music.

"Home, *yaa Sidi*?" asked Kmuzu.

"No rest for the wicked, my friend," I said, leaning my head back and massaging my temples. "Take me back to the eastern gate of the Budayeen. I need to talk with the medical examiner there, and after that I'm going to sit in Chiriga's for a few hours. I need to relax a little."

"Yes, *yaa Sidi*."

"You're welcome to come with me. You know that Chiri will be glad to see you."

I saw Kmuzu's eyes narrow in the rearview mirror. "I will wait for you in the car," he said sternly. He really didn't like the attention he got from Chiri. Or maybe he *did* like it, and that's what was bothering him.

"I'll be a few hours," I said. "In fact, I'll probably stay until closing."

"Then I will go home. You may call me to get you when you wish."

It only took a few minutes to drive back along the boulevard to the Budayeen. I got out of the car, leaned down, and said good-bye to Kmuzu. I stood in the warm drizzle and watched the cream-colored sedan drive away. To be honest, I was in very little hurry to meet the medical examiner. I have a low tolerance for ghastliness.

And ghastliness was just what I saw when I entered the morgue, which was just inside the gate on the corner of First and the Street. The city operated two morgues; there was one somewhere else to handle the city in general, and there was this office to take care of the Budayeen. The walled quarter generated so many dead bodies that it rated its own cadaver franchise. The only thing I never understood was, why was the morgue at the eastern end of the Budayeen, and the cemetery against the western wall? You'd think it would be more convenient if they were closer together.

I'd been in the morgue a few times in the past. My friends and I called it the Chamber of Horrors, because it bore out every horrible expectation one might have. It was dimly lighted, and there was very poor ventilation. The air was hot and dank and reeked of human wastes, dead bodies, and formaldehyde. The medical examiner's office had twelve vaults in which to store the corpses, but natural death, misadventure, and old-fashioned mayhem delivered that many bodies before noon daily. The later ones waited on the floor, stacked in piles on the broken, grimy tiles.

There was the chief medical examiner and two assistants to try to keep up with this constant, grim traffic. Cleanliness was the next greatest problem, but none of the three officials had time to worry about swabbing the floors. Lieutenant Hajjar occasionally sent jailed prisoners over to work in the morgue, but it wasn't a coveted assignment. Because the builders of the body vaults had neglected to include drains, they had to be mopped out by hand every few days. The vaults were wonderful hatcheries for many varieties of germs and bacteria. The unlucky prisoners often returned to jail with anything from tuberculosis to meningitis, diseases which were eminently preventable elsewhere.

One of the assistants came up to me with a harried look on his face. "What can I do for you?" he asked. "Got a body or something?"

Instinctively, I backed away from him. I was afraid he'd touch me. "I have permission from the imam of the Shimaal Mosque to proceed with the exhumation of a body. It was a murder victim who never received an official autopsy."

"Exhumation, uh huh," said the assistant, beckoning me to follow him. I passed through the tiled room. There was a naked corpse stretched stiff on one of the two metal autopsy tables. It was illuminated by a dirty, cracked skylight overhead, and by a row of flickering fluorescent fixtures.

The formaldehyde was making my eyes burn and my nose drip. I was thankful when I saw that the assistant was leading me toward a solid wooden door at the far end of the examination room.

"In here," he said. "The doc will be with you in a few minutes. He's having lunch."

I wedged myself into the tiny office. It was lined with file cabinets. There was a desk piled high with stacks of folders, files, books, computer bubble plates, and who knew what else. There was a chair opposite it, surrounded by more mounds of papers, books, and boxes. I sat in the chair. There was no room to move it. I felt trapped in this dark warren, but at least it was better than the outer room.

After a while, the medical examiner came in. He glanced at me once over the top of his thick-rimmed spectacles. New eyes are so cheap and easy to get—there are a couple of good eyeshops right in the Budayeen—that you don't see many people with glasses anymore. "I'm Dr. Besharati. You're here about an exhumation?"

"Yes, sir," I said.

He sat down. I could barely see him over the litter on his desk. He picked up a trumpet from the floor and leaned back. "I'll have to clear this through Lieutenant Hajjar's office," he said.

"I've already been to see him. I was given permission by Imam Abd ar-Razzaq to have this posthumous examination performed."

"Then I'll just call the imam," said the medical examiner. He tootled a few notes on his trumpet.

"The imam is dead," I said in a flat voice. "You can call his secretary, though."

"Excuse me?" Dr. Besharati gave me an astonished look.

"He was murdered this afternoon. After I left his office."

"May the blessings of Allah be on him and peace!" he said. Then he murmured for a while. I assumed he was praying. "That's most horrible. It's a terrible thing. Do they have the murderer?"

I shook my head. "No, not yet."

"I hope he's torn to pieces," said Dr. Besharati.

"About Khalid Maxwell's autopsy—" I handed him the written order from the late Dr. Abd ar-Razzaq.

He put his trumpet back on the floor and examined the document. "Yes, of course. What is the reason for your request?"

I filled him in on the entire story. He stared at me with a dazed expression during most of it, but the mention of Friedlander Bey's name snapped him out of it. Papa often has that magical effect on people.

At last, Dr. Besharati stood up and reached across his desk to take my hand. "Please give my regards to Friedlander Bey," he said nervously. "I will see to the exhumation myself. It will be done this very day, *inshallah*. As to the autopsy itself, I will perform it tomorrow morning at seven o'clock. I like to get as much work done before the heat of the afternoon. You understand."

"Yes, of course," I said.

"Do you wish to be present? For the autopsy, I mean?"

I chewed my lip and thought. "How long will it take?"

The medical examiner shrugged. "A couple of hours."

Dr. Besharati's reputation suggested that he was someone Friedlander Bey and I could trust. Still, I intended to let him prove himself. "Then I'll come by about nine o'clock, and you can give me a report. If there's anything you think I ought to see, you can show me then. Otherwise, I don't see the need for me to get in your way."

He came out from around his desk and took my arm, leading me back out into the Chamber of Horrors. "I suppose not," he said.

I hurried ahead of him to the outer waiting room. "I appreciate your taking the time to help me," I said. "Thank you."

He waved a hand. "No, it's nothing. Friedlander Bey has helped me on more than one occasion in the past. Perhaps tomorrow, after we've finished with Officer Maxwell, you'll permit me to give you a tour of my little domain?"

I stared at him. "We'll see," I said at last.

He took out a handkerchief and wiped his nose. "I understand completely. Twenty years I've been here, and I hate it just as much now as when I first saw it." He shook his head.

When I got back outside, I gulped fresh air like a drowning man. I needed a couple of drinks now more than ever.

As I made my way up the Street, I heard shrill whistles around me. I smiled. My guardian angels were on the job. It was early evening, and the clubs and cafés were beginning to fill up. There were quite a few nervous tourists around, all wondering if they'd be taking their lives in their hands if they just sat somewhere and had a beer. They'd probably find out. The hard way.

The night shift had just taken over when I walked into Chiri's. I felt better immediately. Kandy was on stage, dancing energetically to some Sikh propaganda song. That was a trend in music that I wished would hurry up and disappear.

"*Jambo*, Mr. Boss!" called Chiri. She flashed a grin.

"Where you at, sweetheart," I said. I took my seat at the far curve of the bar.

Chiri threw together a White Death and brought it to me. "Ready for another wonderful, exotic, exciting night on the Street?" she said, plopping down a cork coaster and setting my drink on it.

I frowned. "It's never wonderful, it's never exotic," I said. "It's just the same damn boring music and the same faceless customers."

Chiri nodded. "The money always looks the same, too, but that don't make me kick it out of bed."

I looked around the club. My three pals, Jacques, Saied the Half-Hajj, and Mahmoud, were sitting at a table in the front corner, playing cards. This was rare, because the Half-Hajj got no kick from watching the dancers, and Jacques was militantly straight and could barely speak to the debs and sexchanges, and Mahmoud—as far as I knew—had no sexual predilections at all. That's why they spent most of their time at the Café Solace or on the patio at Gargotier's place.

I walked over to welcome them to my humble establishment. "How y'all doin'?" I said, pulling up a chair.

"Just fine," said Mahmoud.

"Say," said Jacques, studying his cards, "what was all that excitement in Frenchy's with that girl Theoni?"

I scratched my head. "You mean when she jumped up and started yelling? Well, the customer she was working on so hard gave her a present, remember? After he left Frenchy's, she opened the package and it turned out to be a baby book. Lots of cute pictures of this adorable baby girl, and a kind of diary of the kid's first few months. Turns out the guy was Theoni's real father. His wife ran off with her when Theoni was only eight months old. Her father's spent a lot of time and money tracking the girl down ever since."

The Half-Hajj shook his head. "Theoni must've been surprised."

"Yeah," I said. "She was embarrassed to have her father see her working in there. He tipped her a hundred kiam and promised to come back soon. Now she knows why he acted so uncomfortable when she was trying to get him excited."

"We're trying to play cards here, Maghrebi," said Mahmoud. He was about as sympathetic as a rusty razor. "Heard you was gonna exhume that dead cop."

I was surprised the news had gotten around already. "How do you feel about it?" I asked.

Mahmoud looked at me steadily for a couple of seconds. "Couldn't care less," he said at last.

"What you guys playing?" I asked.

"Bourré," said Saied. "We're teaching the Christian."

"It's been an expensive lesson so far," said Jacques. Bourré is a quiet, deceptively simple game. I've never played another card game where you could lose so much money so fast. Not even American poker.

I watched for a little while. Evidently, none of the three had any thoughts at all concerning the exhumation. I was glad of that. "Anybody seen Fuad lately?" I asked.

Jacques looked up at me. "Not for a couple days at least. What's the matter?"

"That check was stolen," I said.

"Ha! And you got stuck for it, right? I'm sorry, Marîd. I didn't have any way of knowing."

"Sure, Jacques," I said in a grim voice.

"What you guys talking about?" asked Saied.

Jacques proceeded to tell them the whole story, at great length, with many oratorical devices and changes of voice, exaggerating the truth and making me look like a complete and utter fool. Of course, he minimalized his own participation in the affair.

All three of them broke down in helpless laughter. "You let *Fuad* rip you off?" gasped Mahmoud. "*Fuad?* You're never going to live this down! I gotta tell people about this!"

I didn't say a word. I knew I was going to hear about it for a long time, unless I caught up to Fuad and made him pay for his foolish crime. Now there was nothing to do but get up and go back to my seat at the bar. As I walked away, Jacques said, "You've got a datalink in here now, Marîd. You notice? And you owe me money for all the other ones I've sold so far. A hundred kiam each, you said."

"Come in sometime with the signed delivery orders," I said in a cold voice. I squeezed the slice of lime and drank a little of the White Death.

Chiri leaned toward me across the bar. "You're gonna exhume Khalid Maxwell?" she said.

"Might learn something valuable."

She shook her head. "Sad, though. The family's been through so much already."

"Yeah, right." I swallowed more of the gin and bingara.

"What's this about Fuad?" she asked.

"Never mind. But if you see him, let me know immediately. He just owes me a little money, is all."

Chiri nodded and headed down the bar, where a new customer had sat down. I watched Kandy finish up her last song.

I felt a hand on my shoulder. I turned around and saw Yasmin and Pualani. "How was your day, lover?" said Yasmin.

"All right." I didn't feel like going through it all.

Pualani smiled. "Yasmin says you two are gonna get married next week. Congratulations!"

"What?" I said, astonished. "What's this next week business? I haven't even formally proposed. I just mentioned the possibility. I've got a lot to think about first. I've got a lot of trouble to take care of. And then I have to talk to Indihar, and to Friedlander Bey—"

"Oops," said Pualani. She hurried away.

"Were you lying to me this morning?" asked Yasmin. "Were you just trying to get out of my house without the beating you deserved?"

"No!" I said angrily. "I was just saying that maybe we wouldn't be so bad together. I wasn't ready to set a date or anything."

Yasmin looked hurt. "Well," she said, "while you're dicking around and making up your mind, I've got places to go and people to meet. You understand me? Call me when you take care of all your so-called problems." She walked away, her back very straight, and sat down beside the new customer. She put her hand in his lap. I took another drink.

I sat there for a long time, drinking and chatting with Chiri and with Lily, the pretty sexchange who was always suggesting that we get together. About eleven o'clock, my phone rang. "Hello?" I said.

"Audran? This is Kenneth. You remember me."

"Ah, yes, the apple of Abu Adil's eye, right? Shaykh Reda's little darling. What's up? You having a bachelor party and want me to send over a few boys?"

"I'm ignoring you, Audran. I'm always ignoring you." I was sure that Kenneth hated me with an irrational ferocity.

"What did you call for?" I asked.

"Friday afternoon, the *Jaish* will parade and demonstrate against the gruesome murder of Imam Dr. Sadiq Abd ar-Razzaq. Shaykh Reda wishes you to appear, in uniform, to address the *Jaish* at this historic moment, and also to meet the unit under your command."

"How did you hear about Abd ar-Razzaq?" I asked. "Hajjar said he wasn't gonna tell anybody until tomorrow."

"Shaykh Reda isn't 'anybody.' You should know that."

"Yeah, you right."

Kenneth paused. "Shaykh Reda also wishes me to tell you he's unalterably opposed to the exhumation of Khalid Maxwell. At the risk of sounding threatening, I have to pass along Shaykh Reda's feelings. He said that if you go ahead with the autopsy, you will earn his undying hatred. That is not something to dismiss lightly."

I laughed. "Kenny, listen, aren't we already fierce rivals? Don't we hate each other's guts enough by now? And aren't Friedlander Bey and

Abu Adil already at each other's throats? What's one little autopsy between archenemies?"

"All right, you stupid son of a bitch," said Kenneth shortly. "I did my job, I passed along the messages. Friday, in uniform, in the Boulevard il-Jameel outside the Shimaal Mosque. You better show up." Then he cut the connection. I clipped my phone back on my belt.

That concluded the second trip around the village. I looked at Chiri and held up my glass for a refill. The long night roared on.

fifteen

ī got a good four hours' sleep that night. After the short rest I'd got the night before, I felt exhausted and almost completely worn down. When my sleep daddy woke me at seven-thirty, I swung my feet out of bed and put them down on the carpet. I put my face in my hands and took a few deep breaths. I really didn't want to get up, and I didn't feel like jumping into battle with the forces arrayed against me. I looked at my watch; I had an hour before Kmuzu would drive me to the Budayeen for my appointment with the medical examiner. If I showered, dressed, and breakfasted in five minutes, I could go back to sleep until almost eight-thirty.

I grumbled a few curses and stood up. My back creaked. I don't think I'd ever heard my back creak before. Maybe I was getting too old to stay up all night, drinking and breaking up fights. It was a depressing thought.

I stumbled blearily to the bathroom and turned on the shower. Five minutes later, I realized that I was staring straight up into the hot spray with my eyes wide open. I felt asleep on my feet. I grabbed the soap and lathered my body, then turned slowly and let the stinging water rinse me. I dried myself and dressed in a clean white *gallebeya* with a dark red robe over it. As for breakfast, I had a decision to make. After all, I was going back to the Chamber of Horrors. Maybe food could be put off until later.

Kmuzu gave me his blank look, the one that's supposed to pass for emotionless, but was in fact transparently unfavorable. "You were quite drunk again last night, *yaa Sidi*," he said, as he set a plate of eggs and fried lamb patties in front of me.

"You must be thinking of someone else, Kmuzu," I said. I looked at the food and felt a wave of queasiness. Not lamb, not now.

Kmuzu stood beside my chair and folded his well-muscled arms. "Would you be angry if I made an observation?" he asked.

Nothing that I could say would stop him. "No. Please make your observation."

"You've been lax in your religious duties lately, *yaa Sidi*."

I turned and looked into his handsome, black face. "What the hell do you care? We're not even of the same faith, as you keep reminding me."

"Any religion is better than none."

I laughed. "I'm not so sure. I could name a few—"

"You understand what I mean. Has your self-esteem fallen so low again that you don't feel worthy to pray? That is a fallacy, you know, *yaa Sidi*."

I got up and muttered, "None of your business." I went back into the bedroom, looking for my rack of moddies and daddies. I hadn't touched a bite of the breakfast.

The neuralware wasn't in the bedroom, so I went into the parlor. It wasn't there, either. I finally discovered it hiding under a towel on the desk in my study. I sorted through the small plastic squares. Somewhere along the line, I'd really put together an enviable collection. The ones I wanted, however, were the special ones, ones that I'd had ever since I'd originally had my skull amped. They were the daddies that fit onto my special second implant, the daddies that suppressed unpleasant bodily signals. It was the software that had saved my life in the Rub al-Khali.

I chipped them in and rejoiced at the difference. I was no longer sleepy, no longer hungry. One daddy took care of my growing anxiety, too. "All right, Kmuzu," I said in a cheerful voice. "Let's get on the road. I've got a lot to do today."

"Fine, *yaa Sidi*, but what about all this food?"

I shrugged. "There are people starving in Eritrea. Send it to them."

Kmuzu customarily failed to appreciate that sort of humor, so I just made sure I had my keys and went out into the corridor. I didn't wait for him to follow; I knew he'd be along immediately. I went downstairs and waited for him to start the car and bring it around to the front door. During the ride to the Budayeen we said nothing more to each other.

He let me out by the eastern gate. Once more I had a lot of plans that didn't involve Kmuzu, so I sent him home. I told him I'd call when I needed a ride. Sometimes it's great to have a slave.

When I got to the morgue, I had an unpleasant surprise. Dr. Besharati hadn't even started on the corpse of Khalid Maxwell. He looked up at me as I entered. "Mr. Audran," he said. "Forgive me, I'm running a little late this morning. We had quite a bit of business last night and early today. Unusual for this time of year. Usually get more murders during the hot months."

"Uh huh," I said. I hadn't been in the place two minutes, and already the formaldehyde was irritating my eyes and nose. The suppressor daddies didn't help me at all with something like that.

I watched as the M.E.'s two assistants went to one of the twelve vaults, opened it, and lifted out Maxwell's body. They wrestled it awkwardly to one of the two work tables. The other one was already occupied by a cadaver in an early stage of disassembly.

Dr. Besharati pulled off one pair of rubber gloves and put on another. "Ever watched an autopsy before?" he asked. He seemed to be in great spirits.

"No, sir," I said. I shuddered.

"You can step outside if you get squeamish." He picked up a long black hose and turned on a tap. "This is going to be a special case," he said, as he began playing the water all over Maxwell. "He's been in the ground for several weeks, so we won't be able to get quite as much information as we would with a fresh body."

The stench from the corpse was tremendous, and the water from the hose wasn't making any headway against it. I gagged. One of the assistants looked at me and laughed. "You think it's bad now," he said. "Wait until we open it up."

Dr. Besharati ignored him. "The official police report said that death came about as the result of being shot at close range by a medium-sized static pistol. If the range had been greater, the proper functioning of his nerves and muscles would've been interrupted for a brief time, and he'd have been rendered helpless. Apparently, though, he was shot close up, in the chest. That almost always leads to immediate cardiac arrest." While he was talking, he selected a large scalpel. *"Bismillah,"* he murmured, and made a Y-shaped incision from the shoulder joints to the sternum, and then down to the top of the groin.

I found myself looking away when the assistants lifted the skin and muscle tissue and sliced it free of the skeleton. Then I heard them snapping the rib cage open with some large implement. After they lifted the rib cage out, though, the chest cavity looked like an illustration in an elementary biology book. It wasn't so bad. They were right, though: the stink increased almost unbearably. And it wasn't going to get better any time soon.

Dr. Besharati used the hose to wash down the corpse some more. He looked across at me. "The police report also said that it was your finger on the trigger of that static pistol."

I shook my head fiercely. "I wasn't even—"

He raised a hand. "I have nothing to do with enforcement or punishment here," he said. "Your guilt or innocence hasn't been proved in a court of law. I have no opinion one way or the other. But it seems to me that if you were guilty, you wouldn't be so anxious about the outcome of this autopsy."

I thought about that for a moment. "Are we likely to get much useful information?" I asked.

"Well, as I said, not as much as if he hadn't spent all that time in a box in the ground. For one thing, his blood has putrefied. It's gummy and black now, and almost useless as far as forensic medicine is concerned. But in a way you're lucky he was a poor man. His family didn't have him embalmed. Maybe we'll be able to tell a thing or two about what happened."

He turned his attention back to the table. One assistant was beginning to lift the internal organs, one by one, out of the body cavity. Khalid Maxwell's shriveled eyes stared at me; his hair was stringy and strawlike, without luster or resiliency. His skin, too, had dried in the coffin. I think he'd been in his early thirties when he'd been murdered; now he wore the face of an eighty-year-old man. I experienced a peculiar floating sensation, as if I were only dreaming this.

The other assistant yawned and glanced at me. "Want to listen to some music?" he said. He reached behind himself and flicked on a cheap holosystem. It began to play the same goddamn Sikh propaganda song that Kandy danced to every time she took her turn on stage.

"No, please, thank you," I said. The assistant shrugged and turned the music off.

The other assistant snipped each internal organ loose, measured it, weighed it, and waited for Dr. Besharati to slice off a small piece, which was put in a vial and sealed. The rest of the viscera was just dumped in a growing pile on the table beside the body.

The medical examiner paid very special attention to the heart, however. "I subscribe to a theory," he said in a conversational tone, "that a charge from a static pistol creates a certain, unique pattern of disruption in the heart. Someday when this theory is generally accepted, we'll be able to identify the perpetrator's static pistol, just as a ballistics lab can identify bullets fired by the same projectile pistol." Now he was cutting the heart into narrow slices, to be examined more thoroughly later.

I raised my eyebrows. "What would you see in this heart tissue?"

Dr. Besharati didn't look up. "A particular pattern of exploded and unexploded cells. I'm sure in my own mind that each static pistol leaves its own, unique signature pattern."

"But this isn't accepted as evidence yet?"

"Not yet, but someday soon, I hope. It will make my job—and the police's job, and the legal counselors'—a lot easier."

Dr. Besharati straightened up and moved his shoulders. "My back hurts already," he said, frowning. "All right, I'm ready to do the skull."

An assistant made an incision from ear to ear along the back of the neck, just below the hairline. Then the other assistant pulled Maxwell's scalp grotesquely forward, until it fell down over the corpse's face. The medical examiner selected a small electric saw; when he turned it on, it filled the echoing chamber with a loud burring sound that set my teeth on edge. It got even worse when he began cutting in a circle around the top of the skull.

Dr. Besharati switched off the saw and lifted off the cap of bone, which he examined closely for cracks or other signs of foul play. He examined the brain, first in place, then he carefully lifted it out onto the table. He cut the brain in slices, just as he'd done the heart, and put one piece in another vial.

A few moments later, I realized that the autopsy was finished. I glanced at my watch; ninety minutes had sped by while I was wrapped in a kind of gruesome fascination. Dr. Besharati took his samples and left the Chamber of Horrors through an arched doorway.

I watched the assistants clean up. They took a plastic bag and scooped all the dissected organs into it, including the brain. They closed the bag with a twist-tie, pushed the whole thing into Maxwell's chest cavity, replaced the pieces of rib cage, and began sewing him back up with large, untidy stitches. They set the top of the skull in place, pulled Maxwell's scalp back over it, and stitched it back down at the base of the neck.

It seemed like such a mechanical, unfeeling way for a good man to end his existence. Of course it was mechanical and unfeeling; the three employees of the medical examiner's office would have twenty or more autopsies to perform before suppertime.

"You all right?" asked one of the assistants with a sly grin on his face. "Don't want to throw up or nothing?"

"I'm fine. What happens to him?" I pointed to Maxwell's corpse.

"Back in the box, back in the ground before noon prayers. Don't worry about him. He never felt a thing."

"May the blessings of Allah be on him and peace," I said, and shivered again.

"Yeah," said the assistant, "what you say."

"Mr. Audran?" called Dr. Besharati. I turned around and saw him standing in the doorway. "Come back here and I'll show you what I was talking about."

I followed him into a high-ceilinged workroom. The lighting was a little better, but the air was, if anything, even worse. The walls of the room were entirely taken up with shelves, from floor to ceiling. On each twelve-inch shelf were a couple of thousand white plastic tubs, stacked four high and four deep, filling every available inch of volume. Dr. Besharati saw what I was looking at. "I wish we could get rid of them," he said sadly.

"What are they?" I asked.

"Specimens. By law, we're required to keep all the specimens we take for ten years. Like the heart and brain samples I removed from Maxwell. But because the formaldehyde is a danger, the city won't let us burn them when the time is up. And the city won't permit us to bury them or flush them down the drain because of contamination. We're about out of room here."

I looked around at the roomful of shelves. "What are you going to do?"

He shook his head. "I don't know. Maybe we'll have to start renting a refrigerated warehouse. It's up to the city, and the city's always telling me it doesn't have the money to fix up my office. I think they'd just rather forget that we're even down here."

"I'll mention it to the amir the next time I see him."

"Would you?" he said hopefully. "Anyway, take a look through this." He showed me an old microscope that was probably new when Dr. Besharati was first dreaming of going to medical school.

I peered through the binocular eyepieces. I saw some stained cells. That was all I could see. "What am I looking at?" I asked.

"A bit of Khalid Maxwell's muscle tissue. Do you see the pattern of disruption I mentioned?"

Well, I had no idea what the cells were supposed to look like, so I couldn't judge how they'd been changed by the jolt from the static pistol. "I'm afraid not," I said. "I'll have to take your word for it. But *you* see it, right? If you found another sample that had the same pattern, would you be willing to testify that the same gun had been used?"

"I'd be willing to testify," he said slowly, "but, as I said, it would carry no weight in court."

I looked at him again. "We've got something here," I said thoughtfully. "There's got to be a way to use it."

"Well," said Dr. Besharati, ushering me out through the Chamber of Horrors, to the outer waiting room, "I hope you find a way. I hope you clear your name. I'll give this job special attention, and I ought to have results for you later this evening. If there's anything else I can do, don't hesitate to get in touch with me. I'm here twelve to sixteen hours a day, six days a week."

I glanced back over my shoulder. "Seems like an awful lot of time to spend in these surroundings," I said.

He just shrugged. "Right now, I've got seven murder victims waiting to be examined, in addition to Khalid Maxwell. Even after all these years, I can't help wondering who these poor souls were, what kind of lives they had, what kind of terrible stories led to their ending up on my tables. They're all people to me, Mr. Audran. People. Not stiffs. And they deserve the best that I can do for them. For some of them, I'm the only hope that justice will be done. I'm their last chance."

"Maybe," I said, "here at the very end, their lives can acquire some meaning. Maybe if you help identify the killers, the city can protect other people from them."

"Maybe," he said. He shook his head sadly. "Sometimes justice is the most important thing in the world."

I thanked Dr. Besharati for all his help and left the building. I got the impression that he basically loved his work, and at the same time hated the conditions he had to work in. As I headed out of the Budayeen, it occurred to me that I might end up just like Khalid Maxwell someday, with my guts scattered about on a stainless steel table, with my heart and brain sliced up and stored away in some little white plastic tubs. I was glad I was on my way anywhere, even Hajjar's station house.

It wasn't far: through the eastern gate, across the Boulevard il-Jameel, south a few blocks to the corner of Walid al-Akbar Street. I was forced to take an unplanned detour, though. Papa's long black car was parked against the curb. Tariq was standing on the sidewalk, as if at attention, waiting for me. He wasn't wearing a cheerful expression.

"Friedlander Bey would like to speak with you, Shaykh Marîd," he said. He held the rear door open, and I slid in. I expected Papa to be in the car, too, but I was all alone.

"Why didn't he send Kmuzu for me, Tariq?" I asked.

There was no answer as he slammed the door shut and walked around the car. He got behind the wheel, and we started moving through traffic. Instead of driving toward the house, though, Tariq was taking me through the east side of the city, through unfamiliar neighborhoods.

"Where are we going?" I asked.

No answer. Uh oh.

I sat back in the seat, wondering what was going on. Then I had a horrible, icy suspicion. I'd come this way once before, a long time ago. My suspicions mounted as we turned and twisted through the poverty-ridden eastern outskirts. The suppressor daddy was doing its best to damp out my fear, but my hands began to sweat anyway.

At last Tariq pulled into an asphalt driveway behind a pale green cinderblock motel. I recognized it at once. I recognized the small, hand-lettered MOTEL NO VACANCY sign. Tariq parked the car and opened the door for me. "Room 19," he said.

"I know," I said. "I remember the way."

One of the Stones That Speak was standing in the doorway to Room 19. He looked down at me; there was no expression on his face. I couldn't move the giant man, so I just waited until he decided what he was going to do with me. Finally he grunted and stepped aside, just far enough for me to squeeze by him.

Inside, the room looked the same. It hadn't been decorated since my last visit, when I first came to Friedlander Bey's attention, when I was first made a part of the old man's tangled schemes. The furnishings were worn and shabby, a European-style bed and bureau, a couple of chairs with rips in their upholstering. Papa sat at a folding card table set up in the middle of the room. Beside him stood the other Stone.

"My nephew," said Papa. His expression was grim. There was no love in his eyes.

"*Hamdillah as-salaama, yaa Shaykh,*" I said. "Praise God for your safety." I squinted a little, desperately trying to find an escape route from the room. There was none, of course.

"*Allah yisallimak,*" he replied bluntly. He wished the blessings of Allah on me in a voice as empty of affection as a spent bullet.

As I knew they would, the Stones That Speak moved slowly, one to each side of me. I glanced at them, and then back at Papa. "What have I done, O Shaykh?" I whispered.

I felt the Stones' hands on my shoulders, squeezing, tightening, crushing. Only the pain-blocking daddy kept me from crying out.

Papa stood up behind the table. "I have prayed to Allah that you would change your ways, my nephew," he said. "You have made me unutterably sad." The light glinted off his eyes, and they were like chips of dirty ice. They didn't look sad at all.

"What do you mean?" I asked. I knew what he meant, all right.

The Stones kneaded my shoulders harder. The one on my left— Habib or Labib, I can never tell which—held my arm out from my side. He put one hand on my shoulder and began to turn the arm in its socket.

"He should be suffering more," said Friedlander Bey thoughtfully. "Remove the chips from his implants." The other Stone did as he was told, and yes, I began suffering more. I thought my arm was going to be wrenched loose. I let out one drawn-out groan.

"Do you know why you're here, my nephew?" said Papa, coming closer and standing over me. He put one hand on my cheek, which was now wet with tears. The Stone continued to twist my arm.

"No, O Shaykh," I said. My voice was hoarse. I could only gasp the word out.

"Drugs," said Papa simply. "You've been seen in public too often under the influence of drugs. You know how I feel about that. You've scorned the holy word of Prophet Muhammad, may the blessings of Allah be on him and peace. He prohibits intoxication. *I* prohibit intoxication."

"Yes," I said. It was clear to me that he was angrier at the affront to him than the affront to our blessed religion.

"You had warnings in the past. This is the last. The last of all time. If you do not mend your behavior, my nephew, you will take another ride with Tariq. He won't bring you here, though. He'll drive away from the city. He'll drive far into the desert wastes. He'll return home alone. And this time there will be no hope of your walking back alive. Tariq won't be as careless as Shaykh Reda. All this despite the fact that you're my great-grandson. I have other great-grandsons."

"Yes, O Shaykh," I said softly. I was in severe pain. "Please."

He flicked his eyes at the Stones. They stepped away from me immediately. The agony continued. It would not go away for a long time. I got out of the chair slowly, grimacing.

"Wait yet a moment, my nephew," said Friedlander Bey. "We're not finished here."

"*Yallah,*" I exclaimed.

"Tariq," called Papa. The driver came into the room. "Tariq, give my nephew the weapon."

Tariq came to me and looked into my eyes. Now I thought I could see a touch of sympathy. There had been none before. He took out a needle gun and laid it in my hand.

"What is this gun, O Shaykh?" I asked.

Papa's brow furrowed. "That, my nephew, is the weapon that killed the imam, Dr. Sadiq Abd ar-Razzaq. With it, you should be able to discover the identity of the murderer."

I stared at the needle gun as if it were some unearthly alien artifact. "How—"

"I have no more answers for you."

I stood up straighter and looked directly at the white-haired old man. "How did you get this gun?"

Papa waved a hand. It evidently wasn't important enough for me to know the answer to that. All I had to do was find out who owned it. I knew then that this interview was over. Friedlander Bey had come to the end of his patience, with me, with the way I was handling the investigation.

I realized suddenly that he could well be lying—the needle gun might not actually have been the murder weapon. Yet in the vast, complicated web of intrigues that surrounded him and me and Shaykh Reda, perhaps that was irrelevant. Perhaps the only important thing was that the gun had been so designated.

Tariq helped me outside to the car. I maneuvered myself slowly into the backseat, holding the needle gun close to my chest. Just before he slammed the door, Tariq reached in and handed me the suppressor daddies. I looked at him, but I couldn't find anything to say. I reached up and chipped them in gratefully.

"Where shall I drive you, Shaykh Marîd?" said Tariq, as he got behind the wheel and started the engine.

I had a short list of three choices. First, I wanted to go home, climb back in bed, and take a few medicinal Sonneine until my tormented arm and shoulders felt better. I knew, however, that Kmuzu would never permit it. Failing that, I preferred to go to Chiri's and knock back a few White Deaths. My watch told me that the day shift hadn't even arrived yet. In third place, but the winner by default, was the police station. I had an important clue to check out.

"Take me to Walid al-Akbar Street, Tariq," I said. He nodded. It was a long, bumpy ride back to the more familiar districts of the city. I sat with my head tilted back, my eyes closed, listening to the gray noise in my head from the suppressors. I felt nothing. My discomfort and my emotions had been planed off electronically. I could have been in a restless, dreamless sleep; I didn't even think about what I'd do when I got to my destination.

Tariq interrupted my respite. "We're here," he said. He stopped the car, jumped out, and opened my door. I climbed out quickly; the pain suppressor made it easy.

"Shall I wait for you here, Shaykh Marîd?"

"Yes," I said. "I won't be long. Oh, by the way, do you have some paper and something to write with? I don't want to take this needle gun in there. I need to write down the serial number, though."

Tariq searched his pockets and came up with what I needed. I scribbled the number down on the back of some stranger's business card and put it in the pocket of my *gallebeya*. Then I hurried up the stairs.

I didn't want to run into Lieutenant Hajjar. I went straight to the computer room. This time, the female sergeant on duty only nodded to me. I guess I was getting to be a familiar fixture around there. I sat down at one of the streaked and smudged data decks and logged on. When the computer asked me what I wanted, I murmured, "Weapons trace." I passed through several menus of choices, and finally the computer asked me for the serial number of the weapon in question. I took out the business card and read off the combination of letters and digits.

The computer mulled it over for a few seconds, then its screen filled with enlightening information. The needle gun was registered to my pal Lieutenant Hajjar himself. I sat back and stared at the computer. Hajjar? Why would Hajjar murder the imam?

Because Hajjar was Shaykh Reda Abu Adil's tame cop. And Shaykh Reda thought he owned Abd ar-Razzaq, too. But the imam had made a dangerous mistake—he'd permitted me to proceed with the exhumation of Khalid Maxwell, against Abu Adil's strongest wishes. Abd ar-Razzaq had apparently had a few shreds of integrity left, a tarnished loyalty to truth and justice, and Abu Adil had ordered his death because of it. Shaykh Reda was watching helplessly as his plan to get rid of Friedlander Bey and myself slowly unraveled. Now, to save his own ass, he had to make sure that he wasn't connected in any way to the death of Khalid Maxwell.

There was more data on the computer screen. I learned next that the needle gun hadn't been stolen, that it had been properly registered by Hajjar three years ago. The file listed Hajjar's residence, but I knew for a fact that it was long out of date. More interesting, however, was that the file included Hajjar's complete rap sheet, detailing every misstep and misdemeanor he'd committed since coming to the city. There was an extensive recitation of all the charges that had been brought against him, including those for drug dealing, blackmail, and extortion on which he'd never actually been convicted.

I laughed, because Hajjar had worked so carefully to erase all this information from his entry in the personnel files and from the city's criminal information database. He'd forgotten about this entry, and maybe someday it would help to hang the stupid son of a bitch.

I had just cleared the screen when a voice spoke in Hajjar's Jordanian accent. "How much more time you got before the axman takes you, Maghrebi? You keepin' track?"

I swiveled the chair around and smiled at him. "Everything's falling into place. I don't think we've got anything to worry about."

Hajjar bent toward me and sucked his teeth. "No? What did you do, forge a signed confession? Who you pinning the rap on? Your mama?"

"Got everything I need right out of your computer. I want to thank you for letting me use it. You've been a good sport, Hajjar."

"The hell you talkin' about?"

I shrugged. "I learned a lot from Maxwell's autopsy, but it wasn't conclusive."

The lieutenant grunted. "Tried to warn you."

"So I came here and started poking around. I accessed the city's police procedure libraries and found a very interesting article. It seems there's a new technique to identify the killers of victims done by static pistols. You know anything about that?"

"Nah. You can't trace back a static pistol. It don't leave evidence. No bullets or flechettes or nothing."

I figured a couple more lies in a good cause couldn't hurt. "This article said every static pistol leaves its individual trace in the cells of the victim's body. You mean you never read that? You're not keeping up with your homework, Hajjar."

His smile vanished, replaced by a very worried expression. "You making all this up?"

I laughed. "What do I know about this stuff? How could I make it up? I told you, I just read it in your own library. Now I'm gonna have to go to Shaykh Mahali and ask to have Maxwell exhumed again. The M.E. didn't look for those static pistol traces. I don't think he knew about 'em, either."

Hajjar's face turned pale. He reached out and grabbed the material of my *gallebeya* below my throat. "You do that," he growled, "and every good Muslim in the city will tear you to pieces. I'm warning you. Let Maxwell alone. You had your chance. If you don't have the evidence by now, you're just out of luck."

I grabbed his wrist and twisted it, and he let go of me. "Forget it," I said. "You get on the wire and tell Abu Adil what I said. I'm only one step away from clearing my name and putting somebody else's head on the block."

Hajjar reached back and slapped me hard across the face. "You've gone too far now, Audran," he said. He looked terrified. "Get out of here and don't come back. Not until you're ready to confess to both murders."

I stood up and pushed him backward a step. "Yeah, you right, Hajjar," I said. Feeling better than I had in days, I left the computer room and ran down the stairs to where Tariq was waiting for me.

I had him drive me back to the Budayeen. I'd gotten a lot done that morning, but it was lunchtime now and I felt I'd earned myself some food and a little relaxation. Just inside the eastern gate, on First Street across from the morgue, was a restaurant called Meloul's. Meloul was a Maghrebi like me, and he owned another cookshop not far from the police station. It was a favorite of the cops, and he'd done so well that he'd opened a second location in the Budayeen, managed by his brother-in-law.

I took a seat at a small table near the rear of the restaurant, with my back to the kitchen so I could see who came in the door. Meloul's brother-in-law came over, smiling, and handed me a menu. He was a short, heavyset man with a huge hooked nose, dark Berber skin, and a bald head except for thin fringes of black hair over each ear. "My name is Sliman. How do you do today?" he asked.

"Fine," I said. "I've eaten at Meloul's place. I enjoyed the food very much."

"I'm happy to hear it," said Sliman. "Here I've added some dishes from all over North Africa and the Middle East. I hope you will be pleased."

I studied the menu for a little while and ordered a bowl of cold yogurt and cucumber soup, followed by broiled skewered chicken. While I waited, Sliman brought me a glass of sweet mint tea.

The food came quickly, and it was plentiful and good. I ate slowly, savoring every mouthful. At the same time, I was waiting for a phone call. I was waiting for Kenneth to tell me that if I went ahead with the phony second exhumation, Shaykh Reda would condemn me to all the agonies of Hell.

I finished my meal, paid my bill, and left Sliman a hefty tip, and went back outside. Immediately, I heard a boy whistling the child's tune. I was being watched. After the meal, and with the suppressor daddies still chipped in, I didn't really care. I could take care of myself. I thought I'd demonstrated that time and time again. I started walking up the Street.

A second boy began whistling along with the first. I thought I heard a hint of urgency in their signal. I stopped, suddenly wary, and looked around. From the corner of my eye I caught a blur of movement, and when I looked, I saw Hajjar running toward me, as fast as his legs could carry him.

He raised his hand. There was a static pistol in it. He fired, but he didn't hit me squarely. Still, there was a horrible moment of disorientation, a flush of heat through my body, and then I collapsed on the sidewalk, twitching and quivering spasmodically. I couldn't get my body to respond to my wishes. I couldn't control my muscles.

Beyond me, one of the boys also fell to the ground. He didn't move at all.

sixteen

they took out the suppressor daddies and put me to bed, and I was unaware of anything else for about twenty-four hours. When I began to gather my scattered wits the next day, I was still trembling and unable even to grasp a glass of water. Kmuzu tended me constantly, sitting in a chair beside my bed and filling me in on what had happened.

"Did you get a good look at whoever shot you, *yaa Sidi?*" he asked.

"Whoever shot me?" I said in astonishment. "It was Hajjar, that's who. I saw him plain as day. Didn't anyone else?"

Kmuzu's brow furrowed. "No one would come forward with an identification. There was apparently only one witness willing to speak, and that was one of the two boys who were trying to warn you. He gave a sketchy description that is completely without value, as far as identifying the killer."

"Killer? Then the other boy—"

"Is dead, *yaa Sidi.*"

I nodded, greatly saddened. I let my head fall back on the pillows, and I closed my eyes. I had a lot to think about. I wondered if the murdered boy had been Ghazi; I hoped not.

A few minutes later, I had another idea. "Have there been any calls for me, Kmuzu?" I asked. "Especially calls from Shaykh Reda or his peg boy, Kenneth."

Kmuzu shook his head. "There've been calls from Chiriga and Yasmin. Your friends Saied and Jacques even came to the house, but you were in no condition to receive them. There were no calls from Shaykh Reda."

That was deeply meaningful. I'd fed Hajjar the lie about a second exhumation, and he'd reacted violently, even running after me to stop my investigation with a pop from a static gun. I suppose he thought he could make it look as if I'd just had a heart attack right there on the sidewalk in the Budayeen. The trouble with Hajjar was, he just wasn't as hot as he thought he was. He couldn't bring it off.

I'm sure he passed along my plans to his boss, Shaykh Reda; but this time, there was no warning call from Kenneth. Maybe Abu Adil knew I was only bluffing. Maybe he figured that there couldn't be anymore useful information to be gained by examining Khalid Maxwell's corpse again. Maybe he was just so confident that he didn't care.

This amounted to the third trip around the village, and this time there was only one interested party: Hajjar. I was certain in my heart that he was guilty of both murders. It came as no surprise. He'd killed Khalid Maxwell under orders from Abu Adil, and tried to pin the murder on me; he'd assassinated Dr. Sadiq Abd ar-Razzaq; and he'd wiped out an innocent boy, probably unintentionally. The problem was, as well as I knew the truth, I still didn't have anything I could take into court and wave under his nose.

I couldn't even hold a book, so I watched the holoset all afternoon. There was coverage of the slain imam's funeral, which had been held the day before, after he lay in state for twenty-four hours. Hajjar had been right; there were riots. The streets around the Shimaal Mosque were choked with hundreds of thousands of mourners, day and night. Some of them got a little carried away, and stood outside the mosque, chanting and slashing their own arms and scalps with razors. The crowds surged in one direction and then another, and scores of people were killed, either smothered or trampled.

There were constant, shrill outcries for the murderer to be brought to justice. I waited to see if Hajjar had given my name to the newsmen, but the lieutenant was helpless to fulfill his threat. He didn't even have a murder weapon to connect a suspect to the crime. All he had was some extremely thin circumstantial evidence. I was safe from him, at least for a while.

When I tired of watching the coverage, I turned it off and watched a performance of the mid-sixteenth century A.H. opera, *The Execution of Rushdie*. It did nothing to cheer me up.

My inspiration came just as Kmuzu brought in a tray of chicken and vegetable couscous and prepared to feed me. "I think I've got him now," I said. "Kmuzu, would you please ask Info for the medical examiner's office number, and hold the phone up to my ear for me?"

"Certainly, *yaa Sidi*." He got the number and murmured it into the receiver. He held the phone so that I could hear and speak into it.

"*Marhaba*," said a voice on the other end. It was one of the assistants.

"God be with you," I said. "This is Marîd Audran. I was the one who ordered the autopsy on Khalid Maxwell a couple of days ago."

"Yes, Mr. Audran. When you didn't come back, we mailed the results to you. Is there anything else we can do?"

"Yes, there is." My heart started to beat faster. "I was slightly affected by a pulse from a static pistol in the Budayeen—"

"Yes, we heard about that. A young boy was killed in the same attack."

"Exactly. That's what I want to talk to you about. Was an autopsy done on the boy?"

"Yes."

"Now, listen. This is very important. Would you ask Dr. Besharati to compare the cell rupture pattern in the boy's heart with that of Khalid Maxwell? I think there might be a match."

"Hmm. That is interesting. But, you know, even if there is, it won't do you any good. Not in any legal sense. You can't—"

"I know all about that. I just want to find out if my suspicion is correct. Could you ask him to check on that soon? I'm not exaggerating when I say it's a life-and-death matter."

"All right, Mr. Audran. You'll probably be hearing from him later today."

"I am quite unable to express my thanks," I said fervently.

"Yeah," said the assistant. "What you say." He hung up.

Kmuzu put down the telephone. "Excellent reasoning, *yaa Sidi*," he said. He almost smiled.

"Well, we haven't learned anything yet. We'll have to wait for the doctor's call."

I took a short nap, and was awakened by Kmuzu's hand on my shoulder. "You have a visitor," he told me.

I turned my head, realizing that I was beginning to get some control back over my muscles. There were footsteps in the parlor, and then my young Bedu friend, bin Turki, entered the bedroom. He sat down in the bed beside the chair. "*As-salaam alaykum, yaa Shaykh*," he said seriously.

I was overjoyed to see him. "*Wa alaykum as-salaam*," I said, smiling. "When did you get back?"

"Less than an hour ago. I came here directly from the airfield. What has happened to you? Are you going to get better?"

"Someone took a shot at me, but Allah was on my side this time. My attacker will have to do better than that next time."

"Let's pray there is no next time, O Shaykh," said bin Turki.

I just spread my hands. There would be a next time, almost certainly. If not Hajjar, then someone else. "Now, tell me, how was your journey?"

Bin Turki pursed his lips. "Successful." He took something out of his pocket and set it on the blanket by my hand. I cupped it in my curled fingers and brought it closer to get a better look at it. It was a plastic name tag that read *Sgt. al-Bishah.* That was the name of the bastard in Najran who'd beaten both Friedlander Bey and me.

I'd put it out of my mind, but yes, I'd ordered a murder. I'd calmly condemned a man to death, and this name tag was all that remained of him. How did I feel? Well, I waited a few seconds, expecting cold horror to seep into my thoughts. It didn't happen. Sometimes other people's deaths are easy. I felt nothing but indifference and an impatience to get on with business.

"Good, my friend," I said. "You'll be well rewarded."

Bin Turki nodded, taking back the name tag. "We spoke about a position that would provide me with a regular income. I'm coming to appreciate the sophisticated ways of the city. I think I will stay here for a while, before I return to the Bani Salim."

"We will be glad to have you among us," I said. "I wish to reward your clan, too, for their boundless hospitality and kindness, when we were abandoned in the Sands. I was thinking of building a settlement for them, possibly near that oasis—"

"No, O Shaykh," he said. "Shaykh Hassanein would never accept such a gift. A few people did leave the Bani Salim and build houses of concrete blocks, and we see them once or twice a year as we pass through their villages. Most of the tribe, however, clings to the old ways. That is Shaykh Hassanein's decision, too. We know about the luxuries of electricity and gas ovens, but we are Bedu. We would not trade our camels for trucks, and we would not trade our goat-hair tents for a house that bound us to one place."

"I never thought the Bani Salim would live the whole year at the settlement," I said. "But maybe the tribe might like to have comfortable quarters at the end of its yearly migration."

Bin Turki smiled. "Your thoughts are well intentioned, but the gift you imagine would be deadly to the Bani Salim."

"As you say, bin Turki."

He stood up and grasped my hand. "I will let you rest now, O Shaykh."

"Go with safety, my nephew," I said.

"*Allah yisallimak*," he said, and left the room.

About seven o'clock that evening, the phone rang. Kmuzu answered it. "It's Dr. Besharati," he said.

"Let me see if I can hold the phone," I said. I took it from him and was clumsily able to put it to my ear. "*Marhaba*," I said.

"Mr. Audran? Your suspicions are correct. The cardiac rupture patterns of Khalid Maxwell and the boy are identical. There is no doubt in my mind that they were murdered with the same static pistol."

I stared across the room for a few seconds, lost in thought. "Thank you, Dr. Besharati," I said at last.

"Of course, this doesn't prove that the same individual was using the gun in both cases."

"No, I realize that. But the chances are very good that it was. Now I know exactly what I have to do, and how to do it."

"Well," said the medical examiner, "I don't know what you mean, but again I wish you luck. May peace be with you."

"And upon you be peace," I said, putting down the phone. While I was punishing my enemies and rewarding my friends, I decided to think about something I could do for Dr. Besharati. He'd certainly earned some kind of thanks.

I went to sleep early that night, and the next morning I'd recovered enough to get out of bed and shower. Kmuzu wanted me to avoid any kind of exertion, but that wasn't possible. It was Friday, the Sabbath, and I had a parade of the *Jaish* to go to.

I ate a hearty breakfast and dressed in the dove-gray uniform Shaykh Reda had given me. The trousers were well tailored, with a black stripe down each leg, and cut to fit into high black jackboots. The tunic was high-necked, with lieutenant's insignia already sewn on. There was also a high-peaked cap with a black visor. When I was completely dressed, I looked at myself in a mirror. I guessed that the uniform's resemblance to a Nazi outfit was not coincidental.

"How do I look, Kmuzu?" I asked.

"It's not you, *yaa Sidi*. It's definitely not your style."

I laughed and removed the cap. "Well," I said, "Abu Adil was kind enough to give me this uniform. The least I can do is wear it for him once."

"I don't understand why you're doing this."

I shrugged. "Curiosity, maybe?"

"I hope the master of the house doesn't see you dressed like that, *yaa Sidi*."

"I hope so, too. Now, bring the car around. The parade is being held on the Boulevard il-Jameel, near the Shimaal Mosque. I imagine we'll have to leave the car somewhere and walk a few blocks. The crowds are still huge near the mosque."

Kmuzu nodded. He went downstairs to get the Westphalian sedan started. I followed behind him after deciding not to take either narcotics or moddies with me. I didn't know exactly what I was walking into, and a clear head seemed like a good idea.

When we got to the boulevard, I was startled to see just how great the throng was. Kmuzu began weaving through side streets and alleys, trying to inch his way nearer to the *Jaish*'s gathering place.

After a while, we just had to give up and go the rest of the way on foot. We cut our way through the mass of people; my uniform helped me a little, I think, but progress was still very slow. I could see a raised platform ahead, with a speaker's stand draped in flags decorated with the emblems of the *Jaish*. I thought I could see Abu Adil and Kenneth there, both in uniform. Shaykh Reda was standing and chatting with another officer. He wasn't wearing one of his Proxy Hell moddies. I was glad of that—I didn't want to deal with an Abu Adil suffering the effects of a make-believe terminal illness.

"Kmuzu," I said, "I'm going to see if I can get up on the platform to talk with Shaykh Reda. I want you to work your way around to the back. Try to stay nearby. I may need you all of a sudden."

"I understand, *yaa Sidi*," he said with a worried look. "Be careful, and take no unnecessary chances."

"I won't." I knifed slowly through the crowd until I reached the rear most ranks of the *Jaish*, which was arrayed on the neutral ground of the boulevard in orderly companies. From there it was easier to make my way to the front. All along the way, I received nods and salutes from my fellow militiamen.

I walked around to the side of the platform and mounted three steps. Reda Abu Adil still hadn't seen me, and I walked up to him and saluted. His uniform was much more elegant than mine; for one thing, I think his buttons were gold, where everyone else's were brass. On his collar, instead of brass crescents, he wore golden curved swords.

"Well, what is this?" said Abu Adil, returning my salute. He looked surprised. "I really didn't expect you to come."

"I didn't want to disappoint you, sir," I said, smiling. I turned to his assistant. "And how's it going, Kenny?" Kenneth was a colonel, and loving every minute in the jackboots.

"I warned you about calling me that," he snarled.

"Yeah, you did." I turned my back on him. "Shaykh Reda, surely the *Jaish* is a Muslim paramilitary force. I remember when it was a group dedicated to ridding the city of foreigners. Now we proudly wear the symbols of the Faith. I was just thinking: Is your Kenneth one of us? I would have bet that he's a Christian. Or maybe even a Jew."

Kenneth grabbed my shoulder and spun me around. "I testify that there is no god but God," he recited, "and Muhammad is the Prophet of God."

I grinned. "Great! You're coming along real well with that. Keep it up!"

Abu Adil's face clouded. "You two stop your infantile bickering. We have more important things to think about today. This is our first large, public demonstration. If all goes well, we'll get hundreds of new recruits, doubling the size of the *Jaish*. That's what really counts."

"Oh," I said, "I see. What about poor old Abd ar-Razzaq, then? Or is he just a stiff now?"

"Why are you here?" demanded Abu Adil. "If it's to mock us—"

"No, sir, not at all. We have our differences, of course, but I'm all in favor of cleaning up this city. I came to meet the three platoons I'm supposed to be leading."

"Good, good," said Abu Adil slowly. "Splendid."

"I don't trust him," said Kenneth.

Abu Adil turned to him. "I don't either, my friend, but that doesn't mean we can't behave in a civilized manner. We're being watched by a lot of people today."

"Try to hold your animosity in for a little while, Kenneth," I said. "I'm willing to forgive and forget. For now, anyway." He only glared at me and turned away.

Abu Adil put a hand on my shoulder and pointed down to a unit of men assembled at the foot of the platform, on the right side. "Those are your platoons, Lieutenant Audran," he said. "They make up the Al-Hashemi Detachment. They're some of our finest men. Why don't you go down there and meet your noncommissioned officers? We'll be getting ready to start the drills soon."

"All right," I said. I climbed down from the platform and walked up and down before my unit. I stopped and said hello to the three platoon sergeants, then went through the ranks as if I were inspecting them. Most of the men seemed out of shape to me. I didn't think the *Jaish* would make much of a showing against a real military force; but then, the *Jaish* was never intended to go into battle against an army. It was created to bully shopkeepers and infidel intellectuals.

Maybe a quarter of an hour later, Abu Adil spoke into a microphone, commanding the parade to begin. My unit had no part in it, other than to keep the civilians from interfering. Some of the specially trained companies showed off their stuff, marching and turning and juggling rifle-shaped pieces of wood.

This went on for an hour under the hot sun, and I began to think I'd made a serious mistake. I was starting to feel weak and wobbly, and I really just wanted to sit down. Finally, the last showcase company snapped back to attention, and Abu Adil stepped forward to the speaker's podium. He harangued the *Jaish* for another half an hour, going on about the horror of Dr. Abd ar-Razzaq's murder, and how we all had to swear allegiance to Allah and the *Jaish*, and never rest until the brutal assassin had been captured and executed according to the dictates of Islamic law. I could tell that Shaykh Reda had roused every man in uniform to a barely contained frenzy.

Then, surprisingly, he called on me to speak. I stared at him for just a second or two, and then I hurried back up to the platform. I stood at the microphone, and Abu Adil backed away. An anxious hush fell over the uniformed men assembled before me, but beyond them I could see the hordes of tens of thousands of men and women whose pent-up fury was still seeking an outlet. I wondered what I was going to say.

"My fellow Soldiers of Allah," I began, raising my arms to include not only the *Jaish*, but also the mob beyond. "It is too late for anything but vengeance." A loud cry went up from the onlookers. "As Shaykh Reda said, we have a sacred duty, authorized in many places in the noble Qur'ân. We must find the person who struck down our holy imam, and then we must make him taste our keen-edged justice." Another cry, this one a strange, hungry, ululating sound that made me shiver.

I went on. "That is our task. But honor and faith and respect for the law demand that we control our anger, for fear that we revenge ourselves upon the wrong man. How, then, shall we know the truth? My friends, my brothers and sisters in Islam, I *have* the truth!"

This drew a loud shout from the mob, and a surprised sound from behind me, where Abu Adil and Kenneth were standing. I opened a few buttons of my tunic and brought out the needle gun, holding it high for everyone to see. "*This* is the murder weapon! *This* is the horrible instrument of our imam's death!" Now the reaction was long and frightening. The hysterical crowds surged forward, and the foot soldiers of the *Jaish* struggled to keep the people from rushing the platform.

"I know whose needle gun this is!" I shouted. "Do *you* want to know? Do *you* want to know who murdered Dr. Sadiq Abd ar-Razzaq, shamefully in cold blood?" I waited a few seconds, knowing the uproar would not subside, but pausing only for effect. I saw Kenneth start toward me, but Abu Adil grabbed his arm and stopped him. That surprised me.

"It belongs to Police Lieutenant Hajjar, a Jordanian immigrant to our city, a man with many past crimes that have long gone unpunished. I do not know his motives. I do not know why he stole our imam from us. I only know that he did that evil deed, and he sits this very moment, not far from here, in the police precinct on Walid al-Akbar Street, content in his sinful pride, certain that he is safe from the just retribution of the people."

I'd thought of a few more things to say, but it was impossible. From that point on, the mob became a terrifying thing. It seemed to shift and sway and shake itself, and voices were raised in cries that no one could understand, and chants and curses went up all around us. Then, in only a few minutes, I could see that a bewildering organization had taken place, as if leaders had been chosen and decisions made. Slowly, the mob animal turned away from the platform and the *Jaish*. It began to move southward along the lovely Boulevard il-Jameel. Toward the police station. It was going to claim Lieutenant Hajjar.

Hajjar had foreseen the behavior of the outraged mob. He had foreseen the terror of its mindless rage. He had only failed to foresee the true identity of its victim.

I watched, fascinated. After a while, I stepped back, away from the microphone. The afternoon parade of the *Jaish* was over. Many of the uniformed men had broken ranks and joined the wrathful rabble.

"Very well done, Audran," said Abu Adil. "Excellently played."

I looked at him. It seemed to me that he was entirely sincere. "It's going to cost you one of your most useful hirelings," I said. "Paybacks are a bitch, aren't they?"

Abu Adil only shrugged. "I'd written Hajjar off already. I can appreciate good work, Audran, even when it's done by my enemy. But be warned. Just because I'm congratulating you, don't think I'm not already planning a way to make you pay. This whole matter has been a disaster for me."

I smiled. "You brought it on yourself."

"Remember what I said: I'll make you pay."

"I suppose you'll try," I said. I climbed down the steps at the back of the platform. Kmuzu was there. He led me away from the boulevard, away from the surging mob, toward our car.

"Please take off that uniform, *yaa Sidi*," he said.

"What? Ride home in my underwear?" I laughed.

"At least the tunic. I'm sickened by everything it stands for."

I complied, and tossed the tunic into a corner of the backseat. "Well," I said, stretching out, "how did I do?"

Kmuzu turned around briefly, and he gave me one of his rare smiles. "Very fine, *yaa Sidi*," he said. Then he turned his attention back to driving.

I relaxed and leaned back against the seat. I told myself that the slight interruption in my life caused by Abu Adil and Lieutenant Hajjar and Imam Abd ar-Razzaq was over, and now life could get back to normal. The matter was closed. As for Shaykh Reda himself, any plans of paying that son of a bitch back the way he deserved had to be tabled until sometime in the hazy future, after Friedlander Bey was gathered by Allah into His holy Paradise.

In the meantime, Papa and I restored our good names. We met the next day with the amir and presented him with information and evidence concerning the deaths of Khalid Maxwell, Abd ar-Razzaq, and Lieutenant Hajjar. I didn't feel it necessary to go into detail about the sudden demise of Sergeant al-Bishah in Najran, or certain other pertinent points. Shaykh Mahali then ordered one of his administrative deputies to clear us of the false charges, and expunge any mention of Khalid Maxwell's murder from our records.

I was rather gratified by how easily I slipped back into my old routines. I was soon back at my desk, reviewing information concerning a revolutionary party that was gaining strength in my homeland of Mauretania. Kmuzu stood beside my desk and waited for me to notice him. I looked up. "What is it?" I asked.

"The master of the house wishes to speak with you, *yaa Sidi*," said Kmuzu.

I nodded, not knowing what to expect. With Papa, it was sometimes impossible to predict whether you were being summoned to receive reward or punishment. My stomach began to churn; had I earned his disfavor again? Were the Stones That Speak waiting with him to break my bones?

Fortunately, that proved not to be the case. Friedlander Bey smiled at me as I entered his office, and indicated that I should sit near him. "I commanded you to find an elegant solution to our difficulties, my nephew, and I am well pleased with what you accomplished."

"It makes me glad to hear it, O Shaykh," I said, relieved.

"I have what I believe is adequate recompense for all you have suffered, and for all the labor you performed on my behalf."

"I ask no reward, O Shaykh," I said. Well, I like rewards as much as the next guy, but it was good form to offer a token refusal.

Papa ignored me. He pushed a thin envelope and a small cardboard box toward me. I looked up at him questioningly. "Take them, my nephew. It pleases me greatly to give them to you."

The envelope contained money, of course. Not cash, because the sum was too large. It was a bank draft for a quarter-million kiam. I just stared at it for a few seconds, swallowed, and set it down again on the desk. Then I picked up the box and opened it. There was a moddy inside. Friedlander Bey was strongly opposed to personality modules on religious grounds. It was highly unusual for him to give me one.

I looked at the label. The moddy was a re-creation of my favorite fictional character, Lutfy Gad's detective, al-Qaddani. I smiled. "Thank you, my uncle," I said softly. The moddy meant more to me than the huge amount of money. There was a kind of warm significance to it that I couldn't put into words.

"I had the module created specially for you," said Papa. "I hope you enjoy it." He looked at me for a few seconds more. Then his expression grew serious. "Now tell me about how the datalink project is going. And I need a report on the final disposition of the Cappadocian situation. And further, now that Lieutenant Hajjar is dead, we must decide on a reliable replacement."

Months of torment, relieved at the end by a single minute of good cheer. What more could anyone want?

About the Author

George Alec Effinger (1947–2002) was the author of many highly regarded works of science fiction, including *What Entropy Means to Me* and the Hugo and Nebula Award–winning "Schrödinger's Kitten." His novels of Marîd Audran—*When Gravity Fails, A Fire in the Sun,* and *The Exile Kiss*—are widely considered to be among the finest SF in the "cyberpunk" subgenre.

If you enjoyed this book…
Come visit our Web site at

www.sfbc.com

and find hundreds more:
- science fiction • fantasy
  - the newest books
  - the greatest classics

THE SCIENCE FICTION BOOK CLUB

has been bringing the best of science fiction and fantasy
to the doors of discriminating readers for over 50 years.
For a look at currently available books and details on how to join,
just visit us at the address above.